MW00608774

Kathy ♡ Lockheart

# THE LIES WE TELL

KATHY LOCKHEART

Cover design © By Hang Le

978-1-955017-16-9 e-book
978-1-955017-17-6 Paperback
978-1-955017-18-3 Hardcover

Published by Rosewood Literary Press

ROSEWOOD
LITERARY PRESS

# THE LIES WE TELL

This collection includes two full-length, tension-filled romances in the Secrets and the City series: Deadly Illusion and Fatal Cure. Both are stand-alone romances with no cliffhangers.

# DEADLY ILLUSION

*For my husband, for showing me the beauty of true love.*

# DEADLY ILLUSION BLURB

J enna was determined to leave her dark past behind her and build the life she'd always wanted, but just when she thought all her dreams were finally coming true, a shocking incident shattered her fairy-tale life, and now she's hiding a terrible secret—a secret that could cost her everything.

Damian is as gorgeous as he is mysterious, keeping his own dark secrets from everyone he meets. He never thought he'd care about anything again… until he meets Jenna. He knows letting her get close to him will put her in danger, but when he suspects Jenna's in trouble, there's only one thing that matters: protecting her at all costs.

Thrust into a terrifying nightmare where a threat looms in every shadow, Jenna and Damian find themselves in a race for survival. Soon, everyone Jenna loves is in peril, and only the ultimate sacrifice can save them…

# AUTHOR'S NOTE

Deadly Illusion is an emotional, tension-filled romance, and while the main couple gets their HEA, they experience heartbreak before it. If you are looking for a lighthearted read, you will not find it in these pages.

WHILE THE ROMANTIC SCENES ARE NOT EXTREMELY GRAPHIC, THIS forbidden love story contains violence and other content that may be triggering for some readers. I prefer you go into a story without spoilers, but if you would like **a list of detailed triggers**, you can find it posted on my website at KathyLockheart dot com, under DEADLY ILLUSION.

**P.S. MY DARKEST SECRET** INSPIRED THIS NOVEL. BE SURE TO READ **the inspiration at the end, which unveils what it is, and how it shaped this story.**

1

It happened quickly. One minute, I thought all my dreams were finally coming true—dreams I'd desperately clung to when I was a little girl, pressing my hands against my ears to silence the hurt. But the next, I was staring at a man with gritted teeth, fists clenched so tight his knuckles turned white, and eyes that glared like he wanted to annihilate me.

He grabbed my arm and burrowed his fingers into my skin so painfully that my legs buckled, sending me to my knees.

I swallowed over the sudden dryness in my throat, struggling to understand what was happening. Only moments ago, he'd knocked on my door with a charming smile. And now...

*Oh, God.*

I tried to twist away from him, but his fingers squeezed until my bones felt like they would shatter.

This was not happening. He was not doing this, because that would mean nothing was what I thought it was, and that I didn't know him at all—or, more precisely, that I didn't know what he was capable of...

It meant my brother, who was going to be here any second, might stumble onto this scene. Last night he'd called and told me there was something he needed to talk about. Whatever it was, he insisted on coming over and walking me to work this morning because he wasn't willing to say it over the phone. All night I'd worried about what it could be. Had I done something to upset him? Had something happened to Mom or Dad? But now I wished he wasn't coming, because Justin could get hurt trying to protect me.

I wasn't about to let that happen.

Though the pain in my arm begged me not to move, I stood up and locked defiant eyes with him. The air in my apartment stilled, and the noisy hum of Chicago's streets outside my living room window faded to nothing until our breaths were the only sound.

"Get your hands off me," I snarled.

His eyes narrowed, and as he swung his arm to release me, the momentum threw me off balance, and I fell to the carpet—my face crashing into the wall on the way down. Warm liquid dripped from my nose.

Lying on the ground, staring up at him towering over me, I'd never felt so small and vulnerable. Never before had my body felt like such a liability. His six-foot, two-hundred-pound frame was an asset of solid muscle—twice my size and ten times my strength.

What made me think I could protect myself from someone so much bigger than me?

He let out a long breath, and as he stared down at me, the rage dissipated from his face, falling into what seemed to be despair. He ran a hand through his hair and looked like he couldn't believe what he'd just done. His worried eyes glazed over my body, and in a low voice, he asked, "Are you okay?"

I blinked, struggling to digest it all—the violence, the sudden compassion.

He stepped towards me. "Jenna," he said. "I—"

"Get out," I demanded as forcefully as I could manage. I looked at the clock below the TV. Seven fifteen. *Please let Justin run late.*

His eyes trained on the blood dripping from my nose. "Let me get you a tissue."

Yeah, like that would make everything better. Like we could just pretend that this whole time I'd known him, I'd thought he was a nice guy, while deep inside, he was nothing but a monster.

I stood up, trying to steady my trembling hands. "Leave. Now, or… so help me, I'll call the cops."

He took a step forward.

I stepped back, putting my palm up.

I wished it wasn't shaking. I wished I looked stronger, more intimidating, and I wished that it would take more than one real strike from him to take me out.

He stared at my hand as if *he* were the one baffled, confused how this shocking incident had occurred.

"Get out," I said.

"Jenna, I'm—"

"Out!" I snapped.

His body deflated, and he looked like he was on the verge of tears. His mouth remained a gaping hole of unspoken words that could never erase what just happened. After hesitating for what seemed like an eternity, he finally realized the best thing he could do was to leave, ambling out the front door so slowly he must have been hoping I'd change my mind and call him back.

Instead, I quickly locked the door and pressed my back against it. Sobbing into my hands, I wiped my nose and stared at the thin trail of blood on my skin in disbelief.

Why did he do it? How did I let this happen? And why did it have to happen now, a mere eight months after moving to the city?

Envisioning *this* time in my life, eager to experience it in all its blissful glory, was the only thing that had gotten me through my dark early years.

On the outside, my life had looked the same as any child's growing up in a small Illinois town four hours outside of Chicago. I had a stay-at-home mom, a dad with a steady, albeit small, paycheck running the local grocery store, an older brother, and a picturesque bedroom in an eighty-year-old country house. Beyond our front door, the sun brightened freshly cut lawns and sprawling oak trees, and the sounds of birds singing lovely melodies mixed with the laughter of families playing together. But inside, our home was shadowed in tragedy.

My sister's name was Jessica. She had acute myeloid leukemia—AML. Leukemia is the most common form of childhood cancer, and the normal one—acute *lymphoblastic* leukemia—has a ninety percent survival rate, but not AML. AML is more aggressive. I've always felt bad that I couldn't really remember her. I was only a toddler when she died, so I felt like a traitor for evading the grief that eventually destroyed my family. It was sort of like I grew up in a house with a massive crater at its center. Everyone was aware of the devastating cavity, but while the rest of them had lived through its catastrophic impact, I'd merely lived in the aftermath.

I often walked home from school as slowly as possible, dreading the tightrope we'd have to balance with our mother always on the verge of a breakdown. Many times she wouldn't even notice me when I came in. Sometimes our breakfast dishes would still be on the table, untouched, and she'd be sitting in the same spot as when we'd left for school, staring at the wall with glazed eyes. Other times, she'd linger at the kitchen sink full of suds, washing the same dish for twenty minutes. I used to watch her frail shoulders, praying they would stay still. As long as they were still, the days were bearable, but once they started to shake, her chin would tuck down, and she'd rush into her bedroom sobbing for the rest of the night. I felt awful for not knowing what to do to help her and selfish for needing to escape the sound of her cries—it was as if pain engulfed her soul. My favorite place to go was the swing in the backyard, where I'd close my eyes to feel the warm sun on my eyelids and swing as high as possible, imagining we could fly away from it all.

I'd let myself get lost in daydreams of what my life could be like when I was all grown up. In my head it was always perfect: I'd live in a city full of exciting things to do, with friends that loved me unconditionally, unlike the mean girls in school who snickered at me just because I had to wear hand-me-down clothes. I'd find someone who loved me, and we wouldn't avoid eye contact or sit on opposite sides of the couch like Mom and Dad; we'd hold hands and cherish every moment we had together.

But then I'd feel guilty for dreaming of such happiness while Mom was trapped in her mental purgatory, and I'd wonder what my parents had been like before Jessica died. Did they use to dance in the glow of the television light? Scoop our giggling toddler bodies into their arms and smile, while fireflies lit up the backyard? I couldn't wait for them to find their way back to that happiness, and I knew if I was patient enough, one day Mom would move past her grief and we'd have nightly dinners together and spend Christmas mornings smiling and unwrapping gifts as a family.

It's heartbreaking how long a human will hold on to hope, even as evidence mounts against it, even as months turn into years. But when hope is the only thing you have, when giving up on it means allowing eternal despair to devour you, how can you ever let it go?

By force, evidently. A verbal gunshot, delivered after my last day of eighth grade. When Mom and Dad asked Justin and me to sit down, I could tell by the looks on their faces that they were going to say something terrible. My palms began to sweat, no part of me wanting to hear what it was. As Dad twisted his wedding band and Mom folded her hands in her lap the way she did at church, Dad cracked my security with his words: They were getting divorced. A compassionate person would've hugged them and asked if they were okay, but with that one sentence, they destroyed every ounce of hope we had. I knew they were still grieving my sister; they always would, and I felt sorry for them, since they were obviously in incredible pain. But in that moment, I felt angry. Weren't Justin and I enough for them to appreciate what they *did* have, not just what they lost?

The only security my brother and I had back then was that Dad was our shield. With one look, he could warn us to leave the room just before she exploded. And when Mom was in her bed for days, he made sure we were fed and did our homework. But now he was leaving us behind because *he* couldn't take it anymore? And he wouldn't take us with him? So what if his new place was tiny! It felt like he was saving himself, leaving Justin and me on the *Titanic* as he got into a lifeboat.

I'd been so upset by the news that I can only remember glimpses of what followed. Crying, begging them to change their minds, delusional in believing if I just said the right thing, I could stop our family from falling apart. I remember giving them both the silent treatment for days, and refusing to say goodbye to Dad when he loaded black garbage bags that stretched around his belongings into the back of his truck. I refused to visit him that entire summer, pathetically hoping it would force them back together.

But Mom and Dad never got back together. They signed some papers, opting out of their love story as easily as signing our report cards. I didn't understand why my parents couldn't have leaned on each other instead of giving up on their relationship—so help me, if I ever found true love I'd never let any tragedy divide us. But that's when I realized things were never going to get better. If I wanted a happy life, I was going to have to roll up my sleeves and build it myself.

I hated that my only hope to escape the misery meant leaving Mom alone in her anguish, but if I didn't pursue the light, the darkness would consume me forever. So in high school, I got a job, applied for every scholarship I could get my hands on, and with hard work and determination, I managed to put myself through college and move to Chicago.

For the first time in my life, everything was falling into place, and the upside of going through something bad is that it makes you appreciate the good that much more.

But five weeks after I moved here, a sequence of events was put into motion that would jeopardize everything.

It started on a Sunday evening in January. After spending the day with Justin—who'd moved to Chicago a year and a half before me—I took the "L" and walked the last couple blocks to my apartment. Like many people, I relied on public transportation because owning a car was expensive, and parking was difficult to find. Most people complained of the bitterly cold temperatures with subzero wind chills

—harsh even by Midwest winter standards. But I didn't move here to hibernate in my apartment, so I clutched my coat, pulled my hat down over my ears, and leaned into the whipping winds that stung my cheeks.

Even in the unforgiving weather, I still appreciated the beauty of the city. In the ebony night, the hundred-story buildings stretched up to the sky with thousands of windows glowing like Christmas lights, and down here, elegant lamps hung on arched posts, warmly illuminating the walkways. In the distance, the "L" rumbled with a metallic squeak, ferrying people to all sorts of enchanting places throughout Chicago.

By the time I reached my apartment complex, I was so cold that my fingers ached inside my gloves, but when I saw who was just outside the lobby doors, I stopped in my tracks. My neighbor, Stephen, was smoking a cigarette. I don't know why he gave me the creeps. He'd been nothing but friendly, eager to help when he saw my U-Haul, but there was something about him that made me uncomfortable—something I couldn't put my finger on.

Still, there was no reason to turn around and walk away tonight. Yet, that's precisely what I did.

"Jenna?" he called out.

Like a complete coward, I pretended not to hear him and hurried around the corner, unsure how far I'd have to walk before I could go back. How long did it take to smoke a cigarette? Two minutes? Five? Who had that kind of dedication to smoke when it was freezing outside?

Thanks to the frostbite-inducing temperatures, there was almost no one out tonight, which is why I heard it: a faint whimper coming from the alley on my right. It took me a second to place the sound because the only light cutting through the pervasive darkness was from a single, dim bulb. But then I spotted a dog—a German shepherd, I think—about thirty feet away. The poor thing looked horrible, her ribs protruding against mangy fur, but worse, her stomach was distended.

I urgently looked up animal rescue places on my phone, pleased to discover one only two blocks away, but how in the world was I going to get her there? I had no leash and nothing to lure or trap her with. The only thing I could think of was to try and catch her. It wasn't a good plan, but I had to make it work because there was no way she'd survive tonight's brutal temperatures.

I advanced slowly into the alley, which stunk of rotting food. Pipes stretched along the bricks parallel to the road, hissing a hot, white vapor. The dog looked at me with nervous eyes as I moved cautiously around potholes and past an overfilled dumpster.

"You really shouldn't wander into dark alleys."

I jumped to find a guy lurking behind the heap of trash, and when he reached out to grab me, I slammed my knee up.

"Christ!" He grabbed his crotch and fell to his knees.

The dog scurried twenty feet away, assessing the danger.

So was I.

I eyed him writhing in pain and considered bolting, but if I did, the dog would die. I was reasonably confident I could catch her before he was mobile again and, if not, well... I had two knees, and he had two balls.

"Why the hell did you kick me?" he groaned, his chin tucked against his chest.

"It's disappointing when the people you try to attack fight back, isn't it?"

When he lifted his head to glare at me, I noticed he was good-looking. *So was Ted Bundy,* I reminded myself.

"I wasn't attackin' you, for god's sake."

"Your arm reached out to—"

"Feed the dog," he said in annoyance.

And now that I looked, he was holding a bag of chips, and the dog had been angled towards him.

*Oh crap.* What if I just beat up a poor homeless guy who had been sharing his food with his little homeless dog? But he didn't *look* homeless... In the limited light, I could see he was clean-shaven and his clothes didn't look tattered. A drug dealer, then.

I clenched my hand and brought it up, ready to attack if it came to that, but he simply looked at my defensive fist with an amused grin. After a few seconds, he wobbled to his feet, pressing his hands into his thighs for several moments before straightening his spine.

"I don't want any drugs," I clarified.

"What?" After a moment, he tilted his head in offended understanding. "I'm not a drug dealer."

*Yeah, right.* "Okay."

"I'm not. But I could be. Hell, I could be a serial killer for all you know, and you just walked into an alley with a strange guy. You really need to be more careful."

He was right. The smart thing to do was leave. Lingering in a secluded area with a stranger wasn't safe, and the guy was taking care of the dog, so it's not like it would be alone. But what if he didn't try hard enough to save her? What if he just fed her and then left? How could I sleep tonight if there was a chance she might be out here dying?

As we both stared at her quivering body, I said, "I'm going to take her to an animal hospital."

He looked like he found me naively adorable. "And how are you going to do that, exactly?"

"I'm going to catch her."

"She'll bite you."

"I'll be careful."

"She could have rabies."

"You have a better plan?"

He stared at the canine. "We could call animal control."

Suddenly we were a *we.* Why did that make my stomach do flips, and why did his voice penetrate my chest? *Dear diary, I met a handsome gentleman lurking behind a dumpster, and I caused irreparable damage to his reproductive organs.*

"She'll probably bolt before they show up, and even if they do catch her, they'll probably euthanize her," I said.

This was the first time he looked particularly bothered. "Maybe we can buy a leash or something," he suggested. But he clearly saw the flaw in that idea; she had no collar, and would never stick around long enough for one of us to come back from buying one.

"The dog's pregnant," I said, pointing to her bulging belly. "And with the wind chill, it's supposed to get to negative forty tonight. If she runs off, there's no way she'll live through the night. Neither will her unborn pups."

The guy looked at the dog with troubled eyes, then threw another chip down. "*I'll* pick her up," he offered.

"You need to keep her distracted by feeding her."

"We could switch places," he said.

"That could spook her, and since we already spooked her once—"

"When you *assaulted* me." He was teasing now. *I think.*

"Our best chance to save her is for you to keep feeding her, and for me to grab her."

He looked between the dog and me. "If she comes at you, you think you can outrun her?"

"I don't need to outrun her. I just need to outrun *you.*"

The guy grinned, setting my body's microwave to defrost.

As I gingerly made my way towards the dog, he threw chip after chip. As long as she was eating, she didn't worry about my inching closer, but soon he held up the bag, showing me he'd reached the bottom.

This was it. He threw the last chip down and, though nerves bound my muscles into knots, I pounced. Careful not to bump her belly, I threw my arms around her undercarriage and heaved her up.

The problem was, moving that fast made me lose my footing, and, as I fell to the ground, the dog whipped her head around and bared her teeth. *Holy crap!* She lunged for me with a feral growl and snapped at my face, but just before she bit—her mouth so close I felt her hot, rotting breath invading my nostrils—she was yanked up.

She snapped at the guy, but unlike me, he had a good grip and she couldn't reach his skin. He held her safely, until her snapping resolved into a moan.

"You okay?"

"I'm fine," I said, embarrassed.

"You hit your head," he said. "Maybe I should take you to urgent care."

"I'm good," I insisted, hopping up. "Rescue place is this way."

We walked in silence to the animal hospital and stayed with her while waiting for an exam.

"How'd you find her?" I asked.

"Followed her from the main road and saw her circlin' that dumpster," he said, shrugging as if anyone would have done the same thing. But not many people would have gone so far out of their way to help a poor, defenseless animal.

The guy looked at me and, unlike the dimly lit alley, the clinic's light let me finally see his features in detail. Man, he was knee-buckling gorgeous. His radiant blue eyes were lighter on the inside, darker on the outside, his oval face had a sharp jawline, and his skin was the beautiful peach that hinted it darkened quickly in the summers, complementing his light-brown hair. And his body. Holy hell, his body. No longer hiding beneath a coat, the contours of his muscles pressed against the fabric of his gray shirt, his jeans hugging his hips in all the right places.

A warmth cascaded over me.

"I'm Colton, by the way." His husky tone could make women swoon.

"Jenna," I said. "Sorry I annihilated your manhood."

He laughed, and the way he stared at me, like my life's story was of sudden, vital interest to him, made my cheeks flush.

I'd had guys look at me from time to time, but their looks were normally superficial. Colton, however, looked at me deeper, his gaze breaching my skin and plunging to my core. Like he was truly seeing me.

He studied me the whole time they examined the dog and reassured us they'd adopt her out to a good home. And his attention persisted as we provided our contact information to the clinic, put our winter gear back on, and stepped back outside.

In the blistering cold, cars cracked snow salt beneath their tires and people hurried down the sidewalk, hunched over to protect their faces from the biting winds.

"Well, thanks for not slitting my throat or whatever," I said.

A white cloud burst from his mouth as he threw his head back and laughed. And then he stared at me like the thought of letting me out of sight was no longer an acceptable possibility.

"Let me buy you a drink," Colton suggested. "Least I can do. For helpin' with the dog."

I wanted nothing more than to get to know this handsome man who'd gone out of his way to help an animal in need, but Zoey was on her way to my place.

"My friend's coming over."

"Just a quick drink," he suggested with a sexy smile that made me want to run away with him.

I checked my phone. Zoey said she'd text me when she got off the train. If I left then, I shouldn't keep her waiting.

"I'd only have like ten minutes," I said.

He smiled. "If I only have ten minutes to get to know you, we better hurry."

## 2

Across the street, we entered a bar that greeted us with a welcome rush of heat. I was pleased to discover the place was casual, with most people dressed in jeans, and small bowls of popcorn filling the space with a delicious scent. Behind multicolored bottles, wooden arches framed a black chalkboard with white calligraphy displaying the specials, and basketball-sized globes of light dangled above two dozen stools positioned so close together that when we sat down, our legs almost touched.

*Lucky me.*

"Thanks," I said, after Colton bought me a beer.

"To rescuing dogs," he said. He clinked my bottle with his, and as we took a sip, the salty beer prickled my throat.

Good Lord, his ocean-colored gems drew me in so deeply, it was like our eyes wanted to do all the talking.

"So," Colton started. "Where were you headed before you saw the dog?"

I picked at the label's moist corner. "Just out for a walk."

"A walk."

I nodded.

"In dangerous temperatures?" he challenged.

I shrugged.

He tilted his head towards me and gave me a playful smile that could make me spill secret nuclear launch codes. "Where were you really headed?"

I shifted in my seat. "Nowhere. I was just...avoiding a place, actually."

"How come?"

I took a sip. "I'd rather not say."

"Why?"

I hesitated. "'Cause you'll think I'm either a jerk or a lunatic."

His grin stretched wider. "Well, now you have to tell me." Looking between my lips and my eyes, eagerly awaiting my answer, Colton appeared fascinated by me, as if I were an intriguing puzzle he couldn't wait to solve.

"I was dodging someone."

Colton raised an eyebrow. Clearly, this not the answer he was expecting. "Who?"

"A neighbor."

"Why?"

"I think he likes me."

Colton scanned my body and then met my gaze. "I'd say that's a safe bet."

*And I bet Colton's abs are so ripped their ridges could be used for an exfoliation scrub.*

I blushed. "I don't want to lead him on, so when I saw him tonight, I...walked the other way."

When Colton pulled his shirtsleeves up and rested his sexy-ass forearms on the bar, my hormones had a party at my expense. He caught me looking at the lustful lines of muscles that encased his arms and smirked, clearly enjoying how attracted I was to him.

"So, what do you do for a living?" he asked.

"I'm a marketing analyst."

"What does a marketing analyst do? Exactly." He pulled his lips up on one side, revealing an adorable dimple. Goddammit, how was I supposed to *not* stare at that seductive facial belly button?

"I work in the advertising department. We analyze what type of marketing yields the highest ROIs, and then partner with our creative team to develop campaigns for customers."

"Damn," he said with raised brows.

"It's not as sophisticated as it sounds." I loved how he looked at my mouth when I smiled. "It basically means we're data monkeys that figure out the most profitable ways to advertise. I just started a month ago, so I don't know really what I'm doing yet, but I need to learn fast. I heard if you get on my boss's bad side, it's impossible to get a promotion." I took a sip of beer. "What do you do for a living?"

"I work construction."

"Road?"

"Building."

"Like houses?"

"Commercial. Restaurants in the city, mostly. Strip malls in the burbs. Always been good with my hands. Used to do odd jobs when I was a teenager to earn cash, and it just sort of progressed. I started out framing, then drywalling, and started overseeing parts of projects. Got my general contractor license three months ago, and I got my first official job as a G.C. Restaurant's goin' up in Naperville."

"Wow."

"I'm sure I just got it on price. I undercut the hell outta my bid, so I'm barely breaking even on it, but I gotta get a project under my belt as G.C. if I want any more jobs."

"Still, it's impressive."

He paused and seemed to consider his next words. "Truth is, I'm scared shitless. Everything's ridin' on this. If it doesn't go well, no one else'll ever take another chance on me. I'll be stuck as a day laborer for the rest of my life."

Wow. Most people would have pretended to be completely confident, especially in front of someone new. But there was already something about this conversation that felt comfortable, like we'd known each other longer than the space of a single evening.

"Okay, new topic." Colton offered a lighthearted grin. "Name something on your bucket list."

*Easy.* "Going to the Willis Tower."

"You've never been there?"

"Not yet."

"That's a travesty."

*I know.* "I want to see it all—the Willis Tower, Shedd Aquarium, Field Museum. Everything Chicago has to offer."

"Jenna!" a voice shouted from the other end of the bar.

I looked over and spotted Stephen walking towards me.

*This is not happening.*

Colton's smile fell when he registered the look on my face. "Know him?"

"He's my neighbor."

"The one you were dodging?"

When I nodded, Colton's expression morphed to concern. But Stephen made his way over to us, propping his elbow on the empty bar to my left, oblivious. He ran a hand over his blond buzz cut. "Hey," he smiled. "Thought I saw you in here." His winter coat reeked of cigarette smoke, as usual. "Thought I saw you like an hour ago? Outside the apartment complex?"

I feigned confusion and shrugged.

"Anyway. I haven't seen you around in a few days. All moved in?"

"For the most part."

"If you need any help," he offered again.

"Thanks."

"Can I buy you a drink?"

"I'm actually supposed to meet my friend soon," I hedged apologetically.

He tried to hide his disappointment before he noticed my beer. "I'll wait with you."

How frustrating to be *told* he was going to hang out with me rather than be asked.

"She's not meeting me here," I said.

Stephen ignored me and flagged the bartender. Maybe I wasn't being direct enough. Perhaps I was the one causing the problem here. How could I say *go away* without being a jerk? Usually, I'd be more patient, but Colton and I had only minutes left, and Stephen was intruding on our precious time. I shifted. "Look, now's not really a good time."

His smile faltered, and he glanced at Colton for several seconds before looking back at me with an accusation—like if I was having a drink with anyone, it should be him. "Didn't realize you were with someone."

I opened my mouth, wanting to somehow unravel the tension, but before I could think of anything, he huffed away.

I cringed. "Well, that went as crappy as it could've."

"Don't you think that was weird that he came in lookin' for you?"

"I guess. I hope it won't be awkward with him now," I said, staring at the door. I'd been so worried about hurting Stephen's feelings that I'd obviously left him with the impression I might be interested. I should've had the guts to be blunt in the first place.

"How would he know you were here unless he'd followed you?"

My cell chimed with a text from Zoey. "It's my friend," I said. "I have to go." Unable to hide my disappointment, I had to force myself to stand up and put my coat on.

Colton stood up, too.

"You don't have to leave."

His blue eyes penetrated mine. "I'm walkin' you home."

"That's not necessary."

"It's dark," he said.

"This isn't a dangerous neighborhood."

That damn dimple emerged again. "Says who? Google?"

I stood silent, unwilling to admit that, yes, that's exactly where I'd looked up which locations were safe. I relied on the internet to warn me if I'd ever be mugged. "I'll be fine."

"Says the girl who wandered into a dark alley alone." He grinned and followed me to the exit. Once outside, he tucked his hands into his coat pockets and positioned himself between me and the street as we walked. "So, you have a creepy neighbor, you risk your life to save pregnant dogs, and you're a marketing analyst. Tell me more."

"Like what?"

"Do you have any brothers or sisters?"

I typically skated past this question with a partial truth, but with Colton, that didn't feel right. The connection between us could not be denied, nor contained, growing like an avalanche. "I have a brother who lives here in Chicago, and I had a sister, but she died when I was a kid. She was five."

I could tell my answer surprised him and that he felt bad for accidentally asking such a heavy question. "I'm sorry."

"I was too young to remember much of it."

He considered this. "Still. That must have been hard on you."

He was right about that. I remembered, suddenly, one moment in particular.

*I stand in line with the other five-year-olds in our class, standing on tiptoe to see over Molly's pigtails, eager for my name to be called, and when Jenna Christiansen is announced, a rush of sunlight dances through my tummy. As I walk towards Principal Rolland, I glance out at the audience, excited to see Mom's proud smile as her daughter crosses the stage to get her kindergarten diploma. I smile so big because, in this glorious moment, I feel incredibly special. Until I see the look on her face. Mom isn't smiling; she's crying, and not the I'm-so-proud-I-can't-not-cry, cry. Sadness crying, because my every milestone is a reminder of what she's lost: the daughter she wishes was actually here today. I'm a disappointment for not being her, and as I walk across the stage, trying not to let anyone see my lip tremble, I wonder if Mommy wishes I was the one who died.*

"It was harder on my parents."

We walked under the amber glow of a streetlamp, our feet crunching on the salted sidewalk, our cheeks stinging from the wind gusts.

"What about you?" I said. "Any siblings?"

He looked like he wasn't sure if he should let me change the subject or pepper me with more questions. The fact he cared so much about how to best navigate such a sensitive subject made me like him even more.

"No siblings."

I could get lost in time, just staring at him like this. For years, I'd absorbed so many love stories—books, movies, television shows—but suddenly, all those stories came alive in a way they never had before.

"Are you close with your parents?"

Colton's steps became hesitant. "Family thing's always been kind of messed up." His tone had undercurrents of pain. "But then some-thin' terrible happened, and…" He tried to shake off the sadness of the moment with a light smile. "Kind of a long story."

One I wanted to hear. His elusive comment pulled me in even more—perhaps recognizing another soul that didn't grow up like the Brady Bunch.

"I'd love to hear it."

Colton studied my face, looking like he was surprised by his sudden desire to share his background with me. "I'd like to take you out sometime," he suggested, "and plan something really special for you."

I tried to hide the elation in my voice. "I'd like that."

As we crossed the last intersection, I wasn't sure how I'd be able to wait to see him again. "This is my complex."

Colton's eyes hardened. "He always outside waiting for you like this?"

I followed his leer to find Stephen outside smoking again. When he spotted us, he slowly blew out a cloud of smoke, glowering.

*Great.* It would definitely be awkward bumping into him from now on.

Colton pressed a protective hand to my lower back. "Let me walk you inside."

"I'm fine," I assured him, though I wasn't sure I believed it.

Colton looked at Stephen, then back at me, but before he could argue further, my best friend, Zoey, approached us. I introduced her to Colton. She smiled, shook his hand, and after some small talk we said goodbye to him, though saying goodbye was the last thing I wanted to do.

Colton kept his eyes on me as Zoey and I entered the building and climbed into the elevator. I could hardly contain my smitten grin—until Stephen skulked into the lobby, glaring at me as the elevator doors began to close.

## 3

Wearing a black wool coat over a white button-down shirt and gray pants, Colton arrived with an enchanting smile, his indigo eyes even sexier than I remembered. I couldn't believe I was going out on a date with someone so handsome! Getting all dolled up for a night on the town felt like a ribbon-cutting ceremony, opening a new chapter in my life, full of opportunity.

"Hey, beautiful," Colton said.

That. Right there. That longing in his eyes should be bottled and consumed anytime people needed to feel adored.

He handed me a bouquet of roses. "I haven't been able to stop thinking about you." His confession hung in the air, the seriousness of his tone confirming this wasn't just any old attraction.

I waved him in, hurrying to put the flowers in some water. "Let me grab my stuff," I said calmly, even though inside I was squealing.

Colton crossed his arms, leaned against the doorframe, and glanced down the complex's hallway. "That neighbor still givin' you grief?"

"I think he's mad at me."

"Did he do something to you?" Colton asked sharply.

"No, no. He's just avoiding me." It was downright ironic that just when Stephen was finally leaving me alone, I wanted to seek *him* out and smooth things over so it wasn't uncomfortable bumping into each other. "So," I said, changing the subject. "Where are we going?"

He smiled. "You said you want to see the Willis Tower. That's the first place I'd like to take you, if that's okay?"

He'd organized the entire evening around what *I* wanted to do? *Would it be politically incorrect to throw him down and kiss him?* "Where's the second?"

To this, he bit his lip—oh my gosh, was he *trying* to incite a sensual fog with that bite?—and said, "It's a surprise."

THE ENTIRE SIXTY SECONDS IT TOOK FOR THE ELEVATOR TO ASCEND THE hundred and three stories of the Willis Tower, Colton watched my face. I could tell he was excited to take me to the Skydeck—the observation room famous for its views—but when I met his eyes, I could also see that his gaze was laced with desire.

Once the doors opened, we entered a dimly lit space wrapped in floor-to-ceiling windows, where clusters of onlookers observed the city.

Colton guided me to the room's edge, and when we reached the window, I gasped. The magnificent city of Chicago sprawled out beneath us. Buildings of staggering heights with lights glistening against the cobalt sky stretched on forever, hugging Lake Michigan, which was a gradient of black and sapphire after the sunset.

"You can see the entire skyline," I said, in awe.

"On a clear day, you can see fifty miles and four states—Illinois, Indiana, Wisconsin, and Michigan." Colton looked at me like I was the most remarkable thing he'd ever seen, and then he brought his hand to mine. He waited for my silent permission—an intimate smile—before interlocking his fingers with mine.

Something inside me quivered.

"Come here," he said, leading me to a group of people lined up on the far side of the room.

I felt my mouth run dry when I saw what they were waiting for:

The Ledge. Glass boxes extended four and a half feet outside the building, allowing you to walk out, look down, and have nothing between you and the hundred-story free-fall except the pane of glass under your feet.

When it was our turn in line, I hesitated.

Colton noticed my reaction. "You afraid of heights?"

"More like a fear of falling and having my skull explode all over the ground."

Colton's mouth twitched, clearly trying not to laugh at me. "It's perfectly safe," he assured. "Each box is made up of three layers of half-inch-thick glass. The box weighs seven thousand pounds and can hold up to five tons. You could park a car in one of these things."

"Then why's that box closed?" I nodded to the one with yellow caution tape blocking it off. "It has a shattered floor."

"It's not a shattered floor," he said. "Not exactly, anyway. Every once in a while, the protective layer shatters, but that's what it's designed to do. They block it off, replace the protective layer, and it's perfectly fine again."

But in the meantime, it must not have been safe, or they wouldn't have blocked it off. What happened if you were on it when the protective layer went? If you didn't get off fast enough, would it not stand to reason the next layer would crack, and then the other? Given the walls and ceiling were also glass, how would that not suddenly shatter and send its occupants into a death fall?

"How do you know all this?" I asked.

"Used to work here as a tour guide," Colton said. "You're not gonna fall." He put his arm around my hip, encouraging me to step into the box.

Adrenaline surged needles into my fingers as I took a deep breath and glanced down. My feet stood on a transparent plate, and beneath the plate was nothing but air as we hovered over buildings with a helicopter-like view. Once I got past how horrifically terrifying it was, I had to admit, it was the coolest thing I'd ever done in my entire life. I was standing on top of Chicago, and it was even better than I imagined it would be.

I could see Colton processing the emotion on my face, and he must have realized how significant this was for me because he pulled out his cell phone and asked someone to take our picture.

After finishing at the Willis Tower, we took a taxi to the Signature room. It was a white-tablecloth restaurant on the ninety-fifth floor of the John Hancock building, where we sat next to a glass wall over-looking the city—a city that was feeling more and more like home. The restaurant smelled of delicious scents that only skilled chefs could create, and the warmth of the candle sitting on our table lit Colton's face with a romantic glow.

There was so much I wanted to know about him—especially after the cryptic comment about his family on our walk home last week— and finally, we'd have nothing to do but talk.

4

I glanced around the restaurant full of upscale-looking people. The tables were decorated like a wedding reception with layers of china, a pink candle surrounded by fragrant flowers, water glasses covered in condensation, and silverware so shiny that the spoon reflected the candle's flame.

"I've never been somewhere this nice," I admitted. "I feel like someone's going to tell me I don't belong in a place this fancy and kick me out."

Colton's mouth tugged up on one side and he leaned on his elbows, his eyes iridescent. "I'd throw some swings if anyone tried to do that to you."

My cheeks warmed, and I couldn't believe I'd gotten so lucky to be sitting here with him. Though I was eager to learn what tragedy haunted his past, I didn't want to make him uncomfortable by jumping into something so heavy, so, after the waiter took our order, I started with something lighter.

"Okay, I have to ask," I started. "Why are you single?"

Colton cleared his throat. "Got out of a relationship about a year ago."

"By got out...?"

He smiled. "She dumped me."

*I should send her flowers for putting him back on the market.*

"Why?"

Colton looked apprehensive about how I might react. "She was upset because I couldn't say those three little words."

"Oh."

"Oh." He nodded.

As I stared at him, a twinge of worry tightened my stomach. Obviously we were a far cry from the falling-in-love stage, but the idea that Colton might never be open to those deeper feelings had me suddenly insecure. What would be the point of diving headfirst into a new relationship if there was no potential for it to become something bigger?

"Why couldn't you say it?"

He scrubbed his face with his hands and, after a long pause, spoke in a vulnerable tone. "I came from a crappy family. My parents were both drunks, and my dad ran off on us when I was eight to go be with some lady and a kid of her own. Instant new family. He was a real asshole, though, so really, him leavin' was best." Colton took a slice of bread and dipped it into oil drizzled on a tiny plate. I got the impression it was because he didn't like talking about this, and the snack gave him something else to focus on. "My mom wasn't much better. Never said I love you or anything like that —but at least she stuck around." Colton took a bite of the bread.

"I'm sorry you went through that."

"Don't be. I'm fine. But sharin' my emotions wasn't part of my upbringing, so it wasn't natural for me to say it."

I was selfish for worrying about how his painful past might affect *me*—I knew I should be focused on how hard that must be for Colton —but I was unable to stop myself from asking, "Do you think you'll ever be able to say it to someone?"

His energy shifted, his gaze settling on me with certainty as his mouth softened into a smile. "Yeah," he said in a warm voice. "I think you can meet someone that feels completely different than anyone you've ever met." As the candlelight danced across his face, his hypnotic eyes rendered me mute.

*I wish I could reach across the table and touch that little v on his upper lip.*

"So, tell me more about you."

"What do you want to know?" I managed.

"Everything," he said. "Tell me about your parents."

As I recounted the basics of my life over the next several minutes, Colton studied me.

"My brother thinks I still judge my parents for divorcing," I admitted.

"Do you?"

"No," I said. "I don't think so," I added. "Maybe," I allowed. "I just think that… I know what they went through was horrific, and like fifty percent of marriages end in divorce, eighty percent for couples who have lost a child. But they loved each other. And if you really love each other, then no matter how big the problems you face are, I think…" I paused.

"True love should be able to overcome anything," Colton extrapolated.

*Exactly.* "Something like that." And I guess part of me was on a mission to prove it, because if love *wasn't* capable of conquering everything, then its meaning became diluted to nothing more than a temporary companionship. And a life without the magic of true love seemed a depressing shell of an existence.

"Your entrees," the waiter interrupted. As he set down each dish, he explained the way it was cooked, asked us if we needed anything more, and then left us to enjoy the meal.

"So after your dad left," I said. "Did you maintain a relationship with him?"

Colton's lips straightened. "No."

I speared a Brussels sprout with my fork. "Why?"

Colton tried to shrug away his obvious hurt, but his answer was heartbreakingly simple. "Because he didn't want one."

My parents weren't perfect, but they *wanted* me, and imagining what it would feel like if they didn't hurt too much to comprehend. I wanted to undo the pain in Colton's eyes. "Maybe in the future that'll change."

I could tell he found my optimism endearing. "Unfortunately, I'll never know. My dad is dead."

"Oh, god. I'm so sorry."

"Don't be," he said. "It was a long time ago. He was, uh…" Colton fidgeted with his fork. "He was murdered, actually."

I blinked. *"Murdered?"*

"Haven't thought about it in a while," Colton admitted, clearing his throat. "When it happened, I vowed to find the guy who did it, especially since no one was even arrested. I know my dad was an a-hole or whatever, but he was still my dad." He was quiet for a moment, his eyes glazing over. "Never did go after the guy." Another pause. "Some son I am."

Jessica had her life taken from her by an awful disease. I couldn't imagine how it would feel if someone had deliberately taken her life *and* gotten away with it.

"God, I'm so sorry."

I reached out and placed my hand over his, and I could tell the intimacy meant a great deal to him. In fact, it was a defining moment in our date. We held hands and silently stared at each other for so long that it was only when the waiter came to check on us that we remembered we hadn't finished eating.

We focused on our now-cool food but only got a few bites in before an urgent voice interrupted everyone's dining experience.

"Ladies and gentlemen, if I can have your attention please," a thin guy wearing a chef outfit shouted from the front of the restaurant.

Colton glanced in his direction, and then his eyes widened. "Jenna, get up."

"What?"

Colton sprang from his chair and grabbed both our coats, ushering me by my elbow towards a door marked *Emergency Exit* as the chef continued. "Please exit the building immediately. Use the stairwell, not the elevator, and do not run."

While most patrons seemed confused, Colton pulled me into a

concrete staircase and, just as we started our descent, the fire alarms sounded.

"How did you know?" I asked.

"Saw the smoke, and then I saw the look on his face," Colton said.

With each floor we passed, a crowd of people funneled into the stairwell as a blue flashing light and a honking sound filled the space. Some people were quiet, some a little frantic, but all I could do was count as we descended each flight as quickly as possible. Fourteen steps, a left turn, and another fourteen steps completed one floor. It took us twelve seconds to get down each flight, but it took even longer as more bodies packed the stairs. Even if I rounded down to ten seconds per flight, that was 950 seconds to get down ninety-five floors. Ten minutes equaled six hundred seconds, so that meant it'd take fifteen to twenty minutes to reach the bottom.

But there was no need to feel this worried. Giant buildings like these probably had sprinkler systems and other methods to extinguish or—worst case—slow the spread of a fire. An evacuation was probably just a better-safe-than-sorry procedure. Surely the fire wouldn't engulf the entire building.

*Hopefully.*

Colton held my hand, making sure he didn't lose me in the chaos of it all, while I watched the floors' number plates decline. From ninety to eighty-two, to sixty-seven, to thirty-three.

When we reached the ninth floor—my legs so fatigued I worried I'd fall—the beeping and the pulsing light stopped, and a deep male voice came over the speaker system.

"This is the Chicago Fire Department. A small fire has been extinguished. The restaurant on the ninety-fifth floor will remain closed, but it's safe to return to the rest of the building. Thank you."

People stilled.

Colton looked at me and squeezed my hand when he saw my legs quivering. "You okay?"

"I'm going to need to strengthen my quads if this is what it's like to dine in Chicago."

Colton smiled and looked up. "Think we should run back up the stairs and get the rest of our food to go?"

The fact that he could get me to laugh after something so scary was extraordinary.

"Come on," he said, wrapping his arm around my waist. "I'll take you home."

Outside, snowflakes danced through the frosty air and buildings' lights glowed against the black sky, creating a romantic backdrop for our walk home. Before I knew it, we were outside my apartment building, where I tried to memorize Colton's face, hoping I could bring it into my mind at will later on.

"So if rain on your wedding day is supposed to be good luck, what is fire on a first date?" Colton asked.

I noted the word *first* with glee.

"Memorable?"

To this, Colton grinned. "I assure you, every moment of my night with you has been as memorable as that fire."

*If he says things like that, I'm going to have a seriously hard time controlling my hormones around him.*

"I'd like to take you out again," Colton said. "Maybe next weekend I could take you to the Field Museum? And then the next, to the Shedd Aquarium, and eventually to every other place you want to see in this city."

I loved that he wanted to spend the next several weekends with me, because I couldn't imagine *not* seeing him as much as humanly possible. In fact, my heart stirred thinking about all the times I'd imagined what true love might feel like. As crazy as it seemed, I sensed it coming. It was like the emotional equivalent of your hairs standing up on the back of your neck—when you sense something big and powerful is imminent. "I'd like that."

The road was blanketed in light snow, so streetlights reflected off the cars and pavement, creating shadows of light as the "L" rumbled in the distance.

Colton brought his hand up and cupped my cheek. And as he stared at my lips, desire exploding in his eyes, the energy between our bodies magnetized, especially when he traced my mouth with this thumb.

It drove me crazy, having him this close, yet so far away. I needed to feel his lips on mine, to feel his chest against my body.

He took his time, though, delicately lifting my chin with his finger, and then he slowly parted his lips. Finally, he pressed his mouth to mine. I felt a rush of heat as he pulled the small of my back, pressing our bodies together. Twisting my fingers through his hair, I didn't think this moment could get any better, but when Colton opened his mouth and our soft tongues connected, an intoxicating desire overcame me.

We kissed for a long time, and it took a lot of strength to allow it to slow to its unwanted end. As our lips lightly grazed, the lobby door opened, and Stephen came out, glaring at us as he walked past.

IN THE WEEKS THAT FOLLOWED, COLTON AND I SAW EACH OTHER EVERY day. He took me out to all the places I wanted to see in the city, we took winter strolls around the lake to look at the stars, and we spent many nights snuggled on the couch watching movies.

Moments of our romance imprinted themselves into my memory. Like the night he gave me a framed photo of us in the Ledge, saying, "You seemed to be having a moment there, so I wanted you to have that memory forever." Or the time we frantically fanned the smoke alarms with towels, laughing as the burning smell of salmon lingered in the air from Colton's failed attempt to cook me dinner. The snowy March day I tossed a snow blob at his shoulder, inciting a snowball fight full of giggles. Him chasing me as I laughed, pretending not to be thrilled that he caught me around my waist and threw me over his shoulder in a fireman's grip. And other, more tender moments, like getting to know all his smiles: the smile when he thought I was cute, the one that made me feel like the only person on the planet, and the one that said he wanted me in *that way*. With each new memory, my heart melted into my body, and the rest of our lives became background noise with our love at the epicenter. Call it fate, call it what you want—I fell for him, hard and fast.

One night in June—six months after I'd moved to Chicago—we were on a leisurely stroll when Colton squeezed my hand and said, "Wait here."

With a boyish grin, he jogged out of sight. A minute later, I heard the clip-clop of the horse's footsteps before the white carriage came into view. Colton stood up in the open wagon and held up a huge bouquet of flowers.

"Jenna Christiansen!" he shouted. People turned to stare at him, and I covered my smile with my hand. "I'm madly in love with you!"

When the carriage stopped in front of me, Colton extended his hand and pulled me up.

"You're crazy," I said.

He grinned. "I figured if it's the first time I'm gonna say it to someone, I might as well go big or go home."

Colton kissed me and helped me sit down as the horses began to pull us forward.

"I've never felt this way about anyone," Colton said with such seriousness that it seemed the most important thing he'd ever spoken. "When I'm not with you, I'm wondering what you're doing, hopin' you're safe and happy. And then when I'm with you, I find myself watching you—when you're cooking or walking or sometimes even when you're sleeping. I've never been this happy before." And then he added again, in case I didn't hear it the first time, "I love you."

"I love you, too," I said, and I could tell by the tenderness in his gaze that it was the first time anyone had ever said it to him. I'd assumed his ex-girlfriend muttered those three words, but I guess not.

Colton stroked my cheek. "There's nothing I wouldn't do for you, Jenna. I want to give you everything you could ever want."

If I'd had any idea that this was what love felt like, I would have hunted to the ends of the earth for it all the days of my life.

He kissed me again—a passionate, profound kiss heightened by what we'd just said to each other—and then I sat and rested my head on his shoulder as the horse pulled us through the most romantic city in the world. I couldn't believe how lucky I was to have found him, and I couldn't wait for all the firsts that would follow: our first trip home, our first Thanksgiving, our first Christmas.

"I want to introduce you to my family," I said.

Colton kissed the top of my head. "I'd love that."

"And I want to meet your mom."

Colton tensed and was silent for several beats. "I don't know if that's such a good idea. My family isn't like yours."

"She's your mom."

"I don't want you gettin' hurt," he said.

"Why would I get hurt?"

He paused, his tone full of shame. "You'll see."

## 5

W e approached the front door of a tiny home on the south side of Chicago. Sitting in a row of houses on lots so small you could barely park a car between them, Colton's childhood home had light blue paint peeling off the siding, and its once-white windows were now a dingy gray. In the yard, where there should have been grass, there was dead overgrowth littered with buckets, an old grill covered in rust, and an upside-down garbage can, as well as bottles, boxes, and other debris.

When Colton knocked, a dog barked inside and a female voice yelled, "Shut up!"

A woman with Colton's eyes opened the door. She had blond hair, skin wrinkled beyond her years, hollow cheeks, and lanky arms that didn't look well-nourished. Wearing a ratty T-shirt and baggy jeans, she held a smudgy glass of dark liquid in one hand, and a cigarette sagged between her lips. With disdain and ambivalence, she looked from Colton to me and then walked back into the house without a word.

Colton had warned me she'd be like this. I'd hoped he'd been exaggerating, but if anything, he'd sugarcoated it. In that one moment, I felt the despair that a neglected child would've felt in her care, and it made me want to envelop Colton in my arms and rescue him from all of this.

Unfazed by his mother's behavior, Colton squatted down and greeted the dog who ran around in circles, shoving his face into any open hand, clearly deprived of attention. Like Colton had been as a kid. I tried to shake off the growing ache of pity, forcing a smile for Colton's sake.

"This must be Pita," I said, rubbing the dog's mangy fur.

"Best dog in the world." Colton smiled, kissed Pita's head, then talked baby talk to him.

"Pain In The Ass," his mom called out from over her shoulder, "is what that stands for. Damn thing's always gettin' into the trash. One of these days gonna throw the damn thing out on the street."

Poor Pita was oblivious to her nasty threat, happily trotting inside with us.

We entered the living room, which was even more run-down than the outside. It smelled of cigarettes and dog pee, and unlike other parents' homes, there wasn't a single picture of her kid. No trophies, no artwork or handprints or anything else that parents usually cherished over the years. The only photo in the entire space was a small frame containing a younger version of her and a guy with a brown, star-shaped birthmark on his cheek. I looked closer and realized, based on the age, that he had to be Colton's dad.

"Mom." There was hope in Colton's eyes that since this introduction was special to him, maybe it would be to her, as well. "This is Jenna."

His mom took a long pull of her smoke and—looking about as interested as someone meeting a broom—looked me up and down.

"It's good to meet you." I smiled, extending my hand. She ignored it, smirking as she blew out a puff of smoke. Embarrassment warmed my cheeks as I lowered my arm.

"Mom, please." Colton's voice was respectful.

She glared at him with animosity like, *Who do you think you are, walking into my house with your happily ever after when the man that I loved broke my heart? You really think this'll last?*

Being mean to me was one thing, but seeing how cruelly she looked at Colton made me wish I had the guts to dump her booze over her head.

Over the next hour, his mom didn't ask Colton about his first G.C. job or anything about his life at all. She talked about herself instead. She complained about work, about her boss, about her schedule, about the neighbor that kept throwing loud parties, about the city that kept bugging her with complaints about the lawn. On and on she went.

I tried to bring up Colton's job, but she steered the conversation back to herself, which disturbingly didn't seem to surprise Colton. He seemed conditioned to it. He prodded his mom along with questions like a skilled reporter, steering the conversation away from his dad leaving, time and time again.

I felt so bad for Colton, growing up in this house, with no one properly loving him. I might've had some tough parts to my child-hood, particularly in the earlier years when depression created an emotionally absent mother, but I was always loved. That I never doubted. My parents would do anything for Justin and me, and in fairness to my mom, she'd recently made progress with her depres-sion, and our relationship was better than it had ever been. I had a newfound respect for my parents after this experience with Colton's mother.

Exposing this intimate part of his life had to be one of the hardest things Colton had ever had to do. I could see the shame in his eyes, that he wished he had a family he'd be proud to show off to me, and the worry that I'd now think less of him. What he didn't realize was that seeing this made me feel closer to him. I was proud of him for overcoming his past, and I was excited to be the person who'd show him what love should be like.

The experience clearly opened wounds Colton had long ago tried to close because, on the ride home, he stared out the train's window in silence for several minutes. "If he hadn't died, he might've come back, and if he'd come back...she'd have been better."

I wish I knew what to say to erase the hurt in his eyes as he turned to look at me. "No one's ever loved me like you do. It's like I've been broken my whole life, but then you came along, and for the first time, I feel whole. You're the only thing I care about, Jenna," he said, as he brushed his fingers down my jaw. "Not my job, not my friends, just you. I can't live without you."

"I love you," I said.

By the beginning of August, I'd lived in Chicago for almost eight months, and my life seemed almost too good to be true. Things between Colton and me couldn't be better, I was making new friends at work, and I was on the verge of impressing my boss, which was critical before my first performance review.

As I got ready for work, the only dark cloud was a feeling that whatever Justin was going to tell me would be something I wasn't going to like. What was important enough that he had to say it in person, but not urgent enough to tell me yesterday when he'd called? Why make me wait until this morning?

It was a little after seven, and I was almost done getting ready, when I heard the knock earlier than expected. But when I opened the door, I was surprised to find it wasn't my brother; it was my neighbor, Stephen, who had never come by before. Things had been awkward between us for a long time, but that had eventually simmered into polite hellos. In our last few encounters, I sensed there was something he wanted to say to me, but before he'd had the chance, the elevator would open, or another neighbor would interrupt.

"Hey," Stephen said, throwing his thumb over his shoulder. "U-Haul's waiting for me. I just wanted to say goodbye."

"You're moving?"

"To L.A." He nodded. "To be near family."

"Oh," I said, confused that he felt the need to tell me this. "Good luck!" I don't know why he lingered. Did he want to apologize for being mean? Did he want an apology from *me* for "picking" Colton over him? Whatever his reason, he loitered for several uncomfortable seconds before finally walking away.

The encounter left me feeling uneasy, especially when another knock came only a few moments later. This time, though, it was Colton. *Thank goodness.*

"What a nice surprise!" I kissed him, but there was something off about him—and not just that his lips were tight. "I thought I wasn't going to see you until tonight?"

"Rain showers in Naperville put the roofing on hold." Colton glanced at the hall, then stared at me severely. "Saw Stephen on my way."

"Yeah," I said, hooking my final earring. "He stopped by this morning."

Colton's demeanor hardened. "*Excuse* me?"

I froze. He'd never taken that tone with me, nor had Colton ever looked at me like that, as if I'd done something diabolically wrong.

"That guy's been trying to get in your pants since the moment you met him, and you invited him into your place?"

I laughed, because, though I didn't get the joke—what kind of a weird sense of humor would find that funny?—he *had* to be joking.

His face reddened, and he talked through clenched teeth, as if my goal in life had been to offend him. "You think it's *funny* that I show up when you're not expecting me and catch some guy leaving your apartment?"

I blinked, offended and confused. *What is happening?* "What exactly are you insinuating?"

"Did he spend the night?"

"Are you kidding me?" I snapped. How dare he suggest something like that! It was disgusting, and he knew me better than that!

Colton jabbed a finger towards my face. "Did you guys see me coming?" he yelled. *Yelled!* "Is that why he bolted out of here so fast when I walked past him?"

"What has gotten into you?" This felt like an episode of *The Twilight Zone*, one where your boyfriend is replaced by a lookalike monster.

Colton slammed the door with such force it almost cracked the frame.

"Do *not* slam my door!" Seriously, what the *hell* was wrong with him?

He stepped forward, veins bulging in his neck. "Did you sleep with him?"

"Are you serious right now? How *dare* you talk to me like that! You're acting like a complete jealous lunatic!"

Something in his eyes snapped, and he lunged for me, grabbing my arm. I was in shock, angry and hurt all at the same time, but mostly I was terrified because he was out of control, and I had no idea what was about to happen. I demanded he let me go, and when he did, he pushed me, and my face hit the wall on my way to the ground.

It was only then that his demeanor suddenly changed back into the man I recognized.

But it was too late. The damage was done. I didn't want to hear his apology or anything else from him. I just wanted him to get the hell out of my goddamned apartment, so I forced him to leave.

And now, here I was, sobbing as I stared at the blood on my skin, struggling to digest the incomprehensible reality of what just happened. Every cell in my body burned in the inferno of betrayal, turning my heart into dust.

It was too excruciating to allow it to be real. This couldn't have happened. The love of my life—the person who made me feel like I was far more vital than oxygen itself—could not have done this.

*But he just did.*

I stared at my fridge, at all the brochures pinned to it that we'd collected during our romance, and then I marched over, ripped them down, and shoved them into the trashcan with such force, I tore the bag.

My cell phone buzzed with a text.

**Mom: Morning, sweetheart! How are you today?**

My lip quivered.

After the unfathomable tragedy Mom endured, I'd always felt obligated to keep myself safe, to protect her from another heartbreak.

I never imagined I might fail. *Until today.*

A new wave of tears flooded my eyes.

**Me: I'm great, Mom! I miss you. Xoxo.**

A knock made me jump.

If Justin saw me like this, he wouldn't stop asking questions until I told him what happened, and then he might go after Colton like a vigilante. I couldn't risk Justin getting hurt or arrested, and if I were being honest, it was too humiliating to tell him. As far as siblings go, Justin was the overachiever—his life well-planned and perfectly executed. He didn't stumble like I did. He'd never failed a class in college, he hadn't had to do an extra semester to make up the missed credits, and he'd never let something like this happen to him.

I raced to the bathroom mirror and gasped. A small amount of blood smeared across my nose and cheeks, and tears carried black mascara down my face. But worse, there was a red splotch on my cheekbone where my face had hit the wall.

The start of a bruise, with another on my arm.

*Crap.*

In the distance, a siren began to wail.

Another knock.

"Be right there!" I shouted, yanking a washcloth from the shower.

Was it even Justin? Or had Colton come back?

I frantically wet the cloth with soap and water, scrubbing away the crimson and black as fast as I could. The siren grew louder as I shoved a tissue up my nostril, noticing the blood drops on my shirt.

"Open up, Jen!" Justin insisted.

So it was Justin, after all…

"Just a sec!"

His spare key was supposed to be for emergencies only. He wouldn't use it, would he?

I ripped my shirt off on my way to the bedroom, grabbed a long-sleeve replacement, and put it on as quickly as possible. My hands were shaking, not helping with the buttons. Running back to the bathroom, I grabbed concealer. I had no experience covering up bruises, and to make matters worse, this one wasn't done forming yet.

"Jenna." Justin pounded. "Come on!"

When the siren grew louder still, my mind raced. Surely it wasn't headed here. How many people lived in this building? On this block? In this direction? Statistically, there was no way it was coming here.

But what if…? What if a neighbor heard something and called the cops? What if they showed up before I could get Justin out of here?

I blended the makeup as best I could, praying it would hide the mark all day.

Another knock, louder this time.

"Coming!" I stood back, looking at myself in the mirror. I looked okay. My eyes were a little puffy but otherwise good. I ran to the foyer, throwing the tissue from my nose into the trashcan just before I opened the door.

"The hell took so long? We're gonna be late," Justin said, looking at his watch. When he lifted his focus to me, his eyebrows furrowed. "What's wrong?"

"Nothing."

"You look like hell."

"Thanks a lot."

"Have you been crying?"

"No."

Justin looked at me skeptically, then looked past me into my apartment.

Which is when I realized that off to the side, my original blouse lay crumpled on the living room floor, the blood drops—though few—visible on top. I'd tossed it carelessly as I'd run to the bedroom. And the bloody tissue from my nose had missed the trash, lying on the kitchen floor, tiny but clear evidence.

6

**M**y cheek throbbed, warning me that beneath the concealer, the injury might be darkening. Worse, blood crawled down the inside of my nose, threatening to expose everything with its crimson evidence.

Justin returned his eyes to me. He reminded me of Dad—tall and fit, with sandy blond hair and blue eyes—but unlike Dad's relaxed appearance, Justin constructed his image with great care. His haircut was something you'd see in a salon look-book, and his perfectly pressed black pants were hemmed to the perfect length, so they didn't hang over his perfectly shined shoes. Blue tie, crisp navy shirt, no wrinkles.

I, on the other hand, looked like a twenty-three-year-old version of Mom, with green eyes and long, wavy brown hair.

"Your eyes are swollen," he said incredulously.

Great. Evidently his questions were going to take priority over whatever he'd come here to talk about.

"Well, I'm exhausted, and I don't feel well, okay?"

"You don't look sick, you look upset."

"Oh, sorry, was I supposed to take 'you look like hell' as a compliment?"

"What's wrong?" he insisted, firmer this time.

"Nothing." I gathered my keys and phone and slung my satchel over my shoulder. "You called me last night and told me there's something so important you wouldn't even tell me what it was over the phone. Cut to me being up half the night wondering what it could be, feeling like garbage today, then being told I look like crap. Guess I'm not in the best mood this morning."

I edged my way into the hallway and locked my door.

"That's a hell of a lot of attitude for missing some sleep," Justin said.

He searched my face for answers as we rode the elevator down, and the whole time, my nose's blood refused to surrender to my sniffing. Any second, it would spill above my lip. How in the world could I hide this for the entire fifteen-minute walk to work?

Part of me didn't want to. Part of me longed for his soothing arms to wrap around me, just as they had when we were kids trying to escape the echoes of Mom's sorrow.

The elevator opened with a ding.

No police officers were in the lobby, nor could I see any police vehicles just outside its doors, and the sirens had stopped. Which meant the sirens hadn't been coming for me. Thank God.

Justin looked at his watch. "Look, we need to hurry," he said. "Have a critical meeting first thing this morning that I *cannot* be late to."

If Justin had such an important meeting, why did he insist on walking me to work? It was completely out of his way. Justin worked at CME Group, Inc., which formed when the Chicago Mercantile Exchange purchased the Chicago Board of Trade. My place was near Millennium Park—eight blocks in the wrong direction.

"What kind of a meeting?"

We stepped outside, where the August sun assaulted my eyes and exposed Chicago.

The city seemed different today. The seventy-story skyscrapers that once excited me with their endless possibilities now encased me in their tunnel of steel, making me feel like a small, insignificant ant, and the action that once inspired me now felt chaotic. A river of cars clogged the streets, impatient drivers honked, and, as Chicago's "L" train—perched above the roads—rushed by, the metal-on-metal roar was so loud, it eclipsed all conversations. Down here, people swarmed the sidewalks like an insect infestation.

I felt like a fraud walking among them. I'd let eight months of lucky breaks go to my head, eager to tell anyone who asked how well things were going, as if I belonged on a pedestal. And then today, a sledgehammer obliterated the pedestal, and I fell in slow motion, crashing to the ground in disgrace.

What caused Colton to snap like that? Fear over another guy? How could he even think, for one microsecond, he had *anything* to worry about with Stephen or anyone else for that matter? He knew me better than that! And even if, in some alternate reality, he caught me in the *act* of cheating, there was absolutely no excuse to ever lay a hand on me. How *dare* he do that!

I didn't even recognize him; it was like he was possessed, and in that instant, all our breathless moments of falling madly in love were rewritten. Every time he'd professed his love for me, had there always been a monster lurking beneath the surface?

None of this made sense. In an ocean of confusion, the only thing I knew for sure was that Colton loved me with all his heart. But if he loved me, how could he have ever hurt me? You can't love someone and physically hurt them. Those two things cannot co-exist together.

Under the crushing weight of devastation, it wasn't just my heart that began to shatter; it was my *soul*. I could feel all my happiness, my laughter, my smiles, die in hopelessness. I needed to understand why it happened more than I needed oxygen to breathe because it was the only thing that had the power to take away this unrelenting, unbearable pain.

And there was only one human being who could explain this: Colton.

How sick was I to think that the only person who held the power to sew my heart back together was the very person who'd hurt me in the first place?

I was not this weak. I would *not* listen to anything Colton had to say because I was never going to talk to him again.

A horn bellowed.

Something squeezed my arm.

My body yanked backward.

"Jenna!" Justin snarled.

I'd stepped into the crosswalk while traffic was still flowing. Justin had grabbed me, pulled me back just in time.

"The hell is wrong with you?" he said.

I swallowed meekly. "Wasn't looking where I was going..."

"Yeah. Clearly," Justin said, releasing my arm. My brother studied me, suspicion mounting in his eyes. I wished I had a mirror to check if the bruise was getting worse. "What's with you today?"

*I'm breaking. I'm scared. I don't know what to do.* "I told you, I don't feel well."

The walk sign lit up, and people streamed around us like water working around a clogged drain.

"Come on," he said, hurrying me through the crosswalk.

If I had any hope of stopping his interrogation into my weirdness, I needed to act less weird. Pronto. And change the subject. "Are you going to tell me whatever it is you wanted to talk about?"

"So we're just going to pretend you weren't crying," Justin said.

My gut clenched.

It only *felt* like life would never be okay again, but logically, that wasn't true, and I had a lot to be grateful for. Look at all the breaks I'd gotten: the college scholarships, the jobs I landed to fill in the tuition cracks, the ability to move to the most magnificent city on earth. Plus, even though I wasn't ready to talk about what happened with Colton —maybe never would—Justin's presence comforted me in a way no one else could. Having him here meant more to me than it ever did before.

"I'm fine," I repeated. "And we're running out of time." My office was less than a half-block away.

He studied me, gauging if I was really okay. Crying and a lousy attitude were out of character for me, but it's not like I was hysterical, so after a few seconds, he sighed. "A role opened up at a New York firm," Justin said. "Francis Holdings. They're the sixth-largest investment firm in New York and growing. Supposed to be in the top three in the next five years. They have an opening for an investment banker with an upward track. I checked my email yesterday—they confirmed me for a phone interview this afternoon. If that goes well, they'll fly me in for a round of in-person interviews."

The sinkhole of emptiness swallowed me whole, and my stomach fell to my feet. I should be nothing but happy for him. Excited, even, that Justin might get what he'd always wanted—his dream career in New York. Especially since his career meant everything to him.

But evidently, I was selfish and weak. My brother was one of my best friends, and a role like this meant he would move eight hundred miles away, probably for good. And it couldn't be happening at a worse time. It was like falling into a deep chasm, and just when you slam to the bottom, quicksand swallows you. As you reach desperately for the hand above, it only waves goodbye.

"That's awesome!"

We arrived outside my office's building on West Wacker. It was a beautiful, thirty-story building of tan concrete and architectural columns sitting across from the Chicago River.

Justin checked his watch, seemingly displeased with having to cut his interrogation short. "How 'bout we do lunch?"

"Can't. Michael scheduled another one of his mandatory team-building things."

He studied me and gave me one last chance. "You sure everything's okay?"

No. I didn't even know how I could get through the day. "Yeah. Congrats on the interview! Let me know how it goes, okay?" I turned and walked towards the doors.

"Say hi to Zoey for me."

*Crap.*

My only hope of avoiding a breakdown at work was to push this morning's incident into the far corner of my brain, but my best friend would sense something was off with me. And Zoey was far more stubborn than Justin when it came to getting answers.

Answers she might demand during the next nine hours.

Since she was also my coworker.

Before the hour was up, I was going to punch someone in the face —something I'd never done before, but by god, I couldn't wait to do it now. Why the hell hadn't I defended myself this morning? The whole time Colton grabbed me and pushed me into the wall, I just stood there and let it happen.

And why did I call him a *jealous lunatic* in the first place? While nothing could ever justify Colton's actions, it was wrong and mean of me to call him a name. If I hadn't said those *two words*, would every-thing have turned out differently? Would his explosion have never happened—not today, not ever?

I stared at my phone, which I'd set on the bench off to the side, wondering what was going through *his* head right now, furious with the flip-flopping thoughts running through mine. *You better call me so beside yourself with worry that you* have *to see if I'm okay. No, don't you dare call me ever again. It would be cruel* not *to call me after what you did. It would be disgusting if you'd think I'd talk to you after what you did.* God, what was wrong with me?

At least I was at the gym now, with something more than just emails and PowerPoints to distract me from my relentless thoughts. Sticks and Stones—conveniently located in the building next door to our office—looked like it'd been recently remodeled, with the smell of black paint still lingering in the air and crisp red and black mats blanketing most of the cement floor. Unlike a typical gym, this one had punching bags, an open area, a big cage thing, and two boxing rings—all sorts of places to pound the anger right out of you. *Bring it on.*

Standing outside our group's designated boxing ring, which was currently empty, I yanked the red puffy gloves onto my hands while my boss, Michael, gave his *How Team Building Improves Productivity and Profits* speech. He then transitioned into how he'd chosen *this* event—a boxing lesson—and what we were supposed to learn from it, which, today, evidently included "problem solving skills, focus, and strategic thinking." Like learning how to beat people up would make us better marketing analysts.

I seriously couldn't wait to pound on someone, and as an added bonus, I could use this anger to my advantage—to *not* be the weakest link in our group for once. Since I started here, two team-building events preceded this one: a ropes course, where my fear of heights made me look like a trembling baby, and a paintball event, where I got shot in the first two seconds. Since Michael loved these events—and it was apparent that doing well was a ticket to play at this company—I was determined to *not* suck, to be better than at least *one* of my coworkers. Today, especially, I was *not* leaving here feeling defeated.

"This should be totally fun, right?" Emily said. With long red hair, Emily had remarkable features, the most incredible being her porcelain skin. I loved that while Emily's body was quite thick, and some women might hide it in baggy clothing, she didn't. In fact, she had the kind of confidence that every woman wished for, but only came to those who were born unimaginably beautiful and had experienced a lifetime of being treated exceptionally well as a result.

Emily stood on my side of the boxing ring, while our other coworkers—Steve, Harrison, and Zoey—stood fifteen feet away, outside the other end of the ring. I'd managed to avoid Zoey this morning since everyone was busy preparing to miss work to attend this, but now, I wouldn't be so lucky.

"Have you ever done this before?" I managed.

I discreetly checked the athletic shirt I'd changed into again to ensure it was still hiding the bruise. God, I was lucky that when I'd packed this outfit into my satchel last night I'd picked one with long sleeves. I'd almost gone with a short-sleeve one but had decided less skin was better for a work event. This shirt hid my arm's bruise entirely, and my makeup—which I'd touched up every hour—had done a damn good job of hiding the one on my face.

"My sorority took a self-defense class once," Emily said.

*Dang. That's one more class than I've had.*

"Holy crap." Emily's eyes grew as wide as her smile. I followed her line of sight to a guy who'd just walked through the front door. "Holy mother of hotness!"

Emily loved to talk about boys; it was her second-favorite hobby next to dating them.

I could imagine the wheels turning in her head; the guy was tall, with dark hair, tan skin, and a face that belonged on a men's magazine cover. His cotton shirt hugged the contours of his muscular body, and his black shorts hung on his hips, showcasing his flat stomach. He looked like Superman—Clark Kent minus the glasses, plus an attitude —strutting through the space. And as he did, a few gym members nudged each other and pointed as he made his way to the back. I heard muffled phrases that included things like, "That's *him*," and, "This Friday."

Bold Clark Kent didn't seem to notice any of it, or maybe he didn't care because he was too busy scanning the gym. When his gaze stumbled onto me, his eyes lingered.

"Hey!" Harrison interrupted. Walking around the ring to our side, Harrison Price had all-American good looks: blond, perfectly cut hair, and clothes that shouted he'd grown up with money. He stood with a relaxed posture that exhibited complete self-confidence—the spitting image of a CEO in the making. "You missed a great club on Saturday."

A pang hit my ribs when I thought of that night, an ache that intensified when I saw Zoey headed this way.

Everything about her was pretty. Her wavy black hair and her caramel-colored skin, but what most people noticed about Zoey were her lips. Thick and pouty, they were the kind you saw on toothpaste or lipstick commercials.

Her beauty was the first thing I noticed about her when the University of Illinois paired us as dormmates our freshman year. The second was her kindred spirit. It was her bleeding heart that cemented our unshakable bond, a bond that had strengthened during our tenure at college. And then unbelievable luck hit: When I graduated the semester after Zoey did—I had a semester to make up after flunking a class and changing my business focus to marketing—her office had an opening. In her department, no less. Landing a job where your best friend works? I mean, the odds of something like that have to be like winning the lottery. It had been totally amazing. Until a day like today, when she'd sense something was off and would ask me a zillion questions, and those questions had the potential to make me break down in front of everyone.

I clenched my fists inside my gloves, angry that I had to worry about any of this.

"Hi," I said to her, feigning a smile.

She let a purposeful pause pass before she begrudgingly said, "Hey."

I blinked. "Is everything okay?"

"Yeah, why wouldn't it be?" she muttered.

I couldn't think of why she'd be upset with me. The last time I'd seen her was Friday, and everything had been fine. Regardless, I seriously couldn't handle this today, and I didn't appreciate that her voice was laced with so much ice that even Harrison and Emily noticed, exchanging an uncomfortable glance. If I were upset with her, I'd totally give her the respect to pull her aside and talk about it privately.

"Is something wrong?" I asked, which was a stupid question. Obviously something was wrong, the question was what.

While I'd kept my voice discreet, she didn't afford me the same consideration. "I was going to ask you the same thing."

I blanched. "What do you mean?"

"I can tell something's upsetting you."

*Crap.* "Yeah. You seem mad at me."

"That's not it," Zoey challenged.

"So you're *not* mad at me?" I clarified.

"We can talk about it another time."

"So you *are* mad," I confirmed, irritated by her passive-aggressive evasiveness. "Why?"

But she crossed her arms, clearly having zero intention of telling me, which was beyond frustrating.

"Okay, listen up," some big dude said before I could press her further. He was dressed in all black and wore what looked like a ski mask made out of gym mats. "Name's Billy, and this is how it's going to work." He gave clipped instructions: He'd show us boxing moves, and then we'd each get into the ring and take a turn practicing them as everyone else watched from the sidelines.

Maybe when everyone else was distracted, I could pull Zoey aside and find out what her problem was. Hopefully I could manage it without opening myself up to an interrogation.

"Jenna!" my boss bellowed. "Why don't you go first?"

Was he making me go before everyone else because he knew I'd do the worst and that would make everyone else feel better by comparison? *Not today. So help me, for at least one brief moment, I am going to feel like a victor, not a victim.*

"You got this," Harrison whispered.

I attempted to enter the ropes the way the guy showed us—stepping one leg over, bending my body beneath the top rope, and then lifting the second leg over—but the universe is an a-hole. My back foot caught. I tried to defy gravity but only succeeded in flailing my arms like a deranged flightless bird, while my ankle rolled into a lump of tendons and dumped me to the ground.

*You have got to be kidding me.*

My boss put his hand to his forehead in embarrassment. "You okay?" he asked. I could *hear* his expectations of me lowering, and it pissed me off. Being athletic had nothing to do with being good at my job.

"I'm fine," I said. *Calm down, Jenna. Do not tell your boss off, and do not throw a tantrum. Just get back up.*

I tried, but my ankle betrayed me by wobbling.

"Take her to first aid," instructor dude bellowed, nodding to an area on the other side of the gym.

"I'm fine," I growled. I was going to punch that smirking jerk right in his face, and I was certainly not going to leave as the girl who'd injured herself before she'd even started.

"First aid," he repeated, leaving no room for arguments.

I tightened my jaw, furious. As badly as I wanted to argue, I wasn't going to create a bigger scene in front of my boss. I'd get checked out in first aid and then come *right* back.

Harrison helped me hobble in infuriated humiliation to the first aid area, where a guy emerged from a doorway.

The hot guy Emily had drooled over earlier. *Bold Clark Kent.*

"Put her here," he said, nodding to a chair in an office.

Somewhere under the clutter of disorganized piles of papers and a computer monitor was a desk, along with two visitor chairs and a mini fridge in the corner. The room smelled like cologne mixed with sweat, and thanks to the nearby weight bags, the sounds of grunts and thumps reverberated through the space.

After Harrison helped me sit down, Bold Clark Kent looked at me and asked, "What happened?"

*If Emily saw how light his green eyes are, she'd tear a ligament just to get his attention.*

"She hurt her ankle," Harrison said.

Bold Clark Kent glared at Harrison with a look that said, *She can't speak for herself?* "And you are?"

At six foot three, Bold Clark Kent towered over Harrison, who straightened his spine in a blatant attempt to look taller.

"Harrison *Price*." He emphasized his last name, since many people had heard of his well-known CEO father—a guy who'd been credited with saving a Fortune 500 from disaster—but Bold Clark Kent either didn't recognize the name or didn't care.

"Harrison, if you could give us a minute, I'll bring her back when we're done here." He didn't say it as a question. It was a dismissal, and Harrison scowled at him, unaccustomed to anyone other than Michael trying to tell him what to do. Some battle of testosterone raged on between them, jaws tight, eyes unblinking.

"It's fine," I assured Harrison, wanting to get this over with. My window of being allowed to punch someone in the face was quickly closing. "I'll be right there."

Harrison looked leery about leaving me alone with this guy, but after I gave him one last reassuring look, he reluctantly walked away.

"I'm fine," I reiterated to Bold Clark Kent. "That instructor *made* me come over here, but it was completely unnecessary. My ankle's already feeling a lot better."

"Company policy," he said. "Someone gets hurt, they get checked out."

"Yeah, well, I'd like to get back to my group," I said.

His emerald eyes met mine. "Stand up, please."

As I did, the pain in my ankle wasn't as bad as before, but it was enough to make me wince. "Are you a doctor?" Another stupid question; a doctor wouldn't linger in the back office of a gym.

"No. Sit back down," Bold Clark Kent commanded, squatting in front of me. "Now roll your ankle like this," he demonstrated with his hand, causing his shirtsleeve to inch up, allowing a tattoo to peek out. And the tops of his hands had scars on them as if perhaps they'd once been cut up with broken glass or something. "Good. Other way."

I complied. "See? It's fine."

He glanced back up to my face. "What's your name?"

*Great. He's probably going to write up an accident report. Girl hurts self in a matter of two seconds.* "Jenna Christiansen."

He nodded. "First time here?"

*Is it that obvious?* I nodded.

"What brings you in?"

"My boss likes to torture us with team-building events."

A ghost of a smile came across his face.

Why was he examining me if he wasn't a doctor? "Are you the owner?"

I expected him to say no—he couldn't be more than three or four years older than me—but he nodded.

"Damian Stone." *Stone.* As in Sticks and Stones.

"Is that why everyone's been staring at you?" Lesson one in inciting social awkwardness: blurt out any question that pops into your brain, even ones that make no sense. People didn't look at business owners with *holy crap* stares. Hell, people didn't even look at Harrison's big-shot father like that.

Damian Stone unleashed the power of his olive eyes on me. *I wonder if he really can throw lasers from them.* "You're with that corporate group," he deduced. "Work right next door, right?"

"Yeah." A ruckus of cheering drew my attention to the interior office window; it had a clear view of the ring my colleagues were in, who were clapping and having fun. Michael looked ecstatic with whatever'd just happened. And I was missing all of it. "Look," I said. "I need to get back and finish my turn."

"Don't think that's such a good idea."

I squeezed my hands into balls. Damian didn't appreciate how badly I needed to beat on someone. "If you're worried I'll get hurt, just tell the instructor to not break my bones."

Damian raised an eyebrow. "In the ring, there's no such thing as a controlled environment. Reflexes, bodies moving, always risky." Well, there's something to put on the marketing brochures. *Take our class— only mild chance of death.* "Besides. No offense, but I saw what happened, and my instructor didn't do this to you."

I frowned. "I don't want to leave my boss with the impression I'm some weakling who basically knocked myself out."

Damian stood up. "Need to put some ice on that ankle." Lesson two in inciting social awkwardness: don't even attempt to conceal your immense disappointment in front of a stranger, to the point of near tears. "For a few minutes," he reassured me. "Just to be safe." He went to the fridge's freezer and then squatted in front of me and draped a blue rectangle of frost around my ankle. Looking up beneath perfect, dark eyebrows, he asked, "This okay?"

"It's fine," I said, holding the ice pack.

Damian leaned back against his desk, and when he crossed his arms over his chest, his biceps spilled over his fists, trying to escape his shirtsleeves. "So why is impressing your boss so important?"

"Partly a career thing."

"And the other part?"

I swallowed over the tightness in my throat as every hurt from the last few hours lined up in a mental-torture succession. "I guess I needed something to go my way today."

He evaluated me as he chewed his cheek. "Bad day?"

*If by bad, you mean my entire life is imploding, yeah.* "You could say that." I looked out the office door at a couple of guys working a cylinder log. One guy held it still, as the other guy hit and kicked it repeatedly, getting to release all his anger on it. *Must be nice.* "That's probably one of the reasons people come here, right? To punch away frustration?"

He evaluated me. "Someone piss you off?"

*More like shattered my heart.* I repositioned the ice pack on my ankle. "No," I lied.

I could tell he didn't believe me, though. Maybe he'd heard his share of sob stories coming through his door—certainly anyone who liked to box must also like the release it provided. But Damian nodded, pretending to believe me, and that was something I appreciated.

He continued to check on my ankle. It struck me how the entire time he'd never laid a finger on me—instructing me to move my foot, looking at it for possible swelling. "Think your ankle will be okay," he said, taking the ice pack off. "But you really should stay out of the ring."

*Wonderful.* I had no gas in my tank left to argue, but I wasn't able to hide my despair at having nothing left to focus on but what lay ahead: heartbreaking decisions.

I drifted out of the office, but only made it four steps before I heard Damian sigh and call out, "Jab, uppercut."

I turned around and blinked. "What?" *Man, his eyes are intense.*

"You right or left-handed?"

"Right. Why?"

He nodded. "You want to impress your boss? Do a jab, uppercut. Left hand, jab." He demonstrated the move in slow motion. Evidently, a "jab" was what we common folk call a punch. "Immediately followed by the right hand, uppercut." In other words, a punch, aimed upward, landing beneath the chin. "Goal is to punch his head up and back."

"Up and back," I nodded, feeling a wave of excitement. I could do this. I had to do this. I'd go to bed tonight with the memory of kicking this boxing guy's ass, not being *that girl* on my apartment floor. "Thanks," I said.

Damian nodded, watching as I walked back to my coworkers, who were just wrapping up the last person.

"I'd like to go again," I declared.

The dude wearing the boxing garb looked at me, then to Damian, who nodded, and finally to my boss, who shrugged. I took my place in the ring—magically not injuring an appendage this time—and as I did, Damian came closer, crossing his arms over his chest. Watching me.

Giant boxing man scowled at me. "You gonna actually take a turn this time, or get hurt just thinking about it again?"

*Jerk.*

Warming up for the move that Damian showed me, I took a swing with my right arm, but the instructor blocked it with a smirk. I moved to the side and tried to punch him in his face, but again, the prick blocked it, almost laughing at me.

My eyes stung with fury because it was this morning all over again. He was bigger and stronger and thought he could treat me like discarded trash because of it. A fierce rage tightened every muscle in my body as I pretended to punch with my right hand, but instead threw a jab with my left. The thump of it smacking his face pad was almost as satisfying as the shock in his eyes, but just when he realized it connected, my uppercut came with the force of my entire wrath, hitting his chin so hard his facemask dislodged. His headgear *dislodged*! I'm sure it probably had more to do with the guy not tightening it enough or something, but man, I couldn't decide what was better: the stunned "whoa" from my boss or the asswad in front of me looking annoyed that little ol' me had just made him look bad.

Damian Stone's mouth curled into a smile.

I wanted to savor the moment, but before I had the chance, my cell phone rang. With Colton's ringtone.

## 8

All day I'd longed for five o'clock to come, but now that it was here, I dreaded going home. After dodging six of Colton's calls and failing to discover why Zoey was mad at me, I felt too mentally fried to handle my bastard of a brain that'd spin incessantly over one question all night: Did I really need closure with Colton as bad as I thought?

With movies, people say what comes *after* the final battle is what's most important; it's the resolution that ties up all the loose ends into a nice little bow, leaving the audience with a satisfying conclusion. Especially if it doesn't have a happy ending. Would I be able to walk away from our love story without another word, or did I need my emotionally satisfying conclusion?

The question knotted my heart with its thread as I stepped outside.

"Jenna?"

I turned, surprised.

"Damian?" Unlike a few hours ago, his dark hair was wet like he'd just showered, and he now donned gray shorts and a T-shirt. A T-shirt that left his arms bare, revealing tattoos that encased his muscles in gradient flames of orange and black. Something wrapped around the fire, but I couldn't make out what it was without blatantly staring.

*If Emily saw him like this, she'd forget how to speak.* She probably wouldn't even care why he was here.

Was this a random run-in—his work *was* next door—or had he been waiting for me? I sensed it was purposeful, but I couldn't imagine why.

"Hey," he said in a gruff voice, putting his hands into his pockets. "You did good earlier."

I forced a smile; I wasn't in the mood to talk, but I didn't have the heart to be rude after he'd helped me today. "Good instructions. The guy wasn't hurt, was he?"

"Only his ego. Billy bitched and moaned all afternoon over it."

Despite myself, I laughed. The shock of it was almost as severe as the immediate plummet back into sadness, making me question if I'd ever feel whole again. Would this sadness always be waiting in the wings to crush my chest?

"Did you impress your boss?" Damian asked.

I had to pull myself out of my head to answer. "Think so. Thanks again for the tips."

Damian nodded. "So, your ankle's still doing okay?"

Why did I get the sense there was a deeper meaning behind him asking? More importantly, why would he care?

"Totally fine," I assured. "And for the record, I'm not normally that clumsy."

"I'll take your word for it."

Again, I felt my mouth twitch. I appreciated that somehow, a stranger made me feel normal, if only for a moment. A stranger I might've passed on the street countless times, what with his work so close to mine. "How long have you owned the gym?"

He blew out a breath. "Couple years. Been going here since I was a teenager. Well, not to this exact location," he said, looking at the building. "Knew the owner back when it was a few miles south of here. When he retired a couple years ago, it seemed like a good opportunity."

"Seems like it." Based on how busy it had been today. "People pummeling each other must be a good business."

"Boss!" some guy shouted at Damian from thirty feet away. "We really gotta get going."

Damian nodded and turned his attention back to me. "Listen," he cleared his throat. "If you ever want to take some aggression out, you're welcome to come by any time. We've got bags, people, all sorts of things to punch."

Was that what this was? An invitation to spend time with him?

"I have a boyfriend," I announced. *Had. Had a boyfriend, Jenna. Past tense.* Even though we hadn't uttered the words *We're breaking up,* I figured tossing me into a wall conveyed the same thing.

When Damian furrowed his eyebrows, lava filled my cheeks. I shouldn't have presumed he was interested in me. Damian was way out of my league—a thousand times hotter than me and also more successful. A lot of guys in his position would probably point that out.

Instead, he politely said, "Okay... But you don't have to worry, that's not what I meant. I don't date."

*I don't date.* There was a loneliness in his voice, maybe even a broken heart behind it. A girlfriend who'd cheated on him, perhaps.

"Then why'd you…" I looked at his gym, wondering how long he'd been waiting for me out here, why he'd gone out of his way to extend an invitation.

"Let's just say I know how it feels to need an outlet," he said. "Seemed like you could use one."

"Boss!" the guy shouted, more urgently this time.

"I need to get going," Damian said.

And just as Damian stepped away, Harrison came outside.

"Was that the gym douchebag?" he asked. "What did he want?"

"He was just checking to make sure my ankle was okay and invited me to come back and try out his gym." Like any profitable business owner skilled at networking would do.

"Yeah, well, I found out who he really is, and you should stay away from him. The guy's dangerous."

Dangerous? I was about to ask him what he meant, but before I had the chance, my cell phone rang. Colton again.

Clearly, he had no intention of slowing his calls. If anything, their frequency might increase now that he knew I was off work.

Harrison saw the look on my face. "Everything okay?"

*No.* "Yeah. But I have to go."

I walked home in such emotional confusion that by the time I jammed my key into my front door, my head was spinning.

Someone rounded the corner behind me.

"Jenna."

I froze.

It was Colton.

## 9

"What are you doing here, Colton?"

It's remarkable how much information can be revealed without a single word spoken. His face had aged a thousand years since this morning. Dark circles lay beneath his swollen, bloodshot eyes like he'd been crying all day, and his six-foot frame stood hunched in shame. He looked...terrible. Like he was living in his own personal hell.

*Good.* He deserved to writhe in agony after what he did. I embraced my anger; it felt good. But when our eyes locked, I saw more suffering, remorse, and anguish than I'd ever seen in another human being. Clearly destroyed by what he'd done, there was a desperation to him, a fear that he'd sabotaged the only thing in his life that mattered to him: me.

"I've been so worried about you," he said in a pained voice. "Needed to see that you're okay."

I hated what he'd done. It was unforgivable, inexcusable, and yet, even though I didn't want to right now, I still loved him. I hated that I could still feel that love in this moment. It would be easier to despise him.

Fear plagued his face as he scanned my body and braced to ask the question that had clearly haunted him all day. "How badly did I hurt you?"

I opened my mouth, but no words came out. Because I didn't know what to say. The physical pain was nothing compared to the heartbreak. For nearly seven months, my life had been a dream-come-true, my future brighter than I ever imagined. Then, in the span of a few moments, it was all decimated.

Colton inched forward, holding my gaze as though asking for permission, and once he was a foot away, he brought his hand up to my cheek so slowly he must've thought I'd slap it away.

I was surprised I didn't feel repulsed by his touch, but it made me aware of how badly I missed him. Not the *him* that hurt me but the *him* that loved me, who had always made me feel like as long as I was with him, everything was going to be okay. I needed him to wrap his arms around me and whisper that it had been nothing more than a bad dream.

But this was excruciatingly real. With tormented eyes, Colton brushed my jawline with the backs of his fingers—a loving caress he'd done many times before. Only this time, it was laced with heartbreak because I knew I'd never feel his touch again. We'd never again hold each other, kiss, or snuggle, nor would we go ring shopping, see each other on our wedding day, or live happily ever after. I'd never again live in a world where he was still my everything.

It was all gone. And I was gutted.

When his touch reached my chin, he softly took it between his thumb and forefinger and tilted my injured cheek up to towards the light, nervous about what he'd find. No one else had noticed the mark, but no one else had specifically looked for it, either, so makeup had done its job concealing it. But the injury wasn't undetectable to this level of scrutiny. Clearly, he saw the bruise because he let out an anguished breath and his shoulders sank as if he'd been punched in the sternum. Like all day, he'd been replaying this morning in his mind, hoping that it wasn't nearly as bad as he thought, but seeing the indisputable evidence that he'd not only laid a hand on the woman he loved but also injured her was more than he could handle.

His lower lip trembled, and his eyes flooded with tears. I'd never seen him cry before. Not once, not even when he talked about his traumatic childhood. He was silent for several seconds, seeming to will the courage to continue his exam before finally tilting my face the other way. That side had no damage. He scrutinized it to be sure, and then glided his fingers down my arm and slowly picked up my hand.

I sensed the same dread from him as he hesitated, staring at my wrist, clearly hoping that he hadn't hurt me here too when he'd grabbed me. His pained eyes met mine—an unexpected moment of intimacy between us before he looked back down and slowly pushed the fabric of my shirt up to my elbow. When he saw my forearm's bruise, a whimper escaped his lips, and his body deflated.

I expected just to feel angry, but it also hurt seeing him hurt. Even after what he'd done, I wanted to make his grief go away. And yet, part of me was glad he was upset; it meant he cared and that he wasn't a monster. *How can I feel bad for him, when all I should feel is hate for him? How can I want to shove him away, when I want him to wrap his arm around me and love me, erasing those fleeting moments that changed our lives?* This was all so confusing.

"Are you hurt anywhere else?" he growled, clenching his fists.

"No."

He stepped away and held the back of his neck. "I can't believe I did this," he snarled. "You're everything to me. What the hell's wrong with me?"

I considered inviting him inside to talk. Out here we could get interrupted by a passerby, but I couldn't bring myself to let him into my apartment after what he'd done. Yet I couldn't walk away, either. If I had any hope of moving forward with my life—if that's what you could even call it, without him—I needed answers. Otherwise, this would haunt me for the rest of my life.

But I was afraid of the answers I might get. What if the reason it happened was because of *me*? What if there was something wrong with me? I'd never had a long-term boyfriend before. What if the first person who'd gotten close enough to see my most raw, imperfect soul —with all my faults—saw something ugly in me? Something so ugly it incited pure rage?

*What if I'm unlovable?*

"I was terrified of you this morning," I admitted. "I didn't even recognize you…"

His eyes held mine as he whispered shamefully, "I don't want you to be afraid of me."

I wished I was stronger, so these tears wouldn't form. "I thought you loved me."

Colton's eyes widened as if my statement was absurd. He stepped forward and cupped my face again, stroking my skin with his thumb. "I love you more than life itself."

My heart rejoiced, for his words were the medication I'd desperately needed: validation that he really did love me as much as I thought he did. But it also incited my anger, because it meant he'd ruined something *real*.

I jerked away from his touch.

"You completely lost control," I said. "I had no idea what to expect next or what you're capable of. I thought you were the person that would protect me from the outside world if it ever attacked me. I never dreamed you'd be the person I needed protection from."

My words landed a nuclear blow; he looked like he was going to be sick. Part of me felt vindicated by it, but part of me felt terrible that I could feel good about someone else's pain.

"What you did," I continued, "crossed an uncrossable line. I won't allow myself to be treated like that by anyone. Not even you."

"Jenna," he said. "I am so, so sorry." He looked down. "I don't even —" Colton held his temples, allowing the silence to stretch on as he fought back tears.

"I thought you were my true love, Colton. But I don't even know you. The man that I fell in love with would *never* hurt me in a million years."

I don't know what I expected him to say. But I desperately longed for his words to extinguish this burning pain, and I was angry that it wasn't happening.

If he had the power to break my heart, he had the responsibility to put it back together.

"Jenna," Colton said. "I swear on my life—I love you more than anything. I love you so much it overwhelms me," he said. "I've never let myself get this close to anyone before. Ever. Just the *thought* of losin' you made me completely panic."

"So, what, you love me so much you hurt me? Seriously?"

"No," he said, shaking his head. "I'm just...trying to explain. Not doing a good job of it."

No, he wasn't. "Why'd it happen, Colton? How could you have done that to me?"

The space around us was toxic—the air thick with sadness, with disappointment. I wrapped my arms around my aching stomach, the flames of hell licking the walls of my apartment complex, dragging me into its grip.

"There's no excuse for what I did."

"No. But I deserve an explanation." Maybe I'd been full of myself, thinking I deserved some epic love story. Perhaps this was the universe's karmic punishment for criticizing my parents' decision to divorce.

Judging by the look on his face, Colton had spent the day wondering how this could have happened. "You're the first person who ever *truly* loved me," Colton said. "My own parents never wanted me. I was an unplanned mistake. A drunken night they forgot to wear a condom, my dad used to say. Said that one night in the sack cost 'em years of bills and hell. Said he'd planned to open his own biker shop till I came along and ruined it for him. He'd threatened to leave a million times before he finally did." Colton shoved a hand through his hair, tears rolling down his cheeks. After a pause, he stared directly into my eyes. "I'm nothin', Jenna. A low-life loser. Even my mom thinks so. It's just a matter of time before you realize it and leave me."

A new wave of grief strangled my intestines. I had no idea Colton felt that way, but it made sense. Could I really expect him to walk out of his deplorable childhood unscathed? Being rejected by his mom and abandoned by his dad, insecurity had clearly taken root, manifesting into jealousy. For a person like Colton, maybe falling in love was like arming a child with a loaded rifle. Unable to control it, having no idea how to use it, yet given the full power of the weapon.

"You could have any guy you want. And what do I have to offer you? Money? I work construction—blue-collar. Stability? In construction, I have to run from one job to the next, just to make ends meet. I don't have a steady year-round paycheck with good benefits and bonuses. Success? Career track in construction ain't great right now. And I don't have the smarts or money to go to school or do something better. Family? I don't have that either." He paused. "I've got nothin' to offer you."

He cleared his throat. "Every day, I live in constant fear that one of these days, you're going to leave me for someone better. You deserve someone who can give you so much more than I can. So today, when I saw that guy leaving your place, I thought…" He looked at the floor—too ashamed to make eye contact.

"I'm sorry you went through that," I said gently. I really was. If I had known Colton was struggling like this, I would've have handled this morning differently. In hindsight, it must've felt like I was dismissing his biggest fear. "But if you're asking me to excuse—"

"I'm not," he said, still looking down. "What I did was unforgivable."

I hated that his childhood made him feel worthless. I hated that in his mind, he now had confirmation that he was a loser, unworthy of anyone's love. But I still couldn't get past this, even with all that. Even though my heart was begging me to throw my arms around him and forgive him, to let his kisses erase the tears and pain. To not let one awful morning undo seven months of heaven.

A morning that haunted him as he tentatively looked at me again. "Been going over it in my head all day, trying to figure out why it happened. I think it was like the perfect storm or whatever. Last week was the anniversary of my dad's murder. Ever since I introduced you to my mom, I've been angry about it again. Like seeing what it did to her ripped the scab off that wound. And then, on this job I'm doing, the financier is about to go bankrupt. Owner blames me for not going fast enough building the place. Said he was supposed to be open by now, gettin' revenue. The guy's been makin' calls to try to have me replaced. Then I came over here, and I felt like I was going to lose you to Stephen, and that made me panic."

"Panic? Colton, you didn't *yell*," I said. "You *hurt* me. I never thought in a million years that you'd ever do that." I shifted my weight to the other foot. "There's something inside you that I didn't know was there. Something that…"

"That isn't good enough," he said.

"That's not what I mean."

"Yes, you do," Colton added. "Even if you won't admit it."

"Don't try to flip the tables," I said. "I didn't accuse you of not being good enough, so stop putting words in my mouth!"

I didn't realize I was trembling until I noticed Colton looking at my hands with trepidation. I could see him fighting his instinct to envelop me in his arms.

"I'm sorry I grabbed you," Colton whispered.

"You didn't just grab me," I corrected. "You came at me. You pursued me, you grabbed my wrist and squeezed so hard I thought it was going to break. You slammed me into the wall."

I had bruises on my body. Actual bruises. I wasn't okay with that, and I wasn't okay with him thinking that I was okay with that.

Colton shook his head. "I can't believe I did this. I always knew I'd screw this up somehow."

In the long silence that passed, I twisted my fingers together, struggling with what I was about to say.

"Look, I'm really sorry about everything you've been through. But we can't just go back to the way we were. What happened changed everything. There's bound to be another time I make you angry or when you feel insecure about our relationship. I don't feel safe, and I don't trust you. Us." I choked the last part over tears because, in many ways, I felt like I was letting down the eight-year-old version of

Colton who deserved for someone—just *one* person—to not give up on him. "I can't be with you anymore."

I don't know why I felt shocked at my words or why panic pumped through my blood. I guess part of me was afraid that when I told him to leave and never talk to me again, he'd listen.

He brought his hands to his face, shaking his head. "Please don't say that."

The flames around me burned hotter, and inside, a thousand knives sliced me.

Colton fell to his knees, hung his head, and whimpered. My stomach wrenched at the sight of the fragile person in front of me. Each whimper was echoed with one of my own as I stood, frozen in disbelief that we could go from a romance as perfect as a picnic at sunset to this dark hell we were in now.

Colton crawled forward and pressed his forehead into my stomach as we both cried.

"I can't live without you," he sobbed. "You're the only good thing that's ever happened to me."

He might be bigger than me physically, but I was the one with all the power in this moment—the power to destroy him—and I hated it. I threaded my fingers through his hair, wanting to push him away and comfort him all at the same time.

This was so confusing. I thought it would feel black and white, but this was nothing but gray.

When you love someone, the love you have for them isn't a faucet you can just turn off. When you love him unconditionally, you still love him—even when he's done something terrible. With Colton brought to his knees, at my mercy, it wasn't as easy to give up on him as I thought.

"Please don't leave me. I'll get help, therapy, whatever it takes. Just, please, give me another chance. You're the only person who's ever believed in me, and I can't live with myself if I lose you."

My throat tightened as Colton stood up, tracing my jaw with the backs of his fingers.

"I don't think I can do this," I cried.

He took my face between his hands, breathing heavy, panicked breaths as I stared into his bloodshot eyes. Desperation overwhelmed him. "You're everything to me."

Seeing him unravel made it even harder to understand how hurting him like this was the right thing to do.

I looked down at my quivering limbs. There was no good answer here. No path that felt right. I couldn't imagine my life without him; his love was my oxygen. All the dreams we'd made together, the complete and utter happiness. It couldn't be just forgotten. But after what happened, how could we ever be "we" again?

"I swear to you, Jenna, this was a wakeup call for me. Please," Colton begged. "Please, don't give up on me. If I lose you, I don't know what I'll do. Please." He wept. As much as I didn't want to feel something when he did this, I did. My heart cracked open, and all the love I had for him flooded out, no matter how hard I tried to stop it. "I love you," he cried. "Please don't give up on me." He shook his head. "I can't live without you. You're my entire world. Don't have a family that gives a shit about me. Don't have some fancy career. You are all I have, and I can't go on if I don't have you. I'd rather die."

With every word, he drew me deeper into the darkness of confusion, the wind swirling around me, blurring my vision of what was right and what was wrong. What was the right choice, and what would be a mistake. My head pounded. No matter what happened, this decision would be something I'd dissect for the rest of my life because losing him wasn't just losing him now, it was losing the entire future I'd fallen in love with too. This all hurt so bad, I'd give anything to end the pain. Was it really possible to go back to the slice of heaven we had?

"It kills me that I hurt you," Colton said gently. "Please don't throw everything we have away. Give me the chance to earn your trust back. Please. Give us a chance."

He'd given me every reason to walk away, and yet I still wanted him. I wanted to get back to us. I wanted to go back to the life that made sense, the future that was full of color, the love that was so intense he was the epicenter of my universe. Could we get back there? Was it was worth at least trying?

"This is rock bottom for me, Jenna, I swear on my life it is. Please," he said, stroking my cheeks. "Please don't give up on me."

My lip shivered.

"Will you give us a chance?" he whispered.

## 10

Waiting for my answer, Colton stood before me, looking every part the broken bird he was—a product of neglect. The poor guy was this fragile because no one had ever believed in him or loved him the way humans need to be loved. Did he not, for once in his life, deserve a break? I felt this overwhelming sense of responsibility to show him that not everyone abandons you in life—even when you make mistakes. And I knew that if I didn't give him a second chance, no one ever would because no one would be willing to shoulder his demons. Colton would spend his life alone.

He pulled me to his chest, and I could feel him trying to savor it in case it was the last time he'd ever get to hold me. His body quivered with tears, but in his embrace, everything made sense.

What he did was wrong. But if this was the wakeup call he needed to realize he had underlying issues that needed attention, then maybe it was a blessing in disguise and we would really be okay—getting back everything we had. And as for this morning, Colton obviously didn't know he was capable of snapping like that, and now that he knew, he could fix it. We could work on it together. Hadn't I spent the last several years swearing true love could overcome anything? If anything could help Colton conquer his demons, it was our love. And if, after a valiant effort, it still didn't work, we'd be in no worse place than we were right now. *Right?* And at least then, for the rest of my life, I wouldn't question what might have been if I had at least tried.

"I love you," he whispered. "I'm so sorry I let you down."

He kissed my forehead, then searched my eyes. "I swear to you, Jenna, on my life. Nothing like this will ever happen again."

I hesitated, choosing my words carefully. "If you ever…. If this ever happens again, I won't even consider giving us another chance. I love you, Colton, but I'm not going to build a life with someone I'm afraid of."

"I wouldn't want you to." He searched my face with reserved hope. "Does this mean you'll give me another chance?"

I took a deep breath and met his pleading eyes. "Okay."

His eyes filled with tears. "Okay?"

I nodded and wiped the tears off his cheeks, unable to contain the euphoria I felt, for we were *us* again. My world made sense again. The pain was gone—in its place, hope, possibility, and, most of all, love. It wouldn't be easy to put this behind us, but I was willing to work hard at our relationship, and my new goal was to be the first person who showed him unconditional love. Once he truly accepted it, he'd stop feeling insecure and feel safe for the first time in his life.

His eyes drifted to my lips, and, after waiting to ensure I was okay with it, Colton slowly drew his mouth to mine. His lips were warm, familiar yet new, and we kissed as we never had before, as if we'd lost each other and had been searching day and night to find our way back home. We'd died, but by some miracle, we'd come back to life, and our bodies didn't want to take any of it for granted. Our hands were different, our groans were different, even the way he gently guided me through my door and into my apartment was different. His lips moved down my chin, my jaw, my neck with urgency, all the anger and worry and fighting released through blazing passion.

What had I been thinking almost throwing this away?

"I love you," he said, his breathless lips on my collarbone.

And I believed him.

.   .   .

I WOKE UP FEELING LIKE MYSELF AGAIN. BETTER, EVEN, LIKE THE LEAD vest that had trapped my breath broke free. In my living room, I picked up the framed photo of Colton and me standing on the Ledge at the Willis Tower and smiled, remembering how I'd almost let fear prevent me from having one of the best experiences of my life.

Getting ready for work, I hummed in the shower and sang along to music as I styled my hair. This time, covering the bruise on my cheek didn't come with a bucket of bad emotions.

When I finished, I opened the door to leave and was startled to find Colton leaning against the wall opposite my front door, holding stargazer lilies. They were my favorite flower—I loved how pink spread from the white arrow-shaped petals' center, like bleeding dye mixing with dark pink dots—and they were not easy to find. He must've gotten up early to find a florist open already.

"Morning," he smiled, handing me the bouquet and a coffee wrapped in a cardboard sleeve. "Mocha. Extra whip." Another favorite.

"Aren't you supposed to be at work?" I asked. He usually had to be at the job site—at least an hour's drive from here—by seven o'clock. It was now seven thirty, making him at least ninety minutes late and counting on the job that would make or break his career as a G.C.

"Wanted to see you," he said as if nothing else mattered. But there was something else in his eyes that told me there was more to his visit than flowers and coffee.

"Let me put these in some water," I hurried about my kitchen to take care of the lilies and then said apologetically, "I have to get to work."

"Can I walk with you?"

"Sure."

He smiled and didn't take his eyes off of me as I locked up. I felt bad for turning him away last night. I could tell he'd wanted the intimacy, and part of me did, too, especially with how passionate our kissing was. And I believed his promise that nothing violent would ever happen again. But trust took time, and I wasn't willing to rush it.

"Let me carry that," he said, taking my satchel as I locked up.

In the elevator, Colton nervously watched for my reaction as he put his hand into mine. When I wrapped my fingers around his, his posture relaxed.

Outside, the temperature was a perfect seventy degrees, with a light breeze dancing through the cloudless sky. The streets flowed like arteries pumping vehicles through the city's veins, while couples circulated around them, hand-in-hand. As we walked next to the river, I noticed how peaceful the water was. Like, after a storm, its energy had calmed and now lay in anticipation, ready for the adventures that a new day would bring.

"I'm gonna make us reservations at that Italian place you've been wanting to try," he said.

"For tonight?"

"If that's okay?" he asked.

"Sounds great."

"And I looked into that band you've been listening to all the time. They're coming to Rosemont in November. Bought us tickets."

I'd never given much thought to power in relationships, but it was apparent that in the wake of such a horrific fight, I held all of it. I got the sense that anything I'd ask for, he'd do. Everything I said mattered greatly, and, oddly enough, it was comforting. It gave me a sense of control, I think, when just yesterday everything felt so out of my control. Plus, being pursued like this was reminiscent of when we'd first started dating.

His increased affection continued on the rest of our walk, while, among other things, we discussed Colton's upcoming week. He'd have longer hours through Friday, to make up for being late today, and evidently missing all of yesterday—since he'd been too upset to go to work. Before we knew it, we'd crossed the final intersection and stopped in front of my building.

Colton seemed anxious about letting me go. As his thumb rubbed my hand, silent seconds ticked closer to a minute.

"Are you okay?" I asked.

He swallowed. "I barely slept last night." He rubbed the side of his face. "I kept worrying you'd wake up today and change your mind about giving me another chance."

"Is that why you're here?"

He tucked a loose strand of hair behind my ear and grazed my cheek with the backs of his fingers.

How could I convince him that the ground beneath our newly mended relationship was solid? "I love you, and I meant what I said. I want us to rebuild our relationship."

The whole time Colton studied my face and traced my lips with his thumb, he looked tormented. "I almost lost you."

I don't know why, but a sudden unease flooded me when I wondered what Colton would have done if he *had* lost me.

Before I could let the worry take root, Colton pressed his mouth to mine. Our kiss swelled with so much passion we eventually had to *force* ourselves to step back.

"I love you more than you'll ever understand," he said breathlessly. "In fact, there's something that I've been wantin' to ask you. I was gonna do it nicer than this, with candles. Flowers. But I can't wait another second. Jenna—"

"Morning!" Harrison interrupted, thirty feet away. To Harrison, his greeting was a friendly hello, but I could tell it meant something ominous to Colton. His face fell, and even though he tried to disguise it behind a smile, I could see the concern in his posture.

I knew I couldn't make his insecurities go away overnight, but what I hadn't realized until this moment was that the hill to accomplish that became much steeper because now, he had another reason to fear me leaving him: he'd hurt me. And even though I forgave him, he hadn't forgiven himself. He probably never would, though I hoped that didn't mean he'd live in constant fear of me changing my mind.

Colton looked up at the floor where I'd spend the next several hours with coworkers, which is when something must have occurred to him. Something troubling, based on the look in his eyes. He let a long silence pass, and then cleared his throat. "Was Zoey at work yesterday?"

I nodded.

"Does she, uh…" He rubbed his forehead. "Did you tell her?"

"No," I assured him. "She could tell something was wrong, but I didn't tell her."

His face grew apprehensive, several seconds passing as he digested this. "She'd hate me," he realized in a weak voice. "Everyone would."

He was right, and this brought a new problem to light. If anyone found out what he'd done, they wouldn't even try to understand. They'd cast him as an evil villain and never see him as a human again. Everything about who he was would cease to exist in their eyes—a thousand pages of his life's details blurred out, and that one moment of shame bolded and circled in red. A scarlet letter branded on his forehead.

It wasn't fair. Would any of us want to be identified by the worst mistake we'd ever made?

Colton and I had been through something that no one would understand. It was a secret we needed to protect at all costs, else the world would turn against us. "I'll never let anyone find out about what happened," I vowed.

Colton took a deep breath, trying to let go of his anxiety. "You're amazing, you know that?" He looked at me like he wanted to stare at me all day and never let me go. "I know this probably seems like a weird time to ask this, 'cause I know I have to win back your trust." He caressed my cheek. "From the moment you came into my life, my world changed. Before, there was nothin' but hurt, but now, I feel so happy when I'm with you. You're the most remarkable person I've ever met, and I can't imagine a single day of my life without you in it."

He sank to one knee, pulled a small box out of his back pocket, and opened it to reveal an engagement ring. One he must have bought some time ago. A single diamond sparkled in the sunlight atop a silver band.

I covered my mouth with my hand.

"I love you more than anything in this world, Jenna, and I can't imagine the rest of my life without you by my side. Don't answer me now," he caveated. "Just promise me you'll think about it when the time feels right?"

I didn't know what to say, what to feel. We had a lot of work to do on our relationship before I'd consider it, but I appreciated him recognizing that and still having the courage to profess his intentions.

I nodded. Of course I'd think about it whenever things went back to normal.

Colton stood up, and when he kissed me, I could feel how much the agony of almost losing me had made him cherish me that much more.

"I better let you get to work," he said.

Both of our mouths remained curled into a smile as I strolled towards the front doors.

"Jenna?" Colton asked.

I spun around.

"If Zoey asks you any questions about us"—his face fell into apprehension—"what are you going to tell her?"

I swallowed, realizing I had no idea. My best friend could spot me lying a mile away. But I couldn't tell her the truth, either. So how was I going to keep our secret?

"I don't know," I admitted.

## 11

"He proposed?" Zoey's eyes widened.

We sat at a high-top in Ace's—a bar steps away from our office, where two dozen tables were scattered near a line of bar stools that welcomed the Friday-night crowd.

I couldn't believe the weekend was here already and that Zoey had avoided me for three days. Her unprecedented silent treatment left me scared that our friendship might be in peril. A friendship that was too important to me to lose. I hoped that we'd finally be able to air out whatever was bothering her.

The only other time I'd seen her upset for this long was during our sophomore year when she'd discovered her dad had left her mom for another woman. Zoey expected he'd come to his senses and choose his family over his affair, but that first weekend he was supposed to spend with Zoey, he'd canceled to go on vacation with that other woman. He swore it was a simple miscommunication and that his new girlfriend supposedly didn't realize she'd booked the trip on the same weekend as Zoey's visit, but it didn't matter. He'd had a choice—go on vacation or be there for his daughter during the hardest time of her life—and he'd chosen wrong. The one man who was supposed to put her above everything had let her down. Leaving her heartbroken and furious.

This time, however, her anger was directed at me.

Zoey looked at my hand. "Where's the ring?"

I hesitated. "I told him I wanted to think about it."

She furrowed her eyebrows. "What?"

Zoey waited for me to explain myself, but I spotted our waiter heading towards us with our drinks. He passed by the front door just as it opened, and, to my utter disbelief, in walked Damian Stone.

His broad shoulders stretched out a dark gray T-shirt, and his five o'clock shadow made him look even more like *Badass Clark Kent*. Though it made no sense—I'd only met him that one day, and there's no way he could've known I'd be here—when he scanned the space and his gaze met mine, I got the impression he was looking for me.

Meanwhile, several people were looking at *him* with excitement dancing across their faces. I couldn't hear most of what people said over the boisterous bar, but I picked up *Finally* and *Tonight*.

"Here we go," our waiter said. He had a nose ring, and where ear piercings typically go, his ears' skin stretched around quarter-sized discs that reminded me of a tire on a rim. But most noticeable was how badly he reeked of weed. Which is probably why, as he attempted to take my wine off the tray, he spilled half of it—an apple-sized portion landing on my yellow shirt.

"Aw, man, sorry 'bout that." He stared at my boob. Like that would help.

I began blotting at the red wine as he walked away, but it wasn't doing any good; it looked like my right breast had exploded.

Zoey fanned her face with her hands, her forehead glistening. "So, when did he ask you?"

Damian took a seat at the bar.

"Tuesday."

It was at this moment that her demeanor changed from confused to offended. She scowled at me. "He asked you to marry him three days ago? And you didn't tell me until now?"

I stopped dabbing my shirt. "You didn't seem to be in the talking mood at work." And *she'd* been the one who refused to go out with me until tonight.

Zoey leaned forward. "We're supposed to be best friends, and when the biggest thing ever happens in your life, you don't tell me right away? Seriously?"

Whatever tiny fracture existed in our friendship had just cracked wide open. Zoey retreated into her chair, wrapping her arms around her stomach to cage me out. I could feel my best friend floating away from me, like driftwood taken by a current.

"We used to be so close," Zoey said, her eyes filled with deep-seated hurt. "We used to tell each other everything. I thought when you moved to Chicago, we'd hang out every night and we'd be inseparable. But as soon as you got here you found Colton and just left me on the side of the road. Like I don't even matter."

"Of course you matter."

"We never hang out anymore."

"We see each other every day at work," I said.

"So? We can make—what—small talk between meetings? It's not the same." As she took a sip of her drink, I could see her fighting tears.

I blinked, replaying the last few months in my head, realizing to some degree, she was right. I spent most of my time with Colton. "I'm sorry." I'd never meant to hurt her. "Is that what was bothering you on Monday?"

She offered a shrug in silent affirmation, which made complete sense. Saturday I was supposed to meet up with her and Harrison and Emily, but Colton wasn't feeling well. At the time, I thought I was doing the right thing—not making him go out when he felt sick and sparing my friends from catching his germs, but Zoey must have felt rejected. A better friend would have seen this coming. A better friend would have balanced boyfriend and friend time better in the first place.

She ran her hands through her hair and seemed to recalibrate after getting that off her chest. "So, what was bothering *you* on Monday?"

I'd practiced my answer this morning, but before I had the chance to deliver it, my phone rang. I could tell Zoey expected me to ignore it, what with us in the middle of our heart-to-heart. And normally, I would, but it was only five fifteen, and Justin never called during his office hours. Ever. As one ring turned to two, an uneasiness overcame me.

"Justin?"

"Where are you?" There was an undercurrent of anger in my brother's voice.

"With Zoey. Why?"

"Let me guess," he snarled. "At Ace's."

"Yeah. How'd you know that?"

"I'm on my way," he said. "Just stay there. Don't leave."

"Why? What's wrong?"

"I'll explain when I get there. Don't leave," he repeated. And then he hung up.

I stared at the phone. How did he know where I was? A good guess, maybe, since it was close to my work? But Ace's was one of a dozen bars on this block. And why was he so angry? There wasn't any way he'd figured out Colton had hurt me, had he? No. If he *had* suspected anything, he wouldn't have waited this many days to confront me about it.

"What's wrong?" Zoey asked.

I shook my head. "I'm not sure. But Justin's on his way."

"Here?" she asked. "Now?"

I nodded.

"Why?" Zoey seemed annoyed that our time was being cut short.

"He didn't say."

"Great. How long do we have until he gets here?"

"I don't know." His work was a ten-minute walk from here, but he might already be on his way.

Evidently, Zoey wasn't interested in my brother's mysterious phone call—only that the clock was now ticking to get the information out of me. She put her elbows on the table. "Why were you so upset Monday?"

As hard as it was, I had to push Justin's odd phone call out of my head, so I could focus on the words I'd rehearsed. The spotlight was officially on. I needed—more than anything—to keep our friendship glued together by navigating the sinkhole in front of me. Somehow, I needed to get Zoey off the scent of Colton's mistake. If she found out, I couldn't envision a future where she'd ever accept him, and if my best friend hated the man I loved, how would that work? How would our friendship not die?

Not to mention, if I divulged our secret, I'd be completely betraying Colton.

"Colton and I got into a fight," I hedged, adding, "and then Justin said he has an interview in New York, so he might leave." Could his interview have something to do with his anger? But that wouldn't explain how he suddenly became psychic, guessing my location.

She stared at me, her hope bruised. "That's it?"

"What do you mean?"

"That's all you're going to tell me?"

"What else do you want me to say?"

She let out a half-laugh, shaking her head. All the anger she'd just released returned. Exponentially. "Unbelievable."

"Why are you mad?"

"I thought you'd *want* to talk to me."

"I do."

"No," she snapped. "Actually talk. Like friends do."

"We are talking!"

I didn't realize how fragile the ground beneath our friendship was until it crumbled under the weight of each silent second.

"I'm such an idiot," she said, shaking her head. "I've been feeling… whatever…about our friendship, and I kept hoping that things would go back to normal, and when I saw how upset you were on Monday, I thought maybe you were going through something, and that would explain it, and we'd talk—like really talk—and you'd open to up to me."

"I am. I told you, Colton and I had a fight. What else am I supposed to say?"

She glared at me. "In the entire five years I've known you, I have never seen you like you were on Monday. You stared at your computer screen for over an hour without moving, and after the team-building thing, in the ladies' room, you didn't even notice when I came up next to you. You were staring at the water like a zombie. At first, I thought you were just spaced out, washing your hands, but when I came back later, you were in the same position. Something happened that shook you to your core," she said.

"It was a bad fight," I offered. "I was upset!"

"Did he cheat on you?"

"No, of course not."

"Then what made you act like that?"

I shook my head.

"Did something happen?" she pressed.

"Like what?" I asked, regretting it immediately. I stared at the door, worried Justin would walk in any moment.

"Did he threaten you?" she asked.

"No!"

"Did he hit you?"

"What?"

"Did he hit you?"

"No," I said. "Of course not!"

"So the bruise on your arm? That's not from him?"

"What bruise?"

"The one you accidentally showed earlier and then suspiciously yanked your sleeve back down."

"Why would you even *think* something like that?"

"Just answer the question."

I blinked. "I didn't realize when you invited me out tonight that you just wanted to interrogate me."

I stood up to leave.

"Oh my god," she said with wide eyes. The look on her face told me she'd only been fishing around, throwing darts trying to guess what could be going on. Clearly, she didn't expect this dart to hit the bullseye. "It *is* from Colton."

"No, it's not," I lied.

"I can see it in your eyes."

"You're wrong," I said, rummaging in my wallet for money.

Her demeanor softened from anger to concern. "How long has this been going on?"

I ignored her.

"Does Justin know?" She asked.

I put a ten on the table. "There's nothing to know."

"So, if I ask him?"

I glowered at her. "Are you threatening me?"

She leaned back. "If there really was nothing going on, you wouldn't have taken that as a threat."

*Damn.* I swam right into that trap. She outmaneuvered me just to get information. "I thought you were my friend."

"I *am* your friend," she pleaded, her tone empathetic now. "Please stay." She even put her hand on my arm, like our fighting had never happened. Judging by the look on her face, she figured the gap in our friendship finally had an explanation: a bad boyfriend. And I'd finally break down and confide in her that I'd been going through something, and—in her mind—that kind of intimate sharing would bring us back together.

I looked away from her hopeful eyes to the door, worried how long I had until Justin got here. Maybe I could head towards CME and intercept him. Or call him and tell him to meet me elsewhere. Could I ensure he never collided with Zoey and her allegations? My life felt like an out-of-control car. How hard it crashed, how much damage it did, was yet to be seen.

"Stay," Zoey urged, then after a long silence, she asked, "How many times has this happened?"

"You're way off base, Zoey."

"The cat's outta the bag, Jen."

No. It wasn't. And I wouldn't let it. "You're wrong."

"I care about you," she pleaded. "You can tell me what happened."

"Nothing."

But I could tell she didn't believe me. What the hell was I supposed to do now? She knew. Even without me telling her, she figured it out. Was there anything I could say to make her un-figure it out?

"I'm not an idiot, Jenna."

I shook my head, allowing several incriminating seconds to pass. "I'm not talking about this."

She let out a deep breath and, in a gentle tone, asked, "Are you okay? Like physically, do you need to go to a doctor or anything?"

"I'm fine."

Seriously. This was no big deal. If Zoey could understand just how non-big of a deal it was, she wouldn't be looking at me with those big, worried eyes.

I looked at the door, calculating my next move.

"Did you call the cops?" she asked.

"No," I said too quickly.

My half-confession weighed the air down. I took a deep breath, struggling to stop the string of yarn from unraveling.

"Why not?"

This was a pivotal moment. While I never wanted Zoey to find out what happened, I had to decide which was the lesser of two evils: acknowledge it and risk her hating Colton or continue to deny what she'd already deduced, pissing her off so much she might tell Justin— who might not only go after Colton but might also tell my parents. I had to pick the smarter option here.

Contain the damage. Tell her the bare minimum and hope to God I could control her.

"I don't want him to go to jail."

Her eyebrows creased. And it seemed like she was only now remembering the first part of our conversation, about his proposal, and that my answer wasn't a resounding no.

In disbelief, she accused, "You're thinking of taking him back."

I sat down and twisted my hands together. "We had a heart-to-heart. And we're both going to work on this."

She looked at me, mouth gaping, as if I'd just confessed I liked to clobber old ladies for fun.

"I don't understand."

"Understand what?"

"How can you love someone who abuses you?" she asked.

"He's not abusing me, Zoey. It was a one-time thing."

"You did *not* just say that. You're smarter than this."

"Abuse is when you're getting beaten, like on a regular basis or whatever. Colton didn't even hit me. And you didn't see how awful he felt about it."

"Of course he's going to say that! What else can he do? Say you deserved it?"

If she only knew what this was really like, she wouldn't judge.

"Look, I get that sometimes people have blinders on in relationships," she said. "But he hurt you. Physically. So why in the name of God would you even think of staying with him?"

"You're saying that like it's simple. It's not. It's complicated, Zoey. He went through horrible things in his childhood, and he's...broken inside. I love him, and I want to help him."

She glared at me. "He's manipulating you into staying with him, and you're letting it happen."

The more she hated him, the more I wanted to protect him. Everyone in his life had always turned on him, and now Zoey was too. "He's a human being who made a huge mistake."

"A mistake? Seriously, that's what you're calling it?"

"This one fight doesn't define our entire relationship," I said. "He loves me more than anything, and I love him. If you would just listen to me, maybe you would understand."

"I am listening to you. Are *you* listening to you? He *hurt* you. You think it won't happen again? It's like once a cheater always a cheater! How can you even love someone who's done something like that to you?"

That's when I realized her disgust wasn't directed at Colton, it was directed at me. Which hurt more than I could have imagined.

"After my dad left to be with his skank girlfriend, my mom would never have taken him back. Not in a million years, no matter how much he might've begged. She'd have had enough self-respect to kick him to the curb."

"I thought you'd at least try to understand my side of this," I said, my eyes welling.

She shook her head, angry, disgusted by me and my decisions.

"You're putting yourself in danger by staying with him. He could kill you, Jenna."

"You're overreacting."

"And what if I'm not? What if I'm right and you're wrong? What if you're in a lot more danger than you're willing to admit to yourself?"

"I'm not. I know what I'm doing."

"Well, don't come crying to me when he hurts you again," she snapped.

She stood up, took a ten out of her wallet, and threw it on the table.

"You're leaving?"

"It's bad enough that you drop me for a guy, but a guy who's treating you like crap? And you still pick him over me?"

"I'm not picking anybody. You're both important to me."

She began to walk away, but I put my hand on her arm. "Wait."

She stopped and looked at me, letting several seconds tick by.

Desperate to contain the damage, I asked, "You won't tell anyone, right?"

If she didn't look insulted before, she did now. She must have thought I'd suddenly realized she was right about everything, and that I'd stopped her from walking out so we could rebuild our friendship. Instead, I'd only asked about potential blowback.

"Maybe when you have to start lying for your boyfriend, that should be your first clue that something's wrong," she said. Then she stared at me, her eyes full of betrayal and judgment. "I'm not going to keep your dirty little secret, Jenna."

Zoey stormed out of the bar and out of our friendship.

I stared at the front door for what felt like an eternity, shell-shocked. Praying she'd come back.

At some point, an ambulance raced past.

But I thought nothing of it.

12

Sometimes you know something will be bad, but when it happens, it's even worse than you imagined. Any doubt that I needed to keep what happened with Colton a secret was obliterated by Zoey's reaction—a reaction that made me feel even more isolated than I did before. And frankly, it broke my heart. I thought Zoey loved me unconditionally, but she didn't even try to understand what I was going through. She judged, she criticized, and then she wrote me off like I was an idiot.

She *couldn't* be right. Colton becoming violent again wasn't a *certainty*, it was a possibility. An excruciating possibility that he'd never let happen because he loved me too much to lose me. *But what if Colton's actually sick—too sick for him to know it or for my love to fix it?* No. I couldn't let myself doubt him; he needed me to believe in him.

For a while, I sipped my drink over the balloon in my throat, hoping Zoey would return and apologize and tell me that even if she disagreed with me, she would still be my best friend. I watched people enter and leave, and pedestrians walk past the bar's glass wall. I watched rain begin to fall, which sounded like a distant waterfall that grew louder and softer as the doors opened and closed. But no Zoey.

And no Justin either, even though he'd made it sound like he'd be here forever ago. I called him, but it went straight to voicemail for the fourth time. Which was aggravating. If he'd got stuck at work or something, he could at least let me know. I really wanted to get the hell out of here.

Especially since Damian Stone kept glancing at me from his barstool, as if debating coming over.

**Where are you?** I texted Justin. *Again.*

And again, I obsessed over potential dominos. What if Zoey told Emily? Or Harrison? How could I ever be friends with them again if they knew? How could I work with them? What if word got around to Justin?

*Oh my god.* What if the reason Justin wasn't here yet was that Zoey had intercepted him?

I sprang from my chair, flew out the front door into the humidity of a hot shower, and frantically searched for any sign of them. The towers of steel and glass now sheened with water, thick clouds had darkened the sky in gradients of black and indigo, and the city's lamp-posts were a runway of yellow bubbles. Pedestrians peppered the sidewalks with multicolored umbrellas, and a river of white head-lights and red brake lights sat in a traffic jam, car wipers creating a rhythmic swoop-smack, swoop-smack sound. Justin was nowhere in sight.

What if she'd already told him?

I ambled back to my table inside, pulled out my compact, and double-checked that my concealer hadn't melted in the rain. It hadn't; the bruise was still hidden. But now I had another problem: Damian Stone left his post and approached me.

This was the last thing I needed. My mood was at a solid ten on the bitch-meter, and I didn't appreciate that he wasn't giving me space. You don't walk up to someone you barely know when they're visibly upset, you leave them alone and pretend not to notice.

"Hey," Damian said, holding a glass of water. Who comes to a bar to drink water? He put his hand into his pocket, his emerald eyes tight. It was weird how, with one pull of his eyebrows, he could go from looking intimidating to gentle. "You okay?"

Just hearing the question made my eyes sting. If Zoey told Justin, it would be the ultimate betrayal, and I'd never forgive her. Why did she think she knew everything? If you didn't fit into her perfect mold, she would what—abandon you? Was this the friendship I'd invested my whole heart in? "I'm fine."

A line appeared between his brows. "You've been crying."

Both days he'd met me, I was a hot mess. "I assure you, I'm normally a very happy person."

He stared at my miserable face. "If you say so."

Despite myself, I almost smiled. Almost.

He checked the time on his phone. "Let me drive you home."

I couldn't fathom why he'd care that I was upset. "No, thanks."

"My bike's around back."

*In this weather, unless they make motorcycles with roofs, that's not an enticing offer.* "I'm waiting for my brother."

"What time's he supposed to get here?"

"A while ago, actually." I'd give Justin five more minutes. That's it. Then I was going home, punching my pillow, sending Justin a super-annoyed text in ALL CAPS, and when Colton got done with work, I'd snuggle with him under a blanket. In his arms, it wouldn't feel like my life was spiraling out of control.

But how was I going to tell Colton I'd let Zoey discover his biggest mistake? *I failed him, just like I'd failed Zoey.*

Damian hesitated, and then sat down in the chair opposite of me.

"What are you doing?" I asked, annoyed.

"Sitting with you until your brother shows up."

"I'm not in the mood for company."

"Then pretend I'm not here."

"Let's not pretend, let's *for real* have you not here." I quipped. Which was rude. *I should put myself in social quarantine if this is how I acted in public.*

A smile flashed through Damian's eyes as if he found my attitude amusing. "See those guys over there?" he motioned towards a group of frat-types at the bar. "They think you're drunk." Damian's eyes settled onto the stain on my shirt, then my eyes swollen from crying. "Overheard them planning to come over here and take advantage of your vulnerability."

I couldn't decide if I found his gesture kind or insulting. I didn't need anyone to protect me, let alone some guy I didn't know. "Well, I appreciate your concern, but I can take care of myself."

"I know," Damian said. "Just looked like you weren't in the mood to deal with those idiots."

Who now looked like they had zero intention of coming over while the big, tattooed Damian Stone was sitting here. But while *they* looked intimidated by him, others—though they tried to hide it—still gaped at him.

Damian noticed me noticing them, and he looked curious if I knew why they were doing it. I didn't. In fact, there was a lot that wasn't making sense to me right now.

For example, if he didn't want to talk to those people, wasn't with anyone, and wasn't even drinking alcohol, "Why are you here?"

"Someone was supposed to meet me at the bar next door, before an event." Damian frowned at the glass door. The weather forecast called for a thirty percent chance of storms, but, as of a few minutes ago, that thirty percent became a hundred percent. Maybe that's why Justin was late. Taxis were sparse in lousy weather. "But I saw you walk in here, so..." He shrugged. "Told him to meet me here instead."

I blinked. "You *followed* me?" He didn't say, *of course not*. He just sat there, as if admitting to semi-stalking was inconsequential. "Why?"

He considered this. "Guess I wanted to see if you were doing better than you were on Monday."

Okay, I wasn't *that* distraught in his gym. "If this is some sort of a come-on or whatever, I have a boyfriend."

"You told me that already."

"Well, maybe it bears repeating."

He found my comment entertaining. "Your boyfriend has nothing to worry about. I don't date, remember?"

Yeah, well, try telling Colton that. Damian was just sitting there, oblivious to the complication he was adding to my already-crappy night. Talking to a guy at a bar—especially one as attractive as Damian

—would upset Colton, and we were in such a great place that I didn't want to ruin it. Especially not for some guy Harrison warned me about.

"My coworker said I should stay away from you."

"That so?"

"Said you're dangerous." I waited for Damian to flinch, to say Harrison's statement was ridiculous, but he looked neither surprised nor offended at the assessment.

"Let me guess." Damian's mouth curled up on one side. "It was the peacock, Harrington."

"Harrison," I corrected.

"*Price*," Damian accentuated the last name the way Harrison had.

I bit back my smirk. "Why would he say that?"

"I'm the type of guy you don't mess with. Let's just leave it at that."

"Um, how about we do the opposite of leaving it at that."

A trace of a smile came across his face, but I frowned. If he was going to sit here, he could at least explain some things. Like, for example, "Why have people been staring at you?"

But before he had a chance to react, my cell phone rang. I considered not answering it since it was a number I didn't recognize, but maybe Justin's cell phone died, and he'd had to borrow someone's to explain why he'd left me hanging for all of eternity.

"Hello?"

"Is this Jenna Christiansen?" a female voice asked.

"Yes."

"Is your brother Justin Christiansen?"

Cold electricity zapped my organs. "Yes."

"Ma'am, your brother was admitted to Northwestern's emergency department this evening."

*In case of emergency.* Justin mentioned listing me when I moved here. My mind spun. "Is he okay?"

Damian's eyebrows furrowed.

"He's sustained wounds to his head, chest, and arms, and was unconscious when paramedics arrived."

Paramedics? Unconscious? My head lightened into a helium

balloon, and the sounds of the bar diminished until it was just me and the woman on the other end of the line. My lifeline to Justin. "Is he going to be okay?"

"The doctors are with him now."

"What happened?"

"I'm...I'm not at liberty to say, but it would be best if you could get here as soon as you can."

"How badly is he hurt?"

"As I said, the doctors are with him now, and you should make your way over as quickly as possible."

Had he been hit by a car? If that was the case, wouldn't the hospital just tell me that? Why all the secrecy?

"I'm on my way." I hung up and grabbed my purse.

"Everything okay?" Damian asked.

But I didn't answer. I raced out the front door, into the chaos of tall buildings and backed up traffic and horns and car engines. And rain. Pouring rain.

How could buildings be so close together, and yet the hospital seem so far away? I spotted a cab thirty feet ahead and ran to it, but it was occupied. I couldn't see another, so I punched the hospital address into the ride app on my phone. The closest ride was at least twenty minutes out.

*Shit!*

A hand grabbed my shoulder. "What's wrong?"

"Hospital," was all I managed. "I need to get to the hospital."

The streetlight above Damian illuminated rain dripping down his cheeks and darkening his hair to black. He said something that sounded like *bike* and pulled me by my arm behind a building to a parking lot where he threw something onto my head. A helmet. It was too big, but it had a rain shield, so even though my breath felt hot inside, it was dry.

"Which hospital?" he shouted over the rain, which was now an official downpour. It smelled musty, and the sky opened with blasts of lightning, followed by thunder—a cannonball blasting into a metal wall, vibrating with anger.

"Northwestern."

He pointed to the back of his bike. For a second—just a brief one—I contemplated refusing the ride. Colton wouldn't like this. But then I got angry at myself for letting that thought delay me by even one second because this wasn't about Colton. It was about Justin.

I'd never been on a motorcycle before, but I threw my leg over quickly, underestimating its height. Unable to touch the ground, I began to fall to my right. Damian grabbed my shoulders, steadied me, then sat in front—helmetless—and told me to hang on tight. I grabbed the back of my seat.

"No." He grabbed my arms and pulled them around his waist. "Tight," he shouted over his shoulder.

And then the bike rumbled to a start with a deafening roar. We heaved forward, darted into traffic, and raced through the small space between cars. Usually, I'd be terrified of how Damian wove in and out of traffic at such dangerous speeds, in a storm no less. But we couldn't get to the hospital fast enough.

Damian blazed through a yellow stoplight and made a violent left turn, the bike leaning so hard I thought we'd slip from the rain and crash, but he somehow maneuvered it with skill. We plunged ahead through the line of red taillights for several blocks until a large building with an NW logo came into view.

When he stopped under the Emergency awning, I pulled the helmet off, tossed it at him, and charged through the doors.

13

"Why can't you tell me what's going on?" I demanded.

The lady sat at the desk with pointed glasses pushed to the tip of her nose, the answers surely sitting there on her computer screen, while behind me, people sat in the waiting room. The hospital's entrance was a contemporary space with white walls, gray leather chairs, and clean architecture lines, designed to try and make you forget that just beyond those walls, horrifically injured and sick people clung to life.

"Ma'am," she said curtly, "as I said, someone will be out to speak with you as soon as they're able."

"Can you at least tell me if he's okay?" Was that too much to ask?

"I'll tell them you're here. Now, if you don't mind, there's another waiting room around that corner. Follow the signs down the hall to the end. It'll be on your right."

"Why can't I sit in *this* waiting room?" Was she trying to send me to the bad-news area?

With restrained irritation, she said, "*This* room is for people waiting to be seen. *That* waiting room," she said, pointing towards the end of the hall, "is for people waiting for patients who are currently being treated."

Dripping wet, with my clothes glued to my skin, I ambled past *this* waiting room and headed down the linoleum-lined hallway of tragedy until I got to *that* waiting room, which was empty. The smaller space had twenty gray chairs positioned along two walls, faux hardwood floors, and two vending machines: one for drinks, one for snacks. *Not a good sign.* People in *this* waiting area must stay so long they need nourishment. The room smelled like Lysol, and on the far wall, rain pelted two oversized windows, blurring Chicago's lights. I looked out at the ominous sky blanketing the city from inside a building that was the center of heartbreak.

Heartbreak I needed to tell my parents about. I took my satchel off and fished out my phone, grateful it'd been buried deep enough that it didn't get wet. I hovered my fingers over Dad's number, wishing I didn't have to do this to him. He'd already been through too much. I remember hearing about how, when he held his firstborn child, Dad had been so overcome with love that he cried tears of joy and vowed he'd never let anything happen to her. But Dad couldn't protect her, and he cried again when he held his precious girl's five-year-old body as she took her last breath.

"Jenna?" Dad answered, obviously surprised I was calling him on a Friday night. I could picture him at his store right now, restocking the taller shelves, careful to rotate the product, so people never got expired food.

"Dad," I choked out, trying not to scare him more than I already had to. "Justin's in the hospital."

"What? What happened?"

I told him everything I knew.

"I'm on my way," Dad said. "I'll call your mother. Are you okay?"

I could feel myself unraveling, but he needed to drive safely for the next four hours, not get even more distracted worrying about me. "Yeah."

"Call me as soon as you know anything else, okay?"

I couldn't imagine what he must be going through, but I was glad he and Mom would be together so they wouldn't have to drive alone.

As soon as we hung up, I called Colton, but with each unanswered ring, my anxiety grew. Getting ahold of him was always hit or miss when he was at work, and he said he'd be there until eight. It was six forty-five, so with his job site an hour's drive from here, it would be nine o'clock, best case, before he was with me. I left him a voicemail, praying he'd get it right away, praying the storm would also hit Naperville, so his workday would end. Because I couldn't imagine spending the next two-plus hours without him.

I pulled up Zoey's number next, but my thumb hesitated. I'm sure if I called her for something like this, she'd set aside her anger and come. After all, over the years, she'd come home with me for spring breaks and we sometimes hung out as a group in Chicago, so she'd been around Justin many times. But once she got here, there'd be a huge, anxiety-inducing elephant in the room that would either cause us to sit in uncomfortable silence or reignite the fight we'd just had. I couldn't handle either scenario right now.

As I scrolled through my contacts, looking for who was next on my list, I became despondent. Sometimes, life gives you a barometer by which to measure things you don't often think about, and here I was, in a moment of crisis, with no friends to call. I wasn't close enough to Emily or Harrison to bring them into a family emergency, and my friendships in high school didn't stand the test of time.

I looked at the chairs—every one of them empty except for the one I sat down in—and I was sad and disappointed that I put myself in the position of feeling this alone. I should have made more of an effort to make more friends because facing something like this felt a lot scarier without anyone here.

Outside, rain assaulted the window, and in here, a ceiling vent wiggled a cobweb as ice-cold air flooded past it, penetrating my wet skin. But that's not what made me shiver: it was the squeaky shoes coming down the hallway, growing louder as they made their way to the waiting room to deliver the fate of my brother. When the man rounded the corner, I was shocked to discover it wasn't a doctor. It was a very wet Damian Stone.

"Hey," he said. His dark hair looked even more styled wet, like the rain had done it a favor.

"What are you doing here?" I asked.

"What kind of a dick would drop you off and leave you by yourself?"

Um, a normal one? "I appreciate the ride, but..." Any second, a doctor was going to walk in and give me news that could change my life forever. I didn't want some guy I barely knew having a front-row seat to the worst day of my life. "I just want to be alone."

Damian looked down the corridor. "I've done the hospital waiting thing. Trust me, it's not something anyone should go through alone."

Okay, I did *not* expect that.

Damian looked at my tangled mess of hair, wet clothes, the goose bumps on my legs, and the way my body wouldn't stop shivering. "You look awful."

"Gee, thanks." Seriously, his conversational skills. He was literally dripping on the floor, far wetter and more uncomfortable than I was. He didn't need to endure that discomfort—not when it would only cause more problems. "My boyfriend wouldn't be okay with you staying," I pressed.

"Why's that?" he said with ambivalence.

"Because you're a guy." Obviously. And not just any guy. A super handsome guy, who—draped in wet fabric that clung to the contours of his muscles—now looked every part a sexy magazine cover model.

Damian rolled his eyes. "Thought we covered this already."

He didn't understand. If Colton found out I was here with Damian, he'd be seriously pissed. He was already going to be upset when he found out I'd let Zoey discover what happened. The last thing I wanted to do was make him even angrier.

"Maybe you should prioritize your needs over his jealousy."

I balled my hands into fists of frustration. Damian studied me, probably worried I was having a nervous breakdown or something. "Your boyfriend has nothing to worry about," he reassured me gently. "Is he on his way?"

I shook my head. "I left him a message, but his work's an hour away. My parents are coming, but it's a four-hour drive in good weather."

Damian pulled his phone out of his pocket and frowned at the time. I expected him to leave—this was a perfect excuse, realizing how long of a wait I might have—but he stared at my trembling arms, and then punched something into his screen, "I'll leave as soon as someone else gets here."

"I don't need you to stay here. I'll be fine alone." And I didn't have the energy to argue with Damian Stone, who was frustratingly ignoring me. I had more important things to focus on as I began pacing.

There were probably lots of reasons one could wind up with the types of injuries Justin had. A fall down the stairs, a minor run-in with a moving vehicle. And the lady on the phone hadn't said anything like *lungs* or *brain*. So it probably wasn't that bad. But then why would she say, *get here as soon as you can?* And if this was the waiting room for all the families of patients being treated, why weren't any other people here? What if this wasn't the waiting room; what if this was the family-notification room? "If he was going to be okay, they'd have told me by now, wouldn't they?"

I imagine at this moment, most people would assure me Justin would be fine, even though they had no business making such a baseless claim. But once someone makes a promise they have no authority to make, they lose all credibility to comfort you. Their words become hollow, meaningless fluff, and you can no longer decipher between what they truly think and what they'll say to console you. I appreciated that Damian made no such promises.

Instead, he asked, "Mind if I ask who you're here for?"

I blinked. "My brother, Justin." My esophagus constricted. I felt the tears coming again, so I began to chew on my thumbnail. "What if Justin's *not* okay?" I worried aloud. "What if he's dead and they just haven't told me? Or what if he lives, but he's permanently injured or blind or mentally impaired or needs to be in a nursing home?"

"You're panicking."

"You don't understand. He *has* to be okay. My parents couldn't handle it if something happened to him. They've already lost my sister, and it gutted them."

I saw something pass through Damian's eyes that I couldn't place. An emotion, I think, that he was trying to conceal. His phone buzzed again, and again, he ignored it, too preoccupied with scrutinizing me.

"You need to eat. You look like you're going into shock or something." Damian walked to the vending machines. He pulled a wet dollar out of his pocket, put it into the slot, and watched the machine suck it partly in with a winding noise, then spit it out. He flattened the bill and tried again. Same outcome. After three more tries, he walked down the hall and came back a minute later. With dry money he must've exchanged with someone, he successfully retrieved water and a bag of peanuts with a cartoon nut on the front.

"Here," he said, holding them out. "Eat."

"I'm not hungry."

"Eat," he insisted.

"I can't eat when I'm upset. My stomach feels sick."

"Eat anyway. Or you'll wind up in a hospital bed of your own."

I ignored him and stared outside the window at the massive city before me, remembering how excited Justin had been to move here. "He's the one who inspired me to think bigger than our small town." I sniffled. "Encouraged me to go to college." To him, money meant security—paying for things outright rather than taking loans so that no one controlled you, owning your home so no one could take it from you like the bank almost did to us. His desire for financial independence was the driving force behind him becoming an investment banker.

"He has to be okay," I repeated.

I stared at the sheets of rain washing over the city, remembering one night when I was six and a powerful thunderstorm hit. As flashes of light erupted in the dark sky and thunder bombed the house and rattled the windows, I ran out of my bedroom but stopped when I reached Mom's door because, even over the storm, I could hear her weeping. I glanced back at my bedroom, at the broken picture frame the storm had knocked over, and then I ran to Justin's room. Instead of yelling or calling me a baby, he simply looked at the window, scooted over, and tapped the spot next to him. Letting me crawl into his bed. It was only there that I was finally able to sleep, and from that point forward, any time I was too scared of a storm, it was Justin's room where I sought refuge.

I blinked away the memory, unsure what was making my shivering worse: the freezing air conditioning against my drenched body or my stress. Whatever it was, Damian seemed to notice. He stared at my quivering limbs as he bit his lip, and then, out of nowhere, he left. I was surprised that he didn't at least say goodbye, but even more surprised how much emptier the room felt in his absence.

Suddenly, I wasn't so sure I could handle this storm alone.

I tried calling Colton again and again, left another voicemail pleading with him to call me as soon as possible. I texted him. Then I paced for several more minutes, listening to the storm intensify. *God, I hope Mom and Dad get here safe.*

A girl with chocolate brown hair who appeared to be my age walked into the waiting room and plunked into one of the seats. She made eye contact with me, her eyes bloodshot, and she swallowed harshly, as if fighting back a fresh tsunami of tears. But she shoved her face into her hands, and her shoulders shook. It hurt, seeing another human suffering through what must be her own nightmare.

"Sorry. They should have a dedicated crying room where we can break down in private." She wiped her cheeks. "I'm trying to hold it together, but it's hard."

"I hope whoever you're here for makes it out okay," I said.

She stared at her hands. "He will this time, but…"

*This time.* I wondered what that meant. Was her loved one sick?

There was something else in her tone, though, something that told me there was a lot more to it than that.

"Fallon?" A nurse appeared.

*Fallon.* What a unique name.

Fallon wiped tears from her cheeks again and straightened her back before standing up. She offered me an empathetic look before following the nurse out of the room.

Leaving me alone once more.

"Here."

Damian reentered the waiting room with a hospital gift shop bag. He pulled out a purple sweatshirt with the big word *CHICAGO* in capital letters set in front of the skyline. "They didn't have pants or whatever."

"You bought me a sweatshirt?"

"Night's gonna be long enough without freezing to death from your wet clothes."

Damian ripped the tag off and handed me the shirt.

What a simple solution—one I should've thought of myself, yet never would have because my mind was over capacity worrying about Justin. I guess that's the power of not being alone at a time like this. While you're preoccupied thinking about your loved one, the other person can take the role of making sure your needs are being addressed. *Who played that role for Damian when he went through this?*

"Thanks," I managed. I grabbed my satchel and went into the bathroom, peeled my blouse off, and blotted myself down with napkins. I put the sweatshirt on, so incredibly grateful for the warm, dry cotton wrapped around my torso. I stared at the shirt's purple skyline, feeling the warmth move past my skin. This was exceptionally thoughtful of Damian, who was still stuck in dripping-wet clothes, and it was incredibly kind of him to drive me here. Something he'd done without hesitation.

Now that I'd changed, I decided cleaning myself up would distract me for a couple more minutes. I blotted my legs and skirt, and then, as I ran a brush through my hair, I startled when I saw my reflection.

The bruise on my cheek was slightly visible. The rain had washed away some of the concealer, so I grabbed my makeup from my bag and applied it until I was confident Mom and Dad would never see the mark.

When I finished, I returned to the waiting room, where paranoia washed over me as Damian's eyes flitted to my cheekbone. But it happened so fast I couldn't be sure.

He sat in the far chair with his elbows on his knees, ignoring his buzzing phone as he bounced his leg in obvious anxiety. Even though he was trying to hide it, I could see how hard it was for him to be here.

Which made me wonder... "Do you mind if I ask who *you* waited for at the hospital?"

This time, when Damian looked at me, it was the type of stare that soaks past a person's face and into their core. He held it there for three breaths before locking his hands behind his neck and looking at the floor. "My dad and sister. Car wreck. But my situation was...different."

Different. Something awful behind that word. Judging by his brokenhearted tone, maybe Damian didn't leave the hospital with his dad or sister alive.

"When?"

Sometimes the walls we put up are instantly shattered, tragedy pushing social norms to the side. Normally, you don't talk about your life's hardest moments, particularly with someone you barely know. But when life and death hang in the balance, nothing like that matters and one soul shares with another.

Damian scrubbed his hands over his face, and released an exhausted sigh. "I was eight."

Eight. Old enough to understand, but not old enough to cope with the emotions of a tragedy.

"Were *you* in the accident?" I looked at the scars on his hands.

He was silent for long enough to allow two separate nurses to amble past the room. "We all were," he said in a low voice. "Me, my mom, my dad, and my little sister. She was six. We were on our way to my baseball championship when I realized I left my lucky bat at home. Made us go back for it." Damian rubbed his hands together, his eyes unfocused. "If we hadn't, we'd never have been T-boned at that light."

*Good God.*

"Were you hurt?"

He shook his head. "I was the only one who *wasn't* hurt bad."

And then he must've been at the hospital waiting to hear the fate of his family. Evidently alone. I couldn't imagine going through that as an adult, let alone as a kid.

He cleared his throat. "My mom suffered a bad concussion, broken bones. But my dad and sister," he continued, "didn't make it." There was something else in his voice, something else he wasn't saying.

My heart broke for him.

"I'm sorry," I said, suddenly recognizing just how big a sacrifice Damian had made for me tonight. He'd put himself in a place that drudged up horrible memories just to make sure *I* wasn't alone as I waited for possibly life-shattering news.

He looked at the floor. "It was a long time ago." And yet, the anguish was still very much here. And I got the impression the accident was only the beginning of his story...

*What happened after he left that hospital?*

Damian's cell phone buzzed again, and this time, he pulled it out in annoyance and typed something to whoever was trying to get ahold of him. I suddenly remembered he was supposed to meet someone earlier. "You had some event tonight."

He didn't deny it.

"What kind of event?"

He looked at the rain hitting the window, and then wiped his palms on his thighs. "A fight."

"Like tickets to a boxing match?"

He leaned forward in his chair and put his elbows back on his knees. "MMA."

I'd seen mixed martial arts a couple of times when flipping through channels. It was a brutal type of fighting. "Were the tickets expensive?" He'd made it sound more important earlier.

Damian looked up at me without lifting his head. "I wasn't attending, I was participating." He stared at me, waiting for my too-slow brain to comprehend what he'd meant.

"Attending. As in...you're *in* the fight?"

Suddenly the muscles encasing his shoulders, arms, and back took on a whole new meaning. Not just powerful but well trained. Able to hurt—hell, maybe even kill—people in more ways than I'd probably ever know. Making him every part as dangerous as Harrison had warned.

Damian kept his eyes fixed on me, gauging my reaction.

"That's why those people were staring at you at the bar."

He shrugged as if it was no big deal. "I was pretty well-known in the local circuit."

"Was?"

He cracked his knuckles. I sensed he didn't usually talk about this, but after a minute, he cleared his throat. "Six months ago I was in the cage. Guy was good. Got me into a guillotine choke," he said as if I knew what that meant. "Took me a while to get out of it, so I was lightheaded. Didn't block his uppercut. That's all I remember."

"You were hurt."

"I'm told he landed a series of punches to the head."

*Hurt bad, then.* "And you haven't fought since?"

"Put me out of commission for a while."

Wait. Did that mean… "Tonight was your first fight back?"

He nodded.

*A comeback fight?* "Isn't that kind of a big deal?"

No denial.

"Then what are you doing here? You need to go!"

"Fight started ten minutes ago," he said.

My mouth gaped open. "I don't understand. Why would you miss that?"

Damian shook his hair out, letting the last remaining water droplets fall to the ground. "Seemed like life was giving you one hell of a beating." And what *he'd* gone through must've made him feel so broken that he didn't want another human to go through it alone. Not even a stranger.

I felt a rush of empathy for Damian, empathy that heightened when I thought back to him waiting outside my office. Maybe that was the real reason he'd checked on me that day. Maybe after what he'd been through, he could tell the difference between someone having a bad day and someone going through something awful. Because of his past, he cared enough to want to help. That day…

And today. And even though I'd fought it at first, I was glad he'd stayed. "Thank you," I said. But before I could add anything else, my phone rang.

It was Colton.

I delayed answering, taken aback by the unexpected moment that had just passed between Damian and me. It was surprisingly difficult to let it end.

"Jenna?" Colton's distressed tone was evidence he'd heard my frantic voicemail. "Are you okay?" I explained everything. "Holy shit," he sighed. "I'm so sorry. My freaking battery died, and I didn't get your voicemail until I plugged my cell into my truck. Which hospital are you at?"

Hearing his voice, knowing that he'd be here soon, chipped away at my anxiety.

"Northwestern."

"Alright. It'll take me about an hour to get there. You there alone?"

I looked at Damian, who looked puzzled by my abrupt trepidation. "No."

Colton paused. "Who's with you?"

How could I explain who Damian was? A guy I met at a gym who then sat with me at a bar? That was going to sound so suspicious to him. With only a second to think, I settled on, "A guy named Damian drove me."

In the unnerving silence, I sensed Colton's tension.

"Why in the hell are you there with another guy!"

Colton's shriek was so loud I jerked the phone away from my ear for a second.

"I'm on my way," Colton growled, and then, without saying good-bye, he ended the call.

My ribs shrank, shocked he'd hung up on me. He'd never done that before.

Damian stared at me beneath rigid eyebrows and with restrained anger asked, "He always yell at you like that?"

My cheeks flushed. "He wasn't yelling."

"I could hear him all the way over here."

I knew Colton wouldn't conquer all his demons overnight, and I could appreciate how bad it sounded, but it still hurt. Not that I'd tell Damian that. "He's had a rough time at work."

"Really," Damian said incredulously. "*He's* had a bad day."

It would get a thousand times worse if Damian was still here when Colton arrived. I didn't put it past Colton to get in Damian's face, and Damian didn't deserve that.

"You should probably go," I said.

Damian's eyes widened as he looked past me, then stood up. I turned around to see a doctor walking towards me, but he wasn't alone. Two police officers were with him—one in a black uniform and another in dress slacks and a jacket, no tie, badge hanging on his belt.

Just like officers who had to notify the next of kin. *No. No. No!*

My lungs forgot how to breathe, contorted in a panicked knot, causing my legs to wobble. A hand steadied me by my elbow. It was Damian's, who now stood at my side, holding me upright, ready to catch me if I fell as the doctor prepared to speak words that would forever alter my life.

## 14

The doctor, with white cotton hair and dull eyes, rushed his words as if in a hurry to get this conversation off his to-do list. Medically, Justin suffered two broken ribs, a concussion, two broken arms, twenty stitches in his scalp, and many contusions and lacerations. "But I expect he'll make a full recovery."

All the air abandoned my lungs at once. I wished everyone would stop talking so I could have a moment to savor the good news, but *Doctor Hurry* didn't have time to wait. "Now, he had brown glass fragments in the laceration on his scalp, so we'll need to keep an eye out for infection," the doc said as if I were up to speed. He hadn't even told me what happened to Justin yet, for god's sake! Could he slow down?

"Brown glass?" Was he in a muddy car accident?

"Likely from a beer bottle," the officer explained as if that didn't confuse me more.

Doctor Hurry looked at his watch. "Your brother got very lucky tonight." *Lucky.* The word bounced around my mind. "He'll have to spend at least one night here. He's resting now. Someone'll come out to get you as soon as you can see him." When he was done with his bare minimum, he rushed off to be vague with the next person.

Then it was the nonuniformed officer's turn to talk. Introducing himself as Detective Fisher—*"Call me Fisher"*—he ran his hand over his bald, mocha head. Unlike the doctor, Fisher spoke delicately when he told me what happened: Justin had been beaten. Severely.

I felt the grip on my elbow tighten as I swayed.

The assailant attacked him in an alley—*what was Justin doing in an alley?*—and left my brother unconscious.

Justin was on his way to see me after he'd called. Could I have been close enough to help him? If I'd left when Zoey did and headed towards Justin's office, might I have intercepted him? I thought about that ambulance that rolled past the bar—was that his? "Where did this happen?"

Fisher told me the alley's intersecting streets, but it made no sense. That location was two blocks *north* of Ace's. Justin's work was south of Ace's, not north, and there was nothing else and no one else that he'd have been visiting up there.

"According to the calendar on Justin's phone," Fisher said, "Justin had a five thirty appointment for a haircut at a placed called Buzz." Buzz was around the corner from Ace's. That explained why Justin was in the area, but not why he was so upset, nor how he knew I was there—Zoey and I had been tucked back into the bar when he called, so you couldn't see us unless you came inside. "But according to the manager, Justin never showed."

I shook my head. Even if he had shown up to that appointment, that still didn't explain why he'd been found two blocks north of that or why he'd been beaten.

"Why would someone do this to him?" I asked.

Fisher opened a little notebook and said that's what they were trying to figure out. The only thing they knew at this point was that cash and credit cards were still in Justin's wallet, and his phone was still in his pocket, though that didn't necessarily rule out robbery, he noted, since the assault was interrupted by a passerby.

*Interrupted.* What would have happened to Justin if it hadn't been?

I felt like I was in a fog. *This kind of stuff doesn't happen to people like us.*

Fisher fired off questions in rapid succession, which I tried my best to answer because, as it turned out, Justin didn't remember any of it. A common side effect with head injuries, Fisher assured. No, Justin had no enemies. No, he didn't have a roommate or girlfriend or ex-girlfriend. No, he wasn't into drugs or stealing or gangs. No, I couldn't think of anyone that would want to harm him. No, I wasn't aware of anything going on at his work, aside from the interview he had coming up. What does he do for a living? He's an investment banker, I answered.

"Investment banker," Fisher paused. "He handle other people's money, then?"

"Yeah?"

"A lot?"

"Stocks don't trade in pennies."

Fisher wrote something down. "He mention anyone that lost money recently?"

"No. You think this could be related to his job?"

"Not eliminating any possibilities." He proceeded with a few more questions and then closed his little notebook and thanked me. "For the sake of the investigation, I'll need to advise you to keep the details of the attack to yourself. The part about the beer bottle, for instance."

"Why?"

"If we get a confession, we need to get details only the attacker would know. That strengthens the case against them so they can't retract it later."

There was a case. An investigation. A manhunt for a perpetrator that could've killed my brother. Maybe even intended to. "How could something like this happen?"

He stuffed his pen and miniature notebook back into his breast pocket. "That's what we hope to find out." *Hope.* "I'll be in touch, Ms. Christiansen."

When the cops left, I stared at the spot on the floor where they'd stood. The room's edges darkened, and my legs trembled.

"Jenna, sit down, please," Damian insisted. He led me by my elbow to a chair, where he helped me sit and pressed his hand against my shoulder. "Head between your knees."

It wasn't until this moment that I realized how erratic my breathing was. My ribs compressed my lungs so they couldn't get a deep pull of oxygen.

"Breathe," Damian instructed.

But my mind was preoccupied. *Someone did this to Justin. On purpose. Someone tried to kill him, and whoever it was is still out there somewhere.*

After a couple of minutes, my breathing slowed, and I felt well enough to sit up.

Damian held out the water bottle he'd bought when we first got here. "Please take a drink."

I complied. The cold water cascaded down my throat into my empty belly, which ached for food. I wondered if what I'd just experienced was a panic attack, and I wondered how other people coped in these situations. *If this is what it's like for me, what did it feel like for Damian when he was told his dad and sister were dead?*

"You really should eat so you don't go into shock," he advised, handing me the bag of nuts.

He'd endured the worst circumstances imaginable, and here I was, falling apart when my brother would be just fine. "You must think I'm so weak."

"Not even close." His voice infiltrated my bloodstream and pumped through my body with each beat of my heart. "No one can prepare for something like this," Damian sympathized. "Life dealt you a crap set of cards this week."

This *week*?

My eyes snapped to his, and when he registered the alarm in them, he explained. "Bad day Monday. Arguing with that girl at the bar earlier, and now this."

I felt relieved by his clarification, but Damian seemed troubled by my jarring reaction. He scrutinized me in a way he hadn't before.

"Ms. Christiansen?" A nurse appeared. She was young, with a blond ponytail, white sneakers, and blue scrubs. "Your brother's asking for you."

I blinked. "I'm allowed to see him?"

She nodded.

I grabbed my satchel, slung it over my shoulder, and turned towards Damian.

It was surprising how just hours ago, if I'd never seen Damian Stone again, I wouldn't have thought twice about it, but now, everything had changed. A bond had formed, cemented in shared tragedies, that would last long after the sun came back up.

Making it harder to say goodbye to him than I thought it'd be. I never exactly had a stable family environment, nor had I been at the forefront of my parents' devotion. All I had was Justin, and with him being in the hospital, and me not knowing if he was going to be okay, inside, I had been downright panicking. Even if I didn't admit it to myself at first, I needed someone, and Damian was here when no one else was. He made me feel safe and cared for, and for that, I was forever grateful.

Damian tucked his hands into his pockets and offered a slight smile, like he was sincerely glad that, unlike him, I'd gotten news *my loved one would be okay*. *I wish he would've gotten happy news.* I wished I could have been there for him all those years ago.

"Thank you for staying, and I'm sorry you missed your event." My words were inadequate to express the gratitude I felt for the immense sacrifice he'd made for me. "You were right—I'm glad I wasn't alone."

"I'm just happy your brother's going to be okay, Jenna."

I wanted to reach out and hug him.

"Ms. Christiansen?" the nurse asked impatiently.

I bit my lip. "I better…" I hooked a thumb over my shoulder.

"I can hang here?"

I shook my head. "I'm going to stay with Justin, so it's probably best if you go." *So my boyfriend doesn't yell at you.* Damian didn't deserve to be yelled at by anyone.

"What's your cell number?" Damian asked, pulling out his phone. After I gave it to him, I heard a text chime.

"Now you have mine," he said. "Call me if you need anything."

Just as quickly as the relief came that I had a way to stay in touch, so did the disappointment, because there was no way Colton would ever be okay with me befriending a guy. Not until he had his insecurities under control, at least. I wanted to be respectful of Colton's feelings, but I wanted to be friends with Damian, too. How could I do both?

"Thanks," I said.

Damian offered another smile and watched me follow the nurse down a corridor.

As we entered Justin's room, it struck me that almost everything was white. White walls, white linen, white pillows, white sink, a white panel of plugs for any combination of medical equipment they might need. A large window on the far wall had its shades drawn, and fluorescent lights hovered over the bed. Illuminating my brother's broken body in blazing color.

My memory flashed to one of the times I'd seen him the happiest when he was packing up his room to move to Chicago. His excitement had flooded the house, with him singing along to music and even grabbing Mom at one point to dance.

But the eyes that gleamed joyfully that day were now swollen, his left one bulging out of his head in horrendous shades of purple. The mouth that smiled wider than I'd ever seen it was now split open and ghastly scarlet. The hair that he'd proudly asked our hometown barber to cut that weekend was now matted in crimson blood and wrapped in gauze. His once-excited face looked like the raw pot roast Mom put in the crockpot on Sundays—red, gory looking. Inhuman. The left arm that swung mom around dancing was in a brace from shoulder to wrist, his right forearm the same. And the hand that had proudly shut that U-Haul and waved goodbye now beckoned me closer.

Justin looked at me out of his one eye that wasn't swollen shut. I'd never seen him look so vulnerable before.

"Justin," I managed, hoping he couldn't hear my voice crack. I stepped forward and took his hand, and his eye welled with tears.

"He needs his rest." The nurse finished her notes and then left us alone.

"Are you okay?" I asked.

Justin let go of my hand and somehow tapped a spot on the bed. The same place I used to sleep when I was a kid, scared of storms. Only this time, I could tell he was the one seeking comfort.

The role reversal was jarring; all my life, he'd been the one to find me in my hiding spot behind the living room recliner and comfort me in a storm. Now I needed to be the strong one.

"I don't want to hurt you." I looked at his mutilated body in fear, but he tapped the bed again. I worried about his broken ribs, but with incredible care, I climbed up and laid on the sliver of mattress next to him. In disbelief this was happening.

The rasp in his voice testified to the war he'd fought. "Doctors said if there'd been one more blow to my head…" He let his sentence linger in the air, the unspoken, unimaginable conclusion that he would have died, making my heart burn.

"I can't believe this happened to you."

I thought I'd feel better seeing Justin, and part of me did. I was glad he was alive and would recover. But I was also filled with unease.

What happened from the time Justin called me to the time he was attacked?

As I lay there, listening to the pained sounds of his breaths until he drifted into a medicine-induced sleep, I was no closer to an explanation when a soft knock interrupted my thoughts.

Colton peeked at me through the doorway, waiting as I delicately climbed out of bed without hurting or waking Justin, and joined him in the hall.

"Hey." Colton pulled me against his chest. "Are you okay?" He held me tight, kissed the top of my head. "Is Justin okay?"

"Define okay."

Colton peered into Justin's room. "Jesus," he whispered. "Who did this to him?"

"They don't know," I said hopelessly. "Justin doesn't remember any of it."

He kissed my forehead. "I'm so sorry about the way I was on the phone earlier," he said. "You didn't deserve that."

I wanted to tell him off. Out of all the times he could've acted like that, doing it tonight was utterly unacceptable, but I didn't have the energy to get into an argument. It all seemed so insignificant compared to what happened to Justin.

"I'm scared," I admitted. "It feels like one of those moments where life will never be the same again." *I need to call Dad; I promised him an update.*

"Everything's going to be okay," Colton cooed. But he couldn't know that. We didn't even know if this was a random act of violence.

Or if Justin was still in danger.

Mom and Dad arrived at eleven o'clock, and after a sleepless night, we all headed towards the cafeteria for "breakfast," aka giving Justin a break from Mom's well-intended smothering.

As we strolled past the waiting room, Mom and Dad suddenly stopped. With the sun streaming through the window, the once-empty space now contained eight familiar faces.

I could see the telephone game that must have played out. Mom must have called Justin's best friend, Travis, who must have contacted their coworker, Alex, who'd once dated Emily, who knew Zoey, and on and on. And now, Zoey, Harrison, Steve, Emily, Alex, Travis, and two other coworkers of Justin's whose names I'd forgotten were huddled in the waiting room.

Everyone stopped talking and looked at us expectantly.

As touched as I was that Emily, Harrison, and Steve came all the way here, even though they didn't know Justin well, I was also overcome with dread. It was selfish to think about myself at a moment like this, but having Zoey in the same room as Colton and my parents was disastrous. She stood there with my secret sparking on her lips, capable of igniting my own Great Chicago Fire.

The room suddenly became a thousand degrees, launching my body into an instant sweat. Twenty feet away, a ticking bomb stood amongst the rest of my friends in a loose circle, her mouth capable of firing at any moment. Her threat—*I'm not going to keep your dirty little secret, Jenna*—reverberated in my head, and I didn't put it past her to think that telling my parents would be protecting me somehow. If she did that, my parents would hate Colton, and then how would it ever work with Colton and my family? I needed to get my parents out of here before Zoey had the chance to detonate.

Plus, Mom was particularly fragile right now. The purple crescents beneath her eyes exposed her sleepless night of crying. She was almost at her breaking point, and I couldn't let Zoey push her over the edge.

"Mom, I'm starving," I said. "Can we please eat first?"

"Jenna," she whispered. "It's *rude* not to say hello—"

"But—"

"When they were kind enough to come."

Before I could think of any way to stop them, Mom and Dad walked away and joined Justin's friends, while my friends stared at Colton and me.

Had Zoey already told them?

I resented that I had to think about any of this right now, and I was angry that she'd violated the unspoken oath between best friends to never divulge each other's secrets. Angry that she'd rejected me when I needed her most. Angry that *she* should have been there with me when I got the worst call of my life, and *she* should have been the person whose shoulder I'd cried on.

"Come on," Colton said, pulling me towards her. He had no idea he might be walking into a hornet's nest. I needed to pull Zoey aside and find out if she'd told anyone yet, but first, I needed to tell Colton that she knew. Before we closed the distance to my friends. "Colton..."

"What's wrong?" He offered a reassuring smile, and as he looked down to lace his fingers with mine, two things registered simultaneously. First, Zoey's eyes flashed with disapproval at the sight of us holding hands, and second, Colton seemed to notice my sweatshirt for the first time. Or maybe he'd noticed it last night but, in the chaos of everything, hadn't commented about it. "Where'd you get the shirt, by the way?"

My stomach sank. We were almost to my friends, and I didn't want to tell him this now because he'd despise the answer. But lying would be far worse because it would convince him that Damian's act of kindness had a devious explanation. "I was soaking wet from the rain when I got here," I explained. "Damian got it from the gift shop, but I'm going to pay him back."

Colton's face fell to a grimace right as we reached everyone. *Fantastic.*

"Hey," Harrison said. "How's Justin doing?" I looked for clues that they knew what Zoey found out last night. They gave no indication, though I wasn't sure if it was because they were just being polite, allowing the focus to be on Justin.

I filled them in on the basics, answered their follow-up questions, and thanked them for coming.

"Listen," Harrison said. "If there's anything I can do to help, don't hesitate to ask."

"Thanks, Harrison. I appreciate that."

Was it just me, or did Colton seem annoyed by his offer?

"Oh my gosh, I just had the best idea!" Emily clapped her hands. "When Justin's feeling better? We should totally have a party for him to cheer him up!"

"An I-survived-a-mugging party," Steve said flatly.

"It would be fun! And," she added, "there are some seriously cute doctors here. Maybe we could invite some."

"Only Emily uses a hospital experience as a way to pick up men," Steve smirked. "Or maybe you just want to make Alex jealous for dumping you."

"I do not," Emily claimed, running her fingers through her hair. "And he did *not* dump me. It was mutual."

I couldn't care less who dumped who; I cared about whether Zoey had betrayed my confidence.

"Zoey, can we talk?" I asked.

But before she could answer, Travis tapped me on the shoulder. I'd met my brother's best friend many times. Part Irish, he had hair with a slight hue of red to it and a skinny frame. "Hey." When Travis gave me a quick hug, Colton's eyes darkened, which annoyed me. Did he really think Travis would suddenly hit on me, and do it now, of all times?

"How you holding up?" Travis tucked his hands into his pockets.

I shrugged.

"Your parents seem pretty freaked."

"They want to know who did this to him."

"Yeah, they asked me if any of Justin's clients got mad at him lately."

"Have they?"

Travis shrugged. "Comes with the territory. But nothing that would explain what happened."

"Did anything unusual happen at work recently?" I pressed.

"Not that I know of."

"Can you ask around?"

Why did he hesitate before nodding? Didn't he *want* to get to the bottom of it? Didn't he understand that Justin's attack occurred shortly after he left work, so whatever happened leading up to it might be relevant?

Travis's lack of concern disturbed me, but once he was distracted talking to Harrison, I focused on a more time-sensitive issue: my former best friend.

"Can we talk?" I asked her again.

She followed me to the far corner of the room, where I fanned my face from the heat.

"I'm sorry about what happened to Justin," she said. "You should have called me," Zoey accused. As if I owed her an apology.

I gritted my teeth. "Did you tell anyone?"

She blinked. "What?"

"Did you tell anyone?"

"No," she said. "We've only talked about Justin." So she wasn't promising to *not* tell, only clarifying she hadn't had the chance to rat me out yet. "Look, I know we had a fight, but I still care about you. You should have called. I would've come," she whined.

Unbelievable. After all the horrible things she'd said to me, now she was making this about her? Like *she* was the hurt party here?

"I trusted you," I snapped, frustrated that my eyes betrayed me with tears. "But all you did was get on your soapbox and judge me, as if you have any clue what you're talking about." Zoey blinked, surprised by my outburst. "And then you walked out on me. What kind of a friend does that?"

"I'm sorry if I didn't react the way I should have. I just... It didn't make any sense."

"I don't care," I said. "You were my *best* friend. You were supposed to be there for me, whether you understood what I was going through or not. Whether you agreed with my decision or not, you should have been there to listen. And instead, you judged."

She wiped a tear to remind me we were out here to make her feel better about treating me like garbage. "If it came across as judgmental, I'm sorry. I'm sorry I got angry and walked out. I shouldn't have done that. I just got so mad because this seems so black and white to me."

So she hadn't come to a different point of view then. Not even after having the entire night to reconsider it. And then she came here and complained about me not telling her about Justin sooner? What did she think was going to happen? That I'd apologize to her *again,* this time for not calling her after she walked out on our friendship?

"Are you going to tell anyone?" I demanded.

She stared at me, stunned by my tone. "I… No."

"You swear?"

It took her a few seconds to answer. "Yeah."

"Good. Then if you'll excuse me, I need to get back to everyone." So I could tell them goodbye and have breakfast with my boyfriend. I needed to tell him what Zoey knew and figure out where I went from here. It hurt so bad to be in Zoey's company, and I wasn't sure I could endure it every day at work. Maybe it was time for a fresh start.

"Jenna, wait," she said, halting my steps. This time when she spoke, her voice was weak, and I could hear her fighting back tears. "For the record? I hope I'm wrong."

Those four words hurt worse than anything we'd said to each other. It was easier to cope with the loss of our friendship if I cast her in the role of the jerk. But she wasn't a jerk, and feeling her love and concern for me made my eyes sting.

"I think I'm ready for some food," I said to Colton as I rejoined my friends. He must have sensed the tears lurking there, because he wrapped his arm around me, and for that, I was incredibly grateful. He could have held onto his frustration over the shirt, but instead, he was trying.

Harrison's body stiffened. "What's *he* doing here?"

Thirty feet away, Damian Stone entered the waiting room and met my gaze. He looked nervous about imposing, now that I was surrounded by people, but mostly relieved to see me.

I smiled, happy he'd come back. What we'd shared last night had been profound, and yet, a paranoid part of me had worried that maybe I was the only one touched by it. That maybe he'd just get on with his life like it had never happened. But here he was. Smiling.

Until he spotted the arm around my waist. Damian's face darkened into animosity as he glared at the boyfriend he'd overheard yelling at me.

"Is that the gym guy?" Emily asked.

Colton creased his brows. "He looks familiar."

This surprised me. "Do you know him?"

Colton considered this for a few seconds, then shook it off.

"What's he doing here?" Harrison repeated.

"I ran into him, and he was kind enough to drive me here when I got the call about Justin."

"You were hanging out with him *before* the hospital?" Colton asked. His tone was so gentle that no one would think twice. But I did. I sensed his frustration simmering beneath the surface. I could see it in the way he adjusted his jaw, the slight hardening of his eyes cloaked behind his now-fake smile. He was angry.

*I wonder what he'd do if nobody else was here.*

I immediately scolded myself for letting that thought go through my head. All he'd done was ask a question, and my mind immediately betrayed my promise to *not* look at him differently.

"I'm going to say hello."

When I stepped towards Damian, Colton pulled my hand back and, through a strained smile, said, "Just stay here."

I frowned at Colton's hand until he dropped mine.

"Come with me," I invited.

Colton's eyes tightened. In an eerily calm tone, he said, "I don't want to. I want us to stay here."

I was perplexed by Colton's behavior. His jealousy didn't surprise me, but this wasn't a frat party, it was a hospital. Shouldn't Colton be *grateful* to Damian that he'd been here in my time of need? If anything, shouldn't he shake his hand and thank him for helping me?

"It's rude not to at least say hello. It'll just take a second."

Colton silently condemned me for picking my side. It would be easier to *not* say hello to Damian, but he'd helped me, and it was mean to ignore him.

I crossed the room, feeling Colton's glower bore into the back of my skull.

Damian scowled at my boyfriend before offering me a weak smile. "Hey." He scanned me up and down. "You look like hell."

I smirked. "You tell me that a lot."

"How much sleep did you get?"

"None."

Damian frowned. "What have you eaten today?"

"Does my thumbnail count?"

He looked at me disapprovingly, then glanced around the room. "Lot of people here." He looked back at me, assessing my mood. "You look like you want to escape."

I knew he was referring to the room itself, but suddenly, the serenity of something I'd always longed to see sounded like a heavenly distraction. "Maybe when this is all over, I'll take a trip to Florida. I hear the sunsets are supposed to be amazing," I mused.

Damian studied me as I cleared my throat and snapped my mind back to the waiting room. "I wasn't expecting to see you."

He rubbed the back of his neck. "Wanted to make sure you were okay."

I got the impression that making friends was a new experience for him. "Careful. People might find out you're not this scary, unapproachable guy. They might realize that you're actually somewhat tolerable."

He smiled slightly, but I don't think he realized how much I meant it. He was a great guy who'd done something downright incredible for another human being who was suffering. Though I'd thanked him last night, I'd done it in such a hurry, rushing off to follow that nurse, that it didn't feel good enough. I was glad I had another chance at it.

"Thank you," I said. "For everything you did. For driving me here and staying…" *And coming back.*

As he tucked his hands into his pockets, clearly unaccustomed to receiving gratitude, Damian's eyes settled onto Colton. "So that's the boyfriend," he said with an edge. "He doesn't take his eyes off you."

"He's worried about me."

"Seems possessive," Damian said. "Harrison's not doing you any favors ogling you."

"Harrison doesn't *ogle* me."

Damian's jade eyes met mine with a playful challenge. "You're blind."

I glanced over. Yes, Harrison was looking at me, but only out of concern over me talking to the big, scary Damian Stone.

When I turned back around, I was taken aback by the abrupt change in Damian's demeanor. Gone was any trace of casualness, replaced by a rigid posture, and he stopped making eye contact—now staring down with narrowed eyes that fixated on one spot. It took me a second to realize what he was looking at: my forearm. My *exposed* arm. In the midst of talking to people, I'd let exhaustion make me careless and had absentmindedly scrunched up my sleeves from being so hot.

"What's that?" Damian demanded.

I felt a rush of adrenaline. "Believe the technical term for it is a bruise." I lowered my sleeves, playing the nonchalant person who had a nonincriminating mark, and pretended not to notice Damian tighten his jaw.

He stared at me for ten full seconds.

"What?"

"Where'd you get it?" Damian's scrutiny was unyielding.

"I fell."

Damian looked offended that I'd try that line. He took a deep breath through his nose and gave me an opportunity to come back with something better. When I didn't, he pressed, "When?"

"Yesterday," I lied.

"That bruise is almost a week old."

"No, it's not."

"Yellow and green's starting to show. Takes five to ten days after the injury."

"And you're what, a bruise expert?"

"Fighter. Comes with the territory."

I couldn't decide who I was angrier at: him for testing me or myself for failing his test. "Okay? So excuse me for not remembering every time I hurt myself."

He stared at me, and I glared right back, offended. How dare he not accept my lies.

"Color of that one matches the one on your face, which is now lathered up with concealer." *So he did see it last night...* My heart started pounding. "The shape of the one on your arm looks like someone grabbed you. Violently."

*Damn fighters.*

Damian glowered at Colton, then back at me, putting the pieces of something together that wasn't his to assemble. In front of all these people, in front of my parents, in front of Colton.

"Like I said, I fell."

Damian huffed and leaned down to ensure only I could hear. "If you had any idea what happened after that car accident, you'd know you can't bullshit a bullshitter."

This was none of his business, and we certainly weren't close enough for him to confront me on something I didn't even feel comfortable talking about with Zoey. I clenched my teeth, and as fight or flight took over, my tongue unleashed its sword and took a swing. "Screw you and your implications, Damian. I want you to leave."

Damian watched me storm off and rejoin everyone else. He looked conflicted, hesitating for several moments before walking out.

As furious as I was, I was shocked at how much the thought of never seeing him again hurt.

## 16

C an we talk? Damian's text came over three weeks after Justin's attack.

I stared at the text, surprised he'd contacted me and unsure how to respond. For three weeks, I'd tried to focus on the good things that happened. Like Justin getting released from the hospital, Mom and Dad feeling reassured enough to return home, Justin's interview getting rescheduled for early September—so he didn't miss out on his dream job—and Zoey keeping my secret.

But there were also some bad things. They hadn't figured out who hurt Justin, Zoey and I never talked again—something that broke my heart more with each passing day—and I still hadn't told Colton that Zoey found out about our fight. I kept waiting until his mood smoothed over to tell him, but as the days passed, there was a constant undercurrent of animosity radiating from him. It almost felt like Colton was waiting, even hoping, for me to make a mistake. Like when we'd recount our days to each other, for example, he'd ask me probing questions like, "What did you eat for lunch?" And then later, he'd circle back to it as a challenge: *How could you have been in that meeting at one o'clock if you were eating tuna melt at twelve forty-five?* It made me feel like I was walking on eggshells, one wrong word away from him going off on me. Making me lose hope we'd ever get back to a good place. How many times would I have to remind him of his promises to behave better?

As guilty as I felt about not confessing to Colton, I felt even worse for how I'd gone off on Damian. He cared enough about me to return to the hospital on Saturday morning just to see how I was doing, and how I'd treated him was wrong. On more than one occasion, I'd typed the words *I'm sorry*, but stared at the unsent text, worried he'd come back with questions like, *"How often does it happen?"* or *"How long has this been going on?"* Reaching out to him was a bad idea, especially since Colton would go ballistic if he discovered me texting with the very guy he'd tried to forbid me from saying hello to. So I tried to let it go.

It proved harder than I thought, though, which was confusing. Yes, I suspected Damian had shared things with me he hadn't told many others, but still. There was no need to check my phone daily to see if he'd call, there was no explanation for why I looked him up online, combing through social media, and there was certainly no reason to look up his MMA history.

Yet that's exactly what I did. Articles flooded my search results, and I drank it all in, fascinated to learn about that side of him. It turned out Damian was kind of a big deal in the MMA world. Before his head injury he'd carried an undefeated record and was someone many bloggers and sports reporters wanted to interview but rarely got. Ironically, this made him a highly sought-after interview to land, especially after his first loss ended in a career-threatening injury.

When I ran out of articles to read, I found fighting videos of him posted by fans. I watched them, mesmerized. Damian was a god in the cage, with unmatched reflexes, skill, and strength. His kicks could easily kill a human with a single blow, and his punches, I was convinced, could bend even the thickest of metals. He inflicted horrible injuries on his opponents, even by MMA standards, including broken skulls, fractured spines, countless broken bones, and tons of soft-tissue damage. I would've expected to feel afraid or revolted by what I saw, but instead, I was in awe of him. Damian was as fascinating as he was kind.

And I missed him. I missed the peace I'd felt in his presence the night in the waiting room. With Damian, I hadn't had to worry about some ongoing feud, like I did with Zoey, and I didn't have to worry about upsetting him by talking to the wrong person, like I did with Colton. When I'd been with Damian, it had felt so...pure. Like I could breathe and focus on getting through that awful night without other people's drama. And the fact he'd shared some of his most painful experiences with me in the process had made me feel even more comforted by him. Comfort I missed.

As one week turned into two, then three, I distracted myself planning Justin's *I-survived-a-mugging* party, scheduled for this Friday, four weeks after his assault. My plan was to hit the party supply store on my way home.

Until I got Damian's text. **Can we talk?**

I stopped walking next to the evening traffic of Wacker drive, sweating like a beast. Eighty-degree temperatures combined with low wind and high humidity made the end of summer steamy in Chicago. The sun-filled sidewalks were more crowded than ever, the last week for tourists to explore the city before most schools started.

**Me: Sure.**

**Damian: Where can we meet?**

**Me: You know that park area, two blocks east of my office building, south of the water?**

**Damian: Yep. Is now good?**

**Me: Yeah.**

**Damian: On my way.**

I couldn't believe he'd texted me. Why, and why now?

Five minutes later, Damian Stone arrived. In the flesh, truly here. He wore black workout shorts, a light gray T-shirt that stretched across his broad chest, and running shoes. Somehow seeing him was surreal, as if our night at the hospital was ten years ago, yet only moments ago, all at the same time.

"Hey." Damian's eyes flitted to the people lingering by the river. "Wanna walk?"

I had no idea how I'd explain this to Colton later, but I nodded and walked next to Damian along the river, towards the lake.

The path was gorgeous, bordered with iron railings and green trees, and it snaked beneath graceful rust-colored bridges that arched over the water. The sun tilted in the sky and cast shadows on the sides of the towering buildings and people peering out at the river.

"I'm sorry," I said, looking up at him. "For how mean I was to you. You helped me, and I should never have treated you like that."

We took three steps before he responded. "It's okay."

It wasn't, not in the least. "I wanted to apologize sooner. I picked up my phone like ten times, but I...I wasn't sure what to say. I'm sorry."

We walked past a wrinkled man playing jazz music on his saxophone as we crossed under another bridge, getting closer to Lake Michigan. A tourist boat chugged along the river while people took photos of skyscrapers.

"I couldn't stop thinking about you," he admitted. I was surprised how much my heart rejoiced at his profession. "I had to see if you're okay."

I stopped walking. "*That's* why you finally asked to see me?" I snarled.

"Why are you pissed?" Damian asked.

"Because I thought you cared about me as a friend, not just some misguided concern over my safety." Honestly, I was such an idiot.

"Jenna." Damian caught my elbow as I tried to walk away. He turned me to face him. "I do care." He hesitated, dropping my arm. "*And* I'm worried about your safety. Spent the last three weeks agonizing over what might be happening to you, coming up with options for what I was going to do about it."

I blinked, trying to figure out how to convince him he was wrong.

He put his hands into his pockets. "My favorite idea was to go after your boyfriend," Damian admitted with vengeful satisfaction in his eyes. "Fantasized about dislocating his face. That was plan A."

Well, thank god for plan B, whatever the hell it was.

"You're off base," I said. "Nothing's going on."

Nothing like what Damian suspected, at least. Our current problem was Colton's perpetual bad mood, which I'd tried many times to pull him out of. I took him to a show, cooked him his favorite meals, but nothing worked. If anything, he grew tenser, and I was losing my patience with how many bad days were stringing together. I needed evidence that the rising tension between us would go away, or I couldn't imagine this would last. In fact, I'd begun to think of Justin's upcoming party as our final test. If we couldn't have fun, that seemed like proof we'd never get back on track. And we just needed to end things.

"But I worried he'd hold it over you, my going after him. Maybe even take it out on you," Damian said, ignoring my denial. "Figured it was more dangerous for you in the long run, so I decided to try to talk to you."

"There's nothing to talk about," I insisted. "You're wrong about whatever it is you think is going on." Before this relationship, I wasn't a liar, but in the past few weeks, I'd lied to almost everyone, either outright or by omission. Some multiple times. Each lie chipped away at me, making me feel less and less like the person I once was. How could lying feel so right in how it protected Colton and yet so wrong at the same time?

Damian hesitated, cautious with his tone. "With addicts," he said, "you can't help them until they recognize they have a problem. Until then, they tell themselves whatever they need to, to rationalize that they're fine. People who are in...*bad*—" I sensed he'd replaced the word *abusive* "—relationships are similar. Sometimes they don't see it. The manipulation. The control."

I wasn't being manipulated. I *knew* what he'd done was wrong, but I was trying to sort through complicated feelings, and I certainly wasn't going to admit to Damian that Colton and I were in a rocky place. Whatever happened between Colton and me was not going to be because people pressured me.

"You know what?" I said. "I don't have time for this. Thank you for your misplaced concern, but I have to go."

When I tried to walk away, Damian touched my arm.

"Please," he pleaded. "Don't— Just…hear me out."

"With what? You have no idea what you're talking about," I said.

"Yes," he said, tucking his hands into his pockets as he held my stare. "I do."

I needed to ignore my insatiable curiosity about his life and walk away, but it turned out my feet were pathetic traitors. They followed him as we silently crossed the pedestrian tunnel under Lake Shore Drive.

When we reached the water, a grouping of boulders extended into the lake like a pier. They were probably dangerous, not intended to be walked on, but they were private and lovely as the sun softened in the sky.

I kicked off my shoes, and Damian helped me carefully walk across six boulders and sit down next to him. The stones were so hot from being out in the blazing sun all day that they nearly burned the skin on my calves as I dangled my legs over the edge, dipping my toes into the cool water as it lapped against the rocks.

We were silent for a while, staring out at the contradiction of the beach setting—with its boats on dark-blue water and people playing in the sand—against the backdrop of modern skyscrapers towering into the purple clouds.

"After the accident," Damian started, "my mom sank into a deep depression. Wouldn't get out of bed for days at a time. The few family members we had in the area tried to help, but she drove them all away. Went on for over two years, until one day, I finally saw the first hint of happiness in her again. Found out it was because she met someone." Damian cleared his throat. "At first I was angry, because it felt like she was cheating on Dad. But the guy made her happy. And since I was the one who'd destroyed her entire life, if there was anything that made her happy, I was damn sure going to keep my mouth shut."

Damian stared at the horizon. "The guy eventually became my stepdad. Moved in with us." He dragged his bottom lip through his teeth, and it took him several seconds to continue. "First time he hit me was because I'd forgotten to put my shoes away. The rest started after. He was smart. Beating me where clothes would always cover the bruises."

I blinked, horrified that someone had done that to him and had been so wickedly calculated, especially to a little boy who'd already suffered a tragedy.

"Did your mom know?" I asked.

"No."

"You didn't tell her?"

Damian rubbed his jaw. "When we got into the accident, I was eight, and Sophie was six." He watched a small girl on the beach squeal in delight when she caught a frisbee from her dad, who picked her up and twirled her around. When Damian spoke next, his tone was flat, like he was lost in a memory. "She had these big blue eyes. Clutched this ratty stuffed bunny everywhere she went. Hippy, she called it." He sighed. "She looked up to me, wanted to do everything I did. If I was reading a book, she'd go find a book and sit next to me and read it, and if I was going to a T-ball game, she wanted to come with." He locked both hands on the top of his head as he gazed out at the water. "She was alive and awake at the hospital, but they warned us she wasn't going to make it. My mom told Sophie that she might go to heaven. I was holding her hand, and she started crying, saying, 'I want to stay here with you and Mommy.'

"I thought they were wrong. She didn't look good, but she was alert and even talking a little, and that didn't seem like a dying person. But the day after the accident, her vitals started to fail like they warned us they would. Monitors beeped, nurses rushed around, doctors were paged, Mom was crying hysterically. Sophie gasped for air with this rattling sound. I tried to comfort her, but it didn't work." Damian's eyes fixated on something that wasn't here. "Her last words were, 'Please don't let me go.'"

I could tell Damian didn't intend to say that last part; he got caught up in the memory and was talking more to himself. He cleared his fog with a deep breath. "When she stopped breathing, I held my own breath. I decided I wasn't going to breathe again until she did." He swallowed hard. "But she never took another breath, and when she didn't breathe again, I didn't want to breathe again, either."

A lump in my throat grew as we sat in silence, watching a white sailboat drift farther out to sea. I never imagined a guy with so much going for him could have so much pain inside.

"It was my fault she died. My fault that Dad was gone and that Mom's entire life was ruined. My stepdad was an asshole to me, but he made my mom happy, and I wasn't going to ruin that." Damian wiped the sweat from his forehead, the sun warm against our skin. "People don't realize that there's a good side to physical pain. It's all your brain can focus on, and you get to escape the hell on earth that's your mind for a little while."

I considered his tattoos, thinking back to a time in college when I'd gone with a girl who got a heart tattoo the size of a quarter. The needle pierced her skin over and over, and just when she thought the spot was too sore to keep going, it kept stabbing her again and again while she groaned in pain. It took about an hour of what she referred to as *unbelievable agony* for her to get that little heart. Damian had tattoos covering his huge arms. While, to her, the needle's pain was a means to the end goal, to Damian, the needle's pain *was* the end goal.

"Is that why you got into fighting? You liked the pain?"

Damian picked up a pebble, tossed it into the water, and watched the ripples. "When my stepdad first started going at me, I felt like I deserved it for killing my dad and sister. After he'd lay into me, I used to go to Sophie's grave and lay on the ground, wishing he'd have hit me just a little harder."

I gasped silently. A speedboat passed in the distance, its wake leaving a trail of white bubbles on the dark water.

"But after a while, I got pissed, because that's not why my stepdad was hurting me. He was just beating me up because he was an asshole. Guess he thought he was going to make it big with money or whatnot, but I don't think he had the brains to make it happen, and I think that pissed him off. He probably saw me as a kid who had everything handed to him. My dad left a hefty insurance payout in a trust fund for me. Who knows why he did it."

Damian picked up a baseball-sized stone and plunked it into the water before continuing. "Couldn't bring myself to tell my mom, but he was becoming more violent, and I got sick of feeling powerless. I started to join clubs to learn how to defend myself. Wrestling. Boxing. Karate. Became kind of an obsession and I got really good at it. I had all this anger with nowhere to put it, and then someone would willingly get in front of me and let me go after them."

It struck me that someone in his situation might have gotten into drinking or drugs, but fighting became his outlet.

"After a while, fighting became who I am. Everything else went on the backburner, and I was always training for the next fight, a new opponent. New techniques. New practice. When I'm not fighting, I'm thinking about fighting, and when I am fighting, it's the only time I feel alive."

That whole time he was going through that, was his mother aware? "Did your mom ever find out what he'd been doing?"

Damian's lips tightened into a line. "Yeah," he said in a tone that closed down the subject.

If he was willing to talk about something as awful as what his stepdad did, why stop there? What could be worse than that? I wanted to ask how she found out and where his stepdad was today. *In jail or six feet under, I hope.* But the pain in his voice stopped me. Damian might be six-three, two hundred twenty pounds of solid muscle, but inside he was still that vulnerable ten-year-old who grew up in a home where he didn't feel safe, blaming himself for his mother's pain and the deaths of his father and little sister. Letting himself be the punching bag to some asshole for years.

And he thought he deserved it.

The clues behind his personality came together like a puzzle. How he always seemed intense and didn't interact with people or reporters who tried to talk to him. Damian didn't like people knowing him, and yet here he sat, confiding what had to be the most intimate secrets of his past to me. Entrusting me with them.

"Why are you telling me all this?" I asked.

Damian hesitated, careful with his words. "I think you're with someone like my stepdad. And I think, just like I did, you're convincing yourself that staying is the right thing."

And just like that, any hope that Damian could be in my life was destroyed. With him projecting his abuse onto me, he'd never accept Colton as my boyfriend.

"I have to go." I shifted, prepared to leave, even though leaving Damian behind was going to hurt like hell. Our time together may have been brief, but I'd savored how secure I felt with him, especially with Zoey and I not talking and Justin possibly moving to New York.

When I braced myself to stand up, though, Damian took my hand —gently, imploring me to stay and listen.

"You deserve better, Jenna."

With my hand in his, and Damian's face only a foot away, I had the strangest feeling that the look in his eyes wasn't just one of friendship or concern. That it was something else.

But that was silly. He didn't date, therefore there'd never be a question of anything romantic. There was no reason to second-guess that, not even with the way he was looking at me right now.

"My situation is totally different than yours." I pulled my hand away and stood up.

"Maybe," Damian conceded. His caring eyes flooded with apprehension. "Or maybe you're giving that asshole too much credit, and deep down, you know it's not over. No matter what he said to woo you back into a false sense of security, it's going to happen again. And next time, you might get hurt really bad.

Or worse..."

## 17

A lot was riding on tonight. Colton and I *had* to get back on track. There was simply no other alternative, because after my talk with Damian four days ago, the reality sank in: if I was wrong, if Colton and I didn't work out, then that meant I'd lost my best friend *and* rejected a friendship with Damian for nothing. That scenario, though I'd never admit this to another soul, haunted me.

Which is why I'd taken extra steps to ensure Colton would like the party. I went to two different stores to get his favorite beer, and even splurged on a new dress. It was pastel pink, with a fitted bodice, spaghetti straps, and a flowy chiffon hem that came down to my knees. I couldn't wait to see the look on Colton's face when he saw me in it. I could imagine him spinning me around and kissing my neck, groaning that I looked far too pretty to share with everyone else.

Meanwhile, I transformed my outdated apartment into the stage for an incredible night. I lit candles to dazzle the place up with a romantic flair, I set out a bunch of snacks, and I stocked the fridge.

At nine o'clock, Colton arrived. He looked incredibly handsome in his dressy jeans and white button-down.

"Hey!" I smiled as I opened the door. "You look amazing!"

Colton offered a strained smile, seemingly preoccupied as he stepped inside and set a backpack on the counter. "I want to show you something."

*Did he get me a gift? A gesture to smooth over the bumpy last few weeks?*

He unzipped the top and pulled out a gun. "Glock nineteen, semi-automatic."

My mouth became sandpaper.

When I was eleven, my schoolmate, Kyle Reed, accidentally shot and killed himself playing with his dad's gun. The tragedy brought our small town to its knees, and with it, whispers that his brain matter had splattered onto his Lego collection—mental images that plagued my dreams for months. That was my introduction to the destructive force of a weapon I'd forever be afraid of. Something that Colton knew.

"Why do you have that?" I stepped away from the metal death machine.

Colton held it like a shiny toy he was proud of.

"After what happened to Justin, I thought it'd be a good idea to get it for protection."

"I hate guns."

Colton looked offended, as if this violent weapon was a romantic gesture that I should have been flattered over.

"Relax," Colton said. "There's no bullets in it. Magazine's empty. See?" He pulled out a black rectangle from the base with a click, showing me it was hollow.

"I don't care. Just...please get rid of it."

"I thought you'd be happy," Colton said. "I got it to keep you safe."

He shoved the gun back into his bag and put it next to the couch.

"I appreciate the thought. I just..." I was terrified of guns and thought Colton knew that.

"Whatever." Colton snatched a beer from the fridge. If he noticed I'd stocked his favorite kind, he said nothing.

He plopped down on the couch, turned the TV on, and flipped around until he found sports highlights. I wanted to somehow un-offend him, but over the last couple weeks, I'd learned the best course of action was to *not* explain myself; he'd interpret that as the start of an argument. The best strategy was to give him space and change the subject.

*I have the perfect thing to cheer him up.*

I went into my bedroom, changed into the dress and matching pumps, touched up my eyeshadow and lipstick, and walked back into the living room. Eager for Colton's reaction.

When his impassive eyes glided over me, he didn't need to say anything; the disapproval was evident from his face.

"Shows a lot of leg, don't you think?"

My heart sank. I looked down at the dress I thought he'd adore. "It comes down to my knees."

"It's a couple inches from your knees, at least. When you sit down, it'll be even higher," he said. "And it's tight."

He glared at me as if commanding me to change, but when he did that, something inside me grew taller—a stubbornness, and I was unwilling to let him dictate what I wore.

"What'd you want to tell me?" Colton asked.

"What?" I asked.

He took a sip of beer and looked at me in annoyance. "Yesterday, you said there was something you wanted to tell me, but my mom called before we got into it. What was it?"

*Crud.* Bad time. Not now. He was too pissed, and tonight of all nights? No way. Yesterday there was a pocket of time he seemed to be in an okay mood, and the heaviness of keeping it from him got to me. "Let's talk about it tomorrow."

"Let's talk about it now."

"I want us to have a good night."

"So it's somethin' that'll piss me off, then."

I hesitated. "Let's just talk after the party. Emily will be here any second."

"God, just spit it out already."

I clenched my fists. I was in the wrong for not telling him sooner, but I didn't appreciate Colton demanding a discussion as important as this one on his terms only. I walked away into the kitchen area.

"I'm just gonna keep askin' you," Colton threatened, implying he'd do it front of everyone.

Why had I been so incredibly worried about *him* when he clearly didn't give a crap about my feelings? I should hold my ground, out of principle. But my mind flashed to Justin being here, witnessing Colton following me around angrily, demanding I answer him. It'd ruin the party, and worse, it'd risk Justin finding out what Colton had done. I tightened my jaw. "Zoey knows what happened with us."

His eyes said it all—*How dare you.*

"I didn't mean to tell her."

"Just slipped out, eh? How's the weather, oh, by the way, my boyfriend is a complete a-hole."

"It wasn't like that."

"So she understood, then? Supports us?"

I blinked.

"Yeah. Thought so. That's just great," Colton said, adding, "Is she gonna be here?"

"No."

He gave me a chastising look and returned his eyes to the television. I understood why he was upset, but I couldn't let this ruin Justin's night. He'd been struggling to process what happened to him and needed a stress-free evening with friends. "For Justin's sake, please don't ruin the party."

Colton took a sip of his beer, refusing to make eye contact.

If he didn't care enough about Justin, he should care about me. "I've been feeling overwhelmed the past few weeks, and this night is important to me. So please," I said, "don't ruin this."

A knock at the door interrupted our standoff. When I answered it, I stiffened. Emily—who wore a white dress with her red hair in stunning waves—I'd been expecting. What I didn't expect was that Zoey would be with her.

I could *feel* Colton's anger on my back.

"Hey!" Emily chirped. "You look great!"

"Thanks," I smiled. At least someone thought so.

"Hope it's okay I brought Zoey." I made the mistake of looking at Colton, who glared at me like Zoey showing up was my fault, and the ultimate *screw you* to him.

Before I could say anything, Emily pulled Zoey into the kitchen. I didn't know what to do. Asking Zoey to leave would make Colton more comfortable, but kicking Zoey out of a party felt extreme and would hurt her terribly, deepening the divide between us. But how could I get Colton out of his bad mood if she stayed?

"Oh, guess what?" Emily said, going into the fridge to get a drink. "So, I went back to that gym where we had that self-defense, team-building thing? Because there was this super cute guy I wanted to invite to the party tonight, and long story short, he can't make it, but we might go out another time. But while I was there, I ran into Damian. I told him he should swing by tonight and bring some of his hot friends." Emily wiggled her eyebrows at Zoey.

I froze. "You gave him my address?"

Emily blanched at my tone. "Was that bad?"

More like horrific. Damian had already considered dislodging Colton's face once, and the only saving grace had been keeping them apart. If he showed, even if he somehow didn't notice Colton's hostile attitude, Colton had an asshole switch. Capable of lighting the match, and then boom. Explosion city.

"Seriously?" Colton snapped, looking at me as if I'd committed a felony. "Now *that* guy's coming too?"

My face reddened. Did he not care that chastising me like that made Emily uncomfortable too? These past few weeks, it seemed like the more desperately I tried to reclaim our once-perfect connection, the further it slipped from my grasp, and now the tension stretched so wide, I could feel it was about to snap.

Emily blinked, taken aback by Colton's tone. "I don't know," she admitted, apologetically. "He said maybe."

So *maybe* this night would be a catastrophe. At least Colton had no bullets...

By eleven, twenty people filled my apartment, including Harrison,

Steve, Zoey, Emily, Travis, Justin, some of his coworkers—both guys and girls—and some of their dates.

So far, no Damian. I'd given Colton plenty of time to cool down and come to his senses. He couldn't hold me responsible for two people coming I hadn't invited, and even if he did, he should care enough about how important this night was to me to not ruin it. But when I finally made eye contact with him, my heart fell to my feet.

From that one resentful look, I could see that our night wasn't going to be filled with romance and laughter. Instead, he'd remain angry and bitter, sulking on the couch. Obviously, if he was having a bad night, he expected me to feel the same. It was as if his emotions were a prerequisite to mine, and in his eyes, me having fun was disrespectful. Would my needs ever be a priority in our relationship?

"Great party," Justin said, interrupting my train of thought. His right arm hung in a sling, and his left forearm was in a cast.

"I'm glad you're having fun," I said. At least one of us was. "When do you fly out again?"

"Sunday."

For Justin's sake, I forced a smile, pretending Colton wasn't ruining everything.

"Interview's Monday, right?"

Justin nodded. "One round on Monday, another Tuesday, with dinner after."

"You sure you're up for it?" I asked, hoping his ribs weren't still bothering him.

"I'm fine," he rolled his eyes. "Besides. They moved it out as late as they could. Everyone else's been interviewed already."

"I'm excited for you," I said. And this time, I really meant it. If there was one thing I learned from Justin's attack, it was that I wanted him to do whatever made him happy and live his life to the fullest.

*Live life to the fullest...* The phrase echoed in my head. A guy spun a girl around, smiling, dancing. When he wrapped his arm around her waist and whispered in her ear, inciting a playful laugh, something inside me began to ache.

"Worked my butt off for two years to have a shot at this," Justin said. "If you don't get into these firms from the ground up, it's next to impossible to ever get in. Basically, now or never." He adjusted his sling. "I talked to someone who works there. Turns out the upside to this job is even better than I thought. Three-year package with an option for six, and a fast track to vice president."

For someone who just found out his dream job offered even more than he could've imagined, he seemed awfully subdued.

"But?"

"But it'll be longer hours than I work now," Justin said. "Plus, most weekends."

Before his attack, Justin didn't care about working so many hours he barely had time for a social life. But now, the personal sacrifice seemed to weigh on him.

"If they offer you the job, will you take it?"

Justin took a sip of beer and stared at his bottle, but he took too long to answer; Zoey approached us.

"Hey."

Justin smiled at her. "Hey, Zoey."

"How are you feeling?" she asked him, oblivious to how mad Colton would be with her standing here.

Nervous, I glanced at him. To others, it probably looked like he was watching television, but what he was really doing was watching me—scrutinizing everything I did. I could tell that if I smiled too big, laughed too hard, or talked to anyone he didn't approve of, he'd get angry—like he was right now, condemning me for engaging with Zoey. It was suffocating, having this invisible chain connecting me to him where I was never free to roam, be myself, or have any fun.

Not wanting to fuel Colton's fire, I excused myself, pretending to be too busy with hostess duties to talk to Zoey. I collected empty beer bottles, brought them over to the sink, and started to rinse them out before putting them into the recycle bin. Each bottle grew heavy as it filled up with water, then lighter as I dumped it back out. How often in our life would I escape to the sink like this?

I looked over at the happy dancing couple again, and this time, he tucked her hair behind her ear and said something that made her look like she wanted to spend eternity with him. They were blissful, living in their own little bubble as if the rest of the party wasn't happening.

My lip trembled.

"Hey," Travis said, snapping me out of my trance.

"Hey," I said.

"Nice party."

"Thanks. Justin said you wouldn't be able to stay long?"

"Yeah. Training run tomorrow is eighteen miles," Travis said.

"Is this your first marathon?"

He nodded. "Twelve weeks into the sixteen-week training schedule. So far, my longest run has been seventeen miles, tomorrow's eighteen. Twenty-six seems...crazy now that I'm in the middle of it."

Colton was already throwing daggers at me for speaking to the male species.

I probably should have walked away—kept the peace, and all—but part of me was starting to feel downright defiant of his attempts to control me.

Plus, there was a question I'd wanted to ask Travis ever since our conversation at the hospital. I turned off the water and wiped my hands on a towel, leaning my hip against the counter. "Hey, did you ever ask around at work if anything happened before Justin was attacked?"

Travis nodded. "One complaint came out, but nothing earth-shattering."

"What kind of complaint?"

Travis shrugged, popping a baby carrot into his mouth. "Someone came forward claiming improper statements of a Fortune 500's financials. The source came to our firm before they went to the SEC with it."

I blinked. "Why would they come to your firm *before* the SEC?"

"To buy shorts."

Was I supposed to know what that meant?

"With stocks, you can make money two ways. If you hold a normal position, you make money if the stock price rises. Hold a short, you make money if the stock price declines."

"So this source intended to make money off their claim," I realized. "Is that legal?"

"It's not not-legal," he said. What did *that* mean? Justin would never stand by and watch something illegal go on without reporting it.

"When did this happen?"

"That Friday."

"The day Justin was attacked? Don't you think that's—"

"There's no way it had anything to do with his assault. Accusations of fraud are not uncommon, and no one's going to kill over it. If they did, it'd be someone more powerful than Justin. He's just an entry-level investment banker, like me."

Travis started to walk away.

"Hey, Travis?"

He turned around.

"For argument's sake, if someone had proof the report was a lie, what would happen?"

Travis considered this. "Source'd be out millions." He shrugged as if it were inconsequential. "But people gamble in the stock market every day, Jenna. People don't get violent because of it."

He thought I was crazy. Was I reaching here? Or was Travis too dismissive to see a possible connection? What if Justin had uncovered something he wasn't supposed to? What if he discovered the report was a lie and was about to cost that "source" millions of dollars in short positions? Or worse, what if he found out his own company knowingly looked the other way, just to make money? Millions of dollars and the future of two companies could be in jeopardy.

"You two looked chummy," Colton accused, appearing in the kitchen.

I couldn't tell if Colton's jealousy was getting worse, if I was becoming less tolerant of it, or both.

"Don't do this," I said.

"Do what?"

"If we're going to make this work, you have to stop interrogating me any time someone talks to me. And I don't appreciate the way you've been watching me, either."

"If you're not doing anything wrong, you shouldn't care if I'm watching. And you know what I don't appreciate? My girlfriend hanging all over some guy."

I clenched my jaw. "Why do you want to be here? You're obviously not having fun. Maybe it'd be best if you leave."

"You'd like that, wouldn't you?" Colton grabbed another beer from the fridge.

I stared at him in disbelief, insulted at his implication.

"Probably why you never put that ring on," he added.

*No, it's because I wasn't even sure I wanted to stay in a relationship with you, let alone accept your engagement.* He was making my decision pretty damn simple.

Colton stomped off and reclaimed his position on the couch, playing the part of the asshat boyfriend sulking so much it was apparent to everyone we were fighting.

"What was that about?" Justin asked.

"Nothing."

"Everything okay between you two?"

I rubbed my hands on the towel again, even though they were already dry. "I don't know if it's going to work out between us." Admitting it out loud was as terrifying as it was freeing. "Things have been...rocky."

Justin kept his expression guarded as he studied me. "Rocky how?"

I broke eye contact and shrugged. "Up and down. Fighting, making up." I sighed. "I kept telling myself the rocky part was tempo-rary and the real part is the perfect part. But I don't think that's right anymore."

Justin glared at Colton, set his beer down on the counter, and scooted closer to me, so no one else could hear. "Fighting how?"

He stared at me, waiting for me to say more, but thankfully, Emily interrupted us.

"Jenna, I'm sorry about the whole Damian thing. I should have asked first."

Justin held my stare for a few more seconds before throwing a sideways glance at Colton. What exactly Justin suspected, I wasn't sure, but I knew my brother. He wasn't going to stop until he got answers. And now I wasn't sure I'd cover for Colton.

"It's totally fine," I assured her. This wasn't her fault, it was mine for letting Colton's misery make other people feel bad.

"I texted him," she said. "I told him it'd be a bad idea if he showed up tonight."

The sound of glass breaking interrupted us. A guy in the black shirt that I'd seen flirting with several girls earlier stood near the fridge, with a broken beer bottle at his feet. I offered Emily a reassuring smile and slipped away to clean up the mess. I got my hand broom from under the sink and some paper towels.

"I'm sorry," the guy said. He had high cheekbones and a narrow jaw.

"It's not a big deal," I assured him.

When I crouched down to clean up the mess, he joined me. "I'm Tai," he politely reminded me, since we'd only met for a second when he'd arrived. I didn't like how he leaned his body towards me in an openly flirtatious way. Colton got jealous enough when he merely *imagined* someone might be flirting.

"I started at CME last month," he said, picking up a shard I missed.

*Please go away. My boyfriend is in a terrible mood and he's watching everything, and he'll think you're hitting on me and he might explode in front of everyone, and my brother already might be suspicious of my boyfriend, and I can't handle everything falling apart all at once, and I don't want to hurt your feelings, so please, just go away.*

"When Justin told me he had a sister, he never mentioned how pretty you are."

I tried to stop my eyes from glancing at Colton, but it was like driving past an accident, where your eyeballs just have to get a quick look. If I thought he looked angry before, it was nothing like this. This time, Colton was staring at me openly, not out of the corner of his eye, and this time, he looked enraged. He'd even thrown his backpack over his shoulder like he was ready to storm out.

Oblivious to any of this, Tai moved closer, like he was revving up to make physical contact.

"I have a boyfriend," I clarified, taking a step back—a blunt end to the problem. Or so I thought. Tai hesitated, but his smile turned mischievous. Maybe he misconstrued it as a come-on, like I was trying to remind *myself* that I had a boyfriend, or maybe drunk ears hear only what they want to, but he looked at my mouth and raised his hand to brush my cheek. I would have handled it, but Colton didn't let me. He launched himself off the couch and charged towards us.

I reached Colton in three strides.

"Don't," I said, putting my hand on his chest.

Justin's eyes snapped to me from across the room.

I pulled Colton by his hand, outside the apartment and into the hallway.

"Colton, I can't live like this." This wasn't just a bad mood; he always treated me like I was a cheater and he was waiting to catch me in the act.

"Live like what? Acting like a slut?"

I reeled from the verbal slap. He'd never said something so cruel, but even more disturbing was that it didn't even phase him. As the silence stretched between us, the divide in our relationship widened.

"This is never going to stop, is it? You're never going to trust me," I realized.

"Maybe if you'd stop flirting with guys, I'd trust you."

It was at this moment that I could see our dysfunctional future together with complete clarity. All the parties and social functions tainted by his behavior. Him keeping me under surveillance, unleashing criticism and false accusations at every turn. Attempting to control what I wore, who I talked to, and when I was allowed to be happy.

I couldn't live like this. Constantly feeling like I was doing something wrong, being thrown up on the witness stand by a prosecutor determined to find inconsistencies in my story. All while I twisted my hands together, nervous I'd say or do something wrong. This wasn't the kind of love I wanted; it was a prison sentence.

"I can't be with someone who doesn't trust me," I said.

"So what are you saying, we're over?"

I could tell he'd said it as a tactic, in an attempt to rock me back on my heels so I'd say, *no, of course not*, and he'd remain in control. Instead, I just stared at him, watching the realization wash over his face.

Before either of us could speak, my front door opened, and music spilled out as Justin glanced at Colton, then me. "Everything okay?"

*No.* And I now knew it never would be. "Yeah," I said.

Down the hall, a group of strangers ambled off the elevator, impeding on our privacy.

I wished I'd waited until tomorrow to have this talk, but it just sort of happened, and now I was in the middle of it.

"I'll be back in a sec," I said to Justin, and motioned for Colton to follow me down the hall. With trepidation, Justin watched us walk away and vanish into the elevator.

Outside my complex, a group of pedestrians were lingering, probably coming to or from a party of their own, so we walked around the corner and into the narrow alley to have some privacy. The same alley where Colton and I had first met months ago. *How ironic.*

The passage was primarily used for dumpster storage—the ground too pothole-ridden for vehicles or people to comfortably pass through. Here, the sounds of the engines and "L" train faded beneath the night sky.

I walked to the same spot where we'd rescued that dog before I turned around and studied the man I thought I'd be with forever. Somehow, he looked different to me tonight. His thin lips, sharp jaw, and high cheekbones didn't seem charming, but bitter. And behind his eyes was a deeply simmering anger. Anger I could tell he was trying to mask as he ran a hand through his brown locks.

"I know I'm not perfect, Jenna." Colton's tone was completely different now. Soft and apprehensive. "But I love you. I'm trying, I swear I am."

But trying wasn't enough.

How arrogant of me to think my love was strong enough to fix him. To think I was special, that we were capable of overcoming something that was so obviously above our heads. How naive of me to believe I could compensate for years of damage that his childhood had cemented into his DNA.

I hated myself for failing him and knew that I was about to destroy him. All Colton ever wanted was to be loved. The young boy who'd been abandoned by his dad and neglected by his mom needed real love more than oxygen, and now that he'd finally found it, I was going to rip it away and abandon him too. And somehow, I knew—I *knew*—no one else would tolerate his behavior. I wasn't just breaking his heart; I was sentencing him to a life with no love.

My lip quivered. "I'm sorry, Colton, but I can't do this anymore." I looked down at my feet, ashamed of myself for hurting him.

"Please don't do this," he pleaded. Heartbreaking silence stretched on. "I was a jerk tonight, I'm sorry. I won't let it happen again." He stepped closer. "Jenna, I love you more than life itself." The desperation in his voice only made it harder to witness, like watching an animal cornered by a predator, panicked that it was about to be killed. My eyes welled with tears. I'd honestly thought we could make it. I'd thought I could be enough for him.

Colton rummaged his hand inside his backpack. For a second, I thought he'd pull out the gun to scare me, but he pulled out the engagement ring. "I spent every penny I had on this because I love you."

I said nothing.

"I got fired today," Colton blurted out urgently. "And now, no one else'll hire me. I'll be a day laborer for the rest of my life."

I blinked, taken off guard.

"I didn't want to tell you because I knew this night was important, but that's why I've been in a bad mood."

Before tonight, this would have turned everything around. I'd feel too guilty to leave him in his time of need, and frankly, I'd grasp on to any explanation that might convince me his unacceptable behavior was another anomaly. But he'd acted this way about my neighbor, about people in the hospital waiting room, about Damian and people at this party, and I knew it wouldn't stop. This wasn't about a bad mood. It was something much deeper.

"I'm sorry," I said. "I know how much that job meant to you." I took a deep breath. "But it doesn't change this."

Colton's chest rose and fell quickly. "You're the only person that ever made me feel worthy. Please," he said, cupping my face. "Please don't leave me." Colton's voice cracked. "Don't do this."

I stared into the hopeless eyes of a lost little boy. "I'm sorry," I cried.

"But I love you."

"I love you too," I sniffled. "I always will. And I'll always be here for you if you need anything."

Colton no longer resembled the angry guy at the party or even the guy from the early days of our courtship. His eyes were childlike, afraid. "This can't be happening," he said. "I can't live without you."

"Don't say that."

"You told me you believed love could conquer anything," he said, his voice panicked. "It can, Jenna, we just have to be patient. It won't happen overnight. I know I'll make mistakes, but I love you, and I know this can work if you give it a chance."

I shook my head. "I've tried, Colton, but I don't know if you have. Nothing's changed. Everything just seems to be getting worse."

"You're all I have, Jenna. If I don't have you, I'll kill myself."

His threat stunned me, and the weight of the world pressed heavily on my shoulders because I sensed it was true. But I couldn't stay in a relationship because of a threat. If he was serious, I'd call nine-one-one so that they could put him on a psychiatric hold, but first, I needed to be perfectly clear for his sake and mine.

"I'm sorry," I said. "But, it's over."

"No. No!" he shouted, pacing. "No! No! No!"

I could see him trying to process this new reality in which the only person he'd ever truly loved had just left him. I should have ended it a while ago. I'd thought I was doing the right thing, being compassionate, giving us another chance, fighting for true love, and all that. But seeing how upset he was, I realized maybe I'd hurt him more by staying. The way he paced back and forth was like his feet moved the ground beneath him with forcible strength, and his chest labored like an asthmatic.

"I love you," he said, cupping my face again.

When I didn't change my mind, a wildfire of darkness ignited in his eyes. "I love you," he growled. He began breathing differently as his eyes tightened, looking at me with disgust rather than the tenderness from a moment ago. "I always loved you more than you could've imagined," he snarled as he slid his hand down my jaw to my neck.

And begin to squeeze.

Shocked, I tried to pry his hand off, but he added the other, pressing me against the wall. In unjustified disbelief, I stared into the eyes that had been far more dangerous than I'd ever imagined.

I couldn't breathe. I couldn't scream. I pulled at Colton's wrists, pushed his chest, tried to knee him in the groin, but no matter what I did or how I twisted, I could not get his hands off me.

I looked to the sidewalk, but it was empty. I prayed someone would drive past slow enough to see and courageous enough to help.

I pushed against his face, clawed at his hands, twisted and jerked my body, but I couldn't get a breath. Pressure mounted in my head, and my vision began to blur. Nine floors above us, twenty people were sipping drinks and having a good time, but down here, I was being killed and no one was the wiser.

"Jenna?" Justin shouted from a distance. Judging by his voice, he must be by the front entrance, out of eyeshot.

I thought maybe Colton would let me go, but he squeezed tighter; he knew I was almost gone.

"Jenna?" Justin's voice sounded farther away.

It broke my heart to know Justin would blame himself, replaying the moment he let me and Colton walk out of his sight. I wished I could tell him how sorry I was for letting this happen.

Blackness crept up in my vision, my lungs on fire. My body weakened. Colton's face blurred.

*I don't want to die.*

Justin's voice yelled.

The sounds of feet running on the pavement grew closer.

But he was too late.

My body flew through the air, and my head cracked against something hard.

And then there was darkness.

18

My eyes struggled to focus in the murky space that smelled like disinfectant. I was lying down, my legs pinned beneath a heavy blanket. My throat ached, my head throbbed, and something itched the top of my hand, something that felt like tape holding down a thin tube dripping icy liquid into my vein. An IV, I realized. I was in a hospital.

And I was not alone. A male approached me from one of the visitor chairs, his arm crooked across his stomach.

"Hey," Justin whispered. "How're you feeling?"

Blood stained his shirt. "Are you okay?" My voice was hoarse, and my throat felt like sandpaper.

He looked down, then back up. "Yours," he said, nodding towards my head. "Ten stitches. In the back. Had to shave a small section. They said you should be able to hide it until your hair grows back."

I pulled my hand up, wincing.

"You have some minor soft-tissue damage to the right shoulder, from when you went down, but it will heal in a couple weeks or so."

A crushing weight shattered my heart as it all came back—the breakup, the agony in Colton's eyes, the rage as the man who loved me attempted to strangle the life from my body. All my happiness and hope was reduced to dust as my soul burned, scorched of its spark for life. Leaving every cell singed into exhaustion.

It took me a moment to find my voice again, and when I spoke, I hated how small I sounded. "Did anyone at the party see what happened?"

"No," Justin said. "Some guy did show up when they were putting you into the ambulance, though."

"Who?"

"Don't know. Seemed to know you, but he was kind of an asshole, honestly."

Had Damian showed up after all? Or maybe Colton had invited one of his friends to the party?

I could hear a female voice arguing with someone down the hall, reminding me that if Mom found out what happened, she'd argue with me every day to move back home.

"Mom and Dad don't know, right?" I asked, my voice etching into a panic.

"No," Justin said.

"Please don't tell them." God, just weeks ago, they'd been in a room like this. I stared at the visitor chairs, remembering how Colton had fallen asleep holding me in one just like it, refusing to leave me in my time of need. The tender memory wilted, leaving me hollow in this gripping darkness.

"Is Colton...here?" Waiting to make sure I was okay, at least?

"No."

"Does he know I'm here?"

"Don't worry," Justin said with an edge. "He's not getting anywhere near you."

Colton had snapped, but once that momentary rage subsided, the man who cared more about me than anything in this world would need to know—no need to *ensure*—that I was okay. Despite our relationship ending, his love would've sent him rushing into the ambulance, even if it risked him getting arrested.

Was that why he couldn't be here? "Is he in jail?"

"No," Justin said. "He ran off as soon as he saw me."

*He...what?*

I could have sustained brain damage from lack of oxygen, or my neck could've been broken. I could've been lying there dying, for all Colton knew. And he just ran off? And never came back to see if I was okay?

How could the man who'd loved me unconditionally not care if I was alive or dead? How could he have *wanted* me dead in the first place? My breathing quickened as my heart banged against my lungs. It felt like a bomb had exploded, and as the rest of the world moved in silent motion, my brain focused only on the most acute pain.

Pain that had nothing to do with my physical injuries.

I let this happen to me. This was my fault because after he hurt me, I took him back. And even though my words said I'd never tolerate it, my actions said otherwise. Staying with him told him his behavior was acceptable. *I gave him permission to do it again.*

For a moment—just a brief moment—I wished I'd never woken up.

"He almost killed you. If I hadn't shown up when I did..." Justin grabbed his jaw. "You were limp, Jenna. I thought you might be... And then that asshole? When he saw me? He slammed you to the ground. Almost cracked your skull. That's why they're keeping you overnight."

Justin needed to stop telling me this stuff; I was on fire, and each revelation only doused me in more gasoline.

If Colton running off without making sure I was okay was heartbreaking, learning he'd made that *extra* effort to try and kill me was excruciating.

What I wouldn't give to be on that swing in our childhood backyard, feeling the sun on my eyelids as I mentally flew away from it all. But I was trapped in here, with nothing more than a window offering my mind an escape. A window with a windowsill where a curious flash of pink wrapped in clear plastic was tucked in the corner. As if trying to keep it out of sight.

"What's that?"

Justin's reluctance to answer only increased my curiosity, and when I motioned for him to hand it to me, I could tell he was nervous about my reaction. "Nurses weren't sure if you'd want it. I told 'em I didn't think so, but they, uh, said lemon juice should get the stain out."

Inside the transparent bag was the pink chiffon dress I'd worn to the party. The dress I thought would spark a night of romance was now covered in blood. My stomach clenched, rolling bile higher and higher until I began to gag. Justin's eyes widened, and he grabbed a plastic bin, shoving it under my mouth just in time for me to start dry heaving.

Between each heave, I sobbed an inhuman-sounding wail.

How could Colton's rage overpower his love for me? How could the man who'd once made me feel like the most special person on earth have so much hatred for me that he wished me dead?

After our first fight, I thought I was being considerate of his feelings, trying to avoid things that might upset him, but all I'd done was give Colton so much power over my life that I'd become stressed by everyday experiences. Like if a guy said hello to me, I let myself feel like *I'd* done something wrong, knowing Colton would blame *me* for it. How did I become so spineless?

I'd let myself morph from a strong woman I admired to a pathetic weakling who spent her life tiptoeing around a guy who mistreated me. I'd let him demean me.

There never was an *us* to get back to. The first part of our relationship was the lie. It was nothing more than a deadly illusion.

It took a solid minute of severe focus to stop the heaving. When I was done, Justin put the bin by the sink, sat on my bed, wrapped his unslung arm around me, and let me sob into his chest.

I could hear an argument between a man and a woman down the hall, and I wondered if that couple was able to keep things civil when they fought.

Justin ignored it. "I'm canceling my interview."

"No, you're not." I pulled back from his embrace. "The only thing that could possibly make me feel worse than I already do is if you miss that interview."

An angry voice grew louder and snapped, "Sir!" I guess they weren't a couple after all. "If you don't stop, I'm going to call security."

Footsteps stomped closer until a male figure appeared in my doorway, the light behind him creating a silhouette. Justin tensed. The tall figure entered the room, and when the light feathered across his face, I was shocked to see it was Damian. How in the world did he know I was here?

Behind him, a plump nurse scowled at him. "Sir," she barked, but it didn't break Damian's concentration as he scanned my bed, my IV. Trying to figure out how badly I was hurt.

"It's okay," I said to her.

She frowned at me like Damian had pissed her off, and I'd robbed her of the satisfaction of having him hauled off by security guards.

"You know this guy?" Justin asked disapprovingly.

"He's a friend." I turned to Damian. "How did you know I was here?"

"You need to leave," Justin insisted.

Damian didn't budge.

"It's fine," I said, but evidently, no one trusted my judgment anymore.

"No, it's not. You need your rest." Justin stepped around the bed and stood directly in front of Damian.

The nurse lingered for a few seconds—perhaps hoping I'd change my mind and demand Damian leave—and then marched off in annoyance. Without taking his eyes off me, Damian snaked around Justin—either assuming a guy with two broken arms wouldn't punch him or not caring if he did—and stood next to my bed.

Justin looked like he wanted to clobber Damian with my IV pole. "I'm getting security."

"Don't," I pleaded. "Justin!" But he stormed out of the room. *Wonderful.* I sighed and turned my attention to Damian. "You better leave before you get in trouble."

Damian's eyes glided over my body, his voice searing with anger. "What did he do to you?"

My neck and face turned impossibly hot, and the despair expanded within me. "You were right," I said, twisting my hands together. "Zoey was right." I tried to stop my pathetic lip from quivering.

Damian's jaw tensed.

"I should have listened to you," I said. "I should have seen this coming. All the signs were there." I swallowed down another dry heave. "I'm so stupid."

Damian's chest rose. "You're not stupid."

Yes, I was. Incredibly stupid. There had been so many clues. His jealousy, his constant accusations, and as if that weren't enough, I took Colton somewhere *isolated* and broke up with him *in person*. *If that's not the definition of stupidity, I don't know what is.*

"You really should go…" Before security came. But he didn't leave. Instead, he dragged a chair next to my bed, sat down, and rubbed his hands together. "How did you know I was here?"

It took Damian a second to respond, as if answering my question broke him away from some internal fantasy playing in his head of beating Colton's face in. "Emily uninvited me to your party. Said it wasn't a good night for it, and I got worried something was wrong. Decided to come check that you were okay. When I got there…" Damian chewed his lip. "I saw the ambulance."

So it was Damian Justin had seen, not Colton's friend. I could imagine the rest. Damian demanding to know which hospital. Maybe even following the ambulance but being confined to the waiting room because he wasn't family. Getting into an argument with the nurse but somehow figuring out which room I was in, then storming in here to see if I was okay.

"Is he in jail?" Damian asked.

I shook my head.

"Where is he?"

"How should I know?"

"Where does he live?"

"What does that have to do with…" I stopped, picking up on how nefarious Damian's glare was, how aggressively he kneaded his hands together. "You're not going after him."

Two security officers interrupted us when they came into the room. Justin walked in next to them, throwing Damian a dirty look, which Damian reciprocated ten times over. As if Damian's hostility towards my brother was rooted in something more than the security disagreement...

"He can stay," I said, but it fell on deaf, ego-bruised ears. The guards looked excited as they advanced, ready for a battle. This was probably the part of their job they most looked forward to.

Damian glowered at the men with a hardened jaw. "Lay a hand on me," Damian encouraged in a tone that added, *I dare you.* When Damian refused to move, Justin stepped into his space, provoking Damian to stand up as they both tipped their bodies forward, waiting —maybe even hoping—for the other to make the first move.

I was about to remind them how grown humans should behave in a hospital, but suddenly, another man entered the room. And raised an eyebrow when he saw the two guards. It took a second to recognize him—the cop who'd investigated Justin's assault: Fisher.

"You called the police?" I asked Justin, appalled.

"No," Justin said.

"I'm here to take your statement," Fisher explained.

"We were just escorting this guy out," the shorter guard said, nodding to Damian.

"And I was just saying he could stay, and everyone was ignoring me while flexing their biceps," I added in frustration.

"Why don't you guys all wait in the hall," Fisher suggested.

Several moments passed without any movement, so Fisher came farther into the room and pointed towards the door with an impatient hand. After the guards left, Justin waited until Damian walked out before joining him in the hall. Hopefully, they wouldn't fight out there. *At least if they do, they're in a place with immediate medical attention available.*

Fisher sat in the chair on the side of my bed and opened a miniature notebook. "Need to ask you some questions, kid." Questions. Also known as admitting every humiliating detail of what happened.

What were the chances that the same investigator that worked

Justin's case was now assigned to mine? "Does Chicago PD only employ one detective?"

Fisher's lips curled slightly. "Heard the name on dispatch. Raised my hand on this one."

"Why?"

"For one, I met you working your brother's case and was nearby when the call came in."

"And for two?" He looked reluctant to explain his other reason, but, after measuring my curiosity—perhaps sensing that I'd just keep asking, thwarting his questions—he let out a deep breath. "Early days of being a cop, I worked a domestic violence call. The girl had a split lip. By the time we show up, boyfriend's standing next to her, his arm around her, looking like the remorseful guardian. She refuses to press charges. Says he loves her." Fisher clicked his pen open, then shut. Open, then shut. "I had this bad feeling that I shouldn't leave her there, but my partner explained it happens all the time, nothing more we can do. Still. Couldn't shake that feeling. So a couple days later, I stop back over to check on her. No one answers. Door's ajar, so I go in, gun drawn." Silence laced the air with apprehension. "I find her in the living room, in a pool of blood, next to the baseball bat. Dead at least a day, the coroner said."

I had no idea what he expected me to say after that or why he looked like he was waiting to let it sink in.

"Now, can we get started?" He clicked his pen open again.

I blinked. "Do I have to do this?"

"Afraid so."

"What's going to happen to him?"

Fisher held my eyes for a beat. "Let's just take this one step at a time, okay?" He flipped through his pages until he reached an empty one. All those other pages were undoubtedly filled with detailed accounts of other people's nightmares. And now mine would be added to the collection. "What happened?"

I took a calming breath and told him everything. Fisher made notes with tiny, messy letters that were probably designed that way so people couldn't see their humiliating mistakes written in black and white. "If I'd just had a slightly different angle, I could've gotten my knee up. I could've gotten him off me." I wanted him to write that down, too; it was important to me that people didn't see me as a weakling.

Guided by his questions, he also took me back to the first time Colton had hurt me. I confirmed no police report was filed, there were no witnesses, and no, even though Zoey and Damian saw the marks, I hadn't documented the bruises. Throughout it all, his empathetic voice spoke of a man who'd interviewed who-knows-how-many recipients of violence. When he finished, he stood up.

"Okay, kid, I'll be in touch."

Justin and Damian must have been pacing the hall because as soon as Fisher reached the doorway, they came in and claimed two opposite corners of the bed. Damian crossed his arms over his chest, ignoring Justin's immense irritation at his presence.

"What happens now?" Justin asked.

Fisher held the expression of a man who'd seen more than his fair share of justice not being served. "We'll put an APB out on him for his arrest."

Impatience laced Damian's words. "And in the meantime?"

Justin looked annoyed that Damian had the nerve to ask questions.

"File a restraining order," Fisher answered.

"A piece of paper," Damian said.

"That piece of paper makes it illegal for him to come near her, even if he makes bail."

"Bail?" Justin choked.

"And he'll have to turn over any weapons." Fisher put the pen into his breast pocket. "He got any weapons?"

I wished he hadn't asked that. Not in front of the boys. "A gun."

Damian and Justin exchanged a look—this time, their disgust for one another took a backseat to their worry.

"So we're supposed to what?" Damian snarled. "Wait around, and if he comes after her, hope she's not dead by the time cops show up?"

"Can't you put a protective detail on her or something?" Justin pressed.

"I'll put in a request for a car, but the last three requests got denied. Manpower's tight. If we assigned a cop to every domestic violence victim—" Fisher started.

"I'm not a *victim*," I insisted, insulted.

"You might actually *prevent* people from being killed," Damian said.

Offense washed over Fisher's face. "Pretty ironic coming from you," Fisher snapped.

What in the world did *that* mean? Fisher and Damian exchanged a contentious stare.

I chewed my thumbnail. "When he gets arrested, they'll get him help, right? Like counseling?"

The boys furrowed their eyebrows.

"He tried to kill you," Justin said.

"He's got psychological problems that are obviously worse than I realized."

Fisher hesitated. "Right now, we need to focus on you."

"What's there to focus on? It's over."

"Fact is, you're in more danger now than you ever were."

Damian and Justin tensed.

"Seventy percent of domestic violence homicides happen *after* the relationship ends," Fisher explained. "It's called separation violence. Once the abuser realizes he's lost control of the victim—"

"Please don't use that word," I snapped.

"—and can't get her to take him back, he panics." He looked at me, willing me to understand the danger I was in.

"I know Colton." He'd have snapped out of his rage by now. "If anything, he might try to apologize."

"At first, maybe. But it's unlikely he'll let you go."

I didn't think about it until this moment, but Fisher was right: Colton would never walk away and move on with his life. *Ever.* A shiver tore through me.

"When it sinks in that the relationship is truly over, he's likely to snap again. Could happen right away. Might be two months from now. Maybe even longer. I've seen it a hundred times, kid. The fact that he choked you is a significant predictor for future lethal violence."

Damian's eyes tightened as he regarded at my neck with an all-new rage.

"Statistically speaking, you're ten times more likely to be killed than someone who hasn't been choked," Fisher warned.

"Do I have any hope at all, then, or should I just hurl myself off the roof and be done with it?"

Fisher's unamused eyes held mine. "Let's talk options. My recommendation? A shelter," he said. "Many of them are at capacity, but I could make some calls."

"No. Those are for women in, like, major danger." Who have to flee in the middle of the night, with little kids. I didn't need that, and I certainly wasn't about to take a precious spot away from someone whose life depended on getting into one. Especially a spot that might save an innocent child. "I'm going back to my apartment."

"No," Damian and Justin said in unison.

"Bad idea, kid," Fisher said. "He knows where you live."

"As soon as I'm home, I'll lock my doors and windows, and won't open them for anyone."

"Those can be broken down pretty easily."

"If that happens, I'll call nine-one-one."

"Takes three to four minutes for first responders to arrive to a life-threatening call. Only takes a second to shoot you, few seconds to stab you. Besides, he knows where you work. Knows your schedule."

"What about staying with Mom or Dad for a bit?" Justin asked.

"What are you, crazy? They've been through enough. Besides, I need to stay in the city to work."

"Jen—" Justin started to argue.

"I'm going to work, and they're not finding out about this. End of discussion."

Justin seemed to reevaluate the level of stubbornness he was dealing with. "Then stay with me."

"How are *you* going to protect her?" Damian challenged. "Swat him to death with your casts?"

If Justin thought it was possible to assassinate someone with a look, he was trying it right now.

"Do you have any friends you could stay with?" Fisher suggested. "Preferably someplace Colton doesn't know about?"

I shook my head. Colton knew where Zoey lived, and even if he didn't, she was the last person I could handle staying with right now; our friendship needed to be rebuilt. Plus, the humiliation of going to her with my tail between my legs was too much to bear.

"Stay with me," Damian insisted.

"No," I said.

"You're staying with me," Justin declared.

"You fly out tomorrow for your job interview," I started.

"I'll—" Justin tried to interrupt, but I held up my hand.

"And you are *not* canceling it. I'll avoid my apartment, but only if you go to New York."

"And you'll stay where?" Justin challenged.

"I don't know? A hotel, maybe?"

"Alone? No e'ffin way," Justin said.

"Justin—"

"For god's sake, you're staying with me. At least until your brother gets back," Damian snapped. "That piece of shit doesn't know me or where I live, so it's a hell of a lot safer than anyone else's place. And when you start to feel better, I can teach you some self-defense moves if you want."

Fisher cleared his throat. "I'll let you all sort this out," he said. "Wherever you stay, you need to be careful. He could follow you, so you shouldn't be alone until we catch him." Fisher silently implored me to understand the gravity of the battle ahead. "Domestic abusers don't give up. It's not a question of *if* he comes after you, but *when*."

19

"How could you give me that ultimatum?" I demanded.

"She speaks," Justin said. "I was beginning to forget what your voice sounded like."

We sat on the "L" train. An aisle separated rows of black seats flanked by windows, peppered with silver poles that the standing-room-only patrons held on to for balance. The train rocked side to side as it thundered through the buildings with its metallic roar, the air stuffy, smelling like fast food.

"Mom and Dad have been through enough. How could you even think of putting them through this? It'd crush them."

"Not as much as attending your funeral."

I shook my head in frustration. Ultimatums are dirty tactics to control someone else by using their most vulnerable fear against them. Mom and Dad lived in a world where bad guys existed on the periphery. If they thought one had penetrated my inner circle, they'd never feel safe again, and it'd be cruel to take away their sense of security.

"I wasn't going to sneak out and go back to my place," I said, crossing my arms over my chest. "All I said was that I couldn't stay away *indefinitely*."

I mean honestly, threatening to tell them what was going on if I evaded bodyguard duty?

The train opened its doors, allowing *those* people to get off and go where they *wanted*.

The farther the train got from Justin's place, the tenser he became. He ran his unslung hand through his hair. "I don't know how you talked me into this."

"*You're* the one insisting that I can't be alone."

"He's a stranger."

"Damian's not a stranger," I said. "And it's just a couple of days."

"Four. Four days."

"You don't fly out until tonight, and then you fly back Wednesday, so it's like two full days. And I'll be at work most of the time. We talked about this." For hours.

Justin bounced his leg nervously. "Yeah, well, agreeing to it and going through with it feel like two very different things."

I seriously did not have it in me to go over all this again. It took an extreme amount of convincing to get Justin over the hump once; if he changed his mind, he'd miss out on his job opportunity, and that would haunt me for the rest of my life.

My cell phone buzzed with an unknown number.

I ignored it as my brother studied me, a million questions behind his eyes. Questions that had been there since I got released from the hospital yesterday. Questions I saw him trying not to ask as we packed a bag at my place, as I'd stayed at his apartment last night, and all day today.

He rubbed his face. "This wasn't the first time he hurt you," he finally said. "Was it?"

I smoothed wrinkles in my jeans that didn't exist before speaking softly so no other passengers could eavesdrop. "There was one other incident, but it was...minor."

Justin's lips pulled into a straight line. "Why didn't you tell me?"

"Because you'd never see him the same again. To you, he'd be a bad guy for the rest of his life, and at the time, I loved him too much to do that to him." I looked out the window at the people strolling along the sidewalk beneath us, free to go wherever they wanted—a freedom Colton wouldn't have again for a long time. As much as I wanted him to be held accountable for his actions, that realization still hurt. "I'm worried about how this will all turn out for him."

Justin moved his jaw from side to side.

"Colton can't get a do-over from that night," I explained. "He'll have a record that'll follow him forever. Every single job application, every relationship he has from this point forward, he'll have to tell them about this." And that was after he spent time in prison.

I stood in the ashes of the life Colton could have had, holding the torch that had burned it to the ground.

"I don't understand how you can give two shits about him. The guy tried to *kill you.*"

"I know."

"Do you? Realize the danger you're in? Because denial gets people killed."

"I'm not in denial. I get it." I did. And I knew it sounded absurd— even I didn't understand how my emotions could be so contradicting. How could I feel afraid of what he was capable of, feel disgusted and angry by his actions, and yet, at the same time, feel sorry for him, that he'd ruined his life like this? I might not be in love with Colton anymore, but I didn't *root* for his demise, either. I guess, in a way, I was mourning the loss of the life I wanted him to have.

And mourning the loss of my once-optimistic view on the beauty of love.

Perhaps I should have prioritized other things in my life instead of getting lost in our love story. "Maybe you had it right all along, focusing on your career."

My brother repositioned his sling. "I've been thinking the opposite, actually."

His tone had a more profound reflection in it than merely debating a job offer. I waited for him to explain as he picked at his cast.

"You know, the whole time growing up, money was a struggle. The roof would leak, we couldn't fix it right away, and we'd wear shoes long after we'd outgrown them," he mused. "But after the divorce, it got so much worse." Justin shook his head. "Sometimes Mom would wait until she thought we were in bed," he said, "and then spread out all the bills on the table and stare at them like a jigsaw puzzle that would never fit together." My brother's voice lowered. "On the really bad days, I could hear her crying."

My stomach plummeted. How did Justin know this and I didn't? Was I too self-absorbed, too busy feeling sorry for myself that my folks divorced, to notice what was going on around me?

"I always thought if I made enough money, maybe I could help Mom. She can't keep living like that."

His revelation instantly rewrote years of his motivations and magnified my love for him.

"You want to save Mom."

"More than that." He shrugged. "I guess I want to have a positive influence on this life. Leave the world a better place and all that." He gave a rueful smile and blew out such a big breath that his cheeks puffed. "But when I woke up in the hospital, I started to question if I was going about it all wrong. Before, I thought having money was the only way to help people, because growing up that seemed to be the only thing capable of solving our problems. But now..." He tilted his head back on the seat rest and groaned. "I love this job," he said. "I do, and building my career excites the heck out of me. But I don't know if I want to keep up this pace. I let it monopolize my life, you know? Never made much time for friends or even to ask this girl out that I like."

"If you want to make a difference, you don't have to sacrifice your whole life to do it."

Justin chewed the inside of his cheek.

"Please, don't take the job unless you *truly* want it."

"I don't know what I want."

"Then you have to go there and see if it feels right or not. If you don't even try, you'll regret it for the rest of your life."

When the door opened at our stop and Justin followed me off the train, I took it as a good sign he might follow through with our plan after all. But it wasn't over until he got on that plane. And now, something else seemed to bother him—something, perhaps, embroiled in the attack that provoked these life reflections.

"Travis told me about the fraud thing," I said. "Do you think it had anything to do with your assault?"

Justin kept his face neutral. "I think it was a random mugging."

Did he really think that? Or was he lying so I wouldn't worry about him?

I had a gut feeling it wasn't random. Maybe it was something Fisher said, how Justin handles lots of money—money's always a motive. Or how the fraud thing happened at such a critical time, or Travis's suspiciously ambivalent attitude about it. Whatever the reason, it felt like there was something more to this.

In fact, it'd always bothered me how Justin knew where I was that night. It was the one puzzle piece I could never explain, but today it hit me: What if Justin found out about the fraud thing *before* that Friday, and someone was trying to intimidate him because of it? And when it didn't work, they pressured him by threatening his only relative in the city—me. What if they'd been following me and called Justin with proof of it, hoping he'd finally do whatever they wanted him to? It'd explain Justin's anger when he called me, and how he knew where I was.

And maybe that was why he seemed *this* worried about letting me out of his sight.

My cell phone buzzed from that same number, only this time, it was a text. It took everything to hide the shock on my face as I read it.

**I hate myself for what I've done. U r all that matters 2 me. I NEED to know you're okay. PLEASE call me back at this number. I LOVE you. Colton.**

*He's not letting me go...*

## 20

D amian's apartment had a relaxed industrial style with brick walls, exposed pipes on the ceilings, distressed wood floors, and oversized windows that flooded the place with light. In his bedroom, where he'd told me to set my stuff down, everything matched Damian's personality—the black furniture, gray bedding, and a framed poster of a fighter in midswing. But there was one glaring exception: sitting on top of the hardened fighter's dresser was a pink stuffed animal.

"You have my cell," Justin muttered. He and Damian were by the front door while I lingered in here, hoping it'd decrease the chances of Justin changing his mind about leaving. "She leaves this place? You're with her. She leaves work? You're with her. She's at work or here, that's it. If I find out you took her anywhere else…"

I could imagine Damian glaring at him.

Justin needed to hurry; the sunlight was fading fast, and traffic to O'Hare Airport was unpredictable.

"Keep your eyes and ears open," Justin demanded. "If you see him—"

"If I ever see that piece of shit again, he'll get the beating of his life," Damian declared in an eerily calm tone.

My face flushed in embarrassment.

"What's your angle here? You've known my sister, what—a few weeks? If I find out this is some sort of Romeo play to take advantage of her—"

"You'll swat me to death with your casts. Yeah, I know." After a few seconds, Damian sighed. "Look, man, we're after the same thing here. No one's going to touch her."

Unable to listen to their misguided belief that they were suddenly secret service agents, I refocused on the dresser, noticing a framed photo that lacked the sharpness of a modern camera. In it, a little girl and boy with green eyes and dark hair smiled, while the girl hugged a stuffed bunny. The same bunny that was sitting next to the photo. It was Damian and his sister, Sophie, I realized, and the bunny was Hippy—the one she carried everywhere. I'd never seen Damian smile as big as he did in that picture, nor had I ever seen that light brimming from his eyes.

I could imagine their life before the accident. Damian and his father playing catch in the backyard while his mom and sister played dolls, kisses as Damian climbed onto the school bus each morning with his second-grade backpack that probably had a lunchbox note that said, *I love you!*, bedtime stories from a loving father, and family vacations packed full of memories.

The little boy in that photo had no idea that soon, his biggest worry would no longer be his Little League game getting rained out or what Santa might bring for Christmas. He had no idea this was one of the last happy moments of his life.

Damian opened his bedroom door and saw what I was looking at.

"She's beautiful," I said.

Looking from the powerful guy standing before me to the happy boy in the photo, I thought about how I've always believed people come into your life for a reason. Maybe Damian came into my life to show me how to rebuild after something like Colton, and perhaps I'd come into his life to help him open himself up to people. Because I sensed he'd otherwise spend his life alone.

Damian leaned against the doorframe as he studied me. "How're you feeling?"

I touched the scarf on my neck. "I'm fine."

He chewed his cheek. "Need some Advil?"

"I already took some," I said. "But thanks." It was sweet of him to always think of my needs.

Damian tucked his hands into his pockets, so many emotions swirling over his face. "Did the doctors say anything else when you were released?"

"I'll be fine," I assured him. "It's just some bruising."

But he knew better than anyone that the bruises ran deeper than the skin. They ran all the way to your soul and left permanent splinters in your heart.

Damian looked physically pained at the thought of what I must be going through. I wondered what it was like for him, being a kid, hiding his injuries from people, coping with his soul's bruises on his own.

"You okay?" he asked.

I ran a hand through my hair and let out a deep breath. "Emotionally, it's weird and confusing. I'm upset about everything that happened, of course, and I know things ended...terribly. But still. It was a serious relationship." *Shouldn't I be heartbroken over Colton for a long time?* "I thought there'd be at least a small part of me that missed him—the boyfriend him, you know?" I shook my head, shrugging. "But I don't. And not just because of this violence. I don't know what that means, that all I feel is...relieved to be free." I took a deep breath, thinking about the last few weeks, thinking about when everything had changed for me. "I guess if I'm being honest with myself, my feelings were never the same after that first..." I stopped myself.

Damian tried to hide it behind his leg, but I saw him clench his fingers into a fist.

"It's been toxic," I hedged. Maybe all that time I'd been holding on, waiting for that first part of our relationship to come back, I was unknowingly waiting for my heart to feel towards Colton what it once had. "Maybe I fell out of love with him sooner than I realized."

Because now that I was out of it, our love didn't feel like it had ended a few days or even weeks ago. I loved Colton. I always would, and I hoped he'd get the help he needed. But being *in love* with him felt like an ancient memory.

"I'm glad you got away from him, Jenna," Damian said. "You deserve someone great."

I met his gaze, and my eyes stung with tears. It was incredible; I could feel how much Damian cared for me, just in the way he looked at me. Like he wanted to pull me against his chest and hold me.

And the weird thing was? A part of me wouldn't have minded it. Maybe it was because our friendship was the most stable thing in my life. Maybe it was because the only thing I ever felt when I was with Damian was happy, a breath of air after holding it underwater. Whatever the reason, I appreciated it. And him.

"Thank you," I said, "for letting me stay here."

"I want you here." Damian crossed his arms over his chest. "I feel anxious when you're not around."

Anxious?

He must have sensed my unspoken question because he cleared his throat.

"I feel…" He rubbed the back of his neck and stared at me for several seconds before finishing. "Very protective of you."

My eyes stung again because that was just so damn sweet. But I didn't want the guys to feel all this apprehension. "You don't have to worry about me."

His magnetic eyes held mine.

"It's not just because I worry," he professed.

What did that mean? Why did my pulse react to it, and why did it feel like there was something he wasn't saying to me?

I studied him, thinking back to everything he'd done for me. Staying with me at the bar before Justin's attack, when Damian thought those frat guys were going to give me grief. Driving me to the hospital, staying, taking care of me. Even when it meant missing his comeback fight. Opening up to me about his past, when I was in my most vulnerable hour, making me feel like I wasn't alone in this cold world. Warning me about Colton and doing it in such a kind way, he never made me feel stupid in the process. Coming to the hospital to see if I was okay, and now this—opening his home to me. Without question.

"You're a really good person, Damian."

I hoped he knew that. Because he was. And I appreciated the warmth he brought into my life. Saying he was going above and beyond here was the biggest understatement of the century.

"Why are you so nice to me?" I asked.

Damian's jaw tightened.

"What?" Why did my question upset him?

"I hate that when someone's nice to you, it's so outside your comfort zone you don't know what to make of it."

"That's not true. Everyone's nice to me." Justin, Zoey, my parents—they had issues, but they were nice.

"No one's cared for you the way you deserve," Damian growled.

I swallowed. My parents cared about me. I might not have been at the forefront of their love or devotion, but it wasn't because they didn't care about me. And other people cared about me, too. Most poignantly, at this moment... "You do."

Damian's lips curled up slightly to one side, but as he stared at me for several heartbeats, that smile faded. Replaced by the ghost of a frown.

As if something inside him hurt.

It seemed to take him a second to recalibrate.

"You really tired, or were you just saying that so Justin would leave?"

Okay, that had me curious. "Why?"

Damian looked at his phone. "I'm supposed to have a thing tonight. Scheduled it before the party," he added, as if he owed me an explanation for having a life. He rubbed his jaw. "If you'd feel safer here, we'll stay, but I assure you I'll keep you safe no matter where we are."

I blinked. "What kind of a *thing*?"

Damian grabbed a black duffle bag from his closet. "I'll explain on the way. C'mon. We're running late."

. . .

THIS PLACE WAS REMOTE. AFTER AN HOUR ON THE FREEWAY, WE TOOK A two-lane road that became gravel, then dirt. It snaked through a forest with thirty-foot-tall trees and dense shrubs that canopied us on both sides until we came upon a clearing, where a flat-roofed structure with garage doors was surrounded by a hundred cars on its gravel parking lot and lawn.

"Where are we?" I asked.

Damian parked the red pickup truck—his primary vehicle, he'd explained, the motorcycle was for fun—on the bumpy grass with a clunk of the gear shift and eyed the cars. "Maybe this wasn't such a good idea."

"It's fine." I hopped out of the truck. I welcomed the distraction from my train wreck of a life.

"It's not too late to leave." Carrying his bag, Damian surveyed the surrounding area again. The night was chilly but beautiful, with a full moon and clouds hinting at a coming storm. The humid air smelled of pine and grass.

"I don't want to leave." I was excited to be part of Damian's world. Our friendship had been so one-sided so far, and I was eager to see a part of his life that was important to him, eager to support him, just like he'd supported me. And I wasn't going to let him miss another event on account of me.

On the drive over, Damian explained what was at stake tonight. After canceling his MMA-sanctioned fight the night Justin was attacked, he hadn't been able to rebook a professional event. Too big a flight risk, they'd said. Lost money, disappointed fans. Coming back via the underground circuit would put some chatter and online videos out there, hopefully enticing the professional circuit into giving him another chance.

As we made our way towards the building, our feet crunched on the gravel. "Why were you being so tense with Justin?"

He gave me a knowing look as we approached the building.

"What?" I asked.

"He's your brother. Shoulda protected you."

"Seriously? That's what it's about?" He couldn't possibly hold Justin accountable for not knowing about Colton! Before I could argue—this was *my* mess, not Justin's, and I certainly didn't need an older brother safeguarding me from my own mistakes—Damian opened a door, beyond which three guys and two girls stood in a concrete room, illuminated with only one lightbulb.

"'Bout time," the taller guy said. He had buzzed hair and tattoos of ribbons laced around his muscular arms.

"Jenna, this is Sturge." Damian nodded to the buzz-cut guy. "Ricky," he said, nodding to a leaner guy, "and Levi," he added, nodding to the guy with a nose ring. "That's Mallory." He motioned to a girl with severely straight black hair, an exposed belly, and cowboy boots. "And Audrey," he said, looking at a blond. "Guys, this is Jenna."

Levi held Audrey's hand, but Mallory appeared to be a free agent, and it was evident by the look on her face she'd expected Damian to come alone. Oozing with hostility camouflaged behind ambivalence, she stared at me like I was an insect invading a picnic.

"Let's get you taped up," Sturge said.

But Damian didn't move. He looked at me like this had all seemed perfectly safe in his head, but now, the idea of leaving me—even just a few feet away—worried him. He cleared his throat. "I'll need you to keep an eye on her if everything goes to hell."

Five sets of curious eyes made my cheeks warm, but something bothered me more than their stares. What did he mean everything might go to hell?

Sturge assessed me. "Why?"

"Just...keep an eye on her at all times. Make sure no one gets anywhere near her."

Everyone else seemed curious about Damian's secret pet, but Mallory looked at me like she was plotting my demise.

"Sure, whatever," Sturge snarled.

"I have your word?"

"Yeah. Now let's just get on with it already. Crowd's been waiting twenty minutes."

Damian waited for a few moments to see if I'd change my mind before pulling his shirt off. Without a trace of self-consciousness, he undressed down to nothing but a pair of tight black shorts.

*Wow.*

Damian's beautiful muscles layered into each other like a work of art. His olive-skinned body had broad shoulders, a massive chest and back, and thighs that bulged from his shorts. His tattoos stunningly wrapped around the contours of his arms, as if designed around his muscles, but most impressive was his ripped stomach. I didn't know abs like that existed in the real world; I'd only seen them on the cover of fitness magazines and assumed it was thanks to airbrushing.

Damian Stone was exquisitely beautiful, yet he walked around like he was unaware of this fact.

*What is wrong with me, noticing his body like this?* Shame on me when I'd *just* gotten out of a toxic relationship. My life was crumbling, and evidently, my hormones hadn't gotten the memo.

I risked a glance at Damian's face, praying he hadn't caught my ogling, but when our eyes met, his mouth tugged up on one side.

*Dammit. He totally noticed me staring. And he liked it.*

When I blushed, he bit back a smirk.

*Double dammit.*

As Sturge wrapped Damian's knuckles with white tape, Damian didn't take his eyes off me. It made my chest warm because it was as if we were the only two people in the room while a ghost of a smile danced across his face.

Something Mallory very obviously did not appreciate. In addition to glaring at me, she made a show of how unfazed she was by his undressing, making it clear she'd seen it many times before.

Once Sturge finished, Damian closed the distance between us. "Don't leave their sides for any reason. Understood?"

I nodded, pretending not to notice Mallory's scowl as Damian ushered me down a hallway with his hand on the small of my back.

We entered a room forty feet wide with a scattering of lightbulbs, cement floors, tall ceilings with steel beams holding up the roof, and exposed pipes—one of which drip, drip, dripped water onto a growing puddle in the corner. Two hundred bodies packed the mildew-smelling space.

Damian took my hand, and even though he didn't mean anything by it—he was just trying to keep track of me—something inside me stirred.

As Damian snaked down the aisle, the crowd roared, their eyes wild with primal excitement. Not the type of fans who went to fights with protective refs, they clearly got off on not knowing if the guys would make it out of here in one piece. Beneath the decorative scarf that hid my bruises, my neck began to sweat. Maybe I should've talked him out of this… There were no mats, nothing to keep him safe, and this place was grungy—the floor stained and covered with dirt that hadn't been swept in years.

People chanted Damian's name, holding their hands out for high-fives, but Damian ignored it all, alternating his eyes between me and whatever awaited him in the middle of the room: an open space no bigger than a trampoline, marked off by masking tape on the floor. Once we reached the center, Damian cupped my head to ensure I was listening to him over the crowd. "Stay by them at all times." Only after I nodded did Damian let me go and leave me flanked by Sturge and Ricky.

Damian's bald opponent bounced up and down and brandished a menacing smile.

Suddenly, this all felt like a horrible mistake. Now that I was here, seeing two men gearing up to beat each other, the danger seemed visceral, and Damian's words—*if everything goes to hell*—alarmed me. *Damian might get hurt.* An obvious possibility I hadn't thought much about because I'd been too preoccupied with the excitement of getting to see him fight.

As if that weren't bad enough, in my periphery, I saw Mallory glowering at me.

Levi held Damian's arm up and then threw it down. The crowd howled.

Seeing Damian fight online versus in person were two entirely different things. Here, I could feel the intensity of his eyes locked onto his prey, the excitement radiating off his body. His expression reminded me of an addict about to get their fix, and, unlike watching a fight from the past, I didn't know if Damian would come out of this okay.

I chewed my thumbnail.

The fact that Mallory kept looking at me pissed me off, because it showed a callous indifference to the peril Damian was in.

While his opponent was bouncy, Damian was methodically calm, circling the guy, making him move. The other guy swung, but Damian deflected it effortlessly and punched the guy's jaw with a resounding crack. The crowd cheered.

I admired how hard Damian must have worked to become this skilled at boxing and how, when his life had been in danger, he'd taken action.

Damian kicked, but the guy dodged it and punched him in the ribs so hard I thought his fist would penetrate Damian's body. I drew in a sharp breath.

Meanwhile, Mallory inched so close to me, I had to take a step away so our hips wouldn't touch. I clenched my fists, annoyed at her alpha-dog tactics. She put her hands in her back pockets to show off her stomach—the kind all girls envied—tiny, with trim lines, complete with a belly ring.

"So, how long have you and Damian been together?" She didn't even try to hide the poison in her tone.

I didn't have the energy to deal with her hostility. I wanted to focus on Damian, because it felt like if I took my eyes off him, he might get hurt.

"We're not together."

"Then what are you doing here?" Mallory asked it in a way that made it clear I wasn't welcome.

"He invited me."

"I thought you said you weren't together."

"We're not," I said.

In the cage, Damian landed a ferocious blow to the guy's rib cage while out here, a different match now entered round two. And I could feel my patience wavering.

"Then why'd he invite you?" Mallory interrogated.

"Because we're friends."

"Damian doesn't have friends," she snarled. "*We're* the only ones he ever hangs out with, and I've been coming to his fights for over two years. Levi helps Damian with his publicity and Sturge with training. Lotta times, we all grab dinner after."

*Translation: I'm in his inner circle, and you're not, scarf girl, so stay away.*

All those times I'd let Colton push me around emotionally, I'd just accepted it. I cared about *his* feelings, trying to be kind, but in the end I'd let him stomp all over me. Just like Belly Ring was trying to do now, clearly misinterpreting my friendship with Damian as peeing on a fire hydrant she'd been building with him. If she was going to talk to me with such palpable loathing, I wasn't going to be nice back. I was done with that. "Weird, he's never mentioned you. Maybe I'll ask about it tonight when we're back at his apartment."

My uppercut made her nostrils flare. I could see in her little rage-infested face she'd never been to Damian's apartment. "Well," she said in a fake-nice voice, like when someone calls you *sweetheart* but means *witch*, "I think it's nice of you to be his friend. Most people wouldn't, after what he did." She let her words hang in the air, but when I refused to take her bait, Mallory persisted. "I mean, I've asked myself, am I really safe hanging around someone who's done what he has?"

I would not, under any circumstance, give into her tactics.

Damian charged the guy and pinned him down for several seconds before the guy managed to get out of it and bounce back to his feet.

Mallory shook her head for dramatic effect. "I mean, to have actually killed someone before..."

The world stilled beneath my feet, and I wondered if it would disintegrate right under me. I blinked, unwilling to let the shock show on my face because she was obviously not referring to Damian feeling responsible for his dad and sister's death. She meant *killed*, in the active form of the verb. Purposeful.

Damian slammed his fist into the other guy's head with terrifying force.

"Fighting's a dangerous sport," I said.

Now she full-on smirked. "Didn't happen in a fight."

While she gloated, I felt sick. She had to be lying. Or exaggerating. There was no way Damian was a killer, and if—by some small chance —something horrible did happen, it *had* to have been during an MMA fight. A lousy shot gone horribly wrong. Tragic, but a risk in the profession.

But if it were something as honest as that, why'd he keep it from me? And why the ominous threat: *I'm the type of guy you don't want to mess with.* That didn't sound like someone who felt guilty; it sounded like someone who was proud of what he'd done.

I clutched my stomach. Had I trusted him too blindly? Had I learned nothing from my experience with Colton?

Damian cracked his fist into the guy's nose, and I gasped. I'd never seen blood spray like that, and even more came out when Damian hit him again. Stunned, the guy wobbled backward, and the crowd roared as Damian drew his bloodstained hand back and smashed it into the guy's temple.

With closed eyes, he fell to the floor, limp. But Damian didn't stop. A rabid dog with wild eyes and tendons bulging from his muscles, he hit him again and again, each thud cracking his ribs, his face. The crowd's cheering subsided into unease. Sturge and Levi yanked at Damian's shoulders, but he kept hitting, ignoring their shouts. It took them several perilous seconds to overpower Damian and pull him off the bloody body.

I stepped backward, bile creeping into my mouth. No longer recognizing the man before me. His chest was splattered with blood, his once-white-taped knuckles now crimson.

Damian panted for several seconds and then searched the space until he spotted me. His expression fell when he registered the look on my face.

"Jenna!" he called.

In the chaos of the postwin cheering, his friends were distracted. I ran, pushed my way through the sea of people, and escaped out the door we'd come in, ignoring Damian shouting after me. Outside, there was no traffic for miles. I'd have to figure out a ride, but first, I needed to get away before Damian caught me. I'd made the mistake of letting Colton explain his way back into my life once, and I wouldn't do something like that again.

I headed into the protection of the woods as fast as I could.

Away from the building.

Away from Damian.

Away from a killer.

## 21

The forest has a creepy atmosphere at night. Canopied by leaves, it's so dark that everything becomes black shapes—shapes your eyes struggle to identify, especially now that the clouds concealed the moon. The smell of dirt competes with wet moss, and animals howl to each other, hunting for food.

What kinds of animals lived in these forests?

An owl hooted as it perched on a tree, capable of seeing predators lurking in the dark. Vicious snarls erupted in the distance that sounded like a pack of dogs fighting to the death. Sending my heart into convulsions.

This had been a colossal mistake—hiding here, fifty feet from the woods' edge, watching the cars funnel away from the building, waiting until Damian and his friends stopped searching for me, until my phone stopped buzzing with his incessant calls. I needed to get out of here now. Before my biggest danger was no longer the monster I'd arrived with.

As I began walking, rain cascaded over the foliage, making it harder to hear whatever was out here hunting, and its cold drops provoked goose bumps to blanket my skin. There was no need to feel afraid—animals probably didn't even eat humans—but I picked up a stick the size of a baseball bat, just in case.

Cold, wet, with no idea how I was going to get home, I couldn't believe I'd let myself get into this situation. What was wrong with me? Did my magnetic field malfunction, only inviting dangerous lunatics into my life?

Suddenly, something rustled in the brush. It was huge and headed right for me. Unable to see anything more than just blackness, I quickly assessed my other senses: the sound of twigs snapping, the smell of damp bark, and the coldness of wet fabric clinging to my body. None of which helped identify the creature.

I gripped my stick tighter, and when the animal burst through the shrub at me, I swung the stick as hard as I could, smashing it into the beast over and over as it fell to the ground.

"Stop," it moaned.

I rocked back on my heels, and as clouds shifted, the moon's silver glow peppered through the trees, allowing my eyes to identify the shape. I'd thought it was an animal, but it was even more dangerous. Lying crumpled on the dirt was Damian Stone.

"The hell are you *doing?*" Still shirtless and barefoot, he stood up and towered over me. He might as well be a wild beast—sculpted of pure muscle, strong, and lethal.

I pointed my stick at his chest, noticing it no longer had blood splatter on it. Washed or rained off, I had no idea.

"For God's sake, Jenna! Is that really necessary?"

I clutched my weapon tighter.

Damian let out a frustrated sigh. "After what you saw, you really think a stick would stop me?"

"Yeah," I lied.

"If I wanted to hurt you, I'd have done it by now."

"Comforting."

"You *know* I'd never hurt you."

"No, I don't. I don't know anything about you." And I didn't trust my judgment. It'd been wrong before...

Damian rubbed his ribs. Evidently, I'd gotten in some good swings. I shouldn't have felt a rush of triumph. "Leave," I insisted.

He looked at me sharply. "You can't be serious."

"I'm deadly serious."

Damian pinched the bridge of his nose, his hands no longer taped. "I'm *trying* to be patient here, Jenna, but it's been a long night. You're wet and cold, and you need to come back to the truck before you get hypothermia."

"I'm not going anywhere with you."

"Yes, you are."

"No, I'm not," I said, raising the stick when he reached for me.

"I'm not leaving you alone out here, Jenna, so cut it out!" He reached for me again, so I swung, but he dodged it and glowered at me.

*How frustrating it must be to be so strong and yet powerless to move one small girl.*

The rain slowed to a drizzle. Nearby, a creature made a click-click-clicking sound as Damian scrubbed his face and sighed. "Look, I shouldn't have brought you to a fight. I don't know what I was thinking."

He thought seeing him box was what scared me off. He didn't know that I *knew*. I clutched my baton so tight, pieces of wood pierced my palms and stung my skin. "She said you killed someone."

"What?" he managed.

"Mallory. She said you killed someone."

The absence of his denial was deafening.

"So, it's true," I said.

Damian looked up at the sky, then back at me. "Come back to the building, out of the rain."

"No."

"My truck, then. Lock me out if you want, but come out of the woods. It's not safe."

"No."

He scanned my body with a tightened jaw, clearly contemplating just throwing me over his shoulder and carrying me out.

"Don't even think about it," I warned. "I'm not going anywhere with you."

"I'm not leaving you alone out here," Damian said, irritated. The massive chunk of muscles took another step towards me. I raised my bat.

"You go," Damian pointed behind him. "*I'll* stay, for God's sake."

"You might follow me."

"For the love of…" Damian's chest swelled as he ran a hand through his hair. "Why do you have to make this so difficult?"

"Because I don't know who you are!" Except, evidently, a killer.

He held the back of his neck. "What do I have to do to get you to leave?"

Nothing. There was nothing Damian could do to convince me to leave with him. Not tonight, not ever. This whole time he'd been hiding who he really was.

"Have you killed someone?" I stared at him, acutely aware of the air flowing into my lungs and the beating of my heart. Damian took a deep breath and put his hands on his hips. After a few seconds, he looked back towards the building, then up at the sky before returning his eyes to me and sitting down on a log. Suspiciously out of stick-swatting distance.

A light breeze fluttered the leaves overhead as Damian held my eyes, clearly nervous how I'd react. "Yes."

The goose bumps came fast as I stared into the eyes of a confessed killer. "Who?" And why wasn't Damian in prison?

Damian picked up a twig, and after a couple seconds, he began to snap pieces of it off, one by one, as he looked down at the ground. I listened to the snap, snap, snaps, waiting to see if he'd tell me, or if he'd just get up and walk away forever. "You asked what happened when my mom found out what that asshole was doing to me." He tossed the stick and held his temples, taking a couple breaths to help him endure the memory. "When I was fifteen, she came home from work early one day and found him laying into me. She jumped on his back to pull him off, so he started beating the hell out of her. I tried to stop him, but he was too strong, and the force he was using on her…"

Damian shook his head. "If I didn't do something, she was going to die right then and there." Another pause, his tone ominous. "We kept free weights in our living room for my workouts." Damian swallowed. "Picked up the twenty-pounder and cracked him over the head with it."

The contrast between his powerful muscles and his vulnerable soul was profound.

The drizzle ended, silencing the forest as Damian ran a hand over his head. "Cops ruled it self-defense." Cops. Fisher must know. Surely too young to be on the force at the time, but aware of the incident. That must be what Fisher's *Ironic, coming from you* comment meant when Damian said the police should *prevent* someone from getting killed. "Guess I'm supposed to be happy about that or whatever, but my mom lost another person she loved because of me. If I'd handled it differently..." He looked down.

"You saved her life." It was noble. Heroic, even.

When he finally spoke again, his voice was low. "Everyone I've ever cared about has been killed or hurt because of me."

A bird fluttered from one tree to the next, rustling the branches.

"Is that why you don't date? You think you're toxic or something?"

A small pause. "It's part of it."

"And the other part?"

A cloud concealed the moon for a solid minute before shifting its light back to expose Damian rubbing his jaw, once again looking down as if he didn't want to make eye contact. I could tell by the way he hunched his shoulders that whatever he was about to say hurt him terribly. "That hit I took to the head... The doctors said that kind of head trauma makes me highly susceptible to both dementia and rage. With dementia, I could confuse loved ones for fighters in the cage, which means someday, I might direct that rage onto someone close. If I do, there's no telling what I'd do to a girlfriend or my wife." Damian let several seconds tick by, and when he spoke again, his tone was almost a whisper, as if holding back tears. "Trained my whole life to fight, and it's so ingrained that it's as second nature as breathing. Problem is, my blows could be lethal, and when I enter that cage, a switch flips. Animalistic instinct takes over, me versus him. Once I start fighting, it's hard to stop."

As evidenced by his friends having to pull him off that fighter.

I stared at the muscles blanketing Damian's torso, woven together in tight bands, covered by a sheen of rain. The same tools that once offered him protection now served as a curse.

The moon's glow illuminated his apprehensive eyes. "I'm not going to damn the person I love to that fate." He added in a shameful voice, "I don't want to become the monster I've spent my whole life fighting." Damian was willing to sentence himself to a life of solitude, just to prevent any possibility of ever hurting someone he loved. What a horrible burden to bear, an empty, heartbreaking future. "I've never told anyone that before," he admitted.

Yet he told me.

Once again, Damian had opened up his soul to me in a way he'd never done with anyone else. And I felt honored and special he'd shared it with me.

Mallory had undoubtedly employed sneaky tactics to discover that information—no shock there—which angered me because I could tell that Damian had wanted to tell me this in his own time.

"You can't go through life alone," I said.

Damian raised his tormented face to mine. Was it just rain, or were his eyes watery? "If being with someone you loved put them in danger, and risked their life. Would you do it?"

But he was thinking of others. What about *him?* "Isn't it dangerous for *you* to be fighting? Wouldn't another hit to the head be bad?"

No denial.

"Life-threatening bad?" I pressed.

"I would never have fought tonight if I wasn't sure I could take the guy. I wouldn't have left you unprotected like that."

"That's not what I'm worried about! And what about that other fight? The one you canceled the night Justin was attacked. Was that guy dangerous?"

Damian shifted.

He was! Damian knew he was risking his life, and he still did it?

"Then why would you fight?"

"Fighting's all I've ever known."

But there was more, I could tell. I waited for the rest of his answer as he stared at the ground for several moments in shame. Before finally confessing, "When you have nothing left to live for, you're not that worried about a blow to the head."

Icy oxygen hit the bottom of my lungs as my stomach caved in on itself. "You didn't care if you died that night," I realized.

He didn't deny that, either. Maybe not suicidal, technically speaking, not in the *trying* to die way. But by negligence, putting himself in situations where death was likely.

If our paths hadn't intersected, if I hadn't needed a ride to the ER, Damian Stone could've gone to his grave. Willingly, and welcoming it.

The universe really had formed our friendship at precisely the right moment.

Because a world without Damian Stone in it would be a tragedy.

"I shouldn't have brought you tonight," Damian said. "It was selfish of me. I'm sorry."

But I wasn't sorry. Not one bit. Tonight brought me closer to Damian than I ever thought possible, and made me appreciate just how remarkable he was. "I'm glad I came."

He looked cautiously optimistic as he stood up and studied my face. "Does this mean we're good?"

I nodded, provoking a relieved grin from him as he stepped forward and, unexpectedly, wrapped his arms around me. It took me by surprise, but once I settled into the embrace, it actually felt quite natural, having my cheek pressed against his bare chest. More than natural, it felt...lovely. When he rested his chin on my head, the weirdest question went through my head: *If he did allow himself to date, would he choose me?*

I shut my eyes, angry at myself for having such an inappropriate thought at an inappropriate time. No matter what moment Damian and I had just shared, I'd just broken things off with Colton like five seconds ago and had barely escaped with my life. I needed time to lick my wounds, and if I ever dated again—and that was a big *if*—it wouldn't be for a long, long time.

Yet my heart seemed to disagree. It savored having his body pressed against mine, his muscles locking me to him, and it was busy wondering if Damian had been flirting with me earlier. Hoping he had been...

I pulled away from the hug and shook off the intensity.

"Have any other questions for me?" Damian offered. He held his hand near my back as I stepped over a log.

"Yeah," I said. "Is that other fighter okay?"

He smiled as if he found my concern adorable. "He was coming around when you took off. I'm sure he'll be fine."

Once we cleared the forest, Damian opened his truck's passenger door and helped me in. While he walked around the hood, my cell buzzed for the millionth time, but this time, I checked it.

My mouth ran dry.

The seventeen missed calls were not from Damian after all; they were from the same unknown number Colton had texted me from before. And now, bubble after bubble of texts strung together, each one more desperately furious than the next, the last one in all caps: **CALL ME BACK, JENNA, OR SO FUCKING HELP ME! YOU WILL BE SORRY!**

Damian climbed in and registered the look on my face. "What?"

I swallowed. "I need to talk to Fisher."

22

I emerged from Damian's bedroom to find him in his kitchen, where warm sunlight illuminated the brick wall with stunning shades of red and brown. Every stone had its own unique color and distressed edge, yet together, they looked like a polished work of art.

Dressed in gray shorts and a white T-shirt that hugged his muscles, Damian glanced at me over his shoulder, his hair messy. "Morning," he said in a scratchy voice. "Breakfast will be ready in a few minutes. Scrambled okay?"

I nodded, surprised he was cooking for me. It was weird seeing Damian all domestic after what I'd witnessed last night. The ferocious hands that cracked a fighter's face with blood-splattering force now cracked eggs delicately into a pan. And it was equally strange how he could go from a terrifying guy who beat someone mercilessly to a sweetheart who'd given me his shirt to keep me warm on the drive home.

"Coffee?"

"A gallon, please." I took a seat at the breakfast bar.

Damian evaluated me as he poured coffee into a mug that said, *I have O.B.D. Obsessive Boxing Disorder.* As he set sugar and cream next to my cup, I studied the details of his arm tattoos, noticing that the gradient flames were entrapped in barbed wire, dripping with blood.

"Your cheek's bruised," I noticed.

"Work hazard," he shrugged, returning his attention to the sizzling eggs. What an interesting life, where getting punched in the face was such a nonevent.

I looked at my phone. "Looks like last night was a success. Ten thousand views and counting."

Damian said nothing.

"That's good, right?"

"Yeah."

"Why don't you seem more excited?"

Damian retrieved a bag of shredded cheddar from the fridge and sprinkled some into the pan. "I don't know," he sighed. "Just been thinking about something."

His lack of enthusiasm confused me. "Are you upset that Fisher's coming over?" I'd called him last night, and he agreed to meet us here before I had to leave for work, but in hindsight, the two had that tense moment in the hospital.

"Course not. Keeping you safe is priority number one. In fact, I've been thinking about how we should handle the next couple of days. I'll walk you to work and pick you up after, and we'll stay in each night. We should change the time you go to and from work each day, avoid patterns. Sound like a plan?"

A plan, a prison sentence. For both of us.

Damian scooped the food onto two plates, setting one in front of me, and as he did, his eyes drifted to my neck. He stared at the bruises like he couldn't believe how close I'd come to never taking another breath, and as agony cascaded over his face, so did his rage—looking like he wanted to pulverize Colton.

Had anyone been as protective over him as he was of me?

"Can I ask you something?" I said.

Damian set the pan down and took a bite of egg, waiting for my question. I wasn't sure if the subject was off-limits—I had no idea if his mom was still alive, or what their relationship was like, and I didn't want to upset him—but seeing how violent the fight last night was, I pondered what it'd be like for a mother to have a son engage in such a dangerous sport.

"Does your mom worry about you fighting?"

Damian avoided eye contact as he took a sip of water. "My mom has severe dementia," he said. "Early-onset. A brain injury from the accident." Good god, another thing for Damian to feel guilty about. And further validation, in his eyes, that he was destined for the same thing. "She's in a great assisted-living place," he assured, rubbing the side of his face. "But she doesn't know who I am ninety-five percent of the time."

My heart ached for him. What was it like to have your mom not know who you were? My parents might not be perfect, but at least they knew who I was.

"She never liked me fighting. I knew it stressed her out, but it was the only thing I ever had that kept me going." He paused, staring at his plate. "Some son I am."

*Some son I am.* The phrase brought me back to Colton, when he spoke those same four words after we'd visited his mom. Why did Colton become so unacceptably broken, and Damian so incredible, when they both had horrible backgrounds?

I shook the sad thought from my head and forced myself to focus on the present. Here, with Damian, having a breakfast he'd made.

"I could get used to you cooking for me." I took the first bite of eggs, and my eyes about rolled back in my head. "Oh my god, you're like the egg whisperer."

Damian's mouth curled up on one side.

"Where did you learn to cook like this?"

He arched an eyebrow. "It's just eggs."

"It's little fluffs of yellow heaven," I disagreed.

His smile widened. "Did a lot of my own cooking when I was a kid."

Right. Depressed Mom. But I didn't want to let the energy fall.

"What else can you make?"

Damian took a bite and leaned on the breakfast bar across from me. "Make a mean lasagna."

"Seriously?"

"I'll make it for you tonight. I'll pick up a bottle of wine if you want."

"If you keep this up," I said, "I'm not going to want to leave."

He unleashed his bold Clark Kent eyes. "Maybe I don't want you to leave."

My cheeks heated, and he noticed. Of course he did. It made him smirk.

Being with Damian felt so effortless. I wondered why. When I was with Colton, it was nothing but drama, and when I was with Justin, he was so beyond hyper on alert I couldn't just sit and eat eggs and have a moment. That was the thing I needed right now. Moments. It would take a while to recover, but if I could sneak in a smile here, a moment there, maybe this would be bearable.

"You sure you want to go to work today?" Damian asked. "Could take a few days off. I'd take off with you," he clarified. "If you're worried about being alone."

I shook my head. "I don't want my work to get disrupted." And I didn't want him to make any more sacrifices on my behalf.

A knock interrupted our conversation.

Damian peered through the peephole and tried to look cordial as he let Fisher step inside. Today he wore black pants and a red button-down, his badge hanging on his belt. "Morning, kid."

"Thanks for coming over," I said.

Damian glanced at the clock. "I'll be in the shower," he said, shoveling eggs into his mouth as Fisher sat down on the couch. "We need to be ready in forty."

I'd have to make this quick; I still had to shower and get ready for work.

Five minutes later, Fisher was reading through the texts—which had continued rolling in all night—making little notes in that notebook. He'd already called into the station to have someone check on the phone Colton was using, but he didn't seem optimistic that it would reveal Colton's location.

I examined the badge attached to his belt—a silver circle positioned over a star, the word *Detective* on a ribbon on the top, and the phrase *Chicago Police* engraved in black around the crest. Fisher's shirt was crisp, with no wrinkles, his black shoes lacked a single scuff, and he smelled like a sweet cologne that was most potent in the morning. This was a man who paid attention to details.

"Why hasn't he been arrested yet? It's been over forty-eight hours."

"We're trying, kid. There's a lot of people in this city. He hasn't been back to his apartment, far as we can tell. Neighbors haven't seen him. Any idea where he might be staying?"

"You're asking *me*?" God, this was hopeless. "I gave you the list of all his friends and his mom."

"We'll keep checking them," Fisher promised, frowning at my phone. "He's not giving up on you."

"Seriously, why would he think there is even a remote, possible, fractional shred of chance I would ever get back with him?"

"Abusers don't think rationally. Colton wants you, and that's the only thing he can focus on."

"He's insane."

Fisher handed me back my phone. "Abusers tend to be obsessive."

*Great.*

"You need to be careful, kid. Once he realizes you won't answer, he might try to find you in person. Show up to your work or something."

I pressed my fingers to my temples. "So, what are my options? File another restraining order?"

"Already got one, kid. He needs to pop up, so we can nail him."

Pop up. What were the chances Colton would pop up at the right time and place for the cops to catch him? Slim to none, which is why something occurred to me last night when I was lying awake, disturbed by Colton's texts. I'd been thinking about Fisher's warnings that Colton wasn't going to let me go. What if we used that to our advantage?

"What if I can bring him to you?"

Fisher's eyelids ceased to blink.

"You said yourself he wants to talk to me, right? So what if the next time he calls, I answer. I agree to talk. In person. A place we decide in advance, and you're there waiting for him?"

"Bait," Fisher said incredulously. "You want us to use you as bait."

"Exactly."

"Kid, no can do."

"Why?"

"For starters, it's dangerous. A lot can go wrong in even the most well-thought-out plans. He could kill you before we could stop him. One shot, you'd be dead."

"I can keep him talking."

Fisher drew in an impatient breath.

"What? It can totally work, but the best chance we have is if we do it now. His texts are getting more desperate, so the longer we wait, the more dangerous it could be." We needed to get him arrested, and then the court could get Colton into some sort of therapy while he was locked up.

"Sorry, kid, can't do it. We have protocols for a reason." Fisher's phone went off. He answered it and kept his face neutral as he nodded and mm-hmm'd before hanging up. His eyes, when they met mine, said it all.

"The phone's a dead-end," I said, "isn't it?"

"Texts from earlier last night came from a different number than the ones from the middle of the night. Both of them from burner phones."

"So, where does this leave us?"

"He's swapping them out pretty quickly to prevent us from tracking him. He could be anywhere in the city."

I looked out the window at the skyscrapers. "Maybe he's not in Chicago anymore."

"He got any friends or family or anything else outside the city?"

"No."

"Then it's unlikely he left, especially since *you're* here." I appreciated his brutal honesty. I didn't want people to patronize me. "You have Mace?"

I held his eyes. "You're telling me to get Mace? *That's* your advice?"

"No, kid. My advice is to go to a shelter. If you won't do that, lie low until we catch the bastard. Lock your doors, check the windows. Never walk alone, and yeah, might not be a bad idea to get some Mace."

Fisher stood up to leave.

"I'm not going to just sit here and wait for him to get arrested when he's clearly doing a pretty good job of avoiding it. If you won't help me with my plan, then maybe I'll agree to meet him and call nine-one-one once I get there."

Fisher appraised me, softening his frustration on account of my fear. "Kid, you do that, you're walking right into a spider's web. It'll take minutes, best case, for cops to arrive. That's a long time to spend with someone who's tried to kill you once and is coming unhinged. Not to mention, if he sees the cops and figures out it's a trap, he ain't going to be too happy with you."

I clenched my fists. "I'm not just going to stand by and do nothing."

"Jenna, I swear to you, we're working this, and we'll get him. You just have to give us time."

"How much time?"

Fisher shook his head. "Wish I had an answer for you. Meantime, promise me you won't answer his call."

Fine. I'd give the cops some time, but I wasn't going to wait forever before I took action because what I needed more than anything was for this whole thing to be over. And for my life to go back to normal.

But as days crawled into weeks, nothing went back to normal. Turns out, Colton was better at hiding than the cops were at seeking.

I wasn't able to talk my way out of bodyguard duty or convince Justin to drop his ultimatum—only to negotiate a timeshare. Since Damian lived and worked close to my office, I stayed with him

Monday through Thursday, which allowed Justin to work late those nights. Then I'd spend the weekend at Justin's place. Still, this whole thing wasn't fair to them.

It was bad enough that my life was a mess, but worse, the ramifications of my horrible choices entangled Justin and Damian in their destructive tentacles. The poor guys put their lives on hold trying to protect me no matter how hard I tried to convince them otherwise. Which meant having a guest invading their home, running to my apartment with me every so often to pack a bag, and walking me to and from work. I hated the burden I'd become and that the only way Damian and Justin would let themselves have their lives back was if Colton went to jail. A prospect that felt less likely with each passing day.

Meanwhile, Colton's calls continued. It was getting harder for me to *not* pick up and agree to meet him, especially since his texts were incredibly hostile. The only reason I'd waited this long was that Fisher's warning scared me, but I was officially running out of patience.

And my friends at work were probably running out of patience too, waiting for me to finally explain what had happened at the party. While they may not have seen the ambulance, surely they noticed the host and her brother had suddenly vanished and never come back. What my friends thought had caused our unexplained absence, I wasn't sure, but I was grateful they respected my privacy by leaving the topic alone. *At least for now.*

Today was a Tuesday, the second-to-last day in September, and like any other day that Damian walked me home, he was waiting for me in my work's lobby in the exact spot I'd seen him in at the beginning of the workday,—making me wonder if he ever even left. But unlike any other day over the past three and a half weeks, as soon as we stepped outside, something felt wrong. I scanned my surroundings, looking for clues as to why my sixth sense was raising alarm bells. The bright sky showed no hint of a storm, the weather was a perfect seventy degrees with a gentle breeze blowing through my hair, the traffic crawling through the immense structures had no vehicles that seemed out of place, and even the sounds—horns, engines, pedestrians talking—offered no evidence as to why my gut was screaming at me to run. It wasn't until my eyes wandered across the street, that I figured it out.

There, on the other side of the road, looking directly at me, was Colton.

## 23

I hadn't told Justin or Damian that I thought I saw Colton yesterday. I'd only seen him for a second, and then he'd vanished into the crowd of pedestrians, making me doubt what I'd actually seen. How could I be sure that my eyes hadn't been playing tricks on me or that I wasn't becoming paranoid, seeing things that weren't really there? I wasn't going to worry everyone over something that I wasn't even sure of myself, but just in case it had been real, I finally took Damian up on his offer to teach me self-defense.

Tomorrow was our first lesson, and given tonight was a work night, we needed to get ready for bed.

Damian and I had just finished watching a movie in his living room, and I could tell he was braced for our nightly battle. But I had a different trick up my sleeve tonight. I couldn't believe I hadn't thought about it before!

I hated how much he was sacrificing for me, and at the top of that list? His stubborn refusal to let me sleep on the couch and for him to take his bed instead. Each night, I brought it up. Each night, I lost the argument.

But not tonight. I almost couldn't contain my smile. It might seem like a small thing to other people, but knowing Damian would be comfortable would make me feel less guilty; he was so tall that when he slept on the couch, his feet dangled off the edge.

"Why do you look so... weird?" Damian asked.

"You have a way with words. You should be a poet."

"You're being weird."

I took a sip of my wine. "I'm excited about tomorrow."

Damian looked skeptical that I'd be that excited about learning how to fight. But he set his beer down and ran a hand through his hair. "I'm going to brush my teeth. You wanna go first?"

I held up my wine and shook my head.

The second Damian vanished into the bathroom, I made my move. I grabbed a pillow from his bed, a blanket from the closet, and set up my bed on the couch. I lay under the cover and pretended to already be asleep by the time he came out.

A mere two minutes later.

I could only assume he glared at me.

I was totally going to win. It took everything I had to not break out in an ear-to-ear grin.

Until I felt his arms under my shoulders and knees.

I opened my eyes as he lifted me against his chest with a smug look of victory. I tried to ignore the swelling of my heart that came from being in his arms like this, so I could focus on winning the argument.

"I'm sleeping here." I tried to grab the couch.

"No," he said, pulling me effortlessly away from the couch, "you're not."

He carried me, still covered in the blanket, to his bedroom. I tried to grab the wall on the way, the doorframe, but he just looked down at me and laughed—a deep chuckle that reverberated through my chest.

As he placed me on the bed, I groaned, "I'm not sleeping here."

He put his hands on either side of my shoulders and hovered over me.

"Yes," he said, "you are."

But suddenly, I was no longer thinking about the disagreement over our sleeping arrangements. Because Damian's smile fell as he stared at my eyes, at my lips—which were only inches from his own.

I swallowed, reliving a couple of moments we'd shared recently.

A week ago, I'd gotten up earlier than him. It was the first time; Damian claimed his early wakeups were normal for him, but I suspected it was the damn couch, so when he was sleeping later, I tried to be super quiet as I got dressed. His bedroom door was open— I always slept with it open, and I hadn't shut it that morning because it always made a loud squeak, and I didn't want to wake him. So I started getting dressed, figuring I'd hear him wake up.

Wrong.

On his way to the bathroom, he was scrubbing his hair with his hand when he passed the doorway.

And froze.

As did I.

I was in a pink bra and panties.

Damian looked like he tried to pull his eyes away but found it impossible. They glided down my neck, my chest, my abs, my legs, drinking me in slowly, savoring every inch of me before returning to my face and capturing me in their snare.

His eyes said, *Goddamn, you're gorgeous, Jenna.* And the way he looked at me was like I was the most stunning woman he'd ever seen. I'd never felt as desired as I did at that moment, and as he stood shirtless, I couldn't help but feel turned on by his body's exquisiteness as well—his muscles every woman's fantasy.

For a minute, I thought—hell, maybe even hoped—he was going to close the distance between us and kiss me. He sure as hell looked like he wanted to; he stared at me like the prospect of never getting to kiss me was torture, but after a few seconds, he scrubbed his face with both hands and growled into them as he walked away.

Making me think I'd read more into it than was actually there.

Then, Monday, when I was cooking us dinner—god help us, it had turned out awful, and Damian had pretended it didn't taste like the bottom of a shoe—I'd been struggling to reach a spice on the cabinet's shelf. As I'd stood on my tiptoes and stretched my fingers as high as possible, Damian came up behind me, put his hand on my lower back, reached effortlessly above me, and grabbed it. My back had touched his chest, and it had sent this... electric spark through me. He'd looked down at me as if he'd instantly felt it too, and when he'd handed the spice to me, he kept his hand on my lower back and stared at my mouth, which was only inches from his own. *Is he going to kiss me?* My heart longed for him to, and my chest rose and fell with each beat of my heart, craving it as he parted his lips.

But Damian shut his eyes, let out a deep breath, and stepped back.

I'd wondered if it had all be in my head, especially since he'd said he'd never date.

But this. This was not in my head.

I looked at his lips, imagining how intoxicating they'd feel on mine, and Damian looked like he was envisioning the same thing. I was overcome with how badly my body implored him to touch me; I'd never felt chemistry this strongly with anyone before, and I wondered why it was happening. Perhaps it was because Damian had been such an incredible friend before these feelings ever entered my mind, or perhaps it was because his body and soul were the most beautiful I'd ever encountered, or maybe it was because he was the sexiest guy I'd ever laid eyes on. But whatever the reason, just the possibility of his warm mouth pressing against mine left me breathless. Willing him to lean down farther and let me have a taste.

But then, he took a deep breath, growled the same way he'd done when he'd caught me changing, and pushed himself up.

"Sleep," he insisted.

## 24

I emerged from the women's locker room wearing the fitted yoga pants and tank top I'd picked up during a special run to my apartment. Damian said to find clothing that wasn't loose—clothes that couldn't be tugged or used against me.

Damian's impassive gaze lifted from his phone and stopped, clearly taken off guard by my appearance. He'd seen me in a lot of outfits, but nothing that hugged my body's contours like this, and as he looked down my torso and legs, my cheeks warmed. He looked at me the same way he had when I'd been in my undies.

It took Damian several seconds to clear his throat. "Ready?

Counting the day I first met Damian, this was my second time in his gym. I loved that he had taken advantage of his sixth-month hiatus from fighting to remodel the studio, including speakers that carried rock music throughout the space. The Thursday-night crowd was already rolling in, punching cylinder logs and boxing in the rings.

We moved to an open mat, where he peeled off his shirt and jeans and tossed them to the ground.

Oh my gosh, did he have to train me in nothing but a pair of butt-hugging shorts? Was he *trying* to get my hormones to misbehave? I'd seen him shirtless a handful of times now since he sometimes didn't have one on at home, but his beauty still stunned me. And warmed my lower belly.

He smiled when he caught me gawking at his celestial body. *Is he flirting with me?*

Damian motioned for me to come to the center. I felt self-conscious about giving the seasoned fighters around us an unobstructed view of me.

"People are staring at me," I grumbled.

"They've been staring at you since the moment you got here."

I frowned. "They think I don't belong."

Damian raised his eyebrow and flashed an amused grin. "Trust me; that's not why."

I blushed at his teasing eyes. I'd never noticed how many speckles of different-colored greens were in there—the darker tones around the outside, the lighter ones sprinkled near the pupil. I could only hold his stare for another moment before a fluttering feeling returned to my stomach.

"Okay," Damian said. "First thing you gotta do is evaluate your strengths and weaknesses, how they stack up against his, and how you can use 'em to your advantage."

I nodded. "So I can take him down."

"You don't need to take him down, you need to incapacitate him so you have a few seconds to run."

I flinched. "Run? I thought you were going to teach me how to turn someone into a human pretzel."

Damian crossed his arms over his chest. "Let's start with the obvious weakness. You're tiny."

I glared at him while he tried not to smirk.

"He's got twice as much weight and a hell of a lot more muscle."

"You suck at motivational speaking."

"Then there's the strength. You can use your size to your advantage. You can be quick, and he won't be expecting much from you."

I glared angrier.

"And he'll be emotional. Might make mistakes because of it. Now," Damian said. "Women's legs are the strongest part of their body, so we'll focus a lot on that. But first, we'll start with some basic moves." He put his hands on his hips, where his black shorts hung, revealing that V-lined muscle pointing down to his—

I shut my eyes angrily. *Stop staring at him like that. He's gorgeous. So what? You already knew that. Get over it!*

"With every move, I want you to keep your core tight." He moved behind my left shoulder and pressed one hand on my lower back, the other over my belly button. Only a couple people had ever touched me here, and it was hard to not stare at the steel bands of muscles wrapped around his forearms. *He could probably win an entire fight, using nothing more than a forearm.* "It'll make it harder for him to take control of your body," he said, gliding his hands to my hips—another place few had touched. "Keep your center strong," he repeated, then he moved in front of me.

The absence of his touch took a moment to recover from.

"Let's start with what to do if the attack comes from the front. First thing I want you to do is knee him in the balls. Ready?"

"Ready for what?"

"To practice it."

"Practice kneeing you in the balls?" I said incredulously.

"It's why we're here, isn't it?"

"As incredibly complicated as it sounds, I'm pretty sure I can handle a knee-to-the balls maneuver."

"Guy's attacking you, you'd be surprised. Bodies are moving, twisting. You need to practice it."

Seriously? Professional training included a junk-punch?

"Last I heard, being kneed in the balls hurts like hell. Really want me to send you into a puddle of tears?"

"I'm wearing protection."

"I fail to see how a condom will help."

Damian frowned at me, and now *I* couldn't help but smirk.

"I already kneed Colton in the balls."

Pride gleamed in his eyes. "You did?"

I nodded. "First time I met him. It was a misunderstanding."

"Well, still something we'll practice."

I sighed. "Fine," I said. "Prepare to be sterilized."

Damian moved towards me. I threw my knee up, but he twisted and grabbed my thigh behind my knee. I imagine he'd normally throw his opponent down, but instead he held me there for a moment, my right hip touching his body, our chests close as he stared down at me, our face inches apart.

"You knew it was coming," I argued, suddenly aware of how, with each breath, my chest reached for his.

"Again." He released me.

Now I was determined. I tried again, but again, he thwarted the blow.

"You're a professional fighter," I reasoned. "He won't know all the moves you know."

"Tip number one," Damian said. "Never underestimate your opponent."

I officially questioned my sanity for asking a lethal fighter to train me. We continued our package-smash dance two dozen times, until finally—gloriously—my knee connected between his legs. His hand was already holding my outer thigh in a failed blocking attempt as he stared down at me with pride. It was strange, a unique level of intimacy, cup or no cup, to touch him in that area, and to have his hand so close to my backside.

"Good," he growled, and after holding me there a moment longer than necessary, he let me go. "Alright. Another move. Thumbs to the eyes," Damian said.

He took my hands and rested them on his cheeks. Man, his skin was smooth. *Maybe getting punched in the face repeatedly is a crazy-good exfoliant.*

"You'll put your thumbs here," he said, moving my thumbs to the inner corners of his eyes. It was jarring to hold his face between my hands—his strong, yet vulnerable face, with its perfect skin and dark eyebrows. With his eyes closed, I found myself studying his features. His teeth—probably through the help of a skilled dentist—didn't even have a chip in them, and his jaw and nose were perfectly sculpted. How did he stay this handsome getting pummeled for a living?

"And you'll want to dig," Damian said, showing me with his thumbs "Press in, then scoop like ice cream."

I tried to shake off the daze his gorgeousness left me in, a trance that had been growing since the night of the forest, but it wasn't helping to have our bodies so close.

When he stepped back, the air felt instantly cold.

"Okay, let's say he comes at you from behind and he's got his arm around your throat. I want you to do three things to get him off," he said. "Stomp his foot with your heel. Then bring your elbow back as hard as you can," he said, motioning with his arm. "Try to hit here." Damian pointed to an area on his stomach. *What a kissable spot.* "He should be stunned enough that his grip loosens, and when it does, I want you to turn around and knee him in the balls."

"Thank God for balls. Gives a girl a fighting chance."

"Let's practice the first two." When Damian moved behind me, I sensed him there, inches from my back, aware of his body's heat, and as he got himself into position, my body tensed, longing for his touch. For some reason, I imagined what it'd be like to have his lips on my neck.

His arm draped across my stomach, pulling me until I pressed against his warm chest and abs.

My lower belly pulsated.

"Ready?" he asked.

I tried to snap myself out of whatever spell had come over me, but my brain was preoccupied with the feeling of his arm around my body, his bare flesh pressed against me.

I shut my eyes, willing the rush of desire to go away.

Damian draped his right arm around my neck, his elbow beneath my chin. "Go easy on the foot," he said. "But really give it to me with the elbow. Need to get a sense of where you're at with it."

"I don't want to hurt you…"

He lowered his mouth to my ear, and I could hear his smile as he whispered, "Trust me, I can take it. Go."

I stomped his foot, then threw my elbow back, but it felt like it crashed into concrete.

"A little more to the left," Damian said, pulling my elbow against the spot he wanted me to hit.

Had his voice always been that baritone? So soothing, like music. Acutely aware of his breath over my shoulder, my body warmed, his every touch sending an electric charge through me.

"Okay. Go."

And so we did, many times, until Damian felt pleased by my progress.

I shut my eyes, trying to shake off this rising feeling.

"Is this too much for you?" Damian worried.

I blinked. "What?"

"You seem distracted."

Crap! Did he sense *what* was distracting me? My mind raced to cover my tracks.

"I was just thinking about that MMA fight you were trying to get," I hedged. I was *sort of* thinking about it. Picturing his muscles flexing with each blow. "Have you heard any more about it?"

Damian let a suspiciously long silence pass. "Got a couple calls."

"And?"

"And I haven't called them back yet."

"Why not?"

Damian was silent for several seconds. "Lots to consider."

"Like what?"

More silence. Longer this time, even taking a sip from his water bottle. "I'm starting to wonder if fighting might not be the way to go."

Holy unexpected answer. I thought fighting was his whole life?

My shock must have been obvious, because he continued. "It doesn't exactly have long-term career potential."

But that fact wasn't new, and I could tell he was keeping the real reason from me. "Please don't tell me it's because you're worried it'll interfere with *protection detail*, because if that's the case—"

"No," Damian interrupted with a warm smile—*oh my word, that smile could raise someone's temperature from hypothermia to a fever.* "I'd find a way to protect you no matter what." He rubbed the back of his neck. "I'm just...reevaluating things, is all."

I'd seen a change in Damian these last few weeks. He smiled more, and the darkness in him—perhaps the part that needed to beat on people—had seemed to lighten.

"If you don't fight anymore, what'll you do? Focus on running the gym?"

When Damian hooked his thumbs into his waistband, I tried to restrain my hormonal eyeballs from looking at his lower abs. "Been thinking about starting a national self-defense program for people who want to learn more than just the basics. Most places teach you how to do the minimum needed to escape an attack, but I think I think a lot of people, especially anyone who's been attacked, want to learn more. Knowing how to fight is the only thing that can make you feel in control. It'll have different levels to it that clients can advance through and focus areas they can choose from."

Wow. To take a specific set of people on a training journey from victim to victor. It was incredible. And from a business perspective, it was a damn good idea.

"That's awesome," I said. But it still didn't fully answer the question. "You wouldn't want to continue fighting, too?"

Damian's expression turned serious as he allowed a pause to elapse. "When you find something to live for, you start to think that getting hit in the head on a regular basis isn't such a good idea."

Every cell in my body came alive, and the outside world faded to black until it was just me and him and a connection that tethered my spirit to his. Lost in his gaze, my whole life instantly felt different, like gravity had weakened.

"Alright," Damian said. "Let's get back to it."

As his beautiful body approached me, I tried to tame my growing swell of desire.

## 25

C olton's hands squeezed my throat until I was dying. I screamed, but I had no voice, and no one was around to hear me anyway. The clouds blackened, and winds swirled in the alley as I tried to fight him off. I punched his chest and his shoulders, but nothing I did released his grip—not even a little.

"Jenna."

His hands were somehow on my throat and my shoulders all at once.

I hit him again.

"Jenna," a voice boomed as my body shook.

I punched at Colton's chest, but when I opened my eyes, Colton wasn't there.

I'd been punching Damian's chest, who was shaking my shoulders, trying to wake me up.

"Hey," Damian said, cupping my cheek, searching my eyes for awareness. "Just a dream."

I was panting. My mouth dry, my heart pounding, arms trembling.

Damian sat down on the bed, pulled me against his chest, and rubbed his hand up and down my back. "You okay?"

I nodded. I was safe. I was in Damian's bed because the man was the most stubborn person in history—he'd carried me here five times last night before I gave up. It was just a nightmare—one I'd been having a couple of times a week.

"You gonna tell me what they're about?" Damian asked.

I shook my head, but he wasn't stupid—he probably had a damn good idea. He tightened his grip on me and, in a low voice, vowed, "I won't let anything happen to you, Jenna."

The truth was, no one could guarantee my safety, nor was it anyone's responsibility, but I appreciated how badly Damian wanted to protect me. In his arms, everything felt better.

"Tell me what to do," Damian whispered.

I didn't want to go to sleep; Colton would be waiting for me. "Can we watch a movie?"

Damian hesitated, but after a minute, he tried to act like he wasn't worried as he smiled. "Of course."

And so we did.


I WOKE UP WITH MY CHEEK PRESSED AGAINST SOMETHING WARM AND hard. Something that moved my face up slightly, then back down. It took me a second to realize that we'd both fallen asleep on the couch. But it got worse.

During the night, Damian had tipped over and shifted onto his back. And my ovaries evidently jumped at the delicious opportunity in front of them and had flopped me over so I was lying on his chest with my left leg trapped between him and the back of the couch.

My only saving grace was that Damian was still sound asleep. His chest rose and fell slowly beneath my breasts.

*Crap.* This was not friendship zone. This was…

I needed to get up.

Carefully.

Quietly.

Ninja-like.

I moved my right hand to the other side of his body and carefully pushed my chest off of his.

Damian took one of those deep I'm-about-to-wake-up breaths, so I froze, soooooo not wanting to be caught in this position. My face dangled a foot from his, my arms now on either side of his neck.

*Don't wake up. Don't wake up.*

Damian opened his eyes.

*The universe really is an asshole.*

Damian smirked. "What are you doing?"

Damn, he was freaking gorgeous, even when he first woke up. Look at that jaw, those eyebrows, that adorably tousled hair. And that smile… He looked so dang striking when he smiled.

"Nothing." I tried to move, but he grabbed my hips.

Which were basically straddling him. Something he grinned about when he took notice.

And then he arched an eyebrow. "Were you fulfilling some sort of fantasy in your sleep?"

"Har har," I said, trying to move.

He kept me in place, and when my hair fell forward, he reached up and gently swept it over my shoulder. His fingertips grazed my neck in the process.

Ice ran down my spine at his touch, and my lower belly warmed as I stared at him, watching that beautiful smile fall from his face. He bit his lower lip—my ovaries did a hip-hip-hooray about that move—as he stared at my mouth.

Six inches. That's all it would take to close the distance between our mouths and start something I could feel we both ached for. I could feel his desire in the way he looked at me, the way his fingers lingered on my hip, the way his mouth opened slightly like it wanted to consume me.

I wanted his lips on mine, on my neck, my jaw. His tongue in my mouth. I wanted to see the hunger in his eyes when I peeled my shirt off and pressed my chest against his hands, rocking my hips until he unleashed a feral growl and climbed on top of me—touching every part of my body. I wanted him to ravish me, and I could tell he wanted it too.

He stroked my cheek with his thumb and looked at me in a way no one ever had before, as if his soul was reaching for me. Mine bent to his, craving every part of Damian—his lips, his body, his passion, his affection. His chest rose and fell beneath my breasts, and I could feel the electric energy climbing, building to an unstoppable level.

But suddenly, Damian scrubbed his face with both hands, groaned, and sat up.

I hopped off his lap quickly and watched as it appeared to take every ounce of strength he had to walk away and go into the bathroom.

## 26

"Alright. That's enough for one day," Damian said. Our second training session at his gym had gone even better than yesterday's, but there was one thing I still hadn't asked to learn—the only thing that had the power to help with my nightmares. And I needed to hurry; Justin would be here any minute to pick me up for the Friday handoff of guard duty. A handoff that made me ache, thinking of spending the entire weekend away from Damian.

Damian grabbed his shirt off the ground and threw it over his shoulder.

"I..." *How do I say this without sounding pathetic?*

Damian took a swig of water and looked at me, waiting for me to say something coherent.

"Have you ever been in a chokehold...from the front?"

His knowing eyes tightened, and his body tensed. "Yeah."

"So, there's a way to get out of it?"

He tried to keep his face neutral. "Several."

So, I didn't have to just stand there and let him drain the life from me in that alley. "Will you show me?"

Damian looked at my neck, biting the inside of his cheek in

restrained anger, and then set down his water and shirt. "Put your back against the wall."

A mixture of relief and terror swirled within me, but this was Damian, not Colton, so there was no need to feel panicked. I walked to the nearest wall and pressed my back against it, noticing how much it smelled like rubber. The mat was firm and cold against my skin, and amid the *thump, thump-thump-thump* sound of a guy taking his anger out on a punching bag, the song pumping through the speakers ironically sang about going to an early grave.

Damian balled his fists and looked at the ground for several seconds before returning his gaze to me. "You sure you want to do this?"

*No.* "Positive."

After another pause, Damian took my wrists. "Push your hands together, like this. When my hands are around your neck, there's a space between my arms. I want you to bring your hands up fast, hard, punching through it and widening your arms. It'll break my hold on you." He held my stare. "Okay?"

I nodded.

Damian wrapped his hands around my throat. Even though he didn't squeeze, my mind flashed to the moment in the darkened alley when I thought Mom and Dad would add a tombstone next to Jessica's. I tried to breathe through the panic, to hide it, because I wanted to be strong in front of Damian. But my heart was a coward and smashed around my chest like it was trying to escape.

"You okay?" Damian asked firmly.

I nodded and then followed his instructions—rushing my hands up and apart. It took one second. One piece of knowledge that could've saved my life that night.

It was such a relief to know how to get out of that hold, and even though I may never need that knowledge in the future, my nightmares finally had a shot at ending. I wouldn't feel so helpless now when that moment replayed in my mind's eye. I was empowered to defend myself.

Recognizing how hard this had been for me, Damian pulled me to his chest and rubbed his hands up and down my back. "You did good today."

I shut my eyes, realizing how much his opinion mattered to me.

This whole time I'd been staying with Damian, every magnetic moment that had pulled my body to his hadn't been merely a physical attraction. I was captivated by his whole person—his courage, his pain, his warrior spirit, his protective nature, and, most of all, his beautiful heart.

After the moment we'd shared earlier, I *knew* he felt something for me, too, but I also knew he'd fight his feelings so long as he believed that doctor's diagnosis was correct. All the what-ifs were heartbreaking. What if that doctor wasn't very good? Or was having a bad day, or rushed his analysis of Damian's file because his schedule was packed with patients? Had the doctor studied cases like Damian's day and night, insisting on all the medical testing available? Because anything short of that was an unacceptable tragedy.

I stepped back. "Let me find another doctor," I pressed. "We can get a second opinion about your head."

"What?" His confusion morphed to annoyance. "No."

"Why not?"

Damian rubbed his eyebrows. "Jenna, drop it."

"You deserve to be in love with someone, Damian."

"And then what?" he snapped. "Which doctor do I listen to? If there was a chance you'd be dangerous to the people you loved most, would you take it?"

"You don't even know for sure—"

"Jenna, stop!"

"Why?"

"Because I don't *want* anyone like that in my life!"

It felt like my ribs cracked open and my lungs flooded with poison, making it hard to breathe. I could no longer look at those emerald gems after they'd unleashed their power to shatter me.

It wasn't real. His hands *hadn't* lingered longer than necessary, those raised eyebrows and smiles were *not* flirting, he hadn't wanted to kiss me, and his words—*when you find something to live for*—weren't a profession of feelings for me. It had all been in my head.

I couldn't decide who was the bigger traitor: me for being stupid enough to see whatever I wanted to see, or him for breaking my heart.

I looked down so he couldn't see my face as I retrieved my gym bag.

"Jenna," I heard him call out as I retreated into the seclusion of the women's locker room.

Once there, I stripped, grabbed my toiletries, and made my way to the empty shower stalls before I broke down crying. I knew I'd been falling for Damian; I just didn't realize how deeply, how severely I'd fallen until this very moment, until his rejection of any possibility of a future with me as something more than friends had ripped my heart out of my chest.

I was devastatingly in love with Damian. But he wasn't in love with me, and never would be. And I had to be okay with that.

More than that, I needed to make this go away. Damian trusted me to be his friend, and if he found out I'd betrayed it by pathetically falling for him, it might destroy our friendship. I couldn't let that happen. I'd get this under control and, sooner or later, my feelings would become manageable. Right?

Besides, it really was better this way. I'd only been out of my relationship for a month, and logically speaking, I shouldn't allow myself to be in love anytime soon. If my heart could just understand that, it could stop collapsing.

I finished showering, towel-dried my hair, got dressed, and emerged to find a freshly showered Damian waiting for me with an apology written all over his face. "Jenna, I'm sorry, I…"

"Whoa, this place is badass." Saved by the brother. Wearing black pants and a blue button-down with a tie, Justin walked towards us and glanced around the space. Now that he had his casts off, he probably envisioned using the equipment here.

"I didn't mean to get upset," Damian said. "I just need to make sure you, of all people, understand my position."

Me of all people?

Oh my god. As if it weren't painful enough to not be loved back, Damian felt it necessary to make it abundantly clear that he had never felt, and never would feel, that way about me. I felt a dam of tears breaking within my anger. He didn't have to patronize me like a wolf pup that'd imprinted on the wrong adult.

I clenched my fists and bit my lip, trying to prevent myself from punching something. I needed to get out of here. Now. "I'm leaving," I said, hoisting my bag over my shoulder. Both guys looked beyond confused.

"Jenna, we can't let you—" Damian started.

"Ten minutes," I snapped. "Ten goddamned minutes to be alone, okay? Or so help me, I'm going to snap!"

Justin had a right to look shocked, but Damian didn't.

Stupid crush. Stupid ex-boyfriend. Stupid entire drama.

Ignoring them calling after me and leaving them to argue amongst themselves, I stormed out the front door. The sun had set a half hour ago, the city's lights blazing, horns blaring, and rude people not even watching where they were walking. I willed one of them to bump into me, just so I could shove someone. I couldn't go on like this anymore, and I certainly couldn't ever go back to Damian's after what just happened.

I glanced back over my shoulder and, predictably, saw Justin's head poke out the door.

The warning look I gave him must've been convincing because he stopped short of following me. I walked around the corner and crossed the street, but my anger didn't subside. It didn't subside when I crossed another street or another, nor was it gone when my apartment building grew closer. It only intensified when I spotted a cop car heading this way because it was a constant reminder that Colton was a needle in a haystack. A haystack of three million people.

*Whatever.* At least I was alone for a hot minute. It felt nice, and as I crossed the last intersection to my apartment, I was beyond tempted to go inside and lock the boys out. But they'd worry. Incessantly. I'd already walked longer than the ten minutes I'd asked for, and as frustrated as I was about all of this, the least I could do was shield them from further turmoil.

So I slowed my steps and prepared to turn around.

But as I did, I saw someone standing against my apartment building, staring right at me.

Colton.

Un. Freaking. Believable.

## 27

"You're stalking me now?" I snapped.

Colton's face hardened. Dressed in jeans and a wrinkled green shirt, he approached me, glancing behind me to ensure I was alone. We stood on the immense corner, flanked by buildings. People strolled under the city's lights, which glowed brighter as the sky's civil twilight came to its end, and wind tossed hair into my face.

"I really want to talk to you," he said, obviously hoping that this was going to be some heartfelt reunion.

"I have nothing to say to you, Colton. If I did? I'd have answered one of your zillion phone calls or texts. It's over between us. Get that through your thick skull, and leave me the hell alone!"

Speaking of phone calls, my cell was in my gym bag. I hadn't expected to set my plan in place right now, but clearly my life was full of unexpected surprises these days. I began to dig around for it because this was it—I was calling the cops to come arrest his ass.

Colton digested my reaction with darkened eyes. "You can't just blow me off."

"It's called breaking up. Which, by the way, tends to happen when one person tries to *kill* the other!"

He ground his teeth. "I know what I did was—"

"Save it. Hallmark doesn't make an I'm-sorry-for-trying-to-murder-you card. I don't want to hear your excuses, because that's all they are. You had a bad childhood, but that doesn't give you a free pass to abuse me."

"*Abuse?* You fucking kidding me?"

"Just leave me the hell alone!"

It was in here somewhere. I dug in the corners.

"Stop bein' so fucking dramatic! You just want to be the victim. Get people to feel sorry for you, make me out to be a bad guy."

"You did that all by yourself."

"After everything we had together, you're just going to write me off for not being perfect. Cause *you're* so damn perfect?"

I lifted my shirt out, set it on my shoulder.

"What about promising me you'd always be there for me? Was that a fucking lie too?"

*Ha! Found it!*

"You're with that guy, aren't you?" he accused. "That guy from the hospital. Your *friend*," he spat.

Guilt washed over me for having feelings for Damian, but I wasn't going to let Colton turn everything around on me. "No."

"You're with him a lot."

"So, you *are* you stalking me."

"So you *were* cheating on me," he countered. "Was it just that one guy, or were there others?"

"I'm not doing this, Colton," I said, unlocking my phone and hitting nine-one-one. "You can think whatever you want; I don't care anymore."

"Nine-one-one, what's your emergency?"

I gave the operator the address and explained what was going on, as Colton's demeanor stiffened with rage.

"You never even cared about me." He looked at me like a disgusting stain. "You only care about yourself and your perfect fucking life and your delusional fucking fairy-tale romance. And when someone doesn't fit in your perfect fucking mold, you give them the cold shoulder or write them off! You did it to your parents when they broke up. Your best friend. And now me."

I wouldn't give him the satisfaction of knowing that his words were getting to me, making me paranoid part of it might be true. With everything that had been going on, I still hadn't made up with Zoey, and now I was scared I'd let too much time pass.

"You told me you loved me. You said you'd always be there for me," he snapped.

His guilt trips weren't going to work, though. Not this time. "It's over, Colton. I don't ever want to talk to you again."

His jaw clenched so tight I thought his teeth might crack as he stared at me for two long seconds.

And then came the explosion.

He punched my hand, causing my cell phone to fly through the air.

It was in this moment, as I watched my phone crash to the ground, that I saw it: among the vehicles crawling along the street was the police car I'd seen on my way here. It was less than twenty feet from us, and the officer's eyes were on my cell, then my arm.

I wasn't sure if they'd heard the nine-one-one call or were simply reacting to what they'd just witnessed, but it took less than a second for an officer to jump out.

Colton no longer resembled the man who'd just yelled at me, but rather the kind soul who'd saved the dog, the man who'd fallen in love with me so deeply it had driven him crazy. I could imagine his heart pounding, knowing this was it.

As one officer cuffed him, the other picked up my fallen cell phone and examined it before handing it back to me with an impressed eyebrow raised. "Thank God for screen protectors, eh?"

Colton put up no fight. With his rights read and his arms behind his back, he was led to the squad car.

"You have no idea what I've done for you," Colton said.

## 28

"Come on," Emily urged. "We're late."

I probably shouldn't be doing this. It was irresponsible, but after Colton got arrested, I'd decided to reclaim my life. Eight days ago, I moved back into my apartment, despite the arguments from Justin and Damian. I'd fulfilled our agreement—staying with them until Colton got arrested, and even though they might be right—that the danger was "still prevalent"—I refused to keep my life on hold anymore. Five days ago, I finally got the courage to talk to Emily and Zoey and confided that I'd been going through a "bad breakup."

They weren't surprised Colton and I had split. In fact, after witnessing the tension between him and me at the party, they'd assumed my absence that night was because I'd gotten into a drawn-out fight or breakup with him, and that Justin must have been there too—perhaps going off on Colton for treating me like crap. They weren't far off, and they also weren't far off hypothesizing that the reason Damian waited outside work for me was because we'd started spending time together. Regardless of it all, I apologized for being so absent.

The fact they were understanding should have made me feel great, but I couldn't stop thinking about the betrayed look in Colton's eyes as they handcuffed him, and how depressed he must feel facing jail time. For all his flaws and unacceptable behavior, he was merely human and acting out of lost love.

The only way I could endure the guilt was if three things came from this tragedy: first, if this was a wake-up call that motivated Colton to get help. Second, if it rescued Justin and Damian from worry and the disruption to their lives. And third, if I reclaimed the life and the friendships I'd let slip through my fingers.

Which was why I accepted the invitation to go out with my friends tonight and invited Emily and Zoey over beforehand. I hoped a new atmosphere and time with them might free me from the condemning voice inside my head and allow me to begin the rebuilding process with Zoey.

I'd stayed up late the past few nights, replaying moments of our friendship from over the years. Like the first night in my dorm, when I was ironically homesick for the very home I'd spent years longing to escape, and Zoey soothed my tears with popcorn and a comedy movie marathon. When a guy I briefly dated in college cheated on me, Zoey went on social media and tagged pictures of him with captions like, "I'm a cheater! If you enjoy S.T.D.s, call me." And later, as I'd rounded the corner in my moving truck, Zoey cheered in front of my Chicago apartment.

I guess sometimes you don't realize how important someone is to you until their void is so big that it's all you feel. I needed to repair things before it was too late.

"I think this dress is too short," I said, looking in my bedroom mirror. Giving Emily creative control of my look tonight had sounded good in theory. After all, she had incredible style. But now that I'd curled my hair, applied my makeup thicker than usual, and squished my body into the tight, green, cleavage-showing dress I'd bought for a date with Colton but never dared to actually wear, I was second-guessing the whole thing.

"You look amazing," Emily assured behind my left shoulder.

"I might get cold." It was the second week of October, after all.

"It's supposed to be over sixty tonight," Emily argued. "And Harrison's eyes are going to bug out when he sees you. Ever since he found out you and Colton are splitsville, he totally won't stop talking about you."

I blanched. "He knows?"

Emily applied her lipstick. "Only that you're single. Now, come on! The boys are waiting."

I sighed and looked over at Zoey, who was sitting on my bed. She was always looking at her phone these days, way more than she ever had before. What if it was to avoid me? What if I'd waited too long?

"Hey, Zoey?" I asked.

She looked up, reluctantly.

"Are you guys coming?" Emily shouted from my kitchen.

"Can we talk later?" I asked. "Just the two of us?"

The look on her face filled me with apprehension. "Yeah," she said. "There's something I've been wanting to tell you, actually."

Before I could ask what it was, my phone chimed, and Zoey used the opportunity to slip away. If she wanted to tell me something, she could have done it while we'd been getting ready, so why wait? Was she saving it for the end of the night because she thought it'd ruin our evening?

**Justin: Lunch tomorrow? I have news.**

**Me: What news?**

**Justin: In-person news.**

**Me: ☹ I hate when you do stuff like this.**

**Justin: So that's a yes?**

**Me: Can you at least give me a hint? It'll bug me all night.**

**Justin: No. 12:00, at Giordano's?**

I frowned.

**Me: Fine.**

I suspected I knew what it was about, though. Three days ago, Justin told me he'd been formally offered the job in New York, and he owed them an answer on Monday. What I didn't know was what his answer was going to be.

"Come on! The guys are already there!" Emily urged.

I threw my cell into my clutch, grabbed my keys, and followed

Emily and Zoey out of my apartment. It took a second to understand why they froze.

Sitting on the ground in the hallway with his back to the wall was Damian.

"What are you doing here?" I asked sharply.

And why did he have to look so gorgeous all the time? Look at how his ocean-colored shirt brought out the green in his eyes, and draped across his stomach, just to show it off, and how not shaving for a few days created thick stubble that complemented his dark eyebrows and hair. Being around him was impossible; my hormones couldn't be trusted to *not* do something stupid like pull his thick lips to mine.

Damian stood up, and his muscular shoulders broadened as he tucked his hands into his pockets. "Wow," he said with raised eyebrows, his lips in a ghost of a smile. "You look amazing."

*He should be charged with criminal negligence for giving that compliment.* It reactivated the pathetic part of me that had cried over not being special enough to bend his rules for.

My friends looked between Damian and me, and then Zoey said, "We'll wait for you downstairs." The girls tried to pretend they weren't looking at us as they disappeared into the elevator.

"We've talked about this," I said. "I don't need a bodyguard anymore."

"You're gonna need six bodyguards looking like that," he disagreed.

I flushed under his gaze. The look he was giving me was the kind I'd obsessively dissect for the rest of the night, yearning to see meaning behind it that wasn't there. It was a look that warned me if he came with us, any chance of feeling free tonight would disintegrate because his magnetic field would dominate my thoughts, and I'd long for him to see me as more than a friend.

"You're not coming."

"Compromise was that you could stay at your place. Can't leave it without me or Justin."

"I'm not arguing about this again."

"Jenna—"

"Colton's been arrested and charged." So, protection detail and the torture-fest that was daily encounters with an uninterested guy I'd fallen for were over.

"Meanwhile, he's out on bail."

"With a shiny new court order to stay away from me."

"He violated the last restraining order when he came near you."

"And he went on the record that he has a gun, so now he really has to relinquish it."

"Which, as of today, he still hasn't done."

I sighed. "Damian, he was arrested. What more do you want?"

His jaw tightened. "He tried to kill you, and they charged him with a goddamned misdemeanor."

Justin was equally outraged by this. In his eyes, there was more than enough evidence for stiffer charges. He'd been a witness and there were the hospital records and pictures of the bruises around my neck. The case for domestic violence, the prosecutor explained, was strong, but attempted murder? A woman had been resuscitated four times after sustaining thirty stab wounds. *That* was an attempted murder case. And as for the misdemeanor versus felony charge, well, it turns out that in Cook County Illinois, one must have a prior domestic violence charge for it to be a felony. Like, for example, if I'd reported Colton the first time. It was the universe's way of reminding me that my mistakes had a cumulative effect.

Damian scrubbed his face and softened his voice. "I just want to make sure you're safe."

"They put a lot of stipulations on his bail, so he needs to be on his best behavior if he doesn't want to wind up with extra jail time."

"He knows you won't take him back now, and that you're going to testify against him." At his court date in six weeks. "You're more in danger now than you were before."

But therein lay the problem. This whole time, we'd all put our lives on hold with one tollgate in mind: Colton getting arrested. And just as I finally breathed a sigh of relief thinking it was over, Fisher walked us through the next steps. A court date, followed by testimony, and God willing, *if* he was found guilty—if!—a sentencing hearing. Because the charges were lighter than we'd hoped, Colton was looking at a max one year in jail. And even when he was *in* jail, Damian and Justin would be paranoid Colton would somehow get a friend or find some other way to come after me—if not during his stay, then upon his release. I realized it was one big hamster wheel of tollgate after tollgate that'd go around and around for the rest of my life, so what was I supposed to do? Hide in my apartment forever? When, exactly, was I supposed to start living again? When would everyone agree it was "safe enough" to do so?

Never, I realized. Was *now* a little premature? Who knew? Maybe I should wait a few more months, but I was too angry to care anymore. The truth was, when the life you wanted was ripped out from under you, when you fell madly in love with someone who will never love you back, and when you realized this dark cloud will hang over your head for the rest of your life, you just don't care as much as you should about being overly cautious. Because honestly, what was the point of having a life if you can't *live*?

"Please don't go out tonight," Damian pleaded. "I have a bad feeling about this."

"I appreciate your concern," I said, locking my door. "But I can take care of myself." I brought my mace, and I'd keep my eyes open. "Don't follow me."

I could feel him staring at me as I walked away.

At ten o'clock, The Happening—a dance club where music pumped enough bass to vibrate the floor—was in full swing. Beneath a giant silver ball surrounded by purple and blue lights pulsing to the beat, two hundred people danced in the sweltering heat that reeked of cologne. Along the far wall, ten bartenders served patrons enveloped in blue light.

This is where Zoey, Emily, Harrison, Steve, and I stood waiting for a drink.

As far as I could tell, Damian obeyed my command to leave me alone. Maybe he'd decided the threat of Colton had passed, maybe he was trying to respect my desire for space, or maybe he was in bed with some gorgeous blond, appreciating that his temporary stint as a bodyguard was over.

Either way, it had been worth the fight. Being here was exactly what I needed, and I wasn't going to let his baseless warning ruin my night.

*Honestly, why would he say something like that?* Before he'd opened his big mouth, I was in a perfectly good mood, but now my eyes darted around the space in paranoia. So many people kept funneling into the already crowded bar, so anyone who wanted to hide, could, and it was hard to see people clearly because the lighting created blind spots and shadows everywhere. I chewed my thumbnail and glanced up at the glass-enclosed DJ booth on the upper deck, where several people were hanging out.

The silhouette of a man stood along the glass, but unlike everyone else facing towards the DJ, he was looking out, down at the crowd. There was no need to feel creeped out. He wasn't looking at *us;* he was watching people dance, probably scanning the crowd for a possible romantic connection.

I forced myself to look away and focus on my friends, but I couldn't stop my eyes from wandering back up to him.

*He's staring right at me.*

I gasped. The disco ball's light had only illuminated his eyes for that brief second, too short to be sure it was Colton, but long enough to see the man was glaring at me. *His head's not moving.* He continued to stare at me as I tried to hide my panic from my friends.

I turned towards Zoey, ready to tell her everything and beg her to take me home so I wouldn't have to go alone, and my eyes darted back up.

The man turned his back to the glass. If it were Colton, he'd have kept staring or vanished now that he'd been busted, so obviously, it was just some other guy. *You're being ridiculous, Jenna.* That eerie feeling of being watched was an infuriating consequence of having not been alone for weeks—my sense of security a casualty of this entire experience.

I twisted the ring on my finger around and around. If I couldn't get myself to relax tonight, when I was surrounded by friends, I might as well just go home and never come back out.

I took a deep breath, calming my nerves. Everything was fine. I was a little jumpy, and that was understandable.

Emily nodded with her chin. "Harrison won't stop looking at you."

I glanced over and, sure enough, Harrison offered me a charming smile when I made eye contact. Wearing a white button-down that hugged his muscles, fitted jeans, and nice shoes, he'd styled his blond hair so every strand looked strategically placed. Under different circumstances, I might return Harrison's flirting, but tonight, boys were the last thing I was thinking about. I just wanted to try to relax and have some fun.

After Harrison ordered and passed out Patrón shots, he held up his glass and said, "In all this world, why I do think, there are five reasons why we drink: Good friends, good wine, lest we be dry, and any other reason why. Cheers!"

He clinked my glass first, and as we downed our shots, the liquid burned my throat, making me cough. Harrison kept his eyes on me, but my eyes were on Zoey, wondering what she was going to tell me, and if she'd accept my apology.

"Hey," I said to her. "Can we talk for a second?"

As we walked twenty feet from our friends, I tried not to think about how devastated I'd be if this didn't go well.

"I've been wanting to apologize," I said over the music. "For giving you the cold shoulder the last few weeks."

Zoey's soft hair framed her mocha skin, her chocolate eyes settling into understanding. "I deserved it," she said. "I was being super judgy."

The music switched to a new song, and cheers erupted on the dance floor.

"I was just scared that something bad was going to happen to you," she admitted. "And I couldn't handle it if it did."

"I didn't want you to be right about Colton," I confessed. "But you were."

Her eyes softened even more. "I never told anyone," she swore. "I know I said I wouldn't keep your secret, but I said that out of anger. I'd never actually do it. I hope you know that."

I knew that now.

"Can we put this whole ugly mess behind us?" I asked.

Zoey offered a relieved nod, and then she wrapped her arms around me. My eyes stung, as I felt the tension, the bad blood, melting away between us.

We held each other for a solid minute before letting go.

Zoey smiled. "I'm so glad you're here tonight."

I was too, and now I really did feel like I could have a fun night—especially since I was gloriously alone, without Damian or Justin watching my every move and unintentionally suffocating me.

"What's up, sis?"

I stiffened. *You've got to be kidding me.* I turned around with clenched fists.

"Justin, what the hell are you doing here?"

## 29

"How did you know where I was?" I demanded.

Justin took in my appearance. "You look...different."

"I'll take that as a compliment."

"Couldn't find a *whole* outfit to wear?"

I crossed my arms over my chest. "It's a dress."

"It's a tube top."

I yanked the hem down. The problem was, it pulled the top down a bit too, leaving the girls upstairs a little more exposed.

Justin laughed. "Who the hell convinced you to wear that?"

I frowned at Zoey. "Emily."

"Naturally," he said, looking at Emily, who was now flirting with a handsome guy at the bar. "And the 'dress' came from?"

A regrettable internet sale, in which the dress online appeared to have much more fabric than the one that showed up in the non-refundable box. "What are you doing here?" I repeated. *Other than sabotaging my only hope of having a carefree, good time.* If he took that from me, I seriously might break down crying and never stop. A human can only experience so much pressure before they need a release valve.

Justin tilted his head.

"Damian called you."

"Texted."

*Ugh!*

"You should've told me you were going out." Justin looked around the club, thinking that was the end of our conversation, but I wasn't letting him off that easy.

"Answer my question. How did you know I was here?" I'd purposely never told Damian where I was going.

Justin offered Zoey an apologetic frown.

"I'm sorry," she said. "I didn't realize it was a thing, and," she said with narrowed eyes to him, "I didn't know he'd show up."

Perhaps she sensed me considering wrestling my brother to the ground because she sheepishly walked away to give us some space.

Curiously, Justin's eyes followed her the entire time.

"Since when do you text with Zoey?"

Justin flushed with the same look he had when Mom caught him doing something he tried to hide from her. He seemed to evaluate possible explanations as he looked over at Zoey, who stood near the bar looking apprehensive. Uncharacteristically *not* on her phone. So maybe the person she's been talking to this whole time was here...

Justin tucked his hands into his pockets and waited for me to figure it out, so he didn't have to say it.

*Holy. Mother. Mary.*

"She's the girl you like," I realized. And based on their body language, they'd been hanging out. A lot.

I should have seen this coming. She'd had a long history with my family, tagging along on trips home in college when Justin was there, and in Chicago, we sometimes hung out together in the same social circle. Plus, she was beautiful, smart, ambitious, and down-to-earth, so they were totally each other's types.

"How long has this been going on?"

Justin shook his head. "I think I've always felt a way about her. After I got out of the hospital, I bumped into her one night, and one thing just led to another." He evaluated me. "You pissed?"

"Why didn't you tell me before?"

"Because you two have been in some sort of a *thing*, and I knew you'd overthink it. You have enough on your mind."

He motioned for Zoey to return, smiling at her as he took her hand.

Zoey looked at me nervously. "This is what I was going to tell you. Are you mad?"

"No, of course not." I was thrilled that Justin was finally prioritizing more than just his career, and how could I be upset that two of my favorite people were happy together? It was just a lot to digest. "So, was this your news?" I asked Justin, my mind scrambling.

"No." He paused, his mouth curling up on both sides. "I was going to tell you I turned down the job."

Zoey's eyes lit up. "So, you're not moving to New York?"

"I don't want to spend my whole life working. Turns out when you stop and smell the roses," he grinned, smitten with Zoey, "they smell pretty damn good."

I'd never seen my brother all mushy like this; it was impossible to contain my smile. Especially since that was precisely what I wanted to do tonight—stop and smell the roses. And thankfully, Justin didn't seem hellbent on ruining that for me.

"Another round," Harrison interrupted, passing out shots.

Tonight we had a lot to celebrate: Justin and Zoey, Justin staying in Chicago, and starting a new chapter in my life. The Colton drama might not be fully behind me, but if I didn't celebrate the milestones along the way, I'd spend my whole life *waiting* to celebrate.

We all clinked glasses and downed our drinks.

NINETY MINUTES AND TOO MANY SHOTS LATER, MY SMILE WAS ridiculously wide, my muscles soft, and my words slow. We danced in a loose circle as the overhead ball lit up the dance floor in blue and pink lights, alternating people's skin tones from smurf to flamingo. Sheens of sweat coated foreheads and lower backs, and the dance music became a hypnotic rhythm in my veins.

I couldn't believe it, but I was having fun. A lot of fun. I was smiling and dancing and laughing and acting every part the carefree twenty-three-year-old I should be right now. *I almost forgot what this was like!* I felt like Rapunzel on the first day she'd escaped her tower.

Harrison grabbed my hand, and when he spun me around, I laughed so hard I almost fell over.

The music switched to a slow song, which cleared most people off the dance floor, including me, and once I was off to the side, I watched as my brother stayed behind with Zoey. I don't think I'd ever seen him so happy. As he grabbed Zoey's hand and brought her in for a kiss, they looked utterly and madly in love.

The wave of joy that crashed to shore receded with sorrow, hurt, and, if I was honest, jealousy. How could I be this happy for them yet this heartbroken all at the same time?

Damian would never kiss me like that. We'd never lose ourselves on the dance floor, so absorbed in our romance we'd forget everyone else in the club existed. We'd never have our entire future in front of us, full of possibilities and adventures. We'd never experience anything like that.

I thought the reason Damian pushed me away was because of his head injury, but the more I thought about it, the less sure I became. If he loved me, if he wanted to be with me, he'd have gotten second opinions, not accepted one doctor's possible conclusion—and it *was* just possible, not certain—as fact. He'd break down every door looking for a solution for us to be together. That's what *I* would have done if the roles were reversed, but he wouldn't even try.

"You okay?" Harrison asked.

No. I was instantly not okay. I tried to offer a reassuring smile—no one needed to know my heart was on fire—but when I looked over at Harrison, something in my periphery caught my eye. Something that instantly made my neck prickle with fear.

*I'm being watched.*

I searched the spot that sounded my alarm bells, but there was nothing except the line to the bathroom. I scrutinized the DJ booth, the dance floor, the bar, and the other open spaces, but no one was looking at me. No cause for alarm. My sixth sense needed to cease and desist. I was a single girl in a club, so, statistically speaking, maybe a guy had been watching me because he found me attractive. *It's not Colton.*

Was this what it'd feel like forever?

I stared at my brother, willing my joy to return, but it was fruitless. I could either stay and be a downer or count my blessings that I'd had almost two hours of pure, unadulterated fun. And heck, even if this was a little shorter than planned, going out tonight was a massive step in the right direction, and I was grateful for every minute of it.

"I'm going to head out," I said to Harrison.

"Wait," Harrison said, following me as I headed for the door. I'd text Justin in a few minutes. If I told him I was leaving, he'd feel obligated to abandon Zoey to escort me home, and after everything he'd been through, he deserved to celebrate tonight. I wasn't about to ruin this for him.

I emerged into the October night, surprised Harrison had followed me all the way outside.

"I'll order you a ride," he said, pulling out his cell.

"You don't need to do that," I said, opening my purse to retrieve my cell, but he waved it off, punched something into his phone, and showed me the app that confirmed the ride was on its way.

"I'm glad you came," Harrison said. His slur and sagging eyelids made it clear he'd had too much to drink. Especially when, out of nowhere, he reached down and took my hand.

Which was weird, since we weren't even dancing. It made a bead of sweat form on my forehead, a wave of discomfort roll through my stomach. More than discomfort. Something worse... I leaned up against the brick wall, willing the dizziness to stop. I *so* didn't want to get sick in front of the line of people waiting at the door.

"I'm sorry to hear you and Colton broke up," Harrison said. But his eyes told me he wasn't sorry at all. In an unmistakably flirtatious voice, he added, "You deserve better."

I offered a weak smile. It was the best I could do with how sick I was starting to feel.

"I never told you this, but I had a crush on you when you first started," he admitted through alcohol truth serum. I wished I could feel excited by his confession—it was certainly nice to be *wanted*. But Harrison was an oil painting, while Damian was a masterpiece.

Harrison studied my face the way guys do when they want to pull your mouth to theirs. *No, no, no. Horrible timing, Harrison.* He cupped my cheek and slowly drew his lips closer to mine.

I wasn't sure what to do. I didn't want to hurt his feelings, and I was kind of stuck between him and the wall, so I'd have to do something severe to stop him—but before I could do anything, his mouth was on mine. Warm, opening slightly.

*Oh god.* I was going to vomit. I was sure of it. The clammy hands. The swirling liquid in my stomach. I pushed Harrison's chest away, freeing my lips. "Harrison, stop," I warned.

But he pulled my lips back to his again as if my resistance was some sort of sexy foreplay. The thing a good girl says before making out all night, after which she blushes and claims she'd never done this before. Problem was, I wasn't that girl. I was the girl who was actually telling him to stop or I'd barf all over his designer shoes.

"Harrison." I pushed again, wanting so badly to *not* be the girl who vomited inside his mouth.

Suddenly, he was off of me.

"She said stop."

It took me a second to comprehend that Damian was standing there, the veins in his arms bulging, and Harrison was on the ground. Harrison growled and charged his shoulders into Damian's core, but Damian was ready for it and flung Harrison like a ragdoll against the ground.

"Stop!" I jumped in between them but immediately stumbled.

"Jesus," Damian snarled as he caught me. "How much did you give her to drink, you freaking idiot?"

"I'm fine." I snatched my arm from his hand. "And no one *gave* me my drinks. I'm in charge of myself! And I don't need anyone's help!"

I stormed off to show them who was boss. Unfortunately, my ankle rolled over my ridiculously high heel.

"For the love of—" Damian caught me just before I face-planted.

He threw me over his shoulder in a fireman grip, so my face dangled near his lower back, his arm wrapped around the back of my knees, and worst of all, my queasy stomach squished into his shoulder.

The sidewalk moved beneath me.

Oh my god. It was going to happen. "Put me down!" I said. I caught a glimpse of Harrison wanting to come to my defense and restore his bruised ego.

"Let her go!" Harrison barked.

My throat burned with prebarf.

"Go home, Harrison," Damian said without looking back. "Or I'll beat the shit out of you."

And then we were around the corner, away from the people who'd been staring at our spectacle.

With each step, his shoulder sloshed the unstable contents of my stomach.

"Put me down," I begged, swallowing back a gag.

"Out of all the guys you could possibly date, if you go out with Harrison Price, I'm going to shove an ice pick into my eye socket so I don't have to see it."

My stomach lurched, burning up my esophagus.

"I'm gonna barf all over you," I warned.

He ignored me, the pavement beneath us swaying.

"I'm not kidding, Damian, I'm going to puke! Put me down!"

Damian obeyed. I staggered over to the wall and held myself up, convinced my body was about to reject the night's good times onto the pavement. But shockingly, nothing came, not even after standing for a solid minute.

"What are you doing here?"

"Keeping you from being molested by that prick," he said.

"No, *here*. At the club."

He ran both hands through his hair. "Couldn't stop worrying about you."

See, he couldn't say things like that! What he meant and what my heart wanted him to mean were so excruciatingly different that being in his presence was agony. How was I ever supposed to get over him when he was *always* around?

"You already ratted me out to my brother," I snapped. Justin obviously told Damian where I was. "He already invaded my night, so you certainly didn't need to come too."

Why did Damian look so bewildered by my anger, with his sexy brows all smooshed together? And how long had he been lingering here, exactly, watching my *encounter* with Harrison? "You shouldn't have pushed Harrison."

"He wasn't taking no for an answer."

"I had it under control."

"Yeah. I could tell."

"Why do *you* care anyway?" I demanded.

"Because you're my friend."

*Insert knife into heart. Twist, add salt, then acid.*

"You can't keep doing this to me! You can't hang outside a club all night just to protect me! You can't revolve your life around me, but then turn around and not love me back! If I have any hope of getting over you, I need you to leave me alone!"

## 30

B etween the crisp air and my anger, when I stormed away from Damian, I felt instantly sober. I needed to walk—no, stomp—the ten blocks home instead of taking a cab. High heels be damned. Seeing Damian tonight proved being friends would never work, and the only way to get over him was to cut him out completely.

My eyes stung. How could the prospect of living without him hurt *this* much? Like desperately gasping for air but finding yourself at the bottom of the darkened ocean? I couldn't imagine a more sensual mouth to kiss, a more beautiful body to feel on top of mine, and I couldn't imagine a more incredible soul, either. Everything he'd overcome, all the adversity, his drive, his determination to come out of it, and I'd never witnessed someone as caring as he'd been for me. He was someone I couldn't imagine *not* having by my side for the rest of my life.

In the past, I'd always thought of love as binary: you were in love or you weren't. But clearly there were degrees to it, and my love for Damian would shatter any record. I wasn't just in love with him; he was my soul's other half, and without him, I'd never be whole.

I wiped a stray tear and just kept walking.

"Jenna, wait."

"Go away."

It was ridiculously ironic that the sidewalks were packed with couples wearing gowns and suits, attending one of the many Homecoming dances and afterparties that occurred in October—celebrating their never-ending day of love. And here I was, running away from a guy I was in love with, who was afraid the guy who loved me was going to kill me.

"Will you stop?" Damian called out from behind me.

"Leave me alone, Damian."

"I want to talk about what you just said."

"Well, I don't."

"I don't love you *back*?" he challenged.

*Oh god, I said that out loud, didn't I?*

"Jenna."

I crossed an intersection with barely enough time for a car not to hit me and then walked on the path along the river.

"Jenna!" Damian spun me around, his face desperate. "What did you mean by that?"

"It doesn't matter."

"Answer me!"

"Why?" I yanked my arm back from him. "So you can make me feel like a lost puppy again?"

"What are you talking about?"

"At the gym. You said you didn't want anyone like that in your life." *I will not cry.* "And that *I*, especially, needed to understand that."

"I was trying to protect you!"

"You knew how I felt about you, and you slammed the door in my face."

"That's not true!" Damian growled.

"Yes, it is. God, just be honest!"

"I didn't slam the door in *your* face, Jenna; I slammed it in mine!"

Damian shoved an angry hand through his hair and let out a breath so deep, it was as if he'd held it for years. "I knew if you opened that door, I wouldn't have the strength to stay away."

My jaw went slack, and my heart danced. He *did* feel that way about me—the chemistry, the attraction had all been real.

"It kept getting harder and harder to *not* cross that line," he confessed. "Christ, I even went out and found a top neurologist, thinking it'd assure me I was doing the right thing."

And yet, he wasn't throwing it in my face as justification to stay away.

"You got good news," I said. "Didn't you?"

"They could still be wrong."

"They? So you got multiple second opinions that gave you hope we could have a future together, and you still pushed me away?"

Damian's lips tightened, and his tone was tight. "I didn't want you to throw your life away on me."

That's when I sensed the real battle waging inside him, and suddenly everything made sense. "That's what this was really about." Damian latched on to his head injury as justification to remain isolated, but the real reason he was pushing everyone away was much more tragic. "You don't think you deserve to be happy."

He didn't deny it. Instead, he looked down and put his hands on his hips, and when he spoke, his voice was low. "I've hurt everyone I've ever cared about, and I won't let you be next."

This whole time I thought my inability to trust myself meant I needed to listen to my head, ignore my heart. But that wasn't it at all. I just needed to believe I was capable of making the right decision. And now I needed to have enough trust for both me and Damian, because this was the most incredible, epic love I'd ever imagined. If I could just convince him to give us a chance, I knew we could overcome anything together.

When I closed the distance between us, I sensed he was trying to force himself to step away—a plan that was easier when he'd convinced himself I didn't love him, when he wasn't standing in front of me *feeling* what was passing between us.

"I know you think you're doing the noble thing here, pushing me away, but all that'll do is break my heart."

Torment filled his eyes. "Don't say that."

All our moments, everything we'd shared and everything we *could* share together, hung in the balance of what I was about to say—words that meant more than any words I'd ever spoken. "I'm in love with you, Damian."

His shoulders sank three inches.

My profession, I could tell, changed everything. He could no longer deny my feelings, nor could he rationalize them away. I could see his armor collapsing and the anguish in his eyes give way to joy as he brought his hand to my cheek. "You shouldn't be with me," he whispered. But I could tell he was trying to convince *himself* more than me, his last-ditch effort to regain the will power to push me away. Yet it seemed as though a magnetic force drew his body closer, willing our mouths to unite, and I felt his resolve shatter.

"I love you," I said. "And I don't want a future if you're not in it."

Damian's breaths quickened as he studied my eyes, my jaw, my mouth, allowing himself to feel what he'd denied for so long. It took him several beats to digest this new reality standing in front of him, and I could see he was hesitant to cross the line and kiss me. Once we kissed, there'd be no going back; it would unlock passion and emotions impossible to contain.

All the reasons we shouldn't be together lost their meaning as he traced my lip with his thumb, and—looking like he'd dreamed about doing this countless times—he drew his face closer to mine. The anticipation of his lips touching mine was hell and heaven all at the same time.

And then, he took my upper lip between his.

A fire of desire spread down my throat to my stomach. Having our mouths united was a thousand times better than I had imagined it would be, and I could tell it was for him, too, because he growled and pressed his lips harder against mine. He kissed me like a long buildup of a storm that had finally reached its peak and cracked open the sky with its monsoon—pouring love over me. I placed my hands on the back of his head, ran my fingers through his silky hair, and pulled him closer. His thumb moved to the front of my ear, his fingertips lightly cupping the base of my head. Damian pulled his lips back a fraction of an inch, allowing his warm breath to bounce off my mouth, and then surrendered again to our passion. I could feel his resistance—all his justifications to not let himself fall in love with me—disintegrate.

As I raised up on my tiptoes, locking my arms around his neck, his arm tightened around my waist, entrapping me in his steel cage, making me feel secure and loved in his big strong arms. I never wanted this to end.

Damian opened his mouth, and when our tongues connected, fire spread through my entire body. I craved more of his wet, delicious tongue, and I wanted him to touch me. Everywhere.

Desire now entirely consumed me, craving every part of Damian. I squirmed beneath his hold and pressed my body harder against his, thrilled when he groaned. As he pulled me tighter, his lips unleashed weeks of accumulated desire, our passion building, our lips growing more urgent with each other.

I'd never felt anything like this. I struggled to control myself, wanting every part of Damian, right here, right now. I wished we were somewhere private, where I could take his shirt off, pull him on top of me, spend hours—days—with him in bed. Feel his bare skin, his mouth all over my body.

After all the battles over the past few months, this moment seemed too good to be true. Could this really be happening? A happily ever after, getting the love of my life?

How we must look, making out next to the river, with majestic skyscrapers sparkling all around us. Beneath the silver glow of the moon, we kissed for a long time, and then, panting, we pushed our foreheads together, struggling to regain our composure.

When I finally opened my eyes, what I saw—fifteen feet away—made my stomach drop.

It was Colton.

Glaring at us.

I could imagine how this must look to him—the guy he'd accused me of cheating on him with now holding me in his arms, kissing me with the passion that only comes from true love.

Colton's jaw tensed, and he flashed a murderous look.

## 31

I t took only a second for Colton to bolt and Damian to charge after him.

"Stop!" I screamed.

But Damian didn't listen. He was a cheetah locked on his prey, running full-speed to catch the guy who'd almost taken my life. I didn't know how to stop them, but I couldn't let them out of my sight, so I gripped my clutch tightly—inside were my mace and phone— kicked off my heels, and took off running, too.

Colton sprinted across busy lanes of traffic, inciting honks and swerves, and to my horror, Damian followed. I darted after them.

A set of headlights headed straight for me, honking violently, and, seconds before running me down, it turned. And crashed into a sedan.

Damian spun around to ensure I was okay before galloping towards Colton again.

"Damian, stop!"

Colton wove through people, and when a woman got in his way, he shoved her to the ground.

I needed to stop Damian because if he caught Colton, what Damian did to that fighter would look like child's play. What if Colton didn't survive? Damian couldn't exactly claim self-defense if he hunted Colton down like this, could he? He'd be charged with murder. And worse, it'd be another death on his conscience.

I was a horrible person for being more worried about what Colton's death would mean to Damian than to Colton.

Flanked by steel skyscrapers, we ran south, snaking through pedestrians. I screamed for help as I passed. Some looked confused, some gawked, and some snickered, amused by the strange foot chase, but no one answered my cries.

My bare feet pounded on the concrete so hard that sharp pebbles dug into my skin, but I was losing ground. Damian was at least a hundred feet in front of me now, making it harder to keep my eye on him, and pain stabbed my side with each panting breath.

"Damian, stop!" I screamed.

Holy hell. What if Colton had his gun? What if Damian was the one who got hurt—or worse?

I pulled the cell out of my clutch and managed to call nine-one-one, but it slowed me down. When Colton and Damian sprinted around a corner, the building obstructed my view for several terrifying seconds. And once I finally made the turn, they were nowhere to be found.

I kept running, shouting my location to the dispatcher, ignoring her pleas to stop chasing them.

"Which way did they go?" I screamed at a guy with a Mohawk. He scowled at me, then pointed to an alley.

The narrow corridor between two buildings swallowed me in darkness. Rust-colored bricks blanketed the first two stories of the buildings, dingy light fixtures spilled an uneven glow down the wall like paint, and the uneven ground—made up of cracked asphalt with water-filled potholes—stretched at least a half-mile long, but only ten feet wide. It smelled of rotting trash and dry pee, with half a dozen dumpsters overflowing with sacks of garbage peppered along the sides. It was cold in here, and as I pulled the phone away from my ear so I could listen for movement, the sounds of the city were muffled.

The ground felt wet beneath my bare feet. I got halfway through the passage before seeing the other side was blocked with a thirty-foot-high chain-link fence, shut with a titanium lock. There was no way they could've made it over the fence without me hearing it or seeing it. Which meant I'd wasted precious time going in the wrong direction, and somewhere out there, Damian and Colton could be fighting. I needed to get back to the main sidewalk and ask if anyone knew which direction they went.

When I turned around, I was alarmed how deep inside this alley I was—a hundred feet from the protection of the public sidewalk, at least. All those dumpsters and piles of trash not only offered hiding spots for someone lurking in here, but they'd also hide an attack should an unsavory guy want to assault a girl...

My sixth sense was screaming at me to get out—warning me Colton wasn't the only dangerous thing in the city and that Justin had almost lost his life in an alley just like this one. I headed towards the entrance, but something thumped up ahead, stopping me in my tracks. In the limited light, it was hard to tell if the noise came from the dumpster on the right or the metal staircase leading to what must be an underground door on the left.

Something rustled. My heartbeat spiked. Seconds ticked by with me frozen in place, trying to spot the source of the sound. It was too dark. Too isolated. Too dangerous for a girl to be here, alone, at night. If no one paid attention my screams for help when I was on a safe sidewalk, they certainly wouldn't enter an ominous alley to answer the muffled cries of a stranger.

I forced myself to move forward, my feet stinging from the battering they took running, but when a shadow moved, I froze again.

*I'm being watched. I can feel it.*

Another sound—a clank of metal this time.

The closest light flickered off, canopying me in darkness for several seconds and leaving me alone with my breath. Someone could be right behind me and I wouldn't see them.

The light buzzed, and there was a flash of movement ten feet ahead.

I gasped and almost fell over before realizing it was just a rat. The animal stared at me for a second and then scurried back behind the dumpster. Clutching my chest, I let out a huge breath. I needed to get out of here.

But I only made it ten feet before a clank echoed in the metal staircase.

*Run, Jenna.*

Clank, clank.

*Move! Before whoever it is, is all the way up the stairs!*

Clank, clank.

*There's the top of a head!*

Clank.

I ran on my stinging feet.

Clank, clank, clank.

I stopped. A man stood in front of me and blocked my path.

"You were fucking him the whole time we were together, weren't you?" The light shifted when he moved and reflected off something shiny in his hands. I scrutinized it, terror creeping in.

It was a knife.

*Oh, God.*

Where was Damian?

"Weren't you!" Colton roared.

"No."

"That's why he looked so familiar, isn't it?"

I wasn't going to tell him that Damian looked familiar because he was an MMA fighter. It might make Colton even more determined to dominate and hurt Damian if he hadn't already...

"Do you love him?" With trembling fists, Colton paced in front of me, fidgeting with the knife. I tried to see if there was blood on it, but it was hard to tell with the lack of light.

"Do you love him?" he shouted.

I couldn't find my words with my heart attacking my ribcage.

"You made me believe you actually cared about me." He pointed the knife towards me. "That my life wasn't going to be a bag of shit." He paused. "But you never loved me."

"That's not true."

"You threw me away so easily. Even after you had me arrested, I thought maybe…" He looked me up and down in disgust. "But you're not the person I thought you were."

"Where is Damian?"

"That's all you care about, isn't it?" he screamed.

"Where is he?"

"You don't give a damn about me! You never did!"

"Did you hurt him?"

Colton hesitated, and his anger receded behind a smug look of satisfaction. "Maybe I gave him a taste of what I did to Justin."

He waited while his implied confession dawned on me. What a disgusting thing to say. What kind of monster makes up something so horrible? This was low, even for Colton.

In the distance, police sirens wailed.

"You're just saying that to hurt me."

"Yeah," he admitted. "But it's also the truth."

"It's not," I insisted. It couldn't be. When Justin was attacked, Colton and I were together. Blissfully. Hell, he'd proposed that week. There'd be absolutely no motivation to attack my brother. Not to mention, he didn't have the means. "You were at your job site that night."

"Was I?" he challenged. "How do you know? Because I said so?"

What a vile human being, with his sweaty face, red cheeks. He looked puffy compared to the last time I'd seen him, perhaps drinking a lot, drowning himself in delusions of either winning me back or getting revenge. I couldn't tell which anymore.

But I wasn't going to let him win this repulsive game of his. Back then, we were in love, and he wanted a future with me, so he'd have absolutely nothing to gain and everything to lose by hurting Justin. And yet he expected me to believe he was randomly confessing to the crime? That's the line of bullshit he was selling?

"Nice try, asshole. Screw you."

I started to walk around him, but he positioned himself in my way. I reached inside my clutch and wrapped my fingers around the can of mace.

Sirens grew louder.

"Same fucking attitude *he* had that night. Runnin' his fucking mouth, like I was one of those pathetic losers who pine after some chick they'll never get. He acted tough, but he screamed like a bitch when I hit him with that beer bottle. And in the end, he begged for his life like a fucking pussy."

"Justin would have never picked a fight with you, you lying bastard." He'd have had no reason to.

Colton looked defensive. "When he started going off on me, *I* walked away," Colton snarled. *"He's* the one that wouldn't let up. He's the one that followed me, ran his mouth. Threatening *me.* He followed me into that alley and wouldn't shut the hell up about exposing me, saying he'd kick my ass if I ever went near you again. I warned him to back off, but he didn't. What the hell did he think was going to happen?"

I clenched my hands so tight my fingernails dug painfully into my flesh. I focused on that pain because this was too horrific a reality to accept. I needed him to be lying. Justin would never say something like that to Colton. It made no sense because it almost sounded like... like someone accusing Colton of being a stalker.

But at the time of Justin's attack, Colton and I were happy. Yes, Colton had been worried that people would find out what he'd done, that they'd never forgive him, and maybe convince me to leave him. But that wouldn't explain anything.

Unless...

"You were following me," I accused.

"I was protecting us," he snarled. "Making sure people didn't get in your head about what happened between us. How many people would care enough to do that, huh?"

Oh my god.

It *was* true. The clues fastened together like puzzle pieces that never quite fit until this last piece of information provided the glue. His controlling, obsessive jealousy and his fear that someone would find out what he'd done. My inability to get ahold of him at first, probably as he scurried home and washed the blood off his hands—literally—allowing enough time to pass to support his alibi. The look on his face when I invited him into Justin's hospital room that first time. Colton had looked concerned, but looking back on it, it wasn't a concern for Justin. It was concern Justin would remember it was Colton who'd attacked him.

I could see it playing out. Colton following me, paranoid someone might find out that he'd laid hands on me. Justin, on his way to that five thirty appointment, stumbling onto Colton peering through Ace's window. That's why Justin sounded so angry when he called me, confirming I was the one Colton was stalking. He must have then confronted Colton.

A confrontation that evidently involved Colton walking away from him, Justin pursuing, threatening that if he ever came near me again, yada yada, until they entered that alley. Where explosive accusations turned violent.

And that's when something else Colton just said screamed inside my head: *when I hit him with that beer bottle...* Only Justin's attacker would know he'd been hit with a beer bottle, its brown glass picked out of his scalp by the doctor.

I was going to be sick.

Colton was far more dangerous than I'd ever imagined.

"Where is Damian?" I demanded.

Suddenly, the siren that had been growing louder became piercing as a squad car stopped at the end of the alley. A cop jumped out of the passenger side and spotted the knife in Colton's hand.

Colton took off running towards the other end. The officer ran after him, shouting, "Put your hands up!" And, "Stop!"

Colton didn't listen. He reached the fence and climbed several feet before the officer caught his foot. Colton swung his knife at the officer—missing, thank the lord—before swiftly climbing the rest of the way and launching himself over the thirty-foot fence. Once on the other side, Colton glared at me.

Silently promising a rematch. Before running off into the darkness.

"What did you do to Damian?" I shrieked.

## 32

"Where is he?" I demanded. Damian could be hurt or dying, and we were just sitting around talking while Fisher wrote things in his little notebook. As if protecting people required pens rather than handcuffs.

"They're looking for him, kid."

It was kind of Fisher to show up when he'd heard the call on the scan. I was sitting in the back of an ambulance with its doors open—at my insistence, so I could keep an eye out for Damian—while Fisher stood near the opening and an EMT treated my feet. Running through the city barefoot had cut them up pretty good, but at least they didn't need stitches.

Three police cars sat on this side of the alley, with another parked on the other end. Armed with flashlights that turned room-sized areas from night to day, uniformed officers methodically searched the alley from both sides—for Colton, for Damian. Anyone in the skyscrapers could have probably seen the entire thing play out from an aerial view, and down here, traffic bottlenecked around the congestion. To drivers, this potential tragedy was nothing more than an inconvenient traffic delay.

Meanwhile, a large group of onlookers had gathered behind an invisible line manned by two officers. They didn't have the time or interest to help us before, but now, neither the smell of rotting trash nor the difficulty seeing in the dark stopped them from gawking at the cops crawling all over the place.

"It's never been just *me* who's been in danger," I said. "Has it?" The anchor of guilt weighed me down. My bad decisions—the ones I'd told myself were no one's business and only affected me—were a cancer, spreading to the lives of everyone I loved. "This whole time, Damian and Justin have been worried what Colton would do to me if he found me." It felt like a hole burned in my intestines. "I never stopped to think what Colton might do to them."

How could I have been so self-centered to have not thought of this before? He'd tried to kill me; what further evidence did I need that he was a danger to us all? It's like one day you realize everyone you love is in a boat in shark-infested waters, and there's a hole in the bottom —a hole you put there with your own ignorance—and you're staring at the water flooding the vessel with no idea how to stop it.

"Colton's never going to give up," I said. "Is he?"

"Let's just take this one step at a time."

One step at a time, and the next step was filling Fisher in on Colton's confession. "Colton said something you need to hear."

"Jenna!" Damian's voice shouted.

It took me a second to see his panicked face emerge among the onlookers. *Thank God!* He looked okay! I stood up on my gauze slippers, ignoring the stinging in my feet and the EMT chiding me, and moved to the edge of the ambulance as Damian shoved his way through the crowd. He kept his eyes locked on me until a police officer held him back with a hand to his chest.

"Sir, I'm gonna need you to step back."

"Move out of my goddamned way!" Damian snapped.

"Let him come over," I said.

The cop looked at Fisher, who nodded, prompting the officer to reluctantly release Damian. Who rushed to me.

"Are you okay?" he asked, holding my shoulders as he frantically scanned my body, zeroing in on my wrapped feet.

"I'm fine. It's just from running barefoot."

"I'd stay off them for a while," the EMT cautioned, closing his tackle box.

"Why did you go after Colton?" I asked. "He had a knife. He could've killed you!"

Damian's body tensed. "He had a knife?"

Yes. The outcome could've been catastrophic, one jab to Damian's neck or heart, and my world as I knew it would've been over.

It was at this moment that Damian seemed to digest the scene of cops searching. "Where is he?" Damian growled at Fisher. When Fisher didn't answer, Damian scowled. "You had him right there, didn't you? And you let him get away!"

Fisher's jaw tightened, and his face flashed from blue to red, to blue, to red from a nearby squad car's lights. "He took a swing at an officer with a weapon."

"He had a knife," Damian growled. "Your cop had a gun. Mace. A baton. Oh, and a shit-ton of police training!"

"You need to calm down."

"You and your entire goddamned police force have failed to protect her at every turn." Damian stepped towards Fisher. "Every step of the way, that son of a bitch has been one step ahead of you." Damian jabbed a finger towards Fisher's face. "And tonight, he could've killed her!"

"Damian…" I cautioned, and when I put a hand on his chest, I could feel his heart punching his ribs and his chest laboring like a runner. I wasn't sure if Damian would actually strike Fisher, but it looked like it took all of his strength *not* to.

"This has gone on long enough." Damian threw one arm around my back and another under my knees and picked me up.

"What are you doing?" I asked as he started walking.

"She needs to finish her statement," Fisher insisted. His partner grabbed my purse from the ambulance and handed it to me when Damian stopped to glare at Fisher.

"It doesn't matter what you write on some piece of paper. You're completely incapable of protecting her."

The thump-thump of the ambulance doors closing preceded its engine rumbling to life.

Damian stomped away.

"Wait," I pleaded. "I have to file a *different* statement. Colton's the one who almost killed Justin."

Damian stopped and waited for me to explain. "He confessed," I said. "Justin caught him spying on me that night and confronted him."

Fisher exchanged a look with his partner. "Are you sure?"

I nodded. "He knew details that no one else could, like how Justin had been hit with a beer bottle."

I thought this would change Damian's mind about walking away, but, looking even more scared for my safety, he walked faster.

"Damian, stop!" I insisted. "The police—"

"Haven't done a goddamned thing to keep you safe!" It was unsettling, seeing him unravel like this. "Colton got you alone tonight with a weapon, and we can't wait around anymore until tragedy strikes."

"Damian—"

"Jenna." He shut his eyes. "I need you to trust me."

I'd never seen Damian this desperate. I didn't know what to make of it, and I wasn't sure what he was asking me to do, exactly. I couldn't argue that Colton seemed to be a step ahead of the police, but I wasn't sure I agreed that the police couldn't keep me safe. It was starting to feel like no one could keep us safe from Colton, actually.

"We need to go to the police station," Fisher insisted, following us as Damian carried me down the sidewalk.

"We don't have time for that," Damian snapped. "Every second we stand here arguing is a second he's coming up with *his* next move. Please," he repeated. "Do you trust me?"

I swallowed and nodded. "But I want the cops to get my statement." Damian measured the severity in my gaze, how important it was for me to do everything I could to get justice for my brother.

"Fine," he agreed, and then glowered at Fisher. "But you'll have to follow us."

Fisher scowled at him. "I want to do this at the precinct."

"And I want Colton's head on a spike. Looks like we both need to deal with disappointment tonight."

Looking annoyed, Fisher continued to argue with Damian for another half block before begrudgingly accepting it was a lost cause, and then he and his partner followed us in silence for several blocks to my apartment.

I was shocked that Damian had brought me here since it seemed like the most unsafe place in the whole city right now. Fisher argued with him about it, but Damian shut down the conversation, saying we'd only be here a few minutes, and meanwhile, why didn't Fisher *make himself useful and keep his gun out, for god's sake.*

With Fisher and his partner standing in the foyer, Damian stormed into my bedroom, threw open my closet, and rooted around until he found what he was looking for: my suitcase.

"What are you doing?" I asked.

Damian threw it open on the bed and started tossing my clothes into it, in chaotic piles. "Packing. We're leaving town."

"What? I'm not leaving!" I had to stay here to make sure Colton got charged with Justin's assault.

Damian pinched the bridge of his nose. "Jenna, please don't fight me. We let this go on for too long, and now he's following you with a weapon."

"I can't leave! I have a job! And my friends!" And I couldn't let Damian leave his mom or his gym, his life.

I turned to Fisher. "Colton confessed to attempted murder, so now he'll spend the rest of his life in jail, right? You can put more men on him, to catch him or whatever." Surely he was a bigger priority now.

"If they haven't caught him by now, they never will," Damian said, throwing pajamas into the suitcase.

"His court date," I said. "You can have a bunch of extra cops there when he arrives. Take him then!"

Fisher tilted his head at me.

"Why aren't you helping here?" I demanded.

"Because he's useless," Damian snarled, inciting another glare from Fisher.

"I think you *should* leave town," Fisher said.

"What!"

"Hark! The herald angels sing. The incompetent cop agrees with me," Damian said without looking up from his violent packing.

"But his court date—"

"He'll probably skip his court date after what he confessed, and as much as I don't want to agree with anything *he* says, he's right about one thing. Colton's escalating. But you need to leave the right way," Fisher warned, throwing a glower at Damian. "Not some rushed, sloppy job that'll get you both killed. There's a procedure for protecting a witness."

"Did you hear that, Jenna?" Damian said. "They have a *procedure.*"

"I'm not leaving town!" I screamed, in case anyone cared to listen.

"Kid—"

"He tried to kill my brother! He deserves to rot in jail for the rest of his life!"

"Kid, I wish it were that simple. We'll put more people on this, but it's gonna take time, and you can't—"

"We don't have time!" I insisted. "Don't you get it? Colton knows I moved on with another guy. Actually, he thinks I was cheating on him, which is the mafia equivalent of betraying the mob boss. And now that we know he tried to kill Justin, there's no doubt he's capable of hurting other people besides me. He could come after Damian, maybe even anyone else I care about! It's like there's a bundle of dynamite inside a house full of people I love. Someone lit the fuse, and you can see the little flame rush towards the impending explosion, and cops are saying, *give us time.* We don't have time! You need to catch him. Right now!"

"I told you, they're incompetent," Damian said.

"Where were you?" Fisher snapped. "When you left her alone with him!"

"I'll call him from the last number he texted me from. Set up a meeting. You can have, like, a swarm of officers—"

"It's not happening, kid."

"Why?"

"Do I need to state the obvious?" Fisher said.

"No, we know you'd screw it up," Damian said to him, throwing shoes in the bag.

Fisher ignored him. "Because after what happened tonight, he's not going to try to talk to you. We're past that point." *Right, onto the final stage: murdering Jenna.* He paused, trying to deliver his warning with empathy. "He could shoot you before we even spot him."

"You really make it seem like Colton has the upper hand here, you know that? Like it's hopeless."

"I'll take you to a shelter," Fisher offered.

"A shelter," I said incredulously. "And then what?"

"You move."

"How does that help? He could just google until he finds my new address."

"Not if you have a different name."

I huffed. "A new identity," I said incredulously. "Like witness protection? You can't be serious."

No answer.

"I can't leave my job, my friends, my family!"

"One step at a time, kid. But you can't stay here, it's not safe."

"I'm not leaving! That means he wins! He goes to jail, Fisher. That's how this ends. Period."

"This ain't no movie, kid. Good guy doesn't always win."

Yes, they did. They had to. I could still salvage this. Everything in my life was finally moving in the right direction, and I wasn't going to let him take that from me. I'd find another solution to protecting everyone I loved.

Maybe I could talk to Colton's mom. Maybe she *would* give a damn about him, and maybe she *would* know how to get through to him. Or maybe I could get over my phobia and buy a gun, practice shooting, have it with me at all times. Was it really too big a gamble that he'd be faster pulling the trigger? And even if Fisher refused to play ball, a trap could work. He wouldn't kill me in public, would he? Risk his freedom like that?

I walked over and looked out my living room window, willing an idea to come to me that I could actually work with. But Colton's mom would never help me. She hated me more than she hated Colton, and if anything, going to her would piss him off even more, make him even more volatile. A gun would take days to get and longer to learn how to shoot well. And if the cops wouldn't help me with the trap, there'd be no way to make sure Damian or Justin didn't follow me and get caught in the crossfire, never mind other innocent people.

I stared outside, desperate for better choices to come to me. There had to be something I wasn't thinking of. I watched a streetlight turn red—*blood*—then eventually turn green—*run*—but as it cycled through its *blood, run, blood, run* pattern three more times, reality sank in, and my eyes watered in defeat.

When I finally spoke, my voice had no strength. "If I leave, there's no guarantee he won't find me."

"If you stay in the city, he'll find you for sure," Fisher said gently.

"And if *we* leave, and he finds me with Damian..." Fisher didn't need to say anything; the look on his face confirmed it: As long as Damian was with me, he was in danger. Tonight was proof of that. Being by my side when Colton closed in could have cost Damian his life. The safest place for Damian and Justin was as far away from me as possible.

The irony was not lost on me—how long Damian had pushed me away to keep me safe, and just when I convinced him I needed to be with him, risks be damned, I was about to push *him* away. To keep *him* safe.

I wanted to believe that leaving would only be temporary, that with this team of police officers working the case, surely it was just a matter of time before Colton would be picked up.

But a sea of hopelessness pulled me under. *Cops don't tell you to get a new identity for a temporary stay.* This was never going to end. Not the way I wanted it to, at least.

I felt sick to my stomach, and after a few seconds, I grabbed the framed photo of Colton and me taken at the Ledge and threw it against the wall. The sound of breaking glass prompted Damian to poke his head out of the bedroom.

He looked at the glass, the cause of the sound, then back to me. "You okay?"

I nodded my lie. After he hesitated briefly, he returned to his packing, so I went back to staring out the window, tears streaming down my cheeks.

"If I leave, how can I make sure the boys are safe? What if Colton goes after one of them when he can't find me?"

"Colton's after *you*, Jenna. *You're* the one who broke his heart. *You're* the one who's going to testify against him, so right now, we need to focus on getting *you* out. As quickly as possible, and we'll figure the rest out after."

My chin trembled. I had many unanswered questions. Where would I go? How could I alert Colton I'd left the city so he wouldn't keep searching for me when Damian and Justin remained here? What measures would Fisher take to ensure nothing happened to the boys? How would I make sure Damian wouldn't try to follow me? But one thing was certain: "I have to do whatever it takes to keep everyone safe."

I turned around and used a voice low enough to ensure only Fisher could hear. "You can get me out of town?"

Fisher offered a rueful nod. "I'm sorry it came to this, kid."

This wasn't the ending I wanted, not for me or for Damian. He didn't deserve the heartbreak that awaited him, but I'd rather live a life of unimaginable pain and never-ending darkness than let Damian get killed. And a life where he and everyone I loved was safe was, in its own way, a happy ending after all.

"How are you going to get away from him?" Fisher asked, motioning towards my bedroom with his thumb.

"I don't know," I admitted. "But first, I need to talk to Justin. He deserves to know the truth."

## 33

"Jesus." Justin ran a hand through his hair.

"I'm so sorry he hurt you," I said.

"It's not your fault," he asserted.

Of course it was. A smarter person would have left Colton the moment he laid hands on her. Maybe I deserved to lose everything; it was minimal punishment for the destruction I'd brought to everyone.

We were sitting on Damian's living room couch, talking in hushed voices, while Damian packed his bag and researched places to go in his bedroom. Fisher kept watch outside the front door—communicating the *real* plans to me via discreet sidebars. After we left my place and arrived here, I gave a detailed account of everything that happened and what Colton had confessed to. Over and over, it seemed, prodded with a million questions by Fisher and his partner. It took a lot longer than I'd thought, and Damian was already impatient, wanting to leave right away. I convinced him to let me say goodbye to Justin first, but Damian wouldn't let me wait until morning. He interrupted my brother's sleep and insisted on him coming over as soon as possible.

At three thirty in the morning, I was finally sitting across from Justin, explaining everything and preparing to say goodbye. Outside the oversized window, a full moon blanketed the city in silver, which was as beautiful as it was heartbreaking. I couldn't believe this would be my last night in Chicago, and I couldn't believe Damian and I would only have that one kiss to hold on to for the rest of our lives. I wish we could have done so much more. My body ached for him, imagining all the passionate moments we could've had together.

I pulled the gauze off my feet like socks, unable to stand how hot they felt in the bandages any longer, setting the dirty bandages in a ball on the floor.

"There has to be some other way," Justin insisted.

I shook my head. "Colton's never going to give up."

Maybe I should've just let Colton kill me. One life of a naive fool who'd endangered everyone with her recklessness in exchange for several innocent people I loved being able to get on with their lives seemed like a good trade.

"But leaving…" Justin said.

*I know.* I thought I could get this under control. Actually, I initially had thought true love would heal Colton's damaged soul. What a fool I was.

"Turns out love can't conquer everything," I said. Not because love wasn't powerful enough; as it turned out, it was the opposite. Love was *too* powerful, capable of bringing out the demons inside someone, making them act in ways they would have never imagined. Destroying, killing over it.

It was the most beautiful but also the most catastrophic force in the world.

"When do you leave?"

I blinked. "Flight's at noon." It was hard to imagine that I'd be on a plane in less than nine hours, watching my life grow smaller outside the ascending window. *My first plane ride. Maybe my last.*

"Where are you going?"

"Fisher hasn't told me yet." I shrugged. "Probably thinks I'll slip and tell someone. I'll find out when he takes me to O'Hare." I couldn't care less where I was going; the *where* didn't matter. What mattered was that I'd never see Damian again.

Justin leaned his elbows onto his knees and rubbed his hands together. I could imagine how maddening this must be for him, a control freak, unable to control this. "I don't like the idea of you going alone."

"Fisher's team knows what they're doing." I tried to sound reassuring; I didn't want him to debate what had to be done.

"What're you going to tell Mom and Dad?"

I took a deep breath. "The truth. But not until I get there. Mom would come up here and try to fix things." *And it's not fixable.*

I stared at him, unsure what else to say. "Guess this is goodbye."

In the long silence that passed, I could see how much me having to give up my life tore at Justin, yet how badly he wanted me to do whatever it took to stay safe. I wished I could erase the defeat in his eyes. "This isn't forever," Justin insisted, just as much to himself as to me. "It's just temporary."

"Right," I lied, putting on my don't-worry-I'm-okay smile.

"I'll keep the pressure on the cops to catch him. Maybe hire a PI to track him down."

"I don't want you to do that," I said. I wanted Justin to get his life back.

I stared at his sandy-blond hair and blue eyes. What do you say to someone when it might be the last time you ever get to see them? My throat tightened. "Probably don't tell you this enough," I said. "But you've always been my rock." I blinked away the tears. "Growing up in that house…" I twisted my fingers into knots. "It wasn't their fault." It wasn't. They were loving parents coping with an unimaginable tragedy the best they could. "But you were all I had."

Justin allowed the weight of my confession to sink in and then pulled me into a hug. "Love you too, sis."

I'd miss his smell, his voice, his comfort. I wished I could have been here for the next chapter in Justin's life. Maybe he and Zoey would get married—walk down the aisle, celebrate with all our friends at a reception. Perhaps they'd get pregnant, and I'd miss seeing her belly grow, attending their baby shower. Being in the waiting room with Mom and Dad, waiting for Justin to emerge with a huge grin, telling us baby Christiansen was here. I'd miss holding the baby, blowing raspberries on their belly, and listening to the giggles—watching my niece or nephew grow up.

"You do everything they tell you to stay safe. Call me when you get there."

Would I be allowed to call him? I hadn't even gotten that far to understand how this was all going to work. It was like fleeing a burning building; it wasn't until we were safely outside that we could figure out the next steps. I'd *have* to be allowed to call my family. Period. Nonnegotiable.

Justin walked towards the front door.

"You should stay here until the sun comes up," I said. "I don't want you walking the streets at this time of night."

"I'll be fine," he assured me. "My ride's parked outside already," he said, showing me the ride app on his phone. "Besides, Zoey's waiting for me." Justin looked towards the bedroom where Damian was packing. "And you have another goodbye in front of you."

He opened the front door. "Call me tomorrow," he said. "We'll figure out a safe way to visit and whatnot. And that bastard'll be in jail before you know it."

Optimism becomes rhetorical in dire times.

I watched Justin reluctantly amble out of Damian's apartment, and out of my life, possibly forever.

Grief strangled my heart.

I couldn't let myself fall apart. Not until everyone was safe. Later, in the privacy of wherever I was, I could break down and shed all the tears for everything I'd lost.

"Okay, let's go." Damian appeared with suitcases.

34

I blanched. "Can you give me like two seconds to process what just happened?"

Damian set the suitcases next to the interior brick wall. The moon cast a blueish-gray tint onto the normally rust-colored stones, which was particularly beautiful in the dim light. "You can process in the truck. Chicago Marathon starts in four hours, and we need to beat the traffic."

Right. The Chicago Marathon. At seven thirty, forty thousand runners would begin running twenty-six-point-two miles along a predefined route in the world's fourth-largest race, while over a million and a half spectators packed the sidewalks like they were in the front rows of a rock concert, cheering them on. A lot of streets would be shut down, the city would be flooded with people, so the remaining streets would likely be more crowded than the worst rush hour. "We leave now, we can be in Pensacola by dinner."

"Pensacola," I said incredulously. "What's in Florida?"

"Distance. And a condo available at the last minute."

"It's three thirty in the morning."

"And?"

"And that's like a fourteen-hour drive. We need to rest first, or we'll fall asleep at the wheel."

"We need to get as many miles between us and Chicago as fast as possible," Damian insisted.

"Colton doesn't know your full name, let alone where you live. And Fisher's posted right outside your *locked* door."

I walked towards his bedroom, but he blocked my entry with his body, looking impatient. "I'm fine to drive."

"Says every person who fell asleep at the wheel."

His green eyes tightened, and when I tried to step around him, he put his hand on my hip. Obviously, some warped part of my brain wanted to see our disagreement as foreplay because, looking at his hand touching me, I remembered sensual fantasies I'd had of Damian that started with a touch just like this. I needed to *stop* imagining his hands touching other parts of my body.

Damian looked at me looking at his hand and removed it, softening his tone. "Thought you'd be happier about Pensacola. You made it sound like you wanted to go to Florida one day."

"What? When?"

"The first week we met. You said Florida sunsets are supposed to be beautiful."

He remembered that? One random comment I'd made so long ago?

This is why I loved him, and this is the type of thing that sparked those fantasies—that and his gorgeousness. If I could have stayed here, would I have ever gotten used to his smoldering, emerald eyes, his olive skin painted with sexy tattoos wrapped around his lean muscles, and those full lips?

I was *not* going to kiss him. Zero percent chance. Shame on me for even thinking it. We were about to be separated, and kissing would only make it hurt worse. No kiss, period.

"Figured with all you have to give up," Damian explained, "I could at least give you a beautiful sunset."

I was totally going to kiss him. I pushed him until his back thumped against the wall and then crushed my mouth onto his, tasting the mint gum he'd chewed earlier. I could feel his surprised smile as he hesitated, then cupped my head and returned my desire with warm air escaping his nose onto my cheeks, the bristle of his short stubble rubbing on my chin.

I was no longer thinking of all the worry and complications, or if Damian would try to find me once I left. I was no longer thinking about how awful it would be to say goodbye to him or about how hard my parents would take the news that I was in danger. I was only aware of his mouth, his hand on my hip, pulling me closer to him.

I told myself to stop, now, before things went too far, but when our sweet tongues connected, I found my hands in his hair, greedily taking what was no longer mine to take. *To hell with logic.* If this was our last night together, I wanted him. All of him. I wanted to feel him on top of me, feel our bodies unite.

I pressed my chest harder against him, and he groaned, our tongues delicately touching, again and again. Our kiss grew deeper, as if all this frustration and worry and longing and protecting had been restraining a burning passion, and now that it was escaping, it was a train picking up steam, unable to stop.

I traced my fingers down his sides and pulled his shirt up.

He whispered, "We really should get going."

I didn't mean to whimper; I knew he was just worried that waiting longer to hit the road might put us in danger, but when I did, I felt Damian's lips curl into a smile, and I could tell I wasn't the only one who wanted this by the way he became more forceful, pulling me tighter.

When I tugged his shirt higher, we abandoned our embrace just long enough for him to help me get it over his head and toss it aside and for one second, before our mouths found each other again, I got to look at him shirtless. The contours of his celestial body, his pants hanging below his hips almost exposing what was below. If you were to sculpt a man's body out of clay, this would be a masterpiece. Each chiseled muscle was perfectly proportioned stone wrapped in smooth skin and outlined in indented shadows. The feeling of it beneath my hand as I ran it down his torso warmed my body.

"We really need to get on the road," Damian whispered, but his tone wavered, and his body disagreed.

I couldn't stop even if I wanted to, not even if the fire alarms went off. I couldn't *not* put my lips against his chest and taste his salty skin. I needed to feel every inch of him, and I sensed he needed it too.

It looked like it was taking every ounce of his strength not to throw me down and have his way with me right here. I loved that I could have that effect on him. He might be big and strong, but right now, I had the power to make him come undone.

When I hooked a finger in his waistband and tugged it down an inch, he growled, pulled me back up and kissed me with urgency, trailing his caress down my jaw, pulling my T-shirt down so he could graze my collarbone.

His breaths became bursts.

I couldn't take it anymore. I had to feel him, all of him.

I pressed my hips into him, feeling his desire, relishing the groan it incited from him. Unable to fight it anymore, Damian surrendered. He picked me up by my thighs, wrapped my legs around his waist, and —not breaking our kiss—walked me to his bedroom.

He set me down on his bed and climbed on top of me.

I loved the weight of him on me, the warmth of his chest. I loved how the moonlight illuminated him in silver, but the blinds were angled so that no one but the two of us would see what was about to happen.

Damian laced his fingers under my shirt, tugging it up, breaking our kiss as it went over my head. We rolled over so I straddled him as I took my bra off, relishing the way his hungry eyes glided over my body.

He whispered, "You're so beautiful."

His hands traced the curves of my stomach as we stared at each other, breathless, eager for what was about to happen. I guided his hands higher, craving them on my chest. He moaned, locked his hand behind my head, and pulled my face to his, our bodies pressing harder into each other.

Damian started working on my jeans zipper as I tugged at his waistband. In a few quick steps, the rest of our clothes came off.

"Lay down," he growled.

The way he commanded it turned me on. The way he somehow eliminated any trace of my self-consciousness turned me on. The look of unparalleled desire on his face turned me on.

I gladly obeyed, watching his eyes look over my body like it was his playground. I wanted to be his playground.

Warmth intensified in my lower belly.

"I want to know every inch of you," he whispered, climbing on top of me. He cupped my chest, and I sucked in a breath. He kissed my neck, my shoulder. "Every curve." Lips on my collarbone. "Every pleasure point." Teeth grazing my chest. This time I could feel the wetness of his tongue.

Good god, my skin was beyond hypersensitive. It was like every cell was at attention, waiting for its turn to be touched. Lying on my back, watching the moonlight glisten off his shoulders, I saw Damian kiss my chest. Slowly, taking his time to explore with his hand, then with his mouth, before moving down my stomach one inch at a time. Down my leg, then back up along my inner thigh. And then. I sucked in a ragged breath and clutched the bedspread in my fists. *Holy hell.*

With every moan that escaped me, Damian gave one of his own, and I loved that there was no shyness, no reservations, as if our bodies and fantasies had been designed for each other. I couldn't wait anymore for the best part—I needed all of him now—so I whispered his name.

I heard the sound of his bedside table's drawer open followed by a wrapper, and then, in a trail of upward kisses, he climbed on top of me, pausing to look me in the eyes. "I love you," he whispered as he united our bodies.

I gasped. I adored the hint of pride in his eyes, pleased with himself for the gratification he was giving me. Damian placed my hands above my head, locking our fingers. The weight of his arms sank them into the bed, and he looked at me, grazing my jaw with his teeth. He knew, and I knew, he had complete control over me right now.

I loved submitting to his every desire.

I'd wondered—more times than I'd admit to anyone—what he was like in bed, but this...*this* exceeded my wildest expectations. All his sculpted muscles gave him complete control over his body. Damian tailored every move, every touch, to maximize my pleasure. He read the movements of my body as if the only thing that mattered was my ravenous satisfaction and took his time, making the ecstasy last.

It struck me how much power lay within his muscles, what his hands were capable of doing to an opponent in the cage—destroying flesh and bone—yet how gentle they could be now, gliding over my chest.

It was intoxicating, the way he stared at me like he wanted to devour me. The heat of my chest pressing into his when we rolled over, both of us pulling each other tighter, firmer, unable to get enough, and climbing to incredible heights of ecstasy. The smell of him, the weight of his hips on my thighs, the scruff of his cheeks against my skin, his hungry growl, his breathless smiles. I'd never experienced anything like this. I could spend years making love to him, and it wouldn't be enough.

How could I live without this?

"I can't live my life without you," he said, nibbling on my lip.

I swallowed, trying to focus on his words, but his body, his hands, were doing things to me that made it difficult to concentrate on anything other than the sensations running through me.

"Damian," I whispered.

Our bodies climbed higher and higher, dancing all over the bed until we collapsed, and when we finished, we made love again and again until we were depleted.

This was masochistic torture—letting myself experience what we'd just had, knowing I could never have it again.

Damian rolled onto his back and pulled my head onto his chest, his fingertips tracing my arm. His chest was damp, amplifying the smell of his musk cologne.

"I want to spend every minute of my life with you," he said.

I tried to fight the venom in my stomach. I was the worst human being in the world, letting him think that was still a possibility, and even worse for wanting it so severely I was tempted to let him risk his life so I could have it.

All the could-have-beens overwhelmed me with grief. Making love like this, every day with him. Mornings with Damian in his boxers, cooking us eggs while I came up behind him and kissed his back, wrapping my hand around his waist. A look across the room he'd give me that promised ecstasy after a party. Him watching me as I walked down the aisle towards him, him kissing my swollen belly, holding our baby. Us with gray hair, cooing over our grandchildren.

What if I wasn't strong enough to leave him?

No. I couldn't let doubt enter my mind.

As gut-wrenching as leaving would be, I visualized him in a coffin, with a bullet hole to his head. *That* was the real hell.

Damian propped himself up on his elbow and looked down at me, tilting my chin up until my eyes met his. With our nude bodies draped across each other, it was hard to imagine that in a few hours, I'd be alone, in a foreign place, with no idea, or care, what my future held.

"About earlier," he started. "I'm sorry if I seemed too overprotective. I just…" He swept a hair away from my forehead. "Before I met you, I didn't care about anything except fighting. Only time I felt alive was in that cage, and I was chasing that feeling. It's like all these years I've been walking around dead inside, but when I'm with you, I feel more alive than I ever did in that cage." He let a couple seconds pass. "Which is why I turned down an MMA fight offered to me."

He…*what?*

"I don't want you giving up on your dream because of me."

"I'm not," he promised. "I don't *want* to fight anymore." He traced my jaw with the backs of his fingers. "All I want is *you.*"

I bit back the rock in my throat and looked down before he could see the tears in my eyes.

Goddamned Colton. I hated him. Look at the pain Damian was

about to go through when I left him, all because Colton was an over-grown toddler having a lethal temper tantrum.

In the silence, I could hear a cell phone buzzing. If I listened to Damian profess his love any longer, I'd burst into tears. He'd know something was up and would probably get it out of me, and then this entire plan to keep everyone safe would go up in flames. So I used the call as an excuse to jump out of bed and find my phone in the living room.

How was it six thirty in the morning already? Had we really made love for three hours? And why was Zoey calling me at this hour on a Sunday?

"Zoey?" I answered.

Her tone was full of worry. "Is Justin with you?"

I blinked. "No?"

She let out a worried breath.

Damian stepped out of his bedroom and looked from my nude figure to the couch, where he grabbed a blanket and wrapped it around me. "We need to get going," he said, kissing my temple. "I'm gonna get in the shower. Join me when you're done?" I nodded as Damian disappeared into the bathroom.

"Was he supposed to come to your place?" I asked.

"I'm at *his* place. He texted me that he was on his way. That was three hours ago, and he hasn't shown up yet."

Ice frosted my veins. Justin's place was a mile and a half southeast of Damian's. Even if his ride fell through, it was only a thirty-minute walk—not three hours. I glanced out the window, noting how many people were already out. "Maybe he got stuck in traffic."

Even I could hear how ridiculous the explanation was, but fear makes you grasp at straws.

"Not for three hours." She hesitated. "You think he's alright?"

I pulled my phone away from my ear and saw that I'd missed twenty-seven calls and ten texts from Justin, urging me to call him immediately. I guess I didn't hear them buzzing over the sounds of lovemaking, and while it was odd Justin had called so many times, at least that meant he was okay. "Looks like he's been trying to call me," I reassured her.

She hesitated, and now, her tone was hurt and a little pissed. "He's been calling you but dodging me?"

It looked that way, though I couldn't imagine why. Had he and Zoey had a fight?

"I'll call him and figure out what's going on."

In the silence that passed, I could feel her anger. "Yeah," she said tightly. "Thanks." The call ended.

Clutching the blanket against my chest, I called his number, which only rang twice before he picked up.

"Justin?" I demanded. "Where the hell are you? Zoey's worried sick!"

"You tip anyone off who you're talking to, Justin dies."

## 35

My gut plummeted into a freefall, and my hand jolted, causing the blanket to fall to the floor.

"Why do you have Justin's phone?"

"This is what you're gonna do. Go to the parking structure on South Franklin, near Adams Street. *Alone.* If I see anyone with you? He's dead. If I see anyone that even looks like they might be with you? He's dead. If you tip off the cops, or anyone else, he's dead. I'll be watching."

I felt lightheaded. This couldn't be happening. He had to be bluffing. Right? Somehow, he must've found out Justin was MIA and decided to exploit it. But how would he have gotten his phone? He'd had to have come into contact with my brother.

"Is he okay?" He had to be okay. He had to. Maybe Colton just stole his cell and left Justin perfectly unscathed, and Justin hadn't called us from another phone because…well…I didn't know.

"You have ten minutes. Clock starts now."

A text chimed on my phone with a countdown timer. Some incredulous part of my brain wondered why there'd be a need for one human to share a countdown timer with another, let alone enough demand to create an app for it. But there it was. Nine minutes fifty-nine seconds, fifty-eight, fifty-seven...

Franklin and Adams were five city blocks from here. A ten-minute walk—seven if I ran—but my battered feet would slow me down.

"I'm not coming unless I know he's okay."

After a moment, my cell chimed, asking me to accept converting the call to video. It took a couple seconds before the image came. It was dark, but there, lying on the ground, was Justin. His eyes were open and duct tape covered his mouth.

Ice surged through my limbs.

A gun appeared next to Justin's temple. "Ten minutes. If you're not here, alone, by then, I kill him."

"If I come, you'll let him go?"

Hesitation. "Yeah," Colton said. "You come. I'll let him go."

The line went dead.

I felt like I was going to throw up, and my hands were shaking.

Despite Colton's threat to not tip off the cops, should I tell Fisher? Could he figure out how to sneak up on Colton? But what did Colton mean he was watching? Did he have people watching us right now? Was that how he got Justin? If I didn't do exactly what he said, would he really shoot my brother?

*Yes,* my instincts warned. *Look at how dangerous and erratic he's already proved to be.*

I pressed my fingers to my temples.

Meeting Colton alone was a crazy option—one that could end with Justin and I both dead, but what other choice did I have? If there was a chance to trade my life for Justin's, I had to take it. And I had to find a way to leave without Fisher or Damian knowing. I couldn't risk Justin's life by telling them and Fisher needed to stay here and keep Damian safe.

I searched Damian's window. High-rises had two exits in the event of a fire, and this building was no exception. The latch was easy to find.

Then, I entered the bathroom and stared at the foggy glass shower door.

I told myself it was because I needed to delay Damian; if he got out and found me gone, he'd alert Fisher, and police might stop me before I could save my brother. But the truth was, I needed to say goodbye because I sensed this would be the last time I ever saw him.

The poor guy, after a lifetime of heartbreak, had finally let himself feel love, and now, it would destroy him. When he stepped out of that shower calling my name, his confusion would turn to panic as he searched his apartment because I, along with his happily-ever-after, would have vanished without a trace.

As I watched his unsuspecting face rinse under the water, there were a million things I wished I could say to him. *I love you, Damian. More than I've ever loved anyone. Please don't let this destroy your life. Live your life to the fullest. Love, and let people in. Allow yourself to be as happy as you were when you were with me.* But I could say none of those things right now. They'd make him suspicious, and then he'd never let me out of his sight. I had no choice but to say something simple.

"Give me a few minutes and I'll be in," I said as happily as possible.

He wiped the condensation from the shower glass.

I smiled and pretended seeing him like this was what sparked my next words. "I love you."

Damian Stone gave me a genuine, broad smile that showed his teeth. "I love you too." My intestines folded in on themselves. "Don't take too long. I want to get on the road before traffic gets too backed up from the race."

That was probably already too late…

And, with over a million and a half people packed downtown, the police would be spread unusually thin trying to keep everyone safe. What a perfect day for Colton to do this.

With the clock ticking, I forced myself to put my heartbreak over Damian aside. I ran into the bedroom, got dressed, threw on my sneakers—my feet stung as I laced them up—and rooted around a kitchen drawer until I found a small knife that I could hide in my waistband. Then, as quietly as possible, I lifted the latch of the living room window and slid it to the left.

I looked at the front door for any indication Fisher had heard before I climbed onto the fire escape, shut the window, and sailed down each flight. The iron zig-zag staircase blended into the darkness, so it looked like one wrong footing would catapult me into the air. Each step was met with a menacing squeak and wobble—threatening an injury that would jeopardize everything.

The temperature had dropped, and the wind whipped my hair into my face, goose bumps erupting on my skin. Meanwhile, I ignored the million questions rushing into my head. I ignored my gut feeling that I was about to die, because right now, Justin's future, Colton's future, and my future were all tied together in a nightmarish knot.

When I reached the dark sidewalk—the sun hadn't risen yet—I sprinted through the tunnel of skyscrapers and wove through a river of people gathering to watch the marathon. Like a parade, people gathered everywhere along the route, with higher volumes at the various checkpoints, and the further I got from Damian's, the thicker the crowds grew. I had to bob and weave and sometimes push my way through them.

After a few minutes of running so hard that pain stabbed my side, I approached the green self-park sign.

Why did Colton choose *this* place? Didn't he notice that both Franklin and Adams were roped off with no vehicle traffic? That they were not only part of the marathon route wrapping around the Willis Tower, but a super-crowded checkpoint no less? The sidewalks were packed, and a large green sign read, *Chicago Marathon Mile 3!* There would be no way to drive out of this parking structure.

My cell phone went off, and I answered immediately.

"Come to the Skydeck," Colton demanded.

I turned around. Across the street was the Willis Tower, with a big sign in white letters that read, *Skydeck entrance ahead.*

I looked up the black hundred-and-ten-story monstrosity. The base occupied almost a whole city block, ascending so high that the top was small and nearly indiscernible from the sky. The building was as immense as my struggle to stop Colton's destruction. He'd always been one step ahead, holding all the power over my life, and I could imagine him standing up there, looking down at me. An eagle waiting for his prey to come to his nest.

How could he spot me from way up there, and how could he discern me from all these people? Binoculars?

"It's closed," I pointed out. You couldn't exactly mosey on up there.

"Go west on Franklin to the end of the block. Make a right. There's a metal construction fence with a lock that's cut. Go through it and find the back door on the southeast corner. It's unlocked. Take the stairs up two flights, then the elevator to the Skydeck."

You don't come up with an elaborate scheme like this in a few hours. You think about it. You plan. You check doors and maybe even do a practice run. Colton might have waited until today to pull the trigger, but this idea hasn't just popped into his head.

And how did he get Justin up there? There was no way he could've carried Justin down the street without being noticed.

"I'm not coming unless I know Justin's okay."

"Three minutes left." He hung up.

Oh my god. Was Justin *not* okay?

How was I supposed to sneak into the Skydeck—a well-protected building that surely had security guards, alarms, and whatnot—without getting caught? Why was he making this almost impossible? Did he *want* me to fail? Was—please, god, maybe—was Colton just doing all this to get me arrested? Breaking into the Willis Tower on marathon day had to be some sort of act of terrorism, right?

I wasn't sure, but so help me, Colton was going to suffer for taking Justin. As soon as Justin was safe, whatever Colton had planned, I'd disrupt. Whatever he told me to do, I'd do the opposite.

I'd tried talking. I'd tried reasoning. And he'd continued to be a threat to the people I loved. I wasn't sure if what I was about to do was technically self-defense, but I didn't care if I rotted in prison for the rest of my life if it meant eliminating the fatal threat to my loved ones.

I felt the bulge beneath my waistband, ensuring the knife was still there, and then I began to follow Colton's directions.

Around the corner, there were two gates, not one, which made my heart pound even harder. I glanced at the crowds of people, praying they wouldn't stop me, and as nonchalantly as I could manage, I tugged at the lock on the first gate. Nothing. I twisted it—nothing. I glanced over my shoulder, paranoid someone might be watching me as I walked to the second gate and found another lock. This one, though, when I yanked it, swiveled. I snatched it off the latch, opened the gate, and slithered behind it.

I replaced the lock and dashed to the base of the Willis Tower.

I checked my phone. Two minutes, two seconds. *Shit!* I remembered the elevator alone took a little over a minute to ascend!

I ran along the side until I found the right door, the one Colton somehow unlocked.

Then I raced inside and found myself in a service entrance—a double metal door in front of me, and to my right, concrete stairs illuminated with a single bulb. It smelled of commercial-grade Lysol, a yellow triangle warning of a wet floor even though it wasn't. Not anymore, anyway. I sprinted up two flights and emerged into the common waiting area for the Skydeck. The vast space with red velvet ropes and stuffy air had a counter at the far end with prices for *The Skydeck! Citypass!* I followed the arrows to two elevators that had the word *Skydeck* above them.

I shoved the button and glanced at the countdown app.

Seventy seconds.

The elevator on the right opened with a ding. I rushed in and pressed floor 103.

The elevator was not packed with people. It did not play its usual video above the doors that gave you a one-minute history lesson on the Willis Tower, and it did not feel exciting. It was dark, sinister, mounting pressure inside my ears until they finally popped, and as it soared the hundred and three stories, I assessed what I was about to walk in to.

I had a knife; Colton had a gun and probably also the knife he'd had in the alley, too. Justin's mouth would be taped. I had no idea what was about to happen, but Fisher's words echoed through my head. *This ain't no movie, kid. Good guy doesn't always win.*

And then, time seemed to stand still as the elevator doors opened.

36

It took me a second to gain the courage to walk into the darkened space—the only light came through the glass walls from surrounding buildings. The emptiness in the ordinarily crowded place was eerie, no crowds of people peering out the floor-to-ceiling windows, no rumbling of voices. Just silence.

I saw nothing at first until I heard a moan.

There, in the far-right corner, was the Ledge—the glass boxes that protruded four and a half feet outside the building, attracting tourists who'd step inside and have nothing separating them from the one-hundred-and-three-story drop but the glass beneath their feet. A shape lay in the box that was sectioned off with yellow caution tape. A groaning shape.

"Justin!" I screamed.

I ran over and noticed several things at once. His arms were restrained behind his back, and duct tape bound his ankles and mouth. A pool of blood the size of a dinner plate collected beneath his waist, and something else was off about him—something I couldn't quite put my finger on. Something in the way his body was laying, maybe.

He was tucked into the far corner, and the glass beneath him wasn't clear; it contained a million white lines all over it.

*Oh god.*

That's why it was sectioned off. It was already broken, and now, every second that Justin's two-hundred-pound body weighed on its fragile foundation, it splintered more.

"Give me your phone," Colton demanded.

He emerged from behind me and pointed the gun at us.

"What did you do to him?" I'd followed his orders, and he still hurt him!

"Phone." Colton motioned with his fingers.

"We need to get him out of the box. It's going to break!" I looked around, unsure which body part to reach that gave me the best chance of pulling Justin out without making the glass crack faster from the shift in weight.

"Phone," Colton repeated.

"He needs an ambulance!"

Colton pointed the gun at me. "Phone!"

"Screw you!"

He pointed the gun at Justin. "Last chance. Phone."

I ransacked my pocket and slid my phone over to him, and the farther it slipped away, the more alone I felt. I couldn't dial nine-one-one now, which meant I was the only person who could save Justin.

"Passcode," Colton demanded.

"You got what you wanted! Let Justin go!" I cried.

"Passcode." Again, he pointed the gun at Justin.

"Twelve, twenty-twenty." The month I graduated from college and started my life.

He punched it in and held the phone up to his ear.

What exactly was his plan? He got what he needed out of my brother: luring me here. He was mad at *me*. I was the one who betrayed him. *I* was the one who left him. *I* was the one who broke his heart. So why keep Justin here? "The cops already know it was you that hurt Justin, so if that's why you took him—"

"That's not why," he interrupted. "Damian," he chirped into the phone, like a long-lost friend who hadn't seen him in ages.

My blood thinned.

"Listen very carefully. Having a little conversation here with your girlfriend, and I'd like you to join us."

Wait, what? After everything I just went through to make sure Damian *didn't* come, Colton was going to bring him here? Why not let Damian come with me in the first place?

*Because* some part of my brain said. *If you came with Damian, the two of you would've had ten minutes to come up with a plan to take Colton down. Two against one, with time to prep; the odds would have been too much in our favor. Taken separately, with no chance to communicate, well...that gave Colton the upper hand in whatever he was planning.*

And he got to torture me a little more, too, so there was that.

"Don't listen to him!" I screamed. "Call an ambulance! Justin's hurt!"

Colton's arm hurled down, and he smacked the side of my head with the gun.

Searing pain. Warm liquid on my head. God, it hurt so bad.

So help me, he was going to pay for that.

"You bring the cops or anyone else, she dies. I see anyone even remotely..."

As Colton gave instructions to Damian, the sound of splintering glass brought my attention back to Justin. I carefully leaned into the box, trying to reach him without touching the glass. I stretched, growling in frustration.

Justin shifted his head and squirmed his shoulder.

Why wasn't he moving his lower body?

The glass made a louder cracking noise. I didn't mean to retract— it was instinct, pulling myself out of the box before it broke. My heart raced, but I reached in farther, grasped the tape, and ripped it off his mouth.

"Don't move," Justin warned. "Glass is gonna go, and we'll both fall."

"Justin," I cried. I grabbed his shoulder and yanked.

Glass splintered wider and spread its fissure up the wall.

"Stop!" He looked at the glass box's roof.

"We need to get you out!"

"I can't move my legs, Jenna. I think he cut my spinal cord."

*Holy shit.* My soul sank as the seriousness of the situation rose to another level. If Colton had already done permanent damage to Justin, he probably wasn't ever planning to let Justin go.

And now, if I moved my brother, any chance of regaining his mobility would be destroyed. But he couldn't stay in a box that was literally collapsing beneath him.

"Check your screen," Colton said into the phone. He was enjoying this power trip, undoubtedly sending the same countdown clock to Damian. And then he gave Damian directions to get here.

"How did he get to you?" I asked.

"Must've been following me," Justin whispered. *Colton knew that sooner or later, I'd see my brother again.* "Jumped me when I left Damian's place. Stuck a gun in my back, took my cell, told me to walk."

"You didn't run?"

"He said he'd kill you if I ran. He saw me come out of Damian's, so he knew where you were." Guilt swallowed my insides. "Plus, the streets weren't empty of people." And no one paid enough attention to help? "I didn't want someone else to get hit with a stray bullet, so I complied. Planned to go after him as soon as we got into the building, but he hit me in the head enough to stun me, and then as soon as we got up here, he stabbed me in my back before I had the chance. Taped me up. Threw me into the box."

"Skydeck," Colton said into the phone. "Ten minutes." And then he hung up. No pretenses of going to the parking garage. Straight here, then.

I could imagine Damian right now, frantically taking off like a bullet. Racing to rescue the woman he loved.

But first, I had to rescue someone else I loved... I pulled Justin's arm again, willing his heavy body to cooperate.

"Don't move," Colton said, aiming the gun at my head.

I looked into Justin's eyes. "I don't care if he shoots me, just get out."

Colton pointed the gun at the center of the glass floor this time. I wasn't an expert, but I had to imagine one bullet blasting through an already-compromised glass structure would obliterate it, sending Justin to his death.

"You move, I shoot."

"Why are you doing this?" I cried, enraged. He held the gun with a calmness that struck me as psychotic. "You told me you'd let him go if I came."

"Did I?" He scratched his head, pretending to think. "Guess I'm not the only one who breaks promises."

I clenched my teeth. With God as my witness, I was going to kill Colton. "At least let me get Justin out of the box," I pleaded.

"Let's just wait for Damian to arrive, shall we?"

"The box could break before he gets here!"

"Guess he better hurry, then."

But it wasn't just Justin's life in danger. I once read that a penny falling from this height would kill someone instantly. Imagine a ginormous glass box shattering and falling like a bomb on the unsuspecting people below.

"The box weighs over seven thousand pounds." I recalled the fact Colton had cited on our first date when he'd taken me up here. What a sick, twisted person to choose this, of all locations, to terrorize me.

"And?"

"And there's a lot of pedestrians gathering down there for the race. Seven thousand pounds of glass shards will kill a lot of innocent people. You don't want to do this, Colton."

He gave me a defiant look. "You're not going to talk your way out of this."

God, how evil could he be? Risking everyone—even children!—while we waited for all his pawns to get into place.

"Kill *me*," I said. "Not them." Did that not serve his purpose? Making sure Damian and I couldn't live happily ever after?

Colton ignored my desperate pleas to save them; I could see the only thing he cared about was his diabolical plan.

I gritted my teeth. "So Damian shows, and then what?"

No answer.

"What are you going to do with him?"

Colton stared at me with a sinister look.

*Oh god.*

"Just because he loves me?"

He stared at my horror-struck face with arrogant satisfaction. "Cheating with my girlfriend is only part of it."

"I never cheated on you!"

With disturbing ambivalence, Colton reached into his back pocket and unfolded what looked like a photograph, savoring the silence that followed—the anxiety I endured waiting for his explanation.

"After my dad left, my mom hoped he'd come running back. They fought like cats and dogs. But damned if she didn't love him."

I wasn't going to stand here and do nothing. I began taking small steps to the right, hoping to lure his eyes—and gun—off Justin, and when he did, I was going to strike. I'd take him by surprise and lunge for his throat. If I could get to his jugular before he fired, I'd wrestle the gun away. Then I'd get Justin safely out of the box, get my phone back, and call for help. I had no idea what my odds of success were, but I was about to give it my freaking all.

"So, her first birthday after he split, she finds a card from my dad in the mail. Shoulda seen the look on her face," Colton said. "Could tell she thought it was like, some sort of olive branch or whatever. That after months of ignorin' her, he cared enough to remember her birthday. That it'd lead to 'em getting back together or something."

I took three steps.

"So she tears it open with the biggest smile, but then starts to cry. Throws the card down and runs out of the house. Goes on a three-day binge. Drinking, drugs. Gets fired from her job."

I discreetly clutched the knife by its handle beneath the fabric of my jeans. I'd have to do my best to aim because I'd have one shot—at the most—before he'd fight back.

Colton opened the paper. "He wasn't wishin' her happy birthday, he was showing off his new life. New family. Proving he was better off without her." He studied the photo. "Funny how at the time I wished him dead, but then he got dead, and that pissed me off even more, 'cause the sonofabitch that killed him took away any chance of my dad ever coming back around for my mom. And *that's* why she drank every day, *that's* why she became so messed up." Colton stared at the paper for several seconds. "I vowed I'd find the guy that did it one day." He looked up. "Turns out he shuffled into my life a couple months ago. He's older now, and I hadn't looked at the photo for years, which is why I didn't place him till last night."

Colton threw the picture at me and waited for me to look at it.

I studied the faded image, noticing that brown, star-shaped birthmark on Colton's dad's cheek that I'd seen in the photo at his mom's house. He stood next to a woman and a boy, and when I saw the kid, I gasped.

Because I recognized those piercing green eyes.

"I knew he looked familiar," Colton accused.

*oly shit.* Colton's asshole father, who'd left them for another woman and her kid, was Damian's stepdad—the guy who beat Damian. The guy Damian killed.

I stared at the photograph, my head spinning. What were the odds that these two guys' lives were intertwined like this, with me in the middle of it all? And how did we not know it until now?

Damian probably never knew of his stepdad's former family, let alone what they looked like. Colton's dad wouldn't show off his *old* family, just the new one to torment his ex, and Damian wouldn't have recognized Colton because Colton looked like his mom, not his father.

But now that Colton knew, he was obviously going to kill Damian when he got here—which only gave me a few minutes to take Colton down, at best. Damian was in incredible shape and could run a lot faster than me, and he'd already been running for a minute or two.

I stared at the gun and felt the knife in my waistband. What had Damian said? *He'll be emotional, so he might make mistakes.*

Emotional...

"And here you thought *I'm* the bad guy," Colton snarled.

"You *are* a bad guy," I declared.

Internally, I celebrated the anger that washed across his face. "That's what you want everyone to think. But no one knows what you did to me. Always there, rubbing my face in my screw-ups like a dog who shit on the carpet. Everything had to be on your terms and your rules or you'd leave me. You call that love?"

"You call *this* love?"

Colton's face darkened. "You made me think I could be happy! And then you took it all away from me!"

I inched closer to him. Even if he shot me in the process, if I could just get one stab to his neck, I could wound him enough to give everyone else a fighting chance. "And you're going to kill me because of it?"

He stared at me, his eyes shadowed in vengeance. "Not before I show you how it feels to have *your* whole world taken from you."

What did *that* mean?

He aimed the gun at the bottom of the glass box that precariously held my brother.

"Know how long it takes to fall a hundred stories?" he taunted. "Twelve seconds." He paused. "Doesn't sound like that long. But think about that. One-one-thousand, two-one-thousand, three-one-thousand. Bet it's an eternity when you know you're about to die. Especially after watching your brother go first."

*That* was his plan? To kill Justin in front of me—in the most awful, sadistic way—and then throw me to my death? Not only preying on my fear of heights but also picking one of the tallest buildings in the world so we'd suffer the most prolonged torture possible?

Colton offered a victorious glare as he focused on his target and put his finger on the trigger. *This is it.* I charged him and slammed my shoulder into his chest just as the gun went off, causing it to fire upward.

A bullet blasted a small hole in the box's glass ceiling, and the air whistled in as the splintering glass spread.

Colton and I landed on the ground, and the gun slid several feet away. I managed to straddle him.

There he was, my formidable opponent, eyeing me with anger.

This wasn't going according to his perfect little plan. He wasn't in complete control anymore, and that gave me great satisfaction.

His lips were curled back over his shiny teeth, with little droplets of spit in the corners of his mouth. I swung the knife at his throat, but he grabbed my wrists. I thrashed, putting all my weight and adrenaline into my goal.

He stretched my arms high above his head, so my face was almost touching his. I slammed my elbow into his nose. He howled as it oozed blood, and then he sprang me off and got on top, straddling me. His warm blood dripped onto my cheek as he growled and wrapped both hands around my throat. I couldn't breathe, but he obviously didn't realize I still had the knife in my hand.

I speared it into his neck.

Colton roared, but his cut wasn't spurting or gushing the way a hit to the jugular would be. He pulled the knife out and slapped me. Hard. Then plunged the knife into my side.

I screamed, blinded by the burning pain, needing to get him off me, to get to Justin before it was too late. I could hear the glass cracking even more. I pulled the knife out and harnessed the adrenaline rush that came with it, bucking Colton off of me and diving for the gun.

Colton jumped on my back, his outstretched hands competing with mine in a tangle of fingers. I cracked my head back, hearing another howl as my skull connected with his nose, which flowed its wet warmth onto the back of my head.

I could see Justin struggling in the box, glass cracking along the roof and down the sides as he strained to worm his way out using all the strength his upper body had left.

Colton head-butted me back. It felt like getting hit with a tire iron, but I focused on the weapon in front of me. At this moment, I knew whoever won the gun was going to live, and the other was going to die. I touched the gun with my middle finger.

Colton wrapped his arm around my chest and rolled me over. I bit down on his arm, tasting metal as he screamed. I tried to throw my elbow back into him but missed. He straddled me, and as he began to choke me, I brought my arms up the way that Damian had shown me —a sudden thrust and out.

Colton's arms released, and with him off balance, I managed to roll to the side and out from under him.

I reached for the gun.

But his hand got there first.

He grabbed it. Hit me in the head with it. Hard. It stunned me long enough for him to stand and kick me in the ribs repeatedly. I curled into the fetal position, instinctively drawing my arms up over my head to protect it.

Through my grunts and the sharp pain of Colton's blows, I could hear Justin yelling, thrashing his half-paralyzed, tightly bound body to try and get out of the breaking box.

After a few more kicks, Colton pointed the gun at Justin.

Fighting wooziness, I charged his knees. The gun went off, and I heard a pop of glass. It missed my brother, but the bottom of the box now had a two-foot hole in it. A terrifying wind gusted through the unnatural opening, and tentacles of splinters extended from its epicenter.

"Justin!" I screamed, racing to my brother.

I was pulled back by a fistful of my hair, my back locked against Colton's chest just as the elevator dinged. With his left elbow around my throat, his right hand securing the gun against my temple, Colton spun us around as the elevator doors opened.

Damian's gaze instantly met mine. As he looked at the arm around my throat, blood dripping down my head, and the gun pressed to my skull, fury ignited in his eyes, engulfing the rest of his features in its inferno. He tucked his head down and shifted his glare to Colton.

"Step forward," Colton demanded.

Damian showed his palms in surrender as he stepped off the elevator, seeing Justin in the Ledge for the first time.

"Run!" I said. "He's going to kill—"

Colton's hand smothered my words, pressing so hard I thought my teeth might break.

Damian's eyes narrowed.

It was hard not to focus on the gun—how imminent death felt with it pressed against my temple. One little squeeze and my brain would explode.

"On your knees," Colton demanded of Damian.

The glass fractured louder.

Damian complied, falling to his knees, his hands up in surrender. "I'm the one who convinced her to break up with you."

Colton tensed.

"Told her you treated her like shit, and she deserved someone who'd make something of himself, not some pathetic contractor who'd never amount to anything," Damian lied.

Colton's chest swelled.

Justin wiggled closer to the edge, the glass cracking.

"You're a pathetic piece of shit who isn't even man enough to fight other men. You go after women who aren't strong enough to fight you off. You're a fucking coward."

Damian locked knowing eyes with me as Colton's hold loosened slightly.

I stomped on his foot, slammed my elbow back into his abdomen, and spun around, shoving my knee up to his manhood.

Damian charged forward with a growl and tackled Colton to the ground, sending the gun flying.

I raced to the box.

Just before the sun rises, the darkened sky turns amber. The orange pushes its way up into the dark, casting the city in a silhouette, the moon lingering. It was eerie how something this beautiful could be just outside when blood and death were in here.

Justin's head hung over the edge.

"Hang on!" I said.

"Stay back," Justin said.

Like hell.

I pulled Justin's arm. But he was too heavy from the dead weight of his legs. I looked around for something to help, spotting the knife ten feet away. I raced to retrieve it and cut the tape binding his hands, so they were now free.

The floor made a popping sound, as if the wall was about to detach from its base.

I screamed and pulled at Justin's hands.

I could hear grunts and fists connecting with flesh as the chaos of Damian and Colton waged on. In my periphery, I saw Damian land a series of punches, while Colton barely got any in.

On the sidewalk a hundred stories below, people scurried, evidently aware that something terrible was happening up here. Maybe a few fragments of glass from that hole had warned them to run.

And then, to my horror, I heard another gunshot.

I spun around to see Damian fall to the ground, clutching his now-bleeding stomach.

"No!" I screamed.

Damian didn't get up.

"Jenna, watch out!" Justin yelled.

Colton flew towards us with the gun pointed at Justin. I charged and slammed into him just as the gun fired, missing its target. I grabbed the gun's handle and began twisting for everyone's lives. Damian was growling my name, trying to get up, but failing. Justin was trying to roll out of the box.

As I pulled the gun, Colton head-butted me. I almost lost my grip, but we fought for the barrel's aim, which twisted back to the box.

I fought with everything I had and slowly twisted the gun towards Colton's chest.

I moved my finger over his, on the trigger, and pulled back, just as Colton slammed his boot into my stomach.

I heard the gunshot as I flew backward from his kick.

When I crashed into the back of the box, I heard an explosion of glass as the floor beneath us ruptured. Chicago's iconic attraction disintegrated around us. Justin and I barely grabbed on to the metal lip of the car-sized hole in the building, struggling to hold on as glass shards rained down onto us. The chilly wind swayed our bodies with its light roar, and the only thing I could smell was the metallic iron of blood. Beneath the endless wall of glass and steel extending below our feet were the roofs of other skyscrapers. A beetle-sized police car with its blue and reds on raced to a stop at the closest open road. Two black dots emerged.

But they were too far away.

A hundred stories of air beneath my feet warned me nothing could stop the fall.

"Jenna!" Damian shouted in a weak voice.

Dangling with my arms above my head, I couldn't see over the floor, but I could imagine Damian struggling to get up and close the thirty-foot distance to the opening.

"Justin!" I screamed. "Hold on!"

At this height, the gusting wind felt like a mini-tornado.

"Jenna," Justin growled.

"Pull yourself up!" I cried.

But he was in bad shape. Clearly weak from blood loss, and his bound legs must have been terribly heavy from paralysis. Plus, his fingers were wet with blood—glass fragments piercing our fingertips.

He was slipping.

"Hold on," I cried. "Help is coming." It had to be. The cops had to have broken into the building by now. Someone would burst through that elevator any second, strong enough to lift my brother.

The long drop pulled at us, and Justin's fingers fought for leverage on the slippery ledge.

"Listen to me," Justin growled. "I have life insurance."

"Don't talk like that!"

"It's in a blue folder—"

"Focus on holding on!"

"Shut up and listen!" he demanded. "It's in a blue folder in my bedroom closet. Make sure Mom gets the money to pay off the house and live off of, and Dad gets a share too. Promise me."

"We're both hanging here, Justin!" Why'd he think *I'd* live?

"Promise me!" he screamed.

"I promise, but hold on!" I demanded, tears flowing down my cheeks.

Of all the things he could've prioritized saying at that moment, he tried to protect me from the guilt that would undoubtedly eat me alive if I lived and he died.

"This wasn't your fault," he said.

I growled in anger and tried to thrust myself up, but the momentum almost made me fall. Maybe I'd magically get myself up and pull Justin over the top, or Damian would be able to get up and come over, or the police would bust in, or Justin would thrust himself over from pure adrenaline.

One of those things had to happen.

My brother, who used to fish at the local creek, who caught frogs and turtles and kept them as mascots for our treehouse, who protected his sister from his parents' grief, who loved me more than anyone could ever hope to be loved, could not die.

Not today.

Not like this.

Not because of me and my horrible mistakes.

He was going to get married and raise a family and be there for holidays and birthday parties. He was going to grow old.

Justin kept his gaze fixated on me as the unforgiving wind rocked our bodies, jeopardizing our grips. I tried to put my leg under Justin's body as if that would magically keep him up if he fell, but I couldn't get it to stick; the angle was off.

I screamed in frustration, watching my brother's hands shift lower.

Justin's eyes locked with mine. I could tell he knew he was about to die. He knew there was nothing we could do to stop it.

"I love you," he said, his blue eyes surrendering. "You were always *my* rock."

"Hold on," I begged, tears stinging.

But suddenly, Justin's hands slipped off the edge.

I wanted to believe what I was seeing wasn't real, that it was another nightmare, and I'd just wake up and hug my brother. But the pain radiating from my bleeding body robbed me of that delusion.

I screamed, watching my brother's body drift through the air, his body tilting backward, arms above his head. He never even got the duct tape off his ankles, and somehow, that made it so much more heartbreaking. He didn't even have that last little bit of freedom as he plummeted to his death.

As he fell, he stared at me, but he didn't look scared. Or angry. He looked accepting of the fate that awaited him as he watched my face get smaller and smaller above him.

Colton was right: twelve seconds is an eternity when you know death is imminent. There was no safety net, no magic window washer, nothing to save Justin.

He just fell and fell and fell.

And as he did, a memory flashed.

*I'm a toddler, curled up on Justin's lap. We're still in our funeral clothes, sitting on the couch at the funeral home. Mommy and Daddy are in the next room, saying goodbye to people. Crying.*

*"Does it hurt to die?" I ask. My r's sound like w's at this age, and Justin's speech isn't pronounced perfectly either, but to me, it sounds normal.*

*His blue eyes are fixed on his toy car. "I don't know."*

*Jessica didn't live with us. She lived at someplace called the hospital, and now she lives at someplace called heaven. It's making everyone very sad. I'm scared no one will ever be happy again.*

*I clutch Justin's arm. "How come she can't come back?" When I asked Mommy this, she started crying super hard, and then she slammed the door. I hid under my covers for hours after that. I didn't come out of my bedroom for dinner, not even when my tummy was growling. I didn't want to make Mommy upset again. I seem to do that a lot.*

*But Justin doesn't get mad at me when I make mistakes like upsetting Mommy. He's the nicest person in the whole wide world. He lets me snuggle with him, so I don't cry. He shares his toys, and he gets me my sippy cup out of the fridge, so we don't have to bother Mommy or Daddy.*

*I hope he never leaves me.*

*"Promise me you won't ever die," I say to him.*

*His blue eyes look at me.*

And now those same blue eyes were locked on me as he fell a hundred stories, growing smaller and smaller.

And then, way down below, life as I knew it ended when my brother's helpless body slammed into the ground. Even up here, I could hear the collective shrieks of the crowd who'd parted like the Red Sea.

I stopped screaming.

I stopped crying.

I stopped hoping.

I stopped caring about anything.

I didn't even care when my fingers slipped off the edge.

38

I wasn't falling.

Why wasn't I falling?

I was going up, not down.

I could hear panicked shouting. Grunting.

Hands squeezed my arms so tightly it felt like my skin was tearing off the bone as they yanked my torso.

Damian's terrified face appeared.

It took two police officers plus Damian to haul me up and over the side of the building.

Because of the awkward angle and the jagged layers of glass still connected to the metal rim, they couldn't save me from falling *and* prevent my skin from getting sliced up along the way. Broken glass tore my wrist, face, chest, stomach, and legs, and as they laid me on the floor, a warm pool spread over my thighs.

"Jenna." Damian hovered over me as his distraught eyes scanned my body.

"She's in shock," someone said.

Blood squirted out of my wrist. An officer clamped his hand down, but it merely slowed the flow of crimson.

"Her leg," a voice said as the warmth expanded on my thigh.

"Must be her femoral."

My muscles grew so weak, I could barely move them, and as the pressure of the officer's belt around my thigh intensified, my eyelids demanded rest.

"Tighter," someone said.

Blood slithered through the guy's fingers on my arm. I stared at the hole in the wall where that glass box used to be, where moments ago, my brother was still breathing. In my periphery, I saw Colton's lifeless body with a bloody hole in his chest. No one was by him. No one was working on him. Dead, then.

"Bus is parked a half block out. EMTs are on their way."

"She ain't gonna make it that long."

"Jenna, hold on," Damian pleaded.

But I was waning. I tried to fix onto Damian's eyes, and I tried to ask him if he was okay—he'd been shot, why was no one helping *him*? —but my voice wouldn't come and my vision began to blur.

Everything faded: the faces, the voices, the building, the smell of blood.

As gravity evaporated, I saw Justin's smiling face.

## 39

Within absolute darkness, I could hear a faint beeping growing louder, mixed with the sounds of mumbled voices. The smell of disinfectant jabbed my nose, and pain radiated all over my body. Especially my stomach, which felt like it'd been hit by a semi.

I opened my eyes, cringing as brightness flooded in with a burn. But only in one eye; the other remained dark—something blocking it. My vision was fuzzy at first, focusing like a camera on its target, and as it cleared, I could see that there was a figure sitting in the chair in the corner of the room. A figure with tattooed arms, wearing a hospital gown.

When he saw that my eye was open, Damian jumped up and came to the side of my bed. He brought his hand to my cup my face but must've reminded himself not to touch my bandages and pulled it back.

Even with a bruised cheek, split lip, and messy hair, he somehow made a hospital gown look like it belonged on a runway.

"Hey," he whispered. "How you feeling?"

"Was it all a bad dream?" I prayed.

The look on his face said it all.

The beeping accelerated as my eyes stung. "So he's really gone."

Damian gently wiped a stray tear from my cheek. "They said it was painless. Instant."

Except for the hours of torture he endured before the fall, plus glass cutting his hands as he held on for dear life. And then the twelve-second descent, knowing he was going to die.

I wished I was the one who died. Living in a world without Justin seemed an impossibility, and if anyone deserved to lose their life, it was me. I'd brought Colton into our lives. I'd let him stay there, even after he'd become violent, and I'd disregarded everyone's warnings. I should've left town after Colton strangled me. I shouldn't have gone for that walk when Colton saw me kiss Damian. I shouldn't have dated Colton in the first place.

And that didn't even include all the mistakes I'd made once my brother had been kidnapped. Not calling the police. Letting Colton kick me into the box, shattering it and sealing Justin's fate.

I sobbed, my face throbbing with the pain I deserved.

"Hey," Damian whispered, stroking an unbandaged spot of skin on my arm. He let me cry it out, and as I did, I was grateful I didn't have to share this room with another patient who'd witness my despair; there was no space for one.

This hospital room was too stuffed with more medical equipment than a human could ever need—an ICU room, I suspected. With a giant indoor window that separated it from the nursing area, where medical staff kept a close eye on patients at all times. It was out there that I noticed several nurses and nonhospital personnel—visitors of other patients, I presume—staring at me. It looked like they'd abruptly stopped whatever they were doing in that exact second to gawk.

"Why are they looking at me?"

Damian looked over his shoulder and must've given them quite the glower because they all returned to their own business. Immediately.

"Don't worry about it," he said. But I could tell he was keeping something from me. Was it something to do with his injury?

"Are *you* okay?" I asked. "He shot you." Was that why they were staring?

"Through and through. Minor surgery. I'll have a wicked scar on my stomach." He offered a feeble smile.

I studied him. "You're really okay?"

"I'm okay," Damian assured.

I didn't know if he was sugar-coating it, but he was walking on his own and wasn't hooked up to machines. That had to be good, right?

"Was anyone else hurt?" All those pedestrians.

"No one was killed," Damian said. "People scrambled when the first pieces of glass fell. One tore a guy's shoulder up pretty good. Couple other people got cut up bad enough to be admitted, but by the time the box crashed down, they'd all cleared the sidewalk."

Thank god for that. A miracle, truly.

"Colton?" I asked.

Anger flashed through Damian's eyes. "Rotting in hell."

What a tragic end to a troubled life.

I tried to move but winced in pain that seemed to be everywhere, as if my body had been in a blender.

A brunette nurse wearing teal scrubs with an ID clamped to the collar, black-rimmed glasses, and sneakers came into the room. In her midforties, she was lean, with a huge mole on her neck. "Mr. Stone, you really need to get back to your room. I don't want to have to call security."

Damian ignored her and crossed his arms over his chest as he watched at me. "I think she needs pain meds."

"How you feeling, honey?" She looked at my monitor. "Scale of one to ten, ten being the worst pain you've ever felt, what number are you at?"

A million. But no pain medication would numb a shattered heart.

"Seven."

Through the wall's interior window, I noticed nurses looking at me again, though this time they were at least pretending not to.

"My name's Lisa. I'll be your nurse for the next six hours." She checked my IV bags—one yellow, one clear.

"Why is everyone staring at me?" I asked.

Nurse Lisa pursed her lips and flashed an annoyed look outside.

"Don't mind them. You need to rest, honey. You lost over two thousand milliliters of blood. Lose that much blood, and your heart has nothing to pump, so it...stops. You crashed on the ride in."

She adjusted the IV drip and kept talking as she checked the line's connection to my vein.

"Paramedic was doing chest compressions when you came in. Docs hooked up bags of blood, pushing it in as fast as they could as they rushed you to surgery. They had to repair your femoral, though your stab wound wasn't as bad as they feared. You're lucky it didn't hit major organs. If it had..." She shook her head. "You had a lot of deep cuts up and down your body. Docs lost count of the stitches—said there were thousands of them."

"Will she be okay?" Damian pressed.

Lisa leaned down and looked at me. "You'll be just fine, darlin'. You will have scars, though. A plastic surgeon was called to stitch up the laceration on your face, but he said with how jagged it was..." Another head shake. "They were able to save your eye, though."

How could I care about something as trivial as a scar when Justin lost his life?

"Now," she said with a sigh. "I'm going get some pain meds, honey, and they'll make you very sleepy, so you might want to wrap up your conversation." She glared at Damian as she left. I wondered how many times she'd made empty threats to have him removed. Maybe Nurse Lisa had a soft spot for love.

Careful not to bump me, Damian sat on the side of the bed with a grim expression. "How did Colton get to you?"

I could imagine how terrified he must have been. One second, waiting for me to join him the shower, and the next, discovering I was missing. I felt horrible I'd put him through that. And got him shot...

I explained Colton's call, his instructions. "He had Justin. Said he'd kill him if I didn't come alone."

Damian stroked my cheek as if reassuring himself I was okay and then, after a minute, said, "Your parents are down the hall eating because they don't let food in here." He stood. "I better go get 'em.

312 | KATHY LOCKHEART

Your dad'll have my head on a spike if they don't get to see you before the drugs knock you out again."

"How long have I been here?"

"Couple days," he said, kissing the unbandaged portion of my forehead.

"You'll come back, though?"

"I'll come back."

As Damian walked out, I looked down at my body, marrying how it felt with what I saw. My stomach was wrapped in something—surgical bandages, I guessed, though I couldn't see under the blankets or my gown. And I couldn't explore very well; both my hands were mittens of gauze, prickling pain where there must be tons of stitches in my fingers and palms. Moving my head, I could feel the gauze covering half my face from my forehead to my chin. And many other bandages covered most of my body—ones I could see, like on my arms, and ones I could feel, on my legs.

What a mess I was.

"Hey, kid." Fisher walked in and tried to hide his reaction to my appearance.

He had a black eye, and Damian, who came in behind him, had bruised knuckles. Which could've been from fighting Colton, but based on the hostile look they exchanged, I didn't think so.

"I got you in trouble," I realized. My silent escape, leaving Damian out of his mind with worry, and oblivious Fisher standing on the other side of the door, unable to say where I'd gone. "I'm sorry."

Damian didn't look sorry, though. Not even a little.

"He's lucky I didn't charge him with assaulting a police officer," Fisher said, inciting an eye-roll from Damian.

How did Damian manage to evade Fisher and come to the Willis Tower without him?

"Did you know Colton called Damian?"

Fisher threw another glare at Damian. "No, Romeo here went rogue after his tantrum. Went looking for you himself." Fisher glowered at Damian. "Privacy."

Damian glowered right back, but after a minute he turned around to walk out, not at all trying to hide the open hospital gown, with his butt cheeks exposed.

"Gah!" Fisher cringed at the eye assault and sat down on the lone visitor chair.

Just outside the door, a woman with chocolate brown hair lingered.

"I'll wait down the hall," she said to Fisher.

"I'll get you when I'm done," he replied without looking up.

That's when I recognized her. And based on the widening of her eyes, she recognized me, too.

It was the girl from the hospital waiting room. The one with the cool name, Fallon. The one that had been sobbing. And based on the uniform she was now wearing, evidently, she was a Chicago police officer.

I wondered what she'd been going through that day. What could take an officer undoubtedly trained in coping with trauma to her knees?

Fallon looked from me to Fisher, then back to me again—her eyes uneasy.

*She doesn't want me to mention having seen her in the hospital waiting room.*

*Why?*

I had no idea, but she hesitated before walking away.

"I'd like to ask you some questions before your folks come in," Fisher said. "That okay?"

I nodded and spent the next several minutes recounting everything that happened. I shed some tears. Fisher wrote things down in his notebook, asking for clarifications along the way.

"How did Colton get inside the Willis tower?" I asked.

"Had a buddy working janitorial services. Talked him into leaving the door unlocked." The yellow triangle warning of the floor being wet, inside the service entrance that smelled of Lysol. "Buddy thought it was a romantic thing. Proposal. He's been charged with accessory to manslaughter."

"That's a thing?"

"It's a thing."

"All he did was leave the door open."

"Hundreds of people could've died," Fisher growled. He continued with his questions until he finally put his little notebook away and stood up. "Alright, that's good enough for now. I'll go get your folks."

"Fisher?"

He waited.

"Thank you," I said.

He offered me a nod. "Glad you're okay, kid."

A moment later, the woman, Fallon, emerged. She stood only three feet inside the room, as if not wanting to invade my personal space.

"Thank you." Her tone was full of compassion. "For not saying anything."

I nodded.

She stared at me silently for a few beats and then pivoted to walk away, but stopped. Turned back around.

"I'm very sorry for what happened to you. And for your loss. I know what it feels like to lose someone you love."

My entire body tensed.

"I lost my mother," she said quietly. "And it does get easier."

In the hospital that day, I thought she'd said she was there for a guy. But maybe I'd misheard her.

"Is that who you were waiting for in the hospital?" I asked.

She shook her head, a new sadness plaguing her posture. "No. That was my dad. He made it through, but…" But there was something in her eyes, a pain that told me there was more to that story. Much, much more.

This woman had her own secrets.

Was clearly going through something in her own life, yet made the effort to speak words of encouragement.

"Anyway," she whispered. "I'm really sorry for your loss."

She lingered for another moment the way people do when they don't know what else to say, before finally ambling away.

My parents burst into the room with worry and tears and questions. So many questions. Their eyes were reddened from crying.

I told them how sorry I was, and then recounted what happened—from the first time Colton touched me to the confrontation at the Willis Tower.

They were empathetic, which only made me feel worse. I deserved for them to hate me.

The nurse walked in and misunderstood my parents' tears. "She's going to be just fine, Mom and Dad." Lisa pulled at the IV line, finding the connection she was looking for. "This is going to make her sleepy, so we need to let her rest."

The nurse injected my line, and a warmth spread through my limbs. Lightheadedness made my body float, and my eyelids became trap doors.

"Rest," the nurse said, touching my arm before leaving.

Mom and Dad gave me a kiss. "We'll be here when you wake up."

Dad put his hand on the small of Mom's back, guiding her out of the room.

"Hey, Dad?"

He turned around.

Through the immense fatigue, I managed to ask, "Is Damian really okay?"

My dad would give it to me straight. He nodded. "Bullet didn't hit any organs. That guy can take a beating." He added, "He hasn't left your side since he woke up."

I nodded.

"Hey, Dad?"

He turned around again.

"Why has everyone been staring at me?"

To this question, he hesitated and appeared to debate answering.

"Please tell me." Otherwise, I'd imagine all sorts of awful things he might be keeping from me.

Dad chewed the inside of his cheek—would it always be this painful seeing how much he resembled Justin?—and then he finally walked over to the side of my bed. "News coverage on this thing has been…big."

*Big.* Dad said the word as if it were the understatement of the century.

"Spectators. Cell phones these days. Not everyday something like that happens. Videos of the box exploding. Of you up there... hanging on."

Dad pinched his eyes closed, clearly haunted by whatever he'd seen.

"Did they tape Justin..." Dying?

"Let the cops handle that."

I focused on my breathing, my eyelids growing heavy.

"Now, you get some rest." A kiss on my cheek.

I was so tired. "Does Zoey know about Justin?"

Dad nodded. "She's in the waiting room."

"I want to see her." I couldn't imagine what she must be going through.

"Later," my dad said firmly. "Sleep."

One last kiss, and then my dad looked at me over his shoulder and offered a grateful smile that I was alive, before strolling out of the room.

40

In the weeks that followed, I was told an enormous wave of good came from the unimaginable tragedy on the hundred and third floor. News broke around the world from multiple perspectives: the breaking-of-an-iconic-attraction angle, the engineering "failure" angle, the Chicago-Marathon-interruption angle, and, of course, the domestic violence angle. I was told that had Justin not died, the event would not have gotten the coverage it did because an almost-tragedy isn't the same as a real tragedy. News outlets kept the story alive daily, and because of that, shelters had a surge in survivors escaping violence globally. Donations skyrocketed. Hundreds of thousands—millions, some speculated—of lives were saved.

It should've dimmed the pain, but the selfish truth was I didn't care about any of that. I just cared that Justin was dead, and I would have traded all of that good just to have him back.

A few weeks after his funeral, I had Damian take me to the cemetery so I could see Justin's headstone that had finally arrived. I was overwhelmed staring at the engraved letters and dates, because it was heartbreakingly inadequate how something as monumental as a life and death could be summarized so briefly on a stone.

All Justin ever wanted was to leave this world a better place. If he could speak to me now, he'd tell me his life had saved millions, and what greater impact could he ask for? But it wasn't fair that he'd had to die to save them. If anyone had to die, it should've been me.

Damian put his hand on my waist, recognizing the look on my face. "This wasn't your fault."

*Of course it was.*

"Colton did this. Not you. There may be times when you forget how hard you fought to save Justin, but I'll always remind you. You went to the Skydeck, ready to give your life for his, you tried reasoning with Colton, and you fought so hard you almost died, too. *Colton* killed Justin, not you."

It struck me how, out of all the people the universe could have brought into my life, I had the one person who knew what it was like to feel *responsible* for someone's death. Damian knew how the guilt infected every cell of your body, leaving you poisoned.

And as I considered that, I wondered: Did Mom feel responsible for Jessica's death? Did she wonder if she'd overlooked an early symptom that might've caught the cancer sooner, or whether she'd found a good enough doctor, or if she had chosen the wrong treatment option? Every day she held her dying child, was she haunted by all those decisions, feeling like if she had done something different, Jessica would have lived? *Of course she did; she's human.*

"He'd want you to be happy, Jenna," Damian said.

But I didn't *want* to be happy, and even if I did, it felt as possible as asking me to breathe underwater. Plus, moving on with my life would mean I was okay with Justin's death.

Other than the one day at the cemetery, nothing got me out of bed after he died. Some days I sobbed all day—quietly, protecting Damian's ears from it—some days I was too exhausted to shed a tear. Every day, Damian brought me food, reminded me to shower.

I felt ashamed because I was aware of how disappointed my brother must be in me for abandoning my life in favor of lying in bed day after day. Justin died to give me this time on earth, and living in anguish was disrespectful to his life and sacrifice. I also felt terrible for what I was putting my parents and Damian through, yet I didn't have the strength to fix it. I was too exhausted, and failing Damian only deepened my depression.

One day, Damian lingered after seeing yet another untouched plate of food by the bed.

"Jenna, it's been almost two months. You're starting to scare me."

I hadn't *planned* to stay in bed for this long, but losing Justin felt like I'd been put through a woodchipper and dipped in acid, so one day simply blended into the next.

I stayed in bed for another ten days before Damian finally put his foot down and insisted on taking me out of the apartment. It was nonnegotiable, he said. He loaded me into his truck, and for the first time in two months—aside from visiting the cemetery, that is—we left the apartment complex.

It angered me that the sun was shining, that it rose and fell each day. I didn't understand how the world kept spinning, how trains continued to run, how people still sat at restaurants eating, going on like nothing had happened. As if Justin's death was inconsequential.

I had no idea where Damian was taking me. I assumed just for a drive, but when he stopped at a medical office, I was confused.

"Why are we here?" I demanded. "Are you having me committed?"

Damian looked like he couldn't tell if I was joking, and I could see the hope in his face because being able to joke was a serious step in the right direction.

"No." His eyes turned serious, and he rubbed his jaw the way he did when he had to tell me stuff I didn't like to hear. Followed by a clearing of the throat. *Uh oh.* "I took the liberty of making an appointment for you to get a physical. You haven't been taking care of yourself, and I... Well, I thought maybe..." He looked concerned about how I'd react to whatever he was about to say. "Jenna... I think you need to ask a doctor if you should go on medication. I love you, and I'm worried about you."

*Medication.*

I felt a rush of anger because how could anyone think a little pill could help with my brother having been kidnapped, tortured, and murdered right in front of my eyes? It couldn't help. Nothing could.

*This is just how I'll be forever.* And if this was getting to be too much, then maybe Damian should have taken me up on one of my multiple attempts to break up with him. I'd tried to save him from myself.

But right after the anger came remorse, because looking at the concern radiating from his eyes, feeling him stroke my hand tenderly, I knew he wasn't suggesting there was a quick fix. He just...wanted to help. And then I felt awful because him having to care for me must have drudged up bad memories of his mom's depression. I doubted anything could ever pull me out of this, but for Damian's sake, I wanted to at least try.

"Okay."

The doctor was just a primary care physician with our discussion under the guise of a "physical," but of course, after the nurse left and I was alone in the room with the doctor, she branched off from the *How is your incision site?* questions to mental health ones. I was honest. Why not. *So what if they commit me?*

Twenty minutes later, the doctor came back into the room with an odd expression. *She's probably going to put me on an involuntary hold.* At least it would free Damian from having to see me daily.

She sat on her swivel chair and looked at my chart. "Well, Jenna, I don't think medication's a good idea in your condition."

*In your condition.* What the hell was that supposed to mean? I was that much of a lost cause that even the bazillion-dollar drug company thought I was hopeless? Suddenly I wanted those little pills more than anything because they were my only hope to make this easier on Damian, and beneath all my pain and hurt was still an ocean of love for him. I was furious at myself for not being able to tap into that love to ease the pain for his sake.

"Why?" I snapped, as tears threatened to rupture.

She smiled, breaking the news to me delicately. "You're pregnant."

It took me the full thirty seconds that passed to absorb those two words. And by absorb, I mean let them in, and then bounce them right back out. Sadly, Damian and I hadn't made love since Justin's death. We'd only had that one night together before it.

"That's not possible."

"When was your last period?"

My period. Right. Normal life. "I…I've been distracted. I haven't thought about it."

"Have you had a period since your surgery?"

"I…" *Have I?* All those days lying in bed blended into each other. Where did one week begin and the next end? Had it been two months or two years since I'd been in that room?

"Why don't you follow me," she smiled, opening the door.

I complied, lost in thought as I walked down the hall with her, entering a room containing a small machine. She nodded to the exam table. "Lie down. I'll do a quick ultrasound so we can get some measurements, see how far along you are."

*There's no way I'm pregnant. Maybe I have another medical condition that spikes the hormone detected in pregnancy.*

The doctor started the scan, and within a couple minutes of clicking buttons, she pointed to a bean-shaped thing with a pulsating dot. "Measuring at twelve weeks," she said happily.

I looked at the little oval, and then she put another device on my stomach, and I heard the *whoosh, whoosh, whoosh* of the heartbeat.

In that moment, everything changed. I knew it would take me a while to digest the fact that it was real, to get my head wrapped around it, heck even to get excited about it. But what was instant was the mother's bond, created by seeing and hearing my baby's heartbeat for the first time.

*It's real. I'm actually pregnant. There's a tiny bean baby in my belly.*

*And I'd give my life to protect them.*

"I don't understand how this is possible," I admitted. "We used a condom…" Well, now that I thought about it, we'd actually run out of them the last time that night, hadn't we? We got complacent, hoping all the baby-making ingredients had been depleted by that point. At least, that was my thought as his lips traveled down my chest, and I became a hostage to my desires, allowing one careless encounter to pass… But still. This lady owed me some serious medical explanations. "My heart stopped, and I had surgery." People miscarry over slight tumbles down the stairs.

The doctor shrugged like this was a little miracle. "Implantation takes up to twelve days after conception."

*And evidently, I have a uterus of steel.*

"How can I be twelve weeks along?" I pressed. I'd been in Damian's bedroom for two months, so let's say eight weeks, and I was in the hospital for two weeks before that. "I had sex like *ten* weeks ago, and you said implantation doesn't happen until up to twelve days after that?"

"The pregnancy clock starts the first day of your last period, even though it's, on average, three weeks later that the embryo implants."

She calculated my due date as July 4th and then went through way too much information for a human brain to remember.

"How'd it go?" Damian stood up when I entered the waiting room, looking like he'd been running a stressed hand through his hair.

He didn't deserve to learn about something this big in the doctor's waiting room.

"Fine. Can we go home now?"

He tried to hide his worry that maybe I'd refused help, but he didn't pepper me with questions on the ride home, which I appreciated. It gave me time to contemplate this new reality.

Damian finally gained the courage to ask me his burning question when we were back at his place. Well, *our* place now. My lease ended last month, so he'd moved all my stuff here. I looked outside the window at the snowflakes that fell over the glowing skyscrapers, making the city feel like a snow globe. Damian came up behind me.

"So… What'd she say?"

I turned around, feeling his profound love for me. I knew there was nothing he wouldn't do for me, no length of time he wouldn't wait for me to come around. And something inside me awakened when I realized he'd be just as doting—maybe even more so—towards his unborn child.

"She said meds were a bad idea."

Damian tried to appear neutral, as if he wasn't silently screaming that the doctor was insane.

"Did she say why?" *Man, he's smooth.*

I stared directly into his eyes, knowing these words would change the rest of his life. "She said I'm pregnant. Twelve weeks."

Damian stopped breathing. Like, literally stopped breathing, and stopped blinking, and stopped, well, everything. He had to be doing the math in his head, but other than that, I couldn't tell how he felt. A normal unplanned pregnancy would be jarring to learn about. But this was way more complicated.

He was probably worrying whether I was actually capable of being a mother to his child, if I'd be the mother he had, if I'd be the mother *I* had… It was not their fault for being the mothers that they were, but I had other plans.

"I won't be like our moms," I assured. I would give this child everything, and I wouldn't let this depression steal my baby's mother. For the first time since Justin's death, I *wanted* to be happy, because this was not about me anymore. "This is a turning point, I swear." I would make sure of it. I had no idea how—depression wasn't a choice—but I'd put in the work because failure was no longer an option.

Damian walked up to me, looked in my left eye, then my right, and brought his hand to my face. Would our baby have his majestic green eyes? His strong jaw, full lips? Would they feel the strength and gentility within his muscles when he held them?

For the first time since the night we conceived this little miracle, Damian's mouth curled into a wide smile. It only lasted a second before he crashed his lips to mine.

It stunned me for a moment. He'd been so patient with me all these weeks, but I could feel that his desires had never gone away; they'd been building.

His tongue traced my lower lip, and then it was in my mouth, and my back was pressed against the wall. I didn't expect to feel anything. Sadly, I hadn't thought much about *this* in the past few weeks, but now that his mouth was on mine, and his hand was on my hip, something inside me roused. A match lit the flame that quickly became an inferno.

Damian pulled back. "Sorry."

I didn't want him to apologize for his passion or to stop. I pulled his face back to mine, curious if he'd have had the strength to stop again. Judging by the intensity of his tongue, the urgency with which his mouth explored my throat, my jaw, the answer was no. He ran his hand down my stomach and stopped just below my belly button, where there'd soon be a baby bump. He kept his hand there as his tongue trailed up my neck and was back inside my mouth.

I could tell he was trying to gauge how I felt about all this. Making out was one thing—a wonderfully good thing—but he didn't presume it would lead to anything else.

And for that, my love for him swelled even more.

I unbuttoned his jeans, and with the confirmation of my intent, Damian growled, picked me up, carried me to *our* bed, and placed me down gently. He tugged my clothes off quickly and stripped so fast that his shirt got stuck on his bicep. The two seconds it took him to free himself looked like sexual agony to him.

I smiled.

For the first time in weeks, *I smiled.*

He trailed his mouth up and down my skin, exploring every inch of me, and when he climbed on top of me, he held his lips over mine and made sure I was looking right into his eyes as he connected our bodies. With my gasp came his prideful smile.

JUSTIN'S DEATH SPARKED CHANGE IN THIS WORLD, AND WHILE I WISHED that greatness hadn't cost him his life, I was honored he was my brother, and I wanted to live a life honoring him. I knew it wouldn't be easy, but I took one step forward each day, and eventually, the grief that once swallowed me whole released its grip enough to make room for happiness.

On the really good days, Justin would visit me in my dreams. I'd get to hug him, and we'd have long talks about Mom and Dad. I couldn't be sure what to make of the dreams—possibly grief's manifestation, some sort of coping mechanism—but I chose to believe they were his way of visiting me. I needed to hold on to that because it made me feel like he was still here in his own way.

Zoey agreed with my conviction, though I couldn't be sure if it was merely *her* way of trying to hold on to him, too. She'd admitted as much when we'd gone out for coffee one day, her voice full of pain as she looked down and said, "I know I didn't date him for long, but I loved him. And I miss him." I reached out and held her hand and told her I was incredibly grateful that Justin had felt her love. And then, we held each other as we sobbed.

Through it all, Damian stayed by my side—his love the water that helped my happiness continue to bloom. We took a trip to Florida and watched the sunsets on the beach. He started that self-defense program, which was a huge success that quickly became a national sensation. He held my swelling belly, talking to our baby inside. Every morning, without fail, Damian kissed the six-inch scar on my face, and one day, I finally asked him why he did that. He stroked my cheek with the backs of his fingers, and in a tender voice that tried to hide the heartbreak from the memories of that awful night, explained, "Because it reminds me to never take you for granted."

Damian waited until after we'd had the baby—a little girl we named Justine, who quickly became our everything—before he got down on one knee and asked me to be his wife. It was one of the happiest moments of my life, and the next summer, I walked down the aisle in my childhood backyard, with our closest friends and family present.

It was July, the wildflowers in full bloom, a sunsetting sky, cicadas buzzing in the trees. Little lanterns hung on ropes that sectioned off the white chairs on either side of the aisle, while a local high schooler played her violin as background music. It smelled like flowers and freshly cut grass. I wore my hair down, feeling it dance across my neck in the gentle breeze.

Damian stood in a tan tux, his emerald eyes glued to me as I swayed forward with my father. Zoey stood up there as my maid of honor, and Sturge—looking as out of place as possible in a country setting—was his best man.

In the audience was Mom bouncing Justine on her lap, Damian's mom and her nurse, Emily, Harrison, Steve, Fisher, Ricky, and Levi and Audrey, as well as other family and friends. A table, off to the side, had large framed photos of Justin, Jessica, and Damian's dad and Sophie—our way of making sure they were here with us as Damian and I recited our vows.

Missing Justin would never go away, nor would all of the guilt, but looking into Damian's eyes, seeing the smiles on the faces of our loved ones who were rooting for us to have a beautiful life together, I felt the final shackles of sadness fall away. And along with my vows to Damian, I silently pledged to Justin to choose happiness and light, in his honor.

We'd written our own vows, and it was my turn first. Damian held my hands, his gaze on me as I tried to get through the words without choking up.

"I can imagine Justin standing next to you, putting his hand on your shoulder, saying he's grateful to have such an amazing man become his brother-in-law. I know we will see them all again, but in the meantime, I want to make a vow to you, and to all the ones we've lost, that until then, we'll live each day to the fullest." I smiled. "I'm so madly in love with you, Damian. You don't just make my life better— you make it extraordinary. I can't wait to make a home together, to have more babies with you and hold your hand as we watch them grow. I can't wait to be there for each other during life's hard times and celebrate all the good ones. You've given me all these moments to look forward to." I swallowed over the tightness in my throat. Damian squeezed my hand. "If there's one thing we've learned, it's that none of us knows how long we have on earth. But what I do know is that I want to spend every moment I have with you."

Damian's eyes shimmered as he mouthed *I love you*, and after a minute he pulled a piece of paper from his inside pocket and stared into my eyes.

"When I was eight years old, I sat in the backseat of twisted metal that was once our family car and saw my father, and later my sister, take their last breaths. In the wake of that devastation, I died too. The years that followed were a hollow, painful existence, with nothing tethering me to this life. It was as if gravity ceased to exist. Until I met you. The moment I first saw your eyes, something inside of me awakened, and as I got to know you, you became the center of my every thought. You made me look forward to my future for the first time in my life. I vowed to be your friend, your protector, whatever you'd let me be and for as long as you'd allow it. I was utterly and completely in love with you, but I never imagined you'd fall in love with me too."

He swallowed, clearly trying to hold back his tears. "I know that even on wonderful days like today, there'll always be a part of you that's hurting inside. On the days when that hurt is overwhelming, I'll hold you. And on the days when the hurt is small, I'll be there to dance with you. I vow to give you as many dancing days as I can. I will cherish every single moment we have together, and I will love you, honor you, and protect you all the days of my life."

At that moment, Damian stared at me and no one else existed. I loved him so much, and yet I knew somehow our love would only grow with each passing year.

"By the power vested in me, I now pronounce you husband and wife. You may kiss your bride."

Damian gently cupped my cheek and kissed me, igniting the same fire that we'd get to experience for all the days our lives. As our friends and family cheered, it struck me how close I'd come to surrendering to devastation, and how grateful I was that our love had persevered and gotten us through it.

Through unimaginable tragedy came an immense appreciation for the fragility of life and the power of love—both light and dark.

# EPILOGUE

## FALLON

W hen I emerged from the locker room, I didn't notice the two men loitering, let alone suspect they were here to carry out a hit. Or that within minutes, I'd be fighting for my life.

If I had known, I wouldn't be smiling like this, proud that all my hard work had finally paid off.

"Good morning, Fallon," Zoey—a girl I'd met at this gym—called out to me.

"Morning!" I waved and headed towards the elevator.

*I can't believe this day is finally here.*

A day that I had dreamed about since I was a little girl, and had worked my entire life to get to—graduating at the top of my class in the police academy, and gaining seriously intense experience as a Chicago police officer. All of it was to fulfill my one goal in life: to hunt down the criminals who'd destroyed my family and make them pay.

And now, I finally had the chance, reporting for my first official day on an elite DEA task force.

My next stop? Chicago Police Headquarters.

I stepped into the empty elevator.

**When a gorgeous guy joined me, I had no idea that soon, he**

**would kill several men to protect me...**

~

THANK YOU FOR READING DEADLY ILLUSION! **BELOW, I REVEAL MY deepest, darkest secret** that inspired this novel, and the heart-breaking reason a beloved character died, but first, I hope you loved Jenna and Damian's love story as much as I do. They appear again in **FATAL CURE**, which continues next...

## FATAL CURE

**I had no idea that the criminal kingpin I've been hunting, the one I vowed to make pay for decimating my family, is the man I've fallen in love with...** Dillon has a lot of enemies that would hurt anyone he cares about if he makes a mistake. And falling in love with a DEA agent? Is as big as they get.

Now, we're a target of the world's most dangerous criminals. Our only hope to survive... is to work together...

And time is running out...

☆☆☆☆☆ *"Absolutely one of the BEST books I've EVER read!"*

BUT FIRST, WHAT HAPPENED WHEN DAMIAN SAW JENNA GETTING LOADED into that ambulance? More shockingly, what did he do after? As a THANK YOU TO READERS, find out in this **EXCLUSIVE FREE SHORT STORY from Damian's POV**(https://kathylockheart.com/damian-pov-thelieswetell/). Because there's one secret Damian that never confessed to Jenna... And it will make your jaw hit the floor.

. . .

Now onto **the secret** that inspired this novel and the **gripping reason a beloved character died...**

~

## INSPIRATION FOR THIS NOVEL

*This contains **major** spoilers, so please read after the book.*

I'm not going to lie. Writing down the inspiration for this story is scary for me—publicly exposing a secret I'd buried for years. I do it in hopes of inspiring others. So here we go...

The inspiration for this book came to me when I joined coworkers at a happy hour, unaware that the night would change the trajectory of my writing career. As we sipped drinks, the news came on the bar's television, and the top story concerned the latest celebrity couple involved in domestic violence. I overheard people discussing it and forming harsh presumptions about the couple's relationship. They condemned the woman, saying she was in a violent relationship because she "wanted the attention" and that she must have "daddy issues." The whole time I just kept thinking, *If only you knew...*

If you only knew what it was *actually* like, you'd never judge someone in that position. And while the commentators probably didn't know any better, judgment silences people who need help in their most vulnerable hour.

I know firsthand how that vulnerability feels. My experience took place years ago when I fell in love with a guy. The first part of our relationship was so incredible that a bond formed between us and took root so deeply in my psyche, I didn't think anything could ever jeopardize it.

The first time he laid hands on me, it felt like my world shifted on its axis. Up became down, and all the colors of our once-beautiful romance collapsed into black and white. As confused as I was heartbroken, I made the first decision that would keep me with him. A decision that became an unshakable and dangerous precedent. The only person I was willing to discuss the incident with was him. I knew if I talked to my best friend, she'd write him off, and then how could she be my friend anymore? Plus, *she* couldn't explain why my fairy tale had come crashing down. The only person who could was him, and I needed answers as badly as I needed oxygen to breathe. Thus, the only person I allowed to try and explain what happened was him.

I stayed because I believed him, that he was even more shocked and disgusted by his actions than I was. I stayed because I felt sorry for him, for having a childhood that left him broken. I stayed because as I held him whimpering in my arms, I felt the weight of his demons and the responsibility to show him what real love could be like. I stayed because I loved him, and I thought our love was powerful enough to "fix" him.

We then entered what I now know to be a textbook cycle—explosion, the honeymoon period, rising tension, explosion. Weeks, sometimes even months, would pass without explosions, and between them, the highs were so high they fueled my belief that being with him was probably like being with an addict: When he was "on the wagon" with not losing his temper, we both agreed it was an uncrossable line, and when explosions happened, we'd have a come-to-Jesus discussion about the fate of our relationship if it continued.

Meanwhile, by keeping *the secret,* I became emotionally and mentally isolated from everyone I loved, and the longer it continued— the deeper down the rabbit hole I fell—the harder it became to admit what had been going on. Especially when things started to spiral out of control.

As time went on, the explosions got worse and more dangerous. It wasn't until one of his explosions was so dangerous I feared for my life that I broke up with him. I wish I could say that was the end of it, but when he swore that losing me was a rock-bottom wake-up call, I allowed myself to get sucked back in.

When I finally, permanently, ended it, I was heartbroken, for I still loved him, despite all he'd done. But I felt lucky. I'd made it out, and it was behind me.

Or so I thought. What I didn't know then was that 70% of domestic violence homicides happen AFTER the relationship ends. It's called separation violence, and once I left, his behavior became unstable. I'd never felt more afraid for my life. I spent months looking over my shoulder, terrified to open the door, scared to walk out of a building.

No one knew I'd gone through any of this. Other than confiding in my husband, I kept it a secret for years after, afraid no one would look at me the same. But then, with that conversation at the bar, my long-buried secret awakened, and I became disheartened by some people's misconceptions. As the weeks passed, I couldn't shake a growing desire to help people understand, and I thought maybe I could take my passion for writing and do something good with it. While my primary goal was the same as my other stories—to entertain people—I set out to write a novel that meant more to me than anything I'd ever written.

And as I did, I had three goals in mind: First, I wanted to take the reader through one full domestic violence cycle to eradicate misconceptions and underscore why this phenomenon is as widespread as it is deadly. I wanted to show the emotional complexities of abuse because the truth is, when its disease infects you, domestic violence isn't just scary. It's psychologically alarming how it weaponizes compassion and manipulates your logic. Tragically, you often don't realize the danger you're in until it's too late...

Second, I wanted to show the reader that intimate partner violence doesn't have to be horrifically violent for you to be in danger. I've come to believe abuse is a spectrum, much like autism or alcoholism. Even if you're not being beaten, the threat to your life is still very real.

And my final goal was to highlight the dangers of separation violence. I got lucky. But I might not have and wish I'd understood this statistic so I could've protected myself better.

It was this danger that resulted in the saddest part of this story. Killing Justin was gut-wrenching. I cried over it because my characters are very real to me, and I didn't want any *good guys* to die. But I also knew that if no one we cared about died, the novel wouldn't fairly depict the danger of domestic violence, nor would it honor those who died from it. Justin's death broke my heart, as it did Jenna's. But like so many other admirable people, Jenna found the strength to move forward and honor Justin's life. And in doing so, she became an even bigger hero to me.

If intimate partner violence hasn't personally affected you, chances are, it has affected, is affecting, or will affect someone you love. Thank you for reading this. You now know my secret.

*Xoxo, Kathy*

*P.S. I'd like to point out that while statistically most violence is inflicted on women, intimate partner violence can happen to any gender.*

〜

Don't miss seeing Jenna and Damian again in **FATAL CURE**, which starts next.

I had no idea that the criminal kingpin I've been hunting, the one I vowed to make pay for decimating my family, is the man I've fallen in love with…

But first… read what happened when Damian saw Jenna getting loaded into that ambulance and shockingly, what he did after in this **EXCLUSIVE FREE SHORT STORY from Damian's POV**(https:// kathylockheart.com/damian-pov-thelieswetell/).

# FATAL CURE

*For my dad, my hero.*

# FATAL CURE BLURB

Fallon's a survivor who will stop at nothing to catch the drug criminals that decimated her family, but when she lands the opportunity of a lifetime and joins a DEA task force, she uncovers the shocking truth about her past and realizes the criminal kingpin she's hunting is closer than she ever imagined...

Dillon has a lot of enemies—enemies that would hurt anyone he cares about if he makes a mistake. Thus, he has two rules: never fall in love and never get caught. But when he's rescued from certain death by a captivating woman named Fallon, he has no idea that she's about to break them both or that they've become a target of the world's most dangerous criminals.

Worse, a ruthless drug cartel makes a horrifying move that puts the lives of thousands of civilians, and the fate of the entire country, on the line. And time is running out...

# AUTHOR'S NOTE

F atal Cure is an emotional, tension-filled romance. If you are looking for a lighthearted read, you will not find it in these pages.

WHILE THE ROMANTIC SCENES ARE NOT EXTREMELY GRAPHIC, THIS forbidden love story contains violence and other content that may be triggering for some readers. I prefer you go into a story without spoilers, but if you would like **a list of detailed triggers**, you can find it posted on my website at KathyLockheart dot com, under FATAL CURE.

1

When a gorgeous guy walked into the otherwise empty elevator, I had no idea that in a few weeks, he would kill several men to protect me. He didn't strike me as a killer. He looked like a model with dark hair and facial stubble, a tall, muscular body and captivating eyes.

Eyes that locked on to me as he casually rested his hand on a Gucci gym bag slung over his shoulder.

"Morning." His baritone voice rumbled through the space.

I offered a polite smile but said nothing back. Not that I was trying to be rude. I just wanted to stay focused because today, my lifelong dream to dismantle the drug organizations that had destroyed my family was a huge step closer to coming true.

This all-consuming goal had guided my every move leading up to this moment. I'd worked three jobs to get my bachelor's degree from the University of Illinois, graduated at the top of my class from the police academy, moved to Chicago, and after gaining experience as a Chicago police officer, applied to and gotten accepted into a prestigious DEA task force. The first meeting? Was in one hour.

I ran through my checklist for the millionth time.

Police uniform ironed, crisp and waiting for me in the Chicago Police Headquarters locker room? Check.

Workout this morning to burn off nervous energy and help keep my mind alert? Check.

Showered, makeup and hair done here at the gym? Check, check, and check.

I glanced at my phone screen, seeing it was 7:03 a.m. Three minutes past my target time but still plenty of time to get to the precinct, change, and be in the conference room well before eight—nothing left to chance.

"I'm Dillon." The handsome guy extended his hand as the elevator began its slow descent from the fifty-fifth floor to the ground level. His unwavering eye contact and firm handshake brimmed with the confidence normally reserved for someone beyond his mid-twenties age.

"Fallon," I replied.

"Fallon," he said. "Cool name."

My name meant descended from a ruler. My parents, at the time of my birth at least, viewed me as their little princess, a miracle after a battle with infertility. From that moment on, their entire life shaped around me like the careful organization of the planets in our solar system, their baby the center of gravity pulling each decision they made. My mom packed lunches with little drawings, and Dad dedicated every Saturday to Fallon's-choice day, where I got to pick what we did. If I had to assign a word to those earlier years, it would be *bliss*, when I felt completely safe and love penetrated every cell of my body.

That was before it all got sucked into a black hole, and any semblance of life and of the parents who once loved me more than anything was destroyed.

"I've never seen you here before." Dillon snapped my focus back to the present.

"Maybe you have."

"No." His gaze glided over my lean five-foot-four frame, chocolate hair, and sapphire eyes. "I'd definitely remember if I did."

I would remember if I'd seen him, too. With a rugged jaw drawing you into a hypnotic smile, the guy was so hot that women probably literally fainted around him. He probably had to go around checking pulses left, right, and sideways with the hormonal devastation left in his wake. His extraordinary physique contoured his black T-shirt and gray pants like a walking advertisement for workout clothes.

But no matter how hot he was, there was only one priority today, and that was work. I wasn't going to be distracted by the embodiment of sex on legs.

I watched the floor number on the digital panel descend from twenty-eight to twenty-seven. But I allowed my eyes to wander back over to him, curious if he was staring.

He was.

Until the elevator bounced like a yo-yo. It took me a second to realize I was now on the diamond-patterned carpet, thanks to the elevator having jolted to a stop.

"You okay?" Dillon offered his hand.

*Of course Sir Sex Magnet managed to stay upright, the ridiculously perfect specimen that he is.*

On any other day, that charming way he looked down at me and extended his hand like a gentleman would've sent butterflies in my stomach. But not today.

Not. Today.

This first meeting of the task force was vital. First impressions were critical, and if I couldn't be early, I sure as hell couldn't be late, let alone miss it entirely.

"You have got to be kidding me." I jumped back up. "I don't have time for this."

I pushed the open-door button, several of the numbered floors, and the main-lobby button. When nothing worked, I tried the red emergency-call button. "Hello?"

Static. Crackling, like maybe someone was trying to answer.

I tried again. "Hello? The elevator stopped."

More crackling. I tried four more times.

"What the hell?" I held my phone up, irritated to see it had no signal.

I hated these older skyscrapers. Their elevators were like signal-blocking steel bunkers.

I moved around, desperate to hit the right spot so I could make a call. But as I tried each wall—the center, lower, and then higher above my head—I discovered it was fruitless.

"Can you try yours, please?"

Dillon fished his cell out of his back pocket and held it up. "Who would we call?"

"If we can get a signal, the phone number on the panel, for starters. If they don't answer, we call the fire department."

Dillon raised an impressed eyebrow.

His deltoids waged a war against his shirt's fabric as he held the cell above his head, squinting at the screen. After several moments, he sighed. "I'm not getting any bars, but I'm sure the elevator will restart any second. They probably know we're in here."

"I can't bank on *probably*. Can you please turn your cell off and back on?"

His lips curled up as he complied.

"What?" I asked.

He shook his head and ran a thumb over his smile. "Nothing."

After both our cells rebooted, I asked, "Are you getting any bars now?"

He frowned.

"Great." I pushed the emergency-call button again. "Hello?" I tried repeatedly but couldn't get a response.

If I missed this meeting, I might get kicked off the task force before I even started, and then all the work I'd done to get here would go up in smoke. On every future application, I'd have to disclose that I'd been let go from the operation, thwarting any realistic chance of joining another in the future. My ability to succeed on this task force was my ticket to establishing a successful career in the DEA, which was more than just a career move. It meant being able to stop other families from going through what happened to mine.

"Let's try to pry the doors open," I suggested.

Dillon raised his brows. "*Pry* the doors open? It's only been a couple minutes."

"We could be in here for a couple of hours if we don't do something."

Dillon bit back his smile, dropped his gym bag on the floor, and joined me by the doors. We tried to insert our fingertips between them, but after three failed attempts, we accepted it wasn't happening.

Dillon leaned against the wall and studied me with a playful gleam in his eyes as I paced and twisted my hands together, trying to calculate how long it might take them to get up to the twenty-seventh floor. At least, I thought that was what floor we were on. Someone probably heard us on the other end of that emergency button and was on their way. They had to be…

I might be a Chicago police officer trained in de-arming an assailant, firing a weapon with precision, and getting out of some seriously sticky situations, but no police training could help me if I missed the most important morning of my career if this damn elevator didn't start moving again.

"Are you claustrophobic?" he asked. "Because you're suddenly looking pretty freaked out."

"And you find that amusing?"

"Find it kind of adorable."

I glared at him, but it only incited a bigger smile.

Dillon watched me walk from side to side.

"So, is it a heights thing or a claustrophobic thing that's creating this"—he gestured toward my body—"situation?"

"Neither; I'm in a hurry."

I needed to calm down. I left myself a buffer for the unexpected, just in case. I just hadn't thought I'd actually need it. I didn't like cutting things close.

"You're not gonna faint or something, are you?" Dillon asked.

I glowered at him, and at least this time, he cleared his throat to hide his smile.

"You need to get your mind off being trapped in here," Dillon said.

"That's not possible."

"Do you live in this building?"

"No, I just come for the gym. And I don't want to do small talk," I said. "I want to get us out of here."

The lights flickered, and the space—which had been playing jazz music moments ago—grew quiet.

A new unease washed through me; a simple stuck elevator didn't have its lights flicker or lose power to the speakers.

"Why did the music shut off?" I asked.

Dillon shrugged as he continued to observe me.

"I'd really like to know exactly what is malfunctioning here. There's, like, twenty-six floors of air beneath us."

"Elevator crashes are very rare," he assured.

"He says to a girl in a broken elevator that's dangling from a cable."

Dillon bit his lip, clearly trying not to laugh at me. "They have emergency brakes for things like this."

"Do you hear that?" I asked. "It sounds like yelling."

As we listened, the yelling escalated into an all-out symphony of screaming and a stampede of running.

Dillon furrowed his brows.

"Do you smell that?" I asked.

Dillon sniffed and instantly stiffened his muscles just as the fire alarm blared.

I banged the heels of my palms against the cool steel. "Hello!" I shouted. "Two people are trapped in the elevator!"

Dillon pounded louder than I was able to, but our cries for help were drowned out by shrieks and the alarm.

"We're stuck in the elevator!" I pushed the emergency button again and screamed into the speaker. Not even static returned.

Meanwhile, Dillon dug his fingertips between the metal doors and tried to pry them open again. Unlike before, his movements were desperate. When it didn't work, I joined him—him standing on one side, me on the other, both of us pulling in opposite directions. Our fingertips couldn't get enough traction, though. They slipped off again and again.

The smell of smoke intensified, reminding me of something I'd learned in emergency rescue training. It only took three minutes for a normal-sized structure to become completely engulfed, less than that for it to turn fatal. And while the high-rise was bigger, we'd been tugging and pounding at the doors for a couple minutes already. And counting...

We shoved our fingers deeper into the crack and pulled so hard, sharp pains stabbed my fingertips like my nails might rip off. Finally, the elevator doors opened a couple of inches—just enough to see what was on the other side: a wall.

"We're between floors," Dillon said.

"Shit."

Black smoke billowed in from the ceiling hatch's seal. With a click, the space went dark, but a moment later, another click preceded the amber glow of emergency lights.

"How is the fire spreading this fast?" Dillon asked. "This building must have a sprinkler system?"

This was the exact question investigative journalists researched after a fire killed five people downtown a year ago. On one of the news broadcasts covering the story, the reporters explained that all new high-rises built after 2018 required sprinkler systems, and most older buildings were required to phase them in. But there were exceptions. It depended on the year the building was built and its intended use. Based on the pummeling smoke, this building was either one of those exceptions or hadn't come into compliance yet.

"Lift me onto your shoulders." I coughed, looking up at the escape hatch.

"That's where the smoke is coming in."

"It's our only way out."

Dillon only hesitated for a second before he knelt and let me sit on his shoulders, like we were two teenagers about to play a game of chicken in a swimming pool. When he stood back up, I discovered I still wasn't tall enough to reach the ceiling. With the smoke thickening and the screams and alarms blaring, I held Dillon's head as I carefully got my right foot onto his shoulder, then my left. He sensed what I was doing and grabbed my ankles.

As I stood up, I wobbled, trying to find my center of gravity. Dillon leaned forward and backward in sharp jerks to compensate for it until I was stable enough to stand.

Thankfully, I could now reach the escape hatch, but it didn't budge when I pushed.

With my eyes watering from the thickening smoke, I tried again and again until I realized a lever held it shut. I twisted it, and the escape hatch popped open.

Dense smoke flooded the elevator. The only way out was to go deeper into the worst of it, flames flickering a mere twenty feet above me.

*What could be burning inside an elevator shaft? Pipes? Electrical lines covered in years of flammable grease, maybe?*

The fire stung my eyes with its heat, cracking pops as it stretched down the shaft, reaching to take us in its grip.

I pulled myself up and threw my elbow over the lip, and with Dillon's shove, I yanked my knee up, then slithered my chest on top of the box.

I lay on my stomach and dangled my arm through the opening.

"Take my hand!" I shouted.

He was only three feet beneath my fingers, but when he jumped up, it might as well have been a hundred. He jumped again, and our fingers brushed.

"Higher!" I coughed.

He squatted, sprang up higher, and grabbed my hand. But with the heat, my skin was too sweaty to hold it. Dillon crashed to the bottom on his side, making the elevator jerk.

I risked a quick glance above me and saw the only cables that held us up from certain death were engulfed in the inferno. I wasn't an elevator-cable expert; I didn't know how long the fire would take to compromise its structure, but I had to assume not freaking long. And I seriously doubted brakes would withstand the fire's heat.

My lungs burned, my nose recoiled from the smell of burned

rubber and oil, and my eyes stung so badly that I could barely see through the tears.

I leaned down again. "Come on!" I shouted. "You can do this!"

Dillon tried two more times before staring up at me. A minute ago, he looked so powerful and in control, but now, he looked small. Helpless.

"Just go!" he yelled.

"Grab my hand!"

"Get the hell out of here while you still have a chance!" he choked.

Something popped, and the elevator plunged a few inches before it yanked to a stop.

"I'm not going to have your death on my conscience, so hurry up and grab my hand!"

He jumped four more times, our fingers only touching once.

"This isn't working, so just go, Fallon! Now!"

"Get the strap off your bag!"

Dillon looked at his gym bag and must have realized what I was asking. He unclicked the strap, extended it as long as it would go, and then threw it up to me. I wrapped it around my wrists twice and dangled its end down the emergency opening.

I pushed my feet against the wall, and I had to brace my legs, back, shoulders, and arms so that I didn't fall when he jumped up and grabbed the belt. I clenched my muscles and held my body steady, allowing Dillon the seconds he needed to climb up the strap and grab the lip of the opening.

His elbow flung on top of the elevator, followed by the other.

I locked my hand around his wrist and grabbed his collar as he pulled, grunting from the effort until he finally spilled onto the elevator's roof.

The elevator plummeted a foot.

"Climb!" I pointed to metal rungs along the shaft.

I coughed, choking so hard, I thought I was going to throw up. Dillon did, too, and above our heads, the blue-and-orange fire made a whoosh sound.

*Backdraft,* I thought. Not on us, but nearby.

The heat singed my face as we climbed up to the floor above us. Two silver panels on gliders, normally opened with the elevator's doors, rolled apart when I tugged.

*Thank goodness.*

Another earsplitting pop, and the elevator dropped two feet.

Before I could get out of the shaft, though, a powerful snap cracked above our heads.

"Look out!" Dillon screamed as the elevator's cable whipped by our heads.

And then a metallic grinding sound accelerated, and I watched in disbelief as the elevator we'd been on only moments ago sailed into a free fall for twenty-some stories. Until it crashed with the force of a dynamite explosion.

"Come on!" I shouted.

I threw myself into the hallway, where the fire licked its walls. It was as hot as the inside of an oven, making it even harder to breathe through the hostile cloud of smoke. I covered my mouth with my shirt's sleeve, and Dillon pressed his forearm over his lips.

"Stairs!" I screamed and rushed toward the illuminated Exit sign.

The flames roared up the walls behind us and onto the ceiling as we sprinted to our only salvation.

A popping sound preceded Dillon's shriek. "Fallon!"

He tackled me to the ground and protected my head with his arms as a door-sized piece of fiery drywall crashed down from the ceiling. Right next to us.

"Come on!" He rolled off me and yanked me up by my shoulders.

The door was hard to get open—heavy as sin. As we both pushed, Dillon positioned his body behind me, shielding me from the incinerating heat. We coughed so hard, I feared we'd lose consciousness any second.

Finally, we got the door open and ran into the stairwell.

Just as a whoosh incinerated the rest of the hallway.

Several floors above us, the stairwell was already engulfed. We raced down the steps while I prayed we could make it out alive.

2

"F uck," Dillon said, staring at the engulfed skyscraper.

After climbing down the twenty-some floors, we stood on the ground level, where fire trucks, ambulances, and a growing crowd of onlookers amassed around the structure.

Standing against the backdrop of the morning's pastel-pink sky, the seventy-story building chugged ebony smoke out of its top like a chimney, the upper floors glowing orange with flames crackling outside the windows. The putrid smell of burned metal and wood stung my already-raw nose, and the echoes of sirens racing to the scene silenced the cries of victims, whose once stampede of escapes slowed to a trickle. Then stopped completely.

"Do you think everyone made it out safe?" I asked. As a person trained to help protect people, I felt utterly helpless, unable to do anything but watch trained firefighters battle the blaze.

"I hope so," Dillon said.

*Oh gosh. Zoey.* I'd met her at the gym a few weeks ago. The poor girl had been through a lot lately, barely holding it together after suffering a devastating loss. And she was there today. I needed to make sure she'd made it out alive.

I scrolled through my contacts, grateful we'd exchanged numbers.

**Me: Zoey, are you okay?**

**Zoey: I'm fine. With a crowd on the north end of the building. Are you okay?**

I breathed a sigh of relief.

**Me: Yeah.**

**Zoey: Thank goodness! This was so scary!**

**Me: It was. Stay safe, Zoey.**

**Zoey: You too.**

**Me: Let's do coffee soon?**

**Zoey: Absolutely.**

I coughed, which made my esophagus burn even more.

Dillon put his hand on my shoulder. "Are you okay?"

I nodded, hypnotized by the scene before us. A fire truck extended its ladder as high as it would go, allowing a firefighter to climb up, break through the window with an ax, and enter a floor that didn't have flames sticking out yet.

"You go into a building like any other day," Dillon said, his emotions growing dark and reflective. "You never imagine you won't come out of it." He rubbed the back of his neck. "My brother would've never understood."

The gravity of his words weighted his voice down even lower until he read the questions rolling across my face.

"He's intellectually disabled. Needs round-the-clock care, so he lives in a facility. My mom and I are all he's got. I visit him every Sunday, and if I just stopped showing up…"

Dillon swallowed hard.

My eyes watered, but it wasn't from the flames this time. It was because of how touched I was, sensing Dillon's immense love for his brother. If I were honest, it was also because I was envious.

*I wish I mattered to someone the way Dillon matters to his brother.* To know that if you died, someone out there loved you so much, they would be destroyed. My best friend, Shane, would care, of course. At least I had that. And surely, on some level, no matter how much smaller it was than I wished, my dad would care, too. I shouldn't be so hung up on wishing I were someone's *everything*.

A pop drew our attention to another window that blew out and rained shards of scorching hot glass onto the thankfully cleared sidewalk below.

Fifty feet away, a police officer looked down at his pocket-sized notebook, tapped it with his pen, and nodded before walking away from a pedestrian.

"I'll be right back."

I walked away from Dillon and approached the cop. Chicago employed twelve thousand police officers, spread among various precincts, so it wasn't a surprise that I didn't know him.

The guy appeared to be in his thirties. He was thin with high cheekbones and a narrow jaw.

"Officer O'Connor." I extended my arm and shook his hand firmly. "Is there anything I can do to help?"

He shook his head, motioned to the nearby people. "We're taking witness statements." And then his eyes glided over my appearance, which must have been a dirty mess. "You were inside?"

I nodded and gave him an account of everything I witnessed while he jotted down notes and peppered me with clarification questions.

"I would tell the fire department to look into the elevator shaft. I'm not a fire expert, but I found it odd that it was engulfed when there wasn't any wood or drywall in there to burn."

He raised an eyebrow. "You thinking an accelerant was used?"

"I don't know," I answered. "But it was strange."

He nodded, and after leaving him with my information in case he had any other questions, I made my way back to Dillon.

"Make sure you give your statement before you leave," I said.

Dillon's lips twitched in amusement at my assertive tone when my cell phone buzzed with a text from my father.

**Dad: I know you're upset about what I did, but I love you more than anything.**

*Not anything.* If that were true, he would have shown up to my high school graduation, my college graduation, or my graduation from the police academy. Most dads would've shown up to all three, especially when they had no work conflict preventing them from going. I'd have settled for one, and that didn't even count all the ways he'd let me down before then.

Eleven-year-olds weren't supposed to have to raise themselves.

A stronger person would've cut him out of their life a long time ago, but I guess everyone needed to be loved by their parent, some of us having to chase it harder than others. I'd kept up that chase my whole life, pathetically savoring whatever measly crumbs of affection he'd throw my way. How many times had I gotten my hopes up that things would get better, only to be crushed into dust, rocking myself in the fetal position in tears? Yet I'd kept going back.

But this time was different because he'd gone too far.

For the first time in my life, I'd finally taken the experts' advice and cut Dad out. Addicts couldn't be trusted. Helping him the way I had—funding three rehabs, countless other bills, and groceries—was only enabling him, they'd said. Which, logically speaking, made sense. I'd walk out of those Nar-Anon meetings with my spine straight, ready to decline his calls and lay down an uncrossable line. And every time I'd hear his voice, see his face, or think of the dad before the disease changed him, I'd crumble into my pre-pubescent self, wanting nothing more than my daddy to come home. To hug me and tell me from this point forward, things would finally get better. They had to. And when he'd have no food to eat, all the expert opinions couldn't stop the haunting images of my father suffering. When his landlord threatened to kick him out, they couldn't stop me from envisioning him cold, living in an alley in the dead of winter. So, for years, I couldn't stop doing what they said not to.

But he crossed a line there was no coming back from, and, well, it was the wake-up call I needed. I couldn't enable him. As much as it gutted me and as many times as I cried myself to sleep because of it, I drew a line in the sand. If he wanted a relationship with me, he needed to be sober. Maybe, just maybe, it would finally give him the motivation he needed to get clean.

**Dad: PLEASE call me back. There's something I've never told you, Fallon. I need to tell you before I lose my nerve.**

"Everything okay?" Dillon asked, noticing the look on my face.

I swallowed the pain. "Yeah."

A tickle in my voice box made me cough—a barking, burning cough—and once I started, I couldn't stop. It turned into an all-out fit that drew the attention of a first responder.

"Miss." A guy with a Chicago paramedic patch stitched to his blue shirt approached me. He had a confident tone, but he was so young, I wondered if he'd ever worked a crisis of this magnitude before. "Let me look you over."

The appearance of the EMT snapped me out of my fog, making me realize I'd been here and let the clock tick forward for far too long.

"I have to go," I said.

"Fallon, you need to get checked out."

"I can't be late." I coughed, and this one turned so violent, I gagged.

"Let me at least check your oxygen levels," the EMT insisted.

"I'm fine."

"Breathing makes you barf," Dillon argued. "You're not fine."

I cut my eyes to him. *Traitor.*

"Look, no cabs are getting through." Dillon motioned toward the now-blocked-off roads. "And you can't walk unless you can breathe, so let him help you, and you can be on your way."

I coughed, but before I could argue further, I was ushered inside an ambulance, where I sat on a gray stretcher. I glanced around at all the cubbies filled with medical equipment to help save people: oxygen tanks, blood pressure cuffs, bandages, and defibrillators, among other things.

The EMT put a pulse oximeter on my finger and made me take deep breaths as he listened to my lungs with a stethoscope before doing the same for Dillon.

"You need oxygen." The EMT retrieved a mask attached to a green-and-silver tank and turned it on to the appropriate level of airflow.

But before he could place it on my face, a screaming woman burst out of the skyscraper's front doors. The sleeve of her right arm was singed off, exposing crimson welts that caused the EMT's eyes to widen.

I took in the scene around me, counting thirteen ambulances and noting more victims now spilling out of the building. If help didn't arrive soon to assist with the wave of new victims, this already-dire situation was bound to go from bad to worse. And in the meantime, our EMT appeared to have the least critical patients on his hands—us. He needed to help that lady. Now.

"I got this," Dillon assured and took the mask from the hesitant EMT.

In a typical emergency, an EMT would never let Dillon hold the mask, but this was escalating into a triage situation, and I would be considered green (walking wounded with minor injuries). That lady was probably a yellow (medium priority with moderate injuries) or maybe even a red (a high priority with life-threatening injuries). After a few moments, the EMT rushed to the more critically injured patient and guided her to an ambulance that was open, thanks to other paramedics treating victims where they'd fallen on the ground.

Dillon sat on the bench and positioned his body so we sat face-to-face.

Knees touching.

"Hold still, Fallon." He pressed the oxygen mask against my face, the tip of his finger grazing my skin as he did. Based on the rise and fall of his Adam's apple, the touch seemed to take Dillon a beat to recover from. "Now, breathe."

The air felt cool, going down my throat, hitting the bottom of my lungs. I coughed a couple of times, but it didn't deter Dillon from his mission.

"You need oxygen as badly as I do," I said.

He smirked. "You sound like Darth Vader with this thing over your face."

I took deep breaths in and out and had to remind myself to hurry. Though my boss would be the biggest dickwad in the history of dickwads if he didn't understand why I was late or missed it, I didn't want to give him that first impression of me not being there. Nor did I want to miss when assignments were handed out and volunteer hands shot up for the best parts.

Dillon's thick lips curled down into a serious line, full of fresh emotions.

"You really took charge in that elevator." Which, based on the look in his eyes, was something he was unaccustomed to seeing. Or maybe seeing other women do it, at least. "It was...impressive."

More like well-trained and self-sufficient. After taking care of myself for as long as I could remember, I learned the hard way that people weren't going to step in and solve my problems; I had to do it myself.

Dillon studied my eyes for so long, I thought he'd get lost in them. "You saved my life." He looked at my hair, my hands, my irises. "You could've left me, but you stayed. You saved me."

"Watching people burn to death isn't on my bucket list."

But he didn't smile at my joke. Instead, he scanned my face slowly, his breath hitching as his chestnut eyes locked on mine. I'd never had anyone look at me like this—staring as if the most important thing in the world was to learn everything about me.

And I had to admit...I loved it.

I pulled the mask off my face and pressed it to his. "Your turn to breathe."

His lips parted, and a slow smile spread across his face. "I want to take you out."

I couldn't deny my attraction to him. If I'd met Dillon earlier, I'd have gone out with him, no question. Enjoying the lighthearted company of a hot guy from time to time was fun, and romance provided color to an otherwise bleak existence. But I wasn't sure now was the best time to date someone, not with starting this task force.

"What?" Dillon asked. "You don't date?"

"I don't have a lot of time for dating."

"Make time," he implored. Not in a pushy, won't-take-no-for-an-answer kind of way, but a charming, I-promise-it-will-be-worth-your-time kind of way.

I couldn't help but smile. "And if I refuse?"

He pinned me with a seductive stare, his eyes glimmering with hope. "I owe you my life, so I'd have to become your indentured servant. Your love slave. Feed you grapes, massage your feet, whisk you away to an island."

I laughed.

But even if I made time to date, Dillon's good looks and confidence spoke of someone who probably dated normal people. Not someone like me, who couldn't even remember what normal felt like.

"My life is complicated," I said.

"So is mine," he reasoned, probably trying to put me at ease. "My world kind of imploded when I was thirteen." He shrugged. "So, I guess we have that whole complicated-life thing in common."

I raised my eyebrows. "What happened when you were thirteen?"

He grinned. "You'll have to let me buy you dinner to find out."

I hesitated.

"Come on. After saving my life, the least I can do is treat you to some ridiculously overpriced meal. I'll even splurge for dessert."

I sighed. "I don't even know your last name."

"McPherson."

I looked at his pleading gaze. "When did you have in mind?"

Dillon pulled the oxygen mask off his face and stared between my eyes and my mouth. "Is that a yes?"

CHICAGO'S POLICE HEADQUARTERS STRETCHED ALONG MICHIGAN Avenue for an entire city block. Its five stories of sculpted concrete and perfectly spaced windows showcased clean architecture lines, a far cry from the dirty cases investigated inside.

I ran toward the conference room on the third floor. Past a dozen mahogany doors, past the wooden benches that lined the gray hallway, past the grouping of colorful flags perched along the wall, and when I finally arrived, I hesitated behind the door's frosted glass.

I'd managed to clean the soot off myself and change into my uniform in record time, but I was still a few minutes late, and my new boss had a reputation for being harsh. Praying I could contain the fallout, I took a calming breath, pulled the door open, and walked in.

3

Sixteen officers—a mixture of Chicago PD (including my best friend, Shane) and DEA agents—turned their heads and stared at me with tight faces that rolled tension through the air like a fog machine. They sat around an oval mahogany table, peppered with frosted water glasses that sparkled with sunlight from oversize windows, but one officer was standing, introducing himself to the man who stood in the front—DEA Sergeant Marcus Burch.

*The* Sergeant Marcus Burch. In the flesh. I couldn't believe I was standing in the same room as him. The man who'd kept going through a raid, even after a bullet had shattered his kneecap. The man responsible for taking down some of the biggest criminals in America. The man who'd written more training manuals than anyone in DEA history.

Rumor had it, he was three years away from retirement, and with thirty-six months left, he planned to eradicate one more drug organization on his way out. Which was aggressive. That gave him roughly six months to identify all the players, twelve months to investigate and gather evidence, and eighteen months to prosecute. I guess the way he saw it, you could either fade into oblivion at the end of your career or go out in a blaze of glory.

His pale skin reddened along his throat, and his lips tightened into a thin line beneath his silver-speckled mustache.

"Officer O'Connor, I presume?" he said in a gruff voice that reminded me of thunder.

He carried his tall, lean frame with the kind of authority that could make a grown man cower, his meaty hands clenched his hips, and his black hair was still thick, as if too scared of his wrath to succumb to the typical thinning for a man his age. But the most intimidating thing about him was his sharp eyes, which sliced through the room and stabbed me with animosity.

"Yes, sir, I apologize for being l—"

"Have somewhere more important to be than the official DEA task force kickoff meeting?"

"No, sir, I—"

"Meeting started seven minutes ago, O'Connor."

"I was detained by a f—"

"Do I strike you as the type of guy that gives a crap why you're late?"

Based on my research of him, this was a man who'd served his country, obeyed orders, and never taken BS from anyone. Let alone accepted excuses.

"Sir—"

"We'll talk about this after the meeting; I'm not going to waste everybody else's time."

*I wonder what the world record is for the quickest time in destroying one's career.*

I tried to hide my despair as I walked to the only open seat in the room—the one next to Shane, who must have saved it for me. But when I sat, the look Burch gave me—and by look, I mean, a glower that could've made an old lady drop dead from a heart attack—said he hadn't meant for me to wait *inside* this room.

I squared my shoulders, trying to feign confidence that I belonged here. If I missed the meeting, I would miss the entire case and investigation setup, which they hadn't even gotten to yet. They'd still been doing introductions when I walked in. If Burch accepted my apology and let me stay on the team, I couldn't afford to be behind everyone else.

"Sarge," another uniform interrupted from the doorway. "A word?"

Burch tried to murder me for a few more seconds with his death scowl before he exited the room.

Shane leaned closer. His wavy black hair looked a half-inch longer than normal, as if he'd been running a hand through it, his thick brows drew together, and his athletic frame tensed. "Where the hell've you been?" he whispered.

Shane Hernandez had been my best friend since middle school. Clarification: my only friend. We met in sixth grade after I'd moved from our beautiful brick home on its pristinely manicured lawn to the trailer park where I'd served the rest of my childhood sentence. And by trailer park, I don't mean one of those charming manufactured homes. I mean, the trailer park that gave other trailer parks a lousy reputation—disheveled and full of the one in four families that didn't have enough to eat each day. It was at this trailer park that I first saw Shane.

The son of a stay-at-home mother and a police deputy in Blue Island, Illinois, Shane was four when his father was killed. In the years that followed, his mother struggled. Two small kids and a mountain of debt were too big for the death benefits his father had earned, so eventually, she fell behind on their mortgage and rented the trailer next to us.

But at least Shane's mom ensured they always had food. She was good like that. Reliable. Getting food stamps and doing what she needed to do to ensure her kids ate. I, on the other hand, had fought against perpetual hunger during the first half of that school year.

Enter the day I talked to Shane for the first time. We'd been assigned seats next to each other in class, and as the weeks had passed, I pretended not to notice Shane's flashes of worry when my stomach growled. Especially when it still growled after lunch.

And on that day, the ache in my stomach was all I could think about. I watched the other kids with their overabundance of food throw half their lunch away—perfectly good food, thrown away—and bit my lip, wishing they'd just left it on the table so I could've discreetly taken it.

Looking back on it, what I did was stupid. I'd always been careful about dumpster diving *before* school and off school grounds, so I'd have enough to pick at in front of the lunchroom teachers to make them assume I was just a picky eater, not a kid going hungry. But that day, my dumpster dive had failed to produce anything, so when Jessica Roche threw her entire uneaten sandwich away and everyone cleared the lunchroom, I acted on instinct. Hunger was primal, and a clean, untouched sandwich, still in the bag, was too enticing.

It'd been sitting there, right on top of all the other trash. So, after one last glance around, I reached in and took it.

At the precise moment Shane walked in to retrieve his forgotten water bottle.

Instantly, my cheeks became a furnace.

He looked at my hand as it retracted from the can, then my face. His ocean-blue eyes pierced straight through my protective layers and exposed my hidden truth of all of those stomach growls. I felt naked, standing before him, terrified of the power he now had to destroy what was left of my life if he told someone about this.

"Fallon," Mrs. Swanson barked. Because suddenly, she was there, too—because, for the love of all things holy, why wouldn't she also walk in at the worst possible moment? "Did you just pull that from the trash?"

"I—"

"No," Shane said. "I tossed it to her. She missed."

Mrs. Swanson looked from Shane to me. "Lunch is over. Did you not have enough to eat?"

Dad didn't take the best care of me anymore, but he was all I had left in this world. If they investigated, they'd take me away from him and make me live with complete strangers. I'd rather die than have that happen.

"I did. I just..."

"It's for after school," Shane lied. "We have a study hour planned."

Mrs. Swanson looked back to Shane's convincing face before

pursing her lips. "Both of you, get to class."

Shane grabbed his water bottle, and we retreated into the hallway together.

"Thanks," I said quietly.

The next day, he plopped down across from me at the lunch table. I usually sat by myself because being poor made me unpopular. Shane opened his brown sack, pulled half his sandwich out, and placed it on the table in front of me.

"You don't have to tell me anything else," Shane said. "But I need to know one thing."

I looked into his severe gaze as the hum of voices around the lunchroom seemed to fade.

"Is anyone hurtin' you, Fallon?"

I blinked.

"Are you safe?"

I swallowed. "No one's hurting me," I whispered.

Shane tilted his head and chewed his cheek, clearly trying to decide if he believed me, before finally relaxing into acceptance.

"It has grape jelly," he said. "If you're not a fan, I can leave it off tomorrow."

And that was that. As much as I detested taking charity, Shane didn't make it feel like charity at all. He acted like we were just two friends, sharing lunch, and from that day on, we became as close as brother and sister.

Cut to today.

"You left before I was up," Shane continued.

Fun fact: thanks to sky-high rent, Shane wasn't just a friend and fellow cop; he was also my roommate. Two bedrooms, though—totally platonic.

"What happened?" Shane pressed.

"It's a long story." One I wouldn't go into right now. Right now, I had to focus on salvaging my spot on this task force, and I certainly didn't want Burch to catch me talking about this and misconstrue it as me trying to garner sympathy.

"You've never been late to work before. Let alone today."

"I know; I'll explain later."

"Are you okay?"

"Yes."

"Your voice sounds hoarse."

It'd sound a lot worse if Dillon didn't insist that I get an oxygen treatment.

"There was an incident," I hedged.

Before Shane had the chance to ask me more questions, the door swung back open.

"We're going to need to make this fast," Burch declared as he walked back inside. "A group of us needs to head over to a scene. Officers are processing it as we speak."

When he saw me sitting here, his eyes narrowed, and he opened his mouth like he was about to go off on me and kick me out of the room. But he must have seen the determination in my eyes and sensed I'd try again to explain why I was late. So...ticktock. Crime scene.

"See me after, O'Connor," Burch snarled. "We'll discuss your future on this team."

Future. As in career-ending exit, based on his tone.

"We're in the preliminary stages of investigating the largest narcotics group in the United States," Burch began. "They're highly organized, extremely intelligent, and operate more like a Fortune 500 than an organized crime unit. They have a clear strategy, execute it with precision, and trade in volume."

Whoever came up with the idea for DEA task forces should be given the Medal of Honor. By partnering with city counterparts, the DEA could draw on the local expertise in this area, share resources, and increase possibilities with investigations. Plus, it gave us a great experience on our résumés, so I'd have a better chance to land a full-time role with the DEA, and Shane would have a better shot at one day becoming police chief.

"Now, in terms of narcotics," Burch continued, "we have the usual suspects: heroin, cocaine, diverted pharma, cannabis, but the ones that are on the rise right now are fentanyl—a key driver in the current opioid epidemic."

Shane gave me a worried look.

"And methamphetamine. Vast quantities of which are being smuggled in from Mexico. This is where the group we're investigating comes in: The Chicago Syndicates."

Burch moved to an eight-foot-long corkboard in front of the room and flipped it over. On the other side was an organization chart pinned up with rainbow-colored pushpins with two leaders, four headshots beneath it with the word *Captain* over their pictures, sixteen other leaders beneath them, and at the bottom, dozens of faces titled *Soldiers*. Only a third of the portraits, however, were of actual people with names. The others were a dark cartoon-like silhouette with a question mark under them.

"Our first goal in this task force is to put names and faces to every single one of these roles up here." Burch took a drink of water, plunked the glass down on the table. "This case ain't going to be easy. That protective layer they built by only distributing in larger volume means the typical play of going after the dime-store dealers and working our way up won't work. Further, one of our primary tools to vet operations like these is the use of confidential informants. We work with someone on the inside to get a baseline of the organization, but in this case, no one is talking. And when I say no one? I mean, no one. Not a word. One of the reasons for that, more than likely, is because of this guy."

He pinned a photo of a young man's mugshot to the board. "Christopher Cantrell—a soldier in the org—street name: C.C. Picked up on a narcotics charge, he was facing a life sentence due to his priors. After laying out his nonexistent future for him and his family, we offered Cantrell a deal—at which point he'd be moved into immediate protective custody, awaiting a detailed interview, where he was going to give up names, the structure, everything on a silver platter. Two hours before the interview, he's with two of the most experienced protection agents who, between the two of them, kept over sixty witnesses alive. But not in this case. We were never able to thoroughly interview Cantrell because he was executed right there in protective custody."

"How'd they get past those two guards?" an officer asked.

"They were executed first. As was Cantrell's entire family to send a message."

I picked at my thumbnail.

"This group runs a clean operation," Burch said. "No one's talked, and I'm tired of it. We need to find a good CI. Someone that can help us put names with faces if we have any shot at taking them down soon. We'll work leads. Establish rapport.

"Meanwhile, we need to get out there and start identifying these guys. I need names. Street names, legal names—I don't care. Just get me something to work with. The only lead we have right now is this."

Burch took an eight-by-ten photograph out of a manila folder and pinned it to the board.

"This was obtained during a surveillance operation."

He pointed to the image. It was zoomed in and cropped to show the unclothed back of a man. He wore a hat, so we couldn't see his hair color, if he even had any—just his bare-skinned back.

And on it, a basketball-sized tattoo of a scorpion holding an American flag.

*Why would someone tattoo something like that on their body?*

"This picture was taken three weeks ago when my agents observed what was initially believed to be a possible narcotics move," Burch continued. "This tattoo was later shown to someone in interrogation, who confirmed it belongs to one of the captains in the Syndicates. Find the tat, we identify a captain."

Burch rubbed his chin, looking like he debated on adding something that was on his mind. He gazed over the group of agents and officers and put his hands on his hips. "One more thing I need to make clear, to give you a chance to back out now."

Back out now? What could he possibly say to us to make us reconsider being on one of the most elite task forces led by one of the best —if not *the* best—DEA sergeants ever?

"I believe they're about to make a major play," Burch said. He let his proclamation hang in the air, thickening the room with suspense.

With more busts under his belt than most anyone else in the DEA, his experience was something to be taken seriously. I knew there was the scent of an investigation. The gut feeling, hairs standing up in the back of your neck. Burch had seen things, probably started noticing patterns, and saw what ended up happening when those things played out. It didn't mean he was right, of course—only time would tell us that—but if he said they were about to do something big, then I absolutely believed they were.

I bounced my knee to get the excited energy out.

"My hypothesis?" he continued. "They're about to do a major expansion, which could mean war with the crews in New York or Miami, who are just as ruthless. There's never been a more important time to get in front of this," he said. "Now, little chatter that we did have came to a complete stop weeks before C.C. was killed. History says when that happens, it happens for a reason. People cleaning house, getting their ducks in a row for something. Whether it's expansion or something else, we need to figure out what it is."

The task force agents took notes, several nodding their heads.

"We'll be on the front lines, the faces of the people trying to lock up the biggest and most sophisticated narcotics criminals in the country. I don't need to remind you of the dangers."

As Burch looked around the room and allowed his ominous warning to wrap around our throats and strangle us, the cautionary tales they'd gone over in training flashed through my mind—shootouts, agents who had been killed in the line of duty.

"One more thing," he said. "This is not the case to try and be a cowboy. Later in the investigation, we'll be getting closer to the enemy, but listen to me when I say this: if you are not ready for something, do not volunteer. There's no honor in going undercover and getting yourself killed."

Undercover? I didn't realize that was a possibility. I thought this was going to be a ton of investigation. But being undercover and posing as one of them? Nothing would give me more satisfaction than getting to beat them at their own game. Thank goodness I'd taken all that extra undercover training. It'd give me a better chance at getting picked.

I sat straighter in my seat, tasting the opportunity ahead of us. *Well, if I'm still part of the team, that is.*

"All right, that's enough for today. Hernandez, Marks, Proctor, wait in the hall for me. You'll accompany me to a one-ten."

A first-degree homicide? The only reason the DEA sergeant would take his team there was if he thought it had something to do with this case. Talk about starting with a nuclear-sized bang.

I smiled, thrilled that Shane got called in to the action, yet wished I could be at that scene, too.

"Rest of you, you're dismissed for the day. Except you, O'Connor. You get your ass up here."

Shane put a hand on my shoulder before he strolled out the door with the rest of the officers.

I took a deep breath and tried to calm my nerves as I walked up to the front, knowing the fate of my career hung in the balance of what happened next.

As Burch moved the board to the side of the room, he said, "On a case like this, do you know what happens when an officer gets sloppy?"

I opened my mouth to answer, but he cut me off.

"Puts the lives of everyone else working with her in jeopardy." He turned around and flipped the board around so that anyone passing the conference room wouldn't be able to see the information. "I don't tolerate BS on my team, O'Connor."

"I was in a fire, sir."

Burch tensed. *Why?* He kept his back to me, though, refusing to show his cards, I guess. So, I continued.

"After finishing a workout, I was in an elevator with a civilian when it stopped, and the shaft filled with smoke. We gained access to the escape hatch and climbed out. Made it to the stairwell and escaped. I was treated on the scene for minor smoke inhalation and then came here."

Burch turned around and stared at me with the oddest expression. "The one on Wacker?"

"I—you heard about it, sir?"

"Word travels fast."

Why did it seem like he was holding something back?

"I was told I should be at the hospital, getting treated for smoke inhalation, but I refused to miss any more time than I already had. I want to be part of this task force, and I want you to understand how serious my intent is."

Burch tightened his lips and narrowed his hardened eyes, looking like he wanted to fire me. And something told me that from this point forward, he would look for any reason to do it. Inferno or no inferno, *not* letting me go would make him look weak in front of his team. And that was unacceptable. But he also had to know that dismissing somebody with undue cause—and holy crud, if almost dying wasn't undue cause, what was?—would open a ton of bureaucratic red tape for him.

Burch tugged at his ear and took a step closer, making sure he towered over me when he said, "When you're on my team? Don't put yourself in buildings that catch fire."

*Reasonable.*

But Burch earned his unreasonableness. You didn't get the kind of results that he did by being soft. Maybe by the end of the investigation, I could get him to hate me a little less. The more important headline was that I'd spared my job.

*For now.* What I needed to do was stay out of his line of sight. Let him cool down, give him space because Burch held all the power over the one thing that was most important to me—my career. He could end it with one phone call. And I had a feeling that if I did anything else to annoy him or made a mistake, he'd destroy my career, no question.

"Come on," he said. "You can ride with Proctor."

*What?*

I suppressed the panic that warned me that his invitation to work the scene wasn't a compliment; it was a penalty flag. I was officially on probation. Burch was going to keep an eagle eye on me, waiting for me to screw up so he'd have an indisputable reason to dismiss me.

And as if that weren't bad enough, I was about to share a ride with the one person who hated me even more than Burch did.

4

Proctor rested his right wrist on his cruiser's steering wheel and smirked as he peered at me. "Have a buddy who worked the scene of a fire this morning."

*Here we go.*

Proctor, who sported a blond buzz cut and stocky torso, was an officer from my precinct who I'd had the displeasure of working with. The guy's hobbies included weightlifting, checking himself out in the mirror incessantly, and trying to make my life a living hell.

Why did the guy hate me? To start with, Proctor had been offended when I politely turned down an invitation to go to dinner with him. Cue him throwing condescending jabs at me. Then, things got worse when I received high praise from our boss and severely escalated when I made the task force and he didn't. The only reason he eventually made the team was that one of the original officers had to move to Montana for personal reasons. Being waitlisted was a massive blow to his planet-sized ego, and I guess the only way to soothe it was to belittle me.

Constantly.

I usually tried to ignore it, but I was so not in the mood for it today.

"Said you were canoodling with some guy."

"So, you're keeping tabs on me now?" I asked.

"You gonna go out with him?"

He didn't give two craps about my love life; he just enjoyed antagonizing me.

"The light's green."

He took his foot off the brake. "You going to give this sucker a chance? Or shut him out like you do everyone else?" Proctor asked. Not in a sincere way, of course. In a you'll-screw-this-up-like-you-always-do way.

I clenched my jaw. "Still licking your wounds that I turned you down?" Because honestly, that was what this was about, wasn't it? No female could ever turn down Earth's gift to women.

Unfortunately, my uppercut provoked Proctor to double down.

"You've got *one* friend." Proctor tugged his thumb toward Shane's cruiser behind us. "And your longest relationship with a guy's been what, two weeks?"

"Maybe you should pay attention to your own lack of a love life instead of being obsessed with mine," I snarled.

I didn't want Proctor to know his words bothered me. I didn't shut people out; I dated casually because I was a busy, career-minded woman.

"Whatever," Proctor said. "Can't believe you're even on this team after the stunt your dad pulled."

Despite myself, I shrank two inches. I hated that any mention of my father had this effect on me. After all these years, I should have been stronger by now.

My cell phone buzzed with a text.

**Dillon: How are you feeling?**

Dillon's message was a welcome relief in a vehicle laced with so much hostility. I smiled and immediately answered him.

**Me: Throat feels raw. And I'm tired, but otherwise, I'm okay. You?**

**Dillon: If you start to feel sick, call me. I'll take you to the ER. Okay?**

**Me: Okay. Are you all right?**

**Dillon: I'm fine, thanks to you.**

As three dots blinked at the bottom of the screen, indicating that he was typing, I held my cell perfectly still, eager to see whatever text appeared next.

**Dillon: I can't stop thinking about you. I've never had a woman stuck in my head like this. It's very distracting.**

I smiled wider.

**Me: Maybe your fixation with me is just because I pulled you out of that elevator. Maybe it'll fade.**

This time, when he began texting back, I found myself leaning closer to the screen, watching every dot pulse as seconds ticked by.

**Dillon: It's not just because you saved me, Fallon. I noticed you the second I saw you and kept noticing you as everything unfolded. You impressed the hell out of me, even before the fire started. And no, it won't fade. It's only been growing since we parted. Feels like I've been away from you for a lot longer than an hour. I can't wait to see you tonight. Have a great day.**

I hid my grin from Proctor by looking out the window at the skyscrapers passing us by, grateful he kept his big mouth shut for the remainder of the drive.

Proctor parked his squad car behind several others on the south side of the Chicago River, which was flanked by seventy-story buildings that were home to some of the largest businesses in Illinois. Not the usual place for a crime scene. Yellow *Police Line Do Not Cross* caution tape had already established a wide perimeter, causing traffic to bottleneck with curious drivers. Uniformed officers manned the nearby bridge to shoo away lookie-loos who might inadvertently drop something in the water and contaminate evidence. Water that smelled faintly of rotten eggs—a smell that would likely only intensify in this baking heat.

Shane, Proctor, Marks, and I followed Burch as he approached the bald homicide detective wearing a black suit.

"What've we got, Detective?" Burch asked, shaking his hand.

"Adam Terrell. Captain in the Chicago Syndicates," the detective started, looking at a credit card–sized notebook. "Witness out for a jog this morning saw the body under the bridge and called it in. Cause of death TBD. Body couldn't have been there long." The detective pointed to the surrounding buildings with his pen. "Someone would've seen it. Most likely dumped in the middle of the night."

"Still risky to dump it in this part of the city," Proctor said, trying to add his weight in.

"You don't think he was killed under the bridge?" Burch asked.

"No," the detective said.

"Why?"

"I'll show you."

He motioned for us to follow him, and as we walked, Shane positioned himself next to me.

"Heard the news on the way over," Shane whispered. "Please tell me you weren't at the gym this mornin'."

Shane appeared to hold his breath as he waited for my reaction.

"Close call," I admitted. "But I'm fine."

I hated when Shane looked worried like that; he'd done enough worrying for me when we were kids.

Before Shane had the chance to ask me anything else, Burch stopped in the shade of the rust-colored bridge near the waterline.

My stomach twisted. Seeing the crime scene made the worst moment of my life flood back to me.

*I reach for the doorknob of our trailer, hearing that the television is on inside. I twist the knob and then—*

"O'Connor." Burch waved me forward.

It took me a moment to swallow my past and focus on the present.

"What do you see?" Burch asked.

*He's testing me. Get it wrong, and he might deem you incompetent—due cause for termination.*

The body that rested in six inches of water on the concrete base was nude, save for a single blood-soaked sock. His eyes and mouth were frozen open, as if he'd been screaming in agony at the exact moment of death, which, based on the immense amount of lacerations, burns, and other injuries, was probably exactly what happened.

"He was tortured." I finally found my voice, answering Burch's question. "There would have been a lot of screaming, so it had to have taken place somewhere remote. Or soundproof."

Burch nodded. "This is the only captain in the crime ring that we had identified."

"Which can't be a coincidence," I reasoned.

"I questioned this guy a couple weeks ago," Marks said. "I was doing patrol in a fairly abandoned area and saw him walking around. Turned out, he had a quarter of meth on him, so he got charged with possession."

"A quarter?" Proctor choked. "Why would a captain carry around anything, let alone something that small?"

Marks shrugged. "He never gave that up."

"And why torture him like this?" Proctor pressed. "Normal execution is two in the head, and you're dead."

"During his interrogation, he's the one that confirmed the tattoo belonged to a captain," Marks said.

"Why'd he give that up?" Shane asked.

"Was a slipup in a heated back-and-forth," Marks remembered.

Burch rubbed his chin. "Could explain why he was killed. The one thing the Chicago Syndicates do not tolerate is intel leaking."

"Or maybe it was because he got a possession charge," Proctor mused.

"Either way, this guy's been a loyal captain for years." Burch rubbed his mustache. "They could have buried the body where we would never find it." He glanced at the growing crowd of spectators. Then at the torture marks, the loyal captain, the very public location in the heart of the city.

"This isn't a murder," Burch said. "It's a message."

Shane, Marks, and I exchanged glances and then looked back at Burch.

"To the Syndicates?" Shane asked. "Or to us?"

A stylish guy wearing black slacks, a hunter-green button-down, and a detective badge on his belt interjected and waved Burch over.

*That's detective Fisher. In the past, I'd shadowed him for training purposes, but what would he be doing here?*

As they stood, talking twenty feet away, Burch glanced at me with that look people had when they were talking about you.

I twisted my hands together to massage away my anxiety. What could they be saying about me? And why did they look so irritated by whatever it was?

"You okay?" Marks approached me.

Thirty-three years old with blond hair and a thin frame, Marks was my mentor, assigned to me when I'd started the force. He was a man I admired for how much he adored his family, whose pictures blanketed his desk at the precinct.

"How's your wife feeling?" I managed.

I wanted to ask if he noticed Burch glaring at me, but I was too embarrassed to draw attention to Burch's animosity.

"Huge. I could get the call at any second." He held up a picture on his phone of his two little girls—a toddler and his four-year-old, both with baby blond hair, big blue eyes. "Jess took this yesterday."

"They're beautiful."

"They take after their mother. Maddie, the little one, runs up to me the second I walk in the door and hangs on to me like a monkey the rest of the night. Doesn't let me go."

A pang hit my chest. Those girls were so lucky to have a dad like him. But it was obvious that Marks considered himself the lucky one; he clearly went home every night to a house overflowing with love. Which made me think…

This morning, I'd been obsessed with missing out on my coveted seat on this task force, but after nearly losing my life, I was beginning to wonder if maybe I was missing out on so much more.

"Looks like you're being summoned," Marks said, nodding to Burch, who waved me over.

I swallowed my apprehension, straightened my shoulders, and approached the men.

"O'Connor," Burch started. "This is Detective Fisher."

"We've met."

I'd trained with Fisher around the time he'd worked the tragedy that unfolded in the city a while back with that girl Jenna Christiansen. News stories said she'd moved to the city to go after her dreams, only to find herself in a nightmare.

But Fisher was a homicide detective, one who wasn't working this scene, so why was he here?

"Need you to tell us exactly what happened this morning," Burch insisted as he scraped his thumbnails against his fingertips.

I glanced over my shoulder at the murder scene we were supposed to be processing—the urgent murder scene that was deteriorating by the second, thanks to the water. What could be more important than that?

"They *do* think it was arson," I deduced.

Burch exchanged a look with Fisher, who cleared his throat and said, "The initial report just came in. Confirms telltale signs of it, yes."

Okay...

And Fisher must be the lead detective on the case, which sadly meant someone must not have survived.

But why interrupt an active murder scene to talk about this now? And why did Burch take such an interest?

"You told the officer on the scene you were on the fifty-fifth floor, that correct?" Fisher pressed.

I nodded. "The gym. Got a workout in. Why?"

Fisher exchanged a look with Burch.

"Appears the fire started on that floor, right next to the elevator shaft."

Okay, I wasn't an arson expert, so what did that mean? Would it spread faster through the shaft to the other floors?

"You mentioned the stairwell was also engulfed," Fisher said, looking at his notebook. "That correct?"

"Yes. Is that a point in the investigation?"

"So, maybe they wanted someone dead enough to block all escape routes," Burch suggested.

Wanted *someone* dead? Arson was one thing. Attempted murder was another. Attempted murder that risked the lives of thousands? That was a stretch.

"There are a lot easier ways to kill someone than setting fire to an entire building full of people," I said.

"Unless you don't want police to know which person is the target," Burch said.

"Is that the theory you're working?"

"It's early," Fisher said. "Have to wait for the full investigation before speculating." Code for not willing to share his theory.

"And yet I know how important those first gut feelings are," I pressed.

Fisher evaluated me. "Has anyone threatened you recently?"

"Threatened *me*?"

Burch and Fisher exchanged a look. Fisher shook his head, urging him to keep his mouth shut, but Burch measured something else—something more important than this guy's annoyance.

"Eyewitnesses saw two men loitering near the elevator, O'Connor," Burch said. "Where the fire started."

There was something in the way that Fisher looked at me—fixed gaze, leaning into my words—that made me think this was more than just a routine follow-up interview.

"Meaning?"

Burch delivered the news like a doctor giving a sad diagnosis. "They may have been targeting you, O'Connor."

I blinked. "There were a lot of people in that gym," I said.

"We'll look into everyone," Fisher said.

But that would take time. In the meanwhile, I sensed from his tone that I was their focus.

Which didn't make any sense. I didn't have any enemies. "No one would have a reason to target me."

"Being a cop is a reason."

"I'm one of twelve thousand Chicago police officers. I'm too new to have pissed someone off bad enough to try a one-ten on a cop."

"You're on my task force."

*Oh. That's why he cares so much.* That was where his head was going, the hypothesis hitting me loud and clear.

"Along with almost twenty other people, sir, so why me? Why not one of them? And how would anyone even know I'm on the task force?" And why now when we hadn't even started and had done absolutely nothing to pose any threat at all?

I guess when you'd been the leader of many missions, you'd seen some of the craziest stuff that people were capable of. And clearly, that made you a bit paranoid that any coincidence was no coincidence at all, that it was all related to you and your task force's mission.

"May not know the full motive yet, but I never discount facts. First day of this investigation, a Syndicates captain is found tortured, and one of my DEA agents almost gets killed in an arson."

Still.

"Why would *I* be a target?" I pressed.

"I don't know," Burch admitted. "But we better find out."

5

"Do you think it's true?" Shane's eyebrows pulled together.

I put fresh makeup on in our apartment's bathroom while Shane leaned against the doorframe, watching me.

"I don't think it makes a lot of sense," I assured.

"But *they* think you might have been targeted."

"Key word being *might*. I'm sure it had nothing to do with me."

Shane didn't look convinced, but I didn't want him to worry over a mere hypothesis.

"Can we drop it for now?" I asked.

We'd been talking about this for a while already, and all this wondering wasn't productive.

Besides, there was something else I wanted to ask him about before I left for my date with Dillon. I'd told Shane what Proctor had said but hadn't discussed how it'd made me feel.

As Shane scrubbed his face and let out an exhausted breath, I studied him—my best friend. The guy who'd hopefully be honest with me even if I didn't like the answer.

"Do you think I shut people out?" I asked.

Shane's jaw became a statue of frustration. "Don't listen to Proc-

380 | KATHY LOCKHEART

tor; he's just trying to get into your head, hoping it'll make you screw up at work."

"Doesn't mean he's wrong," I allowed.

In fact, now that I thought more objectively about it, what he said was true—I'd never had a boyfriend last longer than two weeks.

I thought the reason I'd always kept things casual was that I was career-focused, but seeing Marks today reminded me that a lot of career-minded people had significant others. Families even. So, what was my hang-up, then? Why, in all these years, hadn't I ever really opened up to anyone?

"I've never told anyone, except you, about my past," I admitted. "Don't you think that's pretty damning evidence that I don't let people in?"

"I think you're a very private person."

*That's a yes.*

I never discussed anything personal. "All I ever talk about on dates is work."

Maybe that was why I didn't get a lot of callbacks for a second date. If I tried to get to know someone but the only thing they would discuss was their career, I wouldn't feel a connection, either.

"Why do you think I do that?"

Shane sighed and regarded me in the mirror. "Honest truth?"

"No, lie to me."

Shane frowned, unamused. "I think it's because you don't like talking about what happened to you. About…"

How my dad being an addict wasn't even the worst part of my childhood.

"I don't like people pitying me, and I don't want to be a Debbie Downer." I evaluated myself in the mirror, and for the first time, I said out loud what I never wanted to admit to myself. "Maybe I'm afraid people will never look at me the same when they find out what I came from."

That tasted awful coming out of my mouth. Giving a damn about what other people thought of me was weak and pathetic.

"Your history shaped you into the warrior you are today, Fallon.

You should be proud of everything you've overcome and wear it as a badge of honor."

My eyes stung as tears threatened to form. "What if other people don't see it that way? What if they look at me like the trailer trash I was when I was younger?"

Shane tightened his lips. "A, you were never trailer trash, Fallon. And B, if someone ever, ever looks at you like that, they don't deserve to be in your presence, or your life. Better to find out the guy's a douchebag now than later."

I bit my lip. "So, this is what normal people talk about on dates? Their super-depressing past?"

"Opening up is a vulnerable thing," Shane said. "You don't have to do it if you're not ready."

*Maybe I'll never be.* But if I didn't change things, I would wind up alone.

Just like when I was a kid…

I didn't want to feel alone like that ever again.

I wasn't sure if I was ready or even wanted anything more than casual dating. Part of me wondered if I was too broken for it, but I was willing to at least approach things differently with Dillon and keep an open mind.

"You going to tell him?"

I sighed. "I don't know."

Knocking on the door interrupted us and made butterflies float through my stomach. Shane stood in the living room, watching as I danced to the front door, and as soon as I opened it, my mouth went dry.

*Holy smokes.*

Dillon was sinfully gorgeous. His dark hair complemented his sexy stubble and eyebrows. Lean muscles pushed against the high-end fabric of his white button-down, as if the cloth were incapable of containing his rugged strength, and each curve of his chiseled face drew my gaze to his magnetic eyes. I'd never dated anyone so danger-ously handsome. No, handsome was an understatement, an insult to someone of his caliber. If sexiness were an Olympic sport, this guy would win the gold medal, hands down.

I'd never had anyone look at me this way, as if he'd thought about me every moment since we'd parted. His brown eyes drifted through my skin, as if able to see every part of me.

"Whoa." Dillon's gaze skimmed my knee-length red dress, my twisted-up hair, and dangling earrings. He leaned down and pressed his lips against my cheekbone—holy moly, the spark from his mouth on my skin unleashed a tsunami of pleasure—and he murmured, "You look amazing."

Dillon handed me a bouquet of two dozen pink roses in a crystal vase. No guy had ever given me flowers before, let alone something this nice.

"They're beautiful, thank you." I looked at Shane standing there and motioned with my chin. "Dillon, this is my friend and roommate, Shane. Shane, Dillon."

Dillon raised his eyebrows, clearly surprised to find a guy in my apartment.

Shane walked up and shook Dillon's hand. Hard, by the looks of it.

"Nice to meet you." Dillon smiled.

"Same." They finished shaking hands, and then Shane went into his bedroom to give us privacy.

"Hungry?" Dillon asked.

"Starving."

This restaurant was gorgeous. White tablecloths. Women in high-end dresses and even higher heels. Champagne flutes, waiters in tuxedos, lighting carefully crafted to replicate the warm glow of candlelight.

Dillon pulled my chair out for me, and as he walked around and took his seat, he didn't even glance at the other women in this restaurant even though many had movie-star looks. In fact, his piercing gaze never left mine, not even when our waiter came by to take our drink order.

"Do you like wine?" Dillon asked me.

I hesitated. "I'll just have water."

The way he tilted his head made me wonder if he'd ask me why I didn't drink alcohol, but I hoped he wouldn't. It would open a depressing explanation before we even opened the menus.

When the waiter scampered off, Dillon leaned forward and rested his elbows on the table as he smiled at me.

"You live with that guy?" he asked, surprised amusement lacing his words.

I nodded. "Shane's a friend. Platonic," I clarified. "We're like brother and sister." Any doubt to the contrary had been answered in tenth grade when we kissed, curious if it might spark romantic feelings. It didn't for either of us, though. We laughed about it, and it never happened again.

"If I lived with you"—his eyes wandered down my body—"there's no way in hell I could keep my hands to myself."

*I wouldn't want you to.*

"He's protective of you," Dillon continued.

"We've been friends since we were kids. Went through some heavy stuff together."

Dillon's gaze cascaded over my face like he wanted to uncover each puzzle piece of me and put it together.

My chest warmed.

"I have a confession to make," I said.

"Just one?"

"I looked you up on social media."

That wasn't the extent of it. I'd run a basic background check, looking for warrants and criminal records, and he had none. And then I thought to myself, *What the heck am I doing?* Investigating my date couldn't be something a normal, healthy person did.

"I'm not really into the social media thing."

"So I gathered. You have, like, five pictures, and four of them are of sporting events."

He offered a smile. "What can I say? I prefer living in the moment versus posting about it to get likes." Then, he added, "I have a confession to make, too."

"Just one?"

"I looked you up on Instagram, too, and you also only have a few photos. I have to say, it was a breath of fresh air. Most women I've dated are obsessed with putting their whole lives up on social media."

Well, cops were a lot like teachers in that regard. One wrong post could cost you your career, so why take the chance?

"I'm not a social media person. And even if I were, the things I find value in are things I'd never post about online."

Dillon tilted his body closer to mine, his energy glistening through the air like embers cast from a flame and gliding across my skin like silk. My stomach flickered as he enveloped me in his gaze, his chestnut eyes like polished amber, so beautiful, they brightened the entire room.

"So, did your day get better?" Dillon asked.

"After escaping certain death?"

"After that." He smiled.

*Houston, we have a dimple.*

I opened my menu. "Not particularly."

Dillon's smile fell. "Why?"

*Take your pick: a pissed off boss, crazy conspiracy theory that the fire was an attempt on my life, and as an added bonus...*

"A guy was a complete dickwad to me. I'm pretty sure he intends to make my life miserable."

A protective edge sliced through Dillon's eyes as his mouth morphed into a tight line.

"Your waters," the waiter said.

As the waiter stood at the side of the table, Dillon seemed to recalibrate, that momentary edge fading as we placed our dinner orders.

Once the waiter left, Dillon held his glass up toward mine and smiled. "To second chances."

He clanked my glass, and I took a drink.

I stared at the ice cubes, his toast to second chances scorching my heart.

Celebrating our escape from the inferno should have felt great, but it brought a tug of sadness. It wasn't fair that we got to sit here and celebrate having lived when others would never get to do this again. How many families were out there, mourning right now?

Dillon read my expression and cleared his throat. "I heard on the news that seven people didn't make it."

Seven families destroyed after losing a mother, father, sister, brother, son, or daughter.

"Would have been eight if you hadn't saved me." Dark sadness lingered in his tone. "I know I said it before, but thank you. I owe you my life."

"Anyone in my position would've done the same thing."

"We both know that's not true," Dillon challenged. Then, after several seconds of silence, he admitted, "I haven't been able to stop thinking about you all day, Fallon."

Dillon's gaze was so intense, it made my nerves crackle beneath my skin.

"I've been waiting all day to get to learn more about you," he said.

I wasn't used to being the source of someone's absolute attention. So acute, it was like an electric current surging through my veins, erupting goose bumps in its path.

"Like what?"

"Everything."

No one had ever had this kind of insatiable curiosity about me before, and it was exhilarating. Because it was *him* wanting to get to know me.

But as I stared at Dillon, I instantly understood how much I had, in fact, used my work as a crutch in the past. Steering every conversation to my career time and time again had created an emotional barrier that prevented anyone from seeing the real me. A crutch that I'd undoubtedly lean on tonight—and any other night—the second talking about myself felt uncomfortable.

I didn't want to be that closed-off person with Dillon.

It was time I pushed myself past my comfort zone because he was different than other guys I'd dated. Selfless. When he almost died, his first thought wasn't of his own life; it was how his death would shatter his brother. A brother he made time for every Sunday. I wanted to try to open up to Dillon, but to do it, I needed to lock my crutch in a closet.

Plus, now that I was on an official DEA task force, it wasn't like I could discuss details about my job, anyway.

"Would it be okay if we didn't talk about work?" I asked.

Dillon blinked. "Tonight? Or in general?"

Based on my tone, he must have sensed the latter.

"I have a stressful job," I hedged.

Dillon's beautiful lips seemed to know exactly what to say. "We won't talk about work," he conceded. "Any other topics you want to keep off-limits on our dates?"

*Dates. Plural*, I noticed. I smiled, knowing he already liked me enough to want to see more of me, but a swelling panic came right behind it. Did I really have the courage to talk about my dark, twisted childhood?

Dillon seemed to sense my apprehension and leaned his forearms on the table. "I just want to get to know you better," he assured.

Right. This wasn't an interrogation. It was a date with him, the guy whose eyes instantly calmed my nerves.

Before figuring out where to start explaining "everything" about me, I got distracted by my buzzing cell phone. When I saw it was another text from my father, I couldn't hide my grimace.

"Everything okay?"

I sighed. "My dad and I aren't speaking right now," I admitted. Some of which was my fault. I'd cut him off, refusing to speak to him. "He's an addict."

A better daughter wouldn't feel embarrassed by his addiction, that she didn't have a normal parent. Yet heat seared my cheeks and tunneled into my chest, scalding my ribs.

When Dillon's eyes touched mine again, though, they extinguished the flames because his expression wasn't pity. It was poignant sadness, the recognition of someone else who must be battling complications. Complications that were easier to admit to someone who must have also gone through something terrible based on his comment earlier.

"He's promising to get clean again. For the millionth time."

"Has he been an addict your whole life?" Dillon asked.

"He started when I was eleven."

That was when those drug dealers murdered him and replaced him with a zombie mutant whose only purpose was to sprinkle the occasional, irrational hope that he might recover. But instead, he had me living in constant fear of every phone call and every knock on the door that it would be *the one* that told me my father overdosed.

"And your mom?"

I twisted my fingers together. "My mom was a stay-at-home mom. In the beginning, they both doted on my every move." I traced my finger along the circular lip of the glass, the happiness of those times now hurting with how much I missed them. "Those were my original parents."

Dillon shifted in his seat, his gaze morphing into worried curiosity. "What changed?"

The winds of my past carried me back to the place I'd tried so hard to leave behind.

"When I was nine, my mom had to have shoulder surgery. We didn't think too much of it." I picked at my nail. "The doctor prescribed pain pills for after. This was before we knew anything about opioids, let alone how addictive they could be."

Dillon's expression grew apprehensive.

"After, something seemed different in my mom."

To say the least.

Nine-year-olds can't reconcile suddenly going from their parents' first priority to their last. They can't understand why a mom used to greet them with a huge hug when they got off the bus but then won't even say hello when they walk in the door. No. Those nine-year-olds blame themselves, wondering what they did to make their parents fall out of love with them. And they pathetically try everything to regain said love, no matter how many times they cry themselves to sleep after failing.

"I was worried something went wrong with the surgery because she just couldn't get out of the pain. Kept going back to the doctor to get more pills. She became withdrawn and stopped taking me to the park. Eventually, she just stayed inside all day, even on the nice days. Our medical bills must've been piling up, too, because my parents would argue about money. By the time I was ten, we had to move into a trailer park. Dad promised it was temporary, that it was just until Mom got better, so he could pay for her to go to a special shoulder treatment place." I shrugged. "I didn't realize until much later she was going to rehab. Or that she'd switched from pills to heroin since heroin has the same opioid base she'd become addicted to."

I nibbled the inside of my cheek before I continued. "I eventually realized she'd become an addict and felt sorry for her because she never saw it coming. She hadn't sought out drugs or done them to party or something. She'd taken pills her doctor gave her for her surgery, and that was it. What I really couldn't forgive was when my dad became an addict. He'd seen exactly what it'd done to my mom and me, and despite that, he became an addict by choice."

Dillon leaned closer and spoke in a gentle tone. "You said he started using when you were eleven?"

I picked at my nail. "Still in the trailer park, of course. Only now, I was basically an orphan. My mom had died, and my dad was almost always high, and when he wasn't high, he was sleeping or coming down. He'd stopped working, so we lived hand to mouth on whatever government assistance he managed to get ahold of, but the drugs came first. Always first."

Dillon watched me straighten all my silverware even though it didn't need tidying.

I worried he'd ask me questions about my mom, but maybe he sensed I would refuse to discuss the circumstances surrounding her death.

That was something I'd never talk about with anyone. Ever.

Instead, he asked, "How long has it been since you've spoken to him?"

"Three months." After he'd humiliated me and almost ruined my career. But if I were honest, my anger ran deeper than that. "I've never understood why he started doing drugs, and he's always refused to answer that question. Like finding out why my whole life crashed and burned around me is of no consequence."

And now, he kept texting me that there was something he needed to tell me. I didn't care that my gut told me this time was different; I didn't trust him. All his empty promises over the years were daggers that would strike the second my hopes got up. He never followed through with any of them. We never even left that run-down neighborhood.

"He still lives in that trailer. Blue Island is a nice enough town, but that trailer park..." I pursed my lips. "Oasis Homes makes it sound like something beautiful."

Dillon paused and took a tight sip of water. "You lived in Blue Island?"

I nodded. "Why?"

He hesitated. "No reason."

But he wouldn't look me in the eye, and before I could ask why, the waiter brought our food over. Each plate looked like a work of art with asparagus crisscrossed in a pinwheel pattern over steak, parsley flaked on top, and a rich oil dripped along the outskirts. It looked too beautiful to eat, but the smell of its rich, buttery flavor moistened my mouth.

As soon as I cut into my steak, however, my shoulders sank.

"What's wrong?"

"Nothing," I lied and even put on a smile. He was treating me to a nice dinner, and I wasn't about to ruin any part of it.

But Dillon looked at the meat and flagged down the waiter.

"Dillon, it's fine."

"She ordered her steak medium-well, not rare. Please have the chef cook it longer."

"I'm sorry, sir."

"Take my plate, too."

"Sir?"

"I won't eat until the lady does," Dillon declared.

I stilled. How could such a small act make me feel so cared for?

The waiter issued apologies and vanished with our plates, returning a few minutes later with both of our dinners cooked the way we had ordered them.

Dillon picked up his utensils and unleashed the electric current of his stare onto me that glided past my skin and magnetized its voltage inside my chest.

"I'm glad you made it out of that fire, Fallon."

My eyes prickled because I understood his double meaning. The fire of my past and the one that almost took my life.

"I assumed you were going to look at me with pity."

But wonderfully, he raised his eyebrows and shook his head.

"Pity? No. Admiration? Hell yes. I respect someone else that had to pull themselves out of a sinkhole."

I blinked. "Someone else?"

## 6

Dillon cut his steak. "My dad took off when I was thirteen without so much as a phone call or a dollar. He claimed he had some big career opportunity, but I think he couldn't handle the responsibility of my little brother.

"Dex's bills—that's my brother's name, Dexter—his bills were adding up. It became quicksand, and it wasn't long before we lost our home and moved into government-subsidized housing. Gangs infested that place. Loved to talk crap just to assert their alpha dominance, and sometimes, they even beat you up for no reason."

*I can't even imagine.*

"They loved to ridicule Dex, who still lived with us at the time. I knew we had to get out of there. Mom did everything she could, but there just wasn't enough money to move, especially since Dex needed care that cost more than my mom could make. I had to wait until I was fourteen to apply for jobs. State law. Spent my fourteenth birthday applying for every job I could. Took years, but I got my mom out of that hellhole and bought her a home in a good neighborhood. Found a great place for Dex, too, where he gets the care he needs."

Wow. I bet most teenage boys would've become bitterly angry and rebelled in his situation. Maybe even run away. No one could've blamed Dillon for doing that, and no one could've expected him to step up and become a surrogate parent at such a young age. But in the face of a crushing situation, Dillon took action. I admired that he refused to accept his circumstances and not only managed to free himself, but freed his mother and brother as well.

My affection for him became a power surge, blazing through my veins and lighting up everything in its path. It was more electrifying than anything I'd ever felt on a first date—or a second or third, for that matter.

"Do you mind if I ask what Dexter's condition is?"

"Complicated pregnancy, followed by oxygen deprivation at birth," he said. "Suffered brain damage."

"I'm sorry."

He offered a weak smile.

"And you visit him every weekend," I remembered.

"I bring him gummy bears." Dillon smiled. "Our mom would never let us have much candy, growing up. We couldn't afford nonessentials. Dex is a perpetual little kid, so when I roll up with a bag of gummies, it makes him so happy, I can't help myself."

*I think my ovaries just exploded.*

My pull toward Dillon only increased through the rest of dinner. Afterward, Dillon drove me home in his silver 2021 Mustang GT Premium Convertible and walked me to my apartment building's entrance.

I hated that our date drew to its end. Saying good-bye felt like being expelled from a warm bubble bath and stepping into the icy air.

"I had a nice time," I said. "Thank you."

Against the blackened sky, towering buildings with checkered lights sparkled in gradients of whites and grays. It almost looked like a sophisticated, life-size Lego set, complete with cars rumbling along the roads as a light summer breeze danced across my arms, leaving goose bumps in its wake.

Dillon bit his lip and, standing a solid ten inches taller, smiled down at me.

My lower belly warmed. His presence pulled at me, his body just inches from my own. I longed to feel his chest against mine, his lips on my mouth, tasting me, his powerful arms holding me.

"I had a great time tonight, too." His voice glided over my skin in a low, sexy rumble. "And for the record?" He brought the back of his fingers up and trailed them down my cheek. His touch was soft and gentle, awakening desires deep within me. "I've never enjoyed a date as much as this one."

*That makes two of us.*

He cupped my cheek, his thumb in front of my ear.

*Lord, his touch.*

My breathing quickened as my body heated. His lips came closer, but they were going too slow. I needed them on mine—now.

*Hurry.*

He looked from my mouth to my eyes as he tilted his head.

And then an explosion of intoxication as he took my lip between his.

I could no longer feel my legs. I swore him grabbing my lower back was to keep me upright. I moaned—holy mother, it was a moaning type of kiss—and wrapped my arms around his neck, pulling our bodies together. He was warm and delicious, and when he opened his mouth, I accepted the invitation. I touched his tongue, relishing *his* moan as our kiss intensified. Our hands wove through each other's hair as our mouths opened and closed, our tongues connecting deeper and deeper.

I wanted him on top of me, under me.

Kissing him and being in his arms made everything feel lighter, the heaviness that once pressed on my chest evaporating.

Dillon eventually pulled back and smiled, bringing his hand up to my cheek. "I'd like to take you out again."

Was I imagining it, or did that slight crease to his brow make him look worried?

*No, not worried*, I realized. Overwhelmed by whatever this was buzzing around us, between us, and through us. It was comforting to know this sensation must have been as unique to him as it was to me.

I'd never been this excited or eager to go on a second date with anyone. It was thrilling, but it also made me a little nervous because, in the past, I didn't care that much if a guy didn't call me back or never wanted to see me again. But if Dillon ghosted me like that, it'd hurt a lot. And that was after *one* date. What would it feel like after two? Six? Thirty?

I leaned into the warmth of his touch and swept my apprehension into the shadows of my mind.

"I'd love that," I said.

S hane scrubbed his face and blew out a breath.

"Are you okay?" I whispered, so no one else in the conference room could hear. "You haven't been yourself lately."

At first, I attributed his stress to work, but now that I thought about it, his smiles had become less frequent over the past few weeks, even outside of work.

Before I could press Shane further, Burch stormed into the conference room.

"May have just caught a huge damn break," he declared.

DEA agents and officers leaned forward in their seats.

"Autopsy results came back from Terrell," he said. "Turns out, Terrell swallowed something before he died." Burch rubbed his chin. "A USB drive." He looked around the room. "Medical examiner says it was ingested about thirty minutes before the first wounds were made."

"Before he was tortured," Proctor clarified.

Burch nodded. "I sent it to our IT team. Stomach acid ain't too friendly on electronics, but the thing was wrapped in rubber, so we have a shot at finding out what was on it."

"You think it could have some intel for this case," Marks said.

"I don't think people swallow digital family pictures," Burch answered.

"Why would he have a jump drive with vital information on it?" Shane wondered.

*Seriously*. Seemed risky to hold on to evidence like that.

"All businesses need to keep records," Burch said. "Even illegal ones."

"Why would he swallow it, then?" I asked.

"Maybe he threatened to leak it, and they fed it to him to make a point," Proctor, the ever-butt-kisser, offered. As an added bonus, he threw me a snarky look as if we were on a high school debate team and he'd just won the round.

"Too risky," I argued. "If they fed it to him, they risked letting the ME find something that could take them down."

Burch's nod agreed with my logic. I was almost mature enough to *not* relish Proctor's frown. Almost.

"Maybe Terrell sensed he was in trouble," Marks offered.

"Still doesn't explain why he swallowed it, though," Shane added.

"Maybe they found out about it. Showed up at his house to get it," Proctor offered. "So, he swallowed it to get rid of it before they'd confirm he had it."

Burch rubbed his face, as if exhausted by this back-and-forth guessing. "We'll likely never know why he did it, but that doesn't really matter. What matters is what's on it and if IT can salvage any of it."

"How long will it take them?" Shane asked.

"They said a few days, maybe longer."

Whatever was on that USB drive had to be pretty damning to the Syndicates. I couldn't wait to find out what it was.

Burch spent the rest of the morning giving us the overview he'd intended to yesterday. It wasn't until I was on a coffee break that I saw a missed text from Dillon.

**Dillon: I have a surprise for you.**

I smiled and replied.

**Me: What kind of surprise?**

I didn't expect him to text back right away, especially since so much time had passed since his first text, but his response was immediate.

**Dillon: I've been thinking about everything you said at dinner, and I planned something special that I think you're going to love.**

Our conversation, though lovely, had been rather heavy. What fun idea could've sparked from it?

*As long as it includes spending time with him, the date will be incredible.*

**Me: What is it?**

**Dillon: I'll pick you up on Saturday.**

Which was only four days from now. How could four days suddenly feel like an eternity?

**Dillon: And, Fallon?**

What was it about this man that could make me stare at my phone with this much anticipation?

**Dillon: I cannot wait to see you.**

8

Dillon picked me up in his convertible—top down, thanks to the city's seventy-degree temperatures—and as the evening sun tilted in the cloudless sky, he struggled to keep his eyes on the road. His hungry gaze glided over my face, my body, making me feel wonderfully desired.

When we arrived at his secret destination, I smirked.

"Seriously?" I smiled.

"What?" Dillon said.

"We're not thirteen."

"First of all, that's a travesty if you're under the misguided belief that only people the age of thirteen can enjoy this place. Second of all? This is fun."

It wasn't Navy Pier itself that I found amusing. Navy Pier was a 3,300-foot-long concrete peninsula that extended from the shoreline out into Lake Michigan, peppered with brick shops and restaurants, emerald-green landscaping around gorgeous walkways, and a 200-foot-tall Ferris wheel that held over two thousand people an hour. It was the temporary carnival that made me grin.

Dillon watched my reaction as I took in the magic of it all. The rows of multicolored booths with games and prizes. The clowns on stilts that wobbled through the packed pedestrians, trying not to get taken out by a rogue child. The sea of people and the rumble of their voices overriding the city traffic. The smell of fried treats and kids clutching prized stuffed animals as they chomped on pink cotton candy. Other than a serious banner that promoted an upcoming awards ceremony—where the mayor would honor Chicago's chief of police—the place had transformed into a childlike fairyland.

My chest tightened as memories of my tween years crept into my mind. A time that should have been filled with innocence, optimism, and dreams of a prince on a white horse sweeping me off my feet. Instead, I'd peered through the gate of a carnival just like this one at the carefree kids overflowing with laughter with their best friends and crushes on boys. I'd felt so alone on the outside of that gate, looking in on the life and feelings I'd so desperately wanted but would never have.

"I've never been to a carnival," I said.

"I figured." Dillon tried to shrug what he said next off with a nonchalant smile, but his words delivered a powerful blow to my heart. "That's why I picked this. Sounded like you kind of got robbed out of your childhood. Thought it'd be fun to give you a little piece of it back."

My eyes watered, and I had to take a deep breath to keep them from leaking.

Dillon's chestnut eyes cut straight through my camouflage, which made me wonder if he saw all the emotions I usually hid from other guys. The hurt that this was what a tween should have been doing on her Saturday nights, playing games at a carnival with a boy she had a crush on, instead of being a prisoner to that trailer, too scared to leave because she was terrified her dad would overdose.

Dillon took my hand and laced his fingers through mine, and instantly, every ounce of sadness washed away. In his embrace, I only felt bliss.

I felt like a piece of my soul was a butterfly in flight, feeling magnificently free for the first time.

"Come on." He smiled, his lighthearted tone back. "Let's have some fun." He pulled me through the crowd until it came to a clearing, where the song "Iko Iko" blasted through speakers while street dancers dressed in white T-shirts, backward baseball caps, and skinny jeans danced to the music.

The street performers were invigorating, rocking their bodies to the thrumming beat as the crowd clapped and shouted along to the lyrics. All the smiles, the kids squealing with laughter. It was as if someone had put pure happiness into a bottle and released it for everyone to breathe. And I wasn't immune to its intoxicating effects.

When Dillon let go of me to clap to the cadence of the music, my hand had never felt emptier. The omission of his touch and the warmth that radiated through my blood was profound.

We watched the street performers for a full minute. Well, I watched them; Dillon watched me, his smile growing wider, the more I enjoyed myself.

"Come here," Dillon shouted, pulling me by my hand to an open space.

"I can't dance," I said, seeing his intention. But dancing meant I'd get to feel him touching me again, so I wasn't about to put up a fight.

"I can't, either!" He smiled as he spun me around and dipped me, holding my hand and upper back for several beats as he gazed into my eyes.

"Liar."

Dang, the sexiness of his mouth and those beautiful full lips when he chuckled.

With one arm, Dillon effortlessly snatched me back to a standing position. I followed the momentum of his hands' pushes and pulls, moving me away from him and pulling me back. Spinning me one direction, then the next.

I laughed as he spun me again, and this time, he pulled my back to his chest and put his hands on my hips, swaying to the music. Geez, his chest and abs were granite ripples yet warm and inviting, a perfect mold around me.

*Heaven help me. I'd volunteer to be a human crash test dummy to see him without a shirt.*

How did it feel this exhilarating, having my body pressed against him?

When the song ended, everyone erupted into applause for the professional dancers, but Dillon continued to hold me, putting his mouth near my ear. The heat of his breath tickled against my neck. "Keep dancing, food, or games?"

I leaned my cheek against his chin's whiskers. "I've never had cotton candy."

"A tragedy we'll rectify immediately. Come on."

The absence of his chest took a second to recover from, but luckily, he slipped his hand into mine and guided me toward a booth.

"Two cotton candies," Dillon said. He pulled his wallet out of his back pocket, slapped a ten down, and handed me a pink cloud on a stick. He examined my face as I took a bite. "Well?"

It was the strangest sensation, a fluff ball that melted into sugar granules. "Heaven on my tongue."

Dillon's lips curled. "Come on. I need to win you a teddy bear to complete the experience."

He pulled me through the crowd.

Amid the rows of carnival games stood an unsuspecting pink booth with upside-down purple cups spread across four shelves. A rainbow cloud of stuffed animals packed the booth's roof, and below them, a gray-haired man with arms like twigs looked about as thrilled to be there as a plumber called in to unclog a toilet.

Unlike the other booths, this one didn't have a single player. Certainly a bad sign. Humans were quick students, spotting which games were unlikely to win prizes.

"Five dollars," the game guy said.

Dillon placed his money down, and the guy handed him a gun.

*Five bucks, and a guy hands anyone a gun. Every officer's worst nightmare.*

"Well, this seems safe," I quipped.

Dillon smirked. "It's just a BB gun," he said, and then he asked the guy, "How many do we have to knock down to get that?" Dillon pointed to the largest stuffed animal—a three-foot-tall pink teddy bear.

"Fifteen."

"How many shots per turn?"

"Twenty."

Dillon arched a mischievous eyebrow at me.

"Ladies first." He handed me the gun and stood behind me.

Like, inches behind me.

I knew how to handle a weapon, but I didn't tell Dillon that. My hormones were having too much fun, letting his hands caress my hips, then glide sensually down my arms to adjust my grip. He tucked a fallen hair behind my shoulder and lowered his mouth next to my ear.

"Relax," he whispered.

*Dang it, is he trying to make me misfire?*

Impossible when I could feel the thump of his heartbeat. But I tried.

I wanted to impress him, so I aimed toward the center shelf, took a breath in, let it out halfway, and pulled the trigger.

A *ding* sounded, but the purple cup didn't fall.

Cup, my butt. Those things were solid steel.

"They're screwed down," I accused.

Game Guy gave me a look of annoyance and lifted one of the cups, trying to make it look like it didn't weigh seven tons.

Dillon tried not to laugh. "They make the games a lot harder than they look."

"Apparently."

"Try again."

I tried two more times with the same infuriating outcome and then frowned. "There's no way to knock them down."

"You have to hit them right in the center."

"You think I'm *not* aiming for the center?" He didn't know that I went to target practice regularly, but evidently, this cup required sniper-level accuracy to knock down the steel drum.

Dillon chuckled a delicious, throaty laugh.

"You think you can do better?" I challenged.

"Without question."

"Ten bucks says you can't knock even one down."

To this, he raised a flirtatious eyebrow. "I have a different wager in mind." He bit his lower lip. *Lucky lip.* "I knock down fifteen of those before my turn is up," he started and lowered his mouth to my ear. "I get to take you home and have my way with you."

*Holy crud.* My lower belly tingled, my hormones grabbing the steering wheel and performing a hostile takeover. They tried to convince me to jump over this counter and sucker-punch fifteen cups, so he could carry me to bed.

"And if I win?"

He put his mouth by my ear again. "I'll let you have your way with me."

He dangled his mouth over mine, and instantly, a nervousness swept through my body. Part of me wanted to go to bed with him—a gigantic part, actually—but we'd only been dating a week. A week that had already been a whirlwind for me, and gunning the gas pedal even harder risked us crashing and burning out. I liked Dillon too much to let that happen. It would be better for us to wait a little longer.

I didn't want to ruin the moment, though, because honestly? I enjoyed this flirtatious, sexy banter too much.

I grazed his lips with mine and answered seductively, "While I admire your confidence, you're not getting me into bed that easy."

His lips pulled into a smile.

"And I know you can't knock down fifteen."

He pulled his beautiful mouth back and offered a sexy grin as he rolled up his sleeves.

Man, he was hot, taking his stance. Feet shoulder-width apart, propping his butt up.

*I could totally build a display shelf and fill it with nothing but molds of that fine ass.*

His shoulders exploded out of his shirt when he raised his arms up to aim the gun, and the bands of muscles covering his forearms tightened.

*Bam.* A purple cup fell.

*Bam.* Another fell.

*Bam, bam, bam.* Three more.

I stood with my mouth falling open as Dillon knocked down seventeen cups in what had to be less than ten seconds.

"How do you know how to shoot like that?"

The game guy looked completely uninterested as he yanked the pink teddy down and handed it to Dillon, who passed it to me.

Dillon shrugged. "Bad neighborhood, remember? After something horrible happened, I needed a way to protect my family. Started going to target practice. Got really good at it."

I wondered what horrific event could have made him so worried about their lives that he became obsessive in learning how to shoot. But I wouldn't spoil his mood with my curiosity. I'd save that question for another day.

"For the record," he said, slinging his arm over my shoulders. His embrace sucked me in like a cyclone, whipping everything around us in gusts while we coiled together in the eye of the beautiful storm. "I was only half-joking with the bet."

"Half, huh?"

"My upper body was joking."

I laughed.

Dillon pulled me over to a line of people. It didn't take long before it was our turn on the Ferris wheel.

"Ever been on one of these?" Dillon asked as the cart slowly ascended.

"No."

Dillon's mouth tightened, but he shook it off with a smile as the Ferris wheel rose to the top. And what a climb it was. As we ascended twenty stories in the air, the gorgeous Chicago skyline sparkled against the now-black night like twinkle lights. Swarms of people swam through the booths like a river beneath us, and just as our cart reached the highest point, a burst of orange and red exploded in the sky and shimmered over the ebony water.

Right. Fireworks in the summer every Saturday. And we had the best seat in the city for them.

"Did you time this?" I asked.

Dillon shrugged. "Tried to. Wasn't sure I could pull it off."

*Geez.* He put so much thought into this night. First, he picked something so special, then made sure I danced, played games, tried cotton candy, and now this. I'd never had anyone do so many thoughtful things for me before.

Dillon's kindness was like a warm blanket on a cold winter night. It enveloped me and dethawed parts of my heart I didn't even realize had been frozen.

Red, white, then blue fireworks lit up the night sky as people cheered and clapped.

With each burst, Dillon's face glowed in various colors, but he wasn't even watching the fireworks. He was watching me, absorbing my glee and wonder. When his gaze settled on my mouth, a hunger flashed through his eyes that lingered until it seemed he couldn't resist his desires anymore. He cupped my face, stroked my cheek with his thumb, and then moved his hand to the back of my head.

*Please kiss me. Please put your mouth on mine, put your hands on my body.*

After one last agonizing second, he finally brought his mouth to mine.

And licked my tongue.

*Good Lord.*

The taste of pure sugar from our cotton candy intensified as our tongues connected over and over.

I licked his tongue and pulled his mouth tighter against mine. Taking things slowly with him would be a lot harder than I thought because right now, I wanted far more than just a kiss. I wanted to straddle him and feel him beneath me.

When Dillon's fingers skated along the base of my shirt, I could tell that he wanted more, too. I wasn't about to deny him, either. We were at the top of the Ferris wheel, two hundred feet above the prying eyes of people below, in a glass-enclosed bubble. We didn't have much time —once we descended a bit more, the people in the cart behind us would be able to see us—but the wheel moved incredibly slow.

Affording us a minute or two.

Beneath the fabric of my top, Dillon's hand slid up my stomach slowly, leaving a trail of fire in its wake. When his grip reached my chest, I squirmed and growled into his mouth as he squeezed.

If his touch felt this good with his hand over my bra's fabric, I couldn't even imagine how good it would feel to have his hands on my bare skin—with no clothes on, when we were alone and had all the time we wanted to caress each other.

I moved my hand to his back and skated it up his shirt, exploring the ridges of his tantalizing muscles with my fingertips.

He pinched me, the sensation jolting through my chest.

Our chemistry was dangerous; it could tempt me to misbehave in ways I never had. I needed to control myself, but it was hard, not just because of our passion, but also because of how special Dillon made me feel.

I ran my fingers through his silky hair, feeling the *boom, boom, boom* of each firework vibrating in my chest while a different explosion erupted through the chambers of my heart.

## 9

B urch stood at the front of the room with an expression on his face I'd never seen before. It almost looked as if he was biting back...a smile?

"IT was able to recover some information off that USB drive."

I sat up straighter. Everyone in the task force's conference room did.

"They're still scrubbing it, hoping to come up with more, but for right now, we got three names off the drive. Which might not sound like a lot, but it might be enough to make a huge freaking dent."

*Giddy-freaking-up, buttercup. Here we go. A break.* A huge break, judging by the look on Burch's face. Maybe we'd take down the Syndicates a lot sooner than we thought.

"Now," Burch said as he flipped over his corkboard of mugshots, "we need to divide and conquer, research everything about these guys. Cross-reference the names with any drug busts in the last thirty years, arrest records—misdemeanor or felony. Also want a team working with the IRS to pull their tax records because my guess is that these guys just happen to make a crap-ton of money. On paper, the earnings might look legit, but let's tear into them to see if we can prove money laundering."

I studied the three names he had pinned to the top of the board.

"One name in particular caught my eye, though." Burch pulled the name off the board and pinned it to the side. "Rodrigo Ramirez," he said. "Ramirez used to run narcotics in the Midwest, but he vanished fourteen years ago. Figured he was dead. He might've changed his name, but the question is: what's his role in the Syndicates? And where the hell's he been for the last several years?"

Out of all the names I could have been assigned in the research, I was thrilled I got his. Because his seemed the most out of place and therefore might be an essential clue in our investigation into how the Syndicates ran their operation.

## 10

"I can't talk right now, Dad. I'm heading out."

I hadn't even wanted to answer his call, but evidently, he wasn't going to stop until I acknowledged him—something I did via text, to no avail.

"I understand." The defeat in his voice tugged at my traitorous heartstrings. "I'd rather talk to you in person, anyway, if that's possible?"

The thought of seeing him again after everything he did made me uneasy. I was just starting to find my stride with work and personal life. A bird taking flight for what felt like the first time, soaring through the clouds and leaving the hurricane behind. But here he was, ready to suck me back into his dark vortex.

"I'm swamped."

"It's important," he insisted.

But my life wasn't. The one time he bothered to show up for something important to me, he almost cost me everything. And now, he expected me to be at his beck and call and, what, drop everything the second he asked?

"I'll look at my calendar for the next couple of weeks and text you a time that might work."

"Thank you." He breathed a sigh of relief. "And, Fallon?"

I waited.

"I love you, sweetheart."

I punched the End button harder than I needed to, just as Dillon pulled up to the curb to pick me up for our date.

He hopped out of his running convertible and opened the passenger door for me, his smile fading when he picked up on my tension.

"You okay?"

He waited for me to talk, not even caring that an impatient driver was already honking at him for holding up traffic.

"Dad drama," I hedged and climbed inside.

A moment later, Dillon entered the car, too. "Want to talk about it?"

I shook my head.

Dillon's lips tightened into a concerned line as he threw the car into gear and jetted out into traffic. As we tunneled through the skyscrapers, my muscles relaxed now that I was with him, and somehow, he knew exactly what I needed. He let me process my dad's call in silence as the city's buildings faded behind us, twilight setting in over the darkened interstate. He had the convertible's roof up this time, which was good, considering he gunned his car.

Dillon evaluated me.

"Could go straight to O'Hare," Dillon suggested. "We could be in the Bahamas by morning."

Despite myself, I smiled.

"You'd go to the Bahamas with me," I said incredulously. "Right now?"

"Wouldn't have to twist my arm."

I rolled my eyes. "We have no luggage," I countered. "I don't even have a swimsuit."

"If you don't want to go, you should stop sweetening the pot."

I laughed this time and accepted his embrace when he took my hand and kissed the back of it.

My tension melted even more.

"No international escape," I said.

"Do you still want to grab food?" he asked. We'd planned to get appetizers somewhere casual.

When I nodded, Dillon smiled and pressed the accelerator harder.

He drove to a smaller town outside the city—away from the noise and the congestion of people. When we arrived at the bar, I couldn't believe how empty the parking lot was. Yes, we'd come at an off-hour, and yes, this place was low-key. But still. In the city, you'd never find a near-empty parking lot like this.

We went inside and found the entire space was gift-wrapped in wood. Seriously, every square inch of the place? Wood. Floor? Wood. Walls? Wood. Counters, stools, and bar? Wood. Heck, even the light fixtures were made out of wood. I felt like I was in a log cabin–slash– biker bar with peanut shells on the floor, grungy rock music blasting over the speakers, and the smell of beer and man wafting through the space.

I was probably overdressed for the place—in my black skirt and emerald top—but I liked being away from the chaos of the city.

"Want a beer?" Dillon asked me.

I straightened hypothetical wrinkles out of my sleeves. "I don't drink," I admitted.

To this, Dillon raised an eyebrow.

"Why don't you drink?" he asked, but when his face fell, I could tell he immediately suspected the reason.

"I don't want to turn out like my parents."

His stare felt like it burrowed past my eyes and into my thoughts, medicating any lingering anxiety about my admission. With Dillon, I didn't feel ashamed or embarrassed by my past. His serene presence made me feel so comfortable with exposing all the layers that made me who I was that I might even tell him the rest of the story someday.

Something I thought I'd take to the grave.

A waitress with flaming red hair and tattooed arms appeared. "Can I get you two something to drink?"

"Water," I said.

"Make that two," Dillon added.

"It doesn't bother me if you drink," I assured.

He waited until the waitress walked away to answer me. "You're more important to me than a beer, Fallon."

My eyes burned as tears formed behind them. He couldn't possibly know how his proclamation both scorched my heart—for it reminded me of when I'd desperately longed to be more important than drugs had been to my parents—and spread soothing balm on it. Because to him, I was the priority.

Dillon leaned his sexy forearms on the table and took my hand in his. It was incredible how he could simply stare at me and make me feel so desired and adored and how his touch was like magic pixie dust, sprinkling calm through my body.

"If you don't mind me asking," he said, "what was it like? Growing up with addict parents?"

I'd never been asked this question. "Your childhood was far more challenging than mine."

He studied my gaze. "Somehow, I doubt that."

The tightness of his eyes showed he was as curious as he was anxious to hear my answer.

I ran a hand through my hair and thought back to that time when the whole world seemed like a scary, unsafe place.

"When I was younger, it felt like they didn't love me enough to stop doing drugs. Like I wasn't important enough to them." I tried to fight the wrenching sadness that still existed in fragments of my heart, splinters from a little girl, broken and sobbing in her bedroom because her mommy would rather get high than play with her.

"Then, I became convinced that my parents did drugs because they couldn't stand to be around me."

Some might find that absurd, but when you were rejected incessantly in favor of drugs, the excruciating fear that no one wanted to be around you cemented itself into your DNA. And when you spent almost every non-school hour in your room, alone...

"It made me feel unlovable, like no one would even notice if I ceased to exist."

And many days, I didn't even want to exist.

"That paranoia still creeps up sometimes," I admitted. "Even now."

Dillon shook his head, as if I didn't see myself clearly. But I guess that was what it was to be human. Beneath the layers of confidence and strength lay hidden insecurities, regret, and self-doubt. On any given day, it was just a question of which one rose to the surface.

"I've never talked about this with anyone," I said. Not even Shane.

Dillon raised his brows slightly, looking as surprised as he was flattered that he was the first person I'd opened up to. "Why?"

I considered this as he rubbed my palm with his thumb in soothing circles. "I put up a strong front with most people, so they don't see how broken I actually am inside. Even with Shane, I find myself putting up my armor because it bothers me that he met me at a time in my life when I was so frail. I guess I feel like, with him, I have this image I need to overcome of me being a weakling. It's all in my head, though, not his," I assured. "He's never done anything to make me feel that way. It's just the reality of our relationship. So, I don't like to talk about any of that stuff that left me vulnerable. But with you…" I looked into Dillon's gentle brown eyes. "When I'm with you, I feel like it's okay for me to be all the pieces of who I am. The strong ones and the weak ones. It's like I can just…exhale and be my raw, imperfect self."

I realized how strange that would sound to anyone else but Dillon —that I felt safer with him than anyone else. But our connection had been virtually instant. Maybe almost dying put a lot of things into perspective for me, including living my truth without caring as much about what people thought of me. And maybe that raw honesty, in turn, broke down some of Dillon's walls, and he opened up to me in ways he normally wouldn't have. Or maybe it had nothing to do with a near-death experience, and this was just what it felt like when you met someone extraordinary.

Regardless of the reason, revealing my hidden truths to Dillon was exceedingly significant to me. The look in his eyes told me the magnitude wasn't lost on him, either. He locked his gaze with mine for several beats of my heart, and it felt like nothing could ever break the intimacy of this moment.

Until a guy walking past our table bumped my shoulder. Hard.

He hadn't meant to do it; he was just texting and walking, but that didn't seem to matter to Dillon. Especially when the guy didn't even acknowledge it.

"Hey!" Dillon snarled.

The guy snapped his head around at the sound of Dillon's tone.

"Dillon…"

"You just hit her!"

A quick glance at the guy's body language warned me this might be a bad night to lecture him on social graces. His muscles were tense, and his face contorted in fury as he squeezed his cell phone in his hand, perhaps arguing with someone on the other end.

"Like I give a shit."

When he turned to walk away, Dillon opened his mouth, but I squeezed his hand.

"Let it go," I insisted.

If there was one thing I'd learned from being a cop, it was that small acts of hostility could escalate quickly over nothing at all. I once worked a scene where a fight had spiraled into a stabbing over a spilled beer. Something like this wasn't worth the fight.

Dillon rubbed the side of his nose with this thumb, trying to annihilate the guy with his eyes. His anger didn't surprise me. After how protective he'd been with his brother, defending me from someone's mistreatment didn't feel malicious or dark. It simply felt protective.

Luckily, Dillon let the guy walk away without a further argument. What he didn't know was that Text Guy circled back and took a seat directly behind Dillon.

And proceeded to glower at us.

Dillon rubbed his now-hardened jaw and recalibrated to what we were talking about before the interruption.

"I hate that you had to go through that," Dillon growled.

"Sadly, a lot of kids have it way worse than I did," I said. Addiction didn't just destroy the user; it hurt everyone they loved, too. Kind of like the addict was the epicenter of a bomb's explosion, but all their loved ones were in its blast radius. "My parents never beat or abused me."

"But there was nobody there to keep you safe. The way you've been treated by people upsets me. Makes me want to beat the shit out of anyone who's ever been unkind to you."

His eyes hardened with a longing for vengeance.

"And for the record," he added as he held my gaze, "you're very lovable."

My chest warmed under the weight of his adoration. I wanted to freeze this moment. Come back to visit it, feel it, anytime I wanted.

Dillon kissed the back of my hand, and I wished he could leave his lips there forever. I studied the curve of his mouth, his affection breaching my skin. How could a simple touch emit so much emotion? Emotion that pirouetted through his eyes as he rubbed his thumb along my palm.

But after a few seconds, his eyebrows pulled together. It was so slight, no one else would have noticed, especially when he tried to camouflage it with a smile. But it almost looked like he was...worried?

"What's wrong?" I asked.

He hesitated. "Nothing," he claimed, and then his momentary change evaporated.

I wondered if I should press him on it, but the guy sitting behind Dillon shifted in his seat and glared at the back of Dillon's head. Judging by the droop in the guy's eyelids and the tightness of his jaw, he'd had too much to drink and looked like he'd been stewing over Dillon's earlier attitude, now wanting to settle a score.

I could taste the sudden energy change in the room. And both my sixth sense and my police experience warned me to get out of here before something bad happened.

"We should go," I said.

Dillon looked at the time on his phone. "Let me use the men's room and settle the check. I'll be right back."

I wanted to tell him to stay and wait to use the restroom until we were out of this place, but I worried that explaining why would only compound Dillon's anger with this guy. That would escalate the tension even further, to a point that there would be no hope of avoiding a brawl.

Text Guy waited until Dillon was out of sight before slurring something. "Tell your boyfriend to mind his damn business."

I wasn't being baited into a fight. "Will do."

"I don't appreciate him talking to me like a damn child."

I stood up to leave. Problem was, I had to walk right next to him to get to the door, and I needed to do it before Dillon came back.

"I'll let him know that." I began walking.

Text Guy stood up and grabbed my wrist. "You're a smart-ass, aren't you?"

"Get your hands off me, or you'll be arrested for battery," I said.

"Threatening me now," he said, as if I'd just made this even more interesting for him.

"Let me go," I warned.

He squeezed harder.

"She said, let her go," Dillon growled, suddenly at my side. The fact that he kept his tone calm and deep made it sound all the more threatening.

"Or what?"

Instantly, the guy was no longer holding my wrist. He was pinned against the wall with Dillon's forearm to his throat.

"Touch her again, I'll knock your fucking teeth in," Dillon growled.

"Dillon!" I shouted.

Dillon stared at the guy for a beat—and by stare, I mean, he looked like he had to convince himself that beating the guy to a pulp wasn't worth it. And then he shoved off the guy.

"Come on," Dillon said to me.

Dillon threw a fifty down on our table, glared at the guy one last time, and then took my hand and led me out the front door and to his car.

As soon as we were safely inside, I made sure the raging lunatic hadn't followed us out before turning my focus back to Dillon. "I don't need you to protect me."

Dillon took a deep breath and put his hand on my cheek. And

this time, when he spoke, his voice was softer. "I know you don't. You're the strongest woman I know. But it's about time someone protects you, anyway, Fallon. And I want to be the guy who protects you."

Instantly, my lower belly warmed, and his touch became fire. He released my face, unaware that his words had tunneled past my skin and through my pulsing heart, sparking desires deep within me.

Dillon put his finger on the push-button start, but before he could press it, I leaned over and crushed my mouth to his.

His head jerked in surprise, but after a moment, his lips tightened into a smile before he kissed me back.

And my goodness, did he kiss me back. Fingers in my hair, tongue slipping into my mouth, but it wasn't enough. I needed more. It was like handing a person dying of thirst a water bottle and trying to get them to stop drinking after just one sip.

A greedy need took over my body, my inhibitions, my logic even. Tucked into a back-corner spot of the dark parking lot—thanks to Dillon not wanting to get it scratched—his car was surrounded by trees on two sides. No one would see us. Even so, this was insane. I was more responsible than this. A cop, for crying out loud.

And yet, with his words and fierce protection, something primal and deeper took over. Water bottle in hand, dying of dehydration, I became desperate to satisfy my thirst.

I climbed on top of Dillon's lap and straddled him. He growled and pushed the button to move the seat back to give me more room. His hands skimmed the skin of my thighs, drifting beneath my skirt, causing a surge of heat to erupt inside of me.

As our kiss deepened—our tongues connecting in perfect, delicious rhythms—his hands worked to my backside and squeezed. Hard.

I wove my hands into his hair as he kept one hand on my butt while the other shifted beneath my shirt, found the front snap of my bra, and unhooked it.

When he cupped my bare chest in the strength of his hand, I arched my back. His entire body tightened like a rubber band demanding a release. His desire swelled beneath me as he lifted my shirt and took me into his mouth.

*Holy...sweet...*

"If you want to stop, we need to do it now," he growled breathlessly against my skin.

I risked a quick glance around to ensure no one was nearby. We *should* stop.

But then his hand slid down my stomach and inside my panties. When it hit its mark, I grabbed his shoulders. Even with my eyes closed and my head tilted back, I could feel his gaze on me, watching my reaction to every pulse of his finger, every movement of his palm, hitting my every cadence with just the right note.

I'd never been with a guy who knew how to incite so much pleasure. It was like he knew my body better than I did, making it feel like this was my first time with a man.

Dillon wrapped his free hand around the back of my neck and brought my mouth back to his.

"Tell me what you want," he commanded against my lips.

I couldn't think about anything but his hand. I couldn't catch my breath, couldn't think. All I could do was feel. And need. And want more.

"I want you," I whispered. And then I took his lip between my teeth and nibbled.

That was all it took. In an almost frenzy, Dillon lifted my hips, undid his zipper, pulled his pants to his knees, and slipped protection onto himself that he'd pulled from his pocket.

Then, he grabbed my hips again with so much force, a flicker of pain preceded the pleasure.

As I slid my panties to the side and lowered myself onto him, I looked him in his eyes and savored the groan that escaped his mouth.

My lips were back on his, his hands roaming beneath my shirt as I began to move.

Man, he felt so, so good. Full, blazing fire raged through me as our bodies moved with each other exquisitely, as if designed perfectly for one another.

I'd never felt anything this incredible. Never felt this connection with anyone, this uninhibited as I rocked my body against his. If it felt this good now, I could only imagine being nude and alone with him in a bed

with hours for us to explore each other's bodies.

As we moved, kissing and touching, pushing and pulling for several glorious minutes, Dillon sensed my rise and grabbed my chest, growling as I leaned back. When I hit my release, I looked right into his eyes, watching him follow with a release of his own.

## 11

"This is so frustrating." I tossed my pen onto my precinct desk, which was cluttered with papers and notes that had proven unhelpful in my research.

"Walk me through it," Marks said. "I'll be your sounding board." He leaned on the edge of my desk and crossed his arms over his chest.

I let out a huge sigh. "Okay, so we know Rodrigo Ramirez was a suspected narcotics criminal fifteen, twenty years ago, right?"

He nodded.

"But then fourteen years ago, he upped and vanished."

"Presumed dead," Marks agreed.

"Right. But now, his name shows up on that USB drive along with other *current* names of the Chicago Syndicates. So, he must still be alive, doing something. But I haven't been able to find anything on him."

"What have you searched so far?"

I pinched the bridge of my nose. "I scrubbed all the criminal databases in the United States, even misdemeanors and traffic tickets. I thought maybe he relocated to the Miami or New York crews."

Marks raised an impressed eyebrow.

"But that turned up empty. So, then I went back and looked at his financial records to see if I could find a clue. What his activity was, leading up to his disappearance."

"And also came up empty," Marks presumed.

"The data is spotty. Not all financial databases go back fifteen years. We could assume they looked at all this when he first disappeared, but if he was presumed dead, maybe law enforcement didn't look as hard as we're looking right now."

"Plus, databases are a lot more sophisticated than they were fifteen years ago."

Exactly. "But I've found absolutely nothing to explain where he's been or why he would turn up on this USB drive."

Marks chewed the inside of his cheek while I tapped my pen twenty times on the desk.

"You know," he said, "in the cartel, sometimes, they have certain members whose identities are a carefully guarded secret, even from within their own organization. Like the bookkeeper, for instance. Those are the guys controlling the money needed to fund wars against police, hire soldiers, and pay hit men. Because money is the lifeblood of the organization, they're often the right-hand man to the leader but work completely behind the scenes. Keeping their identities confidential is another protective layer from law enforcement and any other cartels who might want to overthrow them. Maybe the Syndicates followed the cartel's playbook and buried this guy's identity. Maybe he's been here all along as their bookkeeper or something."

I nodded, chewed the cap of my pen.

"Keep at it. You're doing a great job, O'Connor."

I frowned. I didn't feel like I was doing great. I wanted to contribute to this investigation, not just hit dead ends. I rolled my pen between my fingers, considering what Marks had said.

And then bolted straight up in my chair, my eyes darting from side to side. I clicked around on my computer until I finally found the contact information I needed and placed a call, explaining what I was looking for.

"How many years of data are stored in the database?" I asked.

"Fifteen."

*Hallelujah.* "Can I get an extract of any passengers that departed Chicago O'Hare from 2007 to 2009?"

"That's a lot of data." She paused. "It'll take me some time to put it together."

I gave her my information to send it as soon as possible, and then I hung up with new hope in my chest.

But that hope took a backseat to a new set of emotions when I saw the time and realized I had less than an hour before Dillon picked me up. Dillon invited me over to his place tonight, which was both exhilarating and also a little terrifying because this time, being intimate with him wouldn't be some frenzied, unplanned moment of passion. It would mean something more—a deliberate step in our relationship. One that was important to me.

I'd already grown to care more about Dillon in three weeks than I ever had with anyone else. In fact, I hadn't been able to stop thinking about these feelings that had grown inside of me. A light had cracked open in my chest and flooded with happiness whenever I was with him. His every text and phone call sent my heart into flutters, and I found myself thinking about him before I fell asleep and as soon as I woke up.

And while I was almost certain he felt the same for me as I did him, I couldn't take that deliberate step in our relationship on hope alone. I needed to know where I stood with him.

Tonight, I was going to lay it all out on the table. Tell him how I felt and find out if he felt the same for me, too.

*It's funny how, for weeks, you can feel confident that the emotions you've developed for another person are mutual. Yet when you're about to put it all on the line, you feel incredibly vulnerable. Because opening your heart to that person gives them the power to hurt you.*

## 12

"**H**ey, gorgeous." Dillon cupped my cheek and brought his lips to mine, the rest of the world evaporating instantly.

I tasted his tongue and groaned as he pressed his hand to my lower back. In his arms, my heart floated in ecstasy.

Dillon pulled back and rubbed his thumb over my cheek, making me feel like the most majestic thing he'd ever laid eyes on. "You okay?"

I offered a weak smile and nodded. I loved the way he looked at me, the way he always held me for several seconds after he kissed me, like he couldn't bring himself to let me go. I loved the way he smelled —of clean soap and joy. I loved the feeling of his body against mine when he hugged me.

"You didn't have to pick me up," I managed.

Dillon simply smiled and grabbed my hand as we walked out of my apartment complex to his convertible parked just outside. I savored the feeling of warmth and happiness radiating from his palm to mine.

He held the door open and shut it once I sat down. He walked around the hood, got inside, and held my hand as he drove.

"I've never had a guy cook me dinner before."

That had to be a good sign, right? Surely, you didn't go through that level of effort for any girl.

On the drive over, Dillon cheerfully talked about how his visit with Dexter had gone yesterday, but my mind was only half-listening. It was too busy assuring myself the impending conversation would go the way my heart needed it to.

When Dillon arrived at his apartment complex, he let me out of the car by the building's entrance while he went to park. I cherished his chivalrousness.

As I stood outside the front doors of the building, I looked at the sun dipping behind the skyscrapers, anxious to realize that my next chapter with Dillon would begin by the time that sun set. Hopefully, it would be a good chapter and not an ending.

After parking a block away—which was close, by Chicago standards—Dillon headed toward me. Man, he was gorgeous, wearing jeans and a white T-shirt. I adored how, even a half-block away, he fixed his eyes on me with a commanding stare, as if he were coming to claim me. Amid a chaotic city full of traffic horns, crowded sidewalks, and skyscrapers, I was the only thing he had eyes for.

Suddenly, those eyes abandoned mine, and his grin fell. He halted when a man approached him. An unwelcome man, based on the tightness of Dillon's face. I could only see the guy's back. Six feet tall. Brown hair. Thin, wearing a navy suit.

As he spoke to the guy, Dillon flashed his troubled eyes to me but only allowed them there for a fleeting moment.

*He doesn't want the guy to notice and look my way.*

Did Dillon need help?

I stepped forward, but Dillon flipped his hand around, so his palm pointed to me. He did it discreetly and only held it there for a second, so whoever he was talking to wouldn't see. But I saw it and stopped.

I wasn't sure what to do while the guy talked to Dillon. Why did I get the sense I should hide? I willed the guy to turn around, so I could look at his face, but after a minute, he walked away in the opposite direction.

And when Dillon reached me, his mood was dark and possessive.

"Come on." He guided me by my elbow inside. He smiled and took my hand as he flashed some card that activated his building's elevator, but the tension radiated off of him in waves.

"Who was that?" I asked as the elevator ascended.

"Just a guy from work."

"What did he want?"

Why would he come to Dillon's apartment building instead of, oh, say, his office or call him?

"Just work stuff." Dillon squeezed my hand.

The cop in me knew he was lying.

It made my stomach twist as the elevator rose and opened to Dillon's apartment. As in the elevator opened *into* his apartment.

"You live in the penthouse?" I raised my eyebrow.

"You like it?"

The floor-to-ceiling windows surrounding the central area exposed the city's buildings that stretched out as far as I could see. The roads below had tiny cars and people scuttling around like little bugs while in here, his white kitchen with a sofa-sized center island stretched into the dining room area. Next to that, a navy sectional couch faced a flat screen that hung above a gas fireplace, which crackled flames with fake sounds of burning wood. Gray and black accent colors polished the decor with a shag rug, throw pillows, and black-and-white images of Chicago, circa the early 1900s when the city had rebuilt after the Great Chicago Fire of 1871.

Dillon poured us each a glass of water and handed it to me without a smile.

"I'm going to start cooking," he said. Also sans smile.

"Is everything okay?"

"Yeah," Dillon claimed as he busied himself about the kitchen. "It's fine."

But as I sat at one of the stools along the overhung center island and watched him cook, it didn't seem like everything was fine. Something weighed on his shoulders. He'd stir the sauce and then stop, just staring into the pan. He'd cut up onions and let several beats pass before washing his hands.

I wanted to ask him again who that guy was, but he clearly didn't want to talk about it; doing so might sour his mood even more. I'd come here with a mission, and I needed to fulfill it before I lost my nerve.

I took a deep breath and prepared to speak, but Dillon stopped cooking, shut off the stove, and spoke in a low tone. "Fallon, there's something I need to tell you."

Something bad, by the sound of his voice.

His troubled eyes locked on mine, and he looked like he didn't want to spit out whatever it was.

But suddenly, I suspected what it was—he was going to end things. He had to have sensed my feelings for him—feelings that weren't mutual after all—and he must have prepared this meal as a thoughtful way to let me down and end things.

I'd been so lost in my head when he picked me up that I assumed he was acting normal with his kiss and holding my hand. But he'd been lost in his own head, too, knowing he was going to break it off with me. That was probably why he didn't want that guy to meet me —the pathetic girl who'd fallen for him.

"I was wrong, then," I said, looking down at my hands.

Dillon came to me and pressed his finger to the base of my chin, pulling it up until I looked at him. "Wrong about what?"

I hid my embarrassment. "I was going to tell you tonight. Make sure it wasn't all in my head."

His eyebrows pulled together, and he searched my face for understanding. "Tell me what?"

*Maybe I shouldn't tell him.* What would be the point now?

But as I stared into his eyes, I couldn't stop the pulses of affection or the desire to let him know how much he meant to me. Even if it would be the last thing I ever got to say to him. Especially so.

"I…" I bit my lip. "I'm falling for you."

Dillon looked stunned by my emotional stab, his shoulders sinking.

Not the reaction a girl longed for after professing her feelings. This was a huge mistake. I bit back the stinging in my eyes, grabbed my purse off the counter, and walked to the elevator. Pushed the button.

"Fallon." Dillon turned me around by my elbow, and when he stared at me, the look on his face wasn't sympathy. More like a dark, penetrating sadness. He looked as if he was fighting his own internal war, though his creased eyebrows relaxed as he bit his lip.

Dillon took a step closer, staring at my mouth as he put his palms flat to the wall on either side of my head. And when he spoke, his words sounded strangled. "You shouldn't be with me."

*Shouldn't.*

"Why?" I asked.

But my heart didn't care about *why* at this moment; what it cared about was that, with that one word, I could tell he felt this, too. And that he wanted it—I could see it in his eyes.

He stroked my cheek and confessed, "I'm falling for you, too, Fallon."

His words tunneled through my ears and into my heart, penetrating my soul. I wanted to savor them, put them in a bottle and consume them anytime I wanted to hear them again.

For the first time in my life, I left my comfort zone and embraced the possibility of having a serious boyfriend. In the past, this idea had felt foreign and induced anxiety, but with Dillon, it was like soaking my emotions in a soothing bubble bath.

Dillon stared at my mouth for one, two, three seconds, and then he crashed his lips to mine.

I dropped my purse and welcomed the fire that cascaded down my throat and into my belly. Our hands twisted in each other's hair with urgency, and without breaking our kiss, Dillon turned me around and walked me backward.

Ushering me through a doorway into his bedroom.

The only light came from the fireplace outside the room. The sounds of the city—of rumbling engines and the metallic grind of the "L" train—faded in the distance.

Desire spread through my veins, pulling me to him, making me ache for him to touch and kiss me everywhere. He nibbled my lip, kissed down my jaw and neck, licking my skin with his hot, wet tongue as he tugged at the hem of my shirt and pulled it over my head, tossing it aside, followed by my bra.

Dillon stared at me like I was a gorgeous work of art whose beauty deserved a moment of silence before he kissed me. On my mouth, my jaw. My chest.

I pulled at his shirt in desperate jerks, but with one fluid motion, he reached behind his back and tugged it up over his head like a slow-motion music video.

Heaven help me; he was even more gorgeous than I'd fantasized. A body carved of perfection, his shoulders cut into biceps, a rounded chest with a delicious line drawing my eyes lower, down his ripped abs.

He unfastened my zipper and kept his insatiable eyes on mine as he slowly pulled my pants down, one inch at a time until they finally fell to the floor. Repeating the same intoxicating dance with my panties.

His eyes glided over my body with a hunger to taste every morsel of it. "You're stunning, Fallon," Dillon whispered as he stripped out of the rest of his clothes.

This time, when he kissed me, he was more forceful.

I groaned.

He grabbed the backs of my thighs and wrapped my legs around his waist. When he walked me over to his dresser and set me down, I relished how my body was his trophy. He palmed my chest, making me gasp as he moved his lips down my throat, his mouth needy, kissing me everywhere.

He trailed his kisses down my stomach, along the inside of my thigh, closer and closer to my core. With his lips hovering over my center, he looked me in the eyes as he moved his mouth until it—

*Holy hell.*

I grabbed his shoulders as he worked his tongue on the epicenter of my desire. I ran my hands through his hair and watched him savor my body as my legs began to quiver. Our bodies moved with each other, wanting more—so much more—but he made me wait for it, building me up until he could feel me approaching ecstasy.

And when I hit it, he grabbed my thighs, riding my wave until its ravenous end.

He let go of me, leaving me yearning for him as he reached into the drawer, opened a wrapper, and stood between my legs after a second.

"Fallon," he whispered. "Look at me."

His stare pierced my core as he pushed his hips forward.

*Oh my word.*

I gasped and grabbed the dresser's edge and watched the beautiful pleasure spread across his face as he worked our bodies together, pressing his hips against my inner thighs. Dillon knew how to move, knew how to make the beats hit all the right notes, and as he found his rhythm, I climbed higher and higher.

What he'd done a moment ago was ecstasy, but nothing could top this.

Not breaking our connection, he pulled me off the dresser, laid me down on the bed, and climbed on top of me. He kissed my collarbone and chest. I climbed higher and higher, feeling his lips on mine as I broke over the edge. When a moan escaped my throat, one followed from his.

After, I laid my head on his chest, relishing the warmth of his arms wrapped around my body. It was so peaceful, hearing his heart thump beneath my ear, that I could sleep for days in this position, and it wouldn't be enough.


I AWOKE TO THE SMELL OF BACON AND EGGS AND THE BUZZING OF MY cell phone the next morning.

Burch just sent a group notification that we were not to report to HQ this morning; Instead, he required us to report to an address I didn't recognize. Immediately.

*Something must be going down.* I needed to get home, get into uniform, and be on the scene quickly. The last thing I needed to do was piss Burch off more by being the last one to show up.

I tossed on one of Dillon's T-shirts and went into the kitchen to tell him I had to go. Wearing nothing but a pair of jeans, he rested his butt against the counter next to the stove, sipping coffee as breakfast sizzled next to him. The view gave me an incredible look at his abs, chiseled out of stone, set beneath a broad chest.

When he saw me, he smiled and arched a hungry eyebrow as I approached him. "Just when I thought you couldn't get any sexier." He kissed my neck, ran his hand up my thigh to my backside, and growled. "You're not wearing any panties."

"You're making me breakfast."

"Forget breakfast," he said, cupping my butt harder and planting his lips on my collarbone. "I want to ravage you instead."

I smiled. "I have to get to work."

"I can be quick."

I laughed. "As enticing as that is, I can't be late. But we could get together later?"

Later, I wanted to ask about that creepy guy, his mood after, and why he said I *shouldn't* be with him.

"Do you want to take a shower with me?"

I smiled. "I wish I had the time."

Dillon's lips curled down slightly. "You eat while I shower. Then, I'll drive you home."

"I'll just grab a cab. Save you the round trip." Plus, I needed to hurry.

"What kind of a gentleman would make love to you and not drive you home?"

*Make love...not have sex.* My heart danced.

"The kind who has a woman who has to go."

Dillon cupped my cheek. "My woman," he said. He grazed my lips with his one last time and pulled back, leaving me breathless.

"Don't let breakfast go to waste," Dillon insisted. "Eat. I'll be in the shower, praying you change your mind and join me."

I grinned as Dillon gave me a quick wink. He turned around to lift the food off the stove, and when he did, I froze.

Ice surged through my limbs.

The whole time we'd been nude, I'd been facing him, so I hadn't seen him from behind. Until now.

There, across his skin, was a tattoo I hadn't seen last night—a scorpion holding the American flag.

13

My breath lodged in my throat so severely, I thought I might pass out. Unaware of my sudden shock, Dillon scooped eggs and bacon onto a plate and set it on the dining room table along with a fork and a glass of orange juice. I had to focus on keeping my facial expression composed as he kissed my cheek.

This time, his touch felt completely different—ice instead of fire.

"I'll call you later," he said.

When his mouth pressed to mine, I couldn't move a muscle. Luckily, it was just a quick peck, and he didn't seem to notice my statue-like stance as he walked into his bathroom, stripped naked, and got into the shower.

Which had a glass surrounding. With the door open, he had a full view of the kitchen and me. As the water cascaded over his hair, fogging up the glass with heat, I tried to calm my thoughts.

*There's no way. He can't be a captain of the largest drug organization in America. It's not possible.*

When Dillon found out about this, he'd laugh his butt off. He was probably the vice president of some corporation, maybe a lawyer or something.

It was embarrassing how little I knew of Dillon, though. I had no idea how someone so young earned an apparent abundance of money.

Or why he'd have a giant tattoo of a scorpion holding the American flag.

I sifted through all the conversations we'd had, looking for clues.

Imagine the fallout of a cop, a DEA agent—never mind the technicality that it was a temporary DEA badge for this case—letting the very person they were hunting into their bed. Falling for him, for the love of all things holy. My career would be over. How would I ever tell Burch and my precinct boss how stupid I'd been?

If any of this was true, I didn't deserve to be a cop, let alone a DEA agent.

My blood froze. What if he knew I was on this DEA task force? What if he was working me to see if I'd give up intel?

"You okay?" Dillon suddenly shouted. He peered at me through a spot in the shower he'd wiped free of fog, obviously noticing I hadn't moved an inch.

"Got spaced out," I lied with a smile, walking toward the plate of food.

Sadly, lying had become a strength of mine in life. When you had two parents whose addiction you tried to keep a secret, it became an important tool, one that I was grateful I had now.

My cell phone buzzed with an alarm, reminding me I had to hurry to get to work. If Burch was furious that I ran late from being in a fire, he'd never accept this explanation.

*Oh, sorry, after a night of lovemaking, I started to wonder if my boyfriend might be the drug kingpin that's the target of our investigation, so it slowed me down, sir.*

There had to be some simple explanation for that tattoo. A lot of people got tattoos, and while that seemed unique to me, maybe a scorpion holding the American flag was a symbol of something, a symbol that surely more than one person had.

I'd research it and run a more thorough background check on Dillon to prove he wasn't a drug dealer.

Like the ones that had come to our trailer. I shut my eyes, fighting against the barrage of memories.

*My pulse quickens when the knock comes. Mommy opens the door and lets him in. I don't like how he's dressed in baggy pants with that chain around his neck, and I hate how he dangles that cigarette from his lips like he's forgotten it's there. I want to run into my bedroom and hide under my covers, but I'm scared to leave her alone with him, worried he'll do something to hurt her, like last time.*

*"Got my money?" he snaps. He stares at Mommy like she's an irritating errand he needs to get off his long list of traumas.*

*Mommy blinks rapidly, holding out messy bills. "I have most of it. I couldn't get—"*

*She doesn't finish her sentence. He's backhanded her so hard that she falls to the couch in a yipe, and I hear someone screaming, realizing after a few seconds, it's me.*

*"I made myself clear!"*

*"I'm only twenty dollars short," she cries. "I can get it by tonight, I swear."*

*"That's what you said last time, bitch."*

*He takes out a knife, and I know what he's going to do, and I'm screaming.*

*I'm only ten years old, but I charge him, yelling at the top of my lungs as I smash into him. I'm not strong enough to overpower him or even knock him down, but I bite his arm so hard, the coppery taste of blood pricks my tongue.*

*And then something slams into my head. I'm on the floor, no longer screaming.*

*Mommy is.*

*He hits her again.*

*"Help!"*

*Are any neighbors home? Can they hear my cries? If they can, will they be brave enough to come?*

*I try again to charge him, but he throws me across the room like a rag doll, and now, all I can do is hug my knees and cry as I watch him hit my mommy again.*

*He pulls a gun from his waistband and points it at her. "Next time, I blow your head off in front of your kid."*

*He turns around and glares at me.*

*Even though I'm terrified of him, I refuse to give him the satisfaction of showing how afraid I feel. So, I stare at him. I even consider charging him again to bait him into a fight because, maybe, if he hurts me bad enough, Mommy will call the cops this time, and they'll lock this monster up, so he can't hurt anyone else's mommy. But if he hurts me that bad, Mommy might get into trouble, too, for allowing him in our home. Daddy will probably leave her, and then no one will be able to protect her. So, I don't bait him; I just look at him with pure hatred until he leaves.*

I wasn't able to shield Mom from a fallout, though. I had to get ten stitches from when he threw me across the room. Dad was enraged when he got home. After he thought I was asleep that night, he and Mom had the worst argument yet about the drugs being more important than the "damn safety of your own child," and "if one more thing" happened, that was it. He was kicking her out and getting a divorce for my own protection. A drug dealer was never allowed anywhere near me, he'd said, and if he ever found out otherwise, he'd divorce her.

Drug dealers had turned my once-happy childhood into my own personal horror movie. They ruined my family, sabotaged any feeling of safety I had, and became the bogeyman I spent the last several years training to take down.

And now, I wondered if the man I had fallen for might be one of them.

If he was, I had no idea what he was capable of.

I'd witnessed some of the horrific things drug dealers were willing to do to avoid discovery by the police, let alone a DEA agent.

Alone in his home.

*I should get out of here. Run.*

But I couldn't leave here without answers.

I walked past the bathroom, seeing his foggy frame scrubbing his underarms.

I went into his bedroom, unsure of what I was looking for yet terrified of whatever it was. I pulled out each drawer of his dresser, careful not to leave evidence that I'd rifled through his neatly folded clothes. The drug dealers I'd met in my childhood would never have this kind of clothing or organization. But they were the lower-level people, weren't they? The guys above them probably had all the money.

What was I even looking for, anyway? Did I expect to find a brick of cocaine?

In the fifth drawer, I found a Smith & Wesson M&P. But that didn't mean anything. Lots of people kept guns for protection.

But if it was just for protection, why have a gun that held two seventeen-round magazines?

When the sound of the water shut off, I glanced in the direction of the bathroom, hurried to his nightstand, and pulled out its drawer. There were several watches in a fashionable case. But in the back of the drawer, tucked away as if he didn't want anyone to find them, were three phones still in their packaging.

Burner phones.

My throat became sandpaper. Why would Dillon have burner phones? My police training had taught me there were two primary reasons people bought them: people couldn't afford a cell phone plan or to use the phone for criminal purposes.

Dillon entered the bedroom and eyed the open drawer.

And then his eyes cut to me.

## 14

D illon stood in nothing but a white towel fastened tightly around his hips, his dark hair tousled, casting a few water drops onto his shoulders. The sculpted muscles encasing his arms and chest, which had unleashed pulses of desire only hours ago, now fired off a silent warning—how easily he could overpower or crush me if this confrontation turned violent.

Not to mention that if, Heaven forbid, he was a drug lord, he was in an organization that guarded secrets with bloodshed. And he had a loaded gun a few feet away.

He stood between me and the door—blocking me from escaping the room. On accident or on purpose, I wasn't sure. I looked past him at my purse lying on the kitchen counter, where I kept mace.

Dillon glanced at his nightstand. "Were you going through my things?"

As he waited for my answer, I curled my fists in rage that had taken root at the age of nine.

When drug dealers had brought bag after bag of drugs to my mother and anytime she tried to muster the strength to quit, they capitalized on her weakness by offering a free dose, disguised as a *thank you for being a loyal customer.* She was their ATM, and the price tag? Her life and the welfare of her family.

And then came the incident that draped me forever in darkness and extinguished all my childhood innocence. Leaving me a mere shell of who I once was.

*I've decided to beg Mommy with my whole heart. I will tell her I'm scared every waking second of the day and that I've been having nightmares that something terrible will happen to her. The nightmares wake me up with a pounding heart, and I always have to go into her room and see that she's still breathing before I'm able to go back to bed.*

*I approach my trailer's front door and hesitate when I hear the television on inside. Mommy uses the TV whenever she gets high because she knows it makes me feel less scared to see her spaced out, looking at a TV than staring at nothing. Even though she gave up a long time ago hiding her addiction from us, she never gave up her TV trick, and that means she still cares about me. It's my only evidence she still does. She might not greet me with a warm hug when I get off the school bus anymore, she might not want to spend any time with me, but she still cares enough to leave the television on when she gets high. And right now, that means the world to me because maybe she'll start caring about me a little more each day until she loves me again.*

*But the sound of the television doesn't explain my strong hesitation to open the door.*

*It's so strong, I even wonder if I should wait for Dad to get home from work, but it's three thirty, and he won't be home from work until nine.*

I'm probably being silly.

*I twist the doorknob, and it opens into the living room, if you could call it that. A two-person couch along one wall with the television on the opposite wall, separated by six feet.*

*Mommy is lying on the couch. And the second I see her, my heart gallops like a racehorse.*

*Her face is a ghostly white I've never seen before. Her eyes are open, her mouth ajar, and a needle is hanging out of her left elbow, the skin on top of it bulging slightly from the syringe's weight pulling the tip up.*

"Mommy?"

*She doesn't move. Doesn't even blink.*

*Somehow, my heart beats even faster.* "Mommy!" *I shout louder.*

*No response.*

*I toss my backpack down and approach her slowly, noticing that in her right hand, she's clutching a photograph of Dad and me—like she was missing me when she got high. But I'm here now, and I need to wake her up, so she can tell me if she needs an ambulance.*

*I shake her shoulders, but her head only wobbles. I shake harder, but she's not moving. Her eyelids don't even flutter. What are you supposed to do if someone is so high, they don't respond?*

"Mommy!" *I shout, shaking her harder, so hard, the needle falls out of her arm and onto the floor.*

Overdose. *The word echoes through my mind.*

No. She's fine. She's just, like, so high, she can't feel anything or something.

"Mommy!" *I slap her, but her eyes remain an empty cavern of life.*

*I begin to cry. I shake her so hard, I'm worried I'll hurt her. Her chest isn't moving up and down.*

"Mommy," *I cry, moving the hair away from her face.* "Please wake up! Please, please!"

I don't know what to do. Why isn't she moving?

*I root around the couch cushions in a desperate hunt for her phone, not even caring if I get stabbed with a dirty needle that may lie in the crack, and when I find it, I call 911.*

"Lay her flat," *the operator tells me.*

*I heave her off the couch, which is super hard because she's so heavy.*

*I do the chest compressions they tell me to do, but I don't think I'm strong enough because she isn't waking up. And she's cold.*

*So cold...*

"Please don't leave me!" *I sob.*

*Nothing that I'm doing is working. I'm pushing and pumping and breathing in her mouth and screaming at the operator.*

What is taking the ambulance so long?

*And all this time, Mommy is not breathing. She's not waking up, or moving, or fluttering her eyes or anything.*

*Realization tries to invade my heart, but I fight it. I won't let this reality unfold.*

She can't be gone. It can't be true. It isn't true. I won't let it be.

*I pump her chest harder and faster, and I hear the sirens in the distance, but Mommy is cold and floppy, and her eyes are just...they have no light in them at all. She reminds me of one of my toys that ran out of battery.*

*My arms are so tired, but I keep going, and I hear the siren growing louder, and with each failed pump against her heart, I can't stop the reality from crushing my spirit into dust.*

*I want to run out of the trailer and come back another day when this isn't real. I want to hide under my covers until this scary nightmare stops. But I can't.*

*Because it's too late.*

*My mommy. The woman who was the best, most loving mother in the whole wide world for the first nine years of my life, the mommy who used to write a special note in my lunchbox every single day. Who used to read to me for an hour every single night. Who stood at my old bus stop—rain, snow, or shine—breaking out into a huge grin and hug the second my feet got off the bus. Who reminded me daily that I was her miracle baby and there was nothing she wouldn't do for me. Who I knew would come back to me one day, just as soon as she got this addiction thing under control. Is gone.*

*I was too late to beg her to stop using drugs.*

*"Mommy," I cry. I sob so hard, it feels like my ribs are cracking, and part of me wants to take that needle and jab it into my arm because this hurts too bad.*

*I don't want to be alive anymore, either.*

*I stare at an empty orange prescription bottle that lies in the corner of the room, at what was supposed to be medicine to treat her recovering body from surgery. But that medicine didn't cure her pain.*

*It turned fatal.*

*As the sirens grow closer, I lie down next to her and tuck my head onto her chest, pulling her arm around me the way she used to hold me when I was scared.*

This will be the last time Mommy ever holds me.

*I close my eyes and sob as pain devours me, and I hold my breath, hoping it'll stop my heart before the paramedics arrive.*

"Fallon?" Dillon asked.

The brokenhearted little girl inside me needed confirmation he wasn't the devil I had once hidden from, then hunted down, for most of my life. If he was, my whole world would implode, and my heart would be irrevocably destroyed.

But I wouldn't confront him here.

"Why were you going through my things?" he demanded, and this time, his tone had a flare of anger to it.

"I have to go."

I tried to walk past him, but he stood in front of me.

How dare he block my path. Was this supposed to intimidate me?

"Why were you going through my things?" he asked more forcefully this time.

"Move!" I demanded.

"What were you looking for?"

"Move!"

"Tell me why you went through my stuff!"

"Why are you so upset? Do you have something to hide?"

"You think I'm dating other women? Is that it?"

"As if it were that benign!"

"What the hell does that even mean?"

"Are you a drug dealer?" I snapped.

I wasn't sure who was more shocked at my outburst—him or me.

His head tilted back. "What?"

He'd heard me just fine, and it was too late to retract my accusation. I'd shown my cards, and now, the only hope to get an honest answer was to shove more chips into the center of the table before he had time to overthink his response.

"Are you involved, in any way, in dealing drugs?"

Dillon's chest rose and fell faster than it had before. He looked around his room, clearly trying to figure out what sparked my question.

Or my discovery…

If it was a discovery, would he be honest?

Drug lords surely never told people what they did for a living. It had to be as closely guarded a secret as being in the Mafia.

I thought back to how gladly he'd let me stop the conversation about work, and therefore, we'd come to an inadvertent agreement to not talk about what we did for a living. I thought he was doing that for me since I was the one that didn't want to discuss it, but I'd made it so easy for him to hide his profession.

He rubbed the back of his neck, and I eyed the drawer that concealed his weapon, noting I was closer to it than he was.

"Are you a captain in the Chicago Syndicates?"

His eyes rounded slightly.

He chewed the inside of his cheek, probably sifting through his possible answers, playing each scenario in his head. If he was involved with drugs and yet cared about me as much as he claimed, he couldn't hide this forever. So, if he did want a future with me, he couldn't deny it once confronted.

He stared at me. His voice was low and gentle when he spoke this time. "Yes. But let me explain."

T he numbness was temporary. I knew the avalanche of hurt and pain was headed right for me, but anger came first.

Look at him, staring at me with those worried eyes. He'd let me fall for him, and the whole time, he was the big bad wolf.

Images of Dillon mixed with memories from my childhood in flashes. *The man who stinks of cigarettes chases me to my bedroom, where I dive under the bed. His tattooed arm reaches for me, grabs my ankle, and pulls me out as I scream. Dillon's kissing my neck, his hand cupping my chest. The man slaps Mommy, and she yipes, holding her cheek. Dillon cups my cheek before he kisses me.*

I couldn't picture Dillon doing the awful things that Mom's drug dealer did, but I couldn't picture him being a drug lord, either.

Dillon left the room and returned with a glass of water. "Please drink."

He was clearly worried I was going into shock, but he could wipe that look of concern off his face. Drug dealers didn't have souls. They were the devil in plain sight.

I threw the glass across the room, where it shattered and splattered everywhere.

"Fallon..." he said.

"This whole time we've been dating, you didn't think I had a right to know the kind of person I was falling for?" I demanded.

"We didn't talk about work, and even if we had, this isn't exactly something I can open up about," he said sternly. "People who find out stuff they shouldn't are a liability in my profession, and I didn't want to put you in danger. I was trying to keep you safe. How do you even know about the Syndicates, anyway?"

If he thought that made him noble, he was wrong.

"I lost my family because of someone like you."

I stared into his gaze, struggling to reconcile this. How could the man who seemed like the most caring, wonderful person I'd ever met also be the vile, repulsive drug dealer that he was?

"Fallon, please let me explain."

All the other times the foundation collapsed from under me, I was never afforded the answers as to why it happened. I shouldn't listen to a damn word he had to say, but I needed to know how this could be real. If I had any hope of leaving my broken heart behind me, I needed closure.

"I'll give you five minutes," I said. "Not a second more."

For five more minutes, we could wear our relationship hat. But then I would walk out that door and build a case against him and his criminal enterprise.

I stormed past Dillon and plopped down at his kitchen table at the end, wanting distance between us. But the lack of clothing—me still in nothing but a T-shirt, Dillon nude, save for a towel—was a reminder of the intimacy we'd shared.

Dillon took a seat and scrubbed his face with his hands. "What I'm about to tell you, I've never told anyone. You have to promise me you won't tell anyone, Fallon. No matter how mad you are, my life is on the line here."

*So is mine, asshole.*

He must've interpreted my silence as complaisance. Probably thought he could weasel his way past my new brick wall. Fat chance.

"First of all, I need you to know that I didn't set out with the goal of becoming who I am today," he started. "One decision sort of led to the next, and..."

I crossed my arms over my chest. Four minutes, thirty seconds left.

Dillon studied me. "I told you about my dad leaving us with nothing. My mom worked her butt off, but she couldn't leave Dex unsupervised. We didn't have enough food and certainly didn't have enough to pay Dex's medical bills, not even with the help of Medicaid. And not even close to enough for his therapy, which he needed a lot of," he said. "I had to step in and help."

Dillon ran a hand through his hair, provoking a water drop to plop onto his shoulder. "Fun fact: the system isn't set up for a fourteen-year-old to support a family of three, especially one with medical bills. I tried working mainstream jobs. Worked my ass off to try and make ends meet, but it was impossible. Our neighborhood was infested with dealers on every corner, and they were constantly recruiting kids to join in. Kids make good dealers. Don't get charged as an adult, have clean records, aren't on cops' radar. I resisted as long as I could, but... a couple things happened that were so bad, they made selling drugs an acceptable sacrifice."

He blew out a huge breath when he thought back to it. "Dex didn't understand why we had to ration food the way we did. Food pantries weren't enough, so he was always hungry. Me and my mom gave him part of our meals but it still wasn't enough. He kept crying that he was hungry, and it was just so damn..." Dillon hesitated, clenching his jaw. "His unrelenting hunger was the first domino."

He leaned forward in his chair, put his elbows on his towel-covered thighs, and rubbed his hands together. Then, his face hardened into a rock of disgust at whatever he was about to say. Even thinking about it invited a rage into his darkened eyes that I had never seen.

"Second one came when a gang jumped Dex and me outside our home. Not sure if it was random or if it was a gang initiation, but either way, they held him down and made him watch as they beat me up. Bad. Broke three ribs, my arm, but the worst part was hearing Dex's screams as they did it. I kept trying to get to him, but eventually,

I was in so much pain, I couldn't move. When they were done with me, I didn't even care about that pain. I was just so relieved Dex wouldn't have to endure any more of it. But I had no clue what they were going to do next was even worse..." he choked.

"They laid into Dex so badly, he sounded like a wounded animal being murdered right in front of my eyes. The adrenaline helped me get up, but two of them held me down as the others stomped on Dex's face and torso until he stopped moving." Dillon swallowed over the terrible memory. "I thought he was dead. He was in a coma for two days and in the hospital for almost three weeks. It was in that hospital room that I vowed I would do whatever it took to get us out of that hellhole. Whatever it took even if that meant selling drugs."

Dillon ran a thumb across his lip.

"I got good at it. I wasn't like most dealers; I was methodical. Professional about it because I wasn't in it for the flashy jewelry. It wasn't long before bigger opportunities came calling, which meant more money for Dex's care. Took over an entire Chicago region, and then by twenty-five, I was one step down from running the entire Midwest."

Dillon cleared his throat and looked at me—a person whose family crumbled under the weight of narcotics.

"I never meant to fall for you, Fallon. And not just because it's too dangerous; I tried not to fall for you because after what you've gone through, you deserve someone who isn't wrapped up in the drug trade."

"*That's* what bothers you? That you fell for me? Shoving drugs into people's hands didn't bother you?"

"I never pushed them on anyone, Fallon. They came to me."

"You did not just say that."

"I didn't recruit customers. And the only reason I got into this was to save my family. I can't apologize for that."

"Wow." Just when I thought I had an ounce of empathy for him. "That's just what you told yourself for years, so you could sleep at night. It's the only way that you don't see a monster staring back at you when you look in the mirror."

Dillon cringed at my words. "I'm not exactly proud of what I do for a living, Fallon."

"You certainly fooled me, and in case you forgot? My parents were both addicts, and some of those drug dealers that came around my house? They beat me. They pulled me, kicking and screaming, out from under my bed when I was a nine-year-old girl and terrorized me. They beat my mother in front of me, and got high in front of me, and made me feel scared every second of my life!"

I hadn't realized I'd stood up or that I was shaking until this very second.

Dillon rubbed his jaw harshly. "They beat you?"

Judging by the look in his eyes, the boyfriend in him was enraged by it; the narcotics boss in him looked like he wanted names to find out if the sons of bitches were still within his vengeful reach.

"You hurt people for a living, Dillon. I don't understand how you can be okay with that."

It took him a moment to answer. "In my line of work, when someone breaks the rules—if they steal a large sum of money, for example—we can't exactly go to the authorities. So, you're not wrong. There are enforcers in this organization run by my bosses, but I'm not one of them, Fallon. Fear keeps people in line, and I would argue ninety-nine percent of the time, people don't even try to pull something that'd get 'em hurt. It's that one percent who know the rules, know the consequences, and break them anyway."

"Just because *you* don't pull the trigger doesn't mean the blood isn't on your hands, Dillon," I said. "Those dealers? Their bosses? They didn't wait for my mom to come to them. They showed up, over and over, and gave her freebies to keep her hooked anytime she wanted to quit."

Dillon's jaw hardened, and he licked his teeth. "They came to her?"

"Proactively. Like clockwork."

Dillon recoiled, looking sickened.

*Good. That's how a normal human being is supposed to feel when they realize that they've been delusional in thinking that eating gourmet food, driving nice cars, and keeping distance from the dirty, filthy business that they actually operate in makes them any better than the people who attacked a scared little girl.*

He rubbed his hands together for several silent seconds. "Fallon, I think you should leave."

I blinked. "Excuse me?"

After hearing that story, *that* was his reaction? How many ways could he disappoint me?

"Did you even want to stop doing this?" Or did he like the money too much?

"I tried to get out, for my brother's sake. If something happens to me—if I'm in prison or dead—he'll be thrown out of that home and into a state-run facility, best case. Worst case, homeless. Mentally impaired. You do the math on what would happen to him. But even if that wasn't true, I figured out a long time ago, I have a lot less control than I thought. Didn't realize what I was getting into, Fallon. I'd been so tunnel-visioned on getting Dex and Mom out, I didn't stop to consider what this looked like long-term. I never meant to deal drugs forever. It was a desperate stop-gap that got out of control, and by the time I understood what I'd gotten involved in, it was too late."

Dillon spoke in a low tone. "They don't let people out of the organization. You're in, or you're killed, cleaned up as a precaution. I have to watch my back every single day. They watch people. Just wait for someone to slip up. Three weeks ago? They killed my colleague. He'd dedicated his whole life to the organization. Got hit with bad luck, got busted with minor possession. That was it." He shut his eyes and blew out a breath. "You can't get out. And you can't make mistakes."

And yet here he was, unknowingly having made the biggest mistake he could ever imagine.

I stood up, retrieved my purse, pulled out my badge, and set it on the table in front of him.

Dillon stared at it for several seconds, and then his gaze locked on mine. He blinked. Twice. Rubbed a thumb along his nose. "You're a cop?"

"I'm not just a cop; I'm on the DEA task force investigating your organization."

Dillon's gaze sliced through mine, his mind undoubtedly racing.

A better person wouldn't have taken satisfaction in his squirming.

"I figured it out when I saw your tattoo," I said.

Dillon stood up and paced in his kitchen. "Fallon, you need to leave right now. If they see us together, they'll kill you."

"They'll kill you, too," I pointed out.

"You have to leave. Now."

"Turn yourself in," I insisted.

"What?"

"You're a good person who's trapped, right? So, turn yourself in. Make a deal to keep your brother and mom safe."

"You think I haven't considered that? If you're on the case, you know what they did to the last witness and his family."

I gritted my teeth. Did he really think I'd let him go back to breaking the law? No matter what his reasons, if he wasn't willing to cooperate, he left me with no other choice.

"I'm not leaving until you're in cuffs."

I'd let a drug dealer into my bed. The only way I could make this right was to have Dillon arrested. If I didn't arrest him, it would mean he'd won, that *they'd* won. It would be proof that drug dealers could do whatever they wanted, to whomever they wanted, and get away with it. They couldn't. I couldn't live in a world where the balance of justice always tipped in favor of the criminals.

I reached into my purse and pulled out the metal restraints.

Dillon glared at me. "You're joking."

"Not even a little."

"You have no grounds to arrest me."

"Probable cause of a felony crime; you just admitted to being involved with a drug organization. Last time I checked, that's slightly illegal."

"I wasn't Mirandized."

I tightened my lips. I could already hear the district attorney. *Have any evidence of drugs in his apartment? No. Any other evidence of a crime being committed? No. Any specific evidence at all? No. Then, get out of my office and don't waste my time until you have some.*

"And an officer needs a warrant to arrest someone in their home," he added.

These types studied their rights, didn't they? To keep themselves out of jail.

"Exigent circumstances. You let me in."

"Still no grounds for an arrest."

I glanced at Dillon's bedroom. "You have a permit for that gun?"

"The one you found without a search warrant?"

I clenched my jaw. "Then, I'll detain you until a judge signs an arrest warrant," I said, holding the cuffs.

"On what basis?"

"Reasonable suspicion you're trafficking narcotics with the Chicago Syndicates. The tattoo on your back is sufficient evidence."

"You can't detain me," Dillon said.

"While I wait for an officer to obtain a warrant, yes, I can." Especially with concerns Dillon could destroy evidence while we waited. "Put your hands behind your back."

Dillon put his hands up in surrender and backed away. "I can't let you do that, Fallon."

Dillon backed up closer to the wall.

I pursued him, cuffs in hand.

"I let you bring me in, I'm dead, just like my coworker."

"Well, maybe you should have thought of that before you worked for a bunch of psychopaths."

He looked hurt. "You'd really be okay if I died?"

*No. But I should be.*

I reached for his hand, but suddenly, the room spun, and I wasn't facing him anymore; I was facing the wall, my chest pressed up against it. My hands behind *my* back.

Dillon stood behind me, holding my arms together. He hadn't hurt me; he'd just been quick. Quicker than me.

*Dammit.*

"Fallon." His breath warmed my ear.

I sensed the rise and fall of his pectorals, my wrists wedged against his hard, bare abs, and in the struggle, my shirt's hem had come up a couple of inches.

I turned my chin over my left shoulder and looked up into his eyes. His warmth was back. The warmth that had kissed me last night. He stared at me—at my nearly exposed backside, at my lips—with desire swirling through his eyes.

As if he had to fight the urge to kiss me.

"I can't let you take me in," he whispered.

I yanked my wrists, but he tightened his grip and pressed his chest against my back.

"Don't move," he said. "I don't want to hurt you."

"Let me go!"

"I let you go," he commanded, "you walk out of here and never see me again."

My chest ached as I looked up above my shoulder at his chestnut eyes. "Is that really what you want?"

He looked at my mouth, then back at my eyes, and when he spoke this time, his voice was softer. "I need to keep you safe."

The hurt inside me dulled a little, and then I got mad at myself. I shouldn't care if he cared about me. I was a cop; he was a criminal.

"Just let me go."

My cell phone rang with Burch's ringtone, but I remained Dillon's captive. He held me for several more seconds before backing away, but by then, my cell had gone to voice mail.

He retrieved a black bag and placed it on the counter. Packed a wad of cash and a burner phone into it and shoved it into my hands.

"What are you doing?" I asked.

"You need to leave town. I'm calling you a ride."

"No! And by the way, you think I'm that stupid to get into a car *you* put me in? It'd blow up or drive off a bridge."

He looked annoyed at my accusation. "I would never hurt you, Fallon, but the guys I work for would in a heartbeat. If they find out you were dating me, that you know…"

I'd be killed.

We both would.

"Maybe they already saw us together," I challenged.

A fresh look of alarm flashed across his face. He shook his head. "We'd be dead already."

My cell phone rang with Burch's ringtone. I needed to tell Burch everything. Even if he didn't forgive my stupidity, I'd give him every piece of intel I had to help his investigation and let the cards fall where they may.

"Sergeant," I answered.

My intent must have been written all over my face because Dillon took a step closer.

"Fallon," he whispered.

"O'Connor," Burch snapped. "Ever hear of answering your damn phone?"

"Don't do this," Dillon added.

"Yes, sir," I said. "I have something—"

"An officer is missing."

Silence.

"I...what?"

"He left his house for an early morning meeting. Never made it to the station."

*Holy crap...*

"Get down here—now. Texted everyone the address. I took over as IC, and I want the whole task force on this."

Incident commander meant there was an official crime scene, which meant they thought something happened to him. And if Burch was the IC, then it had something to do with the case.

"And, Fallon?"

"Yes, sir?"

"When I call? You answer."

The call ended.

I tried to call Burch back five times. I wanted permission to stay here and detain Dillon. I wanted Burch to confirm the tattoo was sufficient enough evidence to get a warrant. But Burch didn't answer, and with an officer missing, I was left with two bad options: no-show at the crime scene or rush there and tell Burch everything.

I despised the idea of forgoing my original plan, but leaving wouldn't change one vital fact: I now knew the identity of this Syndicates captain. I had Dillon's name, address, and make and model of his vehicle—all things we could use to find him and put him behind bars.

"Looks like you got a temporary reprieve," I choked. "Key word being *temporary*. As soon as I see my boss, I'm telling him everything."

I walked into his bedroom and threw my clothes on. When I came out, Dillon stood with his arms crossed over his chest.

"I wouldn't do that if I were you."

"Is that a threat?" I grabbed my purse.

"It's a warning. Do *not* tell him. You'll be putting yourself in danger."

"More like your life in danger," I said as I put my shoes on.

"You really think I'm saying this to save my own ass?" he snapped. "I don't give a shit what happens to me! If it weren't for my brother and mom, I'd have done something to just let them..."

He stopped and shoved a hand through his hair.

I couldn't process all this right now. Right now, I needed to go, so I pushed the elevator button.

"Fallon."

I turned around and saw the *boyfriend* Dillon again. The man who had broken down all of my walls and made me think that I had finally found happiness.

"I trusted you," I managed over the lump in my throat. "I never trust anyone, and I trusted you."

He opened his mouth but clearly realized there was nothing he could say to undo any of it. Instead, he held the escape bag out and pleaded, "Please reconsider."

The elevator door opened, and I stepped away from the landscape that once held my happily ever after and into the empty shell that was my heart's future.

16

I couldn't believe I fell for Dillon. Love was complete bull, making you savor it when you thought you had it, only to rip it away each time and watch you bleed. What the hell was wrong with me, letting the wall come down I'd safeguarded for years? I finally let someone in, I trusted him and gave him my heart, and look what happened. My soul was put into a woodchipper.

Why? Was I so broken that I only attracted darkness into my life? Was I cursed?

Or maybe...maybe I didn't *deserve* love.

I bit back the tears.

Right behind the pain came anger at myself because I was stronger than this. This whole experience with Dillon just proved my original priorities were right.

Priorities that did not include love but did include rushing to this crime scene.

When I arrived at the address Burch had texted us, I was overwhelmed by the number of uniforms on the scene. When a cop disappeared? Police took that very seriously and spared no expense in looking for one of their own. The top detectives and crime scene units joined us, ready to comb every square inch of this place.

Before I could join them, my cell phone buzzed with a text.

**Dillon: Fallon, please tell me you're okay. I heard a cop is missing.**

Another buzz.

**Dillon: I know it's not fair of me to be worried about you, but I am. I'm so damn worried, so please. Just text me back one word. Tell me to go to hell, anything to let me know you're safe.**

The audacity of him to act like he cared.

**Dillon: For the record, I would give anything to be the guy you deserve, Fallon.**

But he knew all along he wasn't the guy I deserved. How could he let me fall for him?

I clenched my fists. I wanted to hit something. Beat something. My enraged heart thrashed around in my rib cage, pumping an unhealthy desire for revenge, for vigilante justice, through every cell of my body.

"Sir." I approached Burch, who stood near the command center.

Proctor was near him, of course, lips firmly planted on his butt.

I'd quickly changed into my uniform at home before rushing here, where yellow police tape roped off an abandoned parking lot with asphalt so faded, you could barely make out the yellow stripes. Weeds sprouted between its network of cracks, and its fifty parking spots were all empty, except for one police car. The parking lot was flanked by industrial buildings to the north, a patch of weed-infested land to its south, and Lake Michigan on its east, which had once been home to shipments that arrived on a now-broken boat dock.

Burch glanced around at all the other officers, then returned his steely eyes to me. "You're late, O'Connor."

Proctor smirked, making my cheeks warm in anger. I'd never met anyone who savored someone's suffering like Proctor did.

"I know. I can explain. It has to do with the case. I need to tell you something."

"It'll have to wait," Burch said.

Proctor had to act like he was wiping his lips to keep them from smiling too wide.

"All right, listen up," Burch shouted to everyone else, thwarting any possibility to talk to him.

What if Dillon was telling the other captains right now? Getting the jump on this information? I needed Burch to listen now.

"Officer Anthony Marks was last seen at six o'clock this morning when he left his home."

The shotgun blast of shock rocked me back on my heels. The missing officer was Marks? Kind, family-loving, about-to-have-a-third-child Marks? My mentor?

"Told his wife he was heading to an early morning meeting at work—a meeting his commanding officer confirms was on the books. Marks never showed, which is out of character. An hour ago, his empty squad car was found ten miles away in this abandoned parking lot. Which, as you can tell, is the opposite direction of the precinct. We tried to trace his cell," Burch continued. "But it was shut off ten minutes after he left home."

No cop ever shut off his cell, let alone one with a wife about to have a baby any second.

"Upon an interior search of his vehicle, we found small traces of blood on the steering wheel."

*Oh no.*

"We need to work fast," Burch said. His implication—that the clock was ticking to find him before he was killed—twisted my ribs.

If Burch thought this had something to do with the Syndicates, he needed to know about Dillon ASAP. Dillon could be telling his bosses everything about me right now, jeopardizing our case. Maybe even putting Marks in more danger.

"Sir," I pleaded, "I really need to talk to you."

"I'll come find you in a few minutes," he said with an edge. "Right now, I need to get everybody assigned to their grid because minutes matter."

Burch walked away, and Proctor had the nerve to step into my path like some douchebag excuse of a bodyguard protecting his boss from some crazy woman who might otherwise follow Burch around.

The look of complete satisfaction on his face made me clench my teeth so hard, they might break.

"Did you know you were the last one here out of forty officers?" Proctor sneered. "You're making it pretty clear this job isn't a priority of yours."

"I don't have time for your petty BS today, Proctor," I snapped. "So, leave me the hell alone."

His nostrils flared. "Maybe we should discuss your tardiness with your commanding officer."

"You know what?" I snapped. "Let's set that meeting up. Because there's a very good reason I was late today, but there's no good reason for why you won't stop harassing me at every turn. Maybe we should discuss *that* with our commanding officer."

Proctor's jaw ticced. "You're turning into an embarrassment, you know that?" Proctor spewed. "Just like your dad."

My fingers twitched. It took every ounce of self-control to not shove him to the ground and pummel him.

I walked over toward Shane, but because the universe evidently wanted to make today a living hell, Proctor was assigned to our little group working the grid on the nearby small field.

"Do me a favor," Shane hissed quietly. "Next time you decide not to come home at night, give me a courtesy text, so I'm not worried somethin' happened to you."

Shane had never snapped at me like that before.

"I thought you knew I was with Dillon."

"You've never spent the night before," he spat. "For all I knew, something might've happened to you on your way home from his place. Courtesy text. All I'm askin'."

Before I could apologize for worrying him, Shane stomped away.

I dug my nails into my palms, fighting back tears of fury.

"Maybe Marks took off," Proctor suggested with a dismissive shrug.

I bit down on my teeth. "He wouldn't take off, Proctor. His wife is about to have a baby."

"Exactly," Proctor said. "Nagging wife, screaming baby on the way. What guy wouldn't want out?"

"How can you be so ambivalent about a missing cop?" My voice rose.

If he didn't take this seriously, he might miss clues that could save Marks's life.

"Geez, chill!"

"He's missing, and there's blood in his car. Did you flunk common-sense class?" I demanded.

"I can't wait for Burch to fire your ass. You're such an embarrassment to this force!"

I clenched my fists. "You don't care about Marks! Or any other fellow officer, for that matter!"

"*You* don't care about what a shit stain you're leaving on our uniform. I can't believe I ever asked you out. If I'd known you were the offspring of some lowlife junkie piece of s—"

I growled and slammed my fist into his cheek.

Suddenly, I wasn't standing anymore. I was on the grass, holding my face. He had hit me back—hard.

"The hell is going on?" Burch barked.

I stood up, and Proctor wiped his bloody lip.

"Look, I don't know what the hell is going on, and frankly, I don't care. Both of you, go home now," Burch ordered.

He walked away.

"Sir," I started.

"That's an order," Burch said.

Proctor gave me the look of death before walking off, and as badly as I wanted to just get away from the scene, I couldn't leave yet.

"Sir, before I go, there's something I need to tell you."

Burch's lips tightened. "You'd better make this fast, O'Connor."

Burch marched over to the water and expected me to follow, out of earshot of everyone else.

"Sir, I've uncovered the identity of the captain with the tattoo."

Burch stared at me as I willed the words to come.

"I discovered his identity this morning, but for the past three weeks..." I swallowed. "I've been dating him."

Burch didn't move. Didn't blink. Didn't do anything.

"What the hell are you talking about?" he demanded.

"I had no idea he was involved with drugs."

Burch scrubbed his face. He looked like he couldn't believe what a cluster-F this investigation was turning into.

"This morning, I saw his scorpion tattoo. Confronted him."

"You confronted him without backup?"

"It happened fast."

"And let me guess. He didn't give up any evidence we can work with."

I tensed. "No permit for a weapon."

"A slap on the wrist. You should've waited for us to properly interrogate him. You blew our element of surprise."

Something inside of me swelled up, and my backbone snapped straight.

"Maybe," I allowed. "But my guess is, he'd have never admitted he was a drug captain to anyone else. But he admitted it to me because I built up a rapport with him."

Burch smoothed his mustache as he looked to the side. When he spoke again, his tone lost some of its edge. "You tell him about the investigation?"

"I never even told him I was a cop until this morning. But now he knows I'm on the task force investigating his organization."

"There any chance you slipped and gave up details?"

"No."

"Any chance he was working you this whole time?"

"I don't think so. If anyone in the Chicago Syndicates knew he was dating me, he'd have been killed. So would I."

Burch considered this. "What's his name?"

I hesitated. But the protectiveness that came over me was absurd.

"Dillon McPherson."

"Will he still talk to you?"

What? "I...I don't know. Why? You want me to interrogate him?"

"No. I want you to make him an informant."

An informant. Not only a role where I'd be forced to talk to Dillon regularly, but it'd be an intimate, secret relationship between a cop and a CI on top of that.

"No one talks in this organization," he said. "You've just cozied up to a captain in the Syndicates. This is our best shot to get information."

"But we got names off that USB drive, and IT still might get more."

"A CI would be a game changer that we can't afford to pass up."

"Sir, there's no way he'll tell me anything else now that he knows I'm a cop. And even if he would…" It would be too damn painful to tug at the emotions I'd let myself have for him. "We wouldn't be able to trust a word he says."

"Didn't say it'd be easy to sift through the truth, but we need answers."

He must have assumed my sigh was hesitation.

"O'Connor, Officer Marks arrested a captain, and that captain turned up in the river. If the Syndicates *are* responsible for Marks's disappearance, he might not be the last."

Burch was right. Our team, if successful, would continue to put massive dents in the Syndicates' plans. Which meant more officers could be in danger. Even Shane.

My skin prickled at the thought.

He let the fear bounce around inside my head for a full thirty seconds.

"What do you want me to do?" I asked.

"Call him. Set up a meeting."

## 17

The diner screamed the 1950s with red and black walls, where framed Blackhawk jerseys and autographed pictures of celebrities surrounded the casually dressed crowd in Chicago nostalgia. The undercurrent of voices competed with Elvis Presley music that pumped through the stuffy air. Behind a wall opening, a short-order cook with sweat shining on his forehead slapped a set of white plates piled high with pancakes onto the counter—the scent of eggs mixing with the smell of stale coffee.

Dad stood up when he saw me come in, motioning to the empty chair in front of him.

*Like I need his help.*

I plopped down and tossed my cell on the table faceup. If any word surfaced on Marks—any—I wanted to see it right away.

Yesterday, the techs dusted the entire car inside and out for prints and found it clean. Not a single print, not even one from Marks himself. Which pointed to a professional job, one I prayed was not a hit.

Marks's cell phone remained off and unfound. No suicide note, nothing unusual in the initial review of his financial records. Nothing to suggest that whatever happened was self-inflicted. There wasn't a single clue as to what happened to him or where he was. Not even a hair out of place. And now, a day later, the team was no closer to finding him.

And here I was, having to carve out time for breakfast before work because Dad's incessant calls finally made me cave.

"What happened?" Dad motioned toward my bruised cheek and had the nerve to look worried. The hurt he'd caused me in just one of his episodes was nothing compared to the force of Proctor's fist.

"I'm here, so just say whatever it is you want to say because I really have to get going."

*Geez.* When had I gone from the loving daughter who'd fight to the ends of the earth to help her father conquer his disease to this bitter human?

Dad cleared his throat. "You look good," he said, nodding to my uniform, using the same proud tone as when I'd come home with an all-A report card in grade school.

He reached for my hand just like he used to do when I was a kid— before he'd traded his love for me in for drugs.

At dinners, he'd hold my hand, tell me how much he loved me, and ask me to tell him everything about my day. "Don't leave anything out," he'd say with an eager smile. His affection used to be the brightest spot in my day.

The key phrase being *used to.*

I snapped my hand back before suffering the burn of his once-pleasant touch and crossed my arms over my chest.

"What do you want, Dad? And what was so urgent it couldn't wait a few more days?"

"I've missed you," Dad said. He looked like hell, worse than I'd ever seen him. His eyes had dulled to a gray, as if their luminosity was chained to his dwindling spirit, his skin puddled around his elbows, and his hair had further succumbed to balding.

"Here are the coffees you ordered," the waitress interrupted. She wore her hair in a messy bun and smelled like she'd taken a recent smoke break.

"Thought you might want a cup," Dad explained.

"Will you guys be ordering food?" she asked.

"No," I said. "We won't be here long."

She walked away.

I glared at my dad, becoming more impatient as he gathered himself.

He leaned his arms on the table. "I have something to say. It'll just take a few minutes, and then if you never want to talk to me again, I promise I won't bother you."

The fear of losing him kicked my ribs. I was the one shutting him out, so why did it hurt so much that he might stop trying? Maybe it was because the only constant in our relationship—in my life, really— was Dad's pursuit of my love, his promises to recover echoing through the halls of our lives. The thought of that going away terrified me. It was all I had left of him.

"First of all, I need to apologize, Fallon. Last time you saw me..." Dad ran a hand over his head, unable to finish before his lips quivered.

That was the thing about getting high; when you came down, the hurt you'd caused people crashed through you, unable to hide behind the fog of narcotics.

After what he'd put me through, part of me was glad he fought back tears. Especially since his moment of being the good dad, the dad that actually cared if he hurt me, had become less frequent with each dose of drugs.

The soft old Fallon would smile weakly and accept his apology. Anything to preserve the possibility that a morsel of his affection might be thrown my way. Anything to maintain the delusion that things would get better one day. That the foundation of my world would finally be repaired, and what I'd desperately longed for year after year would finally come back to me—the stability of my father and his love for me. If I were honest, I needed it now more than ever. It felt like my life was spiraling with Marks missing and Dillon's shattering revelation. But each time I'd hoped Dad would start to love me how I needed to be loved, my heart was sliced. And now, I couldn't handle being forsaken again.

"What you did was low," I growled. "Even for you."

Dad gripped the white ceramic mug tighter, staring at the brown liquid in shame.

I was an awful person because at this moment, I wanted him to hurt the way he'd hurt me. I wanted him to feel the suffering of a terrified child, devastated over her mommy's death, desperate for her dad to assure her everything would be okay. Only to discover him using Mom's leftover drugs to get himself high.

I hated thinking about that time, filled with a mixture of terror—how could we live without Mommy?—and hope that Daddy would take care of me.

*I'm holding Daddy's hand, watching Mommy's casket lower underground.*

This is all happening too fast.

*Life doesn't seem like life without Mommy. It feels like my world cracked in half and filled with lava, and nothing is ever going to be okay.*

*But Daddy said we'd be okay. He tells me that every night when he tucks me in. And I trust Daddy. He's never failed me, not once.*

*"Things will be okay, kiddo," he says. "I promise."*

*"I'm scared you'll leave me, too," I say.*

*He looks at me super seriously and squeezes my hand. "I will never leave you. I will always take care of you, Fallon. I promise."*

Fast-forward to reality, sitting in a diner.

"I'm ready to answer your question, Fallon." By the tone of his voice, I knew which question he was referring to.

"Really? So, hell has frozen over, then."

His lips tightened, and he tried to hide the sag of his shoulders. "I deserved that."

"You deserve a lot of things."

He cleared his throat. "In my meetings, they've been telling us we need to accept the anger from our loved ones. You have every right to hate me after what I put you through."

"You're going to meetings," I said incredulously. As in plural. As in more than one, without me shoving him through the door.

"For three months."

I glared at him. He expected me to believe this? The last time I saw him, he was so in love with his next fix that he'd finally destroyed me. Almost cost me my coveted seat on the task force.

"Fallon, after what I did to you..." He rubbed his hands, trying to disguise their trembling. "It was rock bottom. After that day, I went to an NA meeting and never touched the stuff again. Never will, either."

Yeah, right. How many times did I have to get my hopes up before I learned my lesson?

"You embarrassed me," I growled. "In front of my boss. My colleagues. Police officers, for crying out loud! That night was special to me, and you could've cost me my job."

I should've known better than to invite him. But that was me—pathetic old Fallon, desperate for my father to care about me. Desperate to get his attention and his approval, thinking if he saw the celebration of me having made the task force, we would have some kind of a happy moment together for once. A happy moment that would bring us closer. I had pictured him walking in and putting his arm around me proudly, maybe even saying a few words on my behalf. But my boss was the one saying a few words on my behalf when my dad stumbled in, high as a kite. In that instant, I was over-come with dread as I watched him lumber through the group of offi-cers, and once he got close? He was so high, he fell into a waitress and knocked her tray of drinks on the ground. The whole restaurant stared at my dad on the floor. And there, lying next to him? What had fallen out of his pocket for all my fellow law enforcement officers to see?

A baggie of heroin and a needle.

As if that wasn't bad enough, the needle had no protective cap. No cap. He could've infected the waitress with Lord knew what when he bumped into her. He could've infected any colleague there—my boss even—if they'd bumped into his pocket.

*Mortification* wasn't even the right word. All the disappointments he'd caused had been brewing inside like a volcano, and that was it. My anger erupted. I was so furious, I didn't even feel bad for him when he was arrested.

I was angry that he'd made me so angry. He'd unleashed some bitter, horrible version of myself.

"I'm sorry, Fallon."

*I'm sorry.* Two words wouldn't undo everything he'd done.

"Is that it, then?" I asked. "Because I have somewhere I need to be."

Dad offered a sad smile. "I have some things I need to say to you, Fallon. Before it's too late."

"It's already too late. I don't care about your apologies or if you're trying to get clean for the zillionth time. I give up on you, Dad," I declared. "I finally don't give a crap why you picked up the drugs because you know what? It doesn't matter. It took me a while to figure out that I don't care."

Dad's gray eyes shimmered, so he looked down.

Evidently, not all of me was on board with hurting him; a sudden rush of compassion made me want to wrap my arms around him because I'd never seen him look so...broken. Not even when Mom died.

And I'd never seen him look so ashamed. It contorted his face, and his body folded in on itself.

"Fallon, you deserve to know why I started taking the drugs in the first place."

My heart stilled in the silence.

"Before your mom died, I'd argued with her so many times about her addiction. In the beginning, I was patient. Understanding. But it was scary, watching the woman I fell in love with change like that. Sent her to rehab multiple times, but nothing worked; it just kept getting worse. I think the first time I felt true anger was when we lost our house. I guess in my mind, it was one thing for her to lose her job, her friends. She was hurting herself, and I hated that, but it was confined to her. Until it wasn't."

Dad took a sip of his coffee, as if willing it to give him courage. The door to the café opened, and a handful of people stomped in, greeting friends with loud hellos.

"When we lost our house and drained our retirement accounts, I got mad and insisted she get a grip on it. If not for her sake, for yours.

You were just a little girl, and she'd be passed out when you got home from school."

Dad rubbed his face. "No matter how much I tried to understand, she was crossing lines I couldn't tolerate. Endangering you with drugs in the house. The people she brought over." Dad cracked his knuckles. "After you left for school one morning, I went off on her like I'd never done before. The years of anger finally exploded. I told her she was being a horrible mom, destroying your life. If she didn't get clean, I was going to file for divorce, take primary custody, and never talk to her again."

When my dad spoke next, I could hear the tears he choked back. "She said maybe we'd all be better off without her." Dad stopped and squeezed his eyes shut. "I said maybe we would."

The air around me became poisonous, stabbing my lungs because I understood where this was going.

"I'd said it out of anger. I was sick of her playing a perpetual victim and flipping the tables like that. What I'd meant was that I couldn't keep an addict in the house with you. But she..." He gathered himself. "She got this look on her face I'd never seen before. Something about it worried me, but I was too pissed to ask her about it. So, I just stormed out and went to work."

Dad rubbed his eyes, taking several moments to gather his emotions.

"That was the last thing I ever got to say to her," he explained. "And to this day, I don't know if her overdose was an accident."

*Oh my gosh.*

All these years...I had no clue that there was a chance her OD was intentional.

I'd later learned the same statistics she probably did in treatment. While the relapse rate for substance abuse disorders was between forty and sixty percent, the rate for heroin specifically was as high as ninety. With a ninety percent chance she'd continue to hurt her daughter, did she think she was doing me a favor, that a life without her was better for me?

How hopeless must she have felt in her final dark hours, the disease of addiction suffocating her spirit. It had to have devastated her to think of the mom she was once capable of being and seeing the anti-mother she had become. It must have destroyed her, realizing her existence caused so much pain to the two people she loved more than anything in the world.

Even though rational people may have seen that with time and the proper treatment, there was plenty of hope she could beat her addiction, perhaps she'd grown too depressed to believe it.

Maybe when she stuck that needle in her arm, it had not been a selfish act at all. Maybe, in her hopeless mind, it was a sacrifice to free me from unconscionable pain. If I was a mother and the only thing I ever did was hurt my child and thought there was no hope of it ever changing, maybe I wouldn't want to be alive, either.

Then, I remembered it—the photograph of me and Dad that had been in her hand when I found her. I'd never told Dad about it. After we got home from the hospital, I'd put it in my jewelry box. But it had always puzzled me why she was staring at Dad and me as she took her final hit—a hit that was so powerful, it must have killed her before she could even get the needle out of her arm.

That had to be why she was holding it. She was looking at the two people who would be better off without her. Maybe it gave her the final motivation she needed to take what she knew was a lethal dose.

"That's why she had that picture..."

I suddenly felt so ill, I had to focus on my breathing to not vomit. I'd resented her for all these years, never comprehending the depths of her suffering. And all the while, she must have sensed my disappointment in her and my hurt that I wasn't enough for her to want to get clean.

When in fact, I meant so much to her, she'd rather die than cause me any more pain.

"What?" Dad's eyebrows furrowed.

Dad's voice snapped me back to the noisy diner. I'd been so lost in thought, I hadn't meant to say that out loud.

"Nothing."

But I could tell he wasn't about to let this slide.

"Fallon, I can tell it's something, so just tell me."

I took a sip of coffee. It was lukewarm and bitter. "I don't want to upset you."

He'd just blame himself more, and even though a minute ago, part of me had wanted him to hurt, there was a considerable difference between that and giving him news that had the power to destroy him.

"Was there a suicide note?" he pressed, trying to hide his growing edge of panic.

"No."

"Did she do something to you?"

"No."

"Fallon, tell me."

It was strange how we could slip back to father-daughter roles with him in command in a snap. I sipped my coffee, trying to think of a way out of telling him. He already suspected suicide, and maybe the photo didn't confirm it with certainty, but it was pretty damning. I looked at the determination in his eyes and realized there was nothing I could say to get him off the scent. The best I could do would be to soften the blow.

"When I found her, she was holding a picture of you and me."

I didn't need to say more. Gut-wrenching understanding washed across his face.

"It might not mean anything," I insisted.

But I could see my words just bounced right off of him.

"More coffee?" the waitress asked.

I offered her an uncomfortable smile as she topped off our mugs.

Dad looked stunned, like he had been emotionally tasered. I didn't know what to say, but when I opened my mouth, my cell buzzed.

**Dillon: Tonight. 10 p.m. I'll text you the location.**

It had taken him almost a day to respond to my request to meet.

The text must have reminded Dad we were on limited time because he forced himself to resume the conversation where he left off, to finish saying whatever it was he wanted off his conscience.

"When your mom died, I went to a really dark place. Blamed myself for her death. At best, I hadn't gotten her the help she needed in time to save her. At worst, saying we'd be better off without her made her..." Dad blinked back tears. "I should've been stronger. I was all you had, and you were hurting." He paused. "And I swear, I tried to be strong, but my mind...wasn't working right. Felt like I'd been drowning for two years and an anchor pulled me under."

Dad's eyes were haunted at the memory, glazing with tears. "What I did next, there's no excuse for. I should have gotten help, but I was just in so much pain. She was the love of my life, and I couldn't stop thinking about the last thing I'd said to her."

Dad let a more extended silence pass this time. He wouldn't look me in the eye as he repeated in shame, "I should have gotten help."

Unease wrapped its unwelcome blanket around me, sensing a far more sinister explanation for what took place after my mother died.

"A few weeks after her funeral," Dad finally continued, "I couldn't look at her stuff anymore. I went around the house, shoving all her stuff into bags. That's when I found a pill bottle wedged between her nightstand and the wall. It was still full of pills, so obviously, she'd gotten high and forgotten they were there or lost them. I shoved the bottle in the bag so hard, it ripped a hole and fell right back out. Lying there on the carpet, taunting me."

Dad rubbed his eyes.

"Wasn't in my right mind. Wasn't sleeping or eating, and every day hurt worse than the last. I'd find a voice mail from her and listen to it repeatedly for over an hour. I'd find old letters she'd written when we first started dating and read them over and over. It made it hurt so much worse, but I couldn't stop myself. Went into a...kind of spiral, missing her so badly, I'd hunt for any piece of her, but that piece would just rip my heart open wider. It felt like a walking wound that I couldn't stop ripping the scab off." Dad paused, and his voice dropped its pitch in shame. "I just wanted the pain to stop."

He rubbed his thumbs together and braced himself.

"I swallowed the entire bottle of pills, Fallon."

My breath caught in my throat. Of all the hypotheses I had come up with over the years as to why he'd first tried drugs, this was one I had never considered—attempted suicide.

Dad may have disappointed me and hurt me throughout the years, but I would never wish pain so unbearable that you wanted to take your own life on to anyone. And knowing he went through that broke my heart.

I thought back to those dark days, but I was hurting so badly that I assumed Daddy's pain was normal. What was normal, after all, when your world was destroyed by a nuclear bomb?

"Guess it wasn't enough to..." Dad said. "So, it just...got me high instead."

"And the high let you escape your pain," I realized. "That's why you started using."

He shook his head. "I'm not going to say that wasn't a welcome side effect, that it took me away from my pain for a bit. But I've, uh... since learned that some people—and they don't know why it's some and not others—get exposed to drugs, and addiction takes place fast. After just one try..."

I'd read up on addiction, about the theory that some people had an addict gene. It aligned with what Dad had experienced. Some people could take a hit with no problem. But others with the gene...one time, and their life as they knew it ended. Especially if they ingested enough heroin-laced pills to almost die. That flood of narcotics must wreak havoc on brain chemicals.

"Never forgave myself for trying to take my life, for almost leaving you an orphan. And then to become an addict on top of that. To become the very thing I'd fought against for two years..." He bit his lip. "I tried so hard to fight it, for your sake. And each time I failed, I felt guilty. That guilt would eat me alive about how much I was letting you down, and that guilt was so overwhelming, I'd give anything to stop it, and the only way to stop it was to take a hit. The worse I felt about myself and how badly I failed you, the more I sabotaged it to escape it."

On the outside, everything had looked so black-and-white.

*Just don't take the drugs*, I'd thought. *You don't need them to stay alive, and each time you choose them, you are choosing them over me.*

I'd been so wrapped up in my own grief, confusion, and hurt that I hadn't seen what he was going through.

If I had understood, this anger would not have snowballed all of those years, and when he fell down at my celebration toast, I would have felt worried instead of angry. This didn't take away all of Dad's mistakes, but it sure as heck explained a lot of it and opened up forgiveness and compassion in my heart.

I wiped a stray tear from my cheek and took a deep breath.

"I'm sorry for all of it, Fallon. I'm sorry for failing you. For letting drugs ruin our lives."

I battled the tightness in my throat, my eyes stinging harder.

"I'm sorry I didn't ask the doctor the right questions when your mom had that surgery. I should've asked if the drugs could be addictive. It just never crossed my mind. I let it come into our house, and I've never forgiven myself. You deserved better."

I'd just heard everything I'd ever needed to hear and felt so much lighter, as if a vise squeezing my body had released.

I could see Dad had changed. He was clean. He was...Dad.

And while the cautious part of me reminded me he could relapse, I was ready to begin building something that we'd been missing for years. It would take a lot of time, but I was willing to put in the work.

I reached across the table and held his hand. And when I did, Dad sobbed. He looked so fragile, childlike almost, as his shoulders shook.

I could see by his pained stare how badly he needed my forgiveness. And by the shrinking of his shoulders, how unworthy he felt to receive it.

He squeezed my hand. "I love you, baby girl."

We sat like that, holding hands and just staring at each other. I hadn't seen him—the old dad—for years. The him that had been overtaken by his demon, and now, here he was, finally sitting across from me.

He'd been so insistent on meeting with me these past few weeks, and now, I could see why. After undoubtedly getting pushed to apologize and come clean in his NA meetings, this was quite the burden to unload, and he must have needed to do it while he had the nerve.

My cell phone buzzed with the location where Dillon wanted to meet.

"I should let you go," Dad said, glancing at my phone.

I wished I could stay longer, but it was a workday.

"Let's do dinner this weekend?" I suggested. "I can buy some groceries and cook for you. Provided I don't have to work," I clarified.

By then, hopefully—please, for all things holy—Marks would be back home safe with his family.

Dad smiled. "I'd love that."

When we both stood, I walked around the table and wrapped my arms around him. I could feel his bones as he shook in tears, and his hug wasn't as tight as I'd once remembered. But for the first time in a long time, peace came over me. No matter what happened with Dillon later, I could handle it now that I had my dad back.

I let him go and, after saying final good-byes, reluctantly walked away. But quickly turned around.

"By the way," I said, "what are you doing downtown today?"

When he asked to meet, I'd assumed it would be out in Blue Island, which was an hour from here. But he said he would be in the city this morning, which was odd. He didn't own a car, and public transportation was expensive.

Dad hesitated. I didn't like the look on his face as he put his hands into his pockets. "I was getting chemo, Fallon."

18

There was his name. Right there on the list.

I shoved the notebook off to the right side of my desk and typed the name of the airport into my search bar. And confirmed my hunch that it was within driving distance of Baja, Mexico. Then, I searched all the nearby airports until I confirmed that this was the most direct route from Chicago to Baja.

I covered my mouth with my hand. After fighting tears all morning from my dad's revelation, I needed this win.

I hustled to the task force conference room, where Burch stood, huddled with the team of investigators working Marks's disappearance. Chicago Police invited the FBI to help with the investigation, and the rest of us were told to stand down, but it wasn't easy to sit on the sidelines when someone you cared about was out there somewhere. I had a whole new respect for what families went through with missing loved ones.

"Sir, I think I found something."

He looked up at me.

"It's not about Marks," I clarified.

Burch motioned for me to come to the other end of the room, out of earshot of everyone else, where he stood with his arms crossed over his chest.

"After a few dead ends, I cross-referenced Ramirez's name against the PNR."

He raised an eyebrow.

"The US Department for Homeland Security keeps the names of passengers, among other things, in their database for fifteen years. Turns out, Ramirez is on that list. Fourteen years ago, he boarded a one-way flight to Los Cabos International Airport."

Burch looked to the side for a moment before returning his gaze to me. "He went to Mexico."

"And never came back."

Burch rubbed his chin.

"Los Cabos International Airport is the closest international airport to Baja, Mexico." I paused. "I think he joined the Baja Cartel fourteen years ago and has been living there ever since."

Burch picked at his thumbnail. "What's your theory on what this has to do with the Syndicates?"

"At first, I thought maybe he was responsible for smuggling drugs over the border to them." But after I'd put in the request to see the passenger list, I'd had more time to think about it. "If he's been working with the cartel this whole time, he wouldn't still be that low on the totem pole. He would have either moved up the chain of command or been killed, and since his name is on the drive, I think it's the former."

"The DEA doesn't have his name on the list of suspected cartel members."

"Which might suggest he's their bookkeeper."

Burch was silent for several moments before he nodded. "This is excellent work, O'Connor."

The approval in his eyes made my cheeks warm. "Marks planted that idea in my head." He deserved to get credit for that. "In any case, if we're right, it provides further evidence that the Syndicates must be about to make a major move, likely expansion, like you said. The bookkeeper would need to be aware of a huge change in the financials."

Burch rubbed his mustache. "We'll bring in the other two Syndicates we found on that drive for questioning, but it's unlikely they'll talk. You meet with McPherson at ten?"

I nodded. "I don't know if he'll agree to be our CI."

"Get him to agree. Meanwhile, poke around about a possible expansion but come at it from the side at first. Not head-on. We don't want to tip our hand. Expansions often mean promotions for leaders, so feel him out there. But the first priority is to find out anything you can about Marks. We need intel. Fast, if we have any shot of finding him before it's too late."

"I'll try like hell, sir."

"You sure you can handle this?" Burch pressed.

Emotionally? No. Tactically? "Yes."

Burch hesitated. "I'll post a car a block away. Anything seems off, anything at all, you get the hell out of there."

"I will, sir."

When he nodded, I turned to walk away.

"O'Connor."

I turned around.

"Be careful. He's had a day and a half to process this. I don't want to have another missing agent on my hands."

19

Darkness encased the pothole-infested alley, concealing anyone who wanted to hide in its shadows, making it challenging to find the metal door. It rested inside a brick wall with a single bulb dimly illuminating its notebook-sized window, covered with a metal slab. As directed, I knocked three times and then scanned my surroundings with uneasy eyes.

The door's window creaked open, and a set of murky eyes peered at me, waiting for a password.

"Dibs." Today's password was a word frequented by Chicagoans, who used it to claim difficult-to-find parking spaces. And today, the ticket to enter was an homage to the past.

Speakeasies—illicit bars that sold alcohol during Prohibition—were a significant part of Chicago's history, a scattering of them peppering the city today. Like the 1920s, their locations were kept secret, passwords changed daily, making it one of the safer places to meet Dillon.

In theory.

It wasn't foolproof, though. Far from it. The risk of being discovered together surged through the air like electricity during a storm threatening to strike.

And that didn't include another danger: I was about to meet a confessed drug lord, a drug lord who may have admitted his mistake to his bosses. If he did, would they step in to clean up his mess?

Was I really meeting Dillon, or was I walking into a trap?

I touched the bulge under my arm, wishing it were winter so I could've hidden my Smith & Wesson better beneath a baggy sweater.

The door groaned open, and the guy manning the entrance allowed me past him, through a crimson hallway, down a flight of concrete stairs, and through the door marked *Enter at your own risk*.

*Ironic.*

It opened into a room draped in chestnut wood and red velvet. Crimson chandeliers that looked like open umbrellas with yellow tassels hung overhead, illuminating the mahogany bar with soft, romantic light that made all the alcohol bottles glow. The ornamental rug next to the bar drew me toward the back, where Dillon told me he'd be waiting.

As I walked deeper inside, I glanced over my shoulder to ensure no one followed me, looked at me, or gave me any indication something was off. But the place was virtually empty. I slowly made my way through two draped doorways, observing every person and their movements until I finally entered the back room.

It was in here, on the far side of the room, where Dillon stood.

I savored the quick bolt of relief that it was him waiting, not some hit man. But I was instantly overwhelmed with how complicated seeing him made me feel. How could the guy I'd fallen for inhabit the same body as a drug captain? How could I want to punch him in the face yet also want him to kiss me?

It didn't help that he looked so...sexy, dressed in Diesel jeans that hugged his hips, a white T-shirt stretched over his muscles, and a baseball cap that brought attention to his striking eyes. Ordinary choices for another man, camouflage for someone trying to blend in with pedestrians on the streets.

*He's the enemy, Fallon. Enemy. Enemy. Just because he's here doesn't mean it's safe.*

"Fallon." His face flooded with relief to see me, and his mouth—the same one that had explored parts of my body I hadn't even seen myself—turned up slightly.

Until his gaze sliced through the room to my cheek.

Rage rippled across his muscles as he stormed over to me and brought his hand up to my face before catching himself and putting the distance between us that now existed in our hearts.

Why did it feel good to think of him touching me? Did a heart have muscle memory it had to outgrow?

Dillon balled his fists at his sides. "Who did that to you?"

"It wasn't one of your minions, if that's what you're worried about."

"Who did that to you?" he repeated, firmer this time.

I did not have feelings for Dillon anymore.

I didn't.

I couldn't.

"Fallon," Dillon pressed.

"Disagreement with a coworker."

Dillon's jaw locked, and his lips tightened into a line. He took my chin between his thumb and finger and tilted my face to the side for a better look.

"Coworker," he growled.

"What can I say?" I added. "Guy's an asshole."

Dillon's eyes snapped to mine. "A *guy*?"

*Uh-oh.*

"A guy *hit* you?"

"I hit him first."

"What's his name?" Dillon demanded.

"Irrelevant."

"Like hell. Give me a name."

"Why?"

"Because I'm going to find him and fucking pulverize him."

"Unwise."

"Name."

"This isn't what we're here to talk about," I said, moving away from him. Distance would help fight the pheromones' effects.

I stood on the other side of the room, but Dillon followed and put his palm on the wall next to my head.

"Coworker, as in a cop did that to you?"

"Doesn't matter."

"So, that's a yes. Give me his name."

"And then what?" I challenged.

"He'll be dealt with."

"I thought you didn't hurt people."

"Willing to make an exception when some asshole hits my girlfriend."

"I'm not your girlfriend."

"If you think I'm gonna let this slide, you clearly don't know me very well."

"No," I agreed. "I don't."

My emotional slap silenced him for a few seconds, and when he spoke next, he softened his tone. "You might not like what I do for a living," he said, his mouth distractingly close to mine. "But you know I'd protect you with my life."

I'd been so angry ever since I found out who he was. Angry when he confessed. Angry when I worked the crime scene where Marks's car was found. Angry when I met my dad. But now, I was just... exhausted. I guess anger only had so much runway before it ran out of steam, and with Dad's terminal prognosis and Marks missing, my anger dwindled.

"Look," I said. "I asked you to meet with me because I have some urgent questions I need to ask."

Dillon chewed the inside of his cheek. I could tell he wasn't going to let the bruise go, but for now, he appeared to recalibrate. "Does anyone know you're here?"

Only Burch. I hadn't told Shane about Dillon. We'd been too busy, talking about my dad.

I was devastated that Dad only had a year to live, but thank goodness I had that time with him. If he'd been cut out of my life abruptly, it would have been unbearable. We had time. Not much, but enough to bookend our relationship with bonding and happier memories. Well, as happy as they could be, fighting stage four cancer. I'd go to every chemo appointment I could with him, I'd take care of him when he was sick from its side effects, cook for him when he was well enough to eat. We'd flip through photo albums to cement the good memories, to remind him of what he was fighting for. The doctors said we'd have only one more Thanksgiving and Christmas, but maybe his body would respond better to treatments, and we'd have more.

My cell phone rang with Shane's ringtone, which was odd since we were scheduled to meet in an hour. Maybe he had to cancel, but I needed to focus, so I turned my ringer on buzz.

"Fallon, I can't answer your questions. Anything I tell you puts you in even more danger." His voice was steady and calm.

Mine was high-pitched and desperate. "Officer Marks is my friend," I said. "He's missing! He was taken—"

"I don't know where he is," Dillon said.

"You could ask."

"Asking around for something like that won't get answers; it'd just raise suspicion. You've seen what they do to people they don't trust."

"Why did you agree to meet me if you wouldn't answer any of my questions?"

"Because I needed to warn you. Something big is going down." But he didn't know that we already suspected as much.

"What is it?"

He shook his head. "The point is, they're cleaning house, and you can't get in my bosses' way."

"That's why you're here?" I couldn't blink back the tears this time. "Because I'm complicating your business?"

I shoved myself away from the wall and steeled myself to get answers. Dillon must have thought I was about to leave, though, because he grabbed my arm to stop me.

"I don't care about the business. I care about you," he said.

I looked down where his hand gripped my skin. With our faces separated by only inches, I could smell his minty breath ripple across his plump lips. The soft lighting darkened his bronze skin and facial stubble, accentuating his jaw and his eyes, which erupted in desire as he stared at my mouth. It looked like it took every ounce of control he had to stop himself from kissing me.

His brows furrowed, and sadness cascaded through his features as he released me. When he finally spoke, despair infected his tone. "I'm sorry, Fallon," he said. "I shouldn't have let myself get involved with you. In my line of work, anyone that gets too close to me could become a target. Leverage if someone wants to get back at me or punish me." His Adam's apple bulged with a swallow. "But I couldn't stop myself." He hesitated. "The truth is, I felt something the first time I laid eyes on you, and then every moment after crashed into the next. And the more time I spent with you, the less possible it felt to cut you out of my life. I told myself to walk away from you many times." He shook his head. "But I couldn't get myself to do it." Dillon looked down. "It was selfish and reckless of me. I'm sorry."

I thought back to that night I'd told him what it was like, growing up with addicts, how he'd reached across the table and linked his fingers with mine, and then that look of worry flashed across his face. And how he'd said I *shouldn't* be with him the night I finally told him how I felt. Looking back, I could see him struggling.

Maybe he thought he could keep our relationship casual; someone he didn't care deeply for could never be used as leverage against him. But his feelings for me had become a runaway horse.

Just like mine for him.

I realized I believed him, that he never set out with ill intent to knowingly put me in danger. And I felt his sorrow pulsing through my veins.

Especially when he reached his hand up and cupped my cheek and stroked my skin with his thumb. "I still care about you, Fallon. And I'm not gonna let anything happen to you," he vowed.

Dillon's gaze fell to my lips and back to my eyes, as if silently begging for permission. Before he tilted his head and drew his face closer to mine.

I was surprised that any part of me wanted him to kiss me, wanted him to wrap his arms around me, if only for a moment.

But I wouldn't allow that to happen. No matter how confused my heart was right now, Dillon was still a Syndicates captain and I was in law enforcement.

I lowered my head before his lips connected with mine and stepped away from his confusing touch.

Dillon sighed deeply but nodded in unsurprised understanding. Several moments of silence passed before he spoke again. "You need to leave town, Fallon."

"Just because Marks is missing doesn't mean I'll go missing."

Dillon picked up a bag off the ground—the same bag full of cash he'd tried to force on me yesterday—and tried to make me take it. "This is the only way I can protect you."

"If you're so worried about what they're capable of, why aren't you leaving town?" I demanded.

"Because it's too late for me," he said. "There are only two paths ahead of me, Fallon. Prison or a coffin."

My eyes watered at his devastating destiny. And when they did, Dillon's gaze shadowed in sadness.

"I'm sorry I was ever involved with any of this, Fallon."

"You could go into witness protection," I whispered.

Dillon gave a sad smile; he didn't need to say what I already knew. These sociopaths got to the witnesses faster than if they went to prison. At least in prison, they lasted a few months before being slaughtered in the showers.

But maybe there was another option. Maybe Burch's idea would give Dillon the benefit of legal immunity with the discretion of his associates not knowing he was helping us.

"I want you to be my CI," I announced.

His eyes shadowed in anger. "Are you kidding me?" His voice was a cool frost over my skin, a whisper of his darker side percolating beneath the surface.

"Unlike witness protection, a confidential informant is just that—confidential. The only people who would know about it would be me, you, and my boss. That's it."

"It'd never work," he snapped. "They'd find out. They always do, and any cop who worked with a CI? Would get killed, too."

He set the bag closer. "I have a car waiting to take you to O'Hare."

"I'm not going anywhere."

"Yes, you are. You're in danger here."

"So are you."

"*You* don't need to be. There's still hope for you."

"Is that what this is about? You've given up hope?"

"You can't be here," he repeated. "It's too dangerous. The guys I work for have started taking things to a whole new level. That fire you were in? Wasn't an accident."

I blinked. "How do *you* know that?"

"That guy you saw outside my apartment? Heard something he wasn't supposed to—the fire was set on purpose. He didn't know what it meant, but after I thought about it, I did. They started in the elevator shaft, right after *you* climbed in. You, who's on the task force trying to take them down. You, on the same team as another officer who's now missing."

It made no sense, yet the cop in me had to acknowledge if two independent sources—my boss and now a captain in their organization—believed I was the target, discounting its possibility was reckless.

"Maybe they were after you," I said. "You're the captain in a drug organization, not me."

"If they wanted me dead, they'd simply send a car for me and put a bullet in my skull. They wouldn't need an elaborate fire to take me out. And if they wanted to kill me and failed the first time, they'd have tried again; I'd be dead by now."

Still, I'd mention it to Burch to make sure that angle was looked at, just in case.

"If they were coming after you before," Dillon said, "what do you think they'll do now that you're deeper into the case? Or if they find out we've been together? Think about it, Fallon. The stairwell on fire? The elevator? It was to make sure you didn't escape."

"How would they have known about me being on the case to begin with, especially since I hadn't even been briefed on it until later that morning? And how would they have known I was in that building?"

"That's what I'm trying to find out," Dillon said.

So, he was working on some information.

"But in the meantime, can you think of any reason they'd be targeting you specifically, out of all the cops on the task force?" Dillon asked.

I hesitated. Burch had shared a hypothesis he'd been piecing together with me. He said there was a difference between having a *passion* for locking up drug criminals and having it be your life's mission. Ever since the fire, he'd been quietly digging through my cases, trying to find a motive, and recently discovered that my vendetta against drug criminals was evident and frequent. For example, it came out when I gave testimony as the arresting officer of low-level drug charges to push for the maximum sentence. Or in the handful of speeches I'd given. Burch now believed the Syndicates may have vetted the cops joining the task force and saw my crazy level of determination as a threat.

"No," I hedged because Burch's theory was just that—a theory with holes in it. He didn't know how they'd get the names of the people on the task force to begin with.

In any case, if Dillon was willing to snoop around this, maybe there was a way for him to ask questions to the right people to get vital information.

"Be my CI," I insisted.

"No. You're leaving town." He kicked the bag closer to me, clearly accustomed to people obeying his commands.

I kicked the bag back. "I'm staying and working this case."

Dillon eyed me like a caveman about to throw me over his shoulder and drag me out.

"Fallon." He seemed to choose his next words carefully. "My bosses have connections with the cartel."

We'd already suspected this, but still. Hearing Dillon's confirmation was unsettling.

The cartels in Mexico were the most dangerous drug organizations globally, known for brutal violence of not only fellow and rival drug members, but also innocent men, women, and children who had nothing to do with their organization. Murder and torture were their weapons of mass destruction, used to incite fear and keep police so afraid, they would never go against them. One time, a cartel even bombed a school full of children simply to send a message to the police.

It was well known most drugs came from the cartels, but those business transactions concluded once the drugs were across the border. Which meant there *was* something bigger going on with the cartel. Was it expansion, like we suspected? Or something else?

"How is the cartel involved in this?"

My cell phone's buzz burst through the silence, and now that I was looking, it was the *tenth* time Shane had called.

*Oh no. They must have found Marks...*

"Shane?"

"Fallon, where are you?"

"Is he alive?" I could hear it in his voice—something terrible.

"I...come home. I need to tell you something."

"Tell me now."

"I'm not doing it over the phone, Fallon."

"Is Marks alive?" I repeated.

"This isn't about the case. It's about...look, just come home."

"You're scaring me."

Shane's silence only heightened my growing panic.

"Tell me what's going on," I begged.

"Fallon, I—"

"Just say it!"

I could feel Dillon's worried stare.

"Fallon...two uniforms came by, looking for you. It's...your dad. They need you to go down to the medical examiner's office."

Two uniforms—textbook death notification procedure.

Medical examiner, as in morgue.

Dad.

After a sleepless night and barely any food, that was all it took for my blood pressure to plummet and for everything to go black.

20

I n the darkness, the cold floor beneath me wobbled.

"Fallon," a gruff voice echoed.

It took several seconds to open my eyes. Dillon's face stared down at me, his eyebrows crinkled in worry.

He held my cheek. "Fallon, say something."

I was spilled across his lap on the floor of a room decorated circa the roaring twenties, and when I touched the back of my head, I hissed.

"You hit it pretty good. You need to go to the ER."

"I'm fine."

In the warmth of his embrace, everything felt peaceful. For a second, I forgot about the call that had made me pass out.

"I have to go."

I tried to get up, but he held me down with a hint of a smile.

"As if I'd let you in your condition."

But my cell phone was already buzzing.

I yanked myself free from Dillon's protective limbs and stood up. Too fast. I wobbled, so Dillon jumped up and steadied my arm.

"I have to get to the..." I choked over the last word. "Morgue."

When Dillon's eyes grabbed hold of mine, they penetrated my

irises, but after a few seconds, he picked what he believed to be the more urgent priority.

"You could've cracked your skull; you need to get it looked at."

But I was already walking away, willing the dizziness to stop. Through the doorways, the hall, back up the stairs, and out the same door I came in.

Damn, my head throbbed. Each beat of my heart launched a cannon into the back of my skull.

I texted Shane.

**Me: Cook County ME office?**

**Shane: What happened? Your phone cut out.**

It annoyed me that I had to repeat myself.

**Me: Cook County, not Will County?**

It was unlikely he'd traveled outside Cook County, but I wanted to be certain.

**Shane: Let me pick you up and take you. Where are you?**

**Me: Which county?**

**Shane: Fallon, you shouldn't do this alone.**

**Me: WHICH COUNTY??????**

I walked down the alley, intending to hail a cab.

"Wait." Dillon's voice came behind me.

I kept walking.

When Shane's text confirmed it was the Cook County office, I ignored his pleas to let him pick me up and lifted my hand, grateful a cab rolled toward me. I opened the door, but Dillon's palm grabbed the top of it, blocking my ability to get inside.

He had the bag slung over his shoulder. "I'll drive you," he insisted.

Did I seriously need to state the obvious right now? Even if I wanted the company, which I didn't. "If you're seen with me, they'll kill you."

"I'm not letting you go to the morgue alone, Fallon. So, either I'm driving you or I'm coming with."

"Hell-lo?" the cab driver barked impatiently.

"I don't need a chaperone."

"You just knocked your ass out. If you think I'm taking no for an answer, you're sadly mistaken. So, we can stand here in the open, debating this, or we can be on our way."

"Yo! Lady! You in or not?"

With a huff, I got into the cab, and Dillon climbed in next to me.

"Where to?" the cabbie barked.

I told him the address.

When the cab pulled off, Dillon's lips tightened in worry for me. "Is it your coworker?" His concern for me deepened when he noticed my lips quiver and my eyes well with tears.

My voice grew weak. "It's my dad."

Dillon's eyes softened into heartbreaking understanding, and he reached over and gently laced his fingers with mine.

With a black hole swallowing me up, I couldn't refuse his comfort.

The cruelties of having feelings for a person who I could never be with receded behind my wall of suffering. At this moment, we existed in a space where all the complications that remained outside of this taxi temporarily faded to black, where Dillon was simply and wonderfully the guy who cared so much about me that he refused to let me go through this alone.

"Incorrect identifications happen sometimes," I said. "Person carrying someone else's wallet, for example. Like if you got robbed and that robber sort of looked like you and died, they'd preliminarily think it was you."

Dillon didn't say anything.

In desperation to prove my theory, I called my dad, but it went straight to his voice mail. Maybe he forgot to charge his cell phone, or maybe he turned it off, sleeping off the long day of chemo.

Chemo.

Cancer. Could it have snagged him suddenly? Stopped his heart after all those years of drug abuse? But the address Shane gave me was to the medical examiner's office. MEs are for things like gunshots, stabbings, and, well, drug overdoses.

I shook my head.

That couldn't be the case. Dad was fighting cancer, and he'd been clean for three months. You didn't fight cancer and turn around and gamble your life away with a high.

And he couldn't die. Not now. I had been waiting for him, my old dad, since I was eleven. He just finally returned to me, and we had so many years to make up for, so much hurt to eradicate through our long-lost love.

"It can't be him."

When we arrived, a silver-haired man approached me.

"Officer O'Connor?" Wearing blue scrubs and a white lab coat, he carried himself with confidence despite the mustard stain on his collar. He extended his hand. "Dr. Archer. I'm the medical examiner. Normally, I have my assistant do this, but when I heard it was an officer coming in..." He must have seen the blank stare on my face because he appraised Dillon—who lingered near my shoulder like a bodyguard—and then cleared his throat. "I'm sorry we're meeting under these circumstances. Please, follow me."

The white walls of this place reminded me of my childhood elementary school, made of giant bricks, painted with so many layers that the paint itself served as glue. Fluorescents buzzed overhead, turning the doctor's skin a jaundiced yellow.

He led us into a dark room with white ceiling tiles, shut the door, and motioned for us to take seats at an oval conference table, where he placed a manila folder in front of him. The place smelled like stale coffee, and icy air blew down from the vent above my head, coating my skin in invisible frost. Four feet of scratched mahogany wood separated me from the doctor.

I picked at my fingernail, trying to appear calm, but whatever happened in the next few minutes was going to change my life forever.

"Before we proceed"—he opened the folder, pulled out a pair of royal-blue reading glasses from the breast pocket of his coat, and put them on the tip of his crooked nose—"I need you to confirm your father's name, please?"

"Philip O'Connor."

Dr. Archer nodded. "I'm going to show you a photo of the man we brought in, and I need you to tell me if it's your father. Do you understand?"

"I thought I'd get to see his body."

"People prefer photographs. Seeing the body can be upsetting."

"I need to see his body."

No way I was looking at a photograph. What kind of closure was that? No way.

"Officer—"

"I appreciate your concern, but I've been around dead bodies before." My mom's, for one. "I'd like to identify him in person, not in a photograph. It's what I drove all the way here to do."

Dr. Archer was clearly about to put up an argument.

"She'd like to see him in person," Dillon commanded, making it clear he had my back in whatever I needed. And unlike my shaky voice, Dillon's forceful tone came off like a warning.

I could suddenly see this other side of Dillon. The one that could calmly make demands and intimidate people with his dominating presence.

Above the table, he screamed power, sucking all the energy out of the room and using it to silently threaten the man sitting across from me—the man attempting to not give me what I wanted. The hint of danger expanded from Dillon's body and thickened the air like a poisonous fog. Beneath the table, he placed his hand on my knee and squeezed tenderly.

And while the normal response might be fear, his demeanor incited a different and unexpected mix of emotions inside me.

Dr. Archer seemed to process the request for a couple of seconds, pulled a cell from his pocket, and placed a call. "Megan, can you get Mr. O'Connor's body prepared for identification?" There was a long pause. "Thank you." He hung up and returned his attention to me. "It'll be a few minutes, then I can take you down."

"What happened to him?" I asked. "Assuming it *is* my dad, what happened?"

Dr. Archer looked at a report. I knew the drill; he knew what happened but wanted to speak the facts precisely as they were. One didn't play the telephone game when it came to death.

"Says here a neighbor saw him lying on the ground, facedown, through the window of his residence."

That nosy neighbor had moved in two years ago. I couldn't blame the guy for disapproving of my dad's obvious drug use, but I did fault him for treating my father like a less-than, a deadbeat, and for always looking for reasons to call the cops. Peering through his windows, taking pictures of any comings and goings.

"Got worried when he wouldn't respond. Couldn't gain entry because the door was locked from the inside. First responders arrived at the scene approximately six minutes later. Upon gaining forced entry, they found no pulse, and the skin was cold. A n—"

He stopped. Looked at Dillon, as if hesitant to say something that might aggravate him.

"A what?"

He looked back at me and sat up straighter, as if to remind himself he was a doctor, delivering information. "A needle was found in his arm."

"So, he overdosed."

"We won't know until we get toxicology back." Standard jargon for, yes, he overdosed.

It was a good thing I was sitting down because the room swayed.

"Somebody must have gotten to him," I declared.

The ME looked confused.

"Fallon," Dillon started.

But the glare I gave him could have cooked his skin. "You said yourself you thought I was in danger. I'm working on a drug case with violent criminals who have ties to the cartel. If something happened to him, it must have been them because my dad was doing great. I just saw him at breakfast, and he was happy."

Dillon opened his mouth but thought better than to disagree.

"Cause of death can't be determined until toxicology comes back in a few weeks," Dr. Archer said. "But there were no bruises, nothing consistent with a scuffle. Nothing at the scene indicated a struggle. And the dead bolt, it says, was still locked from the inside."

"Maybe you just saw all the track marks and jumped to a conclusion," I insisted.

He frowned.

"He was fine," I continued. "He'd been clean for three months. He was starting a new chapter in his life, so none of this makes any sense! He wouldn't have gotten high, not after our talk."

Dillon was kind enough to tighten his lips and nod, letting me hang on to the delusion that my dad hadn't *actually* overdosed for a little bit longer.

*This is how addicts are, unpredictable, never knowing when they'll go off the wagon, the disease always waiting in the wings to take them from you,* a little voice reminded me.

But I didn't listen to that voice; she was wrong. The medical examiner was wrong. Dad would not do this. Not now, no matter how much denial they'd claim I was in.

"They're ready." Dr. Archer stood up, looking at his phone.

I followed him out the door, down a long hallway, and into a medical area. White linoleum flooring, scuffed white walls, gray cabinets, and air-conditioning so cold, it could double as a walk-in refrigerator filled the room. Which was hauntingly quiet. The place smelled of sour pickles, and in the center, lying on a shiny silver table, illuminated beneath a large bulb, was a body, covered by a white sheet.

"Do you need a minute?" Dr. Archer asked.

When I shook my head, Dillon inched closer to me. He probably would have waited in the hall if I'd asked him, but I could see him bracing to catch my fall.

Dr. Archer slowly pulled the sheet down a couple feet.

And there—with his gray skin the only indication that he wasn't simply asleep—was Daddy.

*"Daddy?" I'm holding his hand, staring at Mommy's body in the coffin. I'm studying her face, desperately memorizing every cell of it, because I'm terrified that someday, I won't remember what she looked like. I cried for hours last night, just thinking about it.*

*"Do you still love people when you're dead?"*

*He looks at me with tears in his eyes. "What do you mean?"*

*I know Mommy hasn't been herself lately, but before that, her love for me was so big, it could fill the whole entire planet. It was like it was its own living, breathing force, but...what happens to it when that person dies? Does the love die, too?*

*"Does Mommy still love me?"*

*Daddy's lips tremble. "Always," he assures.*

*Tears form a river down my cheeks.*

*"Will you always love me?"*

*Because I feel so empty and so very sad. Like the floor could just vanish and the ground could swallow me up.*

*"Always," he promises.*

*"Even when you die?"*

Shock was a good thing. It helped you keep speaking, even when your insides had been gutted and set on fire.

"I don't understand how he could've overdosed. Even if he relapsed...he knew his way around drugs."

Dr. Archer's tone was empathetic. "We'll know more when the toxicology comes in, but sadly, this kind of thing happens all the time. Particularly when someone's been clean. Sometimes, they miscalculate how much they can handle. Sometimes, they get a batch that's purer than what they're used to."

I couldn't move.

"I'll give you a few minutes," he said, vanishing from the little hell room.

All those times I'd worried about something happening to him. I thought I'd built up a thick enough skin, especially after losing Mom, that it wouldn't affect me this badly. But this meant I was an orphan. No one tethering me to this world. Like being on a shipwreck as the lone survivor, floating out into oblivion on a raft.

My knees weakened a heartbeat before Dillon caught me under my arm. He gently lowered me to the ground and helped me sit with my back against the wall.

"Breathe." Dillon squatted in front of me, his eyes round with worry. He put his hand on my cheek. "Breathe, Fallon," he repeated.

Fear gripped my bones like a deep winter freeze, fear that I wasn't sure I could endure. I wasn't sure I had any more fight in me.

I'd tried to be strong my whole life. But right now, with my soul crushed, I needed Dillon to have been a stand-up guy, a person I could have leaned on for support. So he could've held me. Told me I wasn't alone in this, helped me with every step to come—the funeral arrangements, the pain that would continue rolling in.

I needed him to have never been involved with the narcotics organization.

I stared up at my father, thinking of all the drugs he'd pumped into his body, all the money he'd given to people to get those chemicals. Those people who didn't give a rat's ass about him.

People like Dillon.

"How can you be involved with a business that does this to people?" I choked. Betrayal pumped toxins through what was left of my heart.

I was ashamed of myself for crumbling and turning into this pathetic weakling. I never even wanted a Prince Charming, but once Dillon came along, I fell in love with the fantasy that he would sweep me off my feet and we would live happily ever after.

But he wasn't the prince. He was the bad guy.

"Fallon," he whispered. "I'd give anything to go back in time and make different choices."

How dare he look at me with watery eyes.

I slapped him.

"This is what you do." I pointed to my dad's body, wishing I weren't sobbing as I yelled. "Stay the fuck away from me, Dillon. You disgust me. The world would be a better place without people like you in it!"

I stood up and stormed out of the room.

## 21

"Do you think they'll find Marks alive?" I asked.

Shane's lips turned down. "I think the FBI is doing everything they can."

The critical forty-eight-hour window had passed already, and even though I knew what that likely meant, hope was a lot harder to extinguish than I thought.

"Has Burch said anything else about that fire?" Shane asked.

I shook my head. He'd relayed the angle that Dillon was in the elevator to Fisher, but nothing had come of it. Burch echoed Dillon's thoughts; if they wanted to execute one of their own, he'd be dead. And there'd be no reason to set an entire skyscraper on fire to try and pull it off.

Shane's chest rose in frustration. "It's been weeks."

My cell phone's buzz interrupted with a text.

**Dillon: Fallon, I'm so sorry about your father. If there's anything I can do...**

And then a second later.

**Dillon: I don't blame you for never wanting to talk to me again. Please know I'll always be here for you, Fallon. Always. Don't hesitate to reach out to me if there's anything you ever need.**

"That from your boyfriend?" Shane asked, turning off the interstate.

*Boyfriend.* I had never used that term to describe Dillon to Shane, but I guess he could tell that was what it had developed into.

Had.

"We're not dating anymore," I said, tucking the phone into my pocket.

"What happened?"

I laughed over my tears. "That's a long conversation."

"Did he hurt you?" Shane growled.

"Does my heart count?"

Shane gripped the steering wheel tighter. "Tell me what happened."

How did one explain that they'd been cut in half and left to bleed to death in disbelief? Even to themselves? Maybe I shouldn't have expected a happy ending. I mean, even though the circumstances were extreme, did I honestly think that my first relationship wouldn't end in heartbreak after all those years of hiding behind my impenetrable shield?

"Proctor was right; I do shut people out." I looked out the window at all the homes that were probably filled with happy families. "At first, I thought the reason I was afraid to get too close to people was that I was afraid of getting hurt. But it's more complicated than that."

Shane waited patiently for me to choke this out.

"When I was a kid, in many ways, I felt abandoned by my parents." My throat clenched at the memories of their loving arms going from reaching toward me for a hug to reaching for the baggie of drugs while my arms remained open, aching for my parents' embrace. "Opening myself up to people makes me vulnerable because it means I have to trust them to never abandon me like they did."

And that abandonment wound, I discovered, was a deep abyss of suffering, so intense, I'd sink to the Mariana Trench to avoid it. That was why confessing my feelings to Dillon had wrapped my body in icy tendrils of fear. All those drugs my parents had taken poisoned my belief that anyone could ever fully love me.

"And he abandoned you?"

I bit my lip. "No. It just…didn't work out."

He looked at me fiddling with my hands. "But you still care about him."

"I don't want to. I made a huge mistake when I fell for him."

Concern radiated through his face. "Why?"

"It turns out, he's a bad guy."

"Did he cheat on you? If he did, so help me, I'm going to rip his freakin'—"

"No, nothing like that. It's just…" I bit my lip. "Can we talk about it later?" Because telling Shane that Dillon was a drug lord would open an exhausting firestorm, and that was the last thing I could handle right now.

Shane's squad car's tires crunched along the gravel in the trailer park we'd once called home. The rectangle-shaped trailers were surrounded by overgrown oak trees, grass so tall that a small child could hide in it, and abandoned cars with rusted wheel casings that made the dilapidated land look like a junkyard. The loud metallic hum of an ancient window air conditioner buzzed through the baking summer heat as we came to a rest just outside my dad's home.

Next to it sat the brown trailer Shane had grown up in, though his family had long since moved away. I suppose most families didn't make this kind of place their forever home.

But Dad did. This trailer had become his prison of defeat, his self-imposed sentence to solitary confinement. It broke my heart that, out of all the stunningly beautiful landscapes in the world, this sad little trailer was where he'd taken his last breaths.

Shane clunked the gear into park, and we went inside.

Even in broad daylight, the interior was dark, encased in chocolate wood paneling. A coffeepot that looked to be from the 1990s sat on the kitchen counter, still filled with four cups of unconsumed coffee Dad must have made the morning he'd died, saturating the stale air with its bitter smell. The kitchen slash dining room-slash living room was so small, you could make it from the sink to the couch in eight steps. The same couch I'd found Mom slumped on.

Shane ran a hand through his dark hair. "I'll start in your dad's closet. See if I can rustle up something decent for the funeral."

I opened a garbage bag and dropped trash into it. Cans of pop, food wrappers. I had to choke over tears when I washed the dishes in the sink. Based on the can on the counter and the stain on the plate, it looked like the last thing he'd eaten was a can of beefaroni. The cheap brand, at that.

If he had to have a last meal, I wished it had been something special.

"Do you think either of these will work?" Shane came out of my dad's bedroom, holding up two outfit choices—a blue sweater with a pair of gray pants and a long-sleeved black shirt with a different shade of black pants. All of them looked like they'd been plucked off the clearance rack at a thrift store.

I frowned.

"I know," Shane said, looking closer at them. "But it's the best he had."

Again, I had to fight over the tears. I wished he'd had nicer clothes to wear, a nicer place to live.

A better life.

"I'll buy him a suit," I said.

Dad deserved a suit. He might have morphed into the diseased dad, but inside was still the loving father who used to check under my bed for monsters. Bought me ice cream for getting straight As. Did his best to shield me from Mom's addiction.

Shane nodded, put the clothes back into my father's room, and then leaned against the doorframe. He tucked his hands into his pockets and studied me the way he'd been doing all morning, like he was worried I was about to shatter.

Which, in fairness, I was.

"How can I help?" he asked. "Put me to work."

"Would you be willing to help pack up his clothes? I'll donate them to the homeless."

"Of course," Shane said. "Anything you need."

Shane deserved a medal for excellency in friendship; I hoped I was as good a friend to him as he was to me.

"You still haven't told me what's been bothering you," I said.

"Who says something's been botherin' me?"

"I know you, so we can skip the coy part and get to what's been eating you."

"Today's about you."

"And I need to get my mind off this. Distract me with your problems."

Shane tightened his lips.

"Please?"

He sighed and seemed to measure how badly I needed to focus on anything other than my life.

"It's work stuff."

"What stuff?"

He pinched the bridge of his nose. "Feels like we're always one step behind, you know? It pisses me off, the things people get away with. And then the ones that do get caught? Overcrowdin' in prison makes them get out before they've even served their full sentence. Meanwhile, the drugs, the killing...it just never ends."

Shane's biggest obstacle to his career was his heart. Seeing the worst of what people were capable of took a lot out of you. I knew it would be an adjustment for him to join the Chicago PD, but looking back on it, I think I'd missed clues he might not be handling the adjustment very well. Like when he first moved to Chicago, his tone had changed.

"The violence," he'd said. "Can't believe some of the stuff people do to each other here. For, like, nothing. It's insane."

"Are you second-guessing wanting to become chief one day?" I asked.

"I don't know," Shane admitted.

Whoa. That was a big change.

Shortly after joining the force, Shane decided he wanted to move up the ranks and be the one setting strategies to keep the city safe one day. But in this job? Some days, it felt like the bad guys were one step ahead. It was only natural to feel discouraged.

"You don't have to be chief of police to make a difference in this world," I assured.

His cell rang.

"Take it," I insisted.

Shane looked at me like he didn't want to prioritize anything else above me, but even off duty, police work never ended.

"Take it," I repeated.

Shane let it ring one more time and then reluctantly answered. "Hernandez," he said, retreating into my father's bedroom.

I ran my hand through my hair and looked around. For a small place, it sure felt overwhelming—how much I needed to organize. I wondered where to begin, and when I scanned the kitchen and living room with its sea of browns and grays, a flash of purple caught my eye. Curious, I walked closer, picked up the notebook, opened it to the first page, and saw my father's handwriting.

*Kim,*

*My sponsor insists that journaling assists sobriety. According to her, it gives us "freedom to express joy, sorrows, and frustrations without pressure or judgment." She asserts that it helps manage the difficulties of recovery as well as anxiety and triggers that can cause a relapse. I hate the suggestion to focus on emotions I have bottled up because isn't that the ultimate trigger? Nothing else has worked, though, so I suppose I have nothing to lose by giving it a shot.*

*But you know me. Talking to myself about my feelings? I can't do it. But I can talk to you. Because I miss you terribly, and you're the only person who understands what this feels like.*

*Oh my gosh.* The front page was dated nearly a year ago when he had a stint in rehab. The one-subject notebook was filled with his entries. I wanted to sit down and read the entire thing front to back, but it'd take hours, so, for now, I skimmed around, desperate to read it.

My dad—through his messy black handwriting—was still alive on these pages.

*August 27ᵗʰ*

*Kim,*

*Insufferable pain is assaulting my entire body inside and out. I can't stop vomiting or shaking from vicious chills that feel like I'm standing naked in a blizzard. I don't want to get high. I just want to stop this torture. I don't know if I'm strong enough to do this. Was this what it was like every time you tried to quit?*

I skimmed ahead.

*October 25th*

*Kim,*

*Withdrawal never ends. It only gets worse. I may not have muscle cramps or diarrhea anymore, but the subsequent depression that's commenced is unendurable, and I'm told it might not go away. How much of it is because, without a filter, I feel the suffering I've caused? How much is because I destroyed the chemical balance in my brain? I'm not sure. All I know is that I can't even remember what happiness feels like.*

I couldn't hold back my tears. He was hurting so much worse than I ever knew, and then I went and laid into him yesterday? Why couldn't I be more sensitive to him? I thought we left on good terms, happy terms, but what if...oh Lord, what if what I'd said to him sent him over the edge?

I shuffled through the pages until I found the last page, which was dated yesterday.

*Kim,*

*I thought nothing could hurt worse than the day you died, but I was wrong. Today, my grimmest fear was confirmed. You were holding a picture of your daughter when you took your fatal dose. Intentionally. Because you thought she'd be better off without you.*

*Because I made you feel that way. I was your husband, and when you were drowning, I held your head underwater.*

*I deserve to let the anguish of this revelation eat me alive, but I am a weak, pathetic excuse of a man because I cannot endure this. The anchor is pulling me down again, and this time, I want to let it pull me under.*

*I'll try to get clean tomorrow. But right now, I need something to take this pain away. Because I cannot bear it.*

That was the last entry in his journal.

He wasn't killed; he relapsed and accidentally overdosed.

Because of what I'd said to him.

I ran to the bathroom and barely got the toilet lid up before the bile came up.

"Fallon?" Shane appeared at the bathroom door.

Dad had seemed so clearheaded, but clearly, the disease was still the driver in Dad's sick head.

Even in a healthy body, taking drugs was potentially lethal. But a man whose body had been weakened by chemo? Chemo didn't just hurt cancer cells; it also damaged the lungs, kidneys, and heart. I was sure his nurses warned him to stay clean—especially after years of drugs already damaging his body—but an addict clearly couldn't be reasoned with. Any dose was a fatality waiting to happen.

"I'm taking you home," Shane declared as he put a hand on my shoulder.

I didn't have the energy to argue. I didn't have the energy to read the psychological roller coaster my dad had been through in the months leading up to his death. Even though I deserved the painful lash from every word.

Shane helped me into his cruiser and watched the trailer grow smaller in the rearview mirror as he pulled away.

"Tell me about the douchebag."

"What?"

"The ex-boyfriend. Tell me about him."

I took a deep pull of oxygen. "You're just trying to distract me from my dad." I looked at the road passing beneath us, feeling utterly empty. Void of anything.

Numbness. It felt better than before.

"So, what if I am? Tell me what he did."

I laughed, and Shane looked at me like I was going crazy.

*Maybe I am.*

"I screwed up so bad."

"You never screw up," Shane said. "If he made you think that..."

"I fell in love with him."

Shane fell silent.

"I've never been in love before. Not like this. That," I corrected. I huffed my hot breath on the passenger window and traced a heart into the fog. Then, I drew an X over it. "He was"—I sighed—"everything I could want in someone. He made me feel alive and like life was going to be okay. Like as long as I was with him…"

Why was I even explaining any of this? I shut my eyes and got to the part where I screwed up.

"So, I see his back for the first time, and guess what I see."

"Nail marks from another chick?"

"Nope. Tattoo of a scorpion holding an American flag. Turns out, my ex-boyfriend is a captain in the Chicago Syndicates."

Shane jerked to the side of the road so fast, the person behind us nearly crashed into us, honking as Shane threw his cruiser into park.

"What?" Shane snapped.

"Life's a bitch, isn't it? It's like you think you're getting a happily ever after."

Shane's vein on his forehead bulged like it might explode beneath his skin. "He's a fucking drug dealer?"

"Technically, he's a captain, so he's the dealers' boss's boss."

"Does he know you're a cop?"

"He does now."

"Maybe he knew all along. You're on the task force. Maybe he inserted himself to work you. Get info."

"No," I said. "At least, I don't think so. We could both get killed if they knew he was dating a cop."

Shane gripped the wheel so tight, his knuckles turned white. "What's his last name?"

"Why?"

"Because I'm going to hunt him down and stab him in his ear with a screwdriver."

"I don't think that'd look good on your résumé."

"This isn't funny, Fallon!"

"I know, but I'm not going to let you get in trouble over it, so I'm not about to tell you his name."

"First name's Dillon," Shane said, pulling up his phone.

"Or is it?" I challenged.

Shane scowled at me.

"Please," I said. "I don't want to pull the dad-just-died card, but there it is. Flopped down on the table. Please don't give me another thing to worry about."

Shane clenched his jaw and looked out at the windshield. He took deep breaths as a dozen more cars drove past us until he finally glanced back over at me. "So help me, if I ever see that son of a bitch, I'm going to fuckin' kill him."

22

W hat is he *doing here?*
  I stepped out of Shane's cruiser and onto the uneven pavement at Rosewood Cemetery, staring at Dillon in disbelief.

I couldn't believe he'd risk his life by coming, just as I couldn't believe this was happening. *Again.*

The first time I'd buried a parent, I was too little to fully comprehend that this was the last profession of love you'd be able to give your family member. But the adult me understood the gravity of this moment with tragic clarity.

Everything felt different—the texture of the air rolling across my skin, the sun warming my face, even the sounds of birds. A red-winged blackbird's throaty call—a lazy *deeeet-deeeet, yak-yak-yak*—sounded sad. It was as if the earth knew that the only person left that I'd loved since I was a baby, my anchor to this world, was gone. Along with the hope that Dad would one day find his way through the darkness.

"Ready?" Shane asked.

I nodded but welcomed the support of his extended elbow as we walked toward my father's final resting place.

Tucked into a sanctuary of trees, Rosewood Cemetery was tragically stunning. Well-kept emerald lawns sat beneath tidy rows of granite stones, and flowers peppered the area with their rainbow of colors. They worked together to veil death and heartbreak with the illusion that catastrophic loss was somehow beautiful.

The grounds were as lovely as the weather. It didn't seem right to have something so heartbreaking on a gorgeous, sunny July day; it should be raining. Thundering.

The walk around the other tombstones felt like it took forever, yet it was too short, all at the same time. Like time slacked in slow motion and prolonged my anxiety over giving Dad's eulogy yet simultaneously plunged me in fast-forward through the last chapter I'd have with my father.

When we reached the site, I was surprised. Dad didn't work, and he had no friends. All night, I'd been haunted by the hollowness of saying kind words about my father when there'd be virtually no ears to hear it. Dad deserved for people to hear it, and now, thirty people stood in loose groups.

Cops. Some of them I'd known from the precinct, every one of the DEA task force, and even some cops I didn't know.

My lips quivered. "You did this, didn't you?" I whispered to Shane.

He shrugged, as if his thoughtful gesture was no biggie. "Burch invited the task force."

I could picture Burch saying, *You all are invited to come to Fallon's father's funeral. And by invited, I mean, show up. Period. We have each other's backs on this team.*

Even Proctor was here, fat lip and all—though I knew it was more to do with obeying a boss's order than to support me emotionally. Nonetheless, it was another set of ears, so my dad's life wouldn't feel like it had ended in vain.

I made my way over to them, and as I did, I couldn't stop my eyes from sweeping across the field to a tree forty feet away, where Dillon stood, wearing a black suit.

Leaning against the bark of an ancient oak, he blended into the shadows of the trees. People had to have noticed him, but hopefully, they'd assumed it was a strained relative, someone who wanted to pay their respects, but maybe wasn't welcome to sit close. But it was also possible they'd start asking questions and find out the very captain they were hunting was among them today.

Our eyes locked.

The last time I saw Dillon, I told him the world would be a better place without him. Most people would've told me to F off, but Dillon didn't. And I wondered if the tragic reason wasn't just because of how much he cared about me...but because he believed what I'd said. Just like my mother believed what my dad said the day she'd taken her own life.

*I should never, ever have said something so cruel.*

And he shouldn't be here. We couldn't be seen together, not by the cops, not by anyone, or else someone could tip off his bosses and put Dillon in grave danger.

But at the same time, I was...relieved he was here. I needed him— the *him* that was my boyfriend, the him that had feelings for me—to care enough about me to come.

I didn't understand how I could go from wanting to never see him again to feeling comforted by his presence. I guess it was because, though other horrible things about Dillon might be true, his actions and words made it clear that his feelings for me were genuine. I could feel it all the way over here, his affection wrapping around me with his gaze. And it made me breathe easier.

As Shane left my side to talk to the pastor, I noticed Dillon type something on his phone before mine buzzed with a text.

**Dillon: I'm so sorry about your father.**

I met his gaze again.

**Me: You shouldn't be here. As you can see, there are dozens of cops.**

Dillon tilted his head while he typed.

**Dillon: I don't want to make your day more stressful. That's why I'm hanging out back here.**

My chest ached. He was willing to subject himself to standing there like an outcast just to make my day less stressful. To make this easier for me. If the tables were turned, would I have that level of self-lessness for him?

**Me: Well, if any of your colleagues see you at a cop's father's funeral, there'd be no way to explain that.**

Dillon looked at his phone, then up at me, and shook his head.

**Dillon: You lost your father. The only thing I care about right now is being here for you.**

My breaths grew easier still as his words warmed me.

**Dillon: I hope this isn't wrong for me to say, but I wish I could hug you right now.**

My lips trembled. I wished he could hug me right now, too. I wished he could come sit with everyone else. I wished I hadn't told Shane about Dillon because I was hurting so badly right now, I didn't want to be rational. I wanted Dillon to hold me.

**Me: My friend Shane knows about you.**

Another eye lock. Yet he didn't look upset with me. Why?

Before I could ask, Proctor came up to me. Honestly, of all the people in the universe I wanted to see right now, he was the last. He conveniently looked over his shoulder to ensure Burch saw him making nice.

"Sorry for your loss," Proctor said.

How vindictive of me to feel gratified that his injured lip looked worse than my cheek.

"Thanks," I managed.

When I returned my gaze to Dillon, he looked at Proctor as if it hurt, not being able to come closer to me like Proctor could. Not being able to just walk up to me without fear of putting me in danger.

But that envy quickly vanished when Dillon's gaze fell to Proctor's fat lip, to my bruised cheek, then back to Proctor's mouth. And then his free hand tightened into a fist.

*Shit.*

But that wasn't my only problem. As Proctor walked away from me, Shane marched over and threw a death glare toward the oak tree.

"Is that who I think it is?"

Dillon took one step forward but suddenly froze.

So did Shane.

Because a black Mercedes SUV rolled to a stop on the pavement, and a man emerged, wearing a royal-blue suit. A man who didn't appear to belong here. Nor did the guy in the black suit, who also stepped out.

"Hey, O'Connor." Burch approached. Other officers started to look at the men, but the SUV was to Burch's back. "Sorry for your loss."

"Thank you, sir. And thanks for having the team show. Means a lot."

I studied the mysterious guy, who buttoned his jacket and scanned the cemetery. Maybe they were coming to pay respects to someone else?

"If you need anything," Burch said, "you let me know, okay? No one will think less of you if you take some time off, Fallon."

It was the first time he'd used my first name, and it felt wonderfully endearing.

"No," I insisted. "I want to work more than ever." It'd keep me busy, give me somewhere to point my energy.

Pride flashed across Burch's face, pride that meant more to me than he could imagine.

"In that case, you'll be glad to hear we put two of the captains behind bars this morning," Burch said.

"You did?"

"Tax evasion. Still building the narcotics case, but losing two of their leaders will hurt like hell."

*I'll say.*

"I know it feels like we're chipping away at a huge chunk of ice, but we're turning up the heat on these guys, Fallon. Homicide detectives have been pulling people in for questioning. We found the USB drive. Whether they suspect we have it or not, who knows? But they have to know that it's missing—that's for damn sure. And that's a huge blow itself. Plus, they know we've brought in those guys for questioning, related to this narcotics string, so they know we're onto them. They can feel the walls closing in, rest assured. There's anxiety in that organization right now. We all should be proud of that."

I nodded.

"And," he added, lowering his voice, "IT got another hit on that USB drive. An address. Working on getting the warrant now, so we can go in first thing tomorrow. Do a search."

"Seriously?"

"You want in?"

"Hell yes."

He smiled at me, but after a few seconds, his smile faded when he turned and spotted the men in suits lurking in front of their Mercedes. They hadn't gone to pay any respects. They'd locked their hands in front of them and proceeded to stare at us.

"Who is that?" I asked.

Burch tightened his lips and tried to give me a smile, but it didn't reach his eyes. "Don't worry about that. Focus on your dad today."

Like I could just stand up there and ignore them. "Who is it?" They looked familiar.

Burch shoved his hands into his pockets.

Shane approached us, and I dared to take a longer look at the men. "Are those guys from…the Baja Cartel?"

The Baja Cartel was the most ruthless, aggressive drug cartel in Mexico. They didn't just traffic drugs and kill people; they'd go after rivals so aggressively, some of the smaller cartels simply folded up shop as a preemptive strike. But why would they be here?

Cartel members lived in Mexico and didn't show up on American soil like this. Not openly, anyway. Certainly not in front of a group of cops like this. And if they *did* decide to show up in the United States, why at my dad's funeral?

"We're here to pay respects to your father," Burch said. "Let's not allow them to interfere with that."

"Am I right?"

Burch sighed. "That guy sucking the toothpick," he said, nodding to the guy in black, "name's Lopez. Street name: Peeps. He's a falcon in their organization. Eyes and ears of the streets, supervises and reports activities of police, military, and rival groups."

"So, he's here to spy on us?" I asked.

Burch shook his head. "You don't spy out in the open like this." He hesitated. "And you don't bring him." Burch looked at the guy in the blue suit. "Juan Sanchez, aka The Enforcer, is a hit man in the Baja Cartel. Part of an armed group who carries out assassinations, kidnappings, extortions."

"Well, if they wanted to hurt us, they wouldn't send two guys against thirty armed police officers," I reasoned. "So, what does it mean?"

"I don't know," Burch said. "But I need to find out." He turned to me and put a hand on my shoulder again. "*After* today. Try not to let them get under your skin."

*Oh, sure. A cartel hit man and his eyes are just here, stalking us, while my ex-boyfriend is hiding in the trees, waiting for a moment to come after Proctor, while Shane wants to pummel Dillon. No distractions here.*

"I don't like this," Shane said. "We should reschedule and get the hell out of here."

"You guys can leave. Hell, maybe you *should* leave, but I'm saying good-bye to my dad. Those two can flop their dicks on the table in front of police another day."

Burch's mouth curled up.

I marched toward the pastor, and as he asked everyone to take their seats among the rows of folding chairs, I risked a quick text to Dillon.

**Me: Do you know why they're here?**

His answer was quick.

**Dillon: No. But I think I know why they're in the United States.**

I didn't like this, and Dillon could not be anywhere near here.

**Me: Leave. Now, Dillon.**

"Are you ready?" the pastor asked me.

As everyone sat and the pastor began citing Bible verses, I noticed Dillon remained in his position.

The sun warmed my shoulders. I probably should have worn a dress instead of a black pantsuit. As I listened to the pastor talk, the sounds of birds chirping echoed through the nearby trees. They sounded so free, so happy—the opposite of what my poor father's life had been.

The closed coffin's shiny wood reflected the afternoon sun and hovered over the hole they'd pre-dug yesterday.

I placed my hand on the wood grain, noting how warm it was. Knowing it was the closest I'd ever be to touching my dad again for the rest of my life.

And then it was my turn to recite the words I'd written and rewritten twenty-five times over the last few days. I pulled the two pages from my suit's breast pocket and unfolded them, wishing my hands weren't trembling from sadness as I started to say good-bye.

"When people see my dad, many only see the drug addict. They didn't see the person he was before drugs performed a hostile takeover of his life, and they didn't see the guy that battled addiction harder than many battle cancer."

My throat was so tight, it burned as I tried to swallow.

"I'm sorry, Dad, that you endured this terrible battle every day of your life. I'm sorry that in our race for time together, the drugs won. And we lost. And I'm sorry I wasn't more understanding during the storm.

"But I understand now that you were never choosing drugs over me. Just the opposite. You spent every single day battling against an impossible current that was trying to pull you under, and the only reason you fought that hard and that long was to get back to me. How strong is a love to wake up every single day for 5,500 days and fight for someone's love?"

My eyes watered.

I looked over at the cartel guy, who was twisting the toothpick in his mouth, his beady eyes staring right at me as he smirked. Those scumbags had some nerve, showing up here. Like they didn't cause enough hurt in this world, supplying drugs to millions of people. When one of their victims lost his life to their narcotics, they couldn't even let the man rest in peace. They had to take away the last moments I had with my father.

Those were the criminals keeping Dillon imprisoned in his occupation, and the only reason they'd stand there like this was to try and intimidate us. They weren't just killers; they were bullies.

I squared my shoulders.

"I couldn't save you, Dad." I glowered at the cartel guy. "But I'll do everything in my power to stop another family from going through this."

The Enforcer stood there for three seconds. And then he grinned at me like I'd just started the most delicious game and slithered back into the SUV with his thug and drove away.

*Crap, what did I just do?*

Burch approached me. "You sure that was wise?"

I swallowed. "There are a lot of ways to help families with addiction," I reasoned.

"Yeah. But you looked right at him when you said that. Judging by the smile The Enforcer gave, he took what you said as a threat. And the Baja Cartel don't take too kindly to threats."

## 23

I wondered what everyone would do if I walked out the door and never came back. *It'd be rude,* I warned myself.

All the cops had come to this post-funeral dinner to show support for me, which I appreciated more than they could imagine. And with only a handful of cops remaining—Shane, Proctor, and three other officers from our precinct—I only needed to wait a little longer.

But grief was exhausting, and after watching my father's casket get lowered into the earth, after taking a fistful of cool dirt and sprinkling it over his coffin, I could feel myself cracking. I'd had to fight to hold it together on the drive over when I picked dirt residue from under my nails. During every encounter with folks offering condolences. I fought to hold my composure when the officers spent most of the meal talking about the cartel showing up, speculating what it might mean—a topic I'd regain interest in as soon as this awful day was over. But now, my sorrow was like that elevator fire. Spreading. Engulfing me. Weakening me.

All I wanted to do was escape. Go back to my apartment, where I could draw a warm bath and release the pressure of tears building inside me.

The problem was, I didn't think I was going to make it that long.

The longer I sat here, the more memories assaulted my heart.

*I'm on a swing, my shoelaces wiggling through the air as my feet pump up toward the sun. "Daddy!" I squeal. "Higher!"*

*As soon as I come down, his hands push my back again as he laughs.*

*Mommy and I are playing hide-and-seek, and I jump out from behind the door and shout, "Boo!"*

*She holds her chest. And then she gives me that look—the one that says,* I'm going to chase you. *And I take off, running up our staircase, laughing, and when she catches me, she tickles me for a full minute.*

*When she's done laughing, she kisses my forehead and says, "I love you, baby girl."*

*Mommy's at the park with me. "Fallon!" she shouts in horror when she sees I've climbed up on top of the monkey bars, walking across them like a balance beam. "Get down—now!"*

*"I'm fine!" I assure.*

*I'm nine. I'm a big girl now, and I have excellent balance. But Mommy climbs to the second story of the equipment faster than a rocket. She's standing at the opening of the fire pole when my footing slips. Her arms shoot out and grab me, swipe me to safety, but she loses her balance. And after pushing me to the playground's second-story floor, she tries to grab the lip of the wall. But it doesn't stop her from falling through the opening. After a seven-foot drop, she crashes to the ground and onto her shoulder.*

*"It's okay," Daddy says to me as we wait in the waiting room. "It's a simple surgery."*

*"It's my fault," I cry.*

*"It's not," he assures. "It was just an accident."*

*But it wasn't. She fell because of me. And as soon as she gets home from the hospital, I'm going to wait on her hand and foot to make up for it.*

*Daddy pulls me into a hug and kisses the top of my head. "This will all be behind us before you know it."*

What if the reason I'd been so determined to blame drug dealers for my family's demise was because the truth was too painful to accept? That the real person responsible for it all was me?

I bit my tongue. I couldn't hold this in anymore. I didn't care if it was rude. I needed to leave now.

My cell phone buzzed.

**Dillon: Meet me in the women's restroom.**

Confused, I looked around the restaurant.

**Me: What? What restroom?**

**Dillon: The one in the back of this restaurant.**

My heartbeat accelerated. What the hell was Dillon doing here?

I looked at Shane. He'd behaved at the funeral, but if he found out Dillon was here, I highly doubted Shane would hold back his wrath toward him now.

I kept my face neutral as I casually stood up and followed the signs to the restroom. Nobody stopped me as I walked to the other end of the main dining room, down a small corridor, turned left into a narrow hallway, and stood outside the door to the women's bathroom.

I glanced up and down the empty hallway before opening the door and walking inside.

The place was immaculate. Gray porcelain tiles blanketed the floor, butting up against white subway tiles that stretched halfway up the walls, reflecting the pink glow of the bathroom's soft lighting. Three stalls were to my left, two black sinks to my right. Dillon leaned against the far wall between them. He still wore his suit pants, button-down, and tie, but not the jacket.

I held up my finger and did a quick search of each stall.

"No one's in here," he said.

But someone could come in any second, and there was no lock on the door.

"What are you doing here?"

Dillon's eyebrows drew together, and he glanced down at my fidgeting hands. Before locking his chestnut eyes with mine.

"You were trembling when they lowered your dad's casket into the ground," he said. "I wanted to make sure you were all right."

Pain radiated through my nerves. He couldn't be this kind and caring with me. It made it harder to do the right thing and push him away. "How did you know I was here?"

Dillon hesitated. "I followed you."

"Someone could've seen you."

"All the other cops left the cemetery before you." Because I'd stayed behind to say my final good-bye to Dad privately.

Shane had waited for me down the hill, and Dillon was no longer at his post by the tree by that point. He must have been in one of the vehicles we passed in the cemetery's main parking lot on our way out. Maybe if Shane hadn't been preoccupied, attempting to console me, he or I would have seen Dillon.

"The cartel could've followed you," I said.

"I was careful. I'd never put you in danger, Fallon."

"I'm not talking about *me*. Plenty of officers came here." I gestured with my hand. "If the cartel wanted to know where I was, they'd have plenty of people to follow. But you showing up puts you in danger."

"I had to make sure you were all right," he repeated in a tone that declared it was all that mattered right now.

Which made my eyes sting.

As I stared at him, something shifted inside of me.

I realized Dillon had this effect on my heart that could never be tamed by rationalization. I felt warm in his presence. The armor that I worked so hard to keep up faltered around him, no matter how hard I tried to glue it back together.

As he studied me, he could've asked me anything or insisted we talk about the cartel's shocking move today. But the question that took priority for him was, "Are you okay?"

Sometimes, when you're breaking inside and it takes every ounce of energy to hold it together, that one question has the power to shatter your resolve.

And just like that, the rest of my bricks crumbled. The avalanche of suffering I had contained in the four days since my dad's death finally broke free.

My dad was gone. Just like my mom was. They would never hold me again or be there for any holiday or milestone for the rest of my life. I would never get to say all the things I wished I had before it was too late.

*What I wouldn't give for just one more day with them on this earth.*

I brought my hand to my mouth and tried to silence my cries, but the moment the first tear broke over my cheek, a flood rushed out behind them. My entire body dissolved into grief. My bones hurt. My chest burned, and my arms ached for my dad's embrace.

I'd managed to be strong in front of everyone else, but I no longer had the energy to hold up the dam. Instead, I covered my face with my hands. I cried so hard, it suffocated the last of my strength, and I slithered to the floor.

After a few moments, an arm reached around my shaking shoulders, and Dillon's hand pulled my head against his chest.

He sat on the floor next to me and held me in silence as I mourned the loss of everything. He didn't rush me or remind me that someone out there might come looking for me. Nor did he mention what the consequences would be for him if Shane found us together.

Instead, I got the sense that Dillon would hold me for as long as I wanted him to.

When my sobs finally slowed, I could hear his beating heart, feel its slight thump against my ear. I could feel his fingers run through my hair and his lips kiss the top of my head.

"I'm sorry for what I said at the morgue," I eventually managed. "And for slapping you."

Dillon chewed the inside of his cheek. "I deserved it."

No, he didn't. He didn't deserve me blaming him for my dad's death, either, or listening to my radical conspiracy theories about what might've happened, as if I could somehow blame Dillon for that, too.

"My dad's death"—I hesitated—"turns out, it was an overdose after all." I took a deep pull of oxygen to brace myself for the next part. "I finally found out the reason he did drugs in the first place."

Dillon tightened his grip on me, fully aware of how important it had been for me to get that answer.

"It was a suicide attempt."

He tensed.

"He blamed himself for the death of my mom. And when we were talking about it, I basically confirmed his fear." How could I ever forgive myself for that?

"Fallon—"

"I should get back to the dinner," I said even though I wanted to stay in Dillon's arms. I wanted us to be two ordinary people free to date, not hiding out in a women's restroom.

I wished Dillon and I could have pursued our relationship. "I wish you had a different occupation."

He kissed the top of my head again. "I do, too."

I loosened myself from his grip, so I could look up at him.

Geez, I'd almost forgotten how exquisitely beautiful he was. The warmth of the light turned his skin golden and made his facial hair—a few days thicker than a five o'clock shadow—look darker, framing his jaw. His shoulders and biceps tried to break out of his shirt, which was rolled to his elbows, revealing muscular steel bands along his forearms.

Dillon's gentle eyes drew my heart closer, reminding me that beneath his flaws and bad choices was the man I'd fallen for. A man that cared more about me than his own safety.

He brushed his thumb across my left cheek, then my right, wiping away the last of my tears. And then, as he stroked my skin, he allowed his gaze to drift from my eyes to my lips.

In that instant, I wanted his mouth on mine. Maybe it was because it was the only thing capable of momentarily soothing my grief. Maybe it was because the old Dillon was sitting with me right now, and I needed him back, if only for a moment. Maybe it was because we'd never had a proper good-bye. And if this was the last time he touched me, I wanted more of him than just his embrace.

Dillon's chest rose and fell quicker, and then he moved slowly, perhaps waiting to ensure I was okay with it before he finally lowered his face.

And pressed his lips to mine.

The flames of desire sparked my mouth to open, allowing his tongue to connect with mine. I shifted my body, so I could wrap my arms around his neck, relishing it when he deepened the kiss.

I knew it was wrong of me. Made me a lousy agent, at the very least. A traitor to law enforcement even. A hot mess of a person, certainly. But I didn't care. No one could understand how complicated this felt—trying to shove all the emotions we'd developed for each other into a box and never allowing that box to open, if only for a few minutes.

Surrendering to this passion felt like when we'd escaped that fire, bursting through that exterior door—leaving the suffocating smoke behind in exchange for fresh air. It made the agony of loss dim, so long as our lips stayed connected.

I pushed myself up onto my right knee and turned myself around. Dillon's hands clenched my outer thighs, steadying me as I straddled him, and I twisted my hands through his hair.

He didn't deny me when I deepened our kiss, when I opened my mouth wider and let my hands roam down his back. Instead, he followed my lead and let his hands roam, too. Wonderfully so.

Beneath my unbuttoned suit jacket, Dillon tugged at the undershirt until it released from my pants. And then his fingers glided up my stomach, to my chest before he squeezed.

I groaned and moved my hips, rocking against him, feeling his desire beneath me. I wanted to run out the door with him. Go back to his place and be selfish and irresponsible and wrong, if it meant I'd get to spend the night with him.

But just when I allowed myself to escape into that fantasy, a knock ruined it.

"Fallon?" Shane said from the other side of the door.

I pulled back, out of breath, staring at Dillon's bronze eyes.

"Are you in there?"

"I'll be right out," I said.

"Is everything okay?"

"Yeah. I just needed some space. Can you tell the waiter I'm ready for the bill? I want to leave."

Shane hesitated. "Okay. I'll let everyone know we're wrapping up."

Dillon cupped my cheek gently and kissed me one last time.

"I'd better go," I whispered.

If Shane found Dillon in here, it would turn into a massacre. I'd have no idea how to explain what I'd just done with Dillon.

Even to myself.

Dillon and I could never be together. I knew that.

So, why couldn't my heart seem to get the memo?

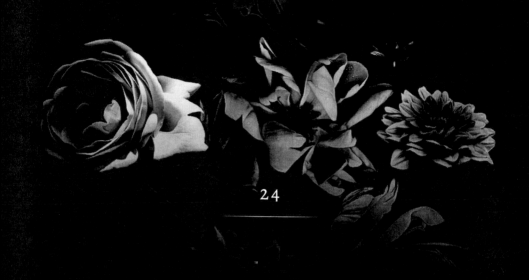

24

The DEA task force gathered with anticipation a block and a half from the address the IT team had recovered. The industrial neighborhood had been abandoned years ago after the real estate crash, its rows of rectangular buildings now empty. That meant the place in question—a three-story brick warehouse—most certainly wasn't being used for legitimate purposes. A sentiment echoed by the men prowling its outside, appearing to guard the place.

The minute we'd arrived at the gathering point, I could tell this wasn't going to be a typical raid. Heck, I'd already gotten that vibe when I heard we'd struggled to secure the warrant. Probable cause was trickier than some people might think—you couldn't simply get one based on an officer's subjective beliefs. Burch was able to provide reasonable suspicion, though, since the three names on that hard drive *were* linked to illegal narcotics, and the officers who'd completed brief surveillance of this address witnessed guards surrounding a box truck as it backed up to the side door. And witnessed what they recognized, based on their experience and training, to be drug activity at two o'clock in the morning.

Now daylight, the cloudless sky offered no shield from the sun, no breeze in the eighty-degree heat. The only sound I could focus on was from the straps of bulletproof vests tightening and quickened breaths from those of us taming our nerves.

I wished this search worked more like the movies and that we'd roll up with dozens of SWAT officers because the ten men walking around the warehouse's perimeter were undoubtedly armed.

Even Proctor seemed nervous.

"Are you okay?" I asked him. He'd winced when he put his vest on.

"Fine," he grumbled.

But he didn't seem fine. It looked like every twist of his ribs caused a great deal of pain. Yet he'd looked fine at the dinner yesterday.

"Remember, everyone is detained *before* we enter," Burch repeated.

He'd gone over this plan in the conference room two dozen times. Had the blueprint of the building pinned up on the wall, broke us up into teams, gave us assignments of where to enter, spreading out teams along the structure. We were to cuff the guards first and detain them for our safety and also so they didn't have the chance to destroy evidence. But planning to do this was nothing compared to this adrenaline of getting ready to possibly confront some of the most dangerous men in the world—armed men who had nothing to lose if they got busted with whatever was inside that warehouse.

"You think Marks could be in there?" I prayed even though I doubted the FBI thought so. If they did, they would have sent more than two men to join us in the raid. Probably reasoned that any address placed on a USB drive *before* Marks went missing was unlikely related to the disappearance case. Still, I hoped otherwise.

"One way to find out," Burch said. "Okay, let's go."

As instructed, we filed into marked police vehicles. It felt like we plunged into the scene at fifty miles an hour, and we had the place surrounded within a minute. Four of us—me, Proctor, and two other officers—jumped out at our mark and pointed our guns at two men on the structure's east side.

"DEA!" Proctor shouted. "Hands up!"

The men stood frozen for a moment, taking in the scene before them with the building now surrounded by cop cars and officers.

There was nowhere for the perps to get away, so the only question was, would they surrender peacefully or go down in a blaze of bullets?

"Hands up!" I repeated.

And then shots rang out on the other side of the building. So much for plan A.

The perps exchanged a look. And then suddenly, the suspect with the square head gritted his teeth, yanked out his gun.

And fired.

His shot missed us, but when his buddy joined him, a barrage of gunshots forced us to take cover behind the SUV and return fire.

*Bam. Bam-bam. Bam. Bam. Bam-bam.*

It was hard to see what was happening. The four of us tried to poke our heads out as bullets sprayed the air with impending death. Gunshots continued to pop on the other sides of the building, too.

Plan B was going to hell.

The suspect on our right jerked and went down, but one of our agents screamed, grabbed his bleeding thigh, and let go of his weapon.

I crawled over him and aimed at the guy to the left. Square Head. I lined up my shot. Fired. And missed.

The other officer positioned himself at the vehicle's back, lined up his shot, and fired.

The second perp thumped to the ground.

Both suspects were down, and within seconds, all the other gunfire ceased. Making me wonder who won the fight on the other sides of the building.

We waited for the all clear—the signal to go inside—but there was nothing.

The sound of silence was haunting when we didn't know what awaited us on the other side of it. All I could hear were my labored breaths, the thumping of my erratic heart beating in my ears.

For what felt like an eternity.

And then, like a rainbow after the storm, Burch's voice commanded us to enter.

When we got inside the building, there were no other suspects. They must've had an escape route. Knew this building and the area better than anyone and had designed ways out in case something like this ever happened.

I'd hoped we'd find Marks inside, but we found something even more shocking.

Surrounding twenty rows of tables were shelving units on all four sides of the massive structure. Where hundreds of white plastic bricks sat. I had no clue how much cocaine we were looking at, but based on the whites of Burch's eyes, I had to assume it was more than any other bust he'd been a part of.

We'd just found the Syndicates' distribution hub.

## 25

I descended the cement stairs, sinking deeper into the darkness of the basement with each step. As the dank smell of mold tickled my nose and my eyes strained to see my footing, the most overwhelming sensation was the room's insidious quietness. I could hear the intake of oxygen flowing into my throat, the thud of my footsteps.

For the millionth time, I looked over my shoulder to ensure I hadn't been followed. I'd been meticulous during my journey here—switching "L" trains two times, walking in circles around three blocks, and walking into the building across the street, only to sneak out its hidden emergency exit to come here. But still. Eyes could be anywhere, especially now that I'd threatened the cartel.

I wondered what Dillon wanted to talk about and why he'd grown so paranoid that he no longer trusted burner phones to do it. If someone was looking for evidence as to who you were communicating with, they'd have to know the identity of *both* phone numbers. And thus far, the Chicago Syndicates hadn't been *that* sophisticated.

Then again, we'd just confiscated a massive amount of narcotics, so paranoia was probably at an all-time high.

At the bottom of the staircase, I turned on my cell phone's flashlight and scanned the space. It was an unfinished basement with concrete walls, stained with years of white and gold mineral deposits settling onto the stone. The concrete echoed each of my breaths in the damp, stale air, steel beams running along the ceiling, propping up the forty-story structure above my head. Save for a small folding table and chairs in the corner, the room was completely bare. I could see why Dillon had picked it—nowhere for someone to hide and eavesdrop.

Or ambush us.

I pulled my .40 caliber Smith & Wesson out as I took a further look around because, hell, maybe I was wrong; maybe there *was* somewhere to hide.

I illuminated the wall by the stairwell, where cobwebs blanketed the corner, and a spider shimmied away from my light. Then, I swept my inspection across to the far wall, where a car-sized water stain bled outward and intensified the smell of must as water dripped from an overhead pipe.

Suddenly, footsteps padded down the stairs, as if the person was trying to obscure the noise of their approach. I shut my light off and tucked myself into the corner with my gun drawn.

The footsteps thumped louder, and then, at the bottom of the staircase, the shadow of a man's outline spun around.

And turned on a flashlight. The light darted around the space until it found me and assaulted my eyes, rendering me blind to whoever was with me down here.

"Will you lower your gun, please?"

He shifted the beam, so it bounced off the wall to my right, illuminating the side of his face.

Dillon.

I let out a gulp of air I'd been unconsciously holding and lowered my weapon as he turned the light off, pulled something out of his backpack, and flipped it on. A portable lantern, the kind that you had for camping, casting off an orange glow.

When he held the lantern up to get a better look at me, Dillon's eyes locked with mine, and something passed between us. Something profound, a bond that hadn't severed despite our opposite positions in this war.

He cleared his throat. "Shall we sit at the table?"

He set the lantern on the folding table in the corner and nodded toward the chairs.

I chose the seat with the best view of the staircase, so I could watch anyone who might come down.

Dillon sat opposite me.

The last time I saw him, he'd held me and comforted me in my time of need. I'd felt grateful and warm, but today, I had a bone to pick with him. And I was going to do it before he had the chance to get into why he'd called this meeting.

I crossed my arms over my chest and said, "You beat up Proctor."

That was why he'd winced in pain the other morning and why he was fine at the dinner. Because he *was* fine. Until someone must have confronted him and changed that. Someone who'd had a score to settle.

Dillon wiped his nose with his thumb. "I'm sure whoever did it wanted to do far worse to him."

"That's not a confession."

"Confessing a crime would put you in an uncomfortable position."

I frowned. "I told you I hit him first."

"I'm sure the only relevant fact to whoever did it was that he laid hands on you."

"Strange that whoever did it was smart enough to leave no bruises on his face to avoid drawing unwanted attention to it. And even stranger that Proctor didn't report it," I said.

"A lot of guys feel embarrassed after getting their ass kicked."

"He could change his mind," I warned.

Dillon locked his steely eyes with mine. "Perhaps the assailant wore a ski mask. So that scumbag didn't see his face."

I glowered at him. "I don't need you to fight my battles for me."

"I know you don't need me to," Dillon said. "But anyone who messes with you can expect to deal with me."

"That's teetering awfully close to a confession."

Dillon tightened his lips. "This isn't what we came here to talk about," he said. "I told you something big is going down..."

I waited.

"I found out what it is."

Okay. He got my attention. "And?"

Dillon reached inside his backpack and set down various items on the table. A stack of cash thicker than the seventh book of Harry Potter. Credit cards. Passport. Plane ticket. I looked closer, examining the passport, realizing it was mine. Kind of. The picture was of me, the stats of my height and weight. But the name was wrong. *Samantha Bowen.* Which was the same incorrect name on the credit cards and plane ticket—which was one way, to Dubai.

"You realize this is all illegal," I said. "And you're handing all this evidence of your illicit activities to a cop."

He was silent.

"How did you even get my picture?"

"The Syndicates will not take that raid lying down. Cost them a lot of money. Plus, those two men at the funeral? The ones leaning against the Mercedes? They belong to the Baja Cartel."

When I said nothing, he tightened his lips and kept talking. "When the Baja Cartel moves into a new area, it becomes extremely dangerous for all the cities and towns nearby. First thing they do is infiltrate the police to get them out of their way. They start with bribes, and if that doesn't work, they resort to violence. Lot of people have tried to stand up to them. Cops. Military. But the Baja Cartel's been too powerful because of how violent they are and the lengths they'll go to, to stay in power. They'll bomb buildings filled with civilians if that's what it takes."

Dillon studied my face. "Those are the people you basically declared war on. So, yeah, if you didn't consider leaving before? You need to now."

I stared at him.

"These guys are vicious. And good."

"So are we," I said. "I trust my people."

A look flashed through his eyes.

"What?" I asked.

Silence.

"What?" I repeated.

Dillon seemed to weigh his next words carefully. "Fallon, I think you have a leak on the inside. Someone leaked that funeral to the cartel."

"Funeral information is public. You found the funeral information without getting it from a cop. Maybe they did, too."

"Maybe," Dillon allowed. "But if someone is under the thumb of the cartel? You need to be careful. They could be just as dangerous if you find them out."

I swallowed.

"You cannot get in these guys' way, Fallon. That cop that was taken?"

Marks...

My stomach rolled with nerves. For ten days, police had completed one of the most thorough investigations in Chicago's history. Street cameras from all over the city were reviewed—even national searches. Airports, parking structures. Thousands of people were interviewed, tip lines worked. And nothing had come of it. His pregnant wife was still in front of the media, keeping his story alive in hopes it would lead to his safe return. But the cops were no closer to figuring out what happened to him.

And now, Dillon knew something about it, which meant he'd stuck his neck out and asked around. Someone might grow quite suspicious of Dillon's loyalty if they hadn't already...

"The one thing the cartel needs to be successful is for the cops to stand down, back off. Not turn up the heat. That cop became a problem the moment he arrested one of our captains."

A captain with a USB drive in his stomach. Was that why they took Marks? To see if the captain had given it to the cops?

"They got nervous the captain mighta given up intel."

Like a USB drive.

So, they eliminated the threat? Or were interrogating Marks to find out?

"And they were trying to expand operations," I deduced. That had to be the big move Burch was sensing.

Dillon nodded.

"And Marks complicated that," I reasoned.

First, when they couldn't find the missing USB drive, and then it only got worse, even after he was abducted. The interrogations. The arrests. The domino had all started with Marks's original arrest of Terrell.

Another nod. "Plus, they'd be damned if they didn't send a message to cops about what happens if you get too close."

I swallowed. In my gut, I knew something awful happened to Marks, but sending a message made it all the more ominous. I thought back to the torture victim in the river and shuddered.

"And they can't *not* send a message after what you said."

Fear turned my voice to a whisper. "Is Marks still alive?"

Dillon blinked. "I don't know."

I leaned back in my seat, my mind taking in the scope of the threat. Marks. The body in the river. The thugs at the funeral.

Dillon rubbed his temples. "Fallon, I know you want to take down these guys. But getting yourself killed isn't going to bring your father back."

I squared my shoulders. "So, we're supposed to what, let the bad guys win?"

"What's happening is so far above all of us that there's nothing we can do to stop it. It's too late. Fighting it will only get yourself killed."

Dillon looked like a thin thread fraying at the edges, deriving its only strength from getting me to safety.

"Please," he whispered. "I need you to know that I really do care about you, Fallon."

My shoulders shrank.

"And I can't exist if something happens to you. Even if you didn't threaten them, you can't be here because I found out what's about to go down. And it's so much worse than I ever imagined."

"What is it?"

He paused. The space seemed to chill with his words. "Fallon, the

Baja Cartel is moving to the United States."

The damp air blanketed my skin in goose bumps. I couldn't imagine a more devastating blow to the war on drugs, nor a larger influx of violence.

"Turns out, your DEA task force has been a little...too successful. The Syndicates were supposed to be expanding, but the DEA's disrupted that. When the cartel saw what a mess we'd made of things, they made a decision. To take over. Here."

"We have some of the best defenses in the world," I said. Best police. Best military. "Our government will never let that happen."

"They'll fight," Dillon agreed. "But the Baja Cartel will fight back, and they don't play by the rules."

I bounced my knee under the table.

Dillon leaned closer to me. "You need to leave—now. Don't go home. Don't collect any of your stuff; just go straight to the airport and buy what you need once you get there," he said, shoving the cash, credit cards, passport into the backpack and setting it next to my foot.

"And what about you?" I didn't agree with what he'd done, but I didn't want him to die over it.

He looked haunted by something as he shook his head.

I studied him. "You're keeping something from me."

He didn't deny it.

"Tell me."

He looked down, shook his head. "You'd never look at me the same."

"Have you killed someone?"

"No."

"Then, what is it?"

"Look, it doesn't matter. What matters is that you need to get the hell out of here."

"And then what?" I challenged. "What happens to Shane? And my colleagues and the innocent people of this country? And what happens to you?"

"Right now, I'm focused on getting you out. I'll figure out my next steps after."

This was a lot of information to process. If what he was saying was correct, it meant a war was coming to this country. With many lives lost.

The balance between good and evil would be as much on the line as the lives of innocent people throughout this country. The face of our nation as we knew it, the sanctuary of freedom.

"Leaving town might be safer for me," I started. "But if what you're saying is true, I'd be abandoning the very people I swore an oath to protect."

"Fallon—"

"I can't leave when my country needs me the most. I have to do everything in my power to stop it from happening."

I shifted the backpack across the floor with my foot.

He stared at me intently, and then he took my hand.

His touch sparked an electric current inside of me.

"For the record?" he said. "What you're doing right now is incredibly reckless."

He brought my hand to his lips. Would my heart ever *not* respond to his touch? Or the way he looked at me like this—his expression brimming with emotion?

"I want you to know something." Sadness choked his words. "I've always known I couldn't let myself get close to anyone." He paused. "But I never felt the weight of that sacrifice until I met you."

My insides wrenched because suddenly, worry for *his* safety ripped through my core.

"I'm sorry for being a bad guy, Fallon. For being any part of this."

"You need to take that cash and bolt," I said.

Amusement danced across his features. "You're encouraging a known criminal to leave the country?"

Was I? Where was *my* moral line?

"I'm going to get my mom and brother out," he said. "But I'm not leaving."

"Dillon—"

"A war is coming, and you're on its front lines. I'm not leaving, Fallon. I'm going to stay and do whatever I can to protect you."

## 26

Blood was splattered across the ash-colored doors. That was what led to the call, what led police to investigate the warehouse that we'd raided only days ago. What led to the discovery of the slaughter inside.

What happened to the victim, however, didn't take place in that building's entrance. Crime scene experts said the blood on the door had been planted there, perhaps to ensure someone would find the body.

New crime scene tape roped off the area along with twenty law enforcement and FBI vehicles, the medical examiner's car, and dozens of cops meticulously marking any possible clue with a yellow cone and a number.

The life this building once had—with its once-immaculate bricks, overflowing light from vast windows wrapping around its three stories—was drained, just like the victim inside of it. The burgundy color of its stones had faded, parts of them flaking off after years of abuse in Chicago's harsh winters, and the first-floor windows were broken and concealed with spray-painted wood.

"O'Connor." Burch waved me inside, where I joined Burch, Shane, and Proctor, who stood in the center while investigators and the rest of the task force scattered about.

The space was vast. Concrete floors echoed my footsteps off its three-story ceilings.

It was there, on one of the ceiling's steel beams, that Marks hung by his neck. The rope was long enough to suspend his nude body four feet off the ground.

Vomit soared into my esophagus, threatening to erupt. I had to focus on breathing for several moments to regain control.

"Fuck," Shane said.

My mind flashed to my first day at the Chicago Police Department when I'd been feeling like a small-town nobody walking into the major leagues.

Officer Marks was the first one to look me in my eye, extend his hand with a warm smile, and say, "Welcome to the team."

Now, that smile was replaced with an open mouth, frozen in the screaming position. His eyes that had welcomed me with kindness were wide enough to show the whites above his irises, and the hand that had shaken mine was bound with the other behind his back.

The state of his body was even worse. His shoulder's skin bubbled with crimson divots—undoubtedly burned slowly, by the looks of it. Nails speckled his arms—so deeply, it had to have been done with a nail gun—and his skin had been shredded with dozens of gashes.

I took a deep breath, shoving the second wave of puke down. And then I clenched my fists with fury.

"How'd they get past the police car parked outside?" Proctor asked, referring to the one that had been assigned there since the raid.

"They knew this place well enough to get out during the raid; probably knew how to get back in without being noticed," Shane reasoned.

"I've seen the work of a lot of drug organizations in my career," Burch said. "But I've never seen anything like this before. It looks like what you'd see from—"

"The cartel," I finished.

Burch looked at me, and then, as the crime scene photographer snapped three more photos of the body, Burch seemed to consider my assertion. He had to see the evidence was insurmountable that the cartel had a hand in this. The blood on the door inciting attention. The dramatic posing of the body, the torture Marks had clearly endured, and the symbolic location—the abandoned warehouse where we'd confiscated their precious narcotics. As if to say, *This is what happens if you mess with our business.*

Seeing Marks should have scared me into accepting Dillon's plan —or at the very least, lying low for a while. But it did the opposite. As I thought of Marks's poor wife and children who would never see him again, a rage grew inside me.

"There has to be something more we can be doing," I said.

"We will," Burch said. "It'll just take time. We'll start putting an undercover team together next week and ramp it up quickly. In a few months, we'll be ready to infiltrate 'em and take every last one of them down."

"We don't have a few months," I said. "I have a credible source that claims the Baja Cartel is planning to move to the United States."

Burch's gaze cut to me.

"I just heard about it," I said.

I could see it in Burch's eyes that he was putting together clues that hadn't quite fit until this piece of the puzzle came into focus. And as it did, an unprecedented reality formed before us all.

Shane's body tensed.

"You think it's true," I said to Burch.

He glanced at Marks's body and rubbed his mustache.

"It would certainly explain some things," he allowed.

"You think they'd really come here?" Proctor asked.

Burch rubbed his jaw. "The Baja Cartel's wanted to move to the United States for years," he said. "More money, domination. They think that if they can take the US, they can take any country and expand their operations exponentially. Kill off all rivals in the market. Chatter has increased about it since last year when a guy named Gutierrez took over."

Gutierrez. I read he'd waged a bigger war than Escobar had.

"And lately, they've been cleaning house, killing off even the slightest perception of a threat to their operations."

Burch looked like he was searching for evidence that would contradict it because the reality of what we might be facing was so dire, no one wanted it to be true.

"This intel," Burch started. "Does this mean we have ourselves a CI?"

"He still won't do it. I got lucky, getting this piece of information."

"If they did plan on it, why come to the funeral then?" Shane pressed. "It blew their cover."

"They wanted us to see them at the funeral," Burch answered. "And they want us to know Marks was tortured for information." Even though he wouldn't have had much to say.

"Marks would never give up anything," I said.

"Body temp says he was killed just a few hours ago; he'd been tortured for ten days."

It took me a second to recover from that and refocus on the conversation. "He'd never talk."

Burch regarded me. "You have kids, Fallon?"

This was undoubtedly a rhetorical question on his part; knowing all the stats of the team he'd assembled, he had to know the answer.

"No."

"Well, I do. A wife, two kids. And one can only imagine the lengths someone's willing to go to in order to save them. Especially if they threatened to do all of this"—he gestured to Marks's body—"to one of his kids."

Seeing Burch rattled made me feel scared.

"We need to get more intel before we run this all the way up the ladder," Burch decided. "Some sort of proof." Burch paced. "This has to be why the Syndicates are hosting that national meeting. They're probably going to discuss it there."

"What meeting?" Proctor asked.

Burch looked like he'd forgotten we were there for a moment. "In six days, Chicago, Miami, and New York are meeting here in Illinois. If the cartel is planning to come, that'd be bad for business for these guys. Could put 'em out of business, maybe even mean their execution —for those that aren't already on the hit list because of the raid, that is. So, maybe that's why the meeting was called."

"Can we get into that meeting?" I asked.

"Undercover? No," Burch snapped.

"Sir—"

"Undercover operations don't work like that," Burch said. "You don't just waltz into a meeting of that caliber on a whim. You slowly build up an identity over months—years sometimes—before you make a play like that."

"But this meeting is happening now," Proctor pushed. "Think about what they'll probably talk about. Those organizations will have some huge decisions to make with the missing contraband and, more importantly, with the cartel coming. They'll surely talk about the timeline they have to play with. How long till the cartel arrives, who's coming, when, and where. We need that information to fight their invasion, and we can't let this opportunity slip by, sir."

Burch didn't disagree with Proctor's assessment. Surely, whatever they discussed at that meeting would be vital. Decisions would be made. Orders given. But he did disagree about an undercover mission on such short notice.

"It's too dangerous," Burch said. "There's a reason we don't do half-assed missions. They fail." His tone closed the door to the conversation.

"This might be the only shot we get," I added. "How long do you think we'd have to wait until they meet up like this again?"

Months, maybe years, based on the look on his face.

"Look, I know this is a long shot," I said. "But it's the only play we have right now, and any chance is better than none. I'm willing to at least try."

"Doesn't matter. Those crews are dangerous. You know how many people they've killed in their careers? Besides, this Saturday's manpower is going to be light; half the task force and hundreds of uniforms will be at Navy Pier for the mayor's award ceremony."

"If we go slow, let someone build up an identity, even if we do get another opportunity like this, by then, it'll be too late. The cartel will have already moved here, planted and watered roots, and started the war. Do we really want to be the team that knew this was coming and didn't strike before it was too late?" Proctor pushed.

I wondered if Burch's legacy flashed through his mind and if he asked himself a tough question. Would he be remembered as the guy that sat back and allowed the most ruthless cartel in the world to move to the United States and didn't do everything in his power to stop it?

"No undercover agent would be willing to jump into something like that in as little as six days," Burch said.

I looked at him intently.

Burch chided, "You've never even been undercover before."

"I have," Proctor said. "I'd like to volunteer."

"No one here is ready," Burch said.

"Sir," I started, suddenly feeling like I was in a job interview, desperate to woo over an objection, "I've taken extensive training on being an undercover operative, both with classes offered by the Chicago Police Department as well as the Undercover Association. I progressed into advanced techniques, including a focus on narcotics, vice, and street crimes. Tactical training, covert missions, human trafficking. All of it." Because I wanted to be on the DEA, and training for their undercover arm increased the chances of acceptance. Not to mention the satisfaction of it. *Think of showing up on those drug criminals' turf, invading their life for once.*

"You haven't logged a single hour of actual experience," Burch argued.

"Maybe not officially, but from the ages of eleven to eighteen, I had to fool every official," I admitted. "Teachers. Principals. Social workers, police officers there to check up on my family. I learned how to be a chameleon, sir. How to think quickly and lie effectively."

Burch had to suspect some of this; he knew about my dad's addiction and was smart enough to imagine what a child would go through, hiding it.

"That, combined with all my training, I'm confident I can handle myself at this meeting."

"This is too dangerous," Shane argued. "We just raided this warehouse and confiscated a shit-ton of cocaine. They might know our faces."

"Their security team is sitting in jail. And there was nobody inside the building," Proctor said.

"Bull," Shane said. "There were most certainly people in the building. They just got the slip on us."

"They were probably too busy getting away to stay behind and memorize faces," Proctor argued.

"They had surveillance all over this place," Shane said, pointing to the cameras posted at every corner.

"Which IT confirmed had been disabled by the time we got in," I said. "To cover their own ass, no doubt, and erase their own faces from the footage."

"They could have footage backed up somewhere. Could be reviewing it as we speak to identify everyone involved in that raid. If they did this"—Shane gestured toward the body—"to Marks because he arrested Terrell, what do you think they're going to do to us? The people that took hundreds of millions of dollars of cocaine from their pocket?"

"I think they have more urgent matters right now," I said. "Namely trying to keep themselves alive after losing all that product. Something they'll surely have to discuss at this upcoming meeting."

"Sarge…" Shane pleaded.

I wondered how many gambles Burch had had to take in his years. Cases didn't always magically align in the perfect sequential order, so leaders were forced to balance risks. Burch had to see the more considerable risk was letting the cartel get an even bigger head start. And I knew how this worked; a threat this big needed more evidence before other agencies would get involved. The word of one unofficial CI wasn't enough for the United States to gear up the military and other forces needed to fight this war. We had to get inside that meeting, find out what they knew, find out a timeline, find out next steps, and get evidence on tape.

Burch rubbed the back of his neck; I could see him strongly considering it.

"We'll wear wires and transmit everything to a nearby command center. If it gets too hot, we'll get out," I said.

Burch chewed the inside of his cheek, took several breaths, and eventually regarded us.

"Proctor, I'll give some thought into sending you in."

Proctor perked up.

"Without an identity, the only way in would be as staff of some sort. Waiter, something like that," Burch pondered. "Still a Hail Mary, at best. We'd have a lot of work ahead of us in the next six days to prepare."

"I'd like to go undercover," I insisted.

"Fallon," Shane chided.

"You're not ready," Burch said. "And in case you forgot, you declared war on the cartel."

"This meeting is between the United States organizations. I'm no more of an enemy to them than anyone else here."

"Unless they're already under the thumb of the cartel," Proctor said. "I'll go, sir."

*Dick.*

"I can do this, sir," I repeated.

"Can't do it, O'Connor. You made a spectacle of yourself at that funeral, and we have no idea if that got back to any of them."

"No one will discuss anything significant in front of a waiter," I insisted.

Burch knew that; he could see the holes. He knew the only legit opening we had, but clearly, he wasn't going to suggest it.

"When I was doing research on these organizations, I read that these 'meetings' are more like parties. And you know who they invite to these parties," I insisted.

Burch stared at me.

"They have a few drinks; they may slip and say something around a hooker," I said.

"Hell. No," Shane snapped, seeing where I was going with this.

"I'm the only female on this task force, sir."

The fact that Burch didn't immediately shoot it down was a good sign.

"You freaking kidding me?" Shane said.

"Maybe one of them will get drunk and sloppy enough to give up something. A name, location. Date. Something to help us fill in the gaps when I'm alone with him. I can get a lot closer than the waitstaff."

"This is absurd," Shane said. "What if those two guys from the funeral circulated your picture to the US members?"

"I'll wear a wig. If I suspect my cover might be blown, I'll leave, and if I can't, I'll use the code word, so reinforcements can come."

"She's not wrong," Burch conceded.

Proctor's shoulders squared in jealousy. "I'm sure I can sly my way into conversations," he protested.

"A female is our best shot."

Proctor scowled at me. "But it's dangerous as hell."

"You know this is our best chess move," I said. "Give me a chance. Worst case, we come out of it with no intel, and we're no worse off than we were before."

His reluctance washed away.

Burch finally said, "Proctor's going in, too."

"What?" I asked. He'd rat me out and enjoy watching my death.

"He has experience undercover, and I'm not sending you in there alone."

"I'll go," Shane said.

"You'd stare at her the whole time, which would only tip them off to her being a cop. And for the record?" Burch looked at me. "Worst case isn't getting no intel. Worst case is that you'll be killed before any of my agents can get to you."

## 27

"Don't do this," Shane demanded. "This is a suicide mission."

Wearing a bathrobe and a towel on my freshly showered hair, I wiped away the mirror's invasive fog and glared at his reflection. Shane leaned against the doorframe of our apartment's bathroom with his arms crossed.

"We have a solid plan." A plan we'd gone over countless times.

The task force had spent days in briefing rooms, preparing for it. Listing out strategies to get information. Undercover operatives gave Proctor and me a crash-course refresher in staying in character, including backstories, details, and the like.

Was it scary? Yes. Did I feel a hundred percent ready? No.

"A million things can go wrong. You know that."

"Six agents will listen in at all times, just a short drive away. If anything happens—"

"They won't be able to get to you quick enough, Fallon! Takes one second to shoot you."

"Proctor—"

"Hates you. I don't trust that piece of shit to save you. And certainly not if it means riskin' his own neck."

I applied the makeup as I'd seen in a tutorial yesterday.

"You're taking this too far, Fallon. What are the odds you get some information that helps stop them tonight? Do you think you're gonna walk into the party and get some nugget of information that all our federal agencies have been unable to get?"

"Maybe you're right, but I still have to try," I said, blending the thick foundation.

"I'm just trying to give you a reality check. Before you get yourself killed on some Hail fuckin' Mary that has a microscopic chance of succeeding. Candidly? I can't believe Burch is crazy enough to go along with this. He's so desperate to end his career on a high note that he's getting reckless."

"Maybe it's reckless, but I'm doing my job."

"This is suicidal, and you know it."

I spun around. "If every cop ran the second things got dangerous, we might as well hand our country over to criminals and be done with it."

"You're takin' this too far!"

"Says someone who doesn't seem to believe the cops can have an impact anymore. If you're reconsidering your police chief career aspiration, that's fine, but stop projecting it onto me!"

"I did reevaluate because it felt like we could never do enough to make a difference," Shane snarled. "But once I realized how close these guys can get to the people that I love? My mind was made up."

He looked at me, letting his silent accusation bounce off the walls.

"I'm super glad you worked through your career-life crisis, but I'm a big girl, and my mind is made up."

Shane stared at me silently for ten heartbeats. Then, he tightened his fists and started to walk off into his room but paused. "Will *he* be there?"

I stiffened. "I have no idea."

I hadn't told Dillon I was going tonight; he might've been able to block my entrance somehow.

And I really hoped he wasn't going to be there. Because the last thing we could afford tonight was for any complication.

## 28

"How come I ain't never seen you before?"

As the windowless white van that reeked of paint fumes bounced along what felt to be an unpaved road, the redhead wearing an emerald-green miniskirt with a blue bikini-style top stared at me with suspicion. Seven sets of eyes joined her.

I gripped the edge of the bench tighter. The other hookers were used to this, being carted into the party's secret location, packed together hip to hip like fresh meat going to a slaughterhouse. But I wasn't. And the farther we got from the remote parking lot we'd been picked up at, the more anxious I grew.

An undercover agent had worked her network of escorts with the cover story that I was her cousin in need of a good gig to bail out my baby's daddy. Luckily, it worked, and one of the escorts vouched for me to get me into this party. But she'd warned it was high pay, high risk. So high risk, in fact, that she wasn't even willing to come tonight.

"Asked you a question," the redhead snapped.

"Don't pay no mind to her," the platinum blonde to my left said. "She just jealous 'cause new girls get the most attention."

Great.

Before the scowling hooker with glossy lipstick clapped back, the van stopped. The front doors opened with a metallic squeak, banged shut, and then footsteps crunched on gravel.

When the doors opened, the girls delivered sexy, come-hither smiles as two men helped us out.

The burly guys with thick beards led us to a gate, where three guards carrying AK-47s began to pat the girls down.

My palms began to sweat. If someone touched me firm enough, they'd feel the button-shaped microphone hiding in my bra that transmitted everything to agents parked nearby. The one that I could use to relay my code word—*Christmas*—if something went horribly wrong.

Guard Man patted down Girl Number Two, touching her hips, looking in her shoes, even feeling her hair. He was thorough. And that was with girls who, based on that *how come I ain't never seen you before* comment, must've come here regularly. I was new.

"Come on," Guard Man snapped.

Someone shoved me from behind so roughly, I almost tripped.

Guard Man gripped my hips, pawed both of my legs, even though they were bare—*a-hole*—and moved to my shoes. Then back up, feeling my stomach. Could he feel my heart punching my ribs? His fingers felt my breasts. Had he done that with the other girls?

"All clear," he said lazily.

The AK-47 squad parted, so all eight of us hookers could glide through the gates like gazelles waiting to be claimed by lions. I tried to mimic the confidence of the other girls.

"Name's Layla," the girl who'd stuck up for me in the van whispered as she walked next to me.

"Candice," I lied. "Got any advice?"

"Keep your eyes to yourself, don't get nosy, and you should make it out in one piece."

*Should.*

My mouth ran dry.

Guards led us to an enormous patio encircled by four buildings.

At first glance, the courtyard looked romantic. Bubble lights swooped between single-story rooftops and ornamental trees, casting the summer night in a soft golden glow. Moss bubbled between uneven patio stones, meeting ivy that crawled up the sides of the stone buildings, and a bonfire tossed embers into the sky in the center of the patio.

But this place was the opposite of romantic. At each of its dozen doors, a guard stood watch with a semiautomatic rifle. More armed guards peppered the space, actively scanning like lifeguards watching a pool for signs of trouble.

"Is there always this much security?" I whispered.

I could see her worry.

"No," she answered quietly. "Not even close."

But then they didn't have three big organizations come together very often, so it was probably just beefed up because of that.

Still, I evaluated my surroundings. The entire area was enclosed by a barbed-wire fence, and the only gate was armed on both sides with several men. Security even flanked the bar.

Where Proctor walked away, carrying a tray of appetizers.

We made eye contact.

And I could see with the slight roundness to his eyes that even he —with his undercover experience—was nervous.

*So am I.*

The door to the main building opened, and three dozen men spilled out into the courtyard.

Between them and the guards, I counted twenty armed men, sixteen automatic rifles, twenty-six pistols, and ten grenades—and that was just what was out in the open.

To protect thirty-some guys? Made no sense. It was overkill; something was off. But then Miami and New York bosses were here. Maybe Chicago was showing off.

I turned to start walking, and that was when I saw him. Standing with his back to me, he said something to the bartender and then leaned on his elbow to look around.

When his gaze reached me, it came to an abrupt freaking halt. To anyone else, his eyes were impassive, but to me, I could see his shock at seeing me here. And then his stare glided slowly, methodically over my legs perched atop stiletto heels, my dress wrapped tightly around my hips and stomach, my breasts pushed up and playing in the air, and my red wig. Before finally returning to my face. Where they lingered in angry disbelief for what felt like an eternity.

Dillon watched as a tall guy with shaggy blond hair, who smelled of cigarettes and whiskey, approached me.

"Hey there." He traced my arm with his finger.

I smiled flirtatiously and had to will my eyes away from Dillon, who now clutched his drink so tightly, I wondered if the glass would break.

"What's your name?" I asked. His face wasn't one I recognized from my studies.

"You can call me John."

"Cute."

"What's yours?"

"You can call me Candice."

"I've never seen you here before."

*So, he's a regular. Must be from Chicago, then.*

He trailed a finger down my collarbone. When his fingertip inched toward my breasts, I had to smile as if I wanted it. And pretend Dillon didn't look like he was going to storm over here and pound the guy's face in.

"You want a little snow?" he asked, motioning toward another bar on the far side of the room, where the other hookers and some men were lined up, sniffing the white powder.

I tensed my lips, nervous that my refusal to participate would make them suspicious. Equally alarming, if these violent men snorted coke, how much more unpredictable would they be?

My throat was instantly dry.

"Maybe later," I managed.

"I'm going to do a quick line," John said. "You get us some drinks. I'll have a whiskey."

I eyed the bar, where Dillon stood alone. I wanted to insist John go with me; approaching Dillon wasn't a smart move. Even though everyone seemed engrossed in conversations and flirting with the escorts, you never knew who could be watching.

But if I pressed the guy to go with me, he might either grow suspicious—why would a hooker be that clingy?—or insist I go with him to the drug table. Where more people could press me to do a line—at which point, I'd get made.

John tilted his head in curiosity at my hesitation, so I smiled and said, "Sure. I'll be right back."

I sashayed over to the bar, careful never to look at Dillon.

"Two whiskeys, please," I ordered.

The bartender nodded and went to the other end of the counter, fishing around for the bottle.

Dillon stared forward, so it wouldn't look like we were talking, his voice quiet when he spoke. "What the hell are you doing here?"

I discreetly glanced around. Made sure no one else had come within earshot, and when I answered, I continued looking at the back of the bar. "Working."

"You can't be here. Not *tonight*," he growled.

*Tonight*. The word bounced around my skull with its implied threat. "Why not *tonight*?"

"You need to get out of here," he insisted.

"I can't leave, so stop wasting your breath. We don't have time to argue about this." I ran a hand through my hair, feeling the thick fibers of the red wig trail between my fingers.

Dillon took an angry sip of his drink.

"He's looking at you," Dillon said, nodding over my shoulder toward the shaggy-haired guy who'd been flirting with me. "It's taking all of my restraint not to fucking kill him."

"You need to behave."

"How the hell am I supposed to do that with you sauntering around in that dress?"

The other women wore even more revealing outfits. I nodded toward them.

"Have you ever partaken?" I asked.

His lips twitched. "I'm glad I'm not the only one jealous tonight."

I pursed my lips.

"No," he answered. "Not that kind of guy."

The bartender set down the two drinks, and when he walked to the other end again, Dillon resumed whisper-talking to me.

"You don't know what you're getting yourself into. You have a weapon on you?" he asked even though he knew it was rhetorical. He could tell there was no place to hide one in this dress. " 'Cause they have several on them and more in the rooms they'll take you to."

"Tell me who to flirt with," I said. "Who has information."

"No one's going to talk to a hooker. Your plan is flawed. You, and that asshole," he said, glaring at Proctor across the room, "put yourself in danger for nothing. Only a matter of time before your cover is blown."

"Thought you were getting us drinks." John appeared by my side.

I smiled, handed him one of the glasses.

But he didn't take a sip; he was too busy, looking over my body, like someone evaluating a car before buying it. Out of nowhere, he grabbed my ass.

Dillon coughed and grabbed the bar's edge.

"Come on," John said. He grabbed my hand and pulled me toward one of the buildings. "You'll get me off in the back room."

In the pre-operation briefings, had I been educated on evasive tactics to avoid sexual acts? Yep. Had I been given a list of excuses to use, depending on the situation? You bet. But it was so dang early in the night that I wasn't sure any of them would work, which created a couple of huge problems.

First, the only kinds of illegal activity the DEA approved for undercovers were for things like buying drugs to catch them in the act. Me having sex with these suspects wasn't authorized. Not that I'd do it if it was; I'd rather light my panties on fire. But the point remained—if I couldn't get this guy to accept no for an answer, the officers listening nearby would terminate this operation immediately. The second, and far more significant problem, was that blowing my cover could get me killed.

The guy tugged me away from the bar, but Dillon stepped into the guy's path, scowling at his hand on my hip. "This one's mine," he claimed.

John looked surprised by Dillon's threatening posture, but he didn't argue. He simply relinquished me and walked away from us.

"That guy reports to you," I realized.

Dillon eyed the other men scattered around the courtyard carefully. "You need to get the hell out of here before it's too late."

"Too late for what?"

Dillon's brown eyes suddenly widened slightly as he stared at the gate, where ten new men strutted into the courtyard like they owned the place.

The guards stiffened.

My hands became clammy.

We were wrong about the real purpose of this evening. This wasn't a meeting between Chicago, Miami, and New York.

It was the welcome party to the Baja Cartel, whose top ten members had just officially arrived in the United States.

And with them were the two men who'd come to my dad's funeral —Lopez, the toothpick-sucking falcon who was the eyes and ears of the organization, and Sanchez, aka The Enforcer, the hit man who'd smirked at me when I threatened the cartel.

## 29

"**F**uck," Dillon whispered. "You need to get out of here. Only way is an underground tunnel in the back that's there in case cops raid the place."

Sanchez's gaze locked on me from his position across the patio. Did he recognize me? I looked nothing like the proper police officer with little makeup and hair twisted into a bun. My red wig was full of sexy waves; my makeup was thick tonight, contouring my cheekbones to look higher and thinner. Not to mention, my outfit made my body look like an entirely different shape than that pantsuit at the funeral. But if he looked close enough, he might make the connection.

The Enforcer walked up to us, coating us with suspicion. If I didn't handle this right, I wasn't the only one in danger; Dillon was, too.

"You look familiar," The Enforcer accused.

Did he know? Was he playing with me or grasping for an explanation?

"I get around," I deflected.

The Enforcer smiled a toothy grin. "Have we partied before?"

"If we had, it would've been memorable."

He remained silent for a second and then smirked. "Funny," he said, though I still couldn't tell if this was lighthearted or if he already knew.

Even if he didn't already recognize me, it felt like it was just a matter of time.

"Was just about to take her in the back for a spin," Dillon said.

The Enforcer traced his fingertip down my breast. "No, this one's mine."

He pulled me by the hand over to his group of men, deeper into his Baja Cartel circle, and just as Dillon's subordinate had to let go when Dillon claimed me, Dillon was lower on the pecking order. And had no choice but to watch me, helpless from across the patio.

I was as scared as I was angry. Facing the Baja Cartel was terrifying, but it was also rewarding. Because I'd get to look them in the eye before helping take them down.

"Can I get you a drink, baby?" I asked.

"Something stronger." He snapped his fingers.

A waiter rushed over with a glass tray containing white lines of cocaine.

"Ladies first." He studied me. My every movement was under investigation.

"I prefer a drink," I said.

"I'm afraid I'm going to have to insist."

It felt like I was under a spotlight, interrogated by The Enforcer. Making me sense that I wasn't in control of this conversation; he was. I was a minor league player trying to outwit the major leagues.

He squinted his eyes and seemed to evaluate my facial expression, my mannerisms. Like he knew that if I was a cop, if he insisted on me doing illegal drugs, the operation would be immediately called off. And I'd either be stuck trying to escape or forced to lead backup into what might become a fatal trap.

"Why's that?"

He leaned in with a smile and whispered, "I have it on good word there's a cop at this party."

Needles surged through my fingers and toes, all while he watched me for my reaction. How would he have it on good word?

"I know all the men here," he said, releasing my hand and trailing his finger down my arm. "So, that leaves the security, the waitstaff, and the hookers."

Someone was hearing this down the street. Assessing the danger. Analyzing the risk. If things were getting too hot, they'd come in.

And even though it felt damn hot, this was fine. It was okay. It felt scary, like he was playing with me, but that didn't mean he was. He could just like to throw his power around and watch people squirm. That was what these types liked, wasn't it? Maybe it was what got him off.

I risked a glance at Dillon, who stood across the courtyard, trying to hide the worry on his face.

"Who do you think it is?" he asked.

"This place is a fortress," I said, keeping my sexy tone in place, like this was part of a hooker's job—to reassure the paranoid leader. "No one could've gotten in here."

"Let's say, for argument's sake, a pig did get in here," he pressed. This time, his tone was tighter. Angrier. His gaze cut through me like a knife to a Jell-O mold. "Who do you think it is?"

I didn't like the way he was smiling, as if he was about to do something wicked. "I think I'll have more fun with someone else."

I made it one step before he grabbed my arm and pulled me back, squeezing it in punishment.

Dillon tensed.

"Point to someone," he demanded.

I yanked my arm, but he wouldn't let it go.

"Why are you asking me? If I thought a cop was here, I'd have to run. I can't get arrested again."

He squeezed my arm harder. "Last time I'm going to say it. Point to someone."

Maybe he assumed I was a frequent hooker here and knew all the faces. Maybe he was asking for help in his bully-like fashion.

"I don't know. What about him?" I nodded toward a random waiter.

The Enforcer motioned to someone, who pistol-whipped the guy in the head.

I gasped and watched blood pool on the guy's face. I could feel The Enforcer's eyes on me as the cartel guy ripped open the guy's shirt, searching for a wire. When none was found, the cartel guy kicked the man in the mouth, cutting open his lips.

Everyone stopped talking, sensing the dangerous shift.

"Try again."

"I'm not playing your sick game," I snapped.

The Enforcer tilted his head, eyeing Proctor across the room. "What about that guy? He looks familiar, too."

If he found Proctor's wire, he'd kill him before anyone could get here.

It was time to abort the mission.

"What is this to you," I said, "some kind of a *Christmas* game?"

The Enforcer smirked at me while I waited for the sounds of the cavalry who were now on their way.

*Hurry. Please hurry.*

"Bring him here," The Enforcer said.

A tall guy grabbed Proctor by the arm and carted him over. Proctor tried to look indifferent, but I could see the panic settling in as they forced him onto his knees.

His white pants ground into the stones.

"Search him."

The cartel guy patted Proctor down.

The Enforcer added, "Remove his shirt."

If they did that, they'd see that one of his buttons was fake—the microphone. I needed to do something. Create a distraction, buy him some time until the agents burst in.

"I know who the cop is," I blurted out desperately. "And it's not him."

The Enforcer looked at me.

"How would *you* know who the cop is?" he asked incredulously.

"I'm a working girl. It's our job to know our johns."

Proctor took deep breaths.

*Where the hell is the cavalry? Maybe they didn't hear my code word.*

"People aren't your own personal *Christmas* gifts to unwrap," I said. It was a lame line. But it had the code word, so whatever.

A hairy guy approached The Enforcer and whispered something in his ear. Whatever it was made him smile wickedly.

"Seems my men found a truck of pigs nearby," he said. "Took 'em to the slaughterhouse."

*What? They found the agents? They...*

*No.*

*No, no, no.*

They were parked in a secure location, nowhere near a road. They had been meticulously careful about that, so they wouldn't be found. Dillon's suspicions of a leak echoed inside my head, but my panicked thoughts prayed The Enforcer was lying, trying to scare me and Proctor. We couldn't be on our own.

With the Baja Cartel onto us.

The cartel guy ripped off Proctor's white jacket, followed by his shirt, sending his buttons flying like M&M's bouncing along the stones. One of which The Enforcer picked up and stared at.

*Shit.*

The cartel guy looked to The Enforcer for an order, who nodded.

When the cartel guy raised his semiautomatic to Proctor's head, I lunged in front of Proctor.

It wasn't a smart move. I could see that now with all the guns that were now aimed at me.

And then came the gunshot.

Warm liquid exploded from my back. I must've been in shock because it didn't hurt. At all. I waited for the darkness to swallow me, but when I spun around, I saw Proctor lying on the ground with a bullet wound to his head.

Blood hadn't exploded from my back; it had splattered *onto* it— from Proctor's wound—and now, it became a crimson river, pooling between the cracks of the stones.

*Proctor!*

A lanky guy grabbed my arm and yanked me through the courtyard, past a horrified Dillon, and into the back building, where he tossed me onto the concrete floor of a storage room, whose shelves were lined with gallon-sized chemical bottles. It smelled like chlorine in here.

The guy padded around my dress and bra until he found my microphone and stomped on it.

Four murderous men surrounded me.

*Why didn't they just kill me when they killed Proctor?*

With a kick to my ribs, The Enforcer asked, "How much does the DEA know?"

How did they know it was the DEA, not the cops or the FBI? A good guess that the DEA would be the division working drug crimes? Still…he'd said it with certainty.

"I'm not going to tell you anything," I declared.

They were going to kill me, no matter what I did, and I certainly wasn't going to help the enemy.

"Wrong answer." The Enforcer grabbed a fistful of my hair and pulled a knife to my neck. "Tell me everything they know, or I'm going to slit your throat from ear to ear and hold your head up, so you watch yourself bleed to death."

"What the hell is going on?" Dillon growled.

*He can't be here. They might sense he's on my side. They'll kill him, too.*

"This bitch is working for the DEA."

The Enforcer kept the knife to my neck while he turned to look at Dillon, as if assessing his reaction.

Was this a test? Did they know Dillon's relationship with me? Or that he'd met with me? Would they murder him, too?

And that was when I saw a different look in Dillon's eyes. He looked at me with disgust. "We'd better find out what she knows, then."

The Enforcer hit me upside the head with his Smith & Wesson, and I thumped to the cold floor. When I regained my bearings, I noticed the guy to my right had an ankle holster.

"Go on. Hit her," The Enforcer said to Dillon.

Silence infected the space as Dillon stared down at me. "What are you going to do with her?"

"Get her to talk," The Enforcer said. "Then slit her throat." He turned to Dillon again. "Go on. Take the first swing."

Was it a test? To see if Dillon's loyalty was with them or me? Or was it some kind of a prize, a welcome-to-the-team gift to partake in the killing of an agent?

Either way, five against one, I knew this was the end for me. But if they thought I'd go down without a fight, they were even more arrogant than I thought. I'd grab the gun from the guy's ankle holster and start firing, killing as many of them as I could.

Starting with The Enforcer, who'd slaughtered so many.

Dillon approached me and raised his left hand.

But just as quickly as he'd raised his left hand, his right suddenly grabbed the gun from his waistband and fired four rapid shots. The four men—who'd been watching my face for the coming blow—slumped to the concrete.

Dillon squatted in front of me and inspected the side of my head, where I'd been pistol-whipped. His lips tightened, and his worried eyes met mine as he cupped my cheek. "Are you okay?"

My thoughts raced, trying to keep up with it all. "I thought you were going to kill me."

His gaze plunged deeply into my eyes, and his body stiffened in shock. "I'd never hurt you, Fallon," he said in a deep voice that sent pulses to my heart. "I'll always do everything in my power to protect you."

He looked at the doorway, where a commotion of shouting grew louder. Killing an unarmed hooker didn't take four shots. Footsteps stampeded down the hallway toward us.

"Come on." Dillon pulled me to my feet. "We need to run."

30

As footsteps grew louder behind us, I grabbed the semiautomatic lying next to The Enforcer, whose blood stretched on the floor toward my high heels, and accepted Dillon's hand.

"The Syndicates have had a few meetings here, but the cartel hasn't. They don't know this place as well as I do," he said.

Dillon led me to a six-paneled white door, which I had assumed was a closet, but when he opened it and ushered me through, I discovered it was a narrow, ventless hallway. Footsteps and voices grew louder as Dillon rushed me through a second door, into what appeared to be an office with two bookshelves overflowing with books and a ten-foot mahogany desk with a bullet hole in its wood.

"Fuck!" a man growled two rooms over. "Where's that girl?"

Dillon grabbed the left bookshelf and slid it three feet over, revealing a rough cutout in the drywall.

"Saw McPherson come in here after her," another voice growled.

Dillon helped me step through the opening and into a dark cavern of uncertainty. My shoes clicked on the stone floor, and cold, damp air that smelled of wet leaves slithered over my skin.

When Dillon quietly pulled the shelf back into position, all light ceased. I could hear my breathing echo off the walls, and I swore I could hear my heartbeat reverberate through this unfinished hallway.

"McPherson's working with that DEA bitch!" a voice shouted.

Dillon activated the flashlight on his phone and pointed down the corridor, motioning for me to follow as he began walking.

I took a step. My high heel clicked against the concrete so loudly, Dillon and I both froze. I looked at the spot we'd entered, praying it wasn't about to open in a sea of bullets.

"This is on fucking Delgado," a voice snarled back in the area of the original room. "If he'd done his job, McPherson wouldn't even be here right now."

Dillon allowed himself a quick look of shock but forced himself to refocus on escaping before it was too late. He motioned toward my shoes.

"What the hell is going on here?" a new voice demanded.

I stepped out of my high heels and onto the cold slab of concrete.

"We have a problem," a voice back in the room said.

"No shit."

"That DEA bitch is missing," he said. "With one of Chicago's captains."

I could only imagine an angry glare preceded, "Who?"

I took my first step, following Dillon.

"McPherson. He and that DEA bitch ran off."

A pause. "Find them. NOW. You," he said. "Go get Delgado, bring him here. Slit his throat for screwing up that fire."

*That fire?*

I tried to hear what they said next, but their voices became harder to hear as the passage descended, and the ceiling's height shortened until we had to crouch. It smelled like dirt, and the air grew colder, sending a shiver across my skin.

Suddenly, Dillon stopped.

We'd hit some sort of dead end. I glanced behind us, watching for any sign of a light breaking through the darkness. I couldn't hear them anymore. Were they still back in that room? Or asking a Chicago crew member where we might escape?

A metallic groan drew my attention back to Dillon, who grunted as he slid an iron circular plate off the floor and revealed another man-made tunnel beneath this one. I looked down into the hole but couldn't see anything. I couldn't tell how deep it was, which direction it went.

Dillon used his phone's flashlight to illuminate it, motioning toward a ring of bars that functioned as a ladder into the space.

"Come on," he said. "Hurry!"

I slipped my lower body through the hole, thighs scraping stone on the way in, and tapped my toes around until I found the rung beneath the ball of my foot. It was bumpy, like its metal had rusted and chipped, and when I began to climb down, those chips stung the skin on my feet and palm of my free hand—my other hand clutching the semiautomatic. I could hear drips of water echo off the underground tunnels' walls. I could feel its dampness in my bones.

After five rungs, my foot couldn't find the sixth.

"Drop," Dillon whispered. The fact that he whispered worried me; it meant he could hear them getting closer. "Ground's, like, three feet down."

I took a deep breath and let go.

I only fell for a moment before the unforgiving ground slammed against my feet and threw me off-balance, tossing my right hip to the floor. My gun scraped against the concrete as it slid from my grip and was eaten by the shadows.

I patted around the pitch-black space, unsuccessful in locating my weapon, as Dillon descended the rungs, replaced the manhole cover, and jumped to the ground. Easily landing on his feet.

Shouting erupted in the tunnel above our heads.

"Come on!"

Dillon grabbed my hand, and we ran.

With his phone light only affording us a few feet of visibility, the darkness swallowed us. The men's voices grew louder. We ran for what had to be twenty seconds, and then my heart lodged in my ribs.

The manhole cover clanked.

"Here." Dillon handed me his phone.

And that was when I saw it—a door. Dillon worked the hatch and shoved it open.

A rush of warm outside air flooded over me as the moon's silver light became our beacon.

Behind us, flashlights cut through the pervasive darkness as men jumped into the passage.

"There!" one of them shouted.

A gunshot blasted off the walls as Dillon and I lunged through the opening and onto a lawn. Dillon slammed the metal door shut behind him and fastened it with a titanium lock that had dangled from its exterior hook. Probably there for the same reason the tunnel was built —to escape a police raid and block their ability to come catch you.

The problem was, *these* people knew where this tunnel system let out—in a field fifty meters behind the property with nowhere to hide. Only grass and trees and a road sixty feet ahead.

A road where an SUV hurtled this way.

"Run!" Dillon demanded.

The vehicle groaned closer while a stocky torso stood through its sunroof, holding a rifle as he scanned the area.

Our only hope of hiding—and that hope was pretty damn dismal— was to make it to the field just behind the road, where the scattering of trees offered a little cover. But getting to it meant crossing the very pavement the SUV thundered down.

My lungs burned, and adrenaline surged through my muscles as my bare feet pounded the cool grass, then thumped against the pavement.

"There!" The guy sticking out of the vehicle pointed at us. Just as the SUV fishtailed to a stop.

We bolted and took cover behind a forty-foot oak tree. Against the backdrop of rustling leaves, the sounds of three sets of footsteps clunked against the pavement as they jumped out, no doubt guns drawn.

Hunting us.

"I lost my gun," I whispered.

Dillon pushed my back against the spiky bark and stood protectively in front of me.

Flashlights swept the air and grew brighter, the closer they got. Judging by the swishing of grass beneath their steps, our hunters were about sixty feet away.

I looked around for another tree, or road, or something, anywhere we could go. But there was nothing, save for the running SUV they'd come in. But to get to it, we'd have to make it past all three of them.

Forty feet away.

And even if there was somewhere to go, running would expose us.

Ten feet away.

I clutched Dillon's back.

Twigs snapped beneath the men's boots as they closed the last steps.

Dillon lunged from the sanctuary of the tree and fired in rapid *pop-pop-pop*s. The taller guy thumped to the ground immediately, but the second and third guys fired back.

In what felt like slow motion, bullets exploded through orange embers from the ends of pistols, cracking the silence. The blasts seemed to echo off the stars that canopied the earth with their beauty.

A second body smacked the ground as the third guy lined up another metal death bomb at Dillon. I charged the figure with my shoulder, but before I made contact, his bang rang out.

Dillon's body jerked.

I wasn't big enough to knock the guy to the ground, but my attempt averted his attention long enough for Dillon to line up his shot.

And pull the trigger.

The man's head snapped back. His body stood hauntingly still for a half-second before dissolving to the ground.

"Come on!" Dillon sprinted toward the SUV.

In the distance, another vehicle plowed toward us. The door to the tunnel lurched with kicks from the people on the other side, and more men ran from the back of the property toward us.

We ran to the vehicle the dead guys had used, and I jumped into the passenger seat just as Dillon threw it into drive. And floored it.

The back window exploded.

As he hurtled the truck away from a mob, Dillon's body pumped blood onto his shirt with every beat of his heart.

## 31

The road flew beneath our tires at a hundred miles per hour as a black Mercedes SUV pursued us a few hundred feet behind. Dillon cut the lights, making it harder for them to see us, but also harder for us to see the road as we thrust into the murky ambiguity that was our future.

The road T'd so sharply, Dillon missed it, thumping into a field before cutting the wheel so tight, we almost flipped over. I looked behind us. The headlights grew smaller and then became taillights as the other vehicle lost sight of us and made the opposite turn.

I sighed, relieved for our reprieve yet unsure of how long it would last.

The only light we had came from the dashboard, illuminating Dillon's eyes that darted between the rearview and side mirrors.

"You okay?" He clutched my hand.

"You've been shot."

"Did they hurt you?"

"You're bleeding. Heavily." I could only see the general location of the wound in his shoulder area, now drenched in blood. "We need to go to a hospital," I insisted.

"We can't. Left a trail of blood on the way to the SUV. They'll look for us there."

I touched his shoulder, which was covered in warm liquid. "You're losing a lot of blood!"

Dillon growled in pain when my fingers explored his chest. "We go to a hospital, they could get to you, Fallon," he groaned. "I'm not risking it. We need to keep moving, get a few hundred miles behind us."

"You're not going to make it a few hundred miles. You might bleed to death before we make it much farther."

He cast his rounded eyes over my face, then the rearview mirror, as if more concerned about leaving me alone and unprotected than he was of his own well-being.

"I don't think it hit anything major," he claimed.

"Well, *that's* comforting. In that case, by all means, just keep driving until you lose consciousness, then. I'll sit here while we both become cartel bait."

Dillon glared at me, and I glared right back.

"A pharmacy," I compromised. "Stop at a pharmacy. I'll grab medical supplies, and we'll stop and clean the wound."

Silence.

"If you don't do it, I'll just jump out of this moving truck, so help me."

Dillon tightened his grip on the steering wheel, looked in the rearview, the side mirrors.

"Let me drive."

"I'm fine," he insisted. "We'll come across a main road in a few minutes, and then it's just a few more minutes to town."

We drove in silence, Dillon constantly glancing at the rearview mirror, watching for any sign of being followed. Eventually, the road bent to the left, then the right, and then we came across a handful of buildings—one of which was a pharmacy.

Dillon parked the SUV behind the building, hidden behind the dumpster, and I grabbed a crumpled T-shirt from the floor, wiping the blood splatter off my back from Proctor's gunshot. Luckily, my dress was dark, so whatever remained would hopefully not be too noticeable.

"You have cash?" I asked.

Dillon fished his wallet out of his back pocket, wincing from the pain of moving his arm. "Less than a hundred bucks."

I grabbed the cash, and he shut the engine off and opened the door like he was about to climb out.

"You can't come in with me," I said.

"I'm not letting you out of my sight."

"You go in, looking like that," I said, pointing to his blood-soaked shirt, "they'll call the cops."

Dillon tightened his lips.

Which, now that I thought about it…

"My opinion? It'd be a good thing."

They could get him an ambulance.

"The cartel has police scanners. Might even have the cops out here on payroll already. We call police, we might as well call the cartel."

Dillon weighed this for a moment, then said, "This was a bad idea."

He shifted to put the truck into gear, but I jumped out first.

"Fallon!"

"You need medical supplies."

"You're not going in there alone!"

"Two minutes, tops," I said.

"You're going to draw attention, dressed like that," he argued. "You don't even have shoes!"

Nothing I could do about that. We needed to stop his bleeding.

Dillon looked at me in exasperation as I walked toward the front door and scanned the road for headlights one more time before ducking inside the building, where I loaded up on medical supplies. Water. Snacks that I grabbed near the register.

Did the cashier look at me funny? Yep. But he seemed too preoccupied, staring at my cleavage, to call the police over my frazzled appearance.

When I exited the building and walked around the dumpster, Dillon's injured shoulder sagged in relief when he spotted me. His eyes shot around in frantic bursts to the road behind me, the parking lot, even the field off in the distance before returning to me. He watched my every step as I neared the truck.

I hadn't seen or heard anyone following us, and while I knew they were out there somewhere, prowling, hunting, the most urgent thing on my mind right now was looking at Dillon's wound. If I thought it was critical, I was going to call an ambulance, whether he liked it or not.

I climbed inside.

He squeezed the steering wheel. "You're the most stubborn person I've ever met, you know that?"

"Says the guy who won't get medical attention for a gunshot wound."

I fished around the bag, reviewing all the medical supplies.

"We need to go somewhere with light and running water, so we can clean your wound."

Dillon started the engine. "We'll drive for a while, and then you can look at it in the truck."

Like I'd let him drive any farther in his condition.

He shifted the gear from park to drive, but I was faster. I opened my door and hopped out, pharmacy bags in hand.

"Where are you going?" Dillon growled.

I walked toward a one-story building just off the main road, turning to explain. "Running water. Light. A place to clean your wound without worrying you're going to pass out at eighty miles an hour."

"We need to put miles between us and them first, so get back here!"

"You can come with me or sit there and bleed to death."

Dillon clenched his jaw. "If they drive past, they could see the SUV."

"So, leave it behind the dumpster. They won't see it from the main road. And if they do"—I pointed to the building across the street—"we'll see them first."

I continued walking, making it clear this wasn't up for debate. His bloodstain was getting bigger by the minute.

"Damn it," Dillon snarled, stomping out of the SUV.

The building appeared to be turquoise, though I couldn't be sure without the benefit of sunlight. Surrounded by trees and an almost-empty parking lot, the structure had six doors separated by fifteen feet. An arrow with red and white letters that said *West Point Motel* pointed to the main door.

I went into the lobby and paid for a room with the leftover cash Dillon had given me.

Room six.

Dillon followed me inside, shut and locked the door, and closed the blinds to the only window, which overlooked the empty parking lot.

I hauled the pharmacy's plastic bags into the bathroom, removed the wig that made me sweat, and quickly organized all the medical stuff from them as well as a washcloths from the motel.

"We need to get your shirt off," I said.

Dillon peered through the blinds, looking to the left before making a slow, methodical sweep to the right. He didn't come into the bathroom until he did his scans twice.

Now that we had some decent lighting, I could see his shirt had a basketball-sized blood-soaked section that was coming from his left shoulder area. It was on the front *and* the back.

I pulled at the hem of his shirt and tugged it up slowly, feeling his gaze on me as the fabric revealed his lined abs with its belly button pulling at the skin stretched around his muscles. When his shirt made it to his chest, sticky crimson peeled with it as Dillon hissed.

"Sorry," I whispered.

I pulled it up delicately, stretching my arms as high as they would go to get it up and over his head. And in that instant, the terrifying reality of his injury slapped me.

The entry hole was a half-inch, penetrating his body roughly two inches below the top of his shoulder, where blood dribbled from the crimson void. I turned him around and found the exit wound behind his left shoulder, in roughly the same position. Blood actively leaked from this one as well, but the location of it made me feel a little better.

Nowhere near the heart or lungs, and if it'd hit an artery, it'd be gushing blood. Hell, he'd be dead by now.

But that didn't mean he wasn't in danger.

"There could be internal damage that we can't see," I said. "We really need to get you to a doctor."

Dillon turned around and stared at me with that damn stubbornness.

"I'm going to clean the wounds," I said. "And it's going to hurt. Sit." I closed the toilet lid and pointed to it.

He obliged, but his lips twitched up on one side.

I pulled out the antibacterial soap. "I don't know what you have to be grinning about. We narrowly escaped death, you got shot, and now, we're kind of up shit creek here."

As I wet a washcloth and doused it in soap, Dillon trapped me in his gaze's snare. Until I wiped the cloth across his chest.

"Gah!"

"Sorry." I put the rag under the sink, waiting for the water to turn from crimson back to clear. Then, I added more soap and, as gently as possible, wiped his skin again.

His shoulder muscles tensed with each pass.

"Is this going to take long?" Dillon asked.

"I don't know. I've never cleaned a bullet wound before; we should ask a *doctor* how long it takes."

I cleaned the washcloth and continued my cleansing on the entrance wound.

"We need to hurry," he said, glancing toward the front door.

"And go where?" I challenged as I pressed the cloth against the wound. "The cartel has targets on both our backs now. Where could we possibly go that we'd be safe?"

"Another country," Dillon hissed through the pain. "Run back to my place, grab some cash, get your passport and mine."

"They've probably got people watching your place."

He tightened his jaw. "The clock is ticking to get you out of town."

"Me?"

Dillon hesitated. "Us. Us out of town." But the look on his face told me there was more to the slip than he was letting on.

"Why did you say me and not *us*?"

"I meant us," he claimed. "Look, we need to hurry," he insisted.

I hesitated but had him turn around, so I could work on the back wound. This one was dripping blood at a more constant pace. A slow drip, which I couldn't decide if that was good or bad. If the wound was slowing its bleeding or if the bleeding was mostly inside his body.

I stared at the tattoo as I cleaned his skin, the tattoo of the scorpion holding the American flag. The one that forever redefined us to each other, on opposite sides of the fight. The drug lord and the DEA agent.

"What does the scorpion mean?" I wondered aloud.

"What?"

"The tattoo. What does it mean?" I asked, wiping his skin.

Dillon allowed a small silence to pass. "Scorpion is an expression of great strength. Ability to control and protect oneself."

Ah. The dad that left his family vulnerable. "And the flag?"

"Asshole father left for some job opportunity in another country. Felt like a *screw you, I'll stay here and protect our family.*"

I rinsed the washcloth and wiped more blood off his skin. Dillon hissed when I had him turn back around to face me and added hydrogen peroxide to the cleaning regime.

"I need to call Burch," I said.

"To hell you do."

"Burch wasn't in that van; he's still alive."

Dillon grabbed my wrist. "I heard what he said to you, about the van of agents being dead. How would they even know about them?"

I blinked.

"They told you about the dead agents within a couple of minutes of spotting you. No way they found them *after* they spotted you. They knew about it all before they even walked in. You have a leak," he said.

"And Burch needs to know that."

I released the cloth. I gathered up all the gauze I'd gotten—squares of it, rolls of it. The antibacterial cream. I pulled the skin glue out of the box, pulled off the safety seal, and wiped Dillon's front wound again. "I don't even know if this'll do any good. This isn't meant for a bullet wound."

I frowned when I had to put the glue on his skin and press the openings together. Dillon tried to hide the pain, but I could see how badly it hurt him. And it didn't even work. Though the opening was small, once I let go of it, the hole opened up again.

"We do need to get you to a doctor. No matter how risky you think it is, your wound is more serious than you think."

I collected the gauze.

"Who knew you were going to be there tonight?"

I smothered some gauze in antibacterial cream. "Everyone involved in the operation."

"Such as?"

I pressed the dressing to the wound and put two pieces of tape on it.

"Me. Proctor. Shane. Burch. Burch's boss. The agents in the van, other agents who've been investigating the cartel's threat to move to the US."

"How much do you know about Burch?"

"I know tonight's going to end his career. He lost seven agents on one mission. There's no coming back from that." I pinched my eyes closed for a moment; I couldn't feel bad over someone's legacy when lives had been lost. "He was reluctant to let me work undercover tonight, but I pushed."

Shane was right: Burch had been too aggressive. Maybe even a bit overconfident after decades of experience, assuming he could thwart any complication.

"He never would have sent us in if he'd had any clue the cartel was going to be there." This one awful night would be the defining moment of his now-dead career.

Dillon hesitated as I bandaged the wound on his back the same as the front. "What about Shane?"

"What about him?"

"He knew about tonight."

*Glare* isn't a strong enough word for the look I shot at Dillon. "Don't even go there."

"I'm just asking if—"

"He's been my only friend for my entire life. He's my only real family, and he'd never, ever do anything to hurt me."

Dillon measured the resolve in my face. "What about Proctor?"

"He got killed."

"Obviously wasn't his plan. Any chance he was working for them?"

I didn't know. "There's another issue we found out about tonight..."

He waited.

"That fire was meant for you."

Dillon didn't reply.

"Why did they try to kill you?" I asked.

"Maybe they were getting ready for the cartel."

"But you hadn't done anything to piss them off? Break one of their rules?"

Dillon shook his head. "No."

"And if they did want to kill you, why'd they do something so unreliable? Why not do something simpler? Like shoot you?"

"No idea."

And when it failed, why didn't they try again?

"We need to find the mole," I agreed. "But we also need to figure out why they wanted you dead."

His troubled eyes looked to the ground, and he was silent for several seconds. When he spoke again, his voice was low. "I'm really sorry that you got tangled up in this," he said. "And it almost cost you your life."

I was in that elevator with him, but everything that came after had been my decision, not his. I was even more eager than Burch had been, more reckless in my determination to take down this organization.

"This is going to hurt," I said, pulling the roll of gauze to his arm. I wrapped it under his armpit, over the entrance wound, over the back, and wound it several more times.

"I need to call Shane."

"No. We need to keep our location off the books."

"We need money, gas, and clothes."

Dillon rubbed his jaw.

"I need your phone," I said. Mine was never part of my hooker outfit.

Dillon chewed the inside of his cheek.

"We can't escape the Baja Cartel all on our own. We need help."

A muscle in his jaw ticced. Breathing through his nose, he pulled the phone from his pocket and gripped it tightly. The muscle in his jaw ticced quicker as his hand slowly opened, and he dropped the phone into my open palm.

## 32

**D**illon peered through the blinds as I called Shane and told him the bare minimum, calming his panic. The force had already heard of the murders and didn't know what had happened to me.

I was declared missing and endangered.

When I was done explaining enough to get him off the phone, I hung up.

"He's on his way," I said.

Dillon walked over to me and brushed the side of my cheek with the backs of his fingers. His lips turned down, and his eyebrows creased, his voice low. "If this doesn't end well," he started.

"Dillon—"

"I need you to know something." His baritone voice drifted across my skin like velvet and encased me in its warmth, his gentle touch against my cheek an ember, igniting everything in its path. "Before I met you, I had no purpose. I wanted to stay alive for my brother's sake, but fighting to exist and fighting to live are two very different things. I was trapped. Waiting for the hammer to finally come down— when I'd be killed. And the thing is, deep down? I really didn't care. Until you came along. You gave me a reason to live again, Fallon. You gave me something to fight for. After all those years of merely existing, you brought me back to life." He rubbed his thumb along my lip. "You saved me," he said. "And not just from burning up in that elevator. No matter what happens, I need you to hold on to that."

He was saying good-bye. Some part of him believed these were our final hours or minutes alive.

"I love you, Fallon," he said. "More than I imagined it was possible to love another person."

I wanted to eat those words. Feel them rush down my throat and live inside my body because his profession hit its mark, lighting the darkness that once shadowed my heart.

We'd almost died. Still might. But no matter what happened, Dillon had saved me; he chose me even though doing so might cost him his life.

Dillon made bad choices. I didn't agree with them, but I'd learned that he was also an admirable, devoted person. And at this moment, I consumed his love, and I let it envelop me and free my caged heart. We were two broken souls that had endured pain and uncertainty, and we saw each other's darkness as well as our light. The feelings we'd fought so hard against had become the cure our diseased hearts had ached for.

"I love you," I said. My eyes watered, and I took his hand and held it to my chest, willing him to feel my heartbeat, to feel how it thumped for him.

Dillon's brown eyes settled on mine.

"Why do you look so sad?" I asked.

He stroked my cheek, and I leaned into his touch.

"This isn't over," I insisted.

His bare chest rose and fell with each breath, and his lips parted as he stared at my mouth. He put his hand on the wall next to my head as if to steady himself, and his mouth was so close, I could feel the heat of his breath. I reached up on tiptoe, and when I grazed my lips against his, Dillon growled. And crushed his mouth to mine, unleashing all our worry, and fear, and pain. With death hanging over our heads, all the times we'd pushed each other away now seemed insignificant.

We kissed passionately, knowing we might never get to kiss again. We held each other for a long while after, knowing it might be the last time, and as I rested my cheek against his chest, a clarity crashed into my heart.

This whole time, I thought taking down narcotics organizations was the only thing that could make me whole. The only thing capable of filling my soul's painful crevices, left from the earthquake of my family's destruction. But no matter how many criminals I helped capture, it would never bring my family back. It would never unwrap the blanket of despair that draped me in pain when I was a little girl, crying in my empty bed, wishing my parents would love me again. I still wanted to help bring people to justice, but I didn't want to sabotage the rest of my life for it.

What I wanted was to feel *this*. This love extinguished the burns of my past and watered the hope for my future. It was the only thing with the power to heal my heart.

I loved Dillon. And despite everything he'd done, I trusted him with my life. I wasn't sure what our future would look like if we even made it out of here with our lives. He'd have to pay for his mistakes, but that wouldn't prevent me from loving him.

I looked up into his eyes, seeing a cloud of worry behind them.

Dillon traced my cheek. "I need you to promise me something."

"Anything."

He drew in a deep pull of oxygen, and the way he looked at me—with a profound, cutting sadness—sent a flood of unease over my skin.

"If something happens to me—"

"Dillon…"

"Promise me you won't go back to shutting yourself out from everyone," he said. "Even if something bad happens."

"Why would you say that?" I pulled back.

He offered a solemn look.

"If you're worried about your bullet wound—"

"I'm not."

"Then, what are you saying?"

Dillon's expression softened, and his voice was low as he grazed my jaw with his hand. "There's something I need to tell you," he started. He swallowed, and I could see his chest rise and fall quicker, his heartbeat clearly picking up in fear. "You're not going to like it, but you need to trust me."

A pounding on the door interrupted us.

## 33

T he pounding came again. Louder this time. Angrier.

Dillon grabbed his gun, opened the blinds an inch, glanced out, and frowned.

"It's a guy in a hoodie," he whispered.

"It's probably Shane."

"He'd have had to drive like a bat outta hell to get here this fast."

"Well, I doubt the cartel would knock," I reasoned.

Dillon ran a hand through his hair and cringed. "You sure you can trust him?" he pressed.

I nodded, but Dillon didn't look convinced. In fact, he looked like he was questioning his sanity for letting Shane come.

If this guy was even Shane...

"This goes to shit"—Dillon grabbed the doorknob—"you take the gun. Kill whoever you have to, take the keys." He reached into his pocket, shoved them into my hand. "And you run like hell."

Someone pounded on the door again.

Dillon grabbed me around the waist and crushed his lips to mine. Before he nudged me behind him, raised his weapon, unlocked the door...

And opened it.

Dillon didn't move, didn't speak. Didn't fire his weapon. I thought he might have a gun to his head, but he didn't lower his weapon, either.

Instead, he opened the door wider and allowed the guy to barge in with a black duffel bag.

"Shane!" I ran to him and wrapped my arms around his neck as Dillon shut and locked the door.

Shane only hugged me back with one arm; the other put the bag on the floor as he scowled at Dillon.

"Put the gun down," Shane demanded.

Dillon didn't move.

"He's not going to hurt you," I said.

"Gun. Down," Shane repeated.

I looked at Dillon, implored him to trust Shane. Grateful when he placed the gun on the nightstand.

"You'd better start telling me what the hell happened tonight because Burch has been calling me every fifteen minutes, demanding to know where you are. He's convinced that I know and that I'm lying to him, and up to an hour ago, I wasn't. So, start talking. Explain to me why I've been lying to my superior for *him*."

I explained everything I hadn't had time to do on the phone and how we needed help. But didn't know who we could trust. Who had tipped them off about the DEA working the party.

"Shit." Shane ran a hand through his hair and took a deep breath.

"Passed three dark SUVs in town," Shane said. "Every second you're here, the cartel gets closer. Probably setting up a grid right now if they haven't already. Get your stuff," Shane said. "We're leaving now. Hurry!"

I ran to the bathroom to get the medical supplies; Dillon's wound would need to be cleaned again in a few hours.

"I'm thinking we head north," I said as I tossed the stuff into the duffel Shane brought. "Once we're somewhere a little safer—"

"I'm taking you to the precinct," Shane announced.

"To hell with that!" Dillon said.

Shane ignored him. "I'm going to tell Burch what's going on. Get him to assign you protection while we figure this out."

I nodded. This made sense. I knew Dillon wouldn't like it, but—

"Screw that! It'll get her killed. We need to get her out of here."

"We need to call this in," Shane said to me. "You know that."

I considered it. "Maybe Dillon's right," I said. "Maybe we should lie low for a little while, do a little more digging before we involve authorities. If we call them right now, we might tip off the leak, and if we do that, we'd be giving the cartel a GPS on our heads."

"Fallon, listen to me," Shane said. "If Burch finds out you've been in bed with a Chicago captain?"

"I already told Burch about Dillon."

"That was before, when you broke it off."

"He wanted Dillon to be a CI."

Shane licked his teeth at that revelation. "But he didn't become one, did he?" He paused. "And now, seven men got killed, and the two of you went missing. When he finds out you've been with him the whole time, do you know what it's going to look like?"

He let a small silence pass.

"It's going to look like you were the leak. You got your agents killed."

"That's ridiculous."

"If you look at this from the bird's-eye, from someone who doesn't know you, it's really not. You got in bed with a Chicago captain, and while seven federal agents were slaughtered, you somehow made it out, unscathed. Bird's-eye view: it looks like you were in on it."

"No one would—"

"Why would they *not* think that?" Shane pushed. "Put yourself in their shoes. Who looks more guilty than you?"

I shook my head and swallowed my shock.

"Think they're not going to look for someone to blame?" Shane pressed. "Someone to bring charges against? Could hold you accountable for the deaths of the men. Manslaughter charges. Maybe even murder."

I wanted to tell him he was crazy. But the scary thing was, he wasn't. Not in the least. Of course that was how it looked.

"You need to get in front of this, Fallon. Come clean now. Surrender yourself while they still view you as the victim, not the mastermind."

*Mastermind...*

"The longer you hide out, the guiltier you look," Shane warned.

"He's right," Dillon said.

I turned around.

"You need to go."

"What?"

Dillon scrubbed the back of his head. "Your odds are probably better, surrounded by federal custody, than running alone, especially if the cartel *and* the feds are hunting you down. And you can't let yourself become the scapegoat for what happened tonight."

That pain in Dillon's eyes returned—the pain that I'd noticed when he said he had something to tell me and that whatever it was, I wasn't going to like it.

"I need you to listen to me," Dillon whispered. "I need you to know I never betrayed you. I never worked you, Fallon. Fact is, I didn't even know you were in law enforcement when we first started dating, and when I found out..." He took a deep breath, looked incredibly depressed. "I'd never do anything to hurt you."

"I know that."

He offered a weak smile, his brows pushed together in pain.

"Fallon..." He closed his mouth, swallowed harshly. "I'm going to turn myself in."

It hurt. Thinking of the risk of him in prison, but I was relieved he'd chosen to do the right thing, taking responsibility for his crimes. And while I didn't know what that meant for our future—if we could even escape to have one—this was the only path that acceptably bridged the person he'd been to the person he'd become.

I nodded. "Burch's team will know what to do. You can go into wit pro."

"We can talk about that later," Shane interrupted, waving an impatient hand. "Fallon, we need to go."

"Wait," Dillon said, pulling me back. He gave me a sad smile, one that didn't reach his eyes, and his posture drooped.

"Fallon, I'm not turning myself in to the *cops*."

"I don't understand—" And then I saw it, the look in his eyes, and I pieced his intention together. That was what his earlier despair was about; he'd already made this decision, perhaps on the drive or when I was in the pharmacy or cleaning his wound. That was why he'd slipped and said *I* should get out instead of *us*.

"You can't." My eyes stung.

"I've thought of a million ways this could go down," Dillon said. "This is the only chance of keeping you safe."

"I see headlights." Shane peered through the blinds. "We need to go, Fallon."

I couldn't believe Dillon was even considering this. There was no way in hell I'd ever, ever let him do this.

"I'll let 'em chase me while you get away."

"They'll catch you!"

"But not you."

"There's no guarantee that sacrificing yourself will get me out of this! And they won't just kill you—you know that! They'll torture you!"

"Fallon!" Shane said.

"Stalling them is the best chance to keep you safe."

"While they torture you!"

"Fallon!"

"No!" I cried. I pressed myself into Dillon's chest, into the chest I'd fallen in love with. The complicated, twisted love that had no clear path forward, yet I couldn't breathe without it.

"It's going to be okay," Dillon lied.

I looked up into his now-tear-filled eyes. I couldn't let him die. Not like that.

"I can't lose another person I love," I said.

His whisper of a voice was full of sorrow. "I'm sorry I failed you."

I wiped a fallen tear from his cheek. "You didn't fail me."

But his lips trembled. "There's something I haven't told you yet."

Whatever it was, it was bad. I could see it plaguing his eyes, haunting him in a way that would keep a person up at night.

"What is it?"

"Fallon!" Shane insisted.

But it was too late.

Headlights swept through the blinds' cracks as tires screeched to a halt. A car door opened, slammed shut.

Dillon pushed me behind him as a fist pounded on the door.

"Open the damn door!"

## 34

D illon grabbed the handgun and aimed its barrel at the hollow metal door that separated us from whoever was on the other side.

Which vibrated with each blow.

*Bam. Bam. Bam.*

"Open up!"

"Looks like it's just one guy." Shane squinted, struggling to see in the night. "But the SUV's dark."

So, who knew how many might be hiding inside of it? Or surrounding the place?

My throat ran dry.

*Bam. Bam. Bam.*

"Hernandez, open up!"

Confusion washed over Shane as he looked at me.

How did *he* know we were here?

"Hide in the bathroom," Shane hissed to Dillon.

"What?" Dillon said.

"Just do it!" Shane demanded.

Dillon looked at me and waited until I nodded my approval to follow Shane's order. He approached me quickly and afforded himself a second to silently proclaim what he didn't dare say out loud in front of Shane right now. By squeezing my hand three times.

*I. Love. You.*

Then, he placed the gun in my hand and vanished into the bathroom.

Shane took a deep breath, unlocked the door, and opened it.

Burch stood on the other side, alone. His eyes cut through the thick tension from Shane to me before he charged into the room. I'd never seen Burch this angry. His jaw set tight, his fists clenched. He barely resembled the methodically calm sergeant he'd always portrayed. Clearly a casualty of losing several men tonight.

Shane shut the door behind him.

"You said you didn't know where she was," Burch accused.

"I didn't until she called me," Shane said and then added, "How did you know we were here?"

Burch unleashed his anger onto me. "Why the hell didn't you call me? You know how many federal officers are looking for you?"

I set the weapon on the nightstand with a clunk.

"I can explain," I said.

"You'd better do it damn fast."

And so I did. I told him everything that happened at the party, how I escaped, and along with my suspicion—leaving out the part about Dillon helping me or being with me. I seriously needed Burch to calm down before offering that little bomb drop.

"You think we have a leak," Burch said when I was done.

"I don't know how else to explain it," I said.

Burch paced, hands on his hips, and as he did, Shane kept watch through a sliver in the blinds.

"Your car's runnin'," Shane said. "We need to turn it off; anyone driving past'll see the activity outside this room."

"Who do you think it is?" Burch asked me.

It had to be a hard consideration to hear because if there was a leak in play, his career wouldn't just end; it would end in disgrace. This would be scrutinized for years and would serve as a warning for investigations from this point forward.

What a horrible way to go down.

"I don't know," I said.

"Proctor?"

"Why would they have killed someone who was helping them?" I asked.

Burch rubbed his jaw. "Anyone else know about your theory?"

"Just Shane and…"

"And?"

I paused. "When I escaped tonight, I had help."

Burch tensed, looked at me like a parent who'd caught his daughter sneaking back into her window in the middle of the night. "From?"

Uneasiness thickened the air around me, and I worried that my boss might misunderstand the situation or look at me differently for accepting help from one of *them*. As pathetic as it might be, I savored his approval—approval that I'd worked so hard to earn. I didn't want to lose it.

But he deserved to hear the whole truth.

"From Dillon."

On cue, Dillon emerged from the bathroom.

Burch pulled the gun from its holster and took aim, provoking Dillon to put his palms up in surrender.

"It's okay," I said. "He helped me escape tonight."

But Burch didn't lower his weapon; if anything, he looked even more enraged.

"He helped you," Burch snapped. "As in the two of you working together?"

"I…no, not like that."

"Have you given him intel?"

"No!"

"How the hell can I trust that?"

"Because it's the truth! I'd never give up information that could jeopardize our case, let alone put people in danger!"

"Would you know if you did?"

"Yes!"

"Seven of my agents got killed tonight, and you think that's a coincidence?"

"I didn't give any info."

"How am I supposed to trust a word you say? You lied to me," he growled. "Said he refused to be our CI. Wouldn't work with us."

"He wouldn't."

"Bullshit! You've been with him the whole time! Feeding him information!"

"I haven't!"

"She hasn't—" Dillon started.

"Shut the fuck up!" Burch said, and then he told me, "Put your hands behind your back."

"What?" I asked.

Burch pointed the gun at me. At *me*. I hadn't just lost his favor; I'd become the enemy.

"Hands. Behind your back!" Burch repeated.

"Sergeant!" Shane started.

"Both of you." Burch motioned for Dillon and me.

"Sarge, Fallon hasn't—"

"Shut up, or I'll arrest you, too," Burch demanded of Shane.

"Then, arrest me," Shane said. "Because she hasn't done anything. I know how this looks, but she's dedicated her entire life to the war on drugs. She didn't flip, Sarge."

But Burch wasn't listening. A shield of anger wrapped around him, and as he stared at me, his right eye began to twitch. He'd lost everything tonight—his career, his reputation—and he looked like he was coming unglued.

Hopefully, at the station, I could prove my innocence. Hopefully, he'd have enough mercy to get Dillon and me some protection, so the cartel wouldn't get to us.

I nodded to Dillon, and then we both turned around and put our hands behind our backs.

As Burch clanked metal cuffs onto Dillon's left wrist, then his right, Dillon's chestnut eyes grabbed mine, emotion radiating with each beat of his heart. We had been through so much together, a war of our own, and I could see his anguish in the sagging of his shoulders and his fear in his widened eyes that, in the custody of someone so furious with us, we might not receive the level of protection required to keep us alive.

*I love you,* Dillon mouthed.

*I love you,* I mouthed back.

"Cuffs." Burch held his expectant hand out to Shane. Evidently, Burch had only come with one pair.

"I didn't bring 'em, Sarge. You don't need to arrest Fallon. Bring her to the station to ask more questions if you want, but—"

"I'm not asking for your damn opinion, Hernandez! You're in enough trouble for lying to me tonight!"

Was this how it was going to be? Burch would turn on anyone involved with tonight and try to throw us under the bus? I screwed up, no doubt. I wasn't ready for an undercover operation of this scale, and I was responsible for having convinced him I was. But Burch couldn't turn *all* of this onto other people and shoulder none of the responsibility himself.

"Sarge—" Shane tried.

Burch squeezed my wrists together and perp-walked me outside.

Dillon followed and kept his eyes on the lot and the main road.

Burch shoved me into the backseat of his SUV and slammed the door. It smelled like sweat in here, like he'd panicked the whole ride down.

How did Burch know we were here? Did Shane lie to me? Did he tell Burch?

"This is bullshit. I'm calling this in," Shane declared as he pulled his cell out.

"I wouldn't do that if I were you." Burch pointed the gun at Shane.

"What are you doin'?" Shane asked.

"Give me your weapon," he demanded of Shane.

"What?"

"Weapon!" Burch screamed.

Dillon glared at Burch.

I yanked the handle and rammed my shoulder into the door repeatedly, but it wouldn't open.

"Weapon!" Burch shouted.

I tried the other side. Same fail.

Shane and I exchanged a look through the window, one that silently communicated our fear. The cartel could come down this road any second, and anyone unarmed would be a sitting duck. As would Dillon, being cuffed. Shane's gaze hardened in disgust as he glowered at Sergeant Marcus Burch. It took several seconds before Shane reluctantly kicked his 0.40 caliber toward Burch, who picked it up and tucked it into his waistband.

We were all disarmed, but on the outside wall of the motel ten feet away was an emergency fire box with a fire extinguisher and an ax. Maybe I could blow the extinguisher in Burch's face or crack him over the head with it, giving us a chance to reclaim Shane's weapon. Get the gun from the motel's nightstand.

I'd have to get out of the SUV first, though.

Dillon took a furious step toward Burch.

"Get in," Burch ordered him.

With his hands behind his back, no shirt, Dillon moved toward the vehicle.

Shane took an aggressive step forward, his shoulders rounded in rage.

"Stay back!" Burch shouted, pointing the pistol at Shane's head.

The inside of the SUV was a sea of shadows with dashboard lights offering the only glow. The engine purred, waiting to move, to take me to my demise.

I tried the door again, but it was locked—child safety locks, I guess. The only way to open it would be from the front. I grabbed the front headrest and heaved myself over to the passenger seat, but before I could do anything else, the driver's door opened.

"Freeze!"

My former hero aimed the barrel of his semiautomatic at my head.

Burch eyeballed the guys, who were momentarily frozen.

I sprang into the driver's seat and threw the running car's gear into reverse. Burch dove inside and landed half on me as the SUV flew backward, its tires squealing along the asphalt. I squeezed the steering wheel, but Burch clenched his sweaty sausage fingers over mine, fighting for control as the vehicle jerked from side to side, careening toward the nearby field.

With the door still open, I elbowed Burch in the nose and kicked him with my free leg, but he hurled himself deeper inside the SUV and maintained his hold on both the weapon and steering wheel.

I tried to jerk the wheel to the right toward the building. If I could crash, maybe he'd fly out the door. But he wrenched the steering wheel back the other way, sending the vehicle into a fishtail toward the road.

Burch hit me in the head with the pistol so hard, it stunned me long enough for him to shove me into the passenger seat, stop, and clunk the gear into drive.

Forward this time.

I tugged the door handle, but it was also locked. I kicked the window.

"Stop."

The icy promise of death pressed against the back of my skull.

And as Burch closed the door, I glanced back at Dillon and Shane, who watched in horror as Burch sped down the country road.

## 35

"Open the glove box," Burch commanded.

As I turned to face forward, he kept his Glock 19 inches from my left temple.

The glove box opened with a click, and the interior yellow light illuminated stacks of papers and the car's owner's manual. On top of which sat a pair of plastic zip ties.

"Put them on. Now."

*I should go for the gun or grab the wheel and make us crash.*

But with death one squeeze away, my instincts cautioned me to wait to make my move. We were driving too fast with no seat belts, so I'd never survive the crash. And with the erratic look in Burch's eyes, I had no doubt he'd kill me.

Even if I had no idea why.

I wrapped the plastic restraint around my left wrist, then added my right. Which was tricky, threading the line through its end and pulling it closed with my teeth.

Burch grabbed the band and yanked it so tight, the ties cut into my skin.

I scowled at him—at the man who I'd once longed to impress.

"You're the leak," I said in disgust.

He said nothing, didn't even have the courtesy to look at me as we plunged ahead on the darkened road into whatever twisted fate awaited me.

"You led your men into an ambush. You sent them tonight, knowing the cartel knew we were coming. Knowing they'd kill us all."

"I didn't know they'd kill you; there was nothing I could do," Burch said.

"Bullshit. There was a lot you could do. They trusted you. Some had families. Kids that'll grow up without a parent."

"This isn't what I wanted, O'Connor."

"What did you want? Money? A cut of the take? What was the price tag for all those families you destroyed tonight?"

"This isn't about money," Burch said.

"Then, what?"

He swallowed. "They have my kids."

He made a left turn and got onto a four-lane road. In the middle of the night, the SUV's headlights pierced through the insidious darkness and lit a couple hundred feet in front of us. Only a few other vehicles sped along this road, and when they grew close in the oncoming lane, their headlights blazed so brightly, it hurt my eyes. No way anyone would see the gun Burch had aimed at me, diabolically hidden beneath the dash.

"Two men showed up at my house," Burch said. "Told me they had my kids." I recalled hearing Burch had two—both of which had graduated college recently. "They had pictures, proof they had them. If I alerted the FBI or anyone, my kids would be tortured and killed."

"What did they want?"

Burch gripped the wheel tighter as a bead of sweat trailed down his temple.

"They needed to know what we knew. What the chances were of being arrested on American soil. What evidence we had."

Right, in order to cross the border safely.

"So, you turned it all over to them," I said. "Including the undercover operation."

"If you have kids someday," Burch started but then caught himself, looking at me with a flash of pity. Realizing I'd never have kids because I wouldn't be alive much longer. "When you have kids, there's nothing you wouldn't do for them."

"So, you're trading me for them."

"When you got away, they offered an exchange." And then he added in a softer tone, "I'm sorry, Fallon."

I bit my lip. "How did you find me?"

He shifted. "Tracked Hernandez's phone."

Then, why didn't they just send someone to the motel to kill me? The thought made me shudder that Dillon and Shane could've gotten killed, too, but why have Burch bring me to them?

"Why didn't they just take a hit out on me?"

Burch sighed. "Can only assume they want to question you about your relationship with McPherson. Find out what he leaked and to who."

My stomach rolled with nausea. Of course that was what they wanted; they'd torture me for days, maybe longer, to figure out what I knew. Uncover any other threat they needed to mitigate to make their big move a success.

My mouth ran dry. "Did they know about us before tonight?" Before we'd been caught, escaping together? Because if they did, why didn't they kill Dillon before the party?

"I had to answer their questions, but I certainly wasn't going to volunteer information they didn't ask for. Protected as much intel as I could. Soon as I have my kids back, I'm going to work the case and personally make sure these animals are put away. Besides," he said, glowering at me, "didn't realize you two were still together."

But now that Dillon helped me escape, they knew. So, what orders had been given for us?

"And Dillon?"

"If I found you two together, I was supposed to snag him, too." Burch looked nervous, clearly worried they might not let his kids go if he only showed up with me. But what choice did he have? When everything went to hell in the parking lot, he at least had me in the car. Returning to the motel to fight with Shane risked me getting away and Burch having nothing to bargain for his kids.

"How long have you been working with them?" I demanded.

He didn't answer.

"My dad's funeral? Were you working with them then?" When I invited Burch as a guest and thought he was honorable?

"No. Funeral was an intimidation tactic," Burch said. "To warn us they can get to any of us. And our families," he added.

Families. Usually present at a funeral, so yeah. That would have sent one hell of a message to everyone.

"How long have you been working with them?" I repeated.

Burch tightened his lips.

"Before we found Marks?"

He didn't look at me.

"And you didn't call off the undercover operation."

"Couldn't do that without tipping my hand."

"But they knew we were going to be there," I challenged.

"They had my kids."

"So, you just let us all walk into an ambush."

"The cartel is playing the long game, collecting people who'll feed them vital intel. If they killed agents tonight, it'd expose their plans, so no, I didn't think it was going to be a massacre."

But obviously, he'd been wrong in his assessment.

"You let your experience go to your head," I accused. All those missions he'd pulled off, with better stats than anyone in DEA history. "You knew it was dangerous, but with all the years under your belt, you thought you could still control this. Save your kids *and* salvage the case." Which wasn't just reckless; it was downright arrogant.

I blinked the stinging of immense disappointment in my eyes. After closing everyone out for years, over the last few weeks, I'd grown to trust two people—Dillon and Burch. And now, this man whose approval I'd savored, who I'd trusted with my life, was driving me to my certain death. His betrayal cut me deep.

Dillon would never betray me; he'd die to protect me.

I guess that was the gamble you took with opening yourself up to people. Some people would hurt you. But others would love you so much, it could make up for all those other hurts combined.

I buried my pain and focused on trying to convince Burch to let me go. "You hand me over," I said, "you really think they'll just let your kids walk?"

He tensed his jaw.

"Untie me, and we can come up with a plan. Maybe I can talk Shane and Dillon into—"

"No."

"You can give me a gun."

"I'm not risking my kids, O'Connor."

"Your kids are in danger, no matter what you do. We work together and maybe—"

"No!" Burch snapped. "I'm doing exactly what they say, period. I'm not deviating."

"You don't have Dillon."

"They can hunt him down themselves."

My throat ran dry. They *would* hunt him down. I had to think of a way to save him, save myself, and Burch was too emotional to listen to reason. Maybe I could get to his cell, call this in, like I should have done to begin with.

As we drove north in silence, Burch didn't take his eyes off the road in front of him. He didn't drive like a cop, looking at his surroundings—hell, the cartel could be following us for all I knew—but rather drove like a crazed father, desperate to get to his children.

I thought I could use that fevered focus to my advantage, but before I had the chance to make a move, he parked the car on a grassy field and led me down a slight hill to a dilapidated pier extending out into Lake Michigan.

The water, almost indiscernible from the dark horizon, was hauntingly calm, barely rocking the hundred-foot-long-foot boat tied to the pier's end. North of us, the city's lights glowed like a beacon of hope, and the moon's silver glow shimmered its reflection off the water, but right here, the shadows of hopelessness swallowed me whole as Burch led me to the armed men guarding the lone vessel.

One of the guys, who brandished spiderweb tattoos on his hands, patted Burch and me down and confiscated his guns before escorting us to the boat. Which had multiple levels to it, including one of those underground quarters.

I wasn't sure exactly where we were, but the area was abandoned, save for the psychopaths standing before us.

"The agent." Burch pushed me forward.

A three-hundred-pound man grabbed my elbow and looked at my face for confirmation.

Burch rubbed his ear. "What are you going to do with her?"

"Ain't no matter to you."

Burch looked at me with a silent apology before focusing on what he really cared about. "My kids," Burch insisted. "They said they'd be here."

"Did they?"

Burch tensed. "Bring them to me."

"Change of plans."

A gunshot blasted, and Burch's forehead split open, and his body collapsed to the wood.

I screamed in horror. When two men grabbed my arms and jerked me forward, I pulled and yanked so hard that I could feel my shoulder muscles tearing. But I was no match for their strength.

Once we reached the boat, one of them simply picked me up and threw me into a room on the lower level of the vessel.

Where I slammed onto the ground in a pool of sticky liquid.

Between two mutilated bodies of who I could only assume were Burch's grown children.

## 36

The bodies—one male, one female—were covered in cuts and bruises. But the most gruesome injuries—on their skin at least —were the inflamed welts that ripped their skin wide open in the shape of a *J*.

The smell was a putrid mix of sweat, blood, and burning flesh. Not decomp. They hadn't been dead long, though I bet they wished they had been.

A guy with two missing teeth pulled me up and shoved me into a wooden chair in the center of the room. A chair sitting on top of a fifteen-foot-wide plastic tarp. He zip-tied each ankle to a chair leg, slithered a zip tie through my currently tied wrists, strapped my right wrist to the right armrest, and cut the original zip tie loose with a knife. I took advantage of the freedom to punch him in his missing-toothed mouth, but he blocked it and shoved my left wrist against the other armrest so hard, I thought the bone cracked. He tied that one, too.

When he was done, he lumbered back up the steps and left me alone to take in my surroundings.

The room shouldn't be empty of furniture; clearly, it intended to hold a living room and maybe a dining room set in what I could only assume was a long-haul fishing vessel. But I guess they didn't need that, only this chair, what appeared to be a fire-burning stove in the corner—which crackled and offered the only light—and two hooks suspended from the ceiling's reinforced beams. One of the hooks splatted drops of blood onto the tarp below.

Footsteps thumped down the stairs.

I rocked the chair, hoping I could slip the tie off the leg, but there was no give with them.

Two men entered the room, but they didn't look at me. Instead, they dragged the bodies off to the side with less care than moving trash bags and jogged back up the steps.

*They wanted me to see that—the fate that awaits me.*

I rocked my chair to the side, getting a couple inches of air beneath the right leg, and I shoved my ankle down hard, trying to slip the zip tie off the peg, but suddenly, new steps descended the stairs. These clomps moved slowly, dragging out each step with measured intention. Whoever it was wore split-toned cowboy boots with a brown base and black top that rested on the calves of his black pants.

The man entered the room with the menacing confidence reserved for leaders, and as three other guys followed, I mentally compared the leader to all the faces of criminals I'd studied. I didn't remember anyone with a dark beard and mustache, bushy eyebrows. Plenty of guys were soft around the middle like this guy, though, like they hadn't seen the inside of a gym in a decade.

He fastened his unblinking gaze onto me.

"Fallon O'Connor." He rolled the sleeves of his blue button-down up to his elbows, seemingly unfazed by the blood splattered across his shirt.

His three henchmen took their stances—one on the wall to my left, near the fire, which popped orange embers from its engulfed logs; one to my right; and one behind me. So I couldn't see whatever horror he might inflict. A total intimidation tactic.

I clenched my jaw. These guys had me at their mercy, and there was nothing I could do about that at the moment. But I wasn't about to give them the satisfaction of showing my fear.

"Twenty-six years old. Police officer with the Chicago Police Department. Member of the DEA task force for less than two months. Career ambition: DEA field agent."

"Wow. You somehow managed to smuggle my task force application offline. Congratulations. If the whole satanic drug lord thing doesn't work out for you, you could become a PI."

He walked around me, pausing over my left shoulder as two more drops of blood from the hook splatted onto the plastic tarp.

The boat's engine rumbled to life, and I could feel the vessel pull away from the dock. Even if, by some miracle, someone figured out where I was, there'd be no way for them to help now.

"No criminal offenses on the books, not even a speeding ticket. Father and mother both deceased. Drug overdoses. Father recent."

"Your drugs kill a lot of people. Prey on the weak. But don't let that stop you," I said, looking up at him. "Money is far more important than having a soul."

"Roommate Shane Hernandez. Best friend since childhood."

I kept my face ambivalent. I wouldn't show him that it made me uncomfortable that he knew something as personal as how long we'd been friends.

"Recent boyfriend, Dillon McPherson." He made a tsking sound as he walked around my back and appeared over my right shoulder. "Federal agent and a drug captain. Not something a good DEA agent would do."

"Guess you kidnapped a dud, then. Sucks for you."

He moved to the front of me. "Shane Hernandez's father was killed in the line of duty, but his mother is still alive."

I scowled at his evil eyes.

"Cares a great deal for her. She lives in an apartment in Rockford these days, near his aunt. It'd be a shame if something happened to her, no?" He smirked. "Mr. McPherson has a mother, too. Must care a lot for her, seeing as how he bought her a house. Must care for his disabled brother, too. Paying for his place in the home."

"Are you ever going to get to your point or just continue with family trees? Because I have a cool family tree I could talk about, too.

The Baja Cartel tree. You're Francisco Gutierrez," I realized now that he was close enough to see his ugly face with that scar on his cheekbone. Probably why he grew the beard—so he didn't show weakness. "Leader of the Baja Cartel and class-A asshole. Killed your own cousin to take ownership of the business *after* you bombed a rival cartel to take over their region."

"You've studied our organization," he said.

"Part of the job description." I looked away from him to his hired guns.

"Then, you know what we are capable of, Ms. O'Connor. And more importantly, what *I'm* capable of."

Yes, I was. Gutierrez murdered hundreds of people in the last few years alone, including innocent children—who he tended to blow up or poison. But the adults...he had fun with the adults. He had a reputation for getting off on the torture, not just using it as a tactic, but enjoying it.

"You took out four of my men tonight," Gutierrez chided.

"Let me kill three more, and we'll call it even." I nodded my chin toward the dudes around us. "These three'll do."

He chuckled and pointed at me with his finger. "I like you."

"Feeling's not mutual."

"I think you may change your mind when you hear my offer," he said, putting his hands into his pockets.

It was hard to not fixate on the blood on his shirt. What exactly had been done to them to make the blood splatter like that?

"You leave here alive. You go back home, live out your life. In exchange for this, you simply provide us with"—he waved his hand—"a bit of information."

"You want me to tell you about the investigations."

"Knowledge is...valuable to any business owner, no?"

"No chance in hell."

He nodded and walked over to the fire-burning stove that didn't belong on a boat; its only purpose appeared to be heating up torture devices. "Thought you might say that. American law enforcement usually needs a little more...*motivation* to listen." He pulled a fire poker out of the flames. The black cast iron stick had a wooden handle that looked like a hot dog, and the bottom six inches of the iron was blazing red in the shape of a *J*.

Threat of branding me or not, I'd never help him. Why would he pick some new cop on a temporary DEA task force to help, anyway?

"Why me?" I asked.

"An agent who's in bed with the person she's supposed to arrest?" He cocked his head. "Is likely to be more...shall we say, willing to cooperate with us. Plus," he added, "you're new, so when you ask many questions for us, it won't raise suspicion."

"It doesn't work like that. I can't ask for details that aren't in my wheelhouse. They won't give me answers."

"You'll get answers," he warned.

"A higher-up would know more than I would."

"We tried that," he said, looking out toward the boat's entrance, where Burch's body had fallen. "Not as...complicit. Failed to disclose your relationship with McPherson. This information would have been quite useful to us."

Which they'd obviously learned about tonight. Yet...

"You tortured his kids for days." Not hours.

"Agreement was to keep them alive. Never said I wouldn't try to get information out of them," he said. "And now, *you'll* provide us with information."

I tightened my lips. "If you'd researched me better, you'd know I'd never work for you. I choose death, thanks." Which was obviously the price of declining his "offer."

"I haven't finished." He blew at the hot poker, watching the steam rise from its bright red tip.

"If you don't cooperate, I'm going to kill your boyfriend. *After* I torture him, of course. I'll start by sawing his legs off with a chainsaw," he declared. "Then, I'll do the same to his mother. His brother who lives in the Cold Springs Home. Poor bastard's mentally...what's the accepted terminology these days? Handicapped? So, when we torture him, he'll have no idea why. Imagine that'll make it scarier for him. Especially since I'll make him watch his mother go first."

An empty pit rolled in my stomach.

"Then, I'll move on to Hernandez. I'll really take my time with him —long line of cops in his family. Make sure he knows you had the option to prevent it."

He paused.

"Then, I'll slaughter his entire family."

He'd probably do that, no matter what I did. But the desire to protect those that you loved could be a dangerous force.

Gutierrez approached me and hovered the hot poker in front of my face. "Lot of death for a simple ask."

He pressed the poker onto my right forearm. The searing pain was so intense, it transcended me to another dimension, where only I and the pain existed. He held it there for what was actually five seconds but felt like an eternity before pulling it off.

Along with the skin it had touched.

The open wound still burned despite the absence of the poker.

"I'll make sure their deaths are...unpleasant," he warned.

I thrashed in my chair, but one of his men put a hand on my shoulder to keep me from tipping over. I turned my chin and tried to bite him but only succeeded in getting slapped.

My blood pumped rage through every cell of my body. If I didn't do what he said, I'd sentence everyone I loved to the most gruesome death imaginable. But I couldn't work with the cartel, either. Even if I could trust Gutierrez—which I never could after what he'd done to Burch—I couldn't help them destroy more lives and ruin this country.

"It's just a little information here and there," Gutierrez insisted. "That's it. You live. People you care about live, and their families live. You don't? We get the information, anyway—we'll convince someone else to cooperate. And everyone you love dies. Seems like a pretty simple choice, if you want my opinion."

## 37

A new man ambled down the stairs. As he entered the room, his impatient eyes assessed me. He was tall and tan with black hair that hadn't sprouted as many grays as someone his age should have, clearly unaffected by this violent line of work. There was something familiar about his face, something I couldn't place—not without getting a better look, at least.

"She gonna do it?" His deep voice possessed only a slight accent.

Gutierrez had spoken to the other men with superiority, but he spoke to this guy like an equal. "About to find out." He stared at me. "You gonna be smart?"

Evidently, my pause tested the new guy's patience because, after a breath, he walked back up the steps. "I'm going to finish setting up."

*Setting up what?*

Before I could speculate what he might be up to, a shorter guy set up something of his own. He wheeled in a metal cart out of the back room. Its wheels thumped along each plank of wood, rattling the instruments that blanketed its four-foot silver top—a Craftsman twelve-inch hacksaw, Black & Decker cordless reciprocating saw, butane blowtorch, Oregon electric chainsaw, cattle prod, hammer, and pliers, among other things. Stained in blood, the tools hadn't even been cleaned yet from their last victims.

I swallowed.

Gutierrez glared at me. "What's your decision, Ms. O'Connor?"

It seemed like such an obvious choice. To never, ever help the cartel. But imagining Dillon and Shane and their families hanging from those hooks, suffering at the hands of those tools until death was a relief...holding the power to prevent it made the decision far less clear.

"And if I say yes, I can leave tonight?" And warn Dillon and Shane, give them a chance to get their loved ones to safety.

"Afraid you'll need to stick with us for a little while until we build up some trust."

"You said I could go home."

"I didn't say tonight. We extended confidence to your boss, and that didn't work out so well."

"I can't help you get answers if I'm held here. I need to go back to the precinct to ask questions."

"One thing at a time, Ms. O'Connor. That's a yes, I presume?"

I hesitated, looking up at the bloody hooks, wondering what exactly Dillon and Shane would endure—if not here, in another torture chamber of their making.

I shut my eyes and remembered everything that happened to my mom, my dad.

I had a choice—to either strengthen the cartel or not. And while they might be right—they might get what they needed, anyway, by kidnapping some other agent—I was not going to give it to them.

I could only hope that Dillon and Shane and their families would forgive me.

There was probably no chance I'd survive the night, but if, by some miracle, I did, maybe I could find out what Gutierrez had up his sleeve, so I could at least give that vital intelligence to the DEA.

"What kind of information would you be asking for?" I asked.

Gutierrez lowered the poker, unsurprised by the likely coopera-tion. I imagine that was why someone as powerful as him handled this; people probably rarely said no to him. And with so much on the line, he needed for this American operation to move smoothly.

"Whatever I ask, whenever I ask for it. After tonight, there'll be a lot of…shall we say, planning the US will do."

My stomach rolled because there was something far more ominous to his tone than the handful of deaths they had already caused this evening. "Why tonight?"

"Do we have a deal?"

"What do you mean, they'll be planning after tonight?" I pressed again.

"Let's just say, we're going to send one hell of a message to Chicago law enforcement. A little…how you say, warning to stop their war on drugs."

What could that mean? What was the guy upstairs setting up for? My mind raced. What could they pull off on a boat? Attacking other vessels—the Coast Guard perhaps? No. Too small. Crashing the boat into some landmark? Still, not enough carnage to send a message. And if the cartel wanted to send a message, it'd be big. The cartel would want to hit law enforcement where it hurt. Bomb a precinct or something, but we were on a boat, not a truck, so that wouldn't work unless…

*Oh my God.* Unless the target was close to the shore, capable of mass casualties.

Like Navy Pier, where hundreds of law enforcement agents—including the chief of police and the mayor—were attending that awards ceremony right now. The mayor, who'd publicly announced a fresh war on drugs.

"You're going to bomb Navy Pier."

A raised eyebrow.

That was what the guy was preparing upstairs—a bomb.

"You're insane."

This boat chugged closer to Navy Pier with each passing second. All those people would be killed, and it wouldn't just be law enforcement. One of the top tourist destinations in the city, Navy Pier attracted two million people from all over the world each year, and on a summer Saturday night like tonight? Thousands of pedestrians would be among the casualties, including children.

I couldn't let this happen.

I stared at Gutierrez and clenched my now-numb hands. "I won't help you," I declared.

His face darkened, and his lips moved into a pucker.

And then, in a move so quick his arm blurred, he raised his gun.

Pain exploded on the side of my head. I was sure I'd been shot. It was only after a few seconds that I realized I'd only been pistol-whipped.

As warmth dripped down the side of my head, he snapped his fingers to one of the guys, who rolled in a different table—a table hidden behind a door—ten feet away. On it was an HP Pavilion laptop.

Gutierrez vanished into a back room while the guy punched a bunch of keys, tilted the laptop's monitor this way and that until he was satisfied. When he walked away, I discovered what he'd done; he'd activated the laptop's camera. The video of me sitting in this chair stared back at me now. It had a white frame around it with an internet bar at the top.

When the cart rolled closer to my chair, it became clear to me what the plan was.

They were going to torture me.

And livestream it on the internet. Anyone watching the undoubt-edly untraceable stream was about to get a front-row seat to the Baja Cartel's leader torturing a United States federal agent. What a horrific moment in American history this would be.

I needed to do something drastic and fast.

I hurled my body to the right and tipped the chair over, bashing my right shoulder into the ground when I landed.

The guy to my right laughed.

On my side, I arched my back and pushed my ankles down the wooden legs. It hurt like hell against the backs of my thighs, which dug into the seat's edge.

More laughter—the morons didn't catch on to what I was doing until my ankles slipped off the chair and freed themselves.

Internet-Setup Guy stopped laughing and marched toward me, but now, I had two free legs.

And I was going to use them.

I kicked him in the shin. Then the groin. And when he went down, holding his crotch, a second guy came at me with a knife.

He managed a swipe on my thigh, but I slammed the heel of my foot into his teeth and felt them break.

He grabbed his bloody mouth, screaming as Gutierrez walked back into the room. Now wearing a white shirt, primed for a bloody show.

Bloody Mouth lunged at me and cracked my temple with his fist as Gutierrez stood next to the instrument tray, debating what he'd use first.

He didn't even flinch when a second man had to join in my struggle, each pinning one of my legs down while the third guy cut my arms free.

I yanked, shoved, and thrashed but couldn't stop the three of them from binding my wrists together with new ties along with a chain.

They hung the chain from the hook and walked away, leaving me dangling directly in front of the camera.

Gutierrez picked his first instrument—a cattle prod.

And then he stood before the camera and pushed the button to start streaming.

"Good evening. My name is Francisco Gutierrez. Today, my colleagues and I were in the middle of a nonviolent business meeting when the DEA invaded and killed four of our men. Unprovoked."

As he lied, I swung my body and tried to kick him upside his vile, lying head.

But it didn't work.

Gutierrez turned around and shoved the cattle prod into my rib. A boiling heat sprinted through my body to my limbs, making my head jerk back. At first, all I could hear was the electric current ringing in my ears, but then screaming sounded in the distance—screaming that grew closer and closer.

It was mine.

Gutierrez looked pleased as he returned to his table, ranting more threats into the camera as he picked up a hammer and an ice pick.

A thump from upstairs made Gutierrez pause momentarily. The guy upstairs had to be almost done, setting up their massive bomb as the boat grew closer to Navy Pier.

I had to warn law enforcement. Maybe the DEA or some other American agency was watching right now. That was the whole point of his plan, was it not? To have them watching? Gutierrez was addressing them, threatening them, showing what would happen if they got in his way. I could use this livestream to warn the United States.

"The Baja Cartel is going to bomb Navy Pier tonight!" I screamed.

Gutierrez snapped his head back.

"They've moved to the United States!"

A hand smothered my mouth from behind. I bit it so hard, it jerked away.

"They killed Sergeant Burch and his kids! And—"

"Get a rag!" Gutierrez snarled.

"They're trying to infiltrate the DEA!"

"Turn that computer off!" Gutierrez snapped.

Another guy sprinted to the laptop and slammed it shut.

Gutierrez narrowed his evil eyes at me. Picked up the electric reciprocating saw and held it up to show off the sharp teeth of its blade.

"That was a foolish thing to do," he growled.

As I hung from the rafters of a boat out in the middle of the water, my executioner approached me.

38

Gutierrez turned the saw on. It buzzed to life with the earsplitting rumble of a lawn mower as its blade jerked back and forth so quickly that Gutierrez's hand vibrated. Tiny bits of what I could only assume were pieces of some poor victim's skin shot out from it, one pelting my cheek.

His three associates shifted into position—two on the wall to my left, one to my right, licking their lips as he prepared to cut me into pieces.

My heart pounded so hard in my chest, it felt like it might break through my rib cage as Gutierrez angled the saw toward my shoulder.

But suddenly, he jerked, and the saw crashed to the floor and stopped buzzing. Gutierrez thumped to the ground, groaning as he grabbed his bleeding shoulder.

The two henchmen on the left wall slumped to the ground with holes in their foreheads before I registered the sounds of gunshots as two silhouettes crouched in the stairway. Dripping wet.

It always amazed me what the police academy had taught us—that guns could fire, even when wet. Technically, they could even fire underwater, but I'd never been more grateful for that until now.

*How did they find me?*

As Gutierrez reached for his weapon, his only living bodyguard pointed his gun at my head.

And this time, when the gun fired, I heard the blast's *bam*.

I waited for the pain to come, but when the guy smacked to the floor, I realized someone else had fired faster.

Dillon. Still cuffed, but the chain connecting them had been broken, so he could move his wrists freely.

Shane approached Gutierrez and kicked his revolver out of reach.

Dillon closed the ten feet separating us in an impossibly fast second, his panicked eyes scanning my body. When he saw the burn on my arm, the cut on my thigh, his every muscle tensed into murderous rage.

Gritting his teeth, he shoved the gun into his waistband, wrapped his arms under my hips, and pushed me up until my wrists were free from the hook.

"I got you, Fallon," he said as he gently lowered me to my feet. Then, he cupped my face with both hands, searched my eyes, desperate for reassurance. "Are you okay?"

I nodded, provoking his shoulders to shrink in relief.

"How did you know I was here?" I asked.

But he was too preoccupied to answer; Dillon's eyes widened in rage-filled horror when he spotted the instruments they'd planned to torture me with.

"What did they do to you?" he growled, his voice primal and protective.

"I'm fine," I assured. "But we need to go."

It took Dillon a second to move. His jaw remained locked in fury as he unraveled the chains around my hands and frowned at the zip ties.

"Fuck, these are tight," he said.

Shane checked the pulses of the cartel members and kicked their weapons out of the way for good measure.

"We need to hurry," I said. "There are other people upstairs somewhere, and they're heading to Navy Pier to bomb it."

Shane and Dillon exchanged a holy-shit look.

Dillon grabbed a knife off the table. "Hold still," he warned and then carefully cut my ties loose. He put his hand on my cheek and asked, "Can you walk?"

"Yeah, we need to hurry," I repeated, bolting toward the stairs, but it was too late.

The man from earlier, the apparent equal to Gutierrez, blocked our path as he descended the steps with two armed men.

One gun pointed at Shane.

One gun pointed at Dillon.

One at me.

## 39

O nce he stepped closer, I finally got a good look at his face. Fourteen years of wrinkles had accumulated since our last photo of him, but I still recognized his eyes. He *had* been working with the cartel, and based on the way Gutierrez spoke to him earlier, he'd become a very high-ranking member of the Baja organization.

Rodrigo Ramirez.

And he stared right at Dillon, whose entire body tensed. I'd never seen Dillon quiver before, and I wondered if it was from anger, fear, or both.

Maybe it was from pain. Dillon was still shirtless, and the gauze I'd carefully wrapped around his wound sagged with water, and his wound lightly bled down his stomach.

Ramirez pointed his gun at my face. Dillon moved protectively in front of me, pointing his gun right back at Ramirez. Shane and the criminal to my left aimed their barrels at each other while the other guy with a bald square head aimed his Glock 19 at me.

Lots of guns. Lots of trigger-happy fingers one squeeze away from ending us along with any hope to stop the Navy Pier massacre.

"You look different," Ramirez said to Dillon.

*Different?*

Dillon's chest rose and fell three times. "I thought you were dead."

Ramirez's mouth twitched up on one side in arrogance. "What made you think that?"

"Not a word, not a dollar, no sign you were alive. Plus, your line of work. Plus, wishful thinking."

Ramirez's nostrils flared, and then he scanned me in a way he hadn't before.

"Your girlfriend's a cop," he accused.

Dillon took a step backward, closer to me.

Ramirez raised his eyebrows. "She know who I am?"

I could see Dillon's shoulders rising and falling faster as his breaths accelerated.

Ramirez smirked at me. "He didn't tell you?"

My stomach plunged.

Ramirez looked at his watch before regarding Dillon again. "You changed your last name," he said.

"You leave, and you think you deserve the honor of sharing a last name with me? Or Dex?"

*Holy crap.*

Ramirez straightened. "You can act as noble as you want, but you're just like me."

"I'm nothing like you."

"You sell drugs. Apple"—he pointed to Dillon, then himself—"tree."

"I sold drugs out of desperation to support Mom and Dex when you left like an asshole coward. You abandoned us. Let us think you were dead, but you've been there all along." Dillon looked between Gutierrez and Ramirez. "Moving up the ranks, evidently."

Gutierrez tried to get up, but Shane kicked him back down.

"Did you order the hit on me?" Dillon demanded of Ramirez.

"We might not be close, but you're still my son. They knew I'd never go along with it, so they tried to conceal it from me by going after you in public, but I wasn't stupid. Saw it for what it was. Dealt with the person who made that call."

*That* was why Dillon wasn't executed in the traditional way.

"Why was I a target?" Dillon demanded.

"They made your tattoo," he said.

I thought back to that first day in the task force when we'd seen the scorpion tattoo. The one Terrell had confirmed belonged to a captain. Terrell had been tortured for days before that fire; he must have confessed to leaking the tattoo detail during his torture session.

"Was only a matter of time before police picked you up."

"I wouldn't have talked," Dillon said in a low voice.

"They didn't want to take the chance. When the hit failed, *I* was the one that stepped in, so they didn't take a second shot at you! I kept you alive, and you jeopardize that chance on what? A girl? A fucking cop, no less? And not just any girl. You know where she lived when she was a kid?"

So, Gutierrez wasn't the only one with my file…

"Shut up," Dillon said.

"He didn't tell you who I am," Ramirez said to me.

No. But I'd caught up.

"You're his father."

"I used to live here," Ramirez said.

"Yeah, I got that by the whole deadbeat-father-walks-out-on-his-family thing."

Ramirez smirked at me. "All Chicago suburbs were part of my region at the time."

*His…region. As in drug region. Of course…*

Ramirez grinned as understanding sank my feet to the ground like anchors.

He was the boss when my parents became addicts, responsible for the drugs making their way into their hands.

"This isn't how I wanted you to find out," Dillon said in a tone only low enough for me to hear. "I was going to tell you."

"How long did you know?" I asked through burning eyes.

He hesitated, breathing only through his nose for several seconds, and with his gun still pointed at his father, his voice hardened. "Suspected it might be him when you told me where you lived. Didn't want to believe it could be…hoped the timing was off."

I thought back to that sickened expression on his face when we both confessed who we were. When he demanded I leave. I'd been so offended at the time, but looking back on it, Dillon must have wondered if his father could have been in charge of the drug region at that time, and that morning, I'd told him how they *pushed* the drugs out, giving freebies to keep them hooked. That was why Dillon looked so ashamed at that moment, carrying the burden of his father's vile choices.

"I wanted to tell you," Dillon said. "But I was hoping I was wrong. And by that point, I was more worried about your safety. That took priority over everything, and I was scared if I told you what I suspected, you wouldn't let me help you."

Ramirez interrupted our moment with a sneer. "Shame about your mom's death."

My mom was one of many to die because of people like him, and if I didn't do something, thousands more would die tonight.

## 40

I quickly assessed the situation in front of us. Ramirez stood with his pistol pointed toward Dillon; Gutierrez still lay on the ground, his breathing labored; a tall dude had his semiautomatic pointed at Shane; and the guy with the square head pointed his gun at me.

All while this floating bomb sped toward Navy Pier.

"You just confessed to dealing narcotics in mass quantities," I said, trying to throw his emotions off-balance. "A confession you made in front of federal agents."

Ramirez's face darkened.

"So, on top of being a piece of shit, not a smart one at that," I added.

His face morphed into full-on rage. "Step aside, son," he said in a tone that implied he wanted to be the one to end my life.

Shane tensed, which caused his rival to tighten his finger on the trigger.

Dillon backed up, covered my body with his. "If you're going to kill her, you're gonna have to kill me first."

An unacceptable outcome. After years of him not giving a crap about his son, I doubted Ramirez's hesitation had anything to do with how much he cared about Dillon. More about his ego. He stuck his neck out to save his son from a second hit, so killing him now wouldn't be a good look. It would undermine Ramirez's authority.

"Step aside!" Ramirez demanded.

Everyone tensed, their fingers tighter on the triggers.

The anticipation of the coming violence broke through the air like the humidity of an approaching thunderstorm, where the air thickened and ominous black clouds rolled through the sky with their threat of the forming tornado.

Dillon was a quick shot; there was a chance he could take out all three of them before this went to hell. But unlike before, when my death was temporarily delayed by an intended interrogation, these guns were one squeeze away from ending our lives.

Ramirez looked at his watch and frowned.

*Ticktock. Clearly, the bomb's live.*

"I'll give you one last chance," Ramirez spat in disgust. "You leave with me now, I'll make you a king in this organization."

Gutierrez groaned, coughed up blood.

"I don't want anything to do with your organization or any of this anymore. I'm out," Dillon declared. "And don't call me *son*."

Ramirez's gaze froze, but his humiliation morphed into vengeance with the widening of his eyes.

"You're just as pathetic as the day I left you." Ramirez's gruff voice was eerily calm.

We saw the intention in his eyes just before the gun fired. Thankfully, Dillon flinched, so the bullet missed center mass, but it still hit Dillon's arm and sent his gun flying several feet away.

The square-headed gangster realigned his shot to Dillon's back— Ramirez clearly wanted to be the one to kill me. I grabbed the hammer from the torture tray, lunged, and smashed it into the gangster's head. The crack of his skull sounded like a twig snapping, and his blood sprayed across my face. The hammer's head stayed lodged in his brain as the whites of his eyes grew larger before he crumpled to the ground.

Meanwhile, Shane tried to fire a shot at his assailant, but when his gun jammed, he tackled the guy to the ground, escaping a bullet himself while sending the other gun sliding. Shane kicked his attacker so hard, his body slammed into the stove. The guy screamed from the burn as it tipped over and ignited the wall.

Dillon shoulder-slammed his dad in his ribs, and the two of them thumped onto the floor as the flames grew.

In the chaos, Gutierrez—who had blood pooling in his lips and smearing across his teeth—managed to crawl and get a nearby Glock 19 that had been lying on the ground. I dove on top of his chest as he lined up the shot with Shane's head, and I grabbed the gun, twisting its aim away. I tried to yank it from his bloody hands, but somehow, his grip remained so tight, I couldn't get it away.

As we wrestled for control, Dillon's lips tightened with years of rage as he pummeled his father in the face with punch after punch. His dad lost the grip on the gun, which lay next to them, but he hit his son in the temple with a blow that stunned Dillon. And followed it with another.

Near the stove, Shane's battle escalated when his attacker jumped on top of Shane and began to strangle him. Shane tried evasive tactics and thrashed his arms up and out, but the man had a death grip on Shane's neck, causing Shane's face to turn purple.

I yanked two more times, got the gun from Gutierrez, and fired one shot. The guy on top of Shane froze for three seconds and then tipped over.

Shane coughed and rolled on the ground to reclaim his breaths.

The fire spread to a second wall. Any second, it would ignite the massive amount of dynamite on this boat, and I didn't know how close we were to the shore—to the thousands of innocent people.

With the flames crawling higher, Ramirez bucked Dillon off and began beating his own son.

I took aim and pulled the trigger.

Ramirez jerked and stilled long enough for Dillon to shove his father off him. Ramirez coughed up blood, a gunshot to his back rendering him a groaning pile of flesh.

"Come on!" I shouted. "We need to get out of here!"

Shane rose to his feet slowly, his nose and lips bloody and eye already beginning to swell.

I winced from the heat of the flames. It was so hot, I wondered if we were technically getting burned right now, and the smoke made it even harder to see and breathe.

I shuffled through the thick cloud toward the only escape—the stairwell ten feet away—and as I approached Dillon on the way, he stood up. Put his hands on his thighs, coughing so hard, I thought he might vomit.

That was when Ramirez made his move. He did it quickly, grabbing the gun and aiming it at my chest.

I pulled my arm up in a hopeless attempt to defend myself, but Dillon was faster.

He dove in front of me, blocking my body with his just as his father pulled the trigger.

Dillon collapsed with a hole in his chest.

"Dillon!" I screamed.

As flames engulfed the third wall, Ramirez's disgusting little lips turned up into a smug look of victory.

As I glared at the villain who'd supplied my mom with her fatal drugs, time seemed to stand still.

He raised his hand to line up another shot at me, but I pulled my trigger faster.

A look of shock spread across his face as a small hole opened above his right eyebrow, and his head thudded to the floor.

Flames engulfed the last wall and spread its heat to the ceiling.

I coughed and knelt by Dillon.

"Dillon!"

"We need to go," Shane said. "I don't know how long we have…"

*Before the bomb explodes.*

"Fallon," Dillon whispered. He was white, making a gurgling sound as he struggled to breathe. "Are you okay?"

"Hang on," I cried. "You're going to be just fine."

"Fallon!" Shane urged as the fire spread toward our only escape—the stairwell.

"Come on." I lifted Dillon's head. But he faded into unconsciousness and became dead weight.

"Help me!" I screamed at Shane.

He grabbed Dillon under his shoulders, and I grabbed his feet.

The fire was three feet from the stairwell now. It burned my skin, my face, my eyes as we lumbered Dillon's body up the stairs.

"Go faster!" I screamed.

I risked a glance at Gutierrez, who had tried to crawl to the stairwell but, choking and bleeding heavily, had collapsed onto the ground.

Fire spat embers onto my shoulder, but I wouldn't drop Dillon's legs. We had seconds, at best, to get off this damn boat before the whole thing went up.

"Arrggghhhh," Shane groaned with gritted teeth. A vein bulged in his forehead as he yanked Dillon's body over the last step and tossed him to the ground.

Dillon's eyes remained closed.

Shane looked over the edge of the boat.

"He's barely breathing!" I shrieked.

"There's an inflatable boat with a motor." The escape boat the cartel was going to take as their bomb sailed into Navy Pier. "Come on!"

I swallowed and grabbed Dillon's feet.

Shane and I could barely manage to put him on the metal banister, aiming the best we could.

"If he falls in the water…" I started. *He'll sink into the darkness.* "One of us needs to get in that boat first, catch him," I said.

Shane huffed an impatient breath; I didn't have the upper body strength to catch Dillon. Only he would.

I held Dillon's body, which was propped awkwardly on the banister, while Shane threw one leg over, then the other, and lowered himself like a pull-up before letting go. I heard a thump and the splash of a wave.

"Okay, drop him!" Shane said.

I looked down, pushed Dillon over, and watched him fall ten feet into Shane's waiting arms. It must have been too heavy, though, because it knocked Shane over, and Dillon landed on the bottom with a belly flop, rocking the lifeboat so hard, it almost tipped over.

But it worked. Both men were safely in the lifeboat.

I risked a glance around, horrified to see Navy Pier only a half-mile away. Within the blast radius, for sure.

And closing.

"You go!" I screamed. "I'll swim to you in a second!"

"What? Fallon!"

"Go!"

I ran to the front of the boat, found the steering wheel. The ship was on some sort of autopilot mode, heading right for Navy Pier.

"Fallon!" Shane shouted.

There was a control panel with the label CPT. A couple dials, one called rudder, one deadpan. Port and starboard side buttons that went from one to ten degrees, and in the center, a little green light beneath a switch that was flipped up to Heading Hold. That had to be the autopilot.

I flipped the switch to standby, and a little red light replaced the green. I could feel the rock of the boat as the autopilot's steering disengaged.

I pulled the steering wheel as far to the right as possible, so tightly, the boat almost tipped over, so I had to release it a bit.

"Fallon! What are you doing?"

The vessel turned out toward the open lake, and once it was pointed toward a safe angle—away from the shore—I flipped the switch back up to Heading Hold and ran to the banister.

Where Shane glared at me. I threw myself over the side and dropped into the boat.

Shane had already untied us from the main boat and started the motor, but he hadn't moved like I'd asked him to; only now, when I was safely inside, did he slam it into gear and speed away.

The buzzing engine increased in pitch as we picked up momentum.

To our left, Chicago's picturesque skyscrapers sparkled against the charcoal sky, branching in staggered heights toward the one-hundred-story John Hancock building with its white antenna-like towers glowing. The smell of musty grass grew faint as the warm summer air whipped past us, and to our right, the cartel boat headed toward the water's distant black horizon.

Shane kept the motor at full speed, so fast, the front end floated above the waterline, and one rogue wave could capsize us. We made it about ninety seconds before the immense blast rocked our boat and shuddered the water. I felt its vibrations all the way to my bones, felt its heat lick my back, and saw the ebony sky light up like a firework as engulfed pieces of the fishing vessel rained down in an array of flaming orange chunks.

One of which came right at us.

Shane jerked the steering so quickly, our boat almost rolled, and when a smaller piece shot toward us, he had to jerk the other way. The farther we got from the explosion, the smaller the balls of fire became until we finally made it far enough away, where we let the engine throttle.

I allowed myself a brief second to look back and see the fiery vessel's back end sticking out of the water as it went down. Balls of orange clouds glowed against the black water and sky so brightly, they stung my eyes, as if staring directly into the sun.

Navy Pier was still in one piece.

"Dillon!"

Shane helped me flip him over onto his back.

He wasn't moving.

His chest wasn't going up and down.

"I don't feel a pulse," Shane said.

41

I gnawed on my fingernail, tapping my foot on the linoleum floor. "We got his heart started very quickly," I reasoned.

Shane said nothing.

"They had oxygen on him the whole time he was in the ambulance." An ambulance that was already on the shore, waiting for us, thanks to the Coast Guard, who had gotten to us within a couple minutes, drawn over by the explosion. "Those are all things working in his favor. Big things."

Shane rubbed my back.

"He's strong," I continued.

He looked dead, completely dead, his skin the color of my dad on that morgue table. And when I'd opened Dillon's eyelids, his eyes were a dull gray, lacking life. But his heart was technically still beating.

No, not technically. Why would I use that word? His heart was beating, period.

"Lots of people survive gunshot wounds to the chest," I continued. "Lots. Like every day."

I stood up and walked to the other end of the hospital waiting room. The space was neat and clean with its architecturally curved ceiling, pristine white walls, perfectly spaced windows, sand-colored carpet, and tidy rows of faux leather chairs. It was all designed to make it look like you were simply here for a medical appointment rather than awaiting the life-or-death news of someone you loved.

There were sixteen strangers in this waiting room, all looking at me. No, not looking. Gawking. I wore teal scrubs the nurse had given me, and I had a bandage on my arm with another hidden beneath the fabric on my thigh. Bandages, courtesy of a nurse that insisted to "at least" wrap the hideous, oozing burn and gash while I waited on news of Dillon. I'd cleaned the blood and dirt off my skin in the ladies' room with wet napkins, but I looked a mess. And I was clearly making the other people uncomfortable.

And Shane didn't look much better.

We'd been here for hours as they rushed Dillon up to surgery in hopes of repairing the damage caused by the bullet meant for me.

The bullet from his father's gun. His father, who'd put his son in the impossible position of supporting his family.

A few weeks ago, I thought I'd never feel an ounce of empathy for anyone who worked with narcotics. I'd judged them, just as I'd judged Dillon for his life choices. But I'd since learned that if I were in his shoes, I could've fallen prey to the slippery slope he did. Desperate to get his family out of the dangerously violent neighborhood—violence that threatened them every day and, on at least one occasion, resulted in the beating of his mentally impaired brother—he succumbed to the financial protection that dealing offered until he was in so deep, there was no way out.

"Fallon"—Shane put a hand on my shoulder—"why don't we go to the cafeteria? Get something to eat?"

"No."

"You look like you're going to faint."

"I'm not leaving until we hear from the doctor."

Dillon shouldn't have been there to get shot in the first place. While the cartel would've gone after him at some point, maybe the United States would have intervened before that could happen. Or maybe Dillon could've run after my death.

"How did you guys even find me?" I asked.

Shane rubbed his neck. "We followed Burch."

"I didn't see headlights."

"Didn't have 'em on."

"I didn't see a car."

"We were careful."

"Burch didn't even notice," I said. Or if he had, he didn't show it.

"Very careful. Watched Burch take you down that dock, to those... guards," Shane said. "When we saw them off Burch, took everything we had not to just go in, guns blazing, but we needed to be smart if we had any chance of getting you off that boat. Dillon and I scoped the place out, looking for a way in, but we had to keep our distance because of the guards. By the time they left the dock, the boat was already moving."

"Did the only thing we could—jumped in the water. Swam after it."

"Dillon had handcuffs on..."

"Used the motel's fire ax on the chain the second Burch left," he explained. "Grabbed the gun from the nightstand and my backup weapon from my trunk. The harder part was getting up onto the damn boat. Not the easiest thing to do. Felt like it took us forever, especially when we could hear you screaming."

And then they charged in, almost got killed themselves, especially when Ramirez showed up.

A doctor—female, short, arms like twigs, black hair in a ponytail—burst through the doors.

"Ms. O'Connor?" she called out.

I jumped up and half-jogged to her.

She took in my appearance but said nothing. "Are you family?"

"Girlfriend." I'd had police finally track down his mom, but she hadn't arrived yet. "And a police officer."

She nodded. "Dillon made it through surgery, but his heart stopped on three separate occasions. The bullet entered his left chest and caused a pneumothorax, which is a full lung collapse. The bullet also nicked his heart, causing a coronary lesion on his left atrium, and also damaged the aortic valve. His status is critical."

She let me process this, gave me a few seconds to try and remember how to breathe.

"We've done what we can, but the next few hours will be critical." She drew out her words slowly, in a quiet voice.

I didn't expect the pessimistic tone. The look on her face to be full of pity.

"What are his chances?" I asked.

"It's difficult to know how any one person's body will respond to trauma."

"But if you had to put a number on it?" Were his odds only, like, sixty percent? Fifty?

She looked from Shane to me before gently answering, "I'd estimate it at five percent."

The world swayed, and Shane was suddenly at my side, holding my upper arm to prevent me from falling over.

She had to be wrong. Dillon was strong, and if anyone could come out of this, he would. She was wrong. Doctors probably lowballed percentages to prepare you, just in case.

"Can we see him?" I asked.

There was that pitiful look again as she pursed her lips and nodded. "I'd advise you to call whoever you need to, so they can say good-bye."

*Good-bye?* I shook my head; there was no way Dillon could die.

Shane said, "I'll check on his mom's ETA."

I nodded.

"You can follow me," she said to me.

Some part of my brain told me that couldn't be good, that she was letting me see him. Visitors were usually confined to family only. Which probably meant she fully believed he wasn't going to make it.

With my head in a fog of dread, I walked with her through the doors, down a long hallway, around two turns, until I was in the intensive care unit.

The outside of the room was dark and intimidating, and the inside was stuffed with so much equipment, it felt like robots lived here, serving the one lone human in their center. The human with tubes coming out of every part of his body.

Dillon had a white tube down his throat, taped over his mouth, and a machine caused his chest to rise and fall with sounds of *shhh* and then *shaaaaaa* in perfect rhythm. Another tube extended out of his left rib cage. He had three IVs and other instruments strapped to his chest beneath his hospital gown. Every machine had colorful lines and numbers and sounds.

But only one phrase came to my mind: *life support*.

"Can he hear me?" I asked the doctor.

"I don't know," she said. "I'll leave you two alone."

Dillon looked so chilly, lying here with so much skin exposed. I pulled the hospital blanket up a few inches higher, making sure I didn't bump anything.

And then I sat next to his bed and reached for his hand.

His hand was cold, and my heart flashed to the other times I'd touched it. In the elevator fire, when he'd told me to save myself even though it meant leaving him behind to die. The first time he'd caressed my cheek, cupped my face before kissing me. The way he'd touched me when I professed my feelings to him, and after, when he touched my body. When he'd saved my life at that party and when he took me down from that hook. And now, this might be the last time I ever held it.

"I don't know if you can hear me," I started. "But I need to believe you can. Because I have some things to say to you."

I took a deep breath and leaned forward, so I could push my cheek against his hand.

"I once told you that the world would be a better place without you in it." My eyes stung, and my throat swelled. "That's not true. The world needs you, Dillon. I need you. Your heart is pure." I wiped a stray tear. "And I'm proud of you. For standing up to your father and having the courage to walk away from that organization."

I didn't want to believe he could die. But I couldn't ignore what the doctor said, either, and if, Heaven forbid, Dillon didn't make it, he couldn't pass away without knowing how much I loved him.

"Before I met you, I'd shut myself off from feeling things for people. I built my walls. Shut people out."

Dillon's heartbeat, beeping on the corner monitor, accelerated. His eyes remained closed, but a lone tear bubbled in the corner of his eye and dripped down his cheek.

I swiped it with my finger as my eyes blurred with tears.

"Maybe part of the reason I obsessed over my career was because it kept me preoccupied, so I didn't have to open myself up for relationships."

I paused. "I blocked everyone out until I met you. You made me feel alive again. And feel loved in a way I never had before. You were the rainbow after my storm, Dillon."

I swallowed the burning in my esophagus. "I don't know how this will all work…" His criminal offenses, my career. "But the only thing I do know is that I love you, and I can't live in this world without you, Dillon. I love you with every cell inside me. So, please, if you need a reason to live? Live for me. Fight for me."

Dillon didn't move. I don't know what I expected, but Dillon didn't open his eyes, his fingers didn't twitch in my hand, nor did he start crying. Maybe the tear I'd seen was nothing more than his body reacting to all the tubes and medication. Maybe he couldn't hear me at all.

Maybe it didn't matter how much his death would destroy his family and me.

A body could only sustain so much damage, and a heart could only take so much physical and emotional pain before it stopped beating.

I hung my head on his bedrail and sobbed.

And as I did, Dillon's hand tightened around mine. Three times.

*I. Love. You.*

## 42

F ive days later, I paced in the halls of the hospital, where noises—sneakers squeaking against linoleum, the rumble of voices talking against the backdrop of monitors beeping—blended together like a now-familiar symphony, the smell of disinfectant growing weaker, the longer I'd been here.

Dillon's vitals had improved enough that the doctor decided to remove Dillon's breathing tube. It was going to take the medical team a few minutes, so I afforded my legs the stretch of walking all the way to the other end of the hospital, which was a treat. Aside from leaving for a shower a couple times and getting minor treatment for my burn and cut, I'd been by Dillon's side, sleeping and existing in the chair next to his bed. I'd even met his mom, who came every single day.

I rounded the bend to head back to the ICU room when something stopped me in my tracks. Well, not something...someone.

Jenna Christiansen.

It was impossible not to recognize her—sadly, the scars on her face were hard to miss. She probably thought that was why I was staring, but it wasn't at all.

It was admiration for the battle she'd fought. A battle that had made global news, the case Detective Fisher had worked. And while some people focused on the romantic aspect of her story—the sexy fighter willing to lay down his life to protect her—most focused on the dangerous side of it, referring to the unthinkable events preceding as a *Deadly Illusion.*

I couldn't believe I was in the same room with Jenna. Every news outlet had failed to get an interview with her. I'd actually met her briefly before, but when she was in the ICU in the aftermath of her tragedy, I didn't know all the details of what she'd endured. And now that I knew? I couldn't let this opportunity pass without telling her, from one woman to another, how proud she should be of what she'd overcome. She'd become a hero to women around the world.

And standing right next to her was another hero: Damian Stone, who kept his arm around her waist. They were in the maternity ward, with a smile that could only come from new parents.

As Jenna ambled down the hallway in a hospital gown, I approached her tentatively.

"Sorry," I said. "I didn't mean to stare. You might not remember, but we met in the hospital."

She must have been used to people approaching her by now because she didn't seem surprised; she simply offered a weak smile, while Damian watched Jenna's face, as if looking for any sign of distress.

"You're very brave," I said. "An inspiration to a lot of people. You saved a lot of lives."

Her eyes held mine for several seconds before she whispered, "Thank you," as if my proclamation chipped away at some of her pain.

She stood there for another moment before they walked to the end of the hall, where they turned out of sight.

I stared at the empty corner for a few moments and then headed back to Dillon's room, where two uniforms were posted outside his door for protection. The cartel was in mad chaos at the moment, but who knew if they might make a move?

Dillon's nurse emerged from the room. "You can see him now."

My pulse quickened as I jogged inside. The sight of him sitting up with a smile on his face was such a welcome relief. Dillon's facial stubble was a few days longer on account of him not shaving, and damn it if it didn't look sexy, complementing his tousled hair and chestnut eyes.

Dillon's voice was gruff, as if the tube rubbed his esophagus raw, but it only made him sound even sexier. "I'm cuffed to the bed." He tugged his right wrist that was handcuffed to the bedrail.

"You're kind of a wanted criminal at the moment."

I bent over and examined his gorgeous cheeks and jaw. The bruises on his face from his dad's blows looked less swollen today, his split lip closing up nicely.

Nice enough to finally give him a light, gentle kiss.

Lord, it felt good, like my center of gravity had returned.

I pulled my lips back, and Dillon tried to cup my cheek, but his wrist clanked to a stop. He frowned at the binding.

"You need to heal quickly," I demanded.

"Working on it."

I smiled and sat down in the chair. It'd be nice once he moved to a non-ICU room, where there'd be a window, where he could see the afternoon sun and the city landscape.

He stared at me, his eyes full of emotions so deep, they could dwell at the bottom of the ocean.

"I'm so sorry your dad's gone," I whispered.

"I'm glad you defended yourself, Fallon. Because I can't even comprehend a world where you don't exist in it. And now that I know everything, I'm glad he left. My mom and brother would've been in danger because the cartel uses family members. I'm just so sorry what he did to your family, Fallon."

I hated hearing the guilt in his voice. It was the same guilt that had laced his words when he insisted I *shouldn't* be with him the night I declared I was falling for him. He must have been battling his feelings for me, fearful of letting me get close to him, given his line of work. And when I met him in that basement after my dad's funeral, he'd said there was something he hadn't told me yet and that I'd never look at him the same. Looking back on it, he must have been trying to get the courage to tell me his suspicions about his father then and again after we escaped the cartel.

I took his hand and kissed it. I couldn't believe how much our tragic pasts were interconnected.

"I don't know how you can look at me and still love me, knowing that my dad is the one that destroyed your entire family."

"Because you're not your dad, and you're not responsible for his actions. I might not agree with some of the choices you made, but I understand why you made them."

I could see my words moving past his skin and the weight on his chest lift with the rise of his shoulders.

A slender nurse in blue scrubs came in and checked Dillon's IV. "Couple more days, Dillon," she said. "Then, you should be moved to a regular room."

When she left, Dillon stared at me in wonder.

"You saved me again." Dillon smiled.

"Shane helped."

"Don't let it go to your head," Shane said, walking in with the food we'd ordered. "I'd have preferred to let you explode. Considered letting your ass drown, too, but I'd have never heard the end of it."

Dillon's smile widened.

Shane set the bags down on the table and unpacked the burgers. The smell made my stomach growl.

"Damn, I missed real food," Dillon said.

"Heard you're going to live," Shane said.

"Sorry to disappoint you."

"Doc thought you were a goner."

To this, Dillon squeezed my hand. "You gave me something to fight for."

And he gave me something to fight for, too. My future would be bright, so long as we were both alive and safe.

Shane cleared his throat. He was probably uncomfortable with the emotional PDA because he changed the subject. "You guys hear of the string of burglaries in the city?"

"The criminals known as the Robin Hood Thieves?" I asked. "Yeah. Why?"

Shane shrugged. "Sounds like an interesting case."

I evaluated him. "You're thinking of leaving the task force?"

"Not right away," Shane said. "But I'm hoping to make detective soon. Those guys haven't hurt anyone yet, but they're escalating. Only a matter of time before someone gets killed."

I smiled, thrilled the passionate, crime-fighting Shane was back. "You'll make a good detective."

Shane's gaze fell to my fingers, laced with Dillon's.

"So, you two are really getting back together?" Shane asked, popping a French fry into his mouth.

I smiled at Dillon. "Yeah."

Shane popped another fry. "How's that going to work with you being in law enforcement and him being a"—Shane waved his hand in the air—"douchebag?"

I glowered at Shane, but he simply smirked and popped another fry into that big mouth of his.

43

"I love you so much." Dillon kissed my hand and my wedding ring that he'd slipped on a year ago at an intimate ceremony on Lake Michigan's beach.

"I love you."

"I'm so damn proud of you, Fallon."

I smiled and relished his lips against my temple.

"I'm going to deliver the good news," he said. "My mom and Shane have been here all night, waiting for an update."

Dillon smiled at me one more time, taking in the scene before him before walking out of the hospital room.

It was hard to believe how much we'd had to overcome to get here. So much had happened in the two years since the cartel's boat exploded.

As soon as the first and second-in-command died, a huge power struggle erupted in the Baja Cartel. All the leaders began killing each other in an attempt to gain control, but what they ended up doing was severely weakening their organization. The cartel members were too busy killing each other to pose a threat to my or Dillon's life, and soon, their organization was left in shreds.

Ripe for the picking when the United States stepped in.

With the cartel weakened, the United States formed a coalition and arrested dozens of cartel and Syndicates members.

The cartel and the Chicago Syndicates had been decimated. It would take decades for another group to take their place, if ever.

Dillon avoided jail time. He was a cooperating witness and received full immunity for it. He even became a consultant to the DEA. He was now on the other side of the fight, helping to stop people dying from drugs.

Still, while Dillon wasn't legally required to do so, he'd completed hundreds of hours of community service, wanting to atone for his mistakes. He'd also set up a community outreach program for families in financial distress, which provided opportunities for employment and prevention for teens who might otherwise get sucked into drug using or dealing. These programs had a significant impact on the Chicago communities.

As for me, I thought I was going to lose my job there for a while, especially when they put me on suspension, pending their investigation. But having a hand in saving the mayor, the chief of police, hundreds of officers, and thousands of pedestrians strengthened my standing with the DEA.

I officially joined a year and a half ago in an amazing role of analyzing cases behind the scenes. The responsibilities were so much more powerful than I imagined, connecting clues, solving mysteries, and investigating things that no one else had done yet. So far, two of my findings solved major cases in this country.

Meanwhile, Dillon and I settled into a beautiful home just outside the city, near his brother and mom, who we saw every Sunday for dinner. And now, we'd be adding another seat at the table.

I looked down, consumed with emotion.

A memory came flooding back.

*I'm two years old, and I'm in Mommy's arms, who's rocking me to sleep. I stare up into her blue eyes and touch my tiny fingers against her smiling cheek.*

*Daddy's face appears over her shoulder behind the rocking chair.*

*"Do you think she'll ever understand how much we love her?"* Daddy asks.

*Mommy shakes her head. "Not until she has one of her own."*

*Love.* A four-letter word, incapable of encapsulating the magnitude of what I felt right now. I never knew anything could be this powerful —more powerful than the strongest earthquake, more majestic than the rising sun. Instantly, my gravitational pull transformed, and the only thing anchoring me to this earth was her.

As I held my infant daughter in my arms, I couldn't explain how she had only come into this world an hour ago, yet it felt as if her beautiful soul had been tethered to mine for all of eternity.

There was nothing I wouldn't do for her.

From this day forward, my love for my child would be as constant as the stars in the sky and as unbreakable as the earth's core. And I knew, without question, that my love for her would even transcend time and space. That even death could not break this everlasting bond. Nothing could.

*You did love me, Mommy. Even when you couldn't show it.*

For the first time in a very long time, I could feel the gravity of how much my parents must've cherished me. I could feel their love wrap around me like a blanket on a winter night, and I now understood that it had been here all along. My eyes stung with the beauty of that realization, but also the sadness of it. To realize how suffocating their addiction had been, disrupting the current of affection between a parent and a child. My heart broke for them all over again, for what they'd lost.

"You know," I said to my newborn daughter, Kimberly, who we'd named after my mom, "there are two extraordinary people who aren't here to meet you. But I know they'd give anything to hold you in their arms." A tear slid down my cheek. "And that they love you so very much. They're your guardian angels, looking down on you right now. And they always will."

I kissed her forehead and then whispered to my parents. "I'll tell her all about you both," I promised. "You'll never be forgotten."

I stroked my daughter's chubby cheek, overwhelmed with affection for her. "I'll love you forever," I vowed. "Even when I'm gone."

Dillon returned to the room, and the smile that reached his eyes was a brand-new one. The smile of seeing his wife holding his daughter. He sat next to me on the bed and opened his arms. Unlike the empty years when I'd pushed everyone away, I accepted his embrace and fell into him, letting his affection wrap around me.

"I love you," he said.

"I love you."

In each other, we found the light we'd always sought. Light we'd searched for in the wrong places, and now that we'd found it, we'd never let it go.

# EPILOGUE

## ZOEY

*She should be here any second.*

As I sat in the restaurant, I looked at the hanging television, and watched the top story on the midday news.

"The manhunt continues for the band of criminals terrorizing the community with a string of brazen armed robberies. Police say they struck again last night in the River North neighborhood, where the suspects broke into a condo, and made out with over fifteen thousand in valuables."

Fallon approached me. "Zoey," she said.

"Hi." I stood up and gave her a quick hug.

Fallon sat down opposite of me and glanced up at the television. "Can you believe these guys? My friend's working on the case. I hope they catch them before anyone gets hurt."

"Can I get you ladies something to drink?" a waiter asked.

We ordered beverages, and Fallon's eyes settled back on me.

"When I said we should do coffee, I didn't mean for it to take two years." Fallon smiled. "I'm sorry."

"Don't be. You've had a lot going on."

We'd had to reschedule several times. Fallon had been swamped with work—with trial testimony, new cases—not to mention getting married and having a baby. Our coffee date kept getting bumped, but that didn't matter. We'd kept in touch via text and it was nice to see her now.

"Based on our texts, you do too," Fallon said. "Is your dad still staying with you?"

"I can't believe it's been months already; feels like he just got released from the hospital yesterday."

"It's admirable you taking him in like that. How's he doing?"

"His recovery's a lot slower than he'd like."

Than I'd like. What I wanted more than anything was for Dad to heal and regain his independence, and to find the bastard who'd hit him with his car, and then fled the scene.

I wanted Dad to get justice. And I would not stop until he got it.

But I had no idea that soon, the struggles that I'd faced over the past couple of years would pale in comparison to what I was about to go through—that three men would hold me hostage intending to kill me...

Nor could I have imagined the shocking truth of who had sent them...

∽

THANK YOU FOR READING THE LIES WE TELL! I HOPE YOU LOVED these stories as much as I do. Don't miss **THE TRUTHS WE HIDE**—a collection of the final two stand-alone romances in the Secrets and the City series, where <u>Zoey gets her HEA</u> in **Lethal Justice** and <u>Shane gets his HEA</u> in **Grave Deception**!

DIVE INTO THIS EMOTIONALLY CHARGED COLLECTION OF TWO STAND-**alone romances filled with betrayal, deception, and the heart-breaking choice between what is right, and what the heart wants.**

. . .

☆☆☆☆☆ *"NAIL BITING, BLOW YOUR MIND & EMOTIONAL ALL WRAPPED up in one phenomenal read!"*

## DIVE IN NOW

WHAT SHOCKING EVENT WAS ABOUT TO UNFOLD WHEN FALLON SHOWED up undercover at that party? And why did Dillon call his brother to say goodbye? As a THANK YOU TO READERS, delve into this **exclusive FREE chapter from Dillon's POV** (https://kathylockheart. com/dillon-pov-the-lies-we-tell/). It will leave you speechless…

*P.S. IF YOU LOVED* **THE LIES WE TELL,** *I'D BE HONORED IF YOU'D consider posting a 2-word* <u>REVIEW</u> *on Amazon.*

# ACKNOWLEDGMENTS

DEADLY ILLUSION

First, **I'd like to thank you, the reader.** You have a ton of options when it comes to books, your time is incredibly precious, and you gave *me* a chance. From the bottom of my heart, THANK YOU. Readers mean the world to me, and I'd love to connect with you! Please find my social media links at www.KathyLockheart.com.

Thank you to my husband for showing me the beauty of true love and being my biggest cheerleader. You are the calming force in my life, my rock, and I love you more than you can imagine. I don't know what I did to deserve you.

Thank you to my children for giving me a love I didn't know existed until you were born and for inspiring me to be the best *me* I can be. Always go after your dreams.

To my family for enveloping me with love, encouraging me, and embracing my idea to become a writer. To my mother, who told an impressionable little girl that she could accomplish anything she wanted in her life. To my dad, for your profound wisdom and for pushing me to keep going when I was about to give up.

To my friends, for your never-ending support, and for being my laugh partners in this crazy thing we call life. For showing up at my house with a bottle of wine when things go wrong, and also when things go right.

To Kristin and Sharon, my first beta readers. Thank you for being a pivotal part of the journey to bring my stories to readers.

To Amy and Kristen, my formal beta readers. Thank you for helping make Deadly Illusion even better.

To my editors, Michelle Mead and Lindsey Alexander, who made this story remarkably better than it was before! To my cover artist, Hang Le, for bringing such beauty to this novel!

To all the authors who came before me—your success paves the road for new writers to do what they love. Thank you.

~ *Kathy*

# ACKNOWLEDGMENTS

FATAL CURE

First, **I'd like to thank you, the reader.** You have a ton of options when it comes to books. Your time is incredibly precious, and you gave *me* a chance. From the bottom of my heart, THANK YOU. **Readers mean the world to me**, and I'd love to connect with you! Please find my social media links at www.KathyLockheart.com.

Thank you to my husband for continuing to cheer me on, even when I wanted to give up. You've always believed in me more than I've believed in myself. Thank you to my children for inspiring me to go after my dream and for the endless happiness you've brought into my life. You are the sun in my solar system, warming my heart and soul.

To my family for loving and encouraging me. To my mother for your unending support, affection, and laughter. To my father, you've always been my hero, but witnessing how you treated people in your darkest hour made you rise to superhero status.

To my friends, Kristin and Sharon, for your never-ending support. You've always encouraged me to go after my passion, even when I was scared to do so. I can't tell you how much that means to me and how much I adore our time together. You guys keep me grounded when I start to spin.

To Katy for reading *Fatal Cure* long before anyone else and giving me honest feedback that motivated me to keep going. Readers like you inspire authors like me!

To my official beta readers and early ARC readers: Tracey (your email made my eyes sting!), Amy, Kristin, Amy, Sara, Kayla, and Ecaterina. Thank you for reading this long before it was ready to put into the dryer and for all your valuable insights that made *Fatal Cure* even better!

To my editors—Michelle Mead, The Novel Triage, Unforeseen Editing, and Judy's Proofreading—who made this story remarkably better than it was before! To my cover artist, Hang Le, for bringing such beauty to this novel!

To all the authors who came before me, your success paves the road for new writers to do what they love. Thank you.

~ *Kathy*

# INSPIRATION FOR FATAL CURE

*This contains major spoilers. Please read AFTER the book.

The inspiration for this novel came from two separate elements: an emotional one and an entertaining one.

I'll start by explaining the emotional inspiration. Addiction is a disease as complicated as it is widespread. I think we all know someone who has suffered from addiction. I personally know someone who was dramatically affected even though they were not an addict themselves. As I thought about this person, I wondered about many things. I wondered what it would feel like to be a child of addicts and what effect it might have on your heart. I wondered what it would be like to be a parent struggling with addiction when you loved your child more than anything yet physically battled against a disease.

My desire to tell a story about addiction increased when I saw the opioid crisis sweeping our nation. I was haunted by stories of everyday people recovering from things like surgeries, only to find themselves physically addicted to the pills that were supposed to cure their pain. Most of these people never saw it coming, and yet, in some cases, their lives were destroyed. My heart broke for them, and I wanted to research this and tell a story about a character struggling with the aftermath of her parents' addiction. In particular, I wanted to take a character through a journey, from anger to compassion, when she unveils the truth of their suffering.

And as I thought about this character's journey, a love interest formed in my mind. This is where the entertaining part of the story comes in. Of all the people Fallon could have fallen for, this one presented the most tension and the most obstacles to their love—a person who made their living, selling the very drugs that destroyed her family. A forbidden romance seemingly doomed to fail.

I couldn't stop wondering how their love story would turn out. What would happen to a DEA agent who fell in love with the drug lord she was hunting? What would happen to her career? What would happen to their love story? Would it end in tragedy? I couldn't stop wondering about all of this, and I had to find out what would happen. Finally, I sat down to write it.

And thus, *Fatal Cure* was born. I hope you enjoyed it!

xoxo,
  Kathy

# RESOURCES

If you, or someone you know, might need help leaving a dangerous relationship, please visit www.thehotline.org.

# LET'S CONNECT!

The easiest way to connect with me is to go to my website, <u>www.KathyLockheart.com</u>, and find my social media links. I interact with readers, so don't be surprised if you see me reply to your post or invite you to join a reader team!

*Xoxo*

*Kathy*

- amazon.com/Kathy-Lockheart/e/B08XY5F2XG
- bookbub.com/profile/kathy-lockheart
- facebook.com/KathyLockheartAuthor
- tiktok.com/@kathylockheart_author
- instagram.com/kathy_lockheart
- twitter.com/Kathy_Lockheart
- pinterest.com/kathylockheart